To Terri & Keith,
   I hope you enjoy this interstellar adventure,

Dan Pekarek

DLPekarek@aol.Com

www.Alcent2092.Typepad.com

Alcent
The Ultimate Adventure
BOOK ONE IN THE ALCENT SERIES

DANIEL L. PEKAREK

Seattle, Washington
Portland, Oregon
Denver, Colorado
Vancouver, B.C.
Scottsdale, Arizona
Minneapolis, Minnesota

Peanut Butter Publishing
an imprint of
Classic Day Publishing
2925 Fairview Avenue East
Seattle, Washington 98102
877-728-8837
info@peanutbutterpublishing.com

Dedication

This story is dedicated to the men and women who risk
their lives to make space exploration happen.

Acknowledgements

Production of this book was made possible through
the efforts of the following people:

Albert Bjorgen
Storyline and Engineering Consultant

Peter Fisher, M.D.
Medical Consultant

Daniel L. Pekarek
Author and Editor

Joan Pekarek
Editor

Beth Mitchum
Editor

David Pekarek
Cover Image

Soundview Design Studio
Book Design

Elliott Wolf
Publisher

Chapter Titles

Cover Illustration

The image on the front cover of this book is a scene from chapter seventeen. Alcent's two moons, Nocturne and Aphrodite, are in a full moon phase as they rise over the entrance to Mystery Lagoon. In *Alcent Adventures*, the second book in the Alcent series, Mystery Lagoon lives up to its name.

ONE

The Long Journey Begins

On July 15, 2092, Captain Jerry Jerontis was in his office onboard the starship Challenger, which was orbiting Earth at an altitude of 280 miles. He was reviewing a list of tasks that remained to be done before leaving Earth on an interstellar voyage to Alcent, a dinosaur-dominated planet orbiting Alpha Centauri A.

Overshadowing the Captain's checklist was the possibility that his starship might be sabotaged. Even though strict security procedures made sabotage unlikely, Captain Jerontis took the threat seriously. He had ordered his security team to do a thorough checkout of the Challenger, and he awaited their report.

If the sabotage existed, Jerry was determined to defeat it. He had always been a tough-minded optimist who never accepted failure, and this time, failure was not an option.

Even Jerry's appearance was that of a strong-willed man. Years of regular physical training gave him a lean, muscular build. He stood six feet three inches tall and had a handsome face set off by bushy brown hair and hazel eyes that always seemed to radiate a bright cheerful attitude.

At age 42, Jerry had been preparing for the mission to Alcent for twenty years. He had accepted employment with the National Interstellar Exploration Administration (NIEA) even before receiving a Master's Degree in Aerospace Engineering. Having been involved in the design, construction, and testing of the Challenger from day one, Jerry knew every inch of the giant starship and felt that it was his creation.

He was eager to depart for Alcent, but before the mission could begin, one major task remained: the Challenger had to be joined to its propulsion stages. In less than an hour, the space tug Goliath would dock with the Challenger. Fueled with antimatter, Goliath's mission was to transport cargo between low Earth orbit and various lunar bases. Shortly, it would transfer the Challenger from low Earth orbit to its propulsion stages in orbit at an altitude of 125,000 miles. The huge quantity of antimatter fuel required for the interstellar mission was accumulated in this high altitude orbit to protect people on Earth from the enormous destructive energy that would be unleashed if an accidental explosion occurred.

1

While awaiting the arrival of the Goliath, Jerry reflected on some major events that led up to his mission. He noted that people had dreamed of flying for centuries before it finally became a reality at Kitty Hawk, North Carolina in 1903. Then, in just 66 years, man had set foot on the Moon. In 2020, the first manned lunar base became operational, followed by a similar base on Mars in 2036. In 2046, NIEA sent Earth's first unmanned interstellar probe, Star Voyager, on a long journey to the Alpha Centauri System. Twenty-six years later, in 2072, it reported the discovery of a life-filled, earthlike planet orbiting Alpha Centauri A. Now, in 2092, people were about to follow the path pioneered by Star Voyager.

Jerry considered his mission to Alcent, the third planet of Alpha Centauri A, a truly epic event in the evolution of the human species. For the first time, people would journey to another planet with a breathable oxygen-nitrogen atmosphere and a temperate climate, a planet where a new civilization could prosper without support from Earth.

However, two extremist groups had vowed to stop the mission. Alcent Environment Preservation Front (AEPF) declared that the arrival of humans on Alcent would pollute the pristine environment and be destructive to the life forms already living there. Also, a fanatical religious cult declared that all of Earth's problems were the result of humans being infected with the devil. It maintained that if the Challenger took people to Alcent, then it would also be infected with the ravages of the devil. These groups had failed to stop the mission in the political arena and had recently resorted to terrorist acts against NIEA facilities, killing thirteen people and seriously injuring thirty-seven. They declared that they had already implemented a fail-proof plan to stop the mission.

Captain Jerontis considered some obvious possibilities. Planting a bomb on a starship orbiting 280 miles above Earth was possible but difficult to do. Their only option to transport the bomb to the ship would have been to conceal it among the ship's supplies or construction assemblies. But Jerry thought this unlikely, because everything had passed through multiple security checks, including intensive inspection by sophisticated bomb detection equipment.

Sabotage by one of the construction workers was possible, but would almost certainly have been discovered, since all work was inspected and tested by three independent crews, who took great personal pride in discovering imperfection. Their goal was to make the huge starship free of malfunction during its long voyage to Alcent. Also, all individuals working on the Challenger had survived thorough security investigations.

With enough money, anti-satellite missiles could be bought from black market arms dealers. However, Jerry doubted that either of the radical groups had the money or expertise to carry out a missile attack. But as a precaution, the USAF had stationed three missile interceptors near the starship.

Jerry's communicator beeped. It was the security chief, who reported:

2

"We've inspected the Challenger, Captain, and we've found no sabotage."

"Have you looked everywhere?"

"Yes! To do a more comprehensive inspection than we've done, we would have to start taking things apart."

"That should not be necessary," responded Jerry. "The security and inspection procedures followed during construction were very strict. Thanks for your report."

Jerry thought about the negative results of the security investigation and wondered if the sabotage threat was nothing more than a psychological ploy, an attempt to save face. Rather than admit that they had failed to stop the mission, extremist leaders could use such a threat as a way to keep their followers fired up, gain additional publicity, and give a starship commander one more thing to worry about.

Totally engrossed in thought, Jerry was startled when the communication system suddenly snapped to life with a loud enthusiastic greeting, "Ahoy there, Captain J.J.! This is your old college football buddy Moose ready to give you a lift to your fuel stop. We expect to dock with the Challenger in ten minutes. Then, we'll light our tail pipes, annihilate some matter, and begin orbital transfer."

While turning to face the rearview screen, so that he could monitor the approach of Goliath, Jerry said, "Sounds like the same old boisterous comic I've known all these years, and I might add, one who seems to be in an exceptionally high-spirited frame of mind."

"Just a natural part of my vibrant personality that you serious types might have a difficult time relating to. However, I am going on a much needed vacation. After all, I've been shuttling payloads to and from the moon for the last six weeks. So after I've delivered you to your fuel stop, I'll have four weeks on Earth, which I'll spend on a warm sandy beach in the South Pacific that is famous for its elegant bikini-clad scenery."

"Sounds like you haven't changed much over the years. Here we are, practically on the eve of mankind's greatest adventure ever, and where is your mind? Somewhere off in a distant, erotic fantasyland."

"That's the kind of comment I'd expect from the predictable, no-nonsense Captain J.J. I've known practically forever. But it's probably not your fault. Who knows, if you hadn't been so dedicated to this Alcent Project, you also might've developed a keen sense of appreciation for some of the more playful aspects of life."

"Getting my starship ready for our long journey has definitely dominated my life, and I really haven't had much time for anything else."

"Before I drop down to Earth for a well-deserved vacation, maybe we could have lunch, and you could give me a tour of your ship?"

"Are you sure you can spare the time? I wouldn't want something as trivial as a tour of Earth's first manned starship and lunch with its Captain to delay your pleasure trip to some exotic beach in the South Pacific."

"In the interest of helping you get into the proper frame of mind for your long voyage, I am willing to make the sacrifice."

Captain Jerontis thought Moose's mild psychological jabs were probably his way of handling the emotions involved in saying goodbye to a life-long friend. Even so, Jerry felt Moose would be disappointed if he didn't make an appropriate response before departing.

Jerry thought back to their college football days when he was starting quarterback and team captain. He remembered his teammates who gave him the title Captain J.J.

Moose, whose real name was John Moosebeck, was the starting fullback. Standing six feet two inches tall, weighing 260 pounds, and having very little body fat, he was an immensely powerful man. He was very quick on his feet and had the habit of running through defenses like a charging bull moose during mating season. His highly vocal fans soon simplified his name to Moose.

Captain J.J.'s mind returned to his mission. With the Challenger only minutes away from leaving its 280-mile orbit to begin the ascent to a new orbit at an altitude of 125,000 miles, nearly all of its twenty-four crew members were at view ports for one last good look at Earth. People had left Earth before, but had always had the option to return. This time, there would be no return. All that had been home would soon be forever left behind.

Over the years, Captain Jerontis had occasionally thought about the emotional impact of leaving Earth. But it never bothered him much, because leaving Earth had always been in the distant future. Now, it was only a few days away, and Jerry allowed his mind to drift into some fond memories. He thought about a hiking trip he had made to a remote wilderness lake in northern Canada. Then, he wondered what it would be like to hike along a lakeshore on Alcent where all lakes would be in wilderness areas.

Jerry's mind was suddenly jarred back to reality when his communicator came to life with a message from Moose: "Captain J.J.! Our instruments indicate the completion of docking. Please confirm."

"Affirmative."

"Our best transfer orbit requires that we have ignition in 15 minutes."

"Okay, let's begin a fifteen-minute countdown. That'll give everyone plenty of time to let us know of any reason to delay engine ignition."

"You got it."

Countdown began and all crew members prepared for 1g acceleration. After having been weightless for several weeks, even acceleration that was only equivalent to Earth's gravity would feel heavy.

The countdown progressed without interruption, and Goliath's antimatter engines ignited on time. When orbital transfer velocity was reached, the engines were shut down, and everyone was again weightless.

An hour and a half later, with nearly half the distance to fuel-stop covered, Captain Jerontis was taking a break in his quarters when Mike

Johnson, the chief engineer, appeared at the entrance and said, "Captain, I need to talk to you."

"Come in Mike. What can I do for you?"

Mike looked into Jerry's eyes and calmly said, "I've decided to leave the mission. I want to stay on Earth."

Mike's announcement hit Captain Jerontis like a bombshell, and for a few moments, he stared into Mike's light blue eyes attempting to sense a motive for his request. "This is a shocking surprise! What has led you to this decision?"

"For the last hour, I've been watching Earth steadily recede in the distance. In a few weeks, we'll be out of the solar system, and Earth will be so far away that we won't be able to see it without a telescope. Thinking about that really bothers me because I have friends and family on Earth that I don't want to leave permanently."

"We're all leaving behind people we love, and that's not easy, but the planet we're going to appears to be at the peak of a dinosaur age. Exploring it and building a home there will be an awesome adventure. Are you sure you don't want to be part of it?"

"I know that will be exciting beyond my wildest dreams, but watching Earth recede in the distance has given me an overpowering gut feeling of emptiness. And we haven't even left yet."

"All of us feel a sense of loss. That's normal; after all, we're leaving everything we've ever known, but we're going to lay the foundation for a new society. In essence, we're going to give birth to a new civilization."

"I've thought about all of that, but that overpowering gut feeling of not wanting to leave everything behind just keeps coming back."

"Have you discussed your feelings with Doctor Nemard?"

"No, but I don't think I need to. They're too strong to be just a passing whim. I think it would be best if you replaced me."

"Very well, but I'll hold your request for a few hours, in case you change your mind. You've been an excellent chief engineer, and I'd like to keep you on the mission, but I'll respect your decision."

"Thank you," responded Mike, as he released his seat belt, gently pushed off, and floated out of Captain J.J.'s quarters. Wanting another look at the receding Earth, Mike went to the observation deck.

Looking down on the Pacific Ocean, he observed a beautiful bluish-green world partly covered with soft white cloud formations that looked like tufts of cotton. The planet had a calm, peaceful appearance, and best of all, it was home. The thought of leaving it revived Mike's earlier feelings of emptiness and forlorn sense of loss. But perhaps the real reason for Mike's distress was the one that he did not discuss with Captain Jerontis, the one that he had to keep to himself for the time being. If his plan worked, the Captain would find out about it soon enough.

Mike drifted across the observation deck to look in the opposite direction. He quickly located Alpha Centauri A and Alpha Centauri B, shining brilliantly in the deep blackness of space. After looking at them for a few moments, Mike tried to turn away, but he could not, because the twin stars had captivated his attention in an almost seductive way. As he continued to gaze at them, they seemed to take on the aura of a pair of beckoning beacons that were trying to entice him into staying on the Challenger for the long voyage to a new home on Alcent. Mike thought about the life-filled planet and the images returned by Star Voyager's video equipment. Some of the images were vividly implanted in Mike's memory, and he was able to visualize them clearly. As he did this, a deep-seated desire rose from the depths of his mind, a desire to go to Alcent, a desire for the exciting adventure of exploring the mysteries of this planet. Mike was so torn between this intense desire and the need to stay on Earth that he decided to reconsider his options.

Meanwhile, back in the Captain's quarters, Captain Jerontis was thinking about Mike's surprise request. Even though regulations permitted anyone on the mission to drop out at any time, Captain Jerontis was puzzled by Mike's sudden move. Everyone on the ship had passed rigorous medical, physical, and psychological tests, along with excelling in the project's arduous training program. After surviving all of that, it simply did not make sense to drop out voluntarily a few days before departure. Captain Jerontis decided to discuss the situation with Doctor Connie Nemard, who was a competent psychiatrist, along with being the ship's medical doctor and a skilled surgeon.

Jerry went to Connie's office and told her about Mike's replacement request. "I don't understand why he's doing this, so I want you to look at his psychological tests and see if there's anything there that might explain his actions."

"I'll do that now. Come back in an hour, and I'll discuss it with you."

"Thank you." As Jerry turned to leave, he felt Connie's eyes fix on him a little longer than appropriate for an office call. That sure looked like a lingering glance, thought Jerry. The possibility caused Jerry's face to light up with just the trace of a satisfied smile.

After leaving, he thought, she is a beautiful woman. Her golden blond hair and those radiant blue eyes are riveting. She might even have a stunning figure, but these loose fitting NIEA uniforms make that hard to determine. But I guess I'd better stop thinking about her. This isn't the right time.

Captain Jerontis returned to the quietness of his quarters. He was a firm believer in personal quiet time and used it to anticipate and solve problems. With the responsibility of getting the big starship ready for its long voyage, he usually didn't have to do much anticipating to find an ample supply of potential problems to be concerned about.

Jerry wondered what difficulties might result from bringing in a new chief engineer so close to departure. While considering the possibilities, he was interrupted by Moose, who floated into his quarters through the open hatch and said, "Ready for lunch? I'm starving."

Moose and Jerry went to the cafeteria and ordered a deluxe combination pizza. When it was ready, they went back to Jerry's quarters to enjoy their meal.

After they started eating, Moose glanced at Jerry. "You are unusually quiet. What are you worried about now?"

Jerry stared into Moose's dark brown eyes. "Didn't you have a complete physical before your current tour of duty?"

"Yeah, I did, but why are you worried about my health when you have a starship to worry about? Do I look ill to you?"

"No, you look perfectly healthy. But did your physical find anything even minutely abnormal?"

"Not a single thing, but why are you so concerned about my health?"

"I'll get to that in a minute, but first, correct me if I'm wrong. You've been Captain of the Goliath for about a year now, and before that, you were its chief engineer for five years. And if my memory serves me right, you are an expert in antimatter propulsion systems."

"Yes, but what's all this leading up to? Are you writing a book about me or a resume for a job I haven't yet applied for?"

"One more question, do you think your ego could handle a demotion from ship's captain to chief engineer?"

Moose's dark complexion lit up with an expression of surprised disbelief, and he blurted out, "What kind of question is that? What do you know about my career that I don't?"

"Mike Johnson has requested that he be taken off this mission, and I'm planning to put you on the mission in his place, instead of following procedure and using the backup chief engineer."

"Hole-e-e-e-e Shit! You are going to stir up a real hornet's nest among the professional bureaucrats at NIEA Command if you make a major change in staff on your own!"

"But that's the beauty of my plan. I won't be acting on my own. You'll be my fellow conspirator. Together, we'll devise a plan to get you on this mission ... if you want it."

"An hour ago, I was relaxing on the Goliath, daydreaming about the wonderful vacation I've been planning, which begins in just a few days. Then, I do nothing more than stop by for lunch, and what happens? You want me to cancel the scenario I'd envisioned for the rest of my life and go jaunting off to another star with you on just a moment's notice."

Jerry grinned rather smugly. "It is all rather sudden, isn't it?"

"Somehow, I get the feeling that you're enjoying putting me on the spot like this. I suppose you want an answer right away."

"Oh no! You can think it over for an hour or two, and then, you can let me know. But right now, you should get back to the Goliath. We need to put the brakes on, or we'll go cruising right on past our fuel-stop."

"What do you mean? Our fuel-stop! I haven't accepted your offer yet."

"No, but I suspect you will. After all, you wouldn't want to admit that this old, serious, worrisome personality type might be a bit too daring and adventuresome for you to keep up with, would you?"

Visibly shaken and deeply lost in thought, Moose floated out of Captain J.J.'s quarters and returned to the Goliath. Shortly thereafter, he started the fifteen-minute ignition countdown sequence.

Meanwhile, Captain Jerontis buzzed the medical lab and when Doctor Nemard responded, he asked, "Have you reached any conclusions about the individual we discussed earlier?"

"Yes, I have."

"Good, I'll be right there."

When Jerry arrived in the medical lab, Connie gave him her report: "The results of the psychological tests Mike has taken over the years show him to be a very stable individual. He should be able to cope with the emotional stress of permanently leaving Earth and living in close confinement with other people during a long interstellar voyage. I believe his replacement request is the result of cool-headed thinking, not fluctuating emotions. A well thought out decision is not likely to be changed, unless the reasons for the decision change. In my opinion, he hasn't given you the complete story behind his request. I think you should honor it and not try to change his mind. However, if he changes his mind, I see no medical or psychological reason to deny him that option."

"I'm not surprised by your findings or by your opinion, which makes his replacement request all the more puzzling. I wonder what he's up to."

"I don't know, but there's one possibility that you need to consider. As you know, there are two extremist groups who've said that they've already implemented a plan to stop our mission. One way to do that would be to have someone on the Challenger sabotage it and then jump ship before we leave. Who on the Challenger would be better qualified to accomplish this than the chief engineer?"

"No one, but surely you don't suspect Mike. I've known him for several years, and he's always been ethical and trustworthy. There's no way I could suspect him of doing anything to jeopardize this mission or the lives of the people on it."

"I agree with you, but under the circumstances, I felt I had to mention the possibility."

"I appreciate that, and I agree with your reasoning. So during the last half-hour before our departure, I want you to roam the ship and make sure that everyone is onboard and at their assigned locations."

Just then, the three-minute pre-ignition warning klaxon blared out its urgent sounding notes forcing Captain Jerontis to head for the command console. He needed to be on station; even though, the Challenger was still under the control of the Goliath. The crucial sequence of maneuvers to carry out rendezvous and docking was programmed into the Goliath's flight control computer, but to guard against malfunction, Captain Jerontis and his flight crew needed to monitor the events leading up to docking.

Fuel-stop was not a fueling station in the sense that fuel would be transferred from storage containers to the Challenger; rather, it was an orbital base where the Challenger would be joined with two fully fueled propulsion stages. Docking maneuvers had to be executed with perfection. Even the slightest deviation from the required flight path and speed could lead to a collision with disastrous results.

When the countdown ticked down to zero, Goliath's antimatter engines ignited, and the burn continued for several uneventful minutes, successfully completing the braking maneuver. Looking at the rearview monitor, Captain Jerontis saw the huge propulsion section, currently about a mile away, very slowly grow larger in appearance as the two modules of the giant starship drifted toward each other at a closing velocity of just a few feet per second. Goliath's flight control computer processed data from laser range finders and other docking sensors. Through precise use of control thrusters, the computer would bring the docking structures of the two modules into perfect alignment and reduce final closing speed to less than an inch per second.

As the two large structures approached each other ever so slowly, time seemed to tick away even more slowly. A full two-and-one-half hours passed by before the habitation and propulsion modules were physically joined in a slow delicate procedure. Now, the Challenger was for the first time a complete starship. However, it would not be allowed to maneuver on its own until its flight control systems were checked out, and the Goliath would remain attached to it until this checkout was complete.

With the checkout underway, Jerry went to his office, where he received a call from NIEA Control. "Captain Jerontis here," he replied.

"Captain, the press conference we discussed earlier has been approved. A crew of three from SNS, a freelance science reporter, an aerospace reporter, and a newspaper reporter are scheduled for liftoff on a personnel shuttle in three hours. They will arrive on the Challenger at about this time tomorrow. We want you to arrange a tour of the ship and work out a schedule with the SNS people for a press conference."

"Have these people been investigated by security for possible association with the fanatics that have vowed to stop our mission?"

"They and their equipment have been cleared. Pertinent information will be transmitted into the security files in your computer."

"You do realize that entertaining them might delay our departure."

"Unavoidable. NIEA wants as much positive publicity as possible to help drum up political support for other NIEA projects. So even though one of the reporters has a reputation for being an antagonistic nag, we want you

9

to avoid making belligerent comments. Try to be a good host."

"That won't be easy if you're talking about old pain-in-the-butt Sam."

"You guessed it. Naturally, we objected to his presence on the news team, but SNS wouldn't back down. So we've delved into his professional life to anticipate the kinds of questions he'll ask. We've generated some appropriate responses, and this info will be transmitted to you shortly."

"We'll review it and be ready for him. Thanks for your assistance."

Reflecting on the next day's press conference, Jerry decided that he would like to bait and then embarrass his least favorite reporter during a live broadcast to a worldwide audience. Since Sam had always been an outspoken NIEA critic, the trick would be to embarrass him in a way that would discredit him. Perhaps, Doctor Nemard would be the right person for this job. As a skilled psychiatrist, she is certainly capable of playing with someone's mind, Jerry concluded.

Turning his thoughts to other matters, Jerry needed final decisions from Mike and Moose. If a new chief engineer had to be brought up from Earth, he would have to be on the personnel shuttle scheduled to take off in less than three hours. Jerry picked up his communicator, entered Mike's number, and received an almost immediate response.

"Hello, Mike here."

"Mike, this is Jerry. Now that you've had a few hours to reconsider, have you decided to withdraw your recent request?"

"I've decided to stick with it."

"Very well; when the new chief engineer arrives, I expect you to give him a full briefing and work with him until our departure."

"Will do."

Having received Mike's final decision, Jerry entered Moose's number into his communicator and waited for a response, but he didn't get the expected one. Instead, Moose appeared at the entrance to his office, held up his communicator, and asked, "Do you prefer to talk through these things, or can I come in?"

"Don't be silly, come in, and sit down."

Moose floated in and strapped himself into a seat. "I've given much thought to your offer, and I've decided to go with you as your chief engineer, if the offer is still open. I only worry that I'm not familiar with the details of this ship, since I've never worked on it."

"But you are a brilliant engineer with 20 years of experience in spacecraft, and our library has detailed specifications of every part of the ship. The computer will give you a 3-D image of any part or assembly by simply asking for it. I have no doubt that if anything malfunctions, you will diagnose the problem and fix it."

"Thanks for the vote of confidence. Obviously, I agree with you, or I wouldn't be here. But is the offer still open?"

"I spoke with Mike just before you arrived, and he confirmed his replacement request. So we have to devise a way to get you on this mission and him off of it without arousing anyone's suspicions. Also, since we're departing in three days, we need to bring you up to speed in a hurry. So I'm going to take you to the engineering library and introduce you to the computer. By the time we leave Earth, I expect that you'll have a basic familiarity with the systems that are mission critical."

"I'll give it my best, and I'll start with propulsion."

PRESS CONFERENCE

One day later, the visiting members of the media were onboard the Challenger and had just completed a partial tour of the starship under the guidance of Dianne Dawson, Life Support Officer. They were now in the cafeteria enjoying snacks and beverages while awaiting the arrival of Captain Jerontis and Doctor Nemard.

When they arrived, Dianne introduced them to the press. Then, she introduced the press: "This is Michelle, a highly respected science reporter. This is Sam from Satellite News Service. This is Caryn, a syndicated aerospace reporter. And this is Patrick with Associated Press."

After exchanging the customary greetings, Captain Jerontis said, "I am pleased to meet each of you. Welcome to our starship! You've already interviewed some of our crew members; now, Dianne, Connie, and I will answer your questions. Michelle, you can be first."

"Captain, what is there about this mission that has motivated you to devote your life to it?"

"I believe that interstellar expansion is human destiny, and I want to help make it happen."

"Why do you think going to the stars is human destiny?"

"It's in our blood. Just take a look at history. Throughout time, our spirit of adventure and thirst for knowledge has always driven us to travel and explore to the limit of our ability. Well, we now know how to go to the stars, and the Milky Way Galaxy alone contains at least 200 billion stars. Eight billion of these stars are similar to our Sun. If only one percent of these sunlike stars have earthlike planets, it will be a very long time before we run out of planets to explore and colonize. Our mission to Alcent is the first step in the interstellar expansion of the human species, and I believe this is a natural part of human evolution."

"That sounds like a paragraph taken from the book *Mankind's Place In The Universe,*" commented Michelle. "But I'd like to know what gives you a burning desire to go to Alcent?"

"I am driven by the human spirit for adventure. This is something that I have to do."

"Why?"

"You're not going to let me off the hook, are you?"

"No, I'm not."

"Okay, here it is. Since I was a teenager, it's been a fantasy of mine to journey seventy million years back in time to explore Earth during the dinosaur age. Well, I can't go back in time, but Star Voyager data indicates that life on Alcent may be similar to what existed on Earth during the dinosaur age. This mission gives me the opportunity to explore a planet that may be in an advanced dinosaur age. Perhaps some of these creatures have even evolved into fairly intelligent beings."

"Why do you say that?"

"The Solar System is believed to be about 4.6 billion years old; whereas, Alpha Centauri A and its planets are believed to be 5 to 6 billion years old. If life started as early in Alcent's history as it did on Earth, then the creatures now living on Alcent may've had an extra billion years to evolve compared to life on Earth. Dinosaurs ruled Earth for 150 million years. If Alcent is in a dinosaur age, it's possible that it started a billion years ago. Intelligence could certainly evolve in that amount of time. But intelligent or not, it will be one super adventure to live among those creatures and study them."

"I can see that you are thrilled by the possibilities, but do you have the training to study dinosaurs?"

"I don't, but Dianne does. She has a PhD in Biology and in Genetic Engineering. She will be in charge of plant and animal research on Alcent."

Next, Captain Jerontis turned to Caryn who asked, "Could you give us a brief summary of your flight plan including speed, time, and distance?"

"As you know, we are going to Alcent, the third planet of Alpha Centauri A. It is 4.35 light-years away. That is 25 trillion 516 billion miles. Before the development of antimatter propulsion, it was impossible to make this kind of journey in a human lifetime. But with antimatter propulsion, the Challenger will accelerate at 1g for nine months to bring us up to .77c, which is 77 percent of light speed. This means that we'll be traveling at 143,220 miles per second. That will be our cruise speed for nearly five years. Then, we'll have nine months of 1g deceleration. In spite of our tremendous cruise speed, it's going to take about six-and-a-half years to go to Alcent."

Caryn argued, "Even with antimatter propulsion, I don't understand how you can carry enough fuel to accelerate to such a tremendous speed and then have enough fuel left to slow down for your arrival at Alcent."

"I know this seems impossible, but you must keep in mind that the energy available from antimatter fuel is about 140 times greater than what is available from nuclear fusion and about 100 million times greater than what is available from chemical rocket fuels. To put this in perspective, if antimatter propulsion had been available in the late twentieth century, thirty-five milligrams of fuel (about the weight of a sugar cube) would've been sufficient to launch the space shuttle."

Caryn seemed satisfied, so Jerry turned to Patrick who asked, "Captain, with twenty-four people on this ship, how can you possibly carry enough food, water, and oxygen to last more than six years?"

Captain Jerontis turned to Dianne. "This question falls into your area of responsibility."

Dianne nodded and faced the media. "We have a sophisticated life support system that recycles all waste materials to produce pure water and oxygen. Also, we are able to grow food from recycled waste."

"Can you tell us briefly how it works?" Patrick asked.

"Genetic engineering is the key to the success of our life support system. Through it, specialized microorganisms were developed to break down the various kinds of waste generated on this ship, and genetically engineered plants were developed to grow the materials that our food synthesizers need to make food. The plants also produce part of our oxygen. Is that brief enough for you?"

"I get the picture, and if you started giving me technical details, I might not understand them anyway."

"I might add that we do have substantial reserves of oxygen, water, and food for emergency use."

"I have one more question," stated Patrick. "How well do your food synthesizers work?"

"With the various kinds of plant materials we feed into them, they are capable of making anything that you can find on any menu on Earth."

"But how well do they work?" persisted Patrick.

"Since arriving on this ship, you've had two meals and a coffee break. How well do you think our food synthesizers work?"

"Amazingly well!" exclaimed Patrick, who just now realized that he had eaten foods made by the synthesizers.

Captain Jerontis turned his attention to Sam and said, "It's your turn."

"Captain, since this project's inception, hundreds of billions of dollars have been wasted on it. Don't you think it would've been better if we'd spent this vast sum feeding the hungry and housing the poor?"

"Sam, that question has been debated by politicians in Washington, D.C. during each year's budget battle since day one. I really don't think there's anything I can say that hasn't already been said many times."

"Captain, you're evading the question. I want to know what your position is on this vitally important issue."

"This is a dead issue. The money has already been spent, and we're almost ready to leave. Why do you persist in pursuing a dead issue?"

"Because it's important for the future! Other expensive boondoggles will come up that need to be stopped, so the money can be invested in social programs. How do you feel about all the money that's been wasted on this project that could've been used to improve the lives of disadvantaged people?"

"Well Sam, as you know, I am devoted to this mission, and during the past 20 years, I've dedicated my life to its success. This hasn't left me with very much time to worry about social programs."

"But Captain, you must have some concern for the plight of the hungry and the homeless and the fact that the money soaked up by this project could've been used to help them."

"Of course I'm concerned about their predicament. But you must realize that the money invested in this project isn't going to disappear into interstellar space when we leave the solar system. We're not taking it with us. It was spent on Earth and provided meaningful jobs and careers for tens of thousands of people for two decades. Much of the money was spent developing technology that can also be used to improve life on Earth. With just a little imagination, even you should be able to figure out that the microorganisms genetically engineered for waste recycling on this ship could be used by the cities of the world to totally recycle their sewage, thereby eliminating a major source of environmental pollution. This technology would also allow cities to recycle their waste water, a very important capability to have in arid and semiarid parts of the world where water is in short supply. The genetically engineered plants we use to produce our food mature rapidly and can produce an abundance of high quality food in a limited space. If grown on Earth on a large scale, hunger could be eliminated as a social problem. All you have to do is overcome the hysterical objections raised by radical environmentalists who claim that genetically engineered plants aren't natural and therefore should not be released into Earth's ecosystem."

Jerry turned to Michelle who said, "Speaking of radicals, they've said that your mission will be stopped. How serious is that threat?"

"Since they've resorted to terrorist acts that have killed or injured several NIEA employees, we must take them seriously. Consequently, our security department has recruited the best professionals in the country. They are organized into two teams, with one team responsible for establishing security procedures, while the other team attempts to breach the system. By trying to outwit each other, they've given us a security system that we believe is nearly impossible to penetrate. Also, we are using the best security equipment that advanced technology has to offer. Sam, you have a question?"

"I want to discuss the population of your ship. You have a crew of twenty-four with twelve crew members under the age of twenty and twelve crew members ranging in age from twenty-eight to forty-two. Why the age difference between the two groups? And what kind of selection process was used?"

Captain Jerontis turned to Doctor Nemard. "Would you like to respond to these questions?"

Connie nodded. "To understand why the people on our ship fall into two age groups, you need to consider the goals and responsibilities of our mission. Those of us in the older group are experienced, highly trained professionals in our respective fields. We are responsible for the operation of this ship and arriving at our destination safely and in good health. Also, we'll provide advanced training to the younger generation.

14

"When we arrive on Alcent, our primary goal will be to establish a new civilization. That means having children and successfully raising them to become competent adults. After a six-year journey through interstellar space, those of us in the older group won't have that many child bearing years left to us. However, those in the younger group will be able to have as many children as they want and thereby give our new civilization a solid beginning and a promising future.

"As to the selection criteria, all applicants for this mission had to take a series of intelligence tests that sought to determine one's ability to learn new material quickly. One's ability to rapidly analyze and solve unexpected difficult problems was also evaluated. To be considered for this mission, an applicant had to score higher than 95% of those tested.

"Also, each person had to pass medical, physical, and psychological tests. Genetics played an important part in this evaluation; in that, a successful applicant had to show a family history free of hereditary diseases that would cause physical or mental disabilities. Also, since we'll be starting a new civilization, the success of which depends on reproduction, only applicants with normal sexual desires were considered.

"Individuals who passed all of these tests faced still more hurdles. Training exercises based on Star Voyager data were developed to help mission candidates learn the survival skills needed to stay alive in the dangerous environment we expect to find on Alcent. Physical endurance, cunning ingenuity, and the ability to handle unexpected situations were all essential to successful completion of this training. Sam, you have a follow up question?"

"Yes, I do. What do you mean by the phrase *normal sexual desires?*"

"I am referring to individuals who want to love and be loved by a member of the opposite sex."

Sam retorted, "But what about people who prefer to live in an alternative lifestyle? Weren't their civil rights violated by being excluded from consideration for this mission? Isn't this tantamount to discrimination on the basis of sexual preference?"

"Yes, it is, but I believe I explained quite clearly why this discrimination was necessary."

"But your earlier statement implied that people living in an alternative lifestyle have abnormal sexual desires."

"I suppose you could interpret my comment that way, but I'm wondering why you're pursuing this line of questioning instead of asking us how we feel about our mission, how we plan to survive and prosper on Alcent, or what we'll do during our long voyage."

"I've just uncovered a flagrant violation of the Civil Rights Act. Also, I've called attention to a socially insensitive comment of yours that is inconsistent with politically correct thinking and that is bound to be offensive to a large group of people in our society, many of whom paid tax dollars to support your mission."

"And that is what you think your viewers from around the world are interested in finding out about the greatest adventure ever attempted. Perhaps after you get back to Earth, one of your viewers could send you a book on human anatomy. After a brief study of male and female body parts, it should become readily apparent to you what would constitute normal sexual activity. Then, with some additional study, you could figure out how human reproduction works and how it is dependent on normal sexual activity. Then, you might be able to understand why discrimination on the basis of sexual preference was necessary for the success of this mission.

"As far as politically correct thinking is concerned, I am still an American, and I do have political freedom as guaranteed by the U.S. Constitution. Not you, or anyone else, is going to tell me what kind of thinking is politically correct. My freedom allows me to decide that for myself. Early in the twentieth century, there was an individual who told millions what politically correct thinking consisted of, and he used lots of guns to enforce his point of view. In case you're not a student of history, his name was Adolf Hitler."

Wanting to end the confrontation with Sam before she lost control and told him where he could go, Doctor Nemard quickly turned to Michelle and said, "Michelle, you have a question?"

"Yes, doctor. The Challenger is a big ship, but you'll be confined to it for more than six years. What are you going to do during all that time? And how are you going to avoid getting cabin fever?"

"Some people would have a difficult time dealing with close confinement for that long a time. One of the purposes of psychological testing was to find and eliminate them from mission eligibility." Connie briefly turned to Sam and said, "I guess you could even consider that a form of discrimination."

Before Sam could comment, Connie turned back to Michelle, "As to your first question, I will monitor the health and well-being of each person and treat any medical or psychological problems that develop. Captain Jerontis and the flight operations crew will monitor the performance of the Challenger's systems, do preventive maintenance, and repair anything that malfunctions. One of the most important responsibilities of the older generation will be to assist the young people with their continued training. For example, by the time we reach Alcent, I will have trained two of them to take over my responsibilities if there is an untimely end to my life."

"But you can't work all the time," protested Michelle. "What about leisure activities?"

"Our responsibilities will keep us quite busy, but we'll find time to have fun."

"But what will you do?"

"We have lots of options available. All the best books, movies, music,

16

and video games produced in the last 150 years are stored in our computer library. Also, we have a large gym. In addition to the exercise equipment located there, it is big enough to play competitive games in. For those who are musically inclined, we have some musical instruments onboard. People who like to design and make things can use the sophisticated equipment in our machine shop."

"That sounds like more than enough to keep people from getting bored and losing their sanity, even during a six-year voyage," noted Michelle.

"That's the plan," stated Doctor Nemard. "Mission planners decided that enjoyable leisure activities are important to personal well-being, and they made sure that much is available to be enjoyed."

After glancing at his watch, Captain Jerontis said, "We have time for one more question from each of you. Caryn, we'll start with you."

"Captain, why was the name Challenger selected for your starship?"

"That name was selected in honor of the seven astronauts who were killed in the explosion of the Space Shuttle Challenger on January 28, 1986. Patrick?"

"In view of all the hazards that you'll face, how do you rate your chance of success?"

"We will succeed! Michelle?"

"Captain, it seems to me that your survival for the next six years is dependent on this ship's waste recycling system. If it fails to function as expected, you could run out of oxygen to breathe, food to eat, or both. How large a safety margin has been built into the system? You have twenty-four people onboard. How many people could you put on this ship before the system becomes overloaded? And what about the microorganisms on which the operation of the system depends, how do you know they'll stay healthy for six years of interstellar space flight?"

Captain Jerontis smiled broadly at Michelle. "That sounds like more than one question."

Michelle returned the smile. "But they're all closely related questions concerning one of your ship's essential systems."

Captain Jerontis nodded in agreement and turned to Dianne, who said, "Our life support system has a safety margin of 35 to 40 percent. So we would have to add eight, nine, or ten people to our crew before we would be in danger of overloading the system and placing our survival in jeopardy. As to your other question, several predecessor versions of this life support system have been in use on our space stations and lunar and Mars bases for several decades. They have proven to be very reliable. However, during our long voyage, I will be using my genetic engineering skills and this ship's research lab to improve the microorganisms and plants on which our survival depends. Sam?"

"AEPF has charged that your presence on Alcent will pollute its pristine environment and that germs carried to Alcent by you will pose a serious threat to the life forms already living there. How do you plan to protect the life on Alcent from this life threatening danger?"

"When we arrive at Alcent, we'll orbit the planet at a low altitude, probably around 200 miles," replied Dianne. "After studying the planet for several weeks, we'll launch sterilized, unmanned landing craft to locations of interest. These landing craft will be complex remotely controlled research labs. With them, we'll study life on Alcent to determine if germs from Earth will be a threat to it. We'll thoroughly evaluate the risks before any of us land on Alcent."

"What if you find out that germs from Earth are a grave threat to life on Alcent?" Sam asked.

"Then, we'll have to find a solution to that problem before we can land," replied Dianne.

"Some environmentalist groups don't believe you can be trusted to be that environmentally responsible," argued Sam.

Dianne glared at Sam and coldly said, "The crew of this starship is a very responsible group, and we will do what is right."

"But AEPF does not trust you and claims that they will stop your mission," stated Sam. "What do you think of that?"

Before Dianne could respond, Captain Jerontis stared at Sam and bluntly said, "AEPF is not a reputable group; they are a radical extremist group, and our mission is not going to be governed by the agenda of a group of terrorists. If they've sabotaged my starship, we'll find that sabotage, and they will fail to stop our mission."

Sam appeared ready to argue the point, but before he could say anything, Captain Jerontis said, "This concludes our press conference. All of you except Michelle will be leaving our ship in three hours to spend the night on the personnel shuttle. Until then, Dianne and Connie will be your tour guides and will introduce you to available personnel for interviews. When you return in the morning, they will again be your guides. Michelle, your request to stay onboard until we depart has been granted. You will stay with the group until they leave the ship. After that, Connie will be your escort and share her quarters with you."

Except for Sam, members of the media thanked Captain Jerontis for his time. Then, he went to the flight deck to check the progress of events leading to departure.

Michelle turned to Dianne and said, "One area you haven't shown us is the hangar deck. I'd like to see the shuttles you'll use to travel to and from the surface when the Challenger is orbiting Alcent."

"Good idea," Dianne responded.

On the way to the hangar deck, Michelle said to Connie, "You are about to depart on a long perilous mission filled with uncertainty. However, when Patrick asked Captain Jerontis to rate your chance of achieving success, he declared, 'we will succeed!' Is this wishful thinking on his part, or is he really that sure of success?"

"He actually is 100 percent confident that we'll be successful."

"But you're attempting to do something that's never been done. How can he be so confident?"

"There's something that you must understand about Captain Jerontis, and that is that he approaches life with a very strong positive attitude. When he decides to do something, he just simply refuses to accept failure. He has more stick-to-it-tive-ness than anyone I've ever met. He just hangs in there and does whatever it takes to achieve his goals."

"But this is a huge complex starship that must function for the next seven years. Any number of things could go wrong."

"That's true, but Captain Jerontis has participated in the design, construction, and testing of this starship from the very beginning. He probably knows more about it than anyone. If he's confident in this starship, so am I."

Michelle thought about the firmness of Connie's comments. Then, she said, "I've talked to several crew members since my arrival, and all of them seem to be as confident in Captain Jerontis as you are. He seems to have the unquestioned loyalty of the crew. How has he won their loyalty?"

"Everyone knows that he's an expert on the intricate details of this ship and how everything works."

"There has to be more to it than that," argued Michelle. "I know many intelligent people, and some of them just don't inspire loyalty in anyone."

"You just mentioned the key word."

"Which word was that?"

"*Inspire*; Captain Jerontis inspires his crew to be confident in him."

"How does he do that?" Before Connie could respond, Michelle said, "Let me make this personal. How does he inspire you to be confident in his leadership?"

"More than anything else, I appreciate his leadership style. He is a strong leader, but he is gentle. He never criticizes anyone; he encourages them. Also, I respect his knowledge, and I like the confident, cheerful attitude that he always displays. Then, there is the seemly limitless energy that he always comes up with when he has a deadline to meet. Perhaps his energy comes from his attitude, determination, and physical strength. He does have a strong athletic build, being six feet three inches tall and 230 pounds. He is lean and muscular, and his energetic, youthful appearance seems to inspire people into thinking that he can do whatever is required."

Michelle noticed that Connie's face lit up when she was talking about Captain Jerontis. Being a professional reporter, she decided to investigate this, so she said, "That was a rather long-winded answer to my question. You seem to know a lot about your Captain."

Not expecting these comments and not prepared to respond to their implication, Connie thought about them for a few moments. Then, rather than respond to what was implied, she said, "I am the mission psychiatrist and medical doctor. I make it my business to know and understand everyone on this ship, especially the Captain."

Michelle sensed that there might be another reason for Connie's extensive knowledge about the Captain, but she decided not to pursue it, because she felt that she wasn't going to get any additional information. Michelle looked into Connie's eyes and smiled in a way that let her know she understood.

A few moments later, the group arrived on the hangar deck, and Michelle said to Dianne, "Those shuttles look like sleek high-speed aircraft. Can you tell me a little bit about them?"

While pointing at them, Dianne said, "The big one is a cargo carrier, and the small one is a personnel shuttle. Both shuttles have NTR propulsion systems that will allow us to travel between the surface of Alcent and the Challenger as many times as we need to without being concerned about running out of fuel."

"What is an NTR propulsion system?" Patrick asked.

"NTR means nuclear thermal rocket," replied Dianne.

Patrick appeared puzzled. "How does an NTR operate?" he asked.

"Its operation is quite simple. A working fluid such as liquefied air or ordinary water is pumped through the nuclear reactor's heat exchanger, where it is heated to a temperature of several thousand degrees. This converts the liquid into an extremely high pressure gas that expands out the rocket nozzle creating enough thrust to accelerate the shuttle to orbital speed and altitude."

"Why were NTRs selected to propel the shuttles rather than antimatter power plants?"

"Antimatter fuel is expensive to produce, and NTRs provide more than enough energy for travel between the surface of Alcent and the low altitude orbit the Challenger will be in. Also, NTRs are rugged, reliable power plants that are easy to operate. The technology involved is mature."

While members of the press asked Dianne additional questions about the shuttles, Captain Jerontis was on the flight deck talking to Mike. "How is our final checkout proceeding?" he asked.

"Very well," replied Mike. "The fact that we're not finding any problems shows just how well-designed this ship is."

"Not only that, but everything has been tested and retested so many times that all problems should've been found and corrected long ago."

"We should be ready to test fire our engines in about three hours, but right now, we've reached a 45-minute break in the checkout schedule."

"Good, let's go to the engineering library. There's someone there I'd like you to meet."

Two minutes later, in the engineering library, Captain Jerontis said, "Mike, meet your replacement, John Moosebeck. He's been glued to the computer since accepting the position and is rapidly becoming an expert on the intricate details of this ship. Right, Moose?"

Moose answered Jerry's question by nodding his head and looking at him with the tired eyes of one who had been involved in hours of intensive study. Moose shook Mike's hand and said, "Pleased to meet you."

"So I finally get to meet the boisterous, flamboyant Moose I've heard so much about," Mike said. Turning to Captain Jerontis, he asked, "How did you manage to motivate the bureaucrats at NIEA Command to allow you to replace me with your life-long friend?"

Seeing the gleam in Captain J.J.'s eyes and the mischievous grin on his face, Mike said, "Never mind. Forget that I asked that question; I really don't want to know."

Turning his attention back to Moose, Mike said, "Attempting to learn the intricate details of this ship in just a few days is a rather tall order. Is there anything I can help you with?"

"So far, I've limited my study to the most crucial systems. I've been looking at propulsion, flight control, and life support; and they aren't much different than on the Goliath, just a bit more advanced. Maybe sometime tomorrow, you could brief me on any peculiarities that you think I should know about."

"Tomorrow's checkout schedule has a two-hour break at lunch time, and that would be the best time for me."

Turning to Captain Jerontis, Mike said, "I am curious to know what clandestine plan you've devised for getting me off this ship and back to Earth without arousing anyone's suspicions."

"The Captain of the personnel shuttle that brought the media up is a friend of mine. Tomorrow, I'll give him a tour of the Challenger and tell him there's been a personnel change and that he is to give you a ride down to Earth. There's no reason for him to be suspicious, and even if he were, I doubt that he'd question NIEA Command about it.

"On another subject, a really sharp-looking reporter named Michelle has requested an interview with our chief engineer. Maybe you could talk with her this evening."

Mike grinned and said, "I don't know if I want to be talking to a good-looking woman when I'm trying to get this ship ready for departure. That might be too big a distraction. Just how beautiful is she anyway?"

Jerry smiled while recalling Michelle's features, "She has an attractive figure, a beautiful face, sandy-brown hair, and a light tan. She's about five-seven, maybe five-eight and probably weighs around 130 pounds."

Noticing that Jerry appeared to be breathing a little faster, Mike said, "It seems that she had quite an effect on you. From your description, it sounds like you took a pretty good look at her."

"She definitely got my attention."

"Well, if she's as outstanding as you say she is, I guess I could find a little time to talk to her."

Acting as though he would be doing Mike a big favor, Jerry said, "If it's going to put too much of a strain on your schedule, I'll tell her that you're busy and handle the interview myself. Depending on how it goes, I might even figure out a way to make her part of the crew."

"That's okay," Mike quickly replied. "I'll talk to her. After all, she did ask for the chief engineer, and I haven't yet been replaced."

Moose grinned at Mike and said, "I heard she has a knack for asking tough questions. I hope she doesn't hit you with something that you're not prepared for. Maybe I should take the interview."

"Thanks for the offer, but I'm sure I can handle it."

Four hours later, all primary propulsion rockets had been throttled up to 65 percent of full power for 15 seconds and then, throttled back down and shut off. Mike, Moose, and Jerry were intently poring over the performance data. The first one to say anything was Mike, "I see no anomalies here. In fact, I don't see how this test run could've been any better. Other than slightly increasing our speed and raising our orbit a bit, not much else happened."

Jerry and Moose agreed, and Mike said, "Since this concludes today's checkout, it's time for me to look up a reporter named Michelle."

Before Mike could depart, Captain Jerontis stopped him and said, "Remember, as far as the press is concerned, and anyone else for that matter, you are the chief engineer for this mission."

Mike nodded and left.

"I haven't eaten in hours," stated Moose, "and I feel like devouring a large combination pizza with extra pepperoni and cheese."

"Do you ever eat anything besides pizza?" Jerry asked, while on the way to the cafeteria.

"Of course I do, but pizza just happens to be my favorite food."

"I would never have guessed that."

A little later, when Moose and Jerry were well into their meal, Moose said, "You sure have excellent food on this ship."

"Yes, we do. We're fortunate to have a chef who is blessed with an intuitive ability in the kitchen. What amazes me is that he does this with the basic ingredients and flavorings produced by our food synthesizers."

"You're lucky that someone with so much talent survived the strenuous training required of people for this mission."

"Actually, he didn't. He is the only person on this mission who didn't do all that well in survival training. However, because of his culinary abilities, NIEA allowed him on the mission anyway, since they consider excellent dining essential to crew morale on a voyage of this length."

"I agree. Good food is a bright spot in anyone's day. But now that I'm here, he isn't the only creative cook."

"What do you mean?"

"Have you forgotten all the good meals you've eaten at my house?"

"No, I haven't, and I'll have to admit that you do know your way around the kitchen. But right now, I'm more in need of a chief engineer than another chef."

"Once we get underway, the engineering workload might not be all that demanding. If that's the case, I wouldn't mind helping out in the kitchen. Your chef can't work around the clock, and he might like some time off now and then."

"True, let's keep that in mind."

"On another subject, are you worried about anything in tomorrow's checkout schedule?"

"Not really. We actually have a fairly light schedule. Our checkout procedures resume at 8:30 AM with a two-hour break at 11:30. If no problems are encountered, checkout will be completed at 4:30 PM. The most crucial event is the full power engine test at 3:30, but I don't anticipate any problems. Our engines are just enhanced versions of the power plants you have on the Goliath, and they've been frequently operated at full power for nine years now. At 1:30 PM the next day, there will be a presidential farewell address, followed by our departure at 2:00 PM. Now that you're part of the mission, are you worried about anything?"

Moose leaned back, briefly pondered the question and said, "Twenty years ago, you and I were part of a football team that won back-to-back national championships. As I see it, our current situation is quite similar. If you can provide the same inspirational leadership now as you did twenty years ago, we should all end up dying of old age on Alcent."

"Now that my all-time favorite fullback is on the team, my job will certainly be easier. When Mike hit me with a replacement request, it threw me for a loop. The backup engineer is a very capable individual, but for some reason, I'm not comfortable working with him. I don't think that he and I would ever have been a smoothly functioning team, and in a time-critical crisis, smooth teamwork is essential."

"That has always been true for us. When we were playing college football twenty years ago, we instinctively worked together. It seemed like we were almost able to sense what each other was thinking."

"Twenty years is a long time, but talking about football brings back fond memories that are so clear, it seems like they happened only yesterday. Have you ever considered that we could be comfortably retired by now if we'd gone into professional football instead of into space? Think about it, we could be having a relatively risk-free life on Earth; instead, we are about to embark on a mission we may not survive."

"We all have choices to make. I believe an individual's state of well-being at any point in his life is the direct result of all the choices that individual made up to that point in his life. Rather than play professional football, I chose to go into space because I enjoy the adventure of it. Facing and conquering the unexpected hazards one sometimes finds in an adventure into the unknown gives me an emotional high like none other. Knowing me as well as you do, you had to know what my decision would be when you gave me the opportunity to go to Alcent with you."

"I was pretty sure you'd accept. After all, my offer to you was just one more unexpected challenge for you to conquer."

"It was definitely unexpected. You dropped it on me right out of nowhere, and it's definitely a big challenge." Moose checked the clock and said, "It's time for me to go back to the engineering library. There are some systems I want to look at before I turn in for the night."

"I'm going to my quarters to call my parents. I can't see them in person before we leave, but the video phone in my quarters has a screen covering one entire wall. A phone call to my parents is almost like being at home with them. I'm also going to call my brother and sister."

"Say hello to them for me," requested Moose, as he headed for the engineering library.

"Will do, see you in the morning."

Mike and Michelle entered the cafeteria just as Moose and Jerry were leaving. Mike introduced Michelle to Moose. After exchanging greetings, Mike and Michelle picked up menus and considered what to order.

"Can we order food to go and eat on the observation deck?" Michelle asked. "Viewing the Universe from above Earth's atmosphere is rather spectacular. It might even be romantic."

Mike assessed Michelle from head to foot. He smiled at her affectionately and said, "I have no objection to eating in such a setting with a beautiful woman."

"Thank you. You have a nice way with words."

A short time later on the observation deck, Mike explained to Michelle, "Here in space, it's easy to become disoriented, especially in the zero gravity situation that we're now in, so let me tell you where we are. To start with, our current orbital position places us directly between Earth and Moon with the Sun at our backs. We can't see the Sun because the shields are in place to protect us from solar radiation and to keep the observation deck in darkness. To our left is Earth with the face that we see half in daylight and half in darkness. The longitudinal axis of the Challenger is currently in upright alignment with Earth's axis of rotation, so that when you look at Earth, the North Pole is at the top. To our right is the Moon, also showing a face that is half in daylight and half in darkness. That brilliant yellow star over there is Alpha Centauri A, and the bright orange star next to it is Alpha Centauri B."

Michelle silently stared into the heavens. She was enchanted by the stunning beauty of the multitude of stars shining in brilliant contrast to the stark blackness of space.

Meanwhile, Mike stared at Michelle. She was enchanting.

After a couple minutes, Michelle's eyes wandered back to home planet.

"Earth looks so tiny from up here," she said. "It really doesn't appear much larger than the Moon."

"We are considerably closer to the Moon than to Earth," Mike said. "In round numbers, we are a little more than 125,000 miles from Earth and somewhat less than 105,000 miles from the Moon."

"When I see Earth suspended against the background of infinite space, it seems so small and fragile. It's hard to believe that it's teeming with life locked in competition for finite living space."

"I get the feeling that you've gained an entirely new perspective in regard to our place in the Universe," noted Mike.

"This is my first trip into space, and viewing Earth and the Cosmos from here makes me feel like I'm a small insignificant part of it."

"That's a fairly normal reaction. I've experienced those feelings more than once. But however inconsequential you may be feeling at the moment, you've become the most important part of my universe."

Mike's words caused Michelle to glow with happiness. After a few moments, she said, "As a science reporter, I've written numerous articles on astronomy, and I've always known that even on a clear dark night, observing the heavens through Earth's atmosphere greatly limits what you can see. But until now, I didn't realize how much beauty is obscured by the atmosphere. For the first time in my life, I'm able to appreciate the vastness of space and truly enjoy its magnificent beauty. The stars are so numerous, it seems like I can see millions of them, and they're so brilliant, sharp, and colorful that I feel like I'm peering into a galactic treasure chest filled with colorful jewelry. And to top it all off, Star Voyager data gives us good reason to believe that there might be an abundance of life out there, making the galactic treasure chest even more precious."

Michelle stopped talking when she felt Mike's arms encircle her from behind. She turned within his arms, so she could face him. In the soft romantic glow of light from the heavens, Mike noted that Michelle's natural beauty took on an almost angelic appearance. He responded by giving her a long tender kiss. He felt an involuntary tremble in Michelle as she responded. With a supreme effort, Mike managed to gain control over his rapidly growing desire, and he said, "Before we get too carried away with this, I think you should tell me your decision in regard to what we've been planning."

"The way I feel right now, I really don't have any choice but to do what you're asking me to do."

Mike kissed her again and softly whispered, "That's what I was hoping you'd say. Now, I need to explain to you what we must do to achieve our objective. Let's go to my quarters, where there won't be any risk of being overheard."

PRESIDENTIAL FAREWELL ADDRESS

Forty hours later, the Challenger and her human occupants were ready to go. All checkout procedures had been completed. The Goliath and personnel shuttle had undocked and moved away to a safe distance.

The security team that had guarded the Challenger during its construction was onboard the personnel shuttle for a ride back to Earth. Its job was now finished because the only people on the Challenger were its personnel, and access to the starship was no longer available.

Before the shuttle could return to Earth, the news team had to cover the starship's departure. TV coverage would be provided by the SNS crew.

With engine ignition less than a half-hour away, the Challenger's personnel had said final goodbyes to friends and relatives in preparation for permanent departure from Earth. All were facing TV screens awaiting the presidential farewell address, which was expected momentarily.

Appearing on TV, the presidential press secretary said, "Ladies and gentlemen, the President of the United States."

The press secretary's image was replaced by that of the president, who said, "Today is truly an epochal occasion as we are about to witness the birth of a new era in human history, the beginning of interstellar expansion. People have dreamed about interstellar travel for centuries, and that dream is about to be realized with the Challenger mission to the Alpha Centauri System. This mission illustrates that what can be conceived by the imaginative human mind can be achieved by free men and women working together when not held in check by a lack of resources or by a stifling political system. Captain Jerontis, we are proud to send you and your personnel, the finest men and women that America has to offer, on this historical mission. Establishing a new civilization is a big responsibility, and I urge all of you to study our history, learn from our mistakes, and not repeat them on Alcent. I urge you to learn from our greatest successes and carry these into your new civilization. Make it a great one that we can all be proud of. Our prayers are with you. Captain Jerontis, you and your crew are ultimate achievers. If you were to leave an inspirational thought with our nation's youth on how to be successful, what would it be?"

"Mr. President, before I do that, I would like to express my sincere thanks and appreciation to all Americans whose hard work, dedication, and sacrifice made this mission possible. I especially want to thank the American taxpayers for funding it.

"To our youth, I will simply say that your freedom makes you responsible for your future well-being. Each day, when you get out of bed in the morning, simply say to yourself: My future depends on the choices that I make today, and then, think about it.

"This simple concept was responsible for turning around the life of a close friend of mine. During his first eight years in school, he was disruptive and rebellious. He studied very little. He was well on his way to becoming an illiterate street thug. When he entered the ninth grade, his science teacher had a fairly large sign on his desk that faced the class. The sign said, MY FUTURE DEPENDS ON THE CHOICES THAT I MAKE TODAY. At first, this simple message didn't mean much to my friend, but as the school year progressed, it started to have a profound effect on his daily activities. Instead of hanging out with the local street gang, he started doing his homework. After a while, he chose to go a step further and spend some time in the school library researching subjects of interest to him. Anyway, he went on to attend a university, where he earned an advanced engineering degree and became a sports hero."

"I like that message," stated the President. "If your new society is based on that simple concept, it should get off to a very good start. In fact, I like that message so much that I think it should be prominently displayed in all of our classrooms and offices. Too many of us forget that freedom of choice is a potent double-edged sword loaded with personal responsibility, and making the right choices in daily life is a personal responsibility. May you and your personnel always make the right choices."

"Thank you, Mr. President."

Captain Jerontis turned to his flight crew and gave the order to start the fifteen-minute countdown. A few minutes later, Connie appeared and handed him a note that said, "All personnel are at their stations."

Jerry made eye contact with Connie and said, "Thank you!"

Shortly thereafter, the warning klaxon blared out its urgent sounding notes indicating that ignition was only three minutes away. A flood of excitement filled Jerry's mind and body with the full realization that twenty years of hard work was rapidly coming down to a climactic moment. With a fresh flow of adrenaline, Jerry's pulse increased, and his mind raced through a series of thoughts: I am leaving Earth, and I will never return. Will I ever regret this? Will our voyage be a safe one? Has the Challenger been sabotaged in a way that has escaped our detection? What challenges will we encounter on Alcent? Will I always make the right choices? I will certainly try. Am I going to miss Earth? Will I miss my family and friends? Of course I will, but I can deal with that."

As the countdown entered the final minute, Jerry hoped that once they had ignition and were underway, his adrenaline flow would get back to normal. Meanwhile, his excited mind continued to race through thoughts of the past and aspirations for the future. Then, the final seconds ticked by: 9 - 8 - 7 - 6 - 5 - 4 - 3 - 2 - 1 - **IGNITION!**

TWO

Sabotage

TIME: 24 Hours ALE. (After Leaving Earth)

While relaxing in his quarters, Captain Jerontis made the following entry into his log: "It is one day after ignition, and the Challenger's antimatter engines have performed flawlessly, giving us a continuous acceleration of 1g. We are 20 million miles from Earth traveling at 527 miles per second. Earth now looks like an exceptionally bright star."

After completing his log entry, Jerry turned to planning his activities and those of his crew. But his thoughts were interrupted by a call from NIEA Command: "Captain Jerontis! We have a serious problem here. When the Goliath arrived at our main orbital base without its Captain, we conducted an inquiry to find out why. The Goliath's pilot explained to us that there had been a last minute personnel change on the Challenger with Captain John Moosebeck assigned to it as Chief Engineer replacing Mike Johnson. We have two problems with this. First of all, we want to know the reason for the change and who authorized it."

"The reason for the change is quite simple. Mike said that he did not want to leave Earth and requested that he be replaced. John Moosebeck is eminently qualified for the position and was immediately available, so I authorized the change."

"But you did not follow regulations. As you know, NIEA has very stringent rules to follow in regard to who is on this mission. You should be disciplined for ignoring the rules."

"I understand the rules. But now that we've left Earth, the success of this mission is my responsibility. John Moosebeck is a very competent engineer with a distinguished service record. He and I work well together, and I am confident that he will do an excellent job.

"Also, I had Doctor Nemard check his medical and genetic background, and she was unable to find any problems of consequence. I believe that I acted in a responsible way. But if you think disciplinary procedures against me are in order, I would suggest that you punish me by canceling my paychecks for the next 30 years or so."

"That's absurd! You're no longer getting paid anyway."

Captain Jerontis leaned back in his seat and smiled in a way that displayed an air of smug satisfaction. "You said that you have two problems with my personnel change. What is the other one?"

"We need to talk to Mike Johnson about his reasons for leaving the mission, but we can't find him. What did you do with him?"

"I asked the Captain of the personnel shuttle to give him a ride back to Earth. Since he's been in space for six weeks working on this ship, I assume he's taking some time off before reporting back to work."

"Time off is okay, but he should've reported in beforehand."

TIME: 48 Hours, 31 Minutes ALE.

Captain's Log Entry: "Our velocity is 1,056 miles per second, and we have traveled 93 million miles, the average distance between Earth and Sun. Earth now looks like just an ordinary bright star."

Captain Jerontis and Moose were reviewing data from the propulsion and navigation systems when they were interrupted by a call from NIEA Command: "Captain Jerontis! We have some disturbing news from an undercover FBI agent attending a national council meeting of AEPF. Council officials said that the end of the ill-fated Challenger mission of a century ago would look like an exploding firecracker compared to the demise of the current Challenger mission. This announcement is ominous because it wasn't made to the press for gaining publicity; it was made at a closed, delegates-only meeting. If we take AEPF seriously, we have to conclude that they intend to explode your antimatter fuel."

"How are they going to do that?"

"The obvious way would be to disrupt the magnetic field in one of the antimatter containment tanks," stated Moose. "The resulting matter-antimatter explosion would certainly make the Challenger accident of a century ago look like an exploding firecracker. A computer virus planted in the field control computers could cause a catastrophic malfunction."

"That's possible, but it would be very difficult to do," argued Captain Jerontis. "To start with, it's a triple redundant system. The virus would have to simultaneously shut down three different computers. If a saboteur makes that happen, there is still the backup system that must be overcome, and it's very simple, consisting of a magnetometer connected to a switch. If the magnetometer detects a dangerous degradation in magnetic field strength, it instantaneously turns on a backup magnetic containment field that can only be turned off by restoring the primary magnetic field. By its simplicity, this system is nearly 100 percent reliable."

"That's all true," acknowledged Moose, "but I believe a determined saboteur, who is a computer expert, could pull it off."

"A cleverly concealed computer virus would be difficult and time consuming to find," stated Captain Jerontis, "and I don't believe we have that much time. I think our best strategy is to block that kind of sabotage by making sure that our backup system has not been tampered with."

"I'll do an immediate inspection," stated Moose, as he left in a hurry.

"I don't think we should rule out the possibility of a bomb," declared NIEA Command.

"With the tight security procedures that have been in effect, I don't see how anyone could've transported a bomb to this ship," Jerry said.

"That's true, but your ship's maintenance shop has some very sophisticated plastics manufacturing equipment in it. With the chemicals and other raw materials that you have onboard, an effective bomb containing plastic explosives could've been made in your shop. By planting it in a critical area, devastating results could easily be achieved."

"If we had some bomb detection equipment onboard, it would sure make searching for a bomb quicker and easier."

"We are already working on that problem. Since we know what kind of chemicals and materials you have onboard, we can determine the kinds of explosives that could be made in your shop. We are designing a detection device you can build in your shop that will be capable of finding these kinds of explosives. This design will be transmitted to you within the hour. In the meantime, you should begin a search of critical areas where even a small bomb could do devastating damage. A plan for a methodical search is being transmitted into your main computer.

"Incidentally, we still haven't located Mike Johnson. If your ship has been sabotaged, his last minute request to leave the mission, along with his disappearance, certainly makes him a prime suspect. Also, no one would be better qualified to sabotage a starship than its chief engineer."

"I've worked with Mike for many years," retorted Captain Jerontis. "I know him very well. I simply cannot believe that he would sabotage this ship. Surely, you must have other suspects."

"Security is considering other possibilities, but you must keep in mind that some of the best saboteurs in history achieved their success by appearing innocent and trustworthy. Therefore, we've initiated an all out effort to find Mike, so we can talk to him. I am signing off for now. You have urgent work to do."

Captain Jerontis quickly assembled all available personnel, explained the situation, and organized them into bomb search teams. In addition, he instructed them to look for anything out of the ordinary that might indicate how the ship had been sabotaged.

Captain Jerontis then turned to the pilot and said, "I want the antimatter engines shut down and the fuel lines emptied."

"Yes sir," replied the pilot, as he started the shutdown procedure.

Captain Jerontis sounded several notes on the warning klaxon to get the attention of all personnel. Then, he addressed them through the ship's intercom. First, he explained the bomb threat for the benefit of individuals not already working on the bomb search teams. Then, he said, "During the next few minutes, we're going to shut off all propulsive

31

power. Prepare for weightlessness. It will continue until we've resolved the bomb threat."

Jerry had two reasons for shutting down the antimatter engines. To start with, the antimatter fuel lines were more readily accessible than the antimatter storage tanks, and therefore, an easier place to plant a bomb. A bomb that could rupture a fuel line would also disrupt the magnetic containment field in the fuel line. This would allow the antimatter in the fuel line to contact ordinary matter resulting in mutual annihilation and catastrophic energy release. This would wreck the nearest antimatter fuel tank causing an explosion powerful enough to detonate all remaining antimatter, resulting in instantaneous incineration of the entire starship. Even at this great distance, the flash from the explosion would be bright enough to be seen in the night sky back on Earth, quite adequately fulfilling the pronouncement made at the AEPF meeting. However, if the fuel line contained no antimatter, then the bomb would only damage the fuel line, which could easily be repaired or replaced.

Jerry's other reason for shutting off propulsive power was to put the ship in a weightless condition. If a bomb were detonated near a load bearing structure, the ship would be far less susceptible to catastrophic failure than if it were under acceleration. A severe structural failure could also lead to the detonation of the antimatter fuel.

Jerry considered the ship's structure and compiled a list of areas where a bomb blast would have the most serious consequences. Further consideration in terms of accessibility allowed him to narrow down and prioritize the list.

Then, Jerry considered some other possibilities. Was there anyone on the personnel shuttle or on the Goliath with the capability to make plastic explosives and assemble a bomb with the equipment in the maintenance shop? If so, could this person have done this without being detected? Then, could this individual have put on a space suit, gone outside, and attached the bomb to the hull close to an antimatter fuel tank without being detected? Not likely, but possible, Jerry concluded.

The Challenger's inventory of maintenance equipment included two external repair vehicles (ERVs) for going outside the ship. These ERVs were equipped with sensors and manipulator arms and could operate under computer control. Alternatively, they could be occupied and controlled by a one or two person crew, or they could be manually controlled from inside the starship. Since computer software was already in place for these ERVs to do a meticulous inspection of the ship's exterior, Captain Jerontis decided to dispatch them on this mission. Any bomb attached to the ship's exterior would show up as a deviation from specifications and be detected by the ERVs.

TIME: 72 Hours ALE.

Captain's Log Entry: "Our speed is 1,085 miles per second and we've traveled 185 million miles, approximately the diameter of Earth's orbit around the Sun. Our antimatter engines have not been restarted.

"Moose has verified that the final backup system to establish magnetic containment fields for the antimatter fuel tanks is fully functional. Our visual bomb search of critical areas has found nothing. The ERVs have finished inspecting the starship's exterior and have found only a few miniature craters caused by collisions with space dust.

"Moose and two assistants are in the machine shop finishing the assembly of a bomb detector. Because of the urgent nature of the project, the design has been kept simple to allow for the use of off-the-shelf components. Even though crude, the device will be sensitive enough to detect the infinitesimal amounts of vapors and particles given off by explosives. A small quantity of plastic explosive is being made to test the detector's capability."

Comfortably seated at the command console, Captain Jerontis was deeply lost in thought, attempting to recall events of recent months in minute detail. He mentally searched for clues as to how his ship may have been put at grave risk. His thoughts were interrupted by the arrival of Dianne Dawson.

Captain Jerontis looked at her and she said, "You asked us to report anything out of the ordinary. I don't know how significant this is, but the composition of our air isn't quite what it should be. The oxygen percentage is slightly lower than normal, and the carbon dioxide level is a little higher than normal. Our environmental control equipment is correcting for the imbalance, but it's operating at a level somewhat higher than it should be."

"Could this small aberration be the result of the increased level of activity on this ship?"

"I've considered that possibility, and I still come to the conclusion that we're consuming more oxygen and generating more carbon dioxide than we should be."

"Do you have any explanation for this?"

"No, but I think I should try to find the cause."

"I agree, and while you're doing that, I want you to also think about the possible ways that a saboteur could either wreck our life support systems or use them against us. For example, could toxic agents be released into these systems in sufficient quantities to be lethal to everyone onboard? For each sabotage technique that you think of, I want you to propose a course of preventive action. Perhaps Doctor Nemard could work with you on this project."

"I'll ask her, and we'll report back to you shortly."

TIME: 75 Hours, 30 Minutes ALE.

Captain Jerontis arrived in the machine shop to observe the first test of the new bomb detector. Moose greeted him and said, "Two hours ago, we placed two ounces of plastic explosive inside that instrument cabinet. If this bomb detector works as advertised, it should easily detect the explosive. All we should have to do is open the small access panel in the back and insert this sensor probe."

"Let's do it," stated Captain Jerontis, as he picked up a screwdriver and opened the access panel.

With the bomb detector's sensor probe in hand, Moose reached toward the open panel. Before he could place the probe inside the cabinet, the red light on top the detector started flashing, the detector started chirping, and the digital readout indicated strong signal strength.

"Wow! That thing is sensitive," exclaimed Captain Jerontis. "If a methodical search of the ship with this detector fails to find a bomb, then I think we can confidently assume that there's no bomb onboard."

"If there's a bomb onboard, we'll find it," declared Moose.

"If we have enough time," commented Captain Jerontis. "Here is a copy of the revised search plan. I suggest you get started immediately. Also, you should periodically test the detector against the plastic explosive you made, just to make sure that it continues to function properly."

TIME: 76 Hours, 15 Minutes ALE.

Captain Jerontis went to the life support lab to consult with Dianne and Connie. After greeting him, Dianne said, "We've examined the difficulties that a saboteur would face in an attempt to use our ventilation system to disperse a poisonous gas or other lethal agent throughout the ship. As you know, the system is equipped with sensitive instruments in key locations to detect the presence of toxins. The area in which the poison is detected is immediately closed off and isolated from the rest of the system until the substance is removed. These safeguards were built in as protection against a localized fire or chemical accident.

"For a saboteur to kill everyone on this ship, he would have to plant a toxic agent in a ventilation shaft and time its release with a shutoff of the isolation equipment. To defeat this kind of attack, we've programmed a backup computer to shut down the entire system if a toxic substance is detected or if any of the sensing instrumentation malfunctions. Also, an alert will be sounded advising all personnel to put on oxygen masks."

"Let's conduct a simple test to make sure everything is working," suggested Captain Jerontis.

"What do you have in mind?" questioned Doctor Nemard.

"Actually, a two-part test; first, we spill a foreign substance, such as ammonia, into the system and see if it does what it's supposed to do. Then, we simulate a malfunction by disconnecting one of the sensors."

"I don't have any ammonia handy," responded Dianne, "but I have some other chemicals that should work just as well."

"Good," stated Captain Jerontis, as he sounded a few notes on the warning klaxon and spoke into the intercom explaining the tests that were about to be conducted.

A short time later, after completing the tests, Captain Jerontis said, "I am satisfied that the system is working well. But to play it safe, we should search the interior of the system for a canister of toxins coupled to a release trigger. For toxins to reach the entire ship, a chemical or biological bomb would have to be planted in the central duct before it starts to branch out. Such a bomb could be rigged to go off if tampered with, so for self-protection, I'll wear my space suit while I conduct the search. Doctor Nemard, I want you to monitor my progress from outside the area. Also, we'll turn off the air circulation and isolate the area."

"While you two are doing that, I'll take another look at the problem of using more oxygen than we should be," stated Dianne.

After putting on his space suit and sealing himself in the central ventilation room, Captain Jerontis opened an access panel to the primary ventilation duct and placed a small remotely controlled inspection vehicle inside it. As he moved the vehicle down the duct, he used its video cameras and sensors to search for suspicious objects. After searching the central part of the system and finding nothing, Jerry closed the access panel, but he left the remotely controlled vehicle inside. He took off his space suit, and said, "I'm satisfied that this part of the ventilation system is clean, but I'm going to have someone search the entire system."

Dianne and Connie nodded in agreement. Then, Dianne said, "In regard to the oxygen/carbon dioxide imbalance, we are consuming seven to nine percent more oxygen than we should be. It's almost as if we have twenty-six people onboard instead of twenty-four."

"Supposedly, everyone not going on this voyage left the ship with the departure of the Goliath and the personnel shuttle," stated Captain Jerontis. "If there are any extra individuals onboard, we should've discovered them during our preliminary bomb search."

"What if they're determined to stay hidden?" Connie asked.

"This is a large ship, so I suppose that's possible. But what prompted you to ask that question?"

"Something we haven't talked about is the possibility that one or two terrorists on a suicide mission might be stowed away on this ship, patiently waiting for an opportunity to strike."

Silence filled the room as Jerry thought about Connie's suggestion. After a few moments, he said, "It just doesn't seem very likely that we have terrorists onboard. Security was extremely tight during those final months of checkout. But under the present circumstances, all possibilities must be investigated, so I'll report this to NIEA Command and ask them to locate everyone who had access to this ship in recent months. Also, I'll get someone to tell everyone on this ship to be alert for terrorists. I don't want to use the intercom for this, because if there are terrorists onboard, I don't want to let them know that we're looking for them. Getting back to life support, we've taken steps to protect our air, but what about the possibility of toxins being released into our food or water?"

"That is the object of our next investigation," responded Dianne.

TIME: 78 Hours, 30 Minutes ALE.

Captain Jerontis returned to the command console to converse with NIEA Command. Normal conversation, however, was becoming increasingly difficult because of the Challenger's great distance from Earth. A radio message traveling at the speed of light now took nearly 19 minutes to reach Earth, which was 210 million miles away. Captain Jerontis transmitted his report and waited 38 minutes for a response.

TIME: 79 Hours, 8 Minutes ALE.

"Captain Jerontis! This is NIEA Command. We've started the investigation you requested, but one thing I can already tell you is that we still haven't located Mike Johnson. The Captain of the personnel shuttle, and several other people, saw him board the shuttle. However, no one recalls seeing him during its descent to Earth. Also, he was not seen getting off the shuttle when it arrived at the spaceport terminal. We think everyone on the shuttle was so preoccupied with your departure that Mike was able to quietly slip off the shuttle unnoticed by anyone and sneak back onto your starship. If this is what he did, we have no explanation for it.

"On another matter, the FBI has arrested the top officials of AEPF for questioning. In an attempt to discover if and how your starship has been sabotaged, these officials will be subjected to brain wave analysis while undergoing intensive interrogation. Under normal circumstances, this would be a violation of their civil rights and would not be allowed, but the President declared an emergency and issued an executive order that it be done. The WWCLU (World Wide Civil Liberties Union) will have a field day challenging this in court. As you know, they have a long history of being more concerned with protecting the rights of criminals than with protecting the rights of their victims. Hopefully, the FBI will be able to ferret out some specific information for you.

"On a lighter subject, a source at SNS has informed us that TV viewers have sent Sam a total of 139,455 books on human anatomy, most of which explain in explicit detail how human reproduction works and how it is dependent on normal sexual activity. Needless to say, Sam is infuriated by this huge response to the comments made by Doctor Nemard during your press conference. Since Sam has always been a nagging antagonist toward us, I thought you might find some humor in the embarrassing situation he now finds himself in. You could probably use a good laugh right about now. This concludes our transmission."

A smile of satisfaction filled Captain J.J.'s face as he visualized the avalanche of books that had descended on Sam at his SNS office. Leaning back in his seat, Jerry closed his eyes, and mulled over the contents of the message just received. He was pleased with the drastic action ordered by the President and hoped that the FBI would do whatever it needed to do to get the information he needed to save his ship and crew from destruction.

Captain J.J.'s thoughts shifted to Mike. Is it true that he's onboard as a stowaway? That would partly explain our extra oxygen consumption. Is it possible that I also have a terrorist onboard? If so, that would fully account for the oxygen/carbon dioxide problem.

As Captain Jerontis thought about the situation, one question kept coming up: was there anything peculiar about Mike's behavior during the last few days before departure? Jerry dropped ever more deeply into thought as he focused his mind on that question. After two minutes of being oblivious to his surroundings, it came to him. Although Mike kept it well hidden, he seemed to display a subtle mood of sadness. His mood suddenly changed for the better when I told him that a reporter named Michelle wanted to see him. Also, they did seem overly comfortable with each other, as if they had known each other for quite some time.

Mike's distant mood could've been the result of having to make a choice between going on an interstellar voyage that had been his dream for many years and staying on Earth with the woman he loved. Is it possible that Mike figured out a way to stay on the mission and bring Michelle along? This possibility brought a smile to Jerry's face.

Jerry was abruptly jarred out of his trance-like mental state by Doctor Nemard who said, "What are you so happy about? This is the first time I've seen you smile in days."

"How long have you been standing there?"

"I arrived a couple minutes ago. I saw you deeply lost in thought and decided not to interrupt. Anyway, what are you smiling about?"

"Two things: first, I think I've figured out why Mike put in his replacement request, and I think I know where he is. Second, the last part of the message from NIEA Command gave me something to laugh about. Old pain-in-the-butt Sam has received 139,455 books explaining how human reproduction works and how it is dependent on normal sexual activity. He is infuriated and blames you for this."

Connie laughed smugly. "I guess I got to him pretty good, and that makes my day. Anyway, what about Mike?"

Captain Jerontis shared his thoughts with Connie, who said, "Your conclusion seems valid and offers a good explanation for Mike's behavior, as well as, the oxygen/carbon dioxide problem. Michelle just might be onboard with Mike. At the press conference, she asked questions appropriate for someone who was trying to decide if she wanted to be on this mission. First, she tried to get into your mind by trying to discover your deepest feelings regarding this mission. Then, she became interested in our life support systems, in particular, how many people could they support before being overloaded. After the press conference, she asked me the questions that she needed answers to in order to assure herself that we'll be successful. It appears that sometime after that, she agreed to whatever plan Mike had devised to bring her along."

"That would explain why Mike was in such an elated frame of mind the day after the press conference," commented Jerry.

"I like Michelle and Mike. I hope they are onboard. Where do you think they might be hiding?"

"We've been underway for several days, and there's only one place where they could be comfortable this long and have a good chance of not being seen, and that's inside one of the shuttles down on the hangar deck. Why don't we go down there and welcome them to the mission. Besides, I could use Mike's help investigating the possible sabotage of this ship."

Connie hesitated for a few moments, as if lost in thought. Then, her cheerful mood was replaced by a look of worried concern, and she asked, "What if we're wrong, and instead of Mike and Michelle, we find some armed terrorists comfortably living in one of the shuttles?"

"That's possible, but what led you to ask that question?"

"If Mike is down there, he would've come out of hiding by now to help us with the bomb search; whereas, terrorists would stay hidden."

"Mike might not know that we're conducting a bomb search."

"But you announced the bomb search on the intercom."

"That's true, but the intercom does not have speakers inside the shuttles. Both the warning klaxon and intercom come through speakers on the hangar deck, but if Mike and Michelle were sound asleep inside either shuttle, they would not have heard me. Those shuttles have thick hulls that are well insulated. Very little sound passes through them."

"But we've been weightless for more than 30 hours. It seems like that would've attracted Mike's attention. It seems like his curiosity would've caused him to investigate this."

"If he thought that we were in critical danger, he would have. However, there are many non-critical reasons that could lead to shutting down the engines for a day or two."

"So you're not the least bit concerned that we might find armed terrorists hiding in one of the shuttles?"

"I'm not trying to say that. I'm only saying that it's possible that Mike and Michelle could be hiding in one of the shuttles and not know anything about our current situation."

"I hope you're right. I haven't known Michelle very long, but I like her. I hope she and Mike are with us."

"I believe we're going to find them in one of the shuttles, but in case I'm wrong, we'd better take some weapons with us and be on guard."

Captain Jerontis also issued weapons to three crew members with security training and took them along. When they arrived at the hangar deck, he said to Connie, "Since you're the only doctor we have, I want you to stay safely out of sight until we find out if this area is safe."

After searching the personnel shuttle and finding no one, Captain J.J. quietly entered the cargo shuttle and went to the flight deck, where he spotted a skirt that he recognized as the one Michelle had worn at the press conference. Quietly, he approached the hatch leading to the cargo hold. Very slowly, he opened it as quietly as he could and peered into the dimly lit cavern. After a few moments, his eyes adjusted to the darkness, and off to one side, he spotted Mike and Michelle sound asleep.

Jerry smiled in satisfaction that his trusted friend was onboard. He glanced at his communicator and punched in the prearranged signal for Connie to join him. When she arrived, Jerry pointed at the innocent looking stowaways and whispered, "Would you like to wake them?"

"Sure," replied Connie, as she drifted over to the sleeping figures. After adjusting the alarm on her wrist watch, Connie held it close to Mike's and Michelle's ears and turned it on. The ringing chimes startled them out of their sound sleep. Both looked around, investigating their surroundings with sleepy eyes. Realizing that they had finally been discovered, Mike made eye contact with Captain Jerontis and said, "Captain! I've changed my mind. If it's not too late, I'd like to withdraw my replacement request and rejoin the mission."

"Since we're more than 200 million miles from Earth, I don't have much choice, do I?"

"I was hoping you'd see it that way, and since you're in such an agreeable mood, is it okay if I bring my wife along?"

"Wife?" questioned Doctor Nemard, as she smiled at Michelle.

"Yes! We were married during Mike's last trip down to Earth."

"Having two additional people onboard won't be a problem," Captain Jerontis said. "Besides, we can use your skills."

Displaying a mischievous smile, Michelle looked at Captain Jerontis. "Actually, there are three of us, because I'm pregnant."

"Congratulations!" Captain Jerontis exclaimed. "This ship's life support systems can easily support the lives of three additional people. The only problem we have is finding you a place to live. The twenty-four apartments on this ship are all occupied."

"I have an idea," stated Mike, looking at Captain Jerontis playfully.

Seeing Mike's expression, Captain Jerontis said, "I'm almost afraid to ask, but let's hear it."

"This is only a suggestion, but I'm thinking that if you were to take a good look at Doctor Nemard and work on developing an appreciation for her feminine beauty and warm loving personality, it's possible that an apartment could become available soon. Also, it might be more romantic to call her Connie instead of always addressing her as Doctor Nemard."

Doctor Nemard's expression indicated obvious personal pleasure and satisfaction with Mike's remark. She was, however, caught off guard as was the Captain by Mike's unexpected suggestion and its implication. She looked at Captain Jerontis, searching for a reaction and was surprised to see him blushing and speechless. He seemed uncomfortable with everyone staring at him in anticipation of his response. I've never seen him like this before, thought Connie with some degree of amusement. With his total commitment to this mission, is it possible that he's never thought about me except in a professional way?

After a few moments, Captain Jerontis recovered his wits and briefly gazed at Connie affectionately. Connie noticed this and thought; maybe he has seen me as a desirable woman. The possibility caused a warm feeling of excitement to well up in her.

Connie's hopes were raised still further when Captain Jerontis turned to Mike and said, "As appealing as your suggestion is, it will have to wait until another time. We still have the urgent problem of finding the sabotage to this ship or proving that it doesn't exist. I have a bomb search team that is nearing the point of exhaustion. Since you are well rested, I want you to take over that job for a while."

Appearing puzzled, Mike asked, "What bomb search?"

Seeing that Mike and Michelle did not know anything about the bomb threat, Captain Jerontis briefed them on recent events. When the briefing was finished, Mike left to take over the bomb search.

Captain Jerontis said to Michelle, "I'm going to put your reporting skills to work by having you transmit regular reports to Earth on the activities onboard this ship. Make an effort to include all of our personnel. In the event that we are destroyed, the video you transmit will be the last images that surviving friends and family back on Earth will see of their perished loved ones. Your first story will, of course, contain an explanation of your presence, as well as, Mike's presence on this ship."

"I'll get started right away. My first report will go out shortly."

TIME: 96 Hours ALE.

Michelle's latest news dispatch to Earth:

"We have been underway for four days and have traveled 278 million miles. During the last forty-eight hours, the people on this ship have had little or no sleep. However, their tenacious resolve to survive seems to be giving them a superhuman strength that allows them to overcome their extreme fatigue and keep the intensive sabotage search moving forward. The question is how much longer can they continue before reaching the point of collapse. Stopping for much needed sleep, however, is not an option. Not knowing how much time we have makes it imperative to continue the effort to the point of collapse.

"To those of you who sabotaged our ship: I want you to understand the

40

futility of what you are trying to do. Even if you succeed in killing us and stopping our mission, you will fail to stop humans from going to the stars, because we now have the technology to go to the stars. Throughout history, human exploration and habitat expansion have always gone as far as allowed by imagination and ability. That is human nature, and you cannot defeat human nature.

"Your leaders are in jail. If you succeed in killing us, they will be tried for murder and executed if convicted. The same will happen to you, because you will be hunted down and brought to justice. You will be executed in the pursuit of a cause that you cannot win. I urge you to come to your senses while there is still time. You can stop your own senseless deaths and ours too by sending an anonymous message to NIEA telling them how you've sabotaged our starship."

TIME: 98 Hours, 20 Minutes ALE.

"Captain Jerontis! This is NIEA Command. The FBI investigation has not yet revealed any specific information. Apparently, AEPF officials have cleverly established code words to conceal the details of their plot. Only these code words were used when communicating with the individuals hired to do the actual sabotage. Given enough time, the mind probing interrogation techniques used by the FBI in conjunction with brain wave analysis will break through the code. They estimate twelve to sixteen hours to accomplish this. I hope this won't be too late.

"WWCLU attorneys have won a restraining order from a liberal minded judge to stop the FBI. Only problem is, they don't know where to deliver it, since the interrogation is being done at a secret location.

"I have just been handed the latest information from the FBI. They do not have concrete proof or specific details, but they believe the sabotage is in one of your flight control computers. We will send you additional information as soon as we have it."

Captain Jerontis thought about this. The flight control system including the computers had already been searched for a bomb. In addition, the computers had been searched for a virus. Nothing had been found. But as tired as everyone is, we could have missed something. I will have both searches carefully redone.

Meanwhile, in the cafeteria, Michelle and Doctor Nemard finished eating their first meal in a long time. "I feel much better now," stated Michelle. "I guess I should have eaten sooner."

"Food is the fuel the body runs on. It's not good to run on empty, especially when you're busy and not getting enough sleep."

After a bit of silence, Michelle asked, "Do you think our ship really has been sabotaged, or do you think the whole thing is just a cruel hoax?"

"Unfortunately, I believe it has been sabotaged. The people who have threatened us are fanatical extremists. They have sick minds and are unable

41

to accept the will of others. They will stop at nothing to achieve their ends. Killing innocent people means nothing to them, as they have shown with their terrorist attacks on NIEA facilities. Even though they are mentally sick, they apparently are quite intelligent. And this combination makes them very dangerous and able to do whatever it takes to stop us."

"It just seems so tragic that a few extremists could thwart the will of a great nation."

"They haven't stopped us yet. Captain Jerontis is very intelligent and capable, as are the rest of us. I am confident that we'll prevail."

"I hope you're right. With a wonderful husband and a child on the way, I'm not yet ready to die. I just wish I could do something to help."

"I think you already have. I heard your last report to Earth. The appeal you made to the saboteurs may get a positive response. Explaining to them the futility of what they're trying to do, along with the consequences, might cause one of them to crack. Sick minds are unpredictable."

"That's true, but these are fanatics who are passionately hoping to destroy us. Before I made that appeal, I decided that I didn't have much of a chance to get a positive response, but I had to try anyway. One other thing that I've been doing is praying for guidance. I've been a practicing Christian my entire life, and I've always prayed for guidance in times of crisis and whenever faced with a difficult decision."

"Has praying for guidance helped you?"

"I believe that it has. I've always made the right choices whenever I've been faced with difficult decisions. Anyway, praying for guidance can't hurt anything, so why not do it?"

"Well, this is a time of crisis," stated Doctor Nemard, as she bowed her head for a few moments of silent prayer. Seeing this, Michelle decided to join her. When they finished praying, Doctor Nemard left the cafeteria and went to the medical lab.

Feeling a need for solitude, Michelle decided to return to the cargo shuttle to rest and think about her next report. When she arrived on the hangar deck, she headed for the cargo shuttle, which had served as a spacious apartment for her and Mike since leaving Earth. As she was about to enter it, she stopped, turned, and looked at the personnel shuttle.

Viewing its sleek shape brought some thoughts to the forefront of her mind. I wonder if I will ever ride it down to our new home. What will it be like to navigate the atmosphere of Alcent and land on its surface? Will we find a place where we can safely live among the dinosaurs?

With her mind pondering the possibilities of the distant future, Michelle became aware of a growing desire to explore the personnel shuttle. Very strange, she thought, that I should feel so compelled to enter it, almost as if I'm being directed by an outside force.

Puzzled by the way she felt so strongly drawn to the personnel shuttle, Michelle approached it with a great deal of suspicion and cautiously peered into the passenger compartment. Not seeing anything of a threatening nature, she entered it and looked around. Nothing unusual here, she thought. I think I'll take a look at the flight deck.

Michelle slowly opened the hatch to the flight deck and cautiously looked in. There's no one here and nothing looks out of place, so why did I feel such a strong compulsion to come here? While she considered the question, Michelle entered the flight crew's compartment and comfortably seated herself in the pilot's seat.

Is it possible that the sabotage to our mission is in this shuttle, and I was guided here to discover it? But what am I supposed to look for? Everything looks normal to me. Perhaps, if I put myself in a state of total relaxation, clear my mind of all anxiety, and leave it open to outside suggestion; maybe, just maybe, the same force that compelled me to come here will guide me to the sabotage. To avoid the possibility of being disturbed at a critical moment, Michelle turned off her communicator. Then, she proceeded to practice her relaxation techniques, and after a few minutes, she became so relaxed that she fell asleep.

TIME: 100 Hours, 45 Minutes ALE.

Moose, Dianne, and Captain Jerontis were in the cafeteria devouring their first meal in a long time. Speaking to Captain Jerontis, Moose said, "I checked in with Mike a few minutes ago, and I promised to relieve him as soon as we've finished eating. He's making good progress. We think we'll be finished with the bomb search of all priority one and two areas in a couple hours."

Captain Jerontis nodded in acknowledgment.

"How far do you plan to go with this bomb search before we restart our engines?" Moose asked. "What I'm getting at is that in order to be certain that there's no bomb onboard, we'll have to open every floor, wall, and ceiling panel; and that will take several weeks."

"I don't think we'll have to do that. The FBI believes that it will have specific information for us sometime during the next several hours. If they fail to do that, and if we fail to find the sabotage, then I don't think we'll be alive twenty-four hours from now."

"What leads you to that conclusion?" Dianne asked.

"For sensational publicity and to satisfy their egos, I believe that our saboteurs wanted the explosion to occur close enough to Earth to be a blinding flash in the nighttime sky. Quite frankly, I'm surprised that the explosion hasn't already taken place. At the present time, we are nearly 300 million miles from Earth. Exploding all of our antimatter fuel at this distance would look like an extremely bright star back on Earth for a few seconds. Although brilliant, it could hardly be considered spectacular."

"But if the explosion is brighter than anything else in the nighttime sky, it might be spectacular enough to satisfy their egos," noted Dianne.

"That means that if there is a bomb onboard, it will explode very soon," stated Captain Jerontis.

While nodding in agreement, Moose said, "We can complete the search of priority three areas in the next twenty-four hours. If we haven't found a bomb by then, and if we're still alive, I think we should consider ourselves the victims of psychological terror and restart our engines."

"I concur with Moose," stated Dianne. "I've been completely through our life support systems, and I'm confident that there's no sabotage there. In regard to a bomb, unless we tear this whole ship apart, there's no way we can be certain that a bomb doesn't exist. Once all mission critical areas have been searched, we should resume acceleration to cruise velocity."

"If there aren't any new developments in the next 24 hours, that would seem to be a reasonable course of action," agreed Captain Jerontis.

"It's time for me to replace Mike," stated Moose.

"Tell him to come to the cafeteria, so I can talk to him about our current situation. He has worked on this ship for so many years that he has a very detailed knowledge of it. I'm going to ask him to think like a saboteur and see if he can come up with something we've overlooked."

"Good idea," responded Moose as he left.

A short time later, Mike arrived, and Captain Jerontis briefed him on what had already been done. Then, he asked Mike to think like a saboteur.

"My mind works much better when I'm not starving," responded Mike. "I'll get some food and think this over while I'm eating. Then, I'll go down to the cargo shuttle and put myself into quiet isolation, so I can sink my mind totally into this problem."

After ordering food, Mike asked, "Have you seen Michelle recently?"

"No! Why? Do you have reason to be worried about her?"

"When Moose relieved me, I tried to reach her on the communicator, but she has it turned off for some reason. Thinking that she might be taking a nap, I stopped by the cargo shuttle, but she wasn't there."

Captain Jerontis entered the intercom number into his communicator and paged Michelle. After waiting a brief period and not getting any response, he sounded a few attention getting notes on the warning klaxon. Then, he said, "Attention all personnel! If anyone has seen Michelle recently or knows where she is, please report immediately."

No one called in except Doctor Nemard who said, "I ate with her in the cafeteria about three hours ago. She said she was going to the cargo shuttle to relax and prepare her next report. I haven't seen her since then. Is there any evidence that something may have happened to her?"

"Mike has just been to the cargo shuttle, and she's not there. She hasn't responded to my page, her communicator is turned off, and no one has seen her in the last three hours. Since we cannot rule out the possibility of an armed terrorist being hidden away somewhere on this ship, we have to consider the possibility that Michelle may have fallen victim to foul play. If that's the case, finding her might lead us to the terrorist. We need to begin an immediate search of the ship."

"I just lost my appetite!" exclaimed Mike. "I will lead the search!"

Without waiting for a response from Captain Jerontis, Mike got on the intercom and said, "Attention all personnel! Search your immediate area for Michelle and report to me!" By a process of elimination, Mike would discover those areas that he needed to search.

Meanwhile, down on the hangar deck, totally oblivious to the consternation Mike was going through, Michelle was sound asleep and in the midst of a vivid dream. In her dream, she was orbiting Alcent, and after seven long years in space, the big day had finally arrived. It was landing day, the day that all had awaited for so long, when humans would finally descend to the surface and begin the adventure of building a new society on a dinosaur planet.

In her dream, she wondered, am I dreaming, or is this real? It seems so real, but I must be dreaming, because we haven't yet left the Solar System. Still, this must be real, because I just heard the warning klaxon signal the beginning of countdown to engine ignition. Also, the instrument panel is lit up and countdown has started, so this must be real and not just a dream. But if this is real, why am I sitting in the pilot's seat? I'm not a pilot. I don't know how to fly this shuttle. There must be some mistake. Lord, please help me. If I'm dreaming, please wake me up. But this can't be a dream; it's just too real... too real... too real...

Suddenly, Michelle awoke with a start and instantly realized that it wasn't a dream. The instrument panel was alive with lighted displays, and a digital countdown clock was ticking down with only 11 minutes and 33 seconds to ignition. Being a science reporter and knowledgeable in how nuclear thermal rockets function, Michelle knew that if the reactor came to full power without any propellant flowing through it to keep it from overheating, there would very quickly be a meltdown and a tremendous explosion. If propellant did flow through the reactor and out the rocket nozzle, it would quickly over-pressurize the hangar deck and blow the ship apart. In either case, all antimatter fuel would be detonated.

Michelle grabbed her communicator, sounded the ship-wide warning klaxon, accessed the intercom, and shouted, "Mike! Captain Jerontis! Moose! Come to the personnel shuttle immediately! I've found the sabotage! The NTR is eleven minutes away from ignition and meltdown!"

In the cafeteria, Mike and Captain Jerontis looked at each other with the kind of eye contact wherein each instantly acknowledged to the other a full awareness of the urgency of the situation. Instantly, they sprung into action, heading for the hangar deck with almost reckless speed.

"Looks like we've found Michelle and the sabotage," yelled Mike, as they left the cafeteria.

"Yes! And what we do during the next eleven minutes will determine whether we live or die."

Captain Jerontis and Mike arrived at the personnel shuttle in less than a minute. Moose arrived just a few seconds later. Turning to Michelle, Captain Jerontis said, "Begin transmitting to Earth a live report on what we're doing. Include every little detail. If we're unsuccessful, I want the FBI to have this information to help bring the saboteurs to justice."

Captain Jerontis then gave his attention to Mike, who was entering a shutdown command into the flight control computer. "Something's wrong here!" cried out Mike. "The computer isn't responding. They've either by-passed it, or they've instructed it to ignore us."

"If we disconnect its power, the countdown should stop," stated Captain Jerontis, as he hit the power shutoff switch. Again, there was no response, and the countdown continued without interruption.

"Evidently, they've installed an auxiliary power source for this computer!" exclaimed Mike. "But where?"

"Finding something that small could take more time than we have," responded Jerry. "Let's go to the reactor room and disconnect all power and control lines leading into the reactor."

"That should work, unless they've found a way to bypass them," stated Moose.

"That's a possibility," agreed Jerry. "And if we fail to shut this thing down by four minutes to ignition, we'll need to jettison this shuttle, ignite our engines, and pull away from it in a hurry."

While Mike and Moose raced to the reactor room, Captain Jerontis contacted the flight deck and told the pilot and flight engineer to eject the shuttle at four minutes to NTR ignition. Then, he went to the reactor room where he found Mike and Moose disconnecting the power and control lines to the electric motor that would soon begin withdrawing the control rods from the reactor's core. Noting that they were making rapid progress and didn't need his assistance, Captain Jerontis checked the control rod safety pins and said, "It looks like the saboteurs would've failed because the safety pins are still in place."

After a moment of thought, Captain Jerontis said, "It makes no sense that they would've overlooked such an important detail. Therefore, the safety pins must have been tampered with."

"I'll inspect them," stated Moose, as he selected a wrench from his tool kit and began extracting one of the pins.

When he had the safety pinhead removed, he held it up for inspection. The saboteurs had neatly cut the safety pin from the pinhead. Then, they turned the pinhead back into the safety pin hole. To outward appearance, the safety pin was in place, but in reality, only the pinhead was in place.

Moose pulled a heavy duty screwdriver out of his tool kit, inserted it into the safety pin hole, and said, "That should take care of this one for now." Moose then inspected the second safety pin, found the same problem, and made the same quick fix.

While Moose did this, Captain Jerontis returned to the shuttle's flight deck. He was greatly relieved to find that the countdown had discontinued at six minutes, thirty-seven seconds. On a display screen, he found the message: "Electric power to control rod drive motor has been interrupted. Countdown cannot resume until power is restored."

Via the shuttle's intercom, Captain Jerontis announced to Moose, Mike, and Michelle: "We've defeated the sabotage. I'm going to the cargo shuttle's reactor room. If it has also been sabotaged, we don't have much time. To be effective, its destruction would have to be timed to coincide with the sabotage we just foiled. Meet me there without delay."

En route to the cargo shuttle, Captain Jerontis cancelled ejection of the personnel shuttle. When he arrived at the cargo shuttle, he passed through its flight deck and noted that all was quiet. He grabbed a tool kit from the shuttle's maintenance closet and headed for the reactor room. It too was devoid of any activity.

As a precaution, Captain Jerontis immediately began disconnecting the control rod drive motor. While he was doing this, Moose and Mike arrived, inspected the safety pins, and found the same situation as on the personnel shuttle.

After the temporary fixes were in place, Moose commented, "It seems strange that they would sabotage these safety pins without also sabotaging the computer."

"How do you know they haven't?" Jerry asked.

"I'm just assuming they didn't. Like you said a few minutes ago, to be effective, it needed to be timed to coincide with the sabotage on the personnel shuttle. The saboteurs should've been smart enough to figure out that if we were fortunate enough to discover the sabotage in the personnel shuttle, we would immediately check this shuttle. Are we giving them too much credit, or are we overlooking something?"

"Whoever was responsible for destroying the safety pins had the easy job," noted Mike. "We haven't yet discovered how they sabotaged the flight control computer as effectively as they did, but I have to believe that it was a time consuming task. Because of tight security, they may not have had an opportunity to get that part of the job done on this shuttle."

"I suspect that your reasoning is correct," Captain Jerontis said. "However, as soon as we have the time, we are going to check out the computers in both of these shuttles. But for the time being, we're going to rely on some new safety pins and disconnected motors to prevent possible disaster. Mike, I want you to take care of making and installing the pins. Moose, you will complete the bomb search of critical areas."

"I'll have that done in an hour or two," stated Moose.

"The new pins will be installed in less than an hour," declared Mike.

"I'm going to assume that the emergency is over and that we've defeated the sabotage," stated Jerry. "I'm going to declare a twelve-hour rest period, so we can get some much needed sleep."

TIME: 4 days, 18 hours AL.E.

"Captain Jerontis! This is NIEA Command. The latest information from the FBI confirms your conclusion that the crisis is over. Until just a few hours ago, the brain wave patterns exhibited by the suspects during questioning were representative of an arrogant attitude based on a firm belief that we were powerless to stop them from destroying your mission. These patterns underwent a dramatic change when we forced them to listen to a recording of Michelle's broadcast of the details of you thwarting their efforts. With the full realization that they had failed to blow up your ship, the brain wave patterns of all suspects became a classic textbook example of what you find in people who have suffered defeat. Additional questions and probing comments by FBI interrogators failed to cause any change in the brain wave patterns, which continued to typify a state of hopelessness."

THREE

Romance and Near-Disaster
on a Seemingly Endless Journey

TIME: 6 Days A.L.E.

Michelle's latest mission update to Earth:

"Our antimatter engines have been restarted, and we are accelerating at 1g. Our current speed is 1,656 miles per second, and we've traveled 492 million miles, Jupiter's approximate distance from the Sun. In the early days of the space age, it took several years for a spacecraft to travel to Jupiter. We've covered the distance in just six days."

After transmitting her report, Michelle went to the cafeteria to have lunch with Connie, who greeted her with a sleepy-eyed smile. Michelle returned the smiled and asked, "Are you ready for lunch, or would you rather go back to bed and sleep for a few hours?"

"It seems like I've done nothing but sleep since the end of the crisis," responded Connie. "And I still feel tired."

"That's understandable. We've just been through a nerve-racking nightmare that I sure don't want to go through again."

"I don't either!" exclaimed Connie. "And now that it's over, maybe we can fall into some sort of comfortable day-to-day life."

"A comfortable daily routine would make our long voyage easier, and life on this starship might even start to feel normal."

"But we're already traveling faster than 1,600 miles per second, and we're still accelerating at 1g. What's normal about that?" Connie asked.

"*What's normal about that* is that it feels normal. Accelerating at 1g feels like Earth's gravity, and that creates the illusion that everything is normal, yet in just nine months, we'll reach three-fourths of light speed."

"That's an incredible speed to travel at. But our journey will still take more than six years, and we're only going to the nearest stars."

"I'm happy we're not going to a more distant star system," stated Michelle. "Six years is a long time to be confined to a starship."

"It sure is, but we have to accept the fact that this starship is going to be our home for a long time and find ways to make it enjoyable."

"What if we succeed in making it such a comfortable home that we won't want to go down to the surface when we arrive at Alcent?"

"I've never considered that possibility," stated Connie. "When we finally arrive at Alcent, I believe everyone will have an undying thirst for the wide open spaces on the planet's surface."

"But this starship will offer a safe, secure home compared to the savage conditions on Alcent, where dinosaurs roam free and pterodactyls rule the sky. If we're happy here, why go down?" Michelle asked.

"Because it will be an incredible adventure to live on a dinosaur planet and explore the place," stated Connie. "But I hope we do become so comfortable on this ship that people won't mind living out their lives on it. There's always the possibility that we won't be able to land on Alcent."

"That would be very disappointing. Despite what I just said, I don't believe anyone would choose to live on this ship rather than on the planet."

"I had the feeling you were arguing just for the sake of debate."

"That is fun, especially when you defend an absurd position and the other person thinks that you're serious." Noticing that Connie was laughing softly, Michelle asked, "What are you giggling about?"

"I was just thinking about how Moose takes pride in his ability to be a jokester and how funny it would be if we could pull some sort of gag on him while convincing him that we're serious."

"That would be fun," agreed Michelle. "Let's watch for an opportunity. Maybe he'll even set himself up for us."

"Moose is rather outgoing in a boisterous sort of way," commented Connie. "I'm sure he'll give us an opening."

"That would be great. After just barely surviving the sabotage to our starship, we could use some lighthearted fun."

"Speaking about survival, there's something that I've been thinking about, and that is that all of us are still alive, seemingly, just by chance."

"What do you mean, just by chance?" Michelle asked.

"What if the chain of events that led to your presence on this mission had been disrupted in some way? Then, you would not be here, and it's unlikely that anyone else would've been in the personnel shuttle when the NTR countdown started. Consequently, we would've all been killed in the ensuing explosion. I think it's ironic that after the expenditure of billions of dollars and twenty years of planning, this mission ends up being saved by something unplanned, namely, the presence of a stowaway."

"Even the best-laid plans cannot account for all contingencies. I'm just happy that I was in the right place at the right time."

"You make it sound like it wasn't any big deal, but we're lucky you found a way to outwit security and be on this ship. How did you do that?"

"There was only one avenue open to me and that was to apply to NIEA to be part of the media team covering your departure."

"It seems like that was a long shot at best."

"Not really! Being a nationally recognized science reporter with a record of supporting NIEA projects made it quite likely that my application would be approved, and it was. By the time I arrived here, Mike had everything planned."

"Even though he had everything planned, you still had a big decision to make. If you don't mind telling me, I'd like to know how you made such a big decision. What was the deciding factor?"

"I love Mike. I'm carrying his child, and I want to be with him."

"But you didn't have to go with us to be with him because he'd requested that he be replaced, so he could stay on Earth with you."

"That's true, but Mike had his heart set on this mission long before he met me. It's been a dream of his to go to Alcent ever since Star Voyager revealed the kind of life that's present there. A year ago, Mike's life became more complicated when he met me during an interview about this project. After the interview, he invited me out to dinner."

"You could've said no."

"I couldn't say no! What I mean is: he invited me out to dinner because I enticed him to do that."

"Even though you knew he was leaving Earth, you wanted to get a romance started! Why?

"I had to! He swept me off my feet during the interview."

"How could an interview about a starship sweep you off your feet?"

"He's tall, dark blonde, and handsome. And I've always had a thing for tall men, especially when they're intelligent and have a cheerful attitude. His lean athletic build also turned me on. I found him irresistible."

"So you enticed him to invite you out to dinner."

"That's right, and that's when things got complicated. A romance started, and we fell in love. Then, a power struggle began. I wanted to stay on Earth where we could have a comfortable life without worrying about being eaten by a dinosaur. But he wanted to take me to Alcent."

"So how did you reach the decision to go with us?"

"I have a feeling you're not going to let this go until I tell you the whole story."

"I am curious, and as you know, I'm not just the ship's doctor, I'm also the mission psychiatrist. It's my job to get into people's heads and understand what makes them tick."

"That's true, but I get the feeling there might also be something personal involved here."

"You might be right, but I'd like to find out how you made the decision to go with us."

"To start with, I am a Christian, and I've always prayed for guidance whenever faced with a difficult decision. I've always believed that the Lord would help me make the right choice. In this case, I was torn between a desire for a safe comfortable life on Earth with family and friends and a desire to please the man I love by going with him on a dangerous adventure.

The night that Mike took me to the observation deck, I was inspired by the spectacular beauty of the Universe, and I felt that I had to experience another part of it. Somehow, I knew that I had to be on this mission and that I would play an important role in it."

"Do you believe that you received the guidance you prayed for?"

"Definitely, but it was still a difficult choice."

"Now that you're here, are you happy to be with us?"

"Yes, but I am sad that I'll never again see my parents, brother, and sister. We've always been a close family. What was bad for them is they had no advance notice that I'd be leaving Earth or that I was even thinking about it. Out of necessity, I had to keep it a secret."

"They must've been shocked when you told them several days after leaving. How are they taking it?"

"They're unhappy at losing me, but they're also proud of me for finding a way to become one of Earth's first interstellar pioneers. They are supportive of my decision and are praying for our success."

"The people on this ship will also support you. We're all dealing with the loss of family and friends, and out of necessity, we'll turn to each other. I believe that we'll become a very close-knit community, like a large family in many respects."

"That will help make our voyage enjoyable," commented Michelle.

"Another thing for you to consider is that we haven't totally lost our loved ones back on Earth. Even though we can't be with them, we can transmit videos back and forth that are quite realistic when viewed in 3-D on a wall-sized screen. So we can stay in close contact, at least for a while. Once we arrive at Alcent, two-way communication will be impractical. It will take 4.35 years for a transmission to reach Earth and 4.35 years for the response to reach us. Videos sent back and forth will be like historical news bulletins by the time they're received."

"But they'll still be welcome," Michelle said. "I know I will enjoy getting news from Earth, and I'm sure they'll be thrilled with the dinosaur video we'll be sending them."

Michelle thought about how much time would be required for communication with Earth, and this put into true perspective just how far from Earth they would be. They would be truly isolated and would be building a new civilization without assistance from Earth.

Then, Michelle thought about her unborn child and how successfully raising children would be essential to getting a new society off to a good start. My child will be the first in the new generation, and Mike and I will have to give our child all the knowledge and training needed to survive and prosper on a hostile planet.

Noticing Michelle's faraway look, Connie waited for a facial expression that indicated Michelle's thoughts had run their course. Then, she said, "You just looked like your mind was a million miles away."

"Actually, my mind was a lot farther away than that. I was thinking about Alcent and raising children there. My child will be nearly six years old when we arrive there and won't have any playmates."

"That's true, but you'll have help raising your child. And that help can start with a physical, so we can begin your prenatal care. If you don't have any plans for the next couple hours, I'd like you to come to the medical lab with me, so I can examine you."

"Thanks, I appreciate that."

Two hours later, in the medical lab, Connie gave Michelle some good news, "All tests indicate that you and your child are in excellent health."

"Did you determine the sex of my baby?"

"Yes, I did. Do you want to know that?"

"Sure, why not?"

"You are going to have a baby boy. I hope that's what you want."

"I really hadn't given it any thought. I just want a normal, healthy baby, which brings up an important question: can a child develop normally when he doesn't have other children to interact with?"

"That is something to think about. If no other children are born until we land on Alcent, your son will be six years older than they are. That will socially isolate him in the sense that he won't have any peers. I don't think that would be a healthy situation, so I will suggest to Captain Jerontis that at least one additional child be borne during our voyage."

Michelle lit up with a naughty grin as she gazed at Connie and said, "Are you going to suggest to him that he get you pregnant, so that my son can have a playmate? Why Doctor Nemard! I think that would be doing the psychologist part of your job far beyond the call of duty."

Connie laughed at the remark. Then, she turned away, breaking eye contact with Michelle, while considering whether to open up to her. A few moments later, Connie turned back to Michelle. "The truth is, I am in love with the Captain, and I'd like to be pregnant with his child. But he doesn't seem to have noticed me in anything other than a professional way."

"Perhaps, he's already involved with one of the other women."

"If he is, it's the best kept secret on the ship."

"Maybe he has avoided making a play for you or any of the other women because this would have made him vulnerable to sexual harassment charges. Imagine the consequences of such an accusation if some radical feminist group decided to pursue it in court and the press made front page headlines out of it."

"Sam from SNS would've had a field day with that story," stated Connie. "He's so opposed to this mission that he would've seized the opportunity to antagonize Captain Jerontis simply because he has been a key individual in putting this mission together."

Michelle nodded. "Whether the charge was justified or frivolous, the end result would've been the same. At the very least, Captain Jerontis would've been faced with a severe distraction while getting this ship ready for departure. At worst, he could've been pulled off this mission; effectively ending a career that he has devoted twenty years to. Even though the possibility of that happening was small, I believe Jerry would've avoided the risk, because this mission is his life. However, we are now a half-billion miles from Earth, and lawsuits carried out for the purpose of destroying someone's career are no longer a threat."

"You may be correct, because Jerry does try to anticipate all possible consequences before taking any action, especially when this mission and his career are involved. I think it's sad that American society has become so concerned with political correctness and being sensitive that someone in a position of authority, like Captain Jerontis, must avoid pursuing an intimate relationship with a subordinate out of fear of putting his career in jeopardy."

"That's well said, but have you ever made an effort to entice him?"

"Because of our intense workload, I haven't had time to do that."

"Are you sure that's the case?"

"What do you mean?"

"Is it possible that you are using your workload as an excuse to cover up the real reason, which might be that you fear rejection?"

Connie thought about Michelle's comment for a few moments. Then, she said, "For a science reporter, you have pretty good insight."

"To become a good science reporter, I had to also become a good investigative reporter. I've never taken anything at face value. When preparing a report, I've always questioned the validity of everything that was presented to me."

"That's a good explanation, but I think there's more to it than that. I believe you have a natural ability to see into other people's feelings. Have you ever considered a career in psychology?"

"No, I just like to understand the people around me, especially those who are important to me. So let's talk about your fear of rejection."

Connie thought about the suggestion for a few moments and decided that Michelle did care and wanted to be helpful, so she decided to trust her. "To start with, I am hopelessly in love with the Captain. I want him so much it hurts. If I'd made a pass at him and been ignored or even outright rejected, I would've been crushed."

"In view of all the training that you had to excel in to qualify for this mission, I am surprised that you would fear rejection."

"Excelling in training made me a professional at what I do; it didn't cancel out my emotions. I still have feelings just like everyone else."

"That makes sense, but is there more to it than that?"

"Had I made a pass at Jerry and been rejected, it would've put a strain on the friendly working relationship we have. With a ship and crew to get ready for departure, we really didn't need any tension between us."

"I sense that you're still not telling me everything."

"If you want the rest of the story, I'll have to go back in time to my childhood days."

"I'd like to hear the whole story."

"Okay, being on this mission is something that I've wanted since age eleven. At that young age, I had a very active imagination that took me on imaginary journeys to Alcent. The wild adventure I enjoyed during those fantasies fed an ever-growing desire to be on this mission, and in my early teens, I made that my number one goal. In my fantasies, I constantly envisioned myself being a doctor, so I set that as a career goal. Somewhere in my teenage years, I concluded that my best chance to be on this mission was to be a better doctor than all others who applied. I also decided that being healthy and in good physical condition was a must. I had such a burning desire to excel and achieve my goals that I spent virtually all of my time studying and exercising. This didn't leave me with any time to get involved with boys and later on, men. I decided that I had to give up many of the social pleasures enjoyed by girls and young women and devote all of my time to achieving my career goals. But now that I've achieved them, I'd like to have an intimate relationship with the man I love, maybe even marry him and have some children."

"That sounds like a challenge you can handle, but if you don't mind my assistance, I could give you a little coaching."

"What do you have in mind?"

"Your fear of rejection is something that you wouldn't have to be concerned with if you could entice him to make a play for you. Let him think that it's all his idea."

"Your story about how you won Mike's love makes me think that you're pretty good at enticing men."

"It's not that difficult. We just need to motivate the Captain to see you as a passionate, desirable woman and not just the ship's doctor. If we can accomplish that, then, if he's a normal man, all you should have to do is send out the proper signals and let nature take its course."

"I have no doubt that he's 100 percent masculine. I've been through his psychological tests with a fine-toothed comb."

"So you have given this some thought, despite your workload?"

"At times, I've torn my heart out over this."

"I think it's time we get started, and the first thing we need to do is get rid of the uniform that you're wearing. While it's loose fitting and functional, it doesn't do a thing to show that you're a woman."

"You're right about that. Apparently, my uniform was designed by the politically correct thinking crowd with the idea of making men and women appear equal in the workplace by concealing their differences with clothing, and they succeeded."

"We are going to undo their success. We are going to put you into something that will knock Jerry off his feet. Fashion design is something I used to do as a hobby. It was fun, and I was even good enough to win some of the contests I entered."

Connie looked at Michelle admiringly. "Your outfit is so feminine; whereas, my uniform could be worn by a man working in a machine shop. I think it's time to pitch my uniforms into the recycling bin."

"That's the spirit I want to hear, but what does this ship have for making clothing?"

"We're in luck. Our computer has an immense amount of information stored in it including the more popular women's fashions. Also, we have equipment for designing and making clothing."

"Do you know how to operate that equipment?"

"I sure do."

"Good! You can teach me, and we'll make you some sexy outfits."

Growing ever more excited as she thought about the possibilities, Connie exclaimed, "This is going to be the most fun I've had in a long time! When can we start?"

"Why not right now, while we're in the mood for it. Also, as long as we're doing this, I'd like to make something for myself. Because of the way I became a part of this mission, I wasn't able to bring much along."

"Good idea," replied Connie.

"Once we get you properly dressed, I want to style your hair into something more glamorous and let you use some of my makeup. When we're finished, the Captain would have to be blind to not notice you."

"It almost sounds like you're planning to totally make me over."

"Not really, we're just going to fix you up in a way that accentuates your natural beauty. After all, you are an attractive woman. You have a beautiful face, enchanting blue eyes, and that great blond hair. I can't tell because of your clothing, but I think you also have a good figure."

"I do, and thanks for the compliments. Hopefully, I will soon get those same compliments from the man I love. I wonder what would be the right occasion to hit him with the alluring new me."

"It would be most effective if you could be alone with him. That way, you can turn on your charm without any distractions."

Connie displayed a naughty grin and said, "I think the recent sabotage ordeal subjected the Captain to a great deal of stress. As the ship's medical officer, I think the responsible thing for me to do would be to call him in for a complete physical."

"You would of course be doing this purely in the line of duty," commented Michelle, returning Connie's naughty grin.

"Certainly! After all, the Captain's health is important to the success of our mission."

Michelle thought about the encounter Connie was planning and said, "What I like about this is that you'll have the element of surprise working

56

for you. He'll be expecting to see you in your sexless uniform and will be caught off guard by the stunning new you. Observing his reaction should give you a good indication if you'll be successful in achieving the relationship you want."

"If the approach we've been discussing fails to achieve the desired response, I may have to use more direct tactics."

With her curiosity immediately aroused, Michelle asked, "What does the good doctor have in mind for the Captain?"

"If he doesn't properly react to the glamorous new me, I might suspect that the stress of recent events has negatively affected his ability to respond to unexpected situations. In that event, to avoid medical malpractice, I will be forced to examine his nervous system to make sure that it's functioning properly. To do that, I will have to check his responses to various kinds of stimulation."

"Why Doctor Nemard, I'm beginning to suspect that you might be planning to deviate from standard medical procedure."

Displaying a broad smile, Connie looked at Michelle and asked, "Whatever gave you that idea?"

"It's your changing attitude. Your fear of rejection has disappeared."

"Not really! Rejection would be painful and put a strain on our friendship, but not knowing his true feelings is putting a strain on me anyway. So which strain do I want to contend with?"

"That's a pragmatic way to look at it. So let's make you a sexy outfit, so you'll have the right medicine to get your love life in order."

"I like the way you put that."

"It seemed appropriate."

"Before we begin, let me tell you about the machine that we'll be using. It not only makes clothing, but it also manufactures the fabric, buttons, zippers, and whatever else that it needs to make boots and garments. Thanks to genetic engineering, we can grow plants that are prolific at producing the fibers the machine uses to make cloth and the polymers it needs to make tough plastics, and it's all recyclable."

"That sounds like a dream machine. Is it difficult to operate?"

"It's computer controlled and user-friendly," replied Connie. "The first step is to give the computer complete data about your body. We can do that right here or from anyone's apartment. It involves giving the computer a 3-D view of your body. This can be done in a number of ways, but one easy way is to let the computer view your body with three video cameras. Here in the medical lab, there is a camera in the corner to your left, in the corner to your right, and up there near the ceiling.

"I will demonstrate how the system works. First, I select the New Clothing Program. As you can see, the computer has turned on the cameras. Now, I step into view of the cameras and remove my clothing. Next, I do a few poses, allowing the computer to see my nude body in different positions. Finally, I do some range of motion exercises. The computer now has exact measurements of all parts of my body, so that whatever clothing we make for me should be a perfect fit."

Connie stepped out of the cameras' field of view and reached for her clothing. As she began putting it on, she looked at Michelle and said, "Now, it's your turn."

Displaying an expression of concern, Michelle said, "I'm not sure I want all those explicit views of my naked body in the computer for just anyone to look at."

"You are the only person who can open the file. Once you've gone through the procedure that I just did, the computer will have enough physical data about you, so that it can identify you. It won't allow anyone else to access your personal file."

"Are you sure about that?"

"Absolutely positive!"

Accepting Connie's assurance, Michelle stepped into the camera's field of view, removed her clothing, posed in different positions, and then did some stretching exercises. When the computer said that it had enough information, Michelle put her clothes back on.

"Specifications for all the popular styles of clothing worn on Earth in recent years are stored in the computer," explained Connie, as she began displaying them in 3-D on the wall-sized video screen. "When we find a fashion design we like, I can instruct the computer to show us what I would look like wearing it."

"What do you think about this evening gown?" Michelle asked, while looking at it.

Connie entered the Display instruction into the computer, and a life-sized, 3-D image of her wearing the gown appeared on the video screen. It showed her gracefully walking, turning, and doing the poses that a professional model would use to sell the dress.

"I like it, but I'm not sure it's what we're looking for. If I am to meet Jerry here in the medical lab, I don't think a party dress is the right outfit."

"True," agreed Michelle, "but I really do like that particular shade of blue. It looks really good on you. Apparently, the computer decided to match the dress color to your blue eyes."

"Color recommendation is one of the features of this program. Based on the colors of my eyes, hair, and skin, the computer will select the shades of the various colors that look best on me. For example, if I want to wear this dress in red, I request that of the computer, and presto, there I am, wearing the same dress, only now, it's red. However, it isn't just any random shade of red; it's the shade of red that looks best on me."

"With equipment like this, coming up with the right outfit for you is going to be easy. Let's see what you look like in a blue jump suit."

Connie entered the request into the computer, and a life-sized, 3-D

58

image of her wearing a blue jump suit promptly appeared on the screen. Again, the computer showed her gracefully walking, turning, and doing the poses that a professional model would do to sell the outfit.

"Let's try some alterations to that design," suggested Michelle. "It fits too loose. Let's change the fabric to an interlock knit. Also, let's change the v-neckline to a scoop neckline, and instead of being sleeveless, let's add sleeves that extend about halfway to your elbows."

When the new image appeared on the screen, Connie exclaimed, "Wow! The way it hugs my body sure doesn't leave much for the imagination, but I'm not sure I'd call it a high-class outfit."

"That's true, but I think we can turn it into an elegant outfit by adding the right kind of trim, starting with the neckline and sleeves. Also, a belt around your waist of the appropriate width, color, and design might be helpful. And we'll fix you up with some attractive jewelry. With this computer, we'll create an outfit that you could successfully model at a high society fashion show back on Earth. Judging from the way you looked in that party dress, and now in this jump suit, I think you could've had a very successful career as a professional model."

"Thank you. That's the nicest compliment I've had in a long time. Imagine how different my life would be if I'd selected that for my career."

Meanwhile, another discussion was taking place in the Captain's quarters between Captain Jerry Jerontis, Mike, and Moose. Captain Jerontis leaned back in his recliner, stretched out, yawned, and said, "With the sabotage ordeal and the intense schedule of recent months now behind us, I'm finally starting to feel relaxed, almost like being on vacation."

Instantly, Moose responded, "Well, if I hadn't allowed you to talk me into going with you on this interstellar voyage, I'd be on vacation right now. Imagine me lying on a warm sandy beach in the South Pacific, surrounded by bikini-clad scenery. I would be faced with the pleasant task of deciding which one to choose."

Mike turned to Jerry and asked, "Is it my imagination, or is it true that Moose's mind wanders off into sexual fantasyland whenever he isn't busy working?"

"Either that, or he's trying to decide what kind of pizza to eat next," Jerry said while grinning.

"Aw come on, you guys are just making fun of me because I like to enjoy life."

"We all like to enjoy life, but some of us have a broader field of interest and consequently, have more options open to us," teased Mike.

"It isn't a question of having a broad field of interest," retorted Moose. "It's just a matter of getting your leisure-time priorities in order. I enjoy life in lots of ways, but I put exciting women and tasty food at the top of my list. Anyway, you're lucky to have a beautiful wife to live with."

"True, I do have a beautiful wife. But she isn't the only attractive woman on this ship. In addition to my wife, there are 12 other good-looking women onboard. With all the stories I've heard from Jerry about how adventuresome you are, I'm wondering why it's taking you so long to get together with one of them."

"How can you tell if they're attractive?" questioned Moose. "All they ever wear are those NIEA uniforms that make them look like they're ready to go to work on a factory assembly line somewhere. Appearance-wise, they're not very exciting to my way of thinking."

Mike turned to Jerry and said, "Apparently, Moose has never developed the masculine art of mentally undressing women."

Much to Moose's displeasure, both Mike and Jerry laughed at Mike's suggestion that Moose lacked imagination. Moose glared at Mike and Jerry; then, he said, "I'm beginning to think this is Pick-on-Moose Day. I make a legitimate comment about the totally-without-style uniforms that women who work for NIEA are required to wear, and what response do I get? You guys decide to have fun at my expense by insulting my imagination. I simply cannot believe that women who are proud to be women, and want to look like women, could find any pleasure in wearing their blasé uniforms."

"You're probably right," responded Jerry. "During recent months, we've all been so preoccupied with making this mission a success that we haven't had much time to be concerned with clothing. And even if we had been, it probably wouldn't have mattered, because our uniforms are a product of the politically-correct-thinking NIEA bureaucracy. But since we're no longer under their control, I'm going to post an order that allows all individuals to recycle their uniforms and dress any way they want. It'll be interesting to see what the women decide to wear."

"Evaluating their outfits will be a good project for me," volunteered Moose. "Since I'm currently on vacation, I'll have ample time for the task. Whoever comes up with the most exciting clothing will receive a prize, namely, the pleasure of my companionship."

"I think all that pizza you've been eating has given you a fat head," declared Mike.

"What makes you think you're on vacation?" questioned Jerry. "This isn't a pleasure cruise on the Caribbean; it's an important mission to start a new society on an alien planet."

"Well, the way I have it figured out, you canceled my vacation to the South Pacific when you coerced me into becoming your chief engineer. But since Mike is still here, I'm not needed in that capacity, and that leaves me free to pursue some of life's finer pleasures, just like I would have on the vacation that I'd planned. Actually, it's probably a good thing that I'm here. I can help you develop a much needed social life for yourself."

"Thanks for the offer, but now that I'm no longer working 24 hours a day, I can take care of my social life on my own. If you'll kindly think back to our college days, I believe you'll recall that my social life was every bit as active as yours. While it's true that you're not needed as chief engineer, I'd like you and Mike to share the responsibilities of the position. This will give both of you ample time off to pursue other activities, such as training for the responsibilities you'll have on Alcent."

"I'm confident that Moose and I can work out a schedule that will allow him sufficient free time for his female fashions evaluation project," commented Mike. "As for me, since I'll be in charge of geological research on Alcent, I intend to continue my geology education."

"Since I'm quite talented at evaluating female fashions, that project shouldn't take much of my time," boasted Moose. "But I still have a lot to learn about the intricate details of this ship, so I intend to continue studying it before I start preparing for a research project on Alcent."

"I agree," stated Jerry, "but I'd like you to decide what kind of research you want to do. Being an unplanned member of the crew, you are free to select a field of study that is of interest to you."

"I'd like to study plants and animals to determine what is edible and what its nutritional content is," stated Moose.

Mike laughed and said to Jerry, "You were right. When he isn't thinking about sex, he's thinking about food, but at least his interests are broadening to include other things besides pizza."

"Someone needs to think about food," retorted Moose. "If we're going to survive and prosper on Alcent, we need to know what's edible and what isn't. I'd love to discover several species of edible fish. Alcent has never been fished on, and the fishing should be absolutely great."

"That's an exciting possibility," agreed Jerry. "But we don't know what kind of aquatic creatures have evolved on Alcent."

"Fish were present on Earth during the Dinosaur Age," argued Moose. "Why shouldn't they be present on Alcent?"

"There might be fish there," Jerry agreed. "More than half of Alcent is covered with water, so there is ample habitat for fish to have evolved in. We do have a small research submarine, and we will be exploring Alcent's underwater world, so we'll find out what lives there."

"What an adventure!" Moose exclaimed. "We have no idea what kind of life exists in the oceans of Alcent. We could find underwater monsters capable of destroying our submarine."

"That's true," agreed Jerry, "but we might also find an abundance of fish that are edible and fun to catch."

"You've sold me," stated Moose. "I definitely want to be involved in underwater exploration."

"Operating that research sub will be one of my responsibilities," stated Jerry. "However, I don't mind sharing that job with you. Also, finding food sources on Alcent will be one of our top priorities. Dianne will be in charge of biological research, and Doctor Nemard has the skills to do nutritional analysis and search for toxic substances, so you'll be working with them. I'm sure they'll appreciate your help."

TIME: 6 Days, 18 Hours ALE.

Dianne Dawson was in the cafeteria eating breakfast when Doctor Nemard walked in, scanned the menu, made her selection, and placed her order. Then, she approached Dianne and said, "You look lost in thought. Do you mind if I join you, or do you need some time to yourself?"

Dianne snapped out of her trance-like mental state and replied, "Please do join me. I could use some company."

Connie sat down. "I sense that something's troubling you. Would you like to tell me about it?"

"I was just thinking about the people I was close to back on Earth."

"We haven't even been gone a week, and you miss them already?"

"I know it's only been a few days, but the finality of our departure is hitting me hard at the moment. I feel a sense of loss because I will never again be able to do anything with the people I left behind."

"That's a normal reaction to our situation."

"I understand that it's normal, but what I'm feeling is still painful. In recent years, I worked so hard at getting a position on this voyage that I never dwelled on the fact that we won't be coming back. But now that we've left Earth, it has really started to sink in that the past is gone. Cherished memories have been pouring through my mind. The things I did with my family and friends, the places that I enjoyed visiting; all of that is now part of the past, never again to be revisited, except mentally."

"You've just done an excellent job of describing the symptoms of an age old disease called homesickness. How do you plan to deal with it?"

"Well, to start with, I can't go back home, not even for a short visit. For the next seven years, this ship is going to be my home, so I'm going to do what I can to turn it into a home filled with warmth and comfort. Maybe while I'm doing that, I'll develop some new relationships to help offset the loss of family and friends. But more than anything else, I need some vacation time. It seems like all I've done recently is work and sleep. I need some time to have fun."

"Now that we're finally underway, your workload should be greatly reduced, and you should be able to do that."

"I think so, and I'll start by organizing some teams for competitive games. We do have a large gym, and it's time to put it to use."

"That should be fun. If you're going to do volleyball and tennis, include me."

"Okay, you're on the list. How about basketball?"

"I'm not very good at that, but I'll try it."

"I was on the starting team in high school. I can teach you some techniques, and then, it'll be up to you to practice them."

"You'll find me to be an eager student, because I like your idea of forming teams to play athletic games. They'll not only be fun, but they'll help us stay in shape, and that will help promote good health."

"That's true, but I'm looking for more than that."

"Like what?" Connie asked.

"I'm interested in the social aspects of team sports. I've always enjoyed group activities, but now that we've left Earth, I'm especially interested in social activities. I need to find new personal relationships."

"That's something we all need to do. It's part of building a new society to replace the one we left behind."

"When we get to Alcent, we'll be giving birth to a new civilization, and that'll be easier if we build a strong society before we get there."

"No doubt about that, and a strong supportive society will also make our long voyage easier."

"Pursuing enjoyable hobbies might also help, especially hobbies that can be shared with others."

"What are you thinking about doing?" Connie asked.

"I like to be surrounded by life. Maybe that's what got me into a career in biology. Anyway, I managed to convince NIEA to let me bring along 3,000 pounds of potting soil and a big variety of plant seeds."

"Three thousand pounds is a big pile of soil. What are you going to do with all of that?"

"I'll use my imagination to create artistic pots to grow plants in. Then, I'm going to turn my apartment into an ornamental garden."

"It seems to me that 3,000 pounds is a lot of soil for just one apartment. If you use all of that, there might not be any room left for you."

"It's not all for me. I plan to share it with others who want to enjoy the soft lines and contrasting colors of healthy plants."

"Even so, I can't believe that you were able to convince the NIEA bureaucrats to let you bring along a ton-and-a-half of soil."

"We're on a very long voyage, and this starship is a cold mechanical machine. Plants can make an apartment feel warm and alive, and they can have a soothing effect on the people caring for them."

"That sounds like a psychological thing."

"You should know. You're the psychiatrist."

Connie laughed. "You are persuasive."

"I try to be when I feel strongly about something. So what kind of plants can I help you grow in your apartment?"

"And the persuasion continues," Connie said while grinning. "But I do love fresh tomatoes that are allowed to ripen on the vine. Did you happen to bring along any tomato seeds?"

"Yes, I did. In fact, I have seeds for several fruits and vegetables. Part of the justification for bringing along so much soil was to be able to produce some fresh food to supplement that produced by our food synthesizers. As for tomatoes, they are one of my favorite foods. I brought along seeds for five varieties."

"Great! I'll find room for a couple tomato plants and some decorative plants. Maybe you could give me some tips on keeping them healthy."

"No problem, I love working with plants. I can even genetically alter the tomatoes to give you the flavor and sweetness you like."

"I like them super sweet with lots of flavor."

"One of the varieties I have fits that description, so genetic altering won't be needed. Maybe sometime tomorrow, we could get together and get your garden started."

"Sounds good to me," responded Connie. "Changing the subject a bit, but still talking about seeds, have you ever thought of this starship as nothing more than a giant seed pod?"

"What do you mean?"

"Let me use an analogy. In the natural life of a plant, there is a sequence of events that begins when a seed germinates. The seed sends roots down into the soil and a tiny plant up through the surface of the soil. This tiny seedling grows and develops until it reaches maturity. Then, it produces seed to begin the cycle all over again. Compare the human species to a plant, and we can see a similar chain of events on a much larger scale. As you know, the human species was born on Earth eons ago. Over the past several hundred thousand years, it has evolved and grown to a level of capability where it has ejected a seed pod. This starship is that seed pod, and we are the seed. When we land on Alcent, a new civilization will be born, which will grow and evolve."

"I've never thought of myself as a seed inside a pod," stated Dianne. "But I like your analogy. To continue it a bit further, when a seedling springs forth from a seed, it can only develop into a strong mature plant if it has a strong root system firmly embedded in fertile soil. Likewise, if we want our new society to grow into something great, we must establish a strong root system to support it. I believe this starts with having a system of government that promotes personal freedom and responsibility. The continued quest for knowledge and practical skills is also essential. And we need to teach all of this to our children."

"I agree, but I think it's also important to have a spiritual life based on a belief in God. I've found that a great deal of happiness, contentment, and peace of mind can be achieved through the pursuit of a positive spiritual life. I believe that religion should be a part of our new society, but it must be a matter of individual choice."

"I've never been a member of any religion," responded Dianne. "But I do believe in God, and I have a very good sense of right and wrong that was instilled into me by my parents. When I have children, I will probably handle the subject with them the same way that my parents taught me."

Dianne paused for a moment. "Getting back to personal freedom, what do you think about the notice posted by Captain Jerontis stating that we're no longer required to wear our uniforms?"

"I think it's great."

"What do you think motivated him to issue that directive?"

"I think the Captain wants us to work together in a relaxed informal atmosphere. Requiring everyone to wear a uniform denotes a sense of formality that I think he wants to dispense with. Also, the uniforms are a product of the NIEA bureaucracy, and when it comes to bureaucrats with their multitudes of regulations, the Captain tends to be a rebel."

"What you're saying is probably true," agreed Dianne. "But I think there's something else involved here."

"What?"

"I think his friend Moose was the instigator of that order. He has quite a playboy reputation, and I think he enjoys being around women who are nicely dressed, even suggestive."

Connie nodded and said, "You might be correct, but how do you feel about wearing your uniform? Wouldn't you like to get rid of it and wear something more stylish?"

"I am going to use any free time that I have today to design and make myself some clothing that is comfortable and feminine."

"You wouldn't be trying to look appealing to Moose, would you?"

"What makes you say that?"

"A moment ago, when you were talking about Moose's playboy reputation, I detected a sparkle in your eyes. I don't think it was there out of interest in me," commented Connie while grinning.

"You're very observant. But then, I guess you should be. You are the psychiatrist."

Dianne thought about Moose for a few moments and her pulse sped up as excitement flooded her system. She admitted, "It's true. I am attracted to him. I especially like his jovial, fun-loving personality. And despite his playboy reputation, I believe he has a solid character and a good set of values. He is obviously very intelligent, and he must be serious and hardworking when he needs to be. Without these characteristics, he could not have advanced as far as he has."

"It appears to me that you've been thinking about him more than just a little bit. Has it occurred to you that a close relationship with him might be exactly what you need to cure the homesickness you're suffering?"

"I haven't thought about it from that perspective, but there might be some merit to that theory. Am I to understand that the ship's doctor is prescribing a relationship with Moose as therapy for my homesickness?"

"Well, I am responsible for the health and psychological well-being of all individuals on this ship. If you need a prescription to get started, I will be more than happy to write you one."

Dianne laughed. "I appreciate your offer, but I think I can manage without written instructions."

At that moment, Moose and Jerry entered the cafeteria. Noticing the presence of Dianne and Connie and that they were both laughing, Jerry turned to Moose and said, "I wonder what they're so happy about."

"It's probably a jubilant reaction to that order you posted about the new dress code," commented Moose.

Having a rather loud booming voice, Moose was easily overheard by Connie and Dianne. They looked at each other with devious expressions and immediately understood what the other was thinking.

When the men arrived at their table, Dianne established eye contact with Moose and asked, "What order are you talking about? Is there something wrong with our uniforms?"

"Captain J.J. issued an order that says we're no longer required to wear our uniforms. We can dress any way we like."

"But these uniforms are loose and comfortable," protested Dianne. "They're functional and easy to work in."

"She's right," stated Connie.

Surprised and disappointed by their comments, Moose shifted his gaze back and forth between them while he considered what to say. Before he could say anything, Dianne smiled at him and said, "I see that you're still wearing your uniform, so can I assume that you agree with us?"

"I like this uniform," replied Moose. "I think I look pretty good in it."

"It sounds like he agrees with us," stated Connie.

"Yes, and he even thinks the uniforms look good," noted Dianne. "So why would anyone want to dress differently?"

"I think they look reasonably good on men," stated Moose.

Looking Moose in the eye and doing her best to display a genuine expression of chagrin, Dianne asked, "Are you implying that we don't look very good?"

Jerry silently observed the conversation with a great deal of amusement at how easily the women maneuvered Moose into a delicate situation. He wondered what they were up to and how Moose would tactfully talk his way out of this one.

With Jerry and both women expectantly staring at him, Moose began to feel uncomfortable as he thought about what to say. Being a quick thinker, after just a few seconds, he politely said, "I wasn't trying to be uncomplimentary. I just like to see good-looking women wear attractive clothing, and these uniforms leave a lot to be desired in that regard."

"That almost sounds like a compliment," noted Dianne. "Thank you."

Dianne said to Connie, "It took a little detective work, but I think I've established that my earlier assertion was correct, wouldn't you agree?"

Connie nodded.

Curious about what they were discussing, and suspicious about whether or not it applied to him, Moose asked, "What assertion are you talking about?"

"Oh, just something we were discussing earlier," responded Dianne.

Moose concluded that he wasn't likely to get an undisguised answer and decided to let it go.

Changing the subject, Connie directed her attention to Jerry and said, "I am concerned about the health of our personnel. It's possible that we could have some medical problems because of the intense pace, high stress level, and lack of sleep during the recent sabotage ordeal. As a precaution, I've decided to give everyone a medical exam."

"That's a good idea," responded Jerry.

"I'm glad you agree, because I want to start with you. How about tomorrow at 9:00 AM?"

"But I feel great. I don't think I need a medical exam."

"You just said that it's a good idea, and since you are the Captain, your health should be closely monitored. Also, you need to set a good example for the crew. Besides that, if you feel great, you have nothing to worry about." Displaying a faint sly smile, Connie added, "Who knows, you might even enjoy it."

Jerry noticed the subtle smile and wondered why Doctor Nemard thought a medical exam would be an enjoyable experience. He figured she must enjoy her job a great deal. "Okay, I'll be there tomorrow at 9:00 AM. On another subject, Moose has indicated a desire to learn the skills needed to evaluate natural sources of food on Alcent."

Dianne turned to Connie and said, "I think the Captain would like us to educate and train Moose in the field of Nutritional Biology."

Speaking to Moose, Dianne said, "If you could stop by the life support lab tomorrow morning, I will help you get started."

TIME: 7 days, 18 hours ALE.

Captain Jerontis arrived at the medical lab for his physical. He entered the front room and announced his presence. From one of the back rooms, he heard Doctor Nemard say, "I'll be right there."

A few moments later, Captain Jerontis saw Connie gracefully walking toward him in her stunning new outfit. Alertly watching him, Connie noticed his eyes light up. Knowing that she had his full attention, she did a graceful turn. The Captain's broad smile of approval told Connie what she wanted to know, but she decided that she also wanted to hear it.

"How do I look?" she asked, with a warm smile.

"Sensational!"

"Thank you. Are you sure there's nothing else?"

Captain Jerontis quickly realized that Doctor Nemard had captivated his full attention. She was so appealing that he simply could not take his eyes off her, and it was obvious that she did not want him to. His body flooded with a desire that had been subdued for far too long, and he wondered what kind of physical Doctor Nemard had in mind.

In a sweet sounding voice, Doctor Nemard asked, "Are you going to just keep staring at me, or are you going to answer my question?"

"You are beautiful, and that's a very sexy outfit you have on. Has anyone else seen you looking like this?"

The possessive tone that Connie detected in Jerry's voice made her feel wanted and filled her with happiness. "Michelle helped me design this outfit. She also styled my hair and helped me with make-up and jewelry. You and she are the only ones who've seen me like this."

"Have you done all of this to please me?"

"Yes."

"That makes me feel special."

"You are special to me. Whenever my mind's not busy with work, it always seems to find you."

"I'm happy you feel that way. By the way, you were right yesterday."

"Right about what?"

"When we were discussing my medical exam, you suggested that I might enjoy the occasion, and you were right."

"I would probably be in tears right now if it had turned out that I was wrong. Should we get started?"

A minute later, while checking Jerry's pulse, Doctor Nemard said, "Your pulse and blood pressure are unusually high this morning. Have you been doing anything that would explain these high numbers?"

Being as obvious as he could, Jerry allowed his eyes to roam over her body with admiration and desire. "You don't need to sound so innocent!" he exclaimed. "You know full well why I'm so excited this morning!"

Toying with him a bit, Connie said, "Please explain."

To comply with her request, Jerry stood up and put his arms around her in a warm embrace. Finding her eagerly responsive, he kissed her passionately. While holding her, he said, "I've wanted to do this for a long time, but for a number of reasons, I've had to keep my feelings suppressed. Now that we're safely underway, none of those reasons exist anymore. I love you, and I have for a long time."

The Captain had just done everything that Connie hoped he would do. Now, her penned up feelings of passion and desire were aroused to the boiling point, and she had difficulty controlling them. Attempting to meld her excited, trembling body even tighter against his, she said, "I feel the same way about you, Captain."

"When we're together like this, maybe you could call me Jerry instead of Captain."

"I will, if you promise to call me Connie instead of Doctor Nemard."

"I can live with that. I know that I came here for a medical exam, but I'm not in the mood for that anymore."

"Your pulse and blood pressure seem to be going through the ceiling. We need to lower them before we can continue with your physical."

"What medical procedure do you plan to use to do that?" teased Jerry.

Connie tilted her head back, looked up into his eyes, and said, "We need to deal with what's causing the high numbers." She kissed him seductively and whispered, "There's a bed in the patient recovery room that we can use, and I believe you are familiar with the procedure. I've never heard it called a medical procedure before, but since it can be quite therapeutic, I guess we could call it that."

Doctor Nemard hung a sign on the medical lab door that said:

**INTENSIVE MEDICAL PROCEDURE IN PROGRESS
DO NOT DISTURB UNLESS YOU HAVE AN EMERGENCY**

Then, she closed the door and locked it.

Meanwhile, in the life support lab, Dianne had completed a review of the life support system's previous twelve hours of performance data. She found no problems, so she decided to move on to her next project: putting together an instruction program to help Moose acquire the knowledge needed for food research on Alcent.

Several minutes into the project, Dianne decided to give up on it. She could not stay focused on putting the program together because Moose kept entering her mind. She couldn't help wondering how he would react when he saw her wearing attractively styled feminine clothing.

Hoping to excite him, Dianne had made a new outfit designed to accentuate her natural beauty. It consisted of a knee-length full-skirt made from soft, colorful material and a tan, somewhat see-through, long-sleeved blouse that revealed the dainty bra under it. Courtesy of Michelle, Dianne wore a flattering new hairstyle, a subtle touch of make-up, and a little perfume. She completed her appearance with some jewelry.

Dianne stood up, walked across the lab, and stood before a large mirror. She looked at herself in self-appraisal. She gazed at her hips and slim waistline. Then, her eyes moved up to her breasts. This is just enough to stimulate Moose's imagination. I hope he thinks I'm attractive. At least, I have a good figure from all the exercise I do.

Dianne took another look at her new hairstyle. "I like it!" she said to herself. "Michelle did an excellent job."

Dianne thought about her maternal grandmother, who had given her the jewelry she was wearing to take with her to Alcent. Dianne treasured the jewelry as a very special gift because her grandmother had worn it on her wedding day. She knew how special this jewelry was to her grandmother and how difficult it must've been for her to give it away. Dianne thought, this may've been my grandmother's way of giving me a part of herself to always remember her by. Maybe she even intended this jewelry to be a tie between the family I will have on Alcent and the family I left behind on Earth. Since this jewelry is likely to be a conversation piece far into the future, it should accomplish that purpose.

Lost in thought, Dianne was startled by the sudden beeping of her communicator, which she immediately picked up and answered, "Life support lab, Dianne speaking."

Almost instantly, she received an exuberant response, "Good morning Dianne! This is Moose. Are you ready to begin turning me into a human nutrition expert, who is fully capable of evaluating biological organisms on Alcent to determine their suitability for human consumption?"

Hearing Moose speak in his high-spirited tone made Dianne tingle with excitement. His constant cheerful attitude was one of the things she really liked about him. She laughed at his longwinded way of asking a simple question and said, "You sound like an eager student with an active imagination, and I am definitely ready to stimulate your imagination."

"Good! I'll be there shortly."

Dianne took one last look at herself and decided that she was ready for Moose. So she turned away from the mirror, walked across the lab, and sat down to await his arrival.

A few minutes later, Moose arrived. Dianne stood up to greet him, not just out of courtesy, but also, to gracefully present herself to him. Total surprise and fascination with the stunning beauty of the woman greeting him left Moose speechless. He intently looked at her in silent appraisal, then in sincere admiration.

Dianne was greatly pleased with Moose's reaction, so she did a graceful turn for him. In a soft tone, she said, "Judging from the way you're staring at me, I get the feeling that you've never seen me before."

"I've never seen you looking like this! After that little masquerade you and Connie put on yesterday, which I naively took at face value, I concluded that I'd never see you in anything other than a uniform. I'm glad I was wrong."

Dianne chuckled at Moose's admission that he had been fooled by their ruse.

"What are you giggling about?" he asked.

"In view of your reputation for being a lady's man with a talent for understanding how women think, I'm amused at how easily we misled you into thinking we were happy with our sexless appearance in our uniforms."

"Well, I don't know either of you very well, so how could I've known that you weren't serious and were just playing with my mind?"

"That's a good point, and I don't know you very well either. Before we get started with work, maybe we should take a coffee break and talk for a while."

"Good idea! Let's go to the cafeteria. I haven't had breakfast yet, and it's been a long time since I last enjoyed a meal with a beautiful woman."

"Thank you for the compliment."

A few minutes later, in the cafeteria, Dianne said, "Except for you and Michelle, all of us had several years to think about whether we wanted to leave Earth and live on Alcent. Michelle had a few months to consider the possibility. You made the choice in just a few hours. Would you mind telling me how you made such a big decision so quickly?"

"I love adventure and this mission is the ultimate adventure."

"I can understand your desire for adventure, but aren't you bothered by breaking your ties to Earth, by leaving family and friends?"

"Not really. I have no wife or children, my parents are both deceased, and my best friend is on this ship."

After a moment of thought, Moose added, "I sense that you are feeling some distress because of leaving family and friends."

"Is it that obvious, or are you just sensitive to my feelings?"

"Maybe a little of both, but I don't think you would've asked that question the way you did, unless it's a problem that you're troubled with. How are you dealing with it?"

"I actually started dealing with it many years ago when I made a total commitment to be on this mission, I've always avoided intimate long-term relationships that could've resulted in marriage and children. That would've put me in an impossible situation. But even though I avoided that problem, I've still left my family and some close friends. The fact that I'll never again be able to do anything with them gives me an empty feeling that I'm having a hard time coping with."

"I understand how you feel. When I lost my parents in a car accident, I grieved for a long time. They were in their late forties, very healthy, and should've had many years of life ahead of them. Losing them was a shock and was very difficult to cope with."

"The grief you felt must've been intense. How did you handle that?"

"Spiritual counseling from their pastor was helpful. The passage of time also helped, but I've never stopped missing them. I wish they were still alive, so I could share with them the thrill of being on this mission."

"What you just said puts a different perspective on my situation. Instead of thinking about the vast distance that separates me from my family, I should be happy that they're alive and healthy and that I can share my experiences with them. As far as close family is concerned, you are alone. That must be difficult for you. Do you ever feel lonely?"

"I am not entirely alone. Jerry and I've been close friends since our college football days. After I lost my parents, he insisted that I accompany him on a vacation trip to Australia. He helped me recover from my grief, and in the process, he became more than just a friend. In many ways, he is like a brother to me. I was an only child, and my parents are dead, so our close friendship has filled an important void in my life."

"I knew that you two are exceptionally close friends, but I didn't realize you thought of yourselves as brothers. With him being white and you being dark, I think it's great that you could think of yourselves as brothers, but it does seem kind of unusual."

"What's so unusual about that? What goes on in a man's brain should not be influenced by the color of his skin."

"I agree, but unfortunately, too many people allow their thinking to be ruled by skin color or ethnic background. In many places on Earth, serious social problems are caused by this, even fighting and killing."

"If I allowed my thinking to be shaped by my ethnic background, my mind would be in a continuous state of confusion."

"What do you mean by that?"

"My ancestry is complicated. One of my great-grandfathers moved to America from Nigeria to do his doctoral work in Nuclear Physics. The woman he married was predominantly French and Native American of Creole descent. One of my grandmothers was Hispanic and Native American of Seminole descent. Her husband was English. If I were to allow my thinking to be ruled by my ethnic background, which of my ancestral cultures would I choose to be the dominant one?"

"That's an interesting question. Have you ever given it any thought?"

"Not much."

"You must have given it some thought, or you wouldn't know your family tree as well as you do."

"Let's just say that I've never made any attempt to live my life in accordance with what was acceptable in any of the cultures in my ethnic background. I've always just thought of myself as an American. I live in the present, and I plan for the future."

"I like that attitude," stated Dianne. "I also have several cultures in my family tree, and like you, I've never made any attempt to preserve any of them. Most of my life has been devoted to achieving the goals that I've set for myself, and that hasn't left me with much time to be concerned about preserving the cultures of my ancestors."

"Which cultures are you talking about?"

"My African heritage is primarily from the Zulu Nation, and I also have French and Creole ancestry."

"I see that we have something in common in our ancestral past, but as complicated as mine is, I'd be surprised if we didn't share some ancestry."

After a few moments, Moose noticed that Dianne was grinning at him mischievously. Wondering what it was about, he asked, "Is there something humorous in what I just said?"

Dianne leaned back into a somewhat enticing posture. "It just struck me that since you don't have any close family, and since we share a few branches in our family trees, you might be tempted to start thinking of me as your sister and pursue a brother/sister relationship."

72

Surprised by Dianne's comment, Moose looked at her with an obvious expression of desire. "It would be difficult for me to have that kind of relationship with you. Besides, I don't think it's what you want either."

"You're right. I have no desire to have a platonic relationship with you. You excite me too much for that to be very satisfying."

"That's encouraging," responded Moose, eagerly.

Dianne looked into Moose's dark brown eyes. "Before you get involved with me, you need to understand that I'm more interested in having a long-term relationship than short-term pleasure. Like I said earlier, I've had to avoid long-term intimate relationships because they would've interfered with my commitment to be on this mission. But now that I've achieved that goal, I'm ready for a long-term relationship."

"I appreciate your honesty. For various reasons, I've never had a long-term relationship with anyone either, but I think it's time I do."

"Why do you think that?"

"Sometimes, I feel alone. I don't have anyone. There's a void in my life that needs to be filled. Recent encounters I had with women back on Earth, although exciting, have not relieved the loneliness that I feel more and more often. I need to belong to someone that I can share the ups and downs of my life with, someone I can be intimate with."

"Now you're being very open with me. I like that."

"I've never revealed these feelings to anyone before, but I feel comfortable with you."

"Because of your jovial attitude toward life, I would've never guessed that you often feel lonely. But I should have, because as far as being dedicated to our careers is concerned, we have much in common. I also feel lonely at times. Sometimes, one's personal life suffers because of dedication to a career. It just can't be avoided."

"Especially, when you have a very time-consuming career," added Moose. "But now, we have partially matching careers, and that will give us time together. En route to Alcent, you'll be helping me learn the skills that I'll need to work with you after we arrive there."

"We'll have more than six years in space, and that'll give us plenty of time to complete your training. Working together should be fun."

"Also, we should have plenty of time for leisure activities. Perhaps later today, we could go down to the gym and play some tennis."

"Great idea," exclaimed Dianne. "I'd love to beat you."

"I'll give you a run for your money, and the exercise will feel good. Let's go." Noticing that Dianne seemed reluctant, Moose asked, "Are you okay?"

Dianne stood up and faced Moose. "I put a lot of time into looking like this. It seems a shame to get out of this outfit and into gym clothes so soon."

Moose slipped his arms around Dianne. "I love what you've done. You are a beautiful woman."

His embrace made Dianne realize that things were happening too fast, so she pulled back. "Thanks for the compliment. And I think we should go play tennis for a while."

Not wanting to push Dianne into something that he sensed she wasn't ready for, Moose released her and said, "Good idea."

"I'll need a little time to change into gym clothes. Can you meet me in the gym in twenty minutes?"

"Sounds good," responded Moose.

TIME: 15 Days, 18 Hours ALE.

Michelle's latest mission update to Earth:

"Nearly sixteen days have passed since we left Earth. During that time, we have accelerated to a velocity of nearly 7,000 miles per second and have traveled just over four billion miles. To put this in perspective, we have traveled a distance slightly greater than Pluto's average distance from the Sun. The first spacecraft sent to Pluto required eight years to make the journey. We have traveled an equivalent distance in less than sixteen days. As fantastic as our speed is, it is only about five percent of the velocity that we will reach in about eight-and-one-half months.

"From this great distance, Earth is no longer visible without a telescope. Although the Sun is still the most brilliant object visible from our observation deck, it is no longer dangerous to view without eye protection. It casts only about as much light into our observation deck as the full Moon did when we were in low Earth orbit."

TIME: 22 Days A.L.E.

Michelle's latest mission update to Earth:

"We have reached a speed of 10,085 miles per second and have traveled just over 8.6 billion miles. Less than an hour ago, we traveled through a region in space called Heliopause. It is a mild shockwave in which the solar wind interacts with the interstellar medium producing low-frequency radio emissions. Heliopause marks the boundary between the solar system and interstellar space. When we passed through it, we became the first humans to enter interstellar space.

"Going back in time to late summer, 1976, Voyagers 1 and 2 were launched from Cape Canaveral on a mission to explore the giant outer planets. In 2010, long after completing their basic missions and traveling in different directions, both spacecraft passed through Heliopause. A journey that required 34 years for the Voyagers has been accomplished by our starship in just 22 days."

TIME: 85 Days ALE.

Michelle's latest mission update to Earth:

"With the flawless performance of our antimatter propulsion system, we continue to gain speed at a steady acceleration of 1g. Our current veloc-ity is 43,273 miles per second. This is approximately 23% of light speed. We have achieved 30% of our planned cruise velocity, and we have traveled 153.8 billion miles. We are now so far away that this message will not reach you until 9.5 days after I've transmitted it.

"At this distance the Sun appears only as an exceptionally bright star in a cosmic background filled with magnificent beauty. Earlier today, on our observation deck, surrounded by a panoramic view of the universe, we car-ried out our first wedding ceremony. Captain Jerontis and Doctor Nemard were joined in holy matrimony. John Moosebeck and Dianne Dawson served as best man and bridesmaid. I was asked to conduct the ceremony, and I did so with great pleasure. This joyful occasion spawned a fun-filled party that lasted for several hours."

TIME: 112 Days, 61 Hours ALE.

Michelle's latest mission update to Earth:

"We are 272 billion miles from Earth traveling at 57,497 miles per sec-ond, 30.9% of light speed. Our antimatter engines were shut down six hours ago, shortly after we collided with a small meteor. Because of our velocity, the meteor vaporized upon impact with our meteor shield. This explosive release of energy blasted a large hole through several layers of the shield. Fortunately, the shield is made up of multiple layers of energy absorbent material, and the explosive impact energy did not reach our starship's hull. The shield is currently being inspected and repaired.

"Because of our tremendous speed, collisions with objects as small as a particle of dust produce the explosive release of a large amount of energy. Some parts of the Milky Way Galaxy are so filled with space dust that a journey similar to ours would be extremely hazardous, if not impossible. The part of the Milky Way that we inhabit, however, is relatively free of dust. This is the result of an event that happened 300,000 years ago. A star located 200 light-years away in the constellation Orion died in a colossal supernova explosion. An enormous shockwave of unimaginable strength swept through interstellar space like a galactic snowplow carrying with it nearly all the gas and dust particles that it encountered, creating a relative-ly gas-free, dust-free bubble in our part of the galaxy. This bubble is com-monly referred to by astronomers as the Local Bubble. It is shaped much like a wind sock and measures some 600 light-years across. This bubble will continue to expand for the next 600,000 years or so before the energy contained in the shock wave has been dissipated. Then, it will begin its col-lapse. The Solar System, the Alpha Centauri System, and a few thousand other nearby stars are contained within the Local Bubble.

"All that remains of the star that died in the supernova is a pulsar named Geminga. It is the burned out core of the dead star. Even though it is less than ten miles in diameter, its mass is comparable to that of the Sun.

Composed entirely of neutrons, it is so dense that a single cubic inch of it has a mass of several thousand tons.

"To our hominid ancestors of 300,000 years ago, the supernova looked far brighter than the full moon. Had it appeared in the nighttime sky, Earth's landscape would have been brightly illuminated, and for a few days, it would have seemed as though Earth had two suns.

"I am astounded by the fact that our journey is relatively safe because of an event that occurred 300,000 years ago. Relative to a human life span, this is a long time, but on a cosmic time scale, 300,000 years isn't much."

TIME: 185 Days ALE.

Michelle's latest mission update to Earth:

"Our current velocity is 95,756 miles per second, approximately 51.5% of light speed. We are continuing to gain speed at a steady acceleration of 1g. At present, we are about 754 billion miles from Earth.

"Captain Jerontis and his wife, Doctor Nemard joyfully announced today that they are expecting to give birth to a baby girl in about seven months. Mike and I are delighted by this news. We are expecting the birth of our son in four weeks and are happy that there will be another child onboard for him to grow up with.

"Because of our great distance from Earth, it will take 46.9 days for this transmission to reach you. By then, my son will have been born and will be several days old."

TIME: 220 Days ALE.

Michelle's latest mission update to Earth:

"We are one trillion miles from Earth, and our speed is 114,194 miles per second, approx. 61.4% of light speed. Mike and I are the happy parents of a healthy baby boy who was born three days ago. He has light brown hair and light brown eyes. His weight at birth was ten pounds. We've decided to name him Matthew in honor of my favorite Gospel writer. By the time you receive this broadcast, Matthew will be 70 days old."

TIME: 261 Days ALE.

Michelle's latest mission update to Earth:

"We have just reached our cruise velocity of 135,793 miles per second, approximately 73% of light speed. We are 1.51 trillion miles from Earth, and our antimatter propulsion system has been shutdown.

"To have a greater fuel reserve, Captain Jerontis decided to travel at 73% of light speed instead of 77% as originally planned. This will increase the length of our journey from 6.40 years to 6.67 years, about 98 days. We believe that the increased travel time is a reasonable price to pay for the added safety and flexibility provided by a larger fuel reserve.

"Because of the nearly perfect vacuum that exists in interstellar space, we will experience very little loss of velocity even though our propulsion system has been shut down. The only force that will slow us down is the pull of the Sun's gravity. However, because of our great distance from the Sun, its gravitational pull is very feeble.

"We are currently weightless because we are no longer accelerating at 1g. Since it would be unhealthy for us to be weightless for the next several years, we will use centrifugal force to create artificial gravity. To achieve this, we will detach stage one of our propulsion system, and move a short distance away from it. Then, we will make a 180-degree turn, so that the nose of our starship faces the top end of the propulsion stage. Next, we will connect the starship to the propulsion stage with a tether that is two miles long. After slowly backing away from the propulsion stage until the tether is tight, we will spin up this configuration to the appropriate rotational speed to give us an artificial gravity of 1g.

"There are two reasons for using a long tether: First, our starship has several decks, and the use of a long tether will reduce the variation in artificial gravity between the top deck and the bottom deck. Second, the use of a long tether allows us to achieve an artificial gravity of 1g with a much lower rotation rate than would be required with a short tether.

"After coasting through interstellar space for five years and three months, we will dock with the first stage of our propulsion system, and begin 1g deceleration. It will take nearly nine months to lose the immense speed that we have gained since leaving Earth. If we are unable to cancel out the tremendous speed that we are traveling at, we will be unable to orbit Alcent. Then, we would be forced to live the rest of our lives onboard this starship. This could happen if we accidentally lose part of our fuel during the next five to six years, or if after our long coast period, our antimatter propulsion system fails to operate at peak efficiency. The serious consequences of these possibilities led to the decision to increase our fuel reserves by traveling at a lower cruise speed.

"Because of our great distance, 94 days will have elapsed by the time you receive this transmission."

TIME: 365 Days ALE.

Michelle's latest mission update to Earth:

"We are 2.73 trillion miles from Earth traveling at 73% of light speed. Today, we are celebrating the second marriage on our starship. Three hours ago, Dianne Dawson and John Moosebeck exchanged vows in a joyful wedding ceremony. Also, today marks our one year anniversary of leaving Earth. We are thankful for the safe journey we have had so far. These two events have created a festive atmosphere onboard our starship. Because of our great distance, 170 days will be required for this brief message to reach you."

TIME: 1 Year, 27 Days ALE.

Michelle's latest mission update to Earth:

"We are 3.05 trillion miles from Earth traveling at 73% of light speed. Nearly 190 days will pass by before you receive this broadcast.

"Today is another joyful occasion for our society. Just a few hours ago, Captain Jerontis and Doctor Nemard became the proud parents of a lovely baby girl. Her name is Denise. She has light blond hair, blue eyes, and weighs eight pounds, seven ounces. She is the first baby to be conceived and born on a starship in interstellar space.

"My son is almost six months old and is a happy, healthy, playful child. He is popular and loves the attention he is getting from everyone."

TIME: 1 Year, 217 Days ALE.

Michelle's latest mission update to Earth:

"We are currently 5.28 trillion miles from Earth traveling at 73% of light speed. It will take 328 days for this transmission to arrive at Earth.

"Today, Mike and I put on a birthday party for Matthew. He is one year old. The light brown hair he was born with has gradually changed to a darker brown, and his light brown eyes have slowly become hazel. He has developed an almost insatiable curiosity making it necessary to watch him constantly, because he has learned to walk and loves to explore.

"Denise is now six months old. Her beautiful blue eyes, golden blond hair, and facial features make her a living image of her mother. Denise is a happy, content child who thoroughly enjoys the attention she constantly receives from everyone. Despite being on a starship moving through interstellar space at great speed and living with artificial gravity, Denise and Matthew are developing normally and are in excellent health."

TIME: 2 Years, 27 Days ALE.

Michelle's latest mission update to Earth:

"I am beginning to develop a deep appreciation for the truly immense size of the universe. We have been in space more than two years, and for well over a year, we have been traveling at nearly 135,800 miles per second. We are seven trillion miles from Earth, a distance so great that this message traveling at the speed of light will require 436 days to reach you. Yet, after all of this time and speed, we have covered only 27.5% of the distance to the Alpha Centauri System, the Sun's nearest interstellar neighbors. Imagine how much time would be required to travel to the more distant stars in the Milky Way Galaxy. Then consider the fact that the universe contains hundreds of millions of galaxies, and you will begin to appreciate the enormous extent of the cosmos and what an insignificant part of it we humans are. But someday in the far distant future, there may be human civilizations thriving throughout the Milky Way. Our voyage to Alcent is the first tiny step in accomplishing this.

"Life onboard the Challenger is comfortable. We have adequate space, privacy when we want it, and all basic essentials, but we are confined. Imagine living in a hotel where different functions are done on different floors. Then, imagine that within this hotel you have everything that you need for a comfortable life. Next, tell yourself that you cannot leave this hotel for seven years. That is what our life is like. We are comfortable, but we are confined, and will be for several more years.

"Denise is one year old today, and there was a birthday party for her. She is a very pretty little girl and continues to enjoy the attention she is getting from everyone. She has learned to walk, and like my son, enjoys exploring her surroundings. Both children display an inquisitive alertness to the activities that go on around them. Also, even at this early age, they are very much aware of each other and enjoy playing together."

TIME: 3 Years, 124 Days, 7.2 Hours ALE.

Michelle's latest mission update to Earth:

"We are now 12.75 trillion miles from Earth moving at 73% of light speed. Today is an important event in our lives because we are halfway to the Alpha Centauri System. From this day forward, we will be closer to our new home on Alcent than the homes we left on Earth. We have decided to make today a special day of thanksgiving, much like the Thanksgiving Holiday that is celebrated in the United States every year. We are thankful that the first half of our voyage has been safe and that we are all in good health. We are grateful that Matthew and Denise are developing normally in this interstellar environment. In fact, they seem quite advanced for their ages. They've learned to talk and are rapidly learning new words because of constant tutoring from everyone."

TIME: 4 Years, 233 Days ALE.

Michelle's latest mission update to Earth:

"We are 18.3 trillion miles from Earth and 7.2 trillion miles from our destination. We continue to travel at 73% of light speed. This transmission will require 3 years and 44 days to reach you.

"Just a few hours ago, our voyage nearly came to a tragic end when we passed through a cloud of interstellar asteroids. Because of our great speed and the large size of the cloud, there wasn't enough time to maneuver around it, so we had to go through it. The asteroids were composed mostly of rock and some ice, and they ranged in size from a few feet across to a few hundred yards. There were several thousand of them, and a collision with even the smallest one could easily have destroyed us. Fortunately, they were spread out over a large volume of space, so that our defensive systems were not overwhelmed and were able to destroy those that we would otherwise have collided with.

"This ship is equipped with radar systems that are so powerful and sensitive that they are able to detect objects out to a range of 100 million miles or more, a distance that we traverse in just over 12 minutes. Radar data is fed into our fire control computer, which tracks all detected objects and determines if we are on a collision course with any of them. If we are, the computer aims and fires our antimatter particle-beam gun at the threatening object. When the high-density beam of charged antimatter particles hits the ordinary matter in the targeted object, a powerful sustained explosion occurs which either annihilates the target, or in the case of a large object, changes its course so that we do not collide with it.

"In all the trillions of miles that we've traveled to date, today was the only time that our particle-beam gun was used. But if we didn't have this defensive equipment, we would no longer exist. The three asteroids that we destroyed were each about the size of a compact car. Colliding with any of them would have destroyed us. We owe our lives to those who insisted that defensive equipment be installed on this starship.

"Because of our great speed, only a half-hour transpired from the time that we detected the asteroid cloud to the time that we passed through it. Needless to say, this was a nerve-racking half-hour. Not knowing from one second to the next whether my life was about to end left me emotionally drained. Every time the computer fired the antimatter particle-beam gun, my mind was filled with anxiety for a few suspenseful moments while I wondered if it would be successful in destroying or deflecting its target. Making the whole experience even more hair-raising was the fact that I could not see any of the asteroids. We were just moving by them too fast. When whizzing by an object at 135,800 miles per second, the human eye simply isn't able to see it. Our lives were dependent on the extremely quick reaction of our defensive equipment. Its flawless performance saved us from certain destruction. Once again, we applaud the excellence achieved by those who designed, built, and tested our starship."

TIME: 5 Years, 352 Days ALE.

Michelle's latest mission update to Earth:

"We are 23.99 trillion miles from Earth and 1.52 trillion miles from Alcent. This message will require 4 years and 33 days to reach you. By the time you receive it, it will almost be ancient history.

"Today is another milestone in our voyage. Our long coast period at 73% of light speed is finally over. It has been a seemingly endless time period of more than five years that we have been traveling at this enormous speed. Although it has been a comfortable home, almost everyone is tired of living on the Challenger. We thirst for the wide open spaces on a planet as opposed to being confined in a starship.

"Two exceptions are Matthew and Denise, who enjoy living on this starship. They have never known any other home. Won't they be surprised by the huge new world that will greet them when we land on Alcent?

"During our long coast period, we added some degree of normality to our lives by providing ourselves with artificial gravity about the same as on Earth. This was done with centrifugal force. The Challenger was secured to its first stage with a long tether, and this configuration was accelerated to the appropriate rotational velocity to provide 1g of artificial gravity. I would have found this long voyage unbearable if I'd had to float around in a weightless condition for more than five years.

"A short time ago, we reduced our rotational velocity to zero and released the long tether that connected us to the first stage of our propulsion system. Then we carried out a sequence of maneuvers to dock with that stage. Its antimatter engines have been ignited, and we are now losing velocity at 1g giving us an artificial gravity equal to that on Earth's surface. Almost nine months of deceleration will be required to reduce our present velocity of 135,790 miles per second down to approximately five miles per second, which will be our orbital velocity around Alcent."

TIME: 6 Years, 1 Day, 3 Hours ALE.

Michelle's latest mission update to Earth:

"We are 24.15 trillion miles from Earth and 1.36 trillion miles from Alcent. The past two weeks of deceleration has reduced our velocity to 128,350 miles per second, approximately 69% of light speed.

"Early in our voyage, Captain Jerontis decided to cruise at 73% of light speed rather than the originally planned 77%. This left a fuel residual in the first stage, which has now been expended. We have separated from stage one and have resumed deceleration with propulsion stage number two. Its antimatter engines are performing normally. Stage one has been discarded and will continue to move through interstellar space at 69% of light speed until it collides with something and is vaporized in a colossal instantaneous release of its tremendous kinetic energy."

TIME: 6 Years, 63 Days A.L.E.

Michelle's latest mission update to Earth:

"We are 24.75 trillion miles from Earth and 760 billion miles from Alcent. Our velocity is 95,757 miles per second, approximately 51.5% of light speed. We continue to decelerate at 1g.

"Today marks our closest approach to Alpha Centauri C, the smallest and coolest of the three stars that make up the Alpha Centauri System. We are currently 941 billion miles away from the star, and we will not get any closer. Since it is a red dwarf of spectral type M5, Alpha Centauri C is too dim and cool to provide the amount of light and heat needed to support life on any planet that it might possess. Also, like many red dwarfs, it is a flare star. Occasionally it has explosive outbursts that double and sometimes even triple its energy output. Any planet close enough to the star to have life during normal times would certainly be torched to death by these explosive outbursts. This is definitely not a place where we would be interested in trying to build a home.

"In contrast to Alpha Centauri C, the Sun is bright, hot, and stable in its energy output making life on Earth not only possible, but comfortable. Alpha Centauri A is like the Sun in many respects. Both are bright yellow main sequence stars of spectral type G2. Only about 4% of the stars in the Milky Way are spectral type G, whereas about 70% are red dwarfs. The Sun and Alpha Centauri A are not average stars; they are members of a small special group where all the conditions are right to support planets filled with an abundance of life."

TIME: 6 Years, 217 Days ALE.

Michelle's latest mission update to Earth:

"We are 25.493 trillion miles from Earth and 17.551 billion miles from Alcent. Our velocity is 14,630 miles per second, approximately 8.15% of light speed. We continue to decelerate at 1g.

"Today is a special occasion for Matthew. It is his sixth birthday, and we put on a birthday party for him. Hopefully, Matthew's next birthday party will be on Alcent.

"Even though we are tired of living on this starship and would like to arrive at Alcent as soon as possible, we have decided to swing by Alpha Centauri B. One of its planets is in the star's life zone. We plan to do a brief orbital exploration of this planet to find out if it is capable of supporting life, if it has any life on it, and if it would be a more suitable home for us than Alcent. We have adequate fuel reserves, and this detour will delay our arrival at Alpha Centauri A and Alcent by only a few weeks.

"Alpha Centauri B is an orange star of spectral type K2. Its mass is about nine-tenths that of the Sun, and its surface temperature is about 8.6% cooler than on the Sun. Although the star's light and heat output are not high enough to be ideal for life, they are intense enough to support life if the right kind of planet is located at the optimum distance from the star. The planet we are going to investigate seems to satisfy these conditions, but we won't know for sure until we get much closer.

"Orange, spectral type K stars make up about 15% of the stars in the Milky Way. Only the largest, hottest, brightest stars in this group are capable of having planets with an abundance of life on them. Alpha Centauri B satisfies these requirements."

FOUR

Rescuing a Planet

TIME: 6 Years, 245 Days ALE.

Michelle's latest mission update to Earth:

"We have just completed our first orbit of Alpha Centauri B's second planet, which we have designated B-2. Our circular polar orbit at an altitude of 230 miles takes us around the planet once every ninety minutes. As B-2 rotates on its axis, our instruments will observe all of it under daytime and nighttime conditions by the time the planet completes one revolution (23 hours, 37 minutes).

"We are currently approaching B-2's equator from the north, and I am on the observation deck looking down on a vast ocean that extends to the north and south polar icecaps and to the eastern horizon. The ocean is dotted with numerous islands. To the west, two major land masses are visible that extend nearly to the western horizon. One of the continents is located north of the equator, and the other is located south of the equator. They are connected by a land bridge with a minimum width of 50 miles."

While Michelle did her mission update, Dianne looked down on B-2, and was fascinated by what she was seeing. She was captivated by the panoramic view of a planet that resembled Earth in many important ways. The planet looked so appealing that she wondered if it might be a better place to live than Alcent with its multitude of dinosaurs. It just seemed so peaceful and inviting. But was this planet filled with life or was it barren? As she pondered the question, a strange feeling gradually pervaded her senses that not only did life exist on this planet, but that it also included intelligent life. The sensation was so strong that Dianne became convinced that it was caused by something other than her imagination.

This unique sensation troubled Dianne and raised a few questions: What kind of life could it be, so that she could sense its presence from a distance of 230 miles? Did these life forms have brains that generated such strong energy fields that she could sense them at such a great distance? Were these life forms doing something to make their presence known? If so, why? Would these life forms prove to be congenial or hostile? So deeply lost in thought was Dianne that she failed to notice Moose sneak up behind her.

Moose silently gazed over her shoulder for a few moments. Then, he startled her out of her mesmerized mental state by loudly asking, "Well, what do you think of it?"

Dianne flinched at the unexpected disruption of her thoughts; then, she turned toward Moose and said, "You sure like to sneak up and startle me. You just never seem to miss an opportunity."

"What do you mean? All I did was ask you a question," declared Moose, innocently.

"It wasn't the question that startled me. It was the way you crept up behind me."

"I did that out of love for you," stated Moose with utmost sincerity.

"Seems like a strange way to express love," retorted Dianne. "Would my dear sweet husband mind giving me an explanation?"

"Simple! It's all part of your training."

"Training?"

"Alcent will be a dangerous place, and you need to develop a greater awareness of your immediate surroundings."

"I am continually amazed at the way you always find a way to justify the things you do to satisfy your overactive sense of humor. Now, you're implying that I need to keep my guard up here on the observation deck, a place that I've always found to be perfectly safe."

"It sounds like my lovely wife no longer appreciates my fun-loving nature."

"On the contrary, your lighthearted attitude is one of the reasons I enjoy being married to you, but maybe you could avoid making me the object of your practical jokes for a while."

"I can do that," replied Moose, giving her a kiss.

Dianne gave Moose a big hug. "I'm glad you're here, because I want to share my feelings with you. This planet reminds me of Earth in so many ways that it really intrigues me. It excites me so much that it has my imagination running wild."

"What has your wildly excited imagination come up with?"

"I have a strong feeling that there's intelligent life down there. Think about it: We've just completed a seemingly endless voyage through the lifeless void of interstellar space, and now, we're facing a planet that might have intelligent life on it. I can't help being wildly excited about that. I'd like to go down there and explore the place."

"That's an adventure I'd like to go on too, but what makes you so convinced that there's intelligent life down there?"

"Call it intuition if you want, but I sense that this planet is inhabited by intelligent life. I know it sounds weird, but I feel its presence. Also, the essentials for life as we know it are there; namely, an earthlike atmosphere, an earthlike climate, and an abundance of water."

"But how can you sense life that is 230 miles below us?"

"I don't know, but we are orbiting an alien planet. Life could have evolved into forms that have mental powers that are different than ours."

"Are you suggesting that there might be intelligent life down there that is trying to communicate with you telepathically?"

"I wish I could answer your question," replied Dianne, "but I don't know. All I can say is that I feel the presence of life. Anyway, the data that we're collecting should give us some answers."

While pointing at two large continents, Dianne said, "They remind me of North and South America."

Moose looked at them and said, "I see what you mean. They're even connected by a land bridge, and the deep green color of the land bridge looks like dense vegetation. It might even be a tropical rain forest."

"Lots of rain is essential for a rain forest, and that heavy cloud cover offshore to the west looks like it could deliver exactly that."

A few minutes later, while passing over the south polar icecap, the Challenger entered B-2's nighttime hemisphere. However, with Alpha Centauri A currently the dominant star in B-2's nighttime sky, nighttime on B-2 just wasn't very dark. At its present distance of 2.45 billion miles, Alpha Centauri A flooded B-2 with far more light than a full moon in Earth's nighttime sky.

Observing this phenomenon, Dianne said, "Having a second star so close that nighttime isn't dark seems strange, almost eerie. The light down there appears to be comparable to what you have on Earth a few minutes after sunset. Imagine having the brightness of twilight all night long."

"Whether we live on this planet or on Alcent, we'll be faced with that situation. Part of the year, the more distant of the two stars will be in the nighttime sky, and it just won't get very dark. But when we get used to that, it'll probably seem normal, and we won't give it much thought."

A few minutes later, Moose said, "It looks like this hemisphere has only one continent, and it's fairly well centered on the equator. It appears to be a couple thousand miles short of reaching either polar icecap."

After a few minutes of silent observation and reflective thought, Dianne exclaimed, "Wow! Look over there! Judging from the size and frequency of those lightning bolts, this planet has thunderstorms just as large and awe-inspiring as any back on Earth."

"That's a large system," commented Moose. "That line of thunder storms must be a thousand miles long."

Preoccupied with their thoughts, Moose and Dianne silently observed the powerful lightning bolts light up the clouds far below them. Dianne wondered if life existed on this continent; and if present, how was it being affected by the awesome forces of nature being unleashed by this storm. As she pondered the life-question, a dreadful feeling of cold fear flooded her senses. The strength and nature of the feeling alarmed Dianne so much that she shook from head to toe as an involuntary tremor passed through her body. She immediately grabbed Moose and cried out, "Moose! It's happening again, and I feel like it wants to torture me."

"What's happening again?"

"I sense the presence of life down there!"

"Are you positive?"

"Definitely!"

"Why do you think it wants to torture you?"

"I don't know why. I don't even know if it has the means to harm me, but it evidently has some capability to communicate telepathically. For some reason, it used that ability to hit me with a wave of cold-hearted hatred so intense that it felt like a vicious attack."

"I wonder why it did that. Since this is its first encounter with humans, it can't possibly know much about us, so why would it hate us? I am especially puzzled that it would express hatred toward you."

"Why is that?"

"Because you have a warm personality and no desire to harm alien life."

"Maybe that's the problem."

"What do you mean?"

"Maybe this creature lives according to a philosophy that's based on hatred and consequently, finds my kindhearted personality repugnant."

"If that's the case, it isn't going to like any of us, because we're all kindhearted. How much danger do you think we're in?"

"I don't know. We know nothing about this creature except that it's down there and has telepathic ability. We don't even know if I'm being targeted by a lone individual or by a large group. If I'm being tormented by a hateful individual who is a member of an otherwise benevolent society, it would seem like that would put us at less risk than facing an entire society that is evil. But whatever the case may be, we don't know what they're capable of doing with their telepathic powers."

"We've never had to deal with a species possessing telepathic ability. What if they're able to use it against us?"

"In what way?" Dianne asked.

"What if they have a very advanced telepathic ability, so advanced that they're able to get into our minds and read our thoughts and memories? Then, our knowledge would become their knowledge."

"I think that's unlikely. Since this is their first contact with humans, they cannot possibly understand our language. If they can't understand the language our thoughts and memories are in, I don't see how they could pick our brains."

"I hope you're right," stated Moose. "When we passed over the other two continents and you first became aware of the presence of life, did you sense any danger?"

"No, I didn't. To the contrary, it was more of a feeling of an awareness of our presence. I felt like we were simply being investigated. Perhaps, it was an effort to find out if we posed any kind of threat."

"Suppose it reached the conclusion that we do pose a threat. What would its response be?"

"That question is difficult to answer. We don't know what kind of life we're dealing with; let alone, what its capabilities are."

"For the sake of discussion, let me speculate a bit," offered Moose. "To me, it seems likely that the life-form that contacted you in a non-threatening way may be of the same species as the one that projected a sense of evil to you. It may be that they differ only in religious philosophy. On the first two continents we passed over, the species may be living in accordance with a religious philosophy that promotes love, trust, benevolence, and tolerance. On the continent below us, the species may be living in accordance with a religious philosophy that advocates hatred, distrust, and intolerance of all who disagree with its teachings. They may even be carrying it to the extreme of tormenting or even killing those who don't accept their philosophy."

"What you're saying is that even though we mean them no harm, they may want to destroy us anyway, just because our philosophy is different from theirs."

"That's exactly what I'm saying. However, wanting to destroy us and being able to destroy us are two different things. We could be in great danger or in no danger at all."

Dianne started to look worried. "If there really are beings down there with an advanced telepathic ability, we could be in big trouble. Suppose they're so advanced in its use that they can telepathically enter our minds and implant suggestions or even take control. At the very least, we could see some strange behavior on this ship. In a worst case scenario, they could cause one of our people to do something that could destroy us."

"Like you said earlier, they're not likely to understand our language, and that should greatly limit what they can do."

"What if they find a way around the language barrier?"

"That's a scary possibility," admitted Moose. "You've just suggested how a race of intelligent beings possessing advanced telepathic ability could seriously harm us, or even destroy us, without the use of high-tech weapons. But if they have high-tech weapons and use them in conjunction with their telepathic ability, we could find ourselves in an extremely serious situation. We need to talk Captain Jerontis about this."

A short time later, Moose and Dianne found Captain Jerontis and Doctor Nemard on the flight deck where they were viewing computer enhanced, high-resolution, 3-D images of small sections of the planet's surface. Skipping a cordial greeting, Moose urgently said, "Captain! We're sorry to interrupt you, but we may be in serious danger from the beings living on this planet, and we should take immediate precautions."

Alarmed by the sense of urgency displayed by the normally carefree Moose, Doctor Nemard and Captain Jerontis quickly turned to face him.

"What beings are you talking about?" Captain Jerontis asked. "Connie and I have been looking at high-resolution images for two hours, and we've seen no evidence of intelligent life, only lots of thick vegetation."

"Intelligent life that does not want to be seen could certainly conceal itself in a jungle," argued Dianne, who proceeded to report her experiences and the conclusions that she and Moose had reached.

"If they don't want to be seen, who are they trying to hide from?" questioned Captain Jerontis. "Is there an ongoing war that would cause them to camouflage themselves, or did they detect us before we arrived here? If they detected us, they could've decided to hide from us while they attempt to discover our intentions. If that's the case, then to have sufficient time to conceal themselves and all evidence of their existence, they would've had to discover us long before we arrived here. But how could they've done that? We haven't detected any radar emissions, and we haven't alerted them to our presence by using our radar. All of our communications transmissions have been beamed toward Earth, directly away from them, so it's unlikely that they could've discovered us by detecting any of our electronic emissions. If they detected us far out in space purely with telepathic ability, then they have an awesome mental power that is far beyond anything we've ever thought possible."

"I find it difficult to imagine that any creature could possess telepathic ability so powerful that it could be effective at distances of hundreds of millions of miles," argued Doctor Nemard.

While facing Jerry, Moose said, "I think your suggestion of an ongoing war is a plausible explanation, especially if it's a worldwide war that's been going on for centuries. If these creatures have any factories and homes, they may be underground. Perhaps they're protecting themselves from their enemies and aren't hiding from us at all. They might not even have discovered us until we started orbiting this planet; at which point, they could've detected us visually."

"That's possible," admitted Dianne, "but the feelings I had were very strong. I believe these creatures do possess telepathic ability and that it has an effective range of at least a few hundred miles."

"Until we know otherwise, we should assume that you're correct," stated Captain Jerontis. "But whether we were discovered visually or telepathically doesn't matter; either way, they know we're here. Consequently, we face the ominous possibility that opposing forces in a major war are investigating us to determine if we are a new weapon invented by the other side. If either side decides that we are, then we could come under attack by whatever weaponry they possess."

"But we might not be attacked by weapons," commented Dianne. "It's possible that they might use their telepathic ability in an attempt to manipulate one or more of our personnel to destroy us from within."

Responding to Dianne, Moose said, "As you pointed out earlier, our language has to be totally alien to them. Because of this language barrier, it seems to me that it would be very difficult for them to telepathically enter our minds and hypnotize or control us in any way."

"The human mind is very complicated," stated Doctor Nemard. "In addition to words and numbers, it contains visual images. By using telepathic images, an alien should be able to find out how our ship is defended. For example, it could project into your mind an image of a large missile on an intercept course with our ship. Your mind might respond by forming an image of our antimatter particle-beam gun destroying the missile. The alien would then know that for a missile attack to be successful; the particle-beam gun would first have to be disabled."

"If they can use telepathically transmitted images to bypass the language barrier, we might be in real trouble," admitted Moose.

"That possibility concerns me," stated Captain Jerontis. "What if they are able to enter our subconscious minds telepathically and explore the images stored in our memories; then, they would be able to obtain a wealth of information about us. How do we defend against that?"

"In normal everyday life, it is the conscious mind that inputs information into the subconscious mind to be remembered for later use," responded Doctor Nemard. "In other words, the normal path to the subconscious mind is through the conscious mind. I think it's very unlikely that an alien being could explore our subconscious minds without us being aware of it, especially if we are alert to the possibility that this might be tried. A danger period would be when we're asleep and the conscious mind is not on guard."

"We need to alert everyone to the risk we're facing," stated Captain Jerontis. "Also, I want all personnel to stay awake and mentally on guard until we leave this planet. That means we'll have to complete our exploration in less than 24 hours, because it's difficult to stay awake longer than that. During that time, I want to find and identify the species with the telepathic powers. I want to determine if they have the ability to endanger us when we're living on Alcent. Since Alcent will never be closer than about a billion miles to this planet, I don't think it's very likely that they'll be able to bother us. But I don't want to take that for granted. We'll face enough dangers on Alcent without having to be concerned about telepathic attack from creatures on this planet."

Captain Jerontis sounded the warning klaxon to get everyone's attention. Since most of them were already there, he directed them to assemble on the observation deck for an urgent meeting. He asked Dianne and Doctor Nemard to conduct the meeting to alert everyone to the current danger and to find out if anyone had been contacted telepathically. In addition, he asked Dianne and Doctor Nemard to report the names of any personnel not present at the meeting. These individuals would be located and investigated to make sure they weren't under alien control.

As they were leaving, Connie said, "I'll ask Michelle to keep the children mentally occupied, because they might be easy targets for mind tampering."

"Good idea, and could you send Mike up here when you're finished with your meeting?"

"Sure can."

Turning to Moose, Captain Jerontis said, "I'd like you to stay here and help me find these creatures. Since we don't know the full extent of their telepathic powers, I believe it's imperative that we find them before anyone needs sleep. That doesn't give us much time, so we need to do this methodically. But where do we start looking?"

"That's a tough question considering that we know nothing about them except that they may have mental powers with enough range to harm us at this altitude. We don't even know if all of them have this ability, or if it's limited to a few special individuals. For that matter, they might even be using high-tech equipment to accomplish telepathic communication."

"That's a possibility, but if they are a high-tech society, we should be able to detect electronic transmissions. Since our arrival here, we've been conducting extensive electronic eavesdropping, and we've detected nothing. Therefore, either they're in a total electronic blackout, which would seem almost impossible to accomplish, or they're a primitive civilization and have not yet discovered electricity."

Looking at the dense jungle displayed on the large video screen, Moose said, "However advanced or primitive they are, they're going to be difficult to find in that."

"We might be able to find evidence of their location with our radar, such as buildings concealed by vegetation. Since they already know we're here, there's no longer any reason to maintain electronic silence, so why don't you put our radar to work and see what you can find."

"Perhaps land areas bordering rivers, lakes, and oceans would be the best place to look," commented Moose. "On Earth, even ancient civilizations tended to build their villages and cities near water for various practical reasons. Unless these creatures are primitive nomadic savages who just happen to have telepathic powers, we should find villages or encampments of some sort near water."

"That sounds reasonable. While you're doing the radar search, I'll study high-resolution images of the rivers we pass over. Even primitive creatures might have canoes for fishing and transportation. If we're dealing with a more advanced society, maybe I'll find a bridge or two."

A few minutes later, Captain Jerontis received a call from his wife, who reported the names of three individuals not present at the meeting. Captain Jerontis noted that all three were currently on duty and asked Connie to contact them after the meeting.

An hour later, with the Challenger beginning its fourth orbit of B-2, an obviously excited Mike Johnson arrived on the flight deck and reported to Captain Jerontis: "Dianne's opening statement at that meeting sure got everyone's attention. What happened these past few hours is a milestone in human history: the first contact with an apparently intelligent alien life-form has occurred. Dianne's experience wasn't unique either. Three other people recounted experiences similar to hers. Doctor Nemard and Dianne are currently meeting with them. They're trying to determine why only four of us were contacted. They'll report to you as soon as they can."

"Thanks for the update," replied Captain Jerontis, who then told Mike what he and Moose were doing.

"Have you found any evidence to confirm the existence of these creatures?" Mike asked.

"So far, we haven't found any indication of intelligent life, just lots of lush vegetation."

"A crazy idea just hit me," stated Mike. "Is it possible that this planet's plant life has evolved some type of collective intelligence?"

"That doesn't seem very likely, but I'll ask Dianne. Maybe she can concoct some wild genetic scheme of events that would allow plant life to develop intelligence. In the meantime, I want you to review our infrared data. Search for something that can only be explained by the presence of intelligent creatures."

"I'll get started right now."

For easier communication, Captain Jerontis decided to give B-2's three continents descriptive names. The two continents connected by a land bridge would be referred to as the Northern Continent and the Southern Continent. The continent centered on the equator and located on B-2's opposite hemisphere would be called the Equatorial Continent.

"Captain, you need to see this!" Moose exclaimed.

When Captain Jerontis joined Moose at his video screen, Moose said, "I think I've found a city, but it's the strangest city I've ever seen. There's a circular area about eight miles in diameter that has almost no buildings on it, but around the circumference of this circle, there are various kinds of structures that extend outward for two to four miles."

"That is very peculiar," agreed Captain Jerontis. "Let's instruct the computer to enhance these radar images for maximum detail."

The Challenger's radar had several features that enabled it to achieve exceptional detail. Being a multi-frequency radar, it could probe its target with radar signals over the entire range from short wave to long wave. The radar images could then be overlaid and compared by the computer to extract maximum detail. Also, the computer could determine the height of a building by measuring the difference in time for a radar signal to return from the top of the building and from the street alongside the building. In addition, because of the Challenger's orbital motion, radar images of the same target could be taken from different viewpoints. By comparing these images, the computer could provide minutely detailed 3-D pictures of the target area. Also, radar signals of the appropriate wavelength could penetrate a forest to reveal buildings concealed by it.

Captain Jerontis asked Mike for a detailed infrared map of the area, while he went back to his screen to study the area with visual images.

A few minutes later, Captain Jerontis said, "My visual images show nothing except a jungle of vegetation."

"My infrared data isn't revealing much either," Mike said. "There just simply isn't much temperature variation over that area."

"Our radar is doing a great job of seeing through the jungle," stated Moose. "This area looks like the remains of city that was destroyed by a nuclear bomb a long time ago, perhaps even centuries ago. All structures have been obliterated inside a circle about six miles in diameter. For an additional two miles outside of this circle, the wreckage of some buildings still exists. Outside of that circle, we start to find structures with less and less damage the farther out we look. Even though they are concealed by vegetation and partly buried by debris, we can see some of the streets in the long-dead city and some of the highways leading into it."

While studying the images, Captain Jerontis said, "If you're correct, there must be other bomb-destroyed cities. Using this set of data as a guide, let's have the computer do a planet-wide search and find them."

"I guess we can scratch the primitive society theory, Moose said.

"Not necessarily," countered Captain Jerontis. "We know only that there was a high-tech society here at the time this city was destroyed. If there was a planet-wide nuclear war, and if there weren't many survivors; then, there might now be a very primitive society living on this planet."

"If there was a planet-wide nuclear war, how were the bombs delivered?" questioned Moose. "If they were delivered by ballistic missiles, then these creatures would've had the capability to launch satellites; however, we haven't found any."

"We haven't looked for satellites," Captain Jerontis said. "But if they had satellites and were involved in a planet-wide war; then, they would've tried to destroy each other's satellites. If any of the weapons used for that purpose are still around, we could be in grave danger. Especially, if the weapons were automatically activated under computer control and fired against any unidentified satellite. We might look like a fat juicy target to that kind of weapon system. Our antimatter particle-beam gun could certainly protect us against a missile attack; however, if we're attacked by a powerful laser, the gun might not be able to knock it out because we don't know if it will be effective shooting through B-2's atmosphere."

"We need to be prepared for all possibilities," stated Mike. "But if anti-satellite weapons existed at the time this city was destroyed, it's difficult to imagine that they could still be functional after all these years."

"We don't know how much time has passed since the war," argued Captain Jerontis. "We only know that one city was destroyed and that it's been overrun by vegetation. We're assuming that it would've taken at least several decades for plant life to overrun a radioactive wasteland, but that's only an assumption."

"Are you suggesting that plant life on this planet is so tough and aggressive that it could overrun a radioactive wasteland in just a few years?" questioned Moose.

"Look at the evidence. Every part of the planet we've passed over is covered with vegetation. It's even possible that the radiation released in a nuclear war could've spawned genetic mutations in plant life that resulted in plants so aggressive, and rapid-growing that they quickly took over the planet. They simply overran everything. My point is that we can't assume that a nuclear war was fought centuries ago. It may've been fought only a few years ago, and anti-satellite weapons might still exist."

Captain Jerontis turned to Mike. "I want our defenses on full alert, and I want our engines ready for ignition in case we have to flee."

Turning to Moose, Captain Jerontis said, "I want you to have someone search for satellites or satellite-debris."

Captain Jerontis sounded the warning klaxon and got on the intercom. He explained the possibility that a laser attack could occur and that the engines could be brought to full power with no warning. With the Challenger currently in a stable orbit, its engines had been shut down since the time the orbit was achieved. With the starship not being subjected to any acceleration, its personnel were in a weightless condition. If the engines were instantly brought to full power, personnel not prepared for the resulting acceleration could be seriously injured or even killed.

As an additional safety precaution, Captain Jerontis ordered all personnel to leave the observation deck because its hull was made of transparent plastic. A laser beam could pass through the transparent hull, and personnel on the deck could be killed or suffer serious burns as well as permanent blindness.

"Captain, I believe our anti-matter particle-beam gun will be effective against ground-based laser weapons," stated Mike. "It's true that the gun was developed for use in space where the antimatter particles that it fires can travel through the vacuum in space without interference. However, there is a theory that claims the particle-beam could penetrate a planet's atmosphere all the way to the surface."

"That theory has never been tested," argued Captain Jerontis. "The problem is very simple: when the antimatter particles fired by the gun contact the ordinary matter in a planet's upper atmosphere, they are destroyed in a process of mutual annihilation. The atmosphere acts like a layer of armor protecting surface targets."

Mike responded, "Granted, when antimatter particles hit the atmosphere, there is an explosion in which the antimatter and the contacted ordinary matter are totally converted into energy. In effect, for a brief period of time, a rapidly expanding sphere of pure energy is created: a sphere which contains no matter, only energy. Since it contains no matter, this energy sphere is similar to the vacuum in space.

"According to the theory, the follow-on antimatter particles in the beam will pass through this energy sphere and strike atmospheric molecules on its other side. Then, the particles will explode and create a second energy sphere, through which following antimatter particles will pass and contact atmospheric molecules to create a third explosion. Theoretically, this chain of explosions will create energy spheres all the way to the planet's surface. Since the antimatter particles in the beam are traveling at 90 percent of the speed of light, the chain of energy spheres is formed so fast that it is in effect an energy tunnel extending to the planet's surface. So in just a few milliseconds, our antimatter particle-beam gun could punch a hole through the planet's atmosphere: a hole that could best be described as a vacuum tunnel filled with energy. A beam of antimatter particles could then pass through this tunnel to the planet's surface to hit and destroy its target.

"To an observer on the ground, it would look like an extremely powerful lightning bolt coming down from space, and it would be very loud, sounding much like the cracking boom of thunder. When the particle-beam gun was turned off, the energy tunnel would collapse with a thunderous boom that would be much louder than the thunder heard in electrical storms."

"That's a great theory," replied Captain Jerontis. "But the critics of the theory argue that the energy field in the tunnel would be so intense that it would tend to scatter the following antimatter particles in the beam and prevent the formation of a vacuum tunnel extending to the planet's surface. To use the lightning bolt analogy, a tunnel with bends and turns might form, which would make targeting impossible. Also, B-2 has an earthlike magnetic field around it. This will bend the antimatter particle-beam and make targeting difficult."

"I can program our fire control computer to compensate for magnetic interference," responded Mike.

"I want you to do that and anything else you think will help make the gun effective against surface targets. I hope your reasoning is correct; unfortunately, the gun was never tested against surface targets. This lack of testing is a direct result of the treaty that banned the testing of space based weapons against targets on Earth's surface."

"So, because of politics, we do not have complete knowledge about how a critical piece of equipment will perform," stated Moose. "Now that there aren't any politicians around, maybe we should test it here. We could shoot at a deserted iceberg in one of the polar seas; then, we'll know if the gun is effective against surface targets."

"I don't believe that will be necessary," responded Captain Jerontis. "We know that the particle-beam gun is effective against an attack carried out with missiles and projectiles in the vacuum of space. The only uncertainty is an attack from the planet's surface with a laser weapon. But a laser can destroy us only by burning a hole through the ship's hull in a critical area. To do that, they have to lock their laser beam onto the targeted area for however many seconds are required to melt down the hull. It seems to me that they would have a difficult time maintaining lock-on if we instantaneously bring our engines to full power and go through a series of erratic maneuvers. Another argument against conducting a test is that they might observe it, and I don't want to give them any information about our capabilities."

Moose and Mike nodded. Then, Mike said, "If we are attacked by laser fire, we can fire the particle-beam gun at the laser. In just a few milliseconds, the computer will know if a straight energy tunnel forms all the way to the target. If not, we can fire antimatter particles in a scatter pattern in the upper atmosphere between us and the attacking laser. The resulting continuous explosion pattern will create a large, intense energy field that will give off brilliant light, intense heat, and a broad spectrum of radiation. I believe this energy field will mask us from them, making it impossible for them to track us while we make our escape."

"Kind of like creating a smoke screen," commented Moose.

"I like that strategy," Captain Jerontis said to Mike. "I want you to modify the fire-control program, so that it'll do what you just proposed."

As Mike left the area, Moose looked at Captain Jerontis and said, "You and I both know that all of this potential danger could be avoided if we just pointed our noses at Alcent, fired up our engines, and hightailed it out of here. After all, Alcent is going to be our new home."

Doing his best to show Moose an expression of exaggerated bewilderment, Captain Jerontis said, "I am puzzled by that comment. My memory tells me that early in this mission you said you were happy to be a part of it because you have a soldier of fortune mentality. You said that you enjoy facing a dangerous challenge and conquering it. Now, you're suggesting that we leave because of the potential danger here. Is old age catching up to you, or has life in space softened you?"

"Aw come on Captain, you know I haven't lost my courage. But I am getting tired of living in a starship, and I have a wonderful wife. We are ready to settle down on Alcent and start building our new home. Old age hasn't caught up to me just yet, but I'd like to start having children before it does."

"I know how you feel, but I think it's important to understand what's happening on this planet before we leave. As you know, Alpha Centauri A and Alpha Centauri B are in a long elliptical orbit about their common center of gravity. Their distance from each other will vary from about a billion miles to about 3.25 billion miles. It takes about eighty years to complete a journey around this orbit. So once every eighty years, when the two stars are closest to each other, if this planet and Alcent happen to be between the two stars, then they will only be about 850 million miles apart. That is less than the distance between Earth and Saturn. Even with the old fashioned rocket technology that existed in the early days of the space age, it was possible to get a probe to Saturn in just a few years."

"You don't need to convince me. I understand the importance of finding out what kinds of creatures live on this planet and what their capabilities are before we leave here. I'm just tired of being in space."

"I am too. I'm sure we won't be here for more than a few days; then, in less than three weeks, we'll arrive at Alcent. Speaking of those wonderful women that we want to settle down with, here they are now."

Moose and Captain Jerontis turned to face Dianne and Connie, expectantly awaiting a report on the results of their meeting. Dianne was the first to speak, "In addition to me, three others experienced telepathic contact by the non-threatening creature. What is interesting about this is all three of them are students of mine. I've been teaching them biology since we left Earth. Also, Connie has been giving them medical training."

"That raises several questions," stated Captain Jerontis. "First, why only individuals skilled in biology and medicine? Second, how did they know which individuals have this knowledge? Third, Connie has in-depth knowledge in both fields; why wasn't she contacted?"

"All contacted individuals were on the observation deck at the time of contact," replied Connie. "I was here on the flight deck with you."

"Why would that make a difference?" questioned Moose.

"I don't know. I was only making an observation."

"The observation deck's hull is almost entirely clear plastic," stated Captain Jerontis. "The rest of the ship's hull is a combination of metal and fiber reinforced plastic. Is it possible that their telepathic messages are unable to reach an individual surrounded by metal?"

"If we knew how their telepathic power works, we could answer that question," responded Connie.

"Give me an educated guess," requested Captain Jerontis.

After a few moments of thought, Connie said, "To have telepathic ability, they must be able to tune into another creature's brain waves and also be able to project their own brain waves into the other creature's mind. As you know, a normally functioning brain generates an energy field that is detectable because of the energy waves created.

"On Earth, the science of brain wave analysis is still in its infancy, but analyzing brain wave patterns does enable us to determine when an individual is lying or telling the truth. Also, the brain wave patterns that go with most human emotions have been identified; for example, we can tell when a person is happy or sad.

"Perhaps the creatures on this planet are way ahead of us in the science of understanding brain waves. Maybe they can even tell what an individual is thinking when language isn't a barrier. It's even possible that they've developed equipment to transmit the brain waves of one individual directly into the brain of another individual, or maybe their brains can do this unassisted by equipment. In any case, if this transmission is anything like a radio transmission, it would not pass through our ship's metal hull, but it would pass through the plastic windows of the observation deck."

"If you are correct, then we would only be at risk to mental tampering if we are on the observation deck," noted Captain Jerontis. "A tired crew member should be able to sleep in his quarters without being concerned about having his subconscious mind rearranged. It would also explain why you weren't contacted, but it doesn't explain why only individuals with medical and biological knowledge were contacted."

"I've been training in biology and medicine," stated Moose. "And I wasn't contacted when I was on the observation deck."

"But you were conversing with me while you were there," noted Dianne. "In contrast, the first time I felt the presence of life, I was looking at B-2 and wondering if it has intelligent life on it. Also, I was in a quiet, relaxed state of mind that I believe was open to outside suggestions. I believe the creature that contacted me picked up on this and made its presence known to me. The other three contacted individuals were in a mental state similar to mine and were also pondering the life question."

"Surely, other people on the observation deck were in a relaxed mental state and wondering if life exists on this planet," stated Captain Jerontis. "Why weren't any of them contacted? Why only individuals involved in the medical and biological sciences? How did they know which of our personnel have extensive knowledge in these fields?"

"People working in these fields would think about life differently than those with other careers," responded Connie. "The aliens might be able to detect and understand the difference in brain waves generated by this difference in thinking. As to your other question, is it possible that they have some horrendous problems that people with knowledge in the medical and biological sciences could help them solve?"

Captain Jerontis displayed radar images of the bomb destroyed city that Moose had discovered. Then, he briefly explained them.

"A planet-wide nuclear war would certainly have created some horrendous medical and biological problems," commented Connie.

"There's no longer any doubt that a nuclear war was fought," stated Moose. "I now have radar images of 37 bomb-destroyed cities, and we've only completed one orbit since I started the search."

"Chemical and biological weapons can be even more dreadful than nuclear weapons," noted Dianne. "If they were also used, survivors could be facing problems so nasty that continued survival is next to impossible."

Speaking to Dianne, Captain Jerontis said, "Maybe the creature that made its presence known to you in a friendly way was trying to get acquainted with the objective of finding out if we can help them. Perhaps it will try to contact you again and try to find out who we are, where we came from, what our capabilities are, and what our intentions are."

"When do you think it will try to contact me?"

"In about six hours, we'll be over the area of the Northern Continent where you were first contacted, but it will be in the middle of the night, and they might be asleep. A little less than twelve hours after that, we will again be over that area, and it will be in the middle of the day. Our best opportunities to learn about these creatures will be for you to be on the observation deck at those times."

"That sounds dangerous," stated Moose. "We know nothing about these creatures, except that they've fought a big war. We don't know what their intentions are, and we know nothing about their capabilities."

"You are correct," Captain Jerontis said, "but I don't believe we should go to Alcent until we find out what's happening here."

Turning to Dianne, Captain Jerontis said, "Attempting to contact these creatures will be risky. If we've guessed wrong about their need for help, we might be attacked. On the observation deck, you will be naked to a possible laser attack against this ship. You could be permanently blinded, severely burned, or even killed. Also, your brain will be open to possible telepathic assault."

"I think I will have to assume the risk," Dianne responded quietly. "There's just too much at stake. If there were going to be any kind of attack, I believe it would come from the creatures on the Equatorial Continent that expressed so much hatred toward me. I have no desire to assume the risk involved in further contact with them. Just thinking about the possibility sends a cold shiver up and down my spine."

Noticing that his wife trembled, Moose said, "I sense that you were more deeply affected by that experience than you realize."

"I've never been a rape victim, but the creature on the Equatorial Continent made me feel like I suffered that kind of brutal attack."

"If these creatures can affect you so deeply using nothing more than telepathic powers, I really do not want you to be on the observation deck contacting one of them," stated Moose.

Dianne looked into her husband's eyes and said, "I understand how you feel, but this is something I must do. Besides, I will be trying to contact the one who was friendly."

"But we don't know what his intentions are. He could be a lion disguising himself as a lamb."

"I didn't get that feeling, but even though you could be right, this is something I must do."

Moose was silent for a few moments; then, he reluctantly nodded in agreement and said, "If you're going to expose yourself to possible risk on the observation deck, I want to be there with you. If anything were to happen to you, my life would be empty; especially now, when we're on the verge of realizing our dream of building a home and raising a family. We've waited a long time for this."

"I appreciate how you feel, but I see no reason why both of us should be exposed to possible risk. Also, I need to be alone, so I can focus my mind on communicating with the alien."

Moose reluctantly nodded in agreement.

Speaking to Dianne, Captain Jerontis said, "I think the best chance to achieve contact is for you to do exactly what you were doing the first time you were contacted. If you are contacted, the first step will be to get acquainted and to establish our peaceful intentions. Since language is a barrier, this will have to be done with images. Since we don't know how advanced they are in their ability to use telepathic communication, we don't know if it's even possible to achieve two-way communication. But if we assume that they are advanced enough so that they can read your mind to the point of being able to see what you see, then it becomes an easy problem. We simply take a large computer video screen to the observation deck and use it to fill your mind with the image you want to convey. For example, ask the computer to display an image of you. Then, clear your mind of all else and focus entirely on the image of you on the screen. Hold the image in your mind long enough for the alien to see it. Then, remove the image from the screen and stare at the blank screen. This will help you clear your mind, so that it is totally blank. If the creature truly wants two-way communication and is able to do it, then it should respond by projecting an image of itself into your mind. If this can be achieved, then we can go back and forth with images until we understand each other."

After considering what Jerry suggested, Dianne said, "The possibility of achieving two-way communication with telepathically transmitted images seems rather far-fetched, like something out of a science fiction movie."

"It seems that way," agreed Captain Jerontis. "But reality always seems to catch up with science fiction. Only a few decades ago, interstellar travel was science fiction, now we've turned it into reality."

"If the alien does communicate with me using images, then what images do I present to him?"

"The first step will be to get acquainted," replied Captain Jerontis. "So I recommend that you keep it personal and show him images of key events in your life. After you've done that, present the blank screen image and see what the response is."

"I like that approach, but to do that, I need to do some preparation. So unless there is more for us to discuss, I'm going to my office to put together a good sequence of images."

Everyone exchanged glances, nodded in agreement, and Dianne left.

Five and one-half hours later, after passing over the eastern shore of the Equatorial Continent, Mike reported, "My infrared data has revealed something very unusual: six volcanic peaks venting jets of hot gas from openings near their peaks."

"What's unusual about that?" questioned Captain Jerontis.

"The jets are all at the same temperature, 115 degrees Fahrenheit."

"That does seem strange."

"Especially, when you consider their locations. The northernmost mountain is on an island 100 miles north of the Equatorial Continent. The southernmost peak is on an island 200 miles south of the Equatorial Continent. The other four mountains are about 100 miles inland along the continent's east coast. How could six volcanic peaks spread out over several thousand miles be venting gas at the same temperature?"

"The probability of that happening because of natural causes has to be close to zero," commented Captain Jerontis. "This has to be the result of activity being done by intelligent beings. But what are they doing inside those mountains that would result in venting gas at 115 degrees?"

"Maybe there's some type of power plant or industrial manufacturing facility inside each of those mountains that was put there before the war for protection from attack," suggested Moose.

"That's a possibility," agreed Mike, "but I don't think dormant volcanoes are a good place to locate underground factories. Dormant volcanoes have a nasty habit of sometimes becoming active."

"That's true," agreed Moose, "but wartime urgency sometimes requires the acceptance of high risk to achieve a desired goal."

With the southernmost mountain still in view, Captain Jerontis instructed the computer to obtain high-resolution optical data of it, while Moose requested radar data. Momentarily, Moose said, "The jet coming out of this mountain is giving a strong radar return. It either contains ionized gases or some type of fine dust that is radar reflective. I am also getting a Doppler Shift that indicates an exit velocity of 900 feet per second. Also, the jet is coming out of the highest point on the mountain."

Quickly examining the optical images, Captain Jerontis found what he was looking for. On his computer screen, he displayed the image of a pipe approximately five feet in diameter rising nearly 100 feet above the mountaintop. A grayish-black jet of gas was spewing out of it. Turning to Moose, Captain Jerontis asked, "What is the altitude of this peak?"

Moose entered the question into the computer and received an immediate answer, which he gave to Captain Jerontis: "My radar data indicates that it is 33,644 feet above sea level."

"Are the other five peaks that high?"

Moose displayed a topographical map of the area, scanned it, and said, "All six volcanic peaks are between 31,000 feet and 36,000 feet."

Turning to Mike, Captain Jerontis said, "We now have a fairly complete infrared map of this planet. Have you detected any mountaintop gas jets similar to these?"

"No! But I will request the computer to do a data search just to make sure I haven't missed any."

"Those mountains have two things in common," stated Captain Jerontis. "They all tower into the stratosphere, and they're all located on the eastern edge of the Equatorial Continent. If the prevailing high altitude wind blows from west to east, they could be using these chimneys to get rid of a toxic by-product of a manufacturing process."

While speaking, Captain Jerontis instructed the computer to display a weather map of the area. After checking it, he said, "As I suspected, we have strong westerly winds blowing across those mountaintops. The wind velocity varies from 110 to 175 miles per hour."

"I wonder what's in those jets?" questioned Moose.

"I don't know," replied Captain Jerontis. "But after your wife completes her communication attempt with the aliens on the Northern Continent, I'm going to adjust our orbit, so that we'll travel directly over these mountains on our next pass over this hemisphere. I want complete data on those exhaust plumes; in particular, I want detailed spectrographic data. If we can determine the chemical composition of the plumes, then we may be able to figure out what's going on inside the mountains."

"Speaking about my wife, I am worried about her being exposed to possible harm," stated Moose. "In her attempt to achieve telepathic communication with the aliens, she will be at the mercy of whatever mental powers they possess."

"That concerns me too. I wouldn't have asked her to assume the risk if there were any other way. But since it's important for us to contact these aliens, we need to compliment her for courageously agreeing to accept the risk, and we need to support her any way we can. The video cameras we installed on the observation deck will allow us to monitor her activities. We'll be just outside the area, so if something bad happens, we can rush in and take action to break the telepathic link. Since my Connie will be with us, medical help will be available if it's needed."

"I think we've taken all the precautions we can," stated Moose. "And I do understand the need for contacting the aliens. I just wish that someone other than Dianne would be making the attempt."

A short time later, the Challenger passed over B-2's equator approaching the Northern Continent from the South. Even though it was nighttime, the planet was fairly well illuminated because of the nearness of Alpha Centauri A.

Dianne was alone on the observation deck hoping to achieve telepathic communication with the aliens living on the Northern Continent. She was viewing the green land mass that the Challenger was rapidly approaching and wondered what kind of life was present and what kinds of problems it was facing in the aftermath of the nuclear war. She felt a mixture of conflicting emotions. She was excited about the possibility of becoming the first human to achieve communication with an alien. However, she was also apprehensive about this, because to achieve telepathic communication, she had to open her mind to the probing of an alien she knew nothing about, and the possibility that the alien could do irreparable damage to her brain was frightening.

A feeling of being alone pervaded Dianne's senses. Even though she had insisted on being alone, the quiet emptiness of the large observation deck that now surrounded her served to enhance her feeling of vulnerability. Dianne appreciated the presence of her husband and two closest friends just outside the observation deck, but wondered if they could rescue her quickly enough to prevent permanent injury if the alien decided to attack and damage her mind.

The Challenger was almost over the area where Dianne first became aware of the existence of life, and she was not yet aware of any attempt to contact her. She wondered if the alien was sleeping or distrusted the personnel on the Challenger and did not wish further contact. She decided to focus her mind very intently on the question of what kind of life existed on the planet below and to surround this intense mental focus with feelings of love, a desire for peace, and a desire to be helpful. So intense was her mental focus that she entered an almost trance-like state in which all else was blocked out.

A few moments later, Dianne became aware of the alien probing her mind. She waited until the feeling became strong. Then, she looked at the large video screen that displayed a 3-D, life-sized image of her, and she focused her mind on it to form a vivid mental image of herself. She held this image in her mind for about a half-minute. Then, she removed her picture from the screen and stared at the blank screen. She closed her eyes and held the blank screen image in her mind.

In just a few seconds, an image of the alien appeared in her mind. Without losing her mental trance, Dianne spoke softly into a small microphone that she was wearing: "I have achieved contact with one of the aliens. Although there are several small differences, he is human in appearance. His skin color is golden bronze. He has blue eyes, dark blond hair, and the beginning of facial lines that would indicate late middle age. He has a muscular build and a masculine appearance. He looks relaxed, healthy, friendly, and intelligent."

A few seconds after Dianne stopped her oral description of the alien, his image faded from her mind. Dianne surmised that the alien was aware that she was orally describing him and kept his image in her mind until she had concluded the description. As the image of the alien faded, it was immediately replaced by a star map showing Alpha Centauri A, Alpha Centauri B, and twenty nearby stars. Dianne spoke softly into her microphone: "He is showing me a star map of local interstellar space. I think he wants to know where we are from."

Outside the observation deck, Captain Jerontis looked at Moose and Connie and said, "I think we should show him. I don't think they can harm the people on Earth. I think he just wants to know who we are and where we came from."

Moose and Connie nodded in agreement; then, Captain Jerontis turned on his microphone and spoke softly to Dianne: "Have the computer place a star map on the screen that is oriented the same way as the map he is showing you. Then, draw a line from the Sun to Alpha Centauri B."

Dianne did this; then, she studied the video screen intently to form a vivid image of it. Almost immediately, Dianne felt a feeling of acknowledgment that she interpreted to mean that the alien had received the image, so she switched to a blank screen and held an image of it in her mind. In just a few seconds, the alien projected an image of the star map into her mind, but it now contained new information. It showed an arrow heading directly back to the Sun, an arrow heading to Alpha Centauri A, and three arrows heading toward other stars. Along with this image, Dianne experienced a sense of alarm, a feeling of danger. The image of the star map was quickly followed by scenes of animals drinking water from lakes and rivers and then, dying. The final scene showed members of the alien's species drinking water and then, dying.

While the alien was presenting these images to her, Dianne described them to her colleagues. She concluded by saying, "I think the alien is trying to tell us to go somewhere else, because this planet is filled with death. I sense that he's concerned about our safety."

"Are you convinced that he's sincere, or do you think he's just trying to get rid of us?" questioned Captain Jerontis.

"I believe he's sincere."

"In that case, show him a star map containing only Alpha Centauri A, Alpha Centauri B, and their planets. On this map show him an arrow extending from this planet to Alcent. Then, show him a sequence of images from your childhood to the present time. A proper selection of scenes from key points in your life will put you on a personal basis with him and establish your professional credentials. Perhaps this will lead him to give us additional information in regard to how the consumption of water is killing animal life."

Realizing that their orbital speed was rapidly moving them away from the alien, Dianne immediately began carrying out Captain J.J.'s orders. Less than ten seconds after forming each image in her mind, Dianne received acknowledgment from the alien that he had seen the image. After completing her sequence of images, Dianne switched to the blank screen.

The alien was very quick to respond. Dianne detected a sense of urgency on his part and surmised that he realized that she would soon be beyond the range of his telepathic powers. The alien rapidly presented a sequence of images from his childhood to the present time. Then, as he started to get into the subject of death caused by water consumption, the images abruptly ceased. Dianne immediately made an entry into the computer, so that the exact time and orbital position would be noted. Then, she said, "I am no longer receiving any images."

Dianne left the observation deck and drifted right into Moose's welcoming embrace. Both Moose and Dianne rejoiced in the fact that communication with the alien had been accomplished without any harm being done to her. Jerry and Connie also expressed their happiness at the outcome of the event and congratulated Dianne for her success.

Upon their return to the flight deck, Captain Jerontis sounded the warning klaxon and announced: "All personnel prepare for acceleration. In three minutes, we'll maneuver the Challenger into a new orbit."

After the orbital maneuvers were completed, Captain Jerontis said to Dianne, "Please give us all the information you can about the alien."

"First, I am happy that he was friendly, polite, and courteous. I felt totally at ease with him. Before the communication began, I felt alone and vulnerable. He may have detected my feelings and made a special effort to put me at ease."

"It sounds like he's sensitive to others," commented Connie.

"I think so," agreed Dianne. "Also, he did show concern for our safety when he warned us not to land on this planet."

"You said that he's human in appearance, but that there are some differences," stated Connie. "What caught your attention?"

"The first thing I noticed was his forehead: it is somewhat larger than ours. With the additional volume in his skull, he may have a larger brain than we have. Perhaps, those additional brain cells give him his telepathic ability. The second thing I noticed was that his ears are a bit larger than ours, which may indicate a more sensitive sense of hearing."

"How tall do you think he is?" Connie asked.

"Since I didn't see him next to anything of known size, I have no way to judge that."

"You keep referring to him as he," commented Moose. "How do you know that he's masculine?"

"I noticed that he had a nicely balanced muscular build like you see in a man who is in good shape. Also, his clothing was nicely tailored and fit him quite snugly. He had the familiar masculine bulge in his groin area, and I saw no indication of breasts on his chest."

"From the tone of your voice, I almost get the feeling that you were turned on by him," commented Moose.

Dianne gave Moose a teasing smile and said, "He may've been sexually aroused by me."

"What makes you think that? Did you do something to excite him?"

"In one of the images I showed him, I was standing on a sandy beach wearing a skimpy bikini. But I showed him that image for purely scientific reasons. I wanted him to see what the human female looks like. That was just to be informative and should not have been arousing to him."

"Why not?" Moose retorted. "You have a great figure."

"Thank you," replied Dianne.

Doing her best to display a naughty grin, Dianne said to Connie, "Isn't it wonderful that my husband is so in love with me that he even worries that I might be sexually arousing to an alien?"

"I wasn't worried about that," stated Moose. "I just think you were a little too personal with an alien that we know very little about."

"I was only trying to show him who we are and what we look like. Also, to indicate to him part of our basic social structure, I showed him a picture of us getting married and some scenes to indicate that we live together. In one of them, you were wearing only your jockey shorts. I believe the alien got the message."

"Again, I hope you weren't too personal with an alien we know very little about."

"I agree with her approach to the alien," Connie said. "I believe the best way to speed up the exchange of information is to be personal. By being open, Dianne may've gained his trust. Also, if he finds Dianne pleasing to look at and pleasant to communicate with, he may feel some affection for her. It seems to me that this set of circumstances would make the alien less likely to censor the information he gives us."

"That's why I was personal with some of the images I presented to him. After I showed him a sequence of images from my life, he showed me a sequence of images from his life, some of which were also quite personal. One of the things that amazed me, was the speed with which he was able to see the images in my mind. At first, I held images for about thirty seconds before I went to the next one, but after we got started, he only needed about ten seconds to read my mind. He let me know when he was ready for the next image by giving me a little mental prod."

"I'm impressed by his ability to communicate telepathically with images" stated Connie. "This form of communication seems to be as easy for him as it is for us to sit here and talk."

"That's the feeling I got. I wish I knew how he does it."

"We may never understand the mechanism involved," Connie said. "But let's be thankful he has that ability. It makes communicating with him easy, and there is so much to learn from each other. I'm curious about the females in his species. Did he show you what they look like?"

"Yes! His parents were present in some images, and except for the differences peculiar to his species, his mother had the same basic anatomy as human females. One of the images showed that his parents were both killed in the war. Apparently, the war occurred shortly after he graduated from a university. I believe he's a veterinarian. If he's in his fifties, then the war took place about 30 years ago. He also showed me what I think is a current family portrait, which indicates that he has a wife who is younger than he is and two children who look pre-teen."

"Did he show you any scenes from the war?" Captain Jerontis asked.

"Yes! When he showed them to me, I felt his deep sadness. If I have correctly interpreted the images he showed me, the war and the poisoned environment that followed it killed 99 percent of all living organisms."

"What did you learn about the war?" Captain Jerontis asked.

"It was brutal. It began with a massive exchange of nuclear bombs delivered by ballistic missiles, cruise missiles, and aircraft. This was followed by chemical bombs. Then, to make the death complete, biological toxins and lethal microbes were unleashed."

"You're right; the war was brutal. It's a wonder anything survived."

"Not much did, but shortly after the war, new kinds of plant life began to overrun everything. Apparently, several new species resulted from genetic mutations caused by radioactive fallout. Evidently, these plants thrive on radiation, because they are growing most vigorously in the areas with the greatest radioactivity."

"That explains the planet-wide jungle that's now down there. Did he show you anything else?"

"No, he didn't. The images came to an abrupt end at the time I noted in the computer. I believe our orbital motion dropped us below the horizon from his viewpoint. Perhaps he can communicate with us only when we're on a direct line-of-sight. If that's the case, we can calculate an approximate location for him. Then, on our next pass over that area, we can take radar and optical data and see if we can pinpoint his location."

"That's a good idea," agreed Captain Jerontis who turned to Moose and asked him to estimate the alien's location and review existing data for the area.

Turning his attention back to Dianne, Captain Jerontis said, "There are three things that strike me about your account of the war. First, I am awestruck by the nearly complete death and destruction caused by this war, which would explain why we haven't seen any ships at sea or aircraft in flight. Second, I am surprised by the rapid growth of vigorous plant life that has overrun this planet in the aftermath of an all out nuclear war. Third, I am amazed by the detail you are able to recall from images that were rapidly run through your mind."

"That amazes me too. Apparently, the alien not only placed images in my conscious mind, but also implanted them in my memory, because I'm able to recall them vividly. It's unfortunate that the science of brain wave analysis is still in its infancy. How convenient it would be if we could have a computer tune in to my brain waves and analyze and interpret them accurately enough to portray the images that the alien transmitted into my mind. Then, everyone could see the images, and we could record them for future reference."

"That would be convenient," agreed Captain Jerontis. "But since we can't do that, I think you should to go to your office and enter into the computer the best description you can of each of the images along with your interpretation. Being alone and quietly thinking about the scenes might give you some additional insight into what he tried tell to you."

"As vivid as those mental images were, I won't have any difficulty entering detailed information into the computer. Also, for the sake of convenience, this alien needs to have a name, so let's just call him Rex."

"That'll work," agreed Captain Jerontis. "In less than an hour, you'll have another opportunity to communicate with Rex. If he needs our help, perhaps, he'll tell us what he thinks we can do for him."

"I'll be ready for that," stated Dianne with a degree of excitement as she turned to leave the flight deck and go to her office.

"Hold on a second," Moose said to his wife. "I think I have an image of Rex's location. If we assume that his telepathic powers are limited by line-of-sight, then he should be living in the area I have displayed on the screen. It measures about 15 by 15 miles. There's a river flowing through the middle of it, and there are two lakes that are about a mile across. Besides all that water, there are several high hills that would make it easy to have an underground home, if there's still a need to live underground."

"That looks like a great area to live in," commented Dianne.

"During your next communication with Rex, you might show him this image," suggested Captain Jerontis. "If he's living in this area, and if he wants us to know his exact location; he can place an X or some other symbol on the image to mark his position."

"If Rex does give us his exact location, that would indicate that he trusts us," stated Connie.

"Or he might be in such desperate need for help that he has no choice but to trust us," commented Captain Jerontis. "In any case, we'll explore that area during our next pass over it."

"Captain! We're approaching the northernmost volcanic peak on the eastern edge of the Equatorial Continent," stated Mike, as he displayed an image of it on the large video screen. "Whatever that stuff is; it's still being vented from the peak at 115 degrees and 900 feet per second. The wind across the peak is blowing from west to east at 160 mph."

"Do we have any spectroscopic data on that exhaust plume?" Captain Jerontis asked.

"I'm getting the first readout on that," replied Mike. "And it indicates an absence of carbon dioxide, carbon monoxide, sulfur dioxide, oxides of nitrogen, and water vapor. Therefore, we're not looking at exhaust from the combustion of organic fuel, and that pipe is not a smokestack for an underground industrial complex."

"I had suspected that this would be the case," stated Captain Jerontis. "There just isn't any logical reason why a power plant chimney would be at the top of a high mountain. Is there enough information in the spectroscopic data to identify the chemicals in that plume?"

"The computer has identified two organic chemicals in the exhaust jet," replied Mike. "Both are composed of large complex molecules. The computer has determined which elements are present, but it is unable to determine the precise geometry of these molecules. Their spectral signatures are different from the spectral signatures of any known chemicals on Earth."

"I think something sinister is happening down there," stated Captain Jerontis. "I can think of only two reasons to eject chemicals into the stratosphere when there's a high velocity wind blowing them away from the Equatorial Continent: either the chemicals are a toxic by-product of a manufacturing process and they want to get rid of them, or the chemicals are being used in a chemical warfare attack against the other two continents. Such an attack can only work if three conditions exist. First, the strong high-altitude winds must blow all the way to the other continents. Second, a significant percentage of the chemical toxins must remain airborne until they reach the other two continents. Third, some of the toxins must precipitate out of the atmosphere when they arrive there."

"We now have the second peak in view," stated Mike. "And it's ejecting an exhaust plume at 900 feet per second with an exit temperature of 115 degrees. Spectroscopic data is identical to that of the exhaust plume from mountain number one. Also, there's a westerly wind at 165 mph."

While Mike reported data for mountain number two, Moose displayed a weather map for the area east of the Equatorial Continent and said, "The high-altitude wind not only extends all the way to the other two continents, but it blows all the way across them before it finally dies out. Also, there are a few thunderstorms over both continents. That is significant, because the tops of some of the storm systems are above 45,000 feet. Those storms are certainly capable of milking chemicals out of the stratosphere and raining them onto the land below."

"We need to find out if those chemicals are still in the stratosphere when the wind arrives over those continents," Captain Jerontis said.

"Now that we have their spectral signatures, we can check for their presence in the atmosphere during our next over-flight," Mike said.

"Suppose we find that these chemicals are there. That still doesn't prove that chemical warfare is in progress," argued Connie. "I can't think of any logical reason for an ongoing chemical attack. The war that was fought thirty years ago was so horrible that there just isn't much left to kill."

"That's true," agreed Captain Jerontis, "so let me propose a sequence of events that could lead to an illogical attack. First, let's assume that those mountains do contain chemical warfare weapons. Then, let's assume that the aliens on this continent started the war with the expectation of winning, but were themselves destroyed by the ensuing retaliation. For whatever reason, suppose that the chemical warfare complexes inside these mountains escaped destruction. Furthermore, let's suppose that for the most part, the only aliens on the Equatorial Continent to survive the war were the ones who were inside the mountains. Now, let's suppose that even though their country started the war, they are blaming their enemies for their own devastation. It's possible that these survivors are so totally consumed by hatred that they now have a fanatical compulsion to continue the war until nothing is left alive on the other continents.

"Perhaps, they've even formed a religious cult based on hatred in which they actually worship the chemical warfare machines inside the mountains. If that's the case, then keeping these machines functioning may be the sole purpose in their lives. They may be so fanatical that they aren't even concerned that an unexpected change in wind direction could cause the poisons they are producing to come raining down on what's left of their continent. Their only purpose in life might be to kill the few remaining creatures on the other continents no matter what the cost."

"Sick minds could fit into that scenario," acknowledged Connie. "But how do we prove your theory?"

"We could enlist Rex's help," suggested Mike.

"How do you propose to do that?" questioned Connie.

"We have Dianne show him a sequence of images of what's happening here," replied Mike. "The first image would be a picture of one of these mountains with its exhaust plume. The second image would be a weather map that would show the locations of all six mountains and the wind direction at their tops. The third image would be a close-up of one of the exhaust plumes with spectrographs along side of it to show the spectral signatures of the two chemicals in the plume. Dianne thinks Rex is a veterinarian. Because of problems caused by the war, he may also be a research scientist. If these chemicals are raining down on him, he might know what they are. He might even recognize their spectral signatures. If these chemicals are causing problems, Rex will find a way to tell us that."

"Suppose he confirms that these chemicals are toxic agents being used in a chemical attack against all living creatures on this planet. What do we do about it?" questioned Moose.

In a strong tone, Connie said, "If that's the case, we'll have to destroy those mountains and the poison factories they contain. We need to give life on this planet a chance to survive and recover."

"I think we should discuss our options and their consequences before we attempt to take out those mountains," stated Captain Jerontis. "We should show Rex some images of what we're planning to do and see how he reacts. He may know something we don't know."

"We've passed over the third peak," Mike said. "And we have the fourth in view. The data for these two are the same as for the first two."

"It looks like the same process is going on inside all six mountains," commented Connie.

"I wonder if they're operating independently, or if they're under the control of one individual," questioned Captain Jerontis. "If they're under the control of one individual, then there must be open communication. That means that if we attack one of these chemical warfare machines, the aliens operating the others will know about it and attack us if they have any defensive systems capable of reaching us at this altitude."

"During their nuclear war, some of the bombs were delivered with intercontinental ballistic missiles," stated Moose. "That means they had the ability to launch satellites and nuclear-armed anti-satellite missiles. This might explain why we haven't found any satellites or satellite debris orbiting this planet. Any satellite incinerated by a nuclear blast would've been reduced to radioactive ash that we might no longer be able to detect. Perhaps they also possessed nuclear-armed antimissile missiles. Maybe these poison factories survived the war not only because they are buried inside mountains, but also because they were very well defended."

"Your analysis might be correct," noted Captain Jerontis. "But do they still have functional, nuclear-armed, anti-satellite missiles?"

"I think we should assume that they do and develop an attack strategy that makes their missiles impotent against us," stated Mike. "For example, we could attack from geosynchronous orbit. That would place us at an altitude of about 22,000 miles. Even if they have anti-missile missiles capable of reaching that altitude, the travel time would give us ample opportunity to detect and destroy them. As far as our attack is concerned, a narrowly focused beam of antimatter particles fired from a high-altitude orbit will be just as lethal as a beam fired from a low-altitude orbit."

"That attack plan does make sense," agreed Captain Jerontis. "And a geostationary orbit will give us time to experiment with the particle-beam gun. We don't know for sure that it'll even work against a surface target."

"We're now over the fifth mountain," stated Mike, "and I'm getting basically the same data as we recorded for the first four."

"Do we have any data that reveals the presence of concrete slabs on or near any of them?" questioned Captain Jerontis. "That kind of construction could indicate the presence of underground missile silos."

"I'll see what I can find," replied Mike.

Captain Jerontis turned to Moose. "I want you to discover how the aliens are getting their raw materials into those mountains. The more we know about our targets; the more efficiently we'll be able to shut them down."

Moose nodded and started working the problem.

Connie turned toward her husband. "It sounds like you've concluded that a chemical warfare attack is being conducted from within those mountains. It also sounds like you've decided to shut them down."

"An ongoing chemical warfare attack is what best explains the information we have. I'll have Dianne present a summary of our data to Rex. If he's awake, this communication will take place in about forty minutes. Hopefully, his reaction will shed some light on the validity of my conclusion. If his reaction supports my conclusion, then I'll have Dianne show him some images of us destroying the poison factories. How he reacts will have a bearing on whether or not we attack."

"Would you like me to prepare the images for her?" Connie asked.

"That would be helpful. Thank you for offering."

Captain Jerontis buzzed Dianne's office. When she answered, he said, "Dianne, I need you to come to the flight deck in fifteen minutes for a meeting about your next contact with Rex."

"I'll be there."

A few minutes later, Mike said, "A computer search of our radar data does reveal numerous concrete missile silos located in and around all six mountains. Most of the silos are empty, but there are a few that still have their concrete lids in place. It's impossible to tell if they contain operational missiles."

"I think we should assume that some of them are functional," Captain Jerontis said.

"Judging from the size of the open silos, it appears that they did contain defensive missiles," commented Mike. "They don't appear large enough to have housed intercontinental weapons."

"They could've contained small ICBMs, but we have to assume that the closed silos contain defensive missiles that are able to reach us at this altitude. I trust that you've already programmed the fire control computer to deal with that possibility."

"I have, and they can't hurt us with a missile attack, unless there's a malfunction in our defensive systems, and I have my engineering crew checking them out."

Satisfied that Mike had the problem under control, Captain Jerontis said, "Perhaps, the biggest danger we face is from a laser attack."

"They could hurt us that way," agreed Mike, "but I don't think they can destroy us unless they're able to detonate our antimatter fuel."

"That fuel will be hard to reach with a laser. They'll have to burn through our meteor shields to get to those tanks, and if we're doing erratic maneuvers, I don't think they can lock on to a spot long enough to burn through it. But a laser attack could still lead to our destruction if they score a lucky hit that cripples our defenses to a missile attack. A direct hit on the particle-beam gun could put us in a serious situation."

"That's the beauty of attacking from geosynchronous orbit. If they even have missiles that can reach that altitude, it'll take them so long to get there, that we can simply leave before they arrive."

"That attack strategy leaves us vulnerable only to laser attack, and we don't know if they even have lasers, but we must assume that they do."

"That's a wise assumption," agreed Mike. "If all those empty silos did contain defensive missiles, then these mountain complexes were heavily defended, and that means that their owners placed great value in them and were determined that they survive the nuclear exchange. If they have lasers, they probably put some of them there too."

"I think the fact that they were so determined to have them survive lends additional credibility to the conclusion that they contain chemical weapons. Perhaps, they thought that if all else failed, they could eventually win the war with chemical weapons."

"Chemical weapons are definitely potent weapons of mass destruction and capable of eventually winning a war."

"But since the two sides have already destroyed each other, there's no longer any need to be conducting a chemical attack. If that is what's going on, it can only be seen as a hideous crime against an entire planet."

"If we're able to determine that that's what's happening, we'll have a big decision to make," commented Mike.

"You're right about that," stated Captain Jerontis.

Thirty minutes later, Dianne was on the observation deck preparing for her next meeting with Rex. Captain Jerontis, Connie, and Moose were outside the observation deck monitoring Dianne's activities.

Observing the planet far below her, Dianne noticed how peaceful it looked. She thought about the horrible tragedy endured by this planet's creatures as a result of the war and wondered how many species had been made extinct. She thought about the creatures presently engaged in a desperate struggle for survival and how this struggle might be doomed to failure because of a planet-wide chemical attack conducted by evil creatures. Dianne trembled at the thought of the cold hatred that she felt during the Challenger's first pass over the Equatorial Continent.

Noticing the approach of the southern shore of the Northern Continent, Dianne started to clear her mind of the sadness that she felt for this planet's creatures. She filled her mind with thoughts of Rex and the things she wanted to accomplish in the anticipated contact with him.

A few minutes later, Dianne achieved a state of total relaxation and entered a trance in which all was blocked out except for a vivid mental image of Rex. Suddenly, she felt a mental prod and immediately replaced Rex's image with a mental image of herself. When she felt a second mental prod, she replaced her self-image with a blank screen image. It had been decided to let Rex open this communication, because it was felt that this would be the best way to discover his top priority problem.

Dianne did not have to wait long; Rex immediately began placing images in her mind. Dianne spoke softly into her microphone and said, "I've just achieved contact with Rex, and he is showing me a temperature scale. On one end of it, there is a block of ice, and on the other end, there is a pot of boiling water. At the point on the scale that represents normal body temperature, he has placed a green mark and the pictures of several creatures, including his picture.

"Now, I'm looking at an animal drinking water. Now, the temperature scale is back in my mind; only now, the animal that just drank water is pictured above the green mark. Evidently, something in the water caused its temperature to go up. Now, Rex is showing me the animal drinking more water. Now, we're back to the temperature scale, but the animal has moved still higher on it. A new image shows the animal drinking still more water.

"I see this doomed animal having convulsions and suffering a painful death. Apparently, it was killed by chemicals that caused its rate of metabolism to run wild and at the same time blocked its natural ability to control its body temperature, which was so high that critical internal organs started to fail. What a cruel way to kill a creature. The natural thing for an animal with an elevated body temperature to do is to drink water, which in this case caused it to ingest more poison and make the problem worse.

"I see an image of Rex analyzing water samples in a laboratory. He is showing me two test tubes full of dark solutions. I think he has isolated two poisons. I see an image of B-2 in orbit around Alpha Centauri B. The two test tubes are pictured next to B-2. I see a new image showing that B-2 has moved half way around Alpha Centauri B; only now, the dark solutions in the test tubes are gone. I believe Rex is telling me that these poisons deteriorate in about half a year.

"I see an image of a spectroscope. I now have an image of a test tube containing a dark solution along with its spectrograph, and now the other dark chemical and its spectrograph. I see a map of this planet with the spectrographs slowly moving around on the map. Rex knows that, since these chemicals deteriorate in half a year, they must be continuously pumped into the environment. He is asking us to find the source. The spectrographs he showed me depict spectral signatures that look identical to what we measured for the chemicals in the exhaust plumes that we've been studying, thus confirming a chemical warfare attack. If I show Rex the source of these poisons, what will the response be? Is it possible that his country may have held a few intercontinental missiles in reserve for this kind of emergency?"

"If they did, that would save us from having to do the job," stated Captain Jerontis. "Show him the mountain images."

Dianne presented the mountain images to Rex, and received a response. "I see Rex in a state of hopelessness. I feel his emotions. He's in a state of despair. I believe he's helpless in this situation. I believe that what's left of his country lacks the capability to stop the injection of these poisons into their environment. Members of his species can probably survive by drinking distilled water, but they'll be unable to save the few wild animals still in existence."

"Show him the images of us destroying the poison factories."

Dianne did as directed, and received an immediate response. "I see an image of Rex wearing an expression of hope, and I feel strong, heartfelt appreciation coming from him."

"Do you have any reason to disbelieve Rex?" Captain Jerontis asked.

"His story about chemicals killing animals confirms the conclusion that we'd already reached regarding the chemicals spewing out of the mountains. His spectroscopic data seems to match ours, and he gave us this information before we presented our data to him. The probability of Rex fabricating his story and showing us two complicated spectral signatures that match the ones we recorded is nil. Also, my intuition tells me that Rex is a benevolent individual who is working hard to promote the survival of his species and what's left of the animal life in his vicinity."

"Your reasoning agrees with mine, and I have a healthy respect for your intuitive judgment. I am going to place a sequence of images on your computer screen that I want you to show Rex."

The first image Captain Jerontis put on the screen showed B-2 and the Challenger's current orbit around it. It also showed a geosynchronous orbit and a dashed line indicating the Challenger's transfer into this much higher orbit. The second image showed the east coast of the Equatorial Continent and the Challenger firing its antimatter particle-beam gun at the poison spewing mountains. The third image showed the Challenger returning to its present orbit. The fourth image showed the Challenger doing a data gathering pass over the destroyed mountains. The fifth image showed B-2 making one-half revolution on its axis of rotation. The sixth image showed a communication scene between Dianne and Rex. Captain Jerontis hoped that the fifth image would tell Rex that one-half day would pass before his next communication with Dianne. After the sixth image, Captain Jerontis switched to a blank screen.

Almost immediately, Dianne reported, "I see an image of Rex nodding his head up and down. I think he's trying to tell us that he understands your message. Also, I'm detecting hopefulness and sincere appreciation on his part. There is now a new image entering my mind. I see Rex and his family on their knees with their heads bowed. Either they are praying for our success, or they are humbly expressing their gratitude to us for what we are going to do for them." This image stayed in Dianne's mind for a full minute; then, it faded away. Feeling the absence of mental energy from Rex, Dianne realized that this communication session had ended, so she and her colleagues returned to the flight deck.

When they arrived, Mike reported: "I've done a spectroscopic study of the atmosphere under our flight path over the Southern and Northern Continent. I've recorded the spectral signatures of both chemicals that are pouring out of the volcanic peaks on the Equatorial Continent. Evidently, the strong high altitude wind has enough turbulence in it to keep a substantial percentage of these toxins airborne until they reach these continents. I've also found these poisons present in lakes by doing a spectroscopic analysis of light reflected from their surfaces.

"Also, I have high resolution optical images of the shores of these lakes. We've located several dead animals next to the water indicating that they were poisoned by the water. In addition, we have a video showing two large animals in the final minutes of their lives."

Mike displayed the video, and it showed the animals lying on the lake shore with convulsive tremors surging through their bodies. The agony continued for several minutes, and then, both lay still. In appearance, the animals had a basic resemblance to elephants. "Our infrared data indicates that these animals had body temperatures above 110 degrees at the time of their deaths."

"Your data validates the testimony Rex just gave us," stated Captain Jerontis. "I believe we now have conclusive evidence that a chemical attack is in progress against these two continents that seeks to kill all living creatures. We have no way of knowing how long it's been going on or how long it will continue. Perhaps, it has been going on intermittently since the nuclear exchange in the opening phase of this war. Maybe, every time they have a strong westerly wind, they eject these poisons into the stratosphere. Most likely, they will continue this insanity for as long as they are capable of continuing it. Maybe it's their intention to kill all life on this planet, and then come out of their mountains and repopulate the planet with life forms of their choosing. In order for life on these two continents to have any chance to survive and prosper, this evil plan must be thwarted. The chemical warfare machines must be shut down, and we are going to do exactly that."

Captain Jerontis sounded the warning klaxon, and announced: "In five minutes we'll begin accelerating into a geosynchronous transfer orbit. During the two hours following engine shutdown, there will be additional engine ignitions to adjust our speed and direction to achieve the desired orbital position."

Five minutes later, the Challenger's antimatter engines ignited on schedule. With the desired orbital parameters entered into the flight control computer, there was little for Captain Jerontis and his crew to do except to monitor the starship's progress. This left them free to relax and to plan an attack on the chemical warfare machines.

Gaining her husband's attention, Connie said, "I agree with your decision to take immediate action. Aren't you glad we don't have instantaneous communication with Earth that would make it possible for government bureaucrats to be in charge of this mission?"

"Do you think they'd handle this situation differently than we are?"

"Well, first they would have to appoint a commission made up of high-salary bureaucrats to study the problem for at least three months. Then, they would appoint a second commission to study the findings of the first commission. After all of this studying had been completed, there would of course be the requirement to file an environmental impact statement which would also have to be studied by a commission to insure its validity. And let's not forget the rights of the killers who are manning the poison factories; after all, we've just imposed a death sentence on them, and they should have the right to at least ten years of legal appeals before we execute them. How much additional death took place on the Southern Continent and the Northern Continent during this long drawn out process wouldn't be as important as making sure that all bureaucratic and legal requirements were met before any substantive action was taken."

Captain Jerontis looked at his wife in amazement, chuckled, and said, "We are 4.35 light-years from Earth and have been in space for well over six years. After all this time, I am surprised that you still harbor all this hostility for bureaucrats and their multitudes of costly, time-consuming regulations and for a legal system that frequently seems more concerned with the rights of criminals than with the suffering of their victims."

"I don't feel any hostility. I'm just happy that we don't have to contend with multiple layers of bureaucratic nonsense anymore and that we can take prompt action when we need to."

"She makes a valid point," stated Moose. "What if we needed congressional approval before we could take action? How many months would we have to sit here waiting for all those endless debates to take place? I like our current situation. We are free to get the job done promptly and move on to Alcent, where we can start building homes."

"I'm beginning to think I have a ship full of anti-establishment renegades who are happy to be free from bearing the burden of a bloated government bureaucracy," stated Captain Jerontis.

"You don't need to sound so innocent," retorted Moose. "You're just as happy as we are to no longer have to try to satisfy multiple layers of conflicting regulations."

Captain Jerontis grinned at Moose while nodding in agreement. Then, he said, "I wonder what kinds of political systems existed on this planet at the time the war started, what part they played in starting it, and if any of them survived."

"Considering the almost total destruction that has taken place, it seems almost impossible that any kind of government could still exist," Dianne said.

"Maybe each little pocket of life that has managed to survive has formed its own self-sufficient social group," speculated Connie. "I wonder how large a social unit Rex is part of."

"Maybe after we destroy those chemical warfare machines, we can explore some societal questions with him," suggested Dianne. "I'd like to know more about the community he lives in. Simple things like how many are in his community, and how they provide themselves with the basic essentials of life. Also, I'd like to get some information about the plants and animals that live down there."

"If he'll show us his exact location, we could land a capsule near him that would deliver a couple video cameras equipped with microphones," stated Captain Jerontis. "Whatever he records with the cameras, he could transmit to us using the capsule's communication equipment. The capsule would also contain a video screen, so we could broadcast to him."

"I like that idea," replied Dianne. "Communicating that way would be faster and more convenient than the use of telepathic images."

After a brief pause in the conversation, Moose decided to change the subject and asked Captain Jerontis, "What do you think is going to be the most efficient way to shut down the chemical warfare machines?"

"As I see it, there are two approaches we can take. We can attempt to shut them down with minimal loss of life, or we can hit them with massive firepower with the intention of trapping and killing all the people who are inside the mountains operating those machines. There are some valid reasons to shut them down with minimal loss of life. First, our recon indicates that their society has been destroyed and that they can no longer produce WMDs. These poison factories are all that remain from the terrible war: destroy them and the war is over. Second, it's possible that some of the operators of the chemical weapons are there because they were forced to serve. Why not give them a chance to escape. Third, there has already been enough killing. If we destroy their ability to attack the rest of the planet, maybe they'll come to their senses and devote their energy to building a better life for themselves."

"I'm not sure they're capable of devoting their energy to constructive activities," argued Connie. "If we judge them by their current activity, it's difficult to reach any other conclusion except that they are insane in a very cruel, sadistic way. They must be aware that the chemical agents they are pumping into the stratosphere are indiscriminately killing water-drinking creatures on two-thirds of this planet. Not to mention that an unexpected change in the wind direction would be hazardous to life on their continent. Since there's no possible gain for them in carrying out this attack, we must conclude that they are insanely cruel. That being the case, they will find cruel ways to prey upon their fellow humanoids if we allow them to live. Therefore, we must not only destroy their chemical warfare machines, but we must also kill them."

"It almost seems paradoxical to hear a medical doctor recommending death for six groups of humanoids," commented Captain Jerontis.

"On the contrary, if you put a medical perspective on this, I believe it is analogous to using radiation therapy to destroy six cancerous tumors that would otherwise destroy whatever normal life still remains on this planet. In regard to the possible presence of innocent individuals forced to serve against their will, if we allow them an opportunity to escape, the insanely cruel will also be able to escape, and this must be avoided. To put this in medical terms, when a malignant tumor is killed, it is sometimes necessary to kill some perfectly healthy tissue along with it to insure that all malignant tissue has been killed."

"I agree with her," stated Dianne. "The monstrous cruelty being committed here is almost unimaginable. What they are attempting is the genocide of several species including the genocide of a large percentage of their own species living on the other continents. I don't see any benefits they can gain by doing this. Therefore, I believe this genocide is being attempted purely to satisfy an insane, hateful desire for revenge. In my opinion, what they're doing qualifies as the ultimate war crime ever committed. It's an atrocity on a global scale. The penalty for a war crime of this magnitude should be death."

"I didn't realize our wives could be so blood thirsty," Moose said to Captain Jerontis.

Staring into her husband's eyes, Dianne said, "I still cringe when I recall the cold hatred that was transmitted into my mind during our first pass over those mountains. The expression of that intense hatred for me at a time when I had no desire whatever to harm them tells me that these creatures will never be beneficial to this planet. They will always be cruel predators looking for ways to satisfy their sadistic desires. We must eliminate them and their poison machines."

"I was with you on the observation deck," recalled Moose. "That was the only time I've ever seen you visibly shaken with fear."

"Given the intensity of the hatred that was expressed, why didn't they attack us at that time?" questioned Captain Jerontis.

After a few moments of thoughtful silence in which no one volunteered an answer, Captain Jerontis spoke in answer to his own question: "There are two obvious possibilities: either they have no way to attack us, or their defensive weapons are few in number and are reserved for use only when they are attacked."

"I think it might be the later possibility," commented Mike. "Our radar exploration did locate a number of missile silos with their concrete lids still in place. They may contain functional defensive missiles or even laser weapons. Perhaps, they no longer have any ability to manufacture missiles and want to conserve what they have."

"Given the degree of hatred expressed, if they have laser weapons, why haven't they attacked us with them?" questioned Captain Jerontis.

"I don't know," replied Mike. "But it's possible they've concluded that we are interstellar travelers. They may've reasoned that if we were from one of the other continents on this planet, we would've attacked them by now. Not knowing where we're from adds a huge uncertainty to their ability to estimate our capabilities. Uncertainty about the potency of our retaliatory capability does have a great deal of deterrent value. It's possible they've decided to leave us alone hoping that we won't interfere with their chemical attack and that we'll eventually leave."

"Now it must look to them like we're leaving," Captain Jerontis said. "Won't they be surprised when we begin our attack?"

"They might be surprised," admitted Mike. "But the risk for us in attacking them is that we don't know what their capabilities are. It would be a tragic ending to our mission if we were destroyed in our effort to save this planet. It took twenty years to design and build this starship and more than six additional years for us to get here. We and the people who made this mission possible have put so much into it that I think we should either attack with the strategy that has the lowest risk for us, or we should simply leave and not interfere with what's happening on this planet."

"In view of everything we've seen here, I won't feel very good about myself if we leave here without destroying these poison factories" stated Captain Jerontis. "I think life on this planet deserves a chance. I've never enjoyed killing, but I think we need to forget the possibility that some of the humanoids inside those mountain fortresses might be there against their will and just take them out as quickly as we can. I think the best way to do this would be to ..."

"Captain! Our infrared instruments have detected the sudden appearance of two hot spots next to the northernmost mountain!" exclaimed Mike. "They're rising rapidly, and are without question the exhaust plumes of missiles. The computer has calculated their acceleration to be 37g, and they will intercept us in just a few minutes. Our fire control computer has already aimed our particle-beam gun at the lead missile."

"They must've taken a look at our flight path and concluded that we're heading for geosynchronous orbit," stated Captain Jerontis. "And they must be convinced that we plan to attack them once we're on station. Since their missiles cannot attack us in a timely manner at that altitude, they're attempting to destroy us now. Let's not fire on these missiles until they reach their maximum speed. I want to know what their performance capability is, and I want to gain some additional altitude before they fire more missiles. However, since they might be nuclear armed, I don't want them getting any closer to us than about fifty miles. After we destroy these missiles, I want to attack the mountain fortress that fired them."

"Understood," responded Mike. "These missiles should be soft targets and easy to destroy. I've programmed the fire control system to hit each one with a ten-millisecond burst of antimatter. But we need to decide how much explosive power to deliver to the mountain fortress that fired them. Also, this gun has never been fired through a planet's atmosphere. I believe it will work, but we don't know that for sure."

"Captain! We have another potential problem," reported Moose. "Our radar has just detected a satellite near the orbital position we're headed for, but I'm not detecting any electronic emissions from it. It could be a dead satellite, a relic from the beginning of this war, or it could be dormant and waiting for an activation signal. The fact that it's positioned directly over the mountains in a geosynchronous orbit makes me suspicious. Whatever its purpose, it could be armed with defensive weapons that could be used to attack us."

"We need to strike the chemical warfare machines before we approach that satellite," stated Captain Jerontis. "I think our lowest risk attack option is to destroy the two incoming missiles and then, immediately attack all six mountain fortresses in rapid succession. If we hit the top of each mountain with an eight-second burst of antimatter, this will be the equivalent of a direct hit from a one-megaton hydrogen bomb. It will take two seconds for the fire control system to target successive mountains, which means that we can attack all six in about a minute. That should inflict enough damage to prevent additional attacks against us. Then, we can deliver additional fire-power if needed."

While Captain Jerontis was speaking, Mike entered the attack instructions into the fire control computer. Then, he said, "The system is ready, and the missiles fired at us have reached their maximum velocity. They are closing on us at eight miles per second and will intercept us in seventy seconds."

Captain Jerontis sounded the warning klaxon and announced: "Our attack will begin in thirty seconds."

Twenty seconds later, all hatches between adjoining compartments were closed and sealed to minimize air loss in the event the ship's hull was pierced. Then a ten-millisecond burst of antimatter particles hit the lead missile causing it to disappear in a blinding fireball followed immediately by the annihilation of the second missile in a brilliant fireball.

Two seconds later, a high-density beam of antimatter particles pierced B-2's atmosphere looking like a blazing lightning bolt from outer space. With awesome destructive power, it struck the top of the northernmost mountain instantly stopping its outflow of poisonous chemicals. The booming, thundering roar of the powerful, continuous explosion lasted for eight seconds. The enormous explosive release of pure energy from the mutual annihilation of matter and antimatter caused part of the mountain top to rise into the atmosphere and begin forming a huge mushroom shaped cloud. Additional massive amounts of mountain top material began cascading down the sides of the mountain in powerful avalanches that swept away and buried everything they encountered. In just a few seconds, several hundred feet of the mountain top was removed.

"The theory is correct!" exclaimed Mike. "The beam does penetrate a planet's atmosphere exactly as predicted. Also, those missiles were nuclear armed, and the antimatter explosions were powerful enough to trigger their nuclear warheads. At least fifty times more energy was released than would have been from the antimatter we delivered to the missiles proving that they had nuclear warheads."

Two seconds after the northernmost chemical warfare complex was blasted, the second poison factory was bombarded with a high-density beam of antimatter particles for eight seconds. Then, two seconds later, the third one was attacked. Four seconds into this attack, the Challenger was hit by a powerful laser beam fired from a weapon located near the base of this mountain. The fire control computer immediately broke off its attack on the mountain top and blasted the laser, instantly putting it out of action. While this was taking place, eight more lasers fired on the Challenger: four from mountain number four, and two each from mountains five and six. During the next twenty seconds, all eight of the lasers were hit with short bursts of antimatter and blasted out of existence. Then, the fire control computer resumed the attack on the chemical warfare machines.

"Captain! We've been damaged by the laser attack," reported Moose. "Four of them melted holes through our micro-meteor shield before we disabled them. Two of these burned holes through our hull."

Using surveillance cameras, Moose displayed the damage on a video screen, and said, "The observation deck was hit, and that hole is about two feet across. Also, the hangar deck was hit, and that hole is about three feet across. The cargo shuttle has a large hole melted through its fuselage. It appears to be far enough forward so that the shuttle's nuclear reactor escaped damage. I don't think we've suffered any casualties because there weren't supposed to be any personnel in those areas."

"There are 39 missiles headed our way," reported Mike. "These might be all they have. It looks like they're making a desperate attempt to destroy us in retaliation for destroying their chemical weapons. By firing every missile they have, they're hoping to overwhelm our defenses."

"We've shut down all six chemical warfare machines," stated Captain Jerontis. "Let's take out those missiles."

Mike entered the appropriate instructions, and the fire control computer began targeting and destroying the incoming missiles. "So far, every missile we've hit has resulted in the detonation of a nuclear warhead," reported Mike. "Apparently, they're all nuclear armed."

"It was no accident that these poison factories survived the war," stated Captain Jerontis. "They were very well defended. Apparently, these aliens placed the highest priority on the survival of their chemical weapons, so they could rain lethal toxins down on their enemies long after the war was over. By subjecting their enemies to a continuing rain of death, they probably hoped to rebuild their society while denying their enemies the same opportunity. They evidently believed that even if the nuclear phase of the war ended in a stalemate, they could still eventually be the victors if their poison factories survived."

"I wonder what could cause a political system to become so insanely malicious that it would be willing to destroy all people and mamals on the

121

rest of the planet, so that it could become the only remaining power," questioned Connie.

"You're the psychiatrist. What do you think would motivate people to do something like that?" Captain Jerontis asked.

"I can only speculate, but it's possible that some fanatical religious cult gained power. Perhaps, it practiced total intolerance of all who refused to accept its doctrines. Maybe the people on the other two continents rejected this religion. Unable to tolerate rejection, the only way the cult-based political system could achieve 100 percent membership was to kill or enslave all the infidels that could not be coerced to join it. On a smaller scale, there are examples of this in human history."

"There isn't any way we can prove your theory, but it's at least a possible explanation for what has happened here," noted Captain Jerontis.

"Maybe after this battle is over, we can establish better communications with Rex, and he can inform us about this planet's recent history," Dianne said.

"Captain, we've completed the destruction of the missiles that were launched against us," reported Mike.

"Good! Let's finish the destruction of the mountain fortresses, starting with mountain number four. Since it was the most heavily defended, it might be their command center. Hit it with a sixty-second burst, and hit the other five with forty-second bursts. When the smoke clears, we'll survey the damage and decide if more attacks are needed."

"Understood," replied Mike, as he entered the instructions into the fire control computer, which immediately began carrying out the attacks.

"Captain, we're still on course for geosynchronous orbit," stated Moose. "Our plan was to attack from there, but our attack will be over long before we arrive in that orbit. Are you planning to investigate the satellite we discovered up there?"

"Since we've already expended most of the fuel needed to reach geosynchronous orbit, we might as well take a look at it. You and I can do that while Mike and his engineering staff repair the damage to this starship. By looking at the equipment on that satellite, we can discover its purpose. Its mass will tell us how much booster power they once had. Studying its instrumentation, electrical power source, and construction materials will give us an indication of the level of technology achieved by the aliens. Who knows, there might be something there we can use."

"There is some risk involved in investigating that satellite," stated Moose. "It could be armed with defensive weapons, or it could be carrying a bomb designed to go off if the satellite is tampered with. In view of the damage we've already suffered, I think we should avoid additional risk, and just go to Alcent. We'll face plenty of danger once we arrive there."

"I don't want to take any unnecessary risk either, but we need to learn as much as we can about these aliens before we leave here. Since you're

122

worried about risk, I want you to devise a plan to investigate that satellite that will minimize our risk. Figure out a way to determine if it's armed; if it isn't, I'd like to capture it and take it with us."

Moose stared at Captain Jerontis in disbelief for a few moments. Then, he said, "You aren't joking! You're serious! You do want to take it with us, don't you?"

"Only if we can determine that it's safe to do that and if our on-site investigation reveals that we might gain some significant knowledge by having additional time to study it."

"I will develop a plan to achieve those objectives with zero risk," declared Moose with conviction.

Captain Jerontis made eye contact with Mike expecting a progress report. In response, Mike said, "Three down and three to go."

"I can't believe you! You're blasting the tops off of mountains, digging deep craters, and creating avalanches that even contain molten rock. And you're acting like doing all this is just a simple, routine matter. You even seem to be enjoying yourself."

"The capability of the fire control system coupled with the astounding power of the antimatter particle-beam gun does make the task rather routine. Having this tremendous power at my fingertips and using it to rescue a planet from genocide makes me a feel good. Having and using the power to give this planet a better future is almost like playing God."

"I can understand why you feel that way," stated Captain Jerontis.

"Can you imagine the horrible consequences, if a weapon system like this fell into the wrong hands?" Mike asked. "A military power possessing a spaceship armed with this system could hold an entire planet hostage, yet it was essential to our survival when we passed through that constellation of interstellar asteroids a few years ago."

"The U.S. developed this gun to increase our probability of survival, but now that they have this technology, I wonder if they've built more of them to guarantee national security. During its multiyear test and development period, this gun was used to annihilate all the unwanted space junk orbiting Earth. This must have made many politicians and military leaders aware of the system's potential. A benevolent power possessing this system could truly become the world's police force."

"At the moment, we are the police force for this planet," declared Mike. "And we've just shut down the largest scale criminal activity I've ever seen."

A short time later, with the Challenger approaching geosynchronous orbit, Moose reported: "We are 400 miles from the alien satellite, and I have some pretty good images of most of it. From the way that it's slowly tumbling, it appears to be out of control, and that would indicate that it's no longer a functional satellite."

Captain Jerontis looked at the images on the video screen and said, "While that could be true, it's also possible that it's simply in a dormant state awaiting an activation signal."

"To cover that possibility, let's aim the particle-beam gun at it and have the fire control system maintain the lock-on," stated Moose. "Then, if it does anything threatening, we can instantly destroy it."

Captain Jerontis looked at Mike, who said, "Already done."

"If it's an armed, functional satellite in a dormant state, maybe we can trick it into activating itself," stated Moose. "We can direct a multi-frequency radar beam at it to make it think that it's being targeted and see if there's any response."

"That's a good idea," agreed Captain Jerontis, "but before you do that, let's illuminate it with a laser beam, so we can get more detail out of our optical images."

Moose hit the satellite with a laser beam, brightly illuminating it. After studying the new images, Captain Jerontis said, "There isn't any obvious damage, so if it's no longer operational, it must be the result of internal problems. Most likely, it was launched 30 or more years ago, and old age may've shut it down. Judging from its antenna configuration, it may've been a communications satellite. Also, it has enough cameras on it, so that it may've been used to monitor the weather in this hemisphere."

Speaking to Moose, Captain Jerontis said, "Proceed with your radar assault, and let's see if there's any response."

After trying various frequencies, Moose said, "There's been no attempt to jam our radar; in fact, there's been no response of any kind."

"So, do you think that it's safe to move in and do a hands-on investigation of that satellite?" questioned Captain Jerontis.

"No! I don't think we should expose ourselves to possible risk. I think we should close to fifty miles. Then, we should launch one of the ERVs to the satellite and use it to do the investigation."

"That sounds like a good plan."

A short time later, the Challenger reached geosynchronous orbit and took up a position fifty miles away from the alien satellite. Moose immediately dispatched one of the external repair vehicles on a course to the alien spacecraft. Mike and his engineering staff used the other one to begin repairing the holes in the Challenger's hull.

In less than an hour, Moose's ERV arrived at the alien satellite. Moose directed it to slowly circle the satellite and send back minutely detailed images of it. Next, he aligned the ERV with the tumbling satellite's axis of rotation. Using the ERV's control rockets, Moose gave it a rotational velocity equal to that of the alien spacecraft, thereby eliminating all relative motion. Finally, he attached the ERV to the alien spacecraft with its grappling arms.

Moose turned to Captain Jerontis and said, "We've captured it. Now, we can look inside."

"Good work," acknowledged Captain Jerontis.

Moose directed the robot to drill a small hole through a side panel in the satellite's body. Then, a tiny video camera equipped with a lamp was passed through the hole into the satellite's interior.

While viewing detailed images of the spacecraft's interior, Captain Jerontis said, "I don't see anything unusual or threatening in this area. I wonder what the rest of its interior looks like."

"We'll soon find out," responded Moose, as he began drilling an access hole into another compartment. "I don't know about you, but I'm thrilled about being the first human to investigate a high-tech piece of equipment that was designed and built by aliens."

"You've undergone quite a change of heart. Earlier, you wanted to ignore this satellite and move on; now, you're excited by the possibility of learning about the aliens who made it."

"Earlier, I felt fortunate to be alive. We'd just had a couple holes burned through our hull. Had one of those laser beams hit one of our antimatter fuel tanks, we would've instantaneously ceased to exist. My hopes and dreams would've vanished in an instant. I'm ready to move on to Alcent, build a home, and raise a family. I don't want to take any additional potentially deadly risks."

"I didn't realize that our near catastrophe affected you so deeply, but I understand how you feel. We should be able to finish up at this planet in a couple days. Then, we can move on."

"Thanks for your understanding," replied Moose. "I appreciate that."

"We've now penetrated another compartment," announced Moose, as the images began appearing on the video screen. While viewing them, both men agreed that everything looked normal and harmless.

An hour later, Moose and Captain Jerontis completed their investigation of the satellite's interior, and Captain Jerontis said, "I believe this satellite is exactly what it appears to be: a communications and surveillance spacecraft that has been out of action for a long time. The fact that its control gyros are not operative, combined with the fact that its station keeping fuel tanks are empty, is enough to convince me that this is a long-dead satellite."

"Those empty fuel tanks point to a fact that we haven't considered," stated Moose. "And that is that this spacecraft has an easterly drift of 12 miles per day. If that drift rate was imparted to it at the time it ceased to function, and if we assume that this satellite has been inoperative for about 20 years; then, this satellite may have been located over the other two continents during its operational lifetime. They could've used it as a communications link between the two continents and for weather information. In other words, it was an unarmed civilian satellite."

"Are you trying to say that it's safe for us to take it with us, so we can study its components and construction materials?"

"Is there any possibility that it could be harboring viable toxic microbes after all these years in the harsh environment of space?"

"To me, that seems impossible, but I think we should have our wives answer that question. Do you have any other objection to taking this satellite with us?"

"None that I can think of," replied Moose.

"Good! Let's attach the satellite and the ERV to external hard points on our hull until our wives complete their search for toxic microbes. Even finding and examining dead microbes would be educational."

"I will begin bringing back the historical artifact that we've so bravely captured," Moose jested in a playful tone.

"You're quite cheerful all of a sudden."

"We're almost home. In just a few weeks, we'll arrive at Alcent. Who knows, we might even find a warm, exotic, sandy beach that we can build our homes next to."

"That's almost guaranteed. Since both of our shuttles are equipped with hydrofoils, we must live on the shore of a body of water that's large enough to land on. Like you, I'm excited about the possibilities."

Captain J.J.'s communicator beeped. It was Mike. "Captain, we've repaired the hole through the hangar deck hull. In about an hour, we'll be finished repairing the hole in the observation deck hull. Also, the hole in the cargo shuttle's fuselage will be easy to repair. Fortunately, none of the shuttle's critical systems were destroyed."

"Thank you for the progress report," replied Captain Jerontis.

Turning to Moose, Captain Jerontis asked, "How long before your project is complete?"

"The ERV will arrive here with our trophy in about 20 minutes. I'll need an additional half hour to secure them both to the hull."

"Good!"

An hour later, Mike arrived on the flight deck and reported: "We've completed repairs to the hull, and both areas have been pressurized. We plan to repair the shuttle on the way to Alcent."

"I assume you did a good job," stated Captain Jerontis. "Do I get any kind of guarantee?"

"I would stake my life on it. By that, I mean I would be willing to roll out a sleeping bag next to either of the repaired holes and camp out for a while; in case of failure, I would be sucked into the vacuum of space."

"Are you telling me that there's no possibility of failure?"

"Absolutely!"

"Moose, do you have the alien satellite and the ERV secured to the hull?" Captain Jerontis asked.

"Sure do!"

"Great work guys. It's now time to drop down to a lower orbit and do a recon run over those chemical warfare complexes. Before we move on, we need to be certain that they are permanently out of action."

Captain Jerontis sounded three blasts on the warning klaxon, and announced: "In three minutes we'll begin 1g acceleration to move into a polar orbit at an altitude of 230 miles."

Three minutes later, the Challenger's antimatter engines ignited on schedule to begin the orbital transfer that would require about three hours. Directing his attention to Moose and Mike, Captain Jerontis said, "During the past hour, I've done a computer analysis of the battle-damage data gathered during our attack. Each mountain is now about a half-mile shorter than it was. Even though the crater in the top of what's left of each mountain is only a quarter of a mile deep, there is a high probability that the beam of antimatter particles penetrated each mountain to a depth of several miles during the attacks. The computer has concluded that the tremendous release of energy in the attacks resulted in a temperature above one million degrees at the leading edge of the particle-beam. Massive amounts of rock melted, reached the boiling point, and evaporated causing extremely high pressure to build up. This extremely hot, high-pressure mixture of liquid and gaseous rock gushed upward around the incoming particle-beam and poured out of the top of each mountain looking like an erupting volcano. When the particle-beam gun was shut off, the eruptions continued until the pressure was dissipated. Then, the sides of the vertical tunnels, being in a super hot state of plasticity, collapsed inward filling the tunnels to the point that they now look like craters that are only a quarter of a mile deep. If the computer is correct in its analysis of the data, then the hollowed out chambers that contained the chemical warfare equipment must have collapsed, bringing about complete destruction of all equipment."

"Is it possible that the particle-beam penetrated all the way to the chambers containing the chemical warfare equipment?" Mike asked.

"I don't know at what level in these mountains the chambers were located, but the computer has calculated that the particle-beam penetrated to a depth of three to four miles. If the manufacturing chambers were located near the base of each mountain, the particle-beam did not reach them, but there is a high probability that molten rock may have poured into and flooded those chambers. The extremely high temperatures and pressures generated by the incoming beam of antimatter particles may have sent a high speed jet of liquid and gaseous rock down the same pipes that the aliens used to pour poisonous chemicals into the stratosphere."

"That would be true justice if the pipes they built to carry poisons into the atmosphere served to transport the fires of hell into their poison manufacturing chambers," stated Moose. "In a matter of a few seconds, everyone and everything in the chambers would've been melted into a liquid state. I don't see any way they could've survived our attack."

"I don't either, but I want our defenses on full alert anyway."

"The programs I put into the fire control computer earlier are still there," stated Mike.

Three hours later, the Challenger began its low altitude pass over the target area. Reviewing high definition optical images of the first mountain, Captain Jerontis said, "Massive avalanches have buried everything around the base of this mountain. All the snow and ice we melted has caused some destructive floods. It looks like a massive volcanic eruption has just occurred. The mountain and the area around its base look like a volcanic wasteland. I wish we could've shut them down without inflicting so much destruction on such a scenic area."

"We did what we had to do," stated Connie.

"In many ways, our attacks were like volcanic eruptions," Dianne said. "As destructive as volcanoes are, nature always recovers. Life is not fragile; it is tenacious. Life around these mountains will recover, and so will life on the rest of B-2, now that the poison factories no longer exist."

Speaking to Dianne, Captain Jerontis said, "In about an hour, you'll have an opportunity to communicate with Rex. Let's show him images of this destruction, so he'll know that the era of poison rain will end once the atmosphere has cleansed itself."

"That should make him and his family very happy," stated Dianne.

"Also, we need to tell him that we'll soon be leaving for Alcent, probably in less than a day. Tell him that if he'll give us his location, we'll send down a capsule that will contain communications equipment. Tell him that we'll station a satellite in geosynchronous orbit over his location that will be capable of relaying information between him and us when we're on Alcent. This satellite will also provide him with weather data. We'll also put a surveillance satellite in a polar orbit at an altitude of 350 miles. These two satellites are mainly for our benefit, because I want to monitor activity on this planet. Also, I believe that Rex will be a friendly, reliable source of information. Giving him access to the data from these satellites will enable him to help us interpret the data, if the need arises."

"Communicating all of this with nothing more than telepathic images is going to be a challenge," stated Dianne. "I'm going to my office to generate the computer images I'll need to accomplish this."

A short time later, Mike said, "We've now looked at all six of our targets, and I see nothing that would indicate anything other than complete and permanent destruction of the poison factories. The job is done."

FIVE

Pioneer Island

TIME: 6 Years, 250 Days ALE.

Michelle's latest mission update to Earth:

"We've left B-2 and are on course for Alcent, a planet where we hope to build our homes. After accelerating at 1g for twenty-four hours, we've reached a velocity of 527 miles per second and are 22,760,000 miles from B-2. We will accelerate for two more days to a velocity of 1,580 miles per second. Then, we'll coast for fifteen days, followed by three days of deceleration at 1g. Even though Alcent is 2.45 billion miles from B-2, we'll be there in less than three weeks."

After transmitting her mission update, Michelle went to the cafeteria to relax over a cup of coffee. Dianne and Doctor Connie Nemard were there and asked Michelle to join them. After the usual small talk, Michelle said to Dianne, "That was quite a feat you pulled off a couple days ago."

"What do you mean?"

"I'm talking about the way you communicated with Rex."

"He did all the work. I just made myself available."

"That might be, but you did communicate with an intelligent alien. How do you feel about that?"

"Pretty good."

Michelle was incredulous, "***Pretty good!*** You've done something that no other human has ever done, and all you can say is a rather matter of fact, ***Pretty good***."

Surprised by the strength of Michelle's reaction, Dianne said, "I wasn't trying to sound like it was just another day at the office. It's just that right now, I feel rather laid back, like I'm on vacation."

"I think you deserve a vacation. You've been involved in some very intense mental and emotional activity, but how do you feel about it?"

"It was thrilling beyond my wildest dreams. I've always believed we aren't alone, but I never thought I'd be the first human to make contact."

"That was an epic event in human history," stated Connie. "You made first contact, and we now know that we aren't alone."

"Just think, if we had gone to Alcent without swinging by B-2, we wouldn't have discovered them," Dianne said. "As eager as we are to start building our homes, we could easily have skipped visiting B-2."

"But if we'd done that, we would've always had that unanswered question about the possible existence of life on B-2," Michelle said.

"That question would've nagged me a lot," admitted Dianne. "I've devoted my career to the study of life, and having an earthlike planet nearby would've always made me wonder if life exists there."

"I would've been curious about that too," stated Michelle. "Then again, I've often been accused of having too much curiosity. That's undoubtedly what motivated me to become a science reporter. Constant exposure to the latest scientific discoveries has always been exciting to me and has served to satisfy and stimulate my curiosity. Being in a starship with the capability to visit a nearby earthlike planet and not doing it would've been disappointing."

"When we're busy building our homes on Alcent, we'll have the satisfaction of knowing that we aren't alone in our little corner of the galaxy," added Connie. "Once we overcome the language barrier, talking with them should be incredibly interesting."

Directing her question to Michelle, Connie asked, "How do you like being responsible for teaching them our language and learning theirs?"

"It'll be challenging, but those satellites we placed in orbit around B-2 and the ground equipment we gave Rex will make the job easier. We're now able to transmit large volumes of information back and forth or do nothing more than just socialize."

"But do you like being responsible for teaching them English?"

"Yes! It'll be fun. I'll be working with Rex's wife, Shannon. We've already started the project, and I've found her to be a warm, intelligent individual filled with enthusiasm. In view of the horrible tragedy inflicted on their planet by the long devastating war, I think her upbeat personality is truly remarkable. I like working with her."

"Much of her positive outlook might be a direct result of us destroying those chemical warfare complexes," stated Dianne.

"That's definitely true," agreed Michelle. "The first words that she taught me from their language is their equivalent of the English phrase, *Thank you.* She has been very emotional in its use. I think they view us as the saviors of their planet. They seem very comfortable with the possibility that we'll be living nearby on Alcent."

"Perhaps, they think that we're willing and able to come back if they need us," commented Connie.

"And they're probably hoping that we'll help them solve the medical and biological problems created by the war," added Dianne.

"That might be one of the reasons why Shannon is so eager to learn our language," Michelle said.

"True," agreed Dianne. "But I think they're just as excited about getting acquainted with us as we are about getting acquainted with them. Finding out that they're not the only intelligent species in the universe has to be an astounding event in their lives."

Facing Dianne, Michelle asked, "How did you feel when you first became aware that an alien was attempting to contact you?"

"I was puzzled. I felt the presence of life, but I didn't understand how I could sense its presence."

"You must've been incredibly excited twelve hours later when Rex transmitted an image of himself into your mind," stated Michelle.

"That did put me on cloud nine," admitted Dianne. "When I was a teenager, I made it my goal to be on this mission. I studied hard to become the best that I could be, but I never dreamed that my hard work would result in me becoming the first human to communicate with an alien."

"Your experience confirms a belief that I've held for a long time," stated Michelle.

"What do you mean?" Dianne asked.

"I believe that individuals who relentlessly strive to achieve excellence will always find unexpected rewards. Your experience with Rex was unexpected and is most definitely a high point in your career. That achievement must be very gratifying."

Beaming with pride, Dianne nodded and said, "It is, and I can't imagine what we might discover on Alcent that will exceed this."

"Alcent is a life-filled planet," stated Michelle. "I am willing to bet that it will hit us with any number of big surprises."

"I'm not going to argue that," responded Dianne.

Speaking to Michelle, Connie said, "Getting back to your belief that unexpected rewards come to those who pursue excellence, I believe that your presence on this ship also tends to confirm that concept."

"Why do you think that?" Michelle asked.

"To me, it's obvious! Your achievement of excellence in your career is largely responsible for you having been selected to be a part of the news team that covered our departure from Earth. And that gave your husband an opportunity to hide you on this ship. I'll bet you never dreamed that your achievement of excellence in your career would result in you becoming a part of this mission."

"That's definitely true," admitted Michelle.

"Your achievement of excellence has also had an unexpected reward for the rest of us," declared Dianne.

"What do you mean?" questioned Michelle.

"Because of your presence, we're all alive. You discovered the sabotage to our ship a few minutes before we would've been annihilated. And because of that, Rex and his people will no longer have to endure poison rain, all because you achieved excellence in your career."

Michelle smiled at Dianne and Connie and said, "I appreciate your recognition. Coming from my best friends makes it more meaningful to me than all of the *Excellence in Reporting Awards* I received back on Earth. Now that we're on the final leg of our journey to our new home, the career that I devoted my life to back on Earth seems very distant. In less than three weeks, we'll begin exploring Alcent in search of an ideal location for our new home. Won't that be exciting?"

TIME: 6 Years, 269 Days, 23 Hours, 15 Minutes ALE.

Michelle's latest mission update to Earth:

"We are 29,000 miles from Alcent and are approaching the planet at a velocity of 21.5 miles per second. Losing speed at a steady 1g, our velocity will be reduced to five miles per second in 45 minutes. At that time, we will enter a polar orbit at an altitude of 210 miles."

After transmitting her brief message, Michelle joined Connie, Matthew, and Denise on the observation deck. The sight of Alcent suspended in space against a background of stars filled Michelle with cheerfulness. Finally, the long journey was nearing an end. "That planet will soon be our new home!" she exclaimed to the children.

Never having been on a planet and not aware of the distance involved, Matthew said, "It doesn't look very big. Will our new home be smaller than our starship home?"

Recognizing how sincere her son was in asking the question, Michelle wondered how to answer it so that the children could get a true appreciation for the enormous difference in size between Alcent and the Challenger. Quickly deciding that this was impossible and that they would not comprehend the vast open spaces on Alcent until they actually experienced them, Michelle simply explained, "Our new home will be much larger than our starship."

"How will we get inside of it?" Denise asked.

"We are going to live on its outside surface," responded Connie.

Being only five years old, and having lived all of her short life inside a starship, this concept presented quite a large problem to Denise. A problem compounded by the fact that she had never experienced planetary gravity or the wide open spaces that exist on a planet. Displaying a puzzled expression, Denise gazed at the small sphere, seemingly suspended in empty space; then, she said, "But it's round like a ball. What will happen if we fall off of it?"

Connie patiently grasped her daughter's right hand, and both sat down on the deck. Interested in the same problem, Matthew sat down next to them and anxiously awaited an explanation. Giving her attention to both children, Connie asked, "Do you remember a few days ago when we were weightless, and we were able to float around in our starship?"

After the children said yes, Connie continued, "Right now, we can't float around, can we?"

After the children said no, Connie said, "That's because we have artifi-

132

cial gravity. It holds us against this floor."

Then, she asked the children to stand up and jump as high as they could. After they had done this several times, Connie said, "Even when you jump as high as you can, the gravity pulls you back down. Our new home on Alcent will have gravity as strong as you feel now. No matter how high you jump or how fast you run, you will never fall off."

After thinking about it for a few moments, the children seemed to grasp the concept and accept the reassurance from Connie. Both stood up, leaned against the crystal-clear plastic hull, and stared at Alcent.

While observing the children, Michelle thought about Christopher Columbus. In 1492, he was warned that the Earth was flat and that when he and his ships reached the edge of the Earth, they would fall off into an abyss. Seeing Alcent from space, Matthew and Denise would have the true nature of their new home impressed into their minds, along with an understanding of gravity and weightlessness.

Michelle's thoughts were interrupted by her son who asked, "Is Alcent like the Earth where you came from?"

Matthew's question stimulated Michelle to recall fond memories from the distant planet Earth, a planet that she would never see again. Michelle remembered the pleasant experience of a passing rain shower on a mild summer day followed by warm sunshine and the fragrance of clean, fresh air accompanied by the sound of wild birds happily singing. In sharp contrast to this were the winter snow storms that turned the countryside into a winter wonderland that on a clear, cold night seemed so bright, quiet, and peaceful under the light of the full moon. Then, she thought about the backpack camping trips through forests over mountainous terrain bordering the vast Pacific Ocean. The pleasant memories flooding through Michelle's mind served to heighten her desire to leave the confinement of the starship that had been her home for so many years.

Michelle was jogged out of her mesmerized mental state by her son, who had lost his patience, grasped her left hand, and tugged on it while saying, "Mother, is Alcent like the Earth you came from?"

Looking into her son's eager upturned face, Michelle said, "I didn't mean to ignore you, but I was thinking about Earth. It was my home for a long time, and I miss it. In many ways, Alcent is like Earth. Living there will be fun and exciting. You will see many of the things that you've only seen in movies from Earth."

Recalling scenes from a movie that he had seen just the previous day, Matthew asked, "Will our new home have big trees?"

"Yes, it will."

"Will there be a tree big enough for Dad to build a tree house in?"

"Some of the trees on Alcent are huge," replied Michelle.

"But will Dad and Uncle Jerry have time to build a tree house for Denise and me to play in?"

Michelle looked at Connie and asked, "What do you think about the possibility of that happening?"

Connie gazed at the children's eager faces and said, "I think your fathers will enjoy building you a tree house."

"Will there be birds in the trees to sing pretty songs like the birds in the movie we saw yesterday?" Denise asked.

"We don't know if there are songbirds on Alcent," replied Connie.

Looking worried, Matthew asked, "Will there be monster bears by our new home that can climb the tree all the way up to our tree house?"

Matthew's question brought a look of fear to Denise's face. Noticing this, Connie said, "We don't know if there are any tree-climbing bears on Alcent, but we do know that there are wild animals. However, you don't need to worry about them, because we have guns to protect you with."

Accepting Connie's reassurance, the children again leaned against the transparent hull to look at the now much larger appearing Alcent. After a few moments, Matthew exclaimed, "Look Mom! It's getting bigger!"

"It's not getting bigger," Michelle said. "It just looks like it's getting bigger because we're rapidly moving closer to it. We'll soon be close enough, so that you'll begin to understand how large it really is."

While Matthew was thinking about what his mother had just said, Denise noticed the deep blue color of a large part of Alcent and the dark green color of a large area bordering the blue area. Turning to her mother, she said, "I like the blue part. It's the same color as my eyes. Will our new home be on the blue part?"

Connie smiled at the innocence and sincerity of the question and wondered how to instill in her five-year old daughter the concept of a vast ocean in view of the fact that the largest quantity of water that Denise had ever experienced was in the bathtub. Connie decided to save the size lesson for a later time and said, "The blue area is a huge body of water. We might build our home next to it but not on it."

"Is the dark green area where trees grow?" Denise asked.

"Yes, and there are also many other kinds of plants growing there."

"What are those bright white areas?" Matthew asked.

"Those are clouds," replied Connie.

"But they look different from the clouds in the movies," objected Matthew. "These clouds are brighter and whiter."

"That's because we are above the clouds, and we can see the brilliant light from Alpha Centauri A that they are reflecting," Connie said. "The people in the movies were below the clouds. When clouds are thick, not very much light passes through them. That's why they looked so dark."

Reflecting on what Connie had just said, the children returned to staring at Alcent. Momentarily, Denise again turned to her mother and asked, "What are those clouds made out of? What do they do?"

Facing Matthew and Denise, Connie said, "Both of you always help me water our plants. Do you know why we give them water?"

"Because plants will die without water," the children replied.

"The wild plants growing on Alcent need water too," Connie explained. "The clouds are made out of tiny droplets of water. Sometimes the clouds have more water than they can hold, and some of it turns into rain and falls out of the clouds. The rain waters all the wild plants."

"I saw rain in the movie we watched yesterday," Denise said.

"I saw the rain too," stated Matthew. "When it started raining, the children went into their tree house, so they wouldn't get wet. After the rain, they had fun running through small pools of water. I think our new home will be fun. When can we go there?"

"In a few minutes, we'll be in orbit," responded Michelle. "By the time we complete one orbit, you'll see just how big Alcent really is. It's so big that we'll have to explore it for several months with our telescopes and other instruments, so we can find a safe place to live. Then, we'll go down and build our new homes."

"Will you show me pictures of the plants and animals that you find with the telescopes?" Matthew asked.

"Yes, we will," responded Michelle.

Denise quickly asked, "Will you show me too?"

"Yes!" replied Michelle.

Pleased with how inquisitive the children were, Connie turned to Michelle and said, "I think our children want to help us explore Alcent and find a place to build our homes."

Before Michelle could respond to Connie, the children exclaimed, "Yes! When can we start?"

"We've already started," replied Michelle.

Fascinated by the view of their new home, the children continued to stare at Alcent, which was now less than 500 miles away. Looking from left to right, they were awestruck by its immense size. It totally dominated the view from the observation deck, and Matthew exclaimed, "It's really big! How long will it take us to go all the way around it?"

"About an hour and a half," replied Michelle.

Turning to Connie, Michelle said, "This hemisphere has only one continent, and it extends from the south polar icecap to the north polar icecap. It looks like it's at least 3,000 miles across at its widest point and no less than 2,000 miles across at its narrowest point."

"It appears to be close to 3,000 miles wide at the north polar icecap," noted Connie. "I'm guessing that the icecap is about 1,500 miles in diameter. That means that animals from this hemisphere could migrate to the other hemisphere without having to traverse the icecap. I wonder how far this continent extends beyond the icecap."

"We'll soon know," Michelle said. "In less than 15 minutes, our orbital speed will take us well beyond the icecap, putting us over the other hemisphere. However, it's probably dark now, since Alpha Centauri A and B are

135

both over this hemisphere."

A few minutes later, Matthew asked, "What is that big, round white area? It looks different than the clouds."

"That's the north polar icecap," replied Michelle.

"But what is it?" questioned Matthew.

"It's ice that's covered with snow," responded Michelle. "When it's too cold for clouds to make rain, they make snow. When it's too cold for the snow to melt, it eventually gets so deep that some of it turns into ice."

Thinking about how cold ice cubes are, Matthew said, "I don't think the icecap would be a good place to live. It would be too cold."

"I want to live some place where it's warm," stated Denise.

"I don't think anyone wants to live on either icecap," Connie said.

A few minutes later, the Challenger was beyond the north polar icecap and over Alcent's nighttime hemisphere. Having completed its deceleration to five miles per second, the Challenger's antimatter engines were shut down, and the big moment had finally arrived. The Challenger and its occupants were now in a polar orbit around Alcent; 6 years, 270 days after leaving Earth.

No longer being subjected to 1g deceleration, the Challenger's occupants were again experiencing weightlessness. Matthew exclaimed, "This is fun! I like to float around."

"Me too!" exclaimed Denise. Pushing off with her legs, she went floating off in pursuit of Matthew.

"They sure enjoy being weightless," commented Connie.

"Yeah, they do," agreed Michelle. "I'm amazed by how quickly they invent games that can only be played in zero-gravity. Their imaginations are very creative."

Noticing that the observation deck was softly illuminated, Connie said, "Considering that it's nighttime, it sure isn't very dark in here. Where is all this light coming from?"

Pointing across the deck, Michelle said, "It's coming from there."

Suddenly, both women realized that they had forgotten that Alcent had two moons. Together, they pushed off and floated across the observation deck to look at them.

"They look just as big as the Moon did back on Earth," Connie said. "What an impressive sight it is to have two moons that look that large."

"With two nearby stars and two moons, we aren't going to have very many dark nights on Alcent," commented Michelle.

"If we end up living in waterfront homes, two full moons in the sky could lead to some romantic evenings on the beach."

The possibilities are exciting, but your romantic episodes on the beach could be dangerous. A hungry dinosaur might come by."

"I haven't even gotten my fantasy going," stated Connie. "And you're already giving me a cold shower."

"I didn't mean to do that, but we will be living on a dinosaur planet."

"Hopefully, we'll find a place to live that'll be free of carnivorous dinosaurs. A small island in the middle of a large lake might be just such a place. It wouldn't provide enough prey to support large predators."

"Unless Alcent has carnivorous dinosaurs that enjoy swimming, the island home you just described might be ideal for us," agreed Michelle. "In any case, we'll have to live near water, because our shuttles are equipped with hydrofoils. A large inland lake would be good for the shuttles to operate from. Who knows, you may have a chance to live the romantic fantasy you just tried to imagine."

"After nearly seven years in space, I'm ready for that."

"Me too!" exclaimed Michelle.

Connie and Michelle drifted across the observation deck to resume visual exploration of Alcent. Even though Alcent was illuminated only by moonlight, its major features were still readily visible.

"The continent we observed earlier not only extends past the north polar icecap, but it also extends southward as far as we can see," Connie said. "And as was the case in the other hemisphere, its width appears to vary from 2,000 to 3,000 miles. I wonder if it extends all the way to, and even beyond, the south polar icecap."

"If it does, that would mean that this planet has one giant continuous continent that encircles the globe from pole to pole like a huge belt."

"If that's the case, the majority of this planet's water is contained in two giant oceans."

"It seems strange that a planet could have only one continent that encircles it like a giant belt," noted Michelle. "If that's what we have here, my geologist husband will have fun trying to figure out how this kind of continent could've formed."

Matthew interrupted Michelle and Connie. "I'm getting hungry," he said. "Can we go to the cafeteria and get some pizza?"

Michelle started to answer Matthew's question, but she was abruptly cut off by Denise who exclaimed, "I'm hungry too!"

Michelle turned to Connie and said, "Care to join us?"

"Pizza sounds good," replied Connie, following them.

Meanwhile, on the flight deck, Captain Jerontis, Mike, Moose, and Dianne were reviewing data from the Challenger's instruments. "I sure hope we don't find any unpleasant surprises like we encountered at B-2," Dianne said, anxiously.

"What do you mean?" Moose asked. "We dealt with that problem quickly and effectively. Rex and his people, along with the animal life, now have a chance to multiply and prosper."

"I can't deny that," responded Dianne. "I am proud of what we did for them, and they are now friendly interstellar neighbors."

"So what is it that you're worried about?" questioned Moose.

"I'm not worried. I just hope we don't find anything that would delay our landing or prevent it entirely. We've been in space for a long time, and I think it's time for us to have the opportunity to multiply and prosper. We've been married five years, and I'd love to have some children. But we can only do that if it's safe for us to go down there."

Giving his wife a tender look of understanding, Moose said, "I share your feelings, and I have some good news for you. Keep in mind that we haven't yet completed one orbit, but computer analysis of our initial radar data doesn't show any evidence of an advanced intelligent species. In fact, I haven't found any kind of construction, not even the kinds of simple huts that primitive creatures might build."

"That supports the conclusions reached from Star Voyager data," commented Mike. "It indicated that Alcent is a primitive earthlike planet inhabited by dinosaurs, and that means we're not going to discover the aftermath of a horrible war."

"Conclusions based on Star Voyager data might not be correct," stated Dianne. "Let's not forget that Star Voyager whizzed by this planet at 20 percent of light speed, and that didn't give it very much time for exploration. It was just good luck that a few of the high resolution photos found dinosaurs. Also, Star Voyager passed over Alcent's northern hemisphere and returned no data at all for the South Polar Region."

"That's all true," agreed Mike, "but the next few days should give us a pretty good idea about what's down there."

Captain Jerontis nodded and said, "In view of what we discovered on B-2, I would be greatly relieved to find that this is a primitive planet that is safe for us to live on. We've been in space for a long time, and I'm ready for some of the simple pleasures available from living on a planet, like diving into a lake and going for a good swim, or catching some fish and grilling them over a campfire."

"I'm with you on that," stated Dianne. "But what about our long NIEA mission exploration plan?"

"Unfortunately, that plan calls for up to two years of exploration of this planet from orbit and with robot landers before we go down. But then, what else would you expect from a plan that was developed by the best bureaucratic brains in the multiple layers of government bureaucracy? Their plan meticulously satisfies all the stifling regulations that would apply if we were still on Earth. But since we're no longer subject to the absurd rules that they've come up with, we are free to just get the job done, and I think we can shorten this exploration period to as little as six weeks. There are only three objectives that we must accomplish before we land. First, we must determine if the immune systems of Alcent's animals can defeat germs from Earth. Second, we must identify the most common microbes on Alcent and determine whether they pose a lethal threat to us. Third, we must find a relatively safe place to live."

"Our robot labs are equipped to achieve the first two objectives," stated

Dianne. "And I think we have a good chance to accomplish them in six weeks, if we quickly find optimum locations to land them."

"What is an optimum location?" Captain Jerontis asked.

"A choice location is one where a robot lab will encounter the greatest diversity of life forms. Time-wise, I'd like to drop the first lander within 48 hours. Then, I'd like to work with it for a few days before we drop additional landers. Depending on what we find, we may want to make some modifications to the follow-up landers. During our long voyage, I trained three assistants. Working as a team, we should be able to operate our remotely controlled labs continuously, thereby greatly reducing the time required to complete our research."

"I like your plan," responded Captain Jerontis. "During the next 48 hours, we'll select a landing site and drop one of your labs on it."

"I'll start working on site selection immediately," stated Dianne.

Speaking to Captain Jerontis, Moose said, "I have an idea on how we can speed up the process of determining what dangers may be present at our selected landing site."

"What do you have in mind?"

"Once we decide where we want to build our homes, we send in Charlie. We have him roam around during the day and sleep next to a campfire at night. If he survives, we pick him up after two or three days and give him a thorough examination."

Giving Moose a puzzled expression, Captain Jerontis said, "I personally know everyone on this ship, and I can assure you that we don't have a crew member named Charlie."

Moose grinned and said, "Charlie's not a real person. He's a human replica, an artificial man of sorts. He doesn't exist yet, but I've figured out a way to build him. All of his key components would either be off-the-shelf equipment or easily manufactured in our shop. I believe I can have him operational in less than six weeks."

"That seems like a very complicated project to accomplish in just six weeks. How do you plan to do it?"

"When I first got the idea, I thought that it would be a difficult, time-consuming project, but the more I looked into it, the more convinced I became that I could do it in just a few weeks. The first question that came up was: How do I make his legs, so that he will be able to walk around easily? As it turns out, the technology for manufacturing artificial limbs is very advanced. Our medical library contains designs for both arms and legs that are almost as good as real arms and legs. They contain artificial muscles that expand and contract like real muscles and are powered by electrical energy from battery packs."

"How do you plan to control the artificial limbs in a way that allows Charlie to maintain his balance when he's walking around?"

"I'll install an inertial guidance system in his upper body. The design used in our robot landers should be able to do the job. All I have to do is change the software, so that it will control the movement of arms and legs instead of firing control thrusters and moving aerodynamic control surfaces. Charlie's eyes will consist of video cameras. Information from them will be fed into his inertial guidance system's computer to prevent him from walking into trees and stumbling over rocks."

"That sounds feasible," agreed Captain Jerontis. "What's the rest of your plan?"

"Since the purpose of building Charlie is to evaluate the dangers to us, we need to convince potential attackers that he's human. For that reason, I want to cover him with artificial human skin that's been coated with human skin oil and perspiration. Since many predators respond to scent, we want Charlie to smell like a human.

"Also, stinging insects and venom injecting creatures are a potential problem that Charlie can help us evaluate. Some creatures find their prey by being able to see in the infrared portion of the spectrum, especially those that hunt at night. To attract them, we need to maintain Charlie's temperature at about ninety-nine degrees. We can do this by covering his frame with an electric temperature control unit like the ones used in our space suits. We cover this with a one-half inch layer of fairly rigid, but pliable plastic foam to simulate flesh. This will be covered with artificial human skin. If Charlie is bitten by a venom injecting creature or stung by a venom injecting insect, the plastic foam will absorb the venom. Then, we can retrieve the venom from Charlie and analyze it."

"You have this design very well thought out," noted Captain Jerontis. "Apparently, you've been working on this for quite some time, but you've never mentioned it. Why all the secrecy?"

"I've only been working on it for a few days, and I wanted to convince myself that the project is feasible before discussing it."

"I like the concept," stated Captain Jerontis. "Small creatures that are able to inject lethal venom could pose a greater threat to our survival than the large carnivores. We do need to find out if they exist, how numerous they are, and what they look like. Charlie is the perfect way to do that. Besides the batteries in his artificial limbs, I suggest that we also fill his body with batteries to give him additional operating time and range."

Mike added, "If we use Charlie in conjunction with a robot lander, then he can periodically plug himself into the lander's power plant to recharge his batteries. Also, the lander could give us video of Charlie's activities when he's near the lander."

"I think we should put microphones in Charlie's ears and equip him with a transmitter," suggested Captain Jerontis. "Then, we can get sound and video from him to complement what we get from the lander."

"I like that idea," stated Mike, "but I think we should also equip Charlie with a radio receiver and install speakers on his chest and back. Then, he

140

can make the sounds that people normally make."

"Those are all good ideas," stated Moose. "But, there's one more thing that we might do to increase Charlie's effectiveness at discovering predators, and that is to give the predators a scent they can't refuse, and that's the scent of blood. Somewhere in Charlie's body we need to make provisions to carry a small amount of human blood. That will enable us to run an experiment in which we send Charlie on a long walk and have him drip blood on his trail as he walks. To properly conduct this experiment, we need to give Charlie a third eye in the back of his head, so that we'll be able to see anything that follows him. We might also have him smear some blood on one of his forearms to find out if that attracts anything."

Obviously pleased, Captain Jerontis said to Moose, "You've come up with a marvelous concept. Charlie will be invaluable to us in discovering and evaluating some of the threats that we'll face. I want you to use all available personnel to expedite the design and construction of Charlie."

"He'll be ready in four weeks," stated Moose.

TIME: 6 Years, 272 Days ALE.

Captain Jerry Jerontis and his colleagues were in the cafeteria discussing possible locations for their new home. They had considered numerous sites, but all except one were rejected. While looking at the winning selection on a wall-sized video screen, Jerry said, "I like it. The lake is large enough for shuttle operations, and the island near the middle of the lake is big enough for us to live on."

"I like the lake's potential for sports fishing," commented Moose.

Jerry grinned at Moose. "I'm not surprised about that being the first thing on your mind."

"You can't tell me that you're not excited about the possibilities. You and I've had some pretty good fishing trips."

"That's true, but we don't even know if this planet has fish on it."

"I can't argue with that, but if fish do live here, a lake that's fifteen miles across and forty-seven miles long has to have fish in it. It's not only a big lake, but it's also connected to other large bodies of water. The river flowing out of the lake's south end enters a huge river in thirteen miles. Forty miles downstream from there, this huge river flows into the ocean. With slow currents, no rapids, and no waterfalls; both of these rivers are easily navigable, which also gives us access to ocean fishing."

"Get your mind off fishing for a minute and agree with me that those rivers will also give our research submarine easy access to the ocean for research purposes," stated Jerry.

"That's great, but what really excites me about those rivers is the possibility of ocean fish migrating to fresh water spawning areas. All the streams flowing into the lake from the mountains to the east might be very attractive to fish in search of a place to spawn."

141

"You're hopeless," commented Jerry.

Speaking to Jerry, Dianne said, "If I could interrupt my husband's fishing fantasies for a few moments, I'd like to point out that the abundant diversity of life in the region around the lake will greatly simplify my job. There are so many species living there that using our robot labs to study them should allow us to reach valid conclusions about whether life from Earth is compatible with life anywhere on Alcent."

"That's especially true when you consider that many of the species in this area aren't unique to the area," Connie said. "We've seen some of them on the other side of the planet."

"This planet's unique geological configuration makes it easy for animals to go anywhere," stated Mike. "Alcent has only one continent, which encircles it like a giant belt. Neither polar icecap gets any closer than seven hundred miles to ocean beaches, so animals can easily migrate entirely around Alcent over a long period of time."

"That freedom to migrate lends credibility to my supposition that if life from Earth is compatible with Alcent life in this region, it should be compatible with life anywhere on the planet," stated Dianne.

"That sounds reasonable," Connie said, "but I think we should drop robot labs in other areas anyway, just to make sure."

"I agree," Dianne said, "but depending on what we learn in this area, we may be able to put that off for a while, thereby shortening the research time needed before we can land."

"I'm ready to go down now!" stated Moose.

"You're just all fired up about going fishing," commented Dianne.

Moose smiled at his wife. "That's true."

"I'm ready to go down too," admitted Dianne. "Once we've selected the area, we'll get the research done as quickly as we can."

"One of the things I like about this area is the pleasant climate that it appears to have," Michelle said. "Being located at thirty-three degrees north latitude, it's close enough to the equator, so that winters will be mild, but it's still far enough north, so that summers won't be too hot."

"I won't have any trouble adjusting to year-round pleasant weather," commented Connie.

"I think constant warm weather is boring," stated Jerry. "I enjoy a changing climate with definite seasons. There's something special about each season that adds interest to daily living."

Speaking to Jerry, Michelle said, "Since this planet's axis of rotation is tilted 23.7 degrees relative to its orbital plane, we'll have definite seasonal weather variations, but all seasons should be quite pleasant."

"Mild winters are important for shuttle operations," stated Mike. "Since we'll land and take off on hydrofoils, we simply can't live on a lake that freezes over in the wintertime."

"My intuition tells me we could live on that big island in the middle of the lake and never see any ice," Michelle said.

"I'm not sure how your intuition arrived at that conclusion," responded Mike, "but I agree with it. I've plugged data into several climate models for this planet, and I've reached the same conclusion."

Michelle smiled at her husband and did not offer any explanation for her intuitive ability. Instead, she said, "I've taken a good look at that big island in the middle of the lake, and I believe I would enjoy living there."

"Did your intuition tell you that?" Mike asked, in a teasing way.

"No! I don't need intuition for this. That island has several appealing features. It's very picturesque. It has several miles of sandy beach, lots of trees, and a pleasant climate."

"It does look like a great place to live," agreed Mike. "And that island also has some characteristics that make it ideal for shuttle operations. First of all, it's four miles long and most of it is about three-fourths of a mile wide. The length is important for wind protection. When the wind is blowing from the west, the water on the east side of the island will be calm and easy to land on. It will be a four-mile stretch of calm water. When the wind is blowing from the east, the water on the west side of the island will be calm and easy to land on. A second feature that facilitates shuttle operations is the way the island narrows to only about a hundred yards across approximately three-fourths of a mile from its south end. This would provide us with a small sheltered bay on both sides of the island in which to anchor the shuttles after landing. A small island just outside each bay shelters them from strong winds."

"This location seems so ideal for our needs that I believe we should concentrate our exploratory research on it," stated Jerry. "If everything goes well, we could be doing a manned landing in as little as four weeks. After we've built our homes, we can explore the rest of the planet in a more leisurely manner."

Turning to Moose, Jerry asked, "How long before Charlie is ready to go down and roam the island?"

"He should be ready in three weeks."

Turning to Dianne, Jerry asked, "Have you been able to locate an ideal landing site for the first robot lab?"

"Across the water east of the island, there's a meadow that extends several miles inland from the lake shore." While speaking, Dianne placed a 3-D image of the area on the large screen for all to see. Pointing at a hill, she said, "If we could place our robot lab on top of this hill, its video cameras would give us an unobstructed view of the forests to the north and south, the open meadow to the east, and the lake shore to the west. When we see something of interest, we can dispatch remotely piloted vehicles from the lab to collect specimens for analysis."

"That does look like a good place to start our research," agreed Jerry. "I see several species of animals peacefully grazing in that meadow, which means there must not be any predators in the area."

"Perhaps the carnivores have had their fill and are sleeping until they get hungry again," suggested Moose. "With that much prey available, predators can't be too far away."

"That may be," agreed Dianne. "But it's a peaceful scene at the moment. I wonder if landing a robot lab in their midst will spook any of those animals."

"The lab will make its final approach suspended from a wing-type parachute," stated Jerry. "The approach and landing will be silent."

"That silent gliding approach might mimic that of winged predators," argued Dianne.

"That's true," agreed Jerry, "but many of the animals grazing in that meadow are too large to be used as prey by winged predators. They shouldn't be spooked into a stampede by our lander."

"While that's true, we need the small animals to stick around too, or if they are spooked, we need them to return to the area. I think we should paint the lander with a camouflage paint scheme with the colors present in that meadow. Then, it will look natural to the area, like it belongs there. But a large collapsed para-wing lying on the ground next to the lander will look unnatural. We need to get rid of it."

"I have a way to do that," stated Mike. "The lander is programmed to release the parachute after landing. All we need to do is pack a balloon and a bottle of hydrogen in the lander and attach them to the para-wing's suspension lines. When the para-wing is released, the hydrogen bottle will inflate the balloon, which will carry away the para-wing."

"Good," stated Dianne.

"How long will it take you to make that modification to the lander and give it a camouflage paint job?" Jerry asked.

"Less than two days," replied Mike.

"We can live with that," responded Jerry.

Turning to Dianne, Mike asked, "Would you like to help me select the colors and layout of the camouflage paint scheme?"

"Yes, I would. In fact, I could do that part of the job while you make the modification to carry away the parachute."

"Thank you, I appreciate the help."

TIME: 6 Years, 274 Days ALE.

A mood of excitement, tempered by anxiety, pervaded the personnel of the Challenger. A robot laboratory was in the final phase of its descent to its resting spot on Alcent. The lab would provide specific information about Alcent's microorganisms and hopefully prove that it would be safe for humans to live on Alcent.

The euphoric mood on the Challenger was restrained by the possibility that the lab might find that life from Earth was incompatible with life on

Alcent. This would be the case if Alcent's microbes were fundamentally different from Earth's microbes. Some microbes cause diseases and are called germs. Some germs are bacterial, others are viral. With immune systems developed over hundreds of millions of years of evolution, animal life on Alcent was able to cope with Alcent's germs.

If the Challenger's personnel landed on Alcent, germs from Earth would land with them, because it's impossible to totally cleanse microbes from the human system. If the various species of microbes from Earth were basically similar to the various species of microbes on Alcent, then the immune systems of Alcent's animals would be able to effectively deal with them. If microbes from Earth were basically different from microbes on Alcent, then the microbes from Earth could pose a lethal threat to Alcent's animals with entire species potentially being wiped out by disease. Likewise, the immune systems of the Challenger's personnel might not be able to cope with Alcent's microbes, and exposure to them could result in serious disease and even numerous fatalities.

Whether or not the Challenger's personnel would be able to inhabit Alcent would be determined by living organisms too small to be seen without a microscope. The big question would soon be answered by a robot laboratory that had been meticulously sterilized to protect Alcent's animal life from potential danger from Earth's microbes.

"The para-wing has just deployed," stated Mike.

With the Challenger's powerful optical instruments trained on the site, a sharply detailed image of the slowly descending robot lab was displayed on video screens throughout the starship. The para-wing's white upper surface made it easy to see from space. To make it less visible to the grazing animals below, the para-wing's lower surface was dyed a shade of blue that it was hoped would be close to the color of Alcent's sky.

"That sure is a smooth, graceful descent," Michelle said. "I like the way it's slowly circling its hilltop destination."

"There's a reason for the circling descent," stated Mike. "Using data from its flight control instruments, the robot's computer is continuously calculating wind velocity during its circling descent. From this, the computer will calculate the altitude and distance from its destination from which it will need to begin its final approach glide for an on-target landing. To minimize forward velocity on impact, the final approach will be made directly into the gentle wind on the surface. Also, the para-wing will pitch up into a stall just prior to impact. That should kill nearly all forward velocity and give the lab a gentle landing."

"It's amazing how you can take a robot lab that's moving five miles per second in orbit at 210 miles and land it at a specific location on Alcent's surface," Michelle said.

"That hasn't yet been accomplished, but it looks like it soon will be," stated Mike. "Although, I'll have to admit that we did pick a difficult target in that it's very small."

"That hill doesn't look all that small to me," joked Michelle.

"The hill isn't all that small," stated Mike. "But what we're trying to do is land on that rock at the top of the hill."

Mike pointed at the rock displayed on the video screen. "That rock formation rises about 35 feet above the hilltop and has a fairly flat top that measures approximately 35 by 60 feet. I know that it's a small target, but if we're successful, the lab will be protected from being run over by charging dinosaurs attempting to escape a predator."

"That rock is a small target," Michelle said. "Do you really think the robot will be successful at landing precisely on top of it? If the approach is too low, it will crash into the side of the rock and be wrecked."

"Using its radar altimeter and its forward distance measuring radar, the flight control computer will determine if it will be successful at landing on that rock. If it concludes that it will fail, then it will turn away to avoid a collision. The lab is now on its final approach, so we'll soon know where it will land."

A few seconds later, a cheer resounded throughout the Challenger as the robot lab made a perfect landing. At the instant of touchdown, the lab released its para-wing, and the bottle of hydrogen began inflating the attached balloon, which carried away the discarded para-wing.

Feeling a great deal of admiration for him, Michelle turned to her husband. "What a perfect landing. I marvel at the way you always seem to find a way to do things that seem to be almost impossible."

"All I did was ensure that the flight control system was healthy and properly programmed," responded Mike. "We were lucky that the wind didn't play any tricks on us."

Speaking to Mike, Dianne said, "You're being too modest. You did an excellent job delivering my lab to a perfect landing, and now, it's time for me to put my skills to work. But before I start identifying and classifying microorganisms, let's take a look at the area around the lab."

A few moments later, a telescoping pole supporting video cameras and microphones started extending above the robot lab. In just a few seconds, the cameras reached their maximum height of 20 feet above the lab. Using one of the cameras, Dianne surveyed the top of the rock. After determining that it was devoid of life except for lichens, moss, and grass that had established a foothold in cracks and crevices; Dianne turned to Mike and said, "You've delivered my lab to what appears to be a safe, secure area. It'll be nice to be able to conduct our research without being disturbed by the creatures that live down there."

Mike smiled at Dianne and nodded in silent acknowledgment of the sincere appreciation that she had just expressed to him for a job well done.

Dianne raised the camera angle a bit and started a panoramic scan of the area around the rock. But she halted the camera's rotational movement after just a few seconds, because an absolutely breathtaking view filled video screens throughout the Challenger. The camera had spotted a giant sauropod calmly lumbering out of the forest to the north of the lab.

"Look at the size of that creature!" Dianne exclaimed. "He must be at least a hundred feet long!"

"That's a huge animal!" exclaimed Jerry. "He must weigh at least a hundred tons!"

The giant sauropod stopped and swung his head from side to side surveying the open meadow for signs of danger. Then, he repeated the scan of the open meadow more slowly, and this time, he moved his rather large ears around as if to cup them in an attempt to hear indications of danger. After doing this, he pointed his head in the direction of the lake, flared his nostrils, and took a deep breath of the gentle breeze blowing towards him. Apparently satisfied that there wasn't any danger present, the giant sauropod bent his long neck completely around, so that his head was facing the forest; then, he let out a soft call that sounded like: "hoot, hoot, hoot." After this, he turned toward the lake and resumed walking.

Immediately following the hooting sound, an infant sauropod emerged from the forest with its mother walking behind him. Behind them, two more infants emerged from the forest staying close to their mothers. Bringing up the rear of this column was a large male, although not as large as the leader.

The people of the Challenger were totally fascinated by what they were watching. Mesmerized into a state of silence, they watched the herd of sauropods calmly make its way to the lake where they drank large quantities of water. All were drinking except the male at the rear of the herd. He stood guard, alertly watching for danger. After the dominant male had quenched his thirst, he took up a position of guard duty while the subordinate male drank.

The only sounds heard on the Challenger were sounds from Alcent. The camera's directional microphone enabled the Challenger's personnel to listen to the herd of sauropods. These sounds were heard against a background of other sounds from the surface picked up by the lab's other microphones. The scene and its sounds had a profound effect on the Challenger's personnel as they considered the reality of living with creatures so large and powerful that they could effortlessly knock down even a stoutly built house.

Finally, Moose turned to Jerry and said, "Even though we knew that creatures of such enormous size might exist on this planet, I must admit that this foreknowledge did little to prepare me for the reality of actually seeing them. I hope that I'm never standing between them and wherever it is they want to go."

"Just from the few minutes that we've observed their behavior, three things are obvious," stated Mike. "First, the fact that one of them is always on guard indicates that carnivores live in this area. Second, these carnivores must be truly awesome if creatures as large as these respect them to the point that one of them is always on guard. Third, these sauropods' behavior indicates that they are quite intelligent, disciplined, and able to communicate effectively."

"Not only are these creatures huge, but they're also very well equipped to defend themselves," Jerry said. "They have three horns growing out of their heads: one on each side and one on top. These must be deadly effective weapons when you consider how long and strong their necks are. In addition, they have three horns near the ends of their long, strong tails, which also must be deadly effective weapons. What kind of carnivores could these creatures possibly fear? I doubt that even the ferocious Tyrannosaurus Rex from Earth's Cretaceous period could overcome this group's leader."

"If this planet does have predators that are similar to the T-Rex, that would explain why these animals are constantly on guard," stated Moose. "Even though they're huge, if a charging T-Rex caught one of them off guard and managed to clamp its huge teeth-filled jaws onto the sauropod's neck, it seems that death would be inevitable. But if they're constantly on full alert, the T-Rex never has an easy opportunity."

"There are some other things to consider," stated Dianne. "First, they have three infants to protect, and parental instinct could be causing them to be extra wary. Second, the degree of caution they're exhibiting could be the result of intelligence, perhaps even thinking."

"Are you suggesting that these animals might be capable of analytical thought?" questioned Connie.

"To answer the question, Dianne narrowed the field of view to just the herd leader and showed him on half of the video screen. On the other half of the screen, she showed an image of a sauropod from Earth's dinosaur age. Then she said, "When you compare these images, it's obvious that this herd leader's head is proportionally much larger than the head on the sauropod from Earth. This raises the possibility of a much larger brain, which increases the probability of intelligence."

"How intelligent do you think they are?" Connie asked.

"I don't know. I'm only suggesting that head size relative to body size indicates that there is potential for a considerable amount of intelligence. Simply knowing the difference between eight objects and six objects would put these creatures a step above animal life on Earth. I certainly would not expect them to have any kind of technical knowledge, but an understanding of simple numbers is possible."

"They might even be smarter than that," speculated Connie. "We must keep in mind that the Alpha Centauri System is 500 million years older than the Solar System. With all that additional time for evolution to proceed, some of the animals on this planet could be quite intelligent."

"That herd leader might even have a good enough memory to remember the various ways that different predators like to attack," stated Jerry. "In

148

addition, he may even be able to think about those attack methods and devise defensive strategies to defeat them."

"If he's capable of all of that, then he's much more intelligent than any animal on Earth," commented Dianne.

Jerry said, "Given the enormous size and potential intelligence of these creatures, I think we should ..."

Jerry's comment was interrupted by an extremely loud bloodcurdling roar that blasted from every speaker on the Challenger because they were all tuned in to the broadcast from the robot laboratory. The terrifying scream reverberated throughout the Challenger with such intensity that it caused nearly everyone's heart to skip a beat.

After recovering from the horrifying roar, Dianne aimed the second camera on top of the long telescoping pole at the source of the scream, which came from a creature that had just emerged from the forest south of the lab. The scene picked up by this camera was displayed on a video screen next to the one displaying the sauropods.

"In case anyone had any doubts about predators being here, they don't have to speculate any longer," stated Jerry. "They are monsters, and they look like extremely capable killing machines."

"They certainly do," agreed Moose. "And they look very similar to the Tyrannosaurus-Rex."

"What is disturbing about this is that there are three of them," stated Mike. "If they hunt in packs, the danger posed by them is greatly increased. If one of us were alone and encountered a pack of these killers, death could be the end result, even with the kinds of guns we have."

"I don't think this group is hunting," Moose said. "All the creatures that had been peacefully grazing next to that forest are madly fleeing the scene. If these T-Rexes were hunting, I think they would've used stealth to sneak up on a victim. That bloodcurdling scream may've been an arrogant challenge, as if to exclaim: We are here! We are coming through! And you can either flee and stay alive or remain and be killed!"

"Arrogance is an attitude found primarily in the human species, especially among politicians and government bureaucrats," stated Connie. "Are you suggesting that this high-and-mighty, better-than-thou attitude might also exist among animals?"

Pointing at the video screen showing the T-Rexes fearlessly stomping through the open meadow, Moose declared, "There is my proof."

"Take a look at what the sauropods are doing," directed Jerry. "This is very interesting."

Not intimidated by the challenge from the T-Rexes, the herd leader was confidently walking toward them as if to give himself some fighting space. Then, while swinging his head from side to side, he bellowed out some sounds that sounded very crisp, almost like a drill sergeant issuing orders. The largest female stepped forward, taking up a position on his right. The other male took up a position to her right. The remaining two females kept the three infants between them and stood guard over them.

Looking at the other screen, Jerry noted that the three T-Rexes had halted their march and had turned to face the sauropods. The largest T-Rex was at least fifty feet long and was apparently the leader. The other two were slightly smaller and looked like immature adults, or perhaps, they were females following a large male.

Without removing his eyes from the screen, Jerry said, "I believe some of our questions have been answered. I have no doubt whatever, that these sauropods are able to think and devise defensive strategies. Furthermore, they are able to communicate, and the subordinates in the herd have the discipline to follow orders."

"I wonder how intelligent the T-Rexes are," questioned Moose. "Are they smart enough to know that the sauropods are ready for them? If they know this, will they attack anyway? Did they even come here to attack? Is it possible that they're intelligent enough to be here for no other reason except to scout the defenses of this herd of sauropods?"

"That would be a scary situation, if they're that smart," replied Jerry.

What happened next came as a complete surprise to the people on the Challenger. The 100-ton sauropod herd leader reared up on his hind legs and let out a deafening, deep-throated roar that froze the inhabitants of the Challenger with a spine-chilling effect. When the huge sauropod's front feet slammed back onto the ground, he lowered his head and charged with the seven-foot horn on top of his head now horizontal and pointed directly at the T-Rex leader. Quickly reaching a speed of 30 mph, the stout horn backed by 100 tons of bone and muscle became an extremely deadly weapon. The female and the male to her right participated in the charge.

Quickly realizing that they were in a deadly no-win situation, the T-Rexes turned and fled. The sauropods gave chase for about a quarter of a mile; then, they gradually lumbered to a halt. After stopping, the herd leader again reared up on his hind legs and issued an extremely loud deep-throated roar; as if to say, don't come back. The sauropods watched the fleeing T-Rexes for a few moments; then, they returned to the lake.

An eerie sound of silence permeated the Challenger as all were deeply lost in thought about the awesome scene they had just witnessed. To observe a scene in which such massive animal power and ferocity were in play only a few minutes after their first robot lab had settled down on the surface of Alcent provided a sobering display of what they would face in their efforts to survive and prosper on this planet.

Eventually, the silence was broken by Moose. "I can't believe that we're seriously planning to go down there and live among those brutes! We must be crazy!"

Doing his best to present Moose with a genuine expression of bewilderment, Jerry said, "I'm surprised that you would say something like that.

150

You must be just kidding."

"How could I possibly be just kidding? It's going to be extremely dangerous down there."

Faking the most sincere tone he could come up with, Jerry said, "Ever since we left Earth, you've been constantly reminding me about how I coerced you into canceling your exciting, adventurous vacation trip to an exotic, warm, sandy beach in the South Pacific. Right down there on the shore of that lake is a warm sandy beach, and it's definitely exotic. I'm willing to bet that time spent on it would be a very exciting adventure. I'm surprised by your reluctance to take advantage of the opportunity."

Having overheard the conversation, Dianne was enjoying the brief diversion from the confrontation they had just observed and now had to evaluate. Also, she wondered how her husband would respond to these playfully provocative comments from his best friend.

Having good peripheral vision, Moose noticed without looking in her direction that his wife was listening to the conversation. Choosing his words carefully, he said, "Captain J.J., old buddy, you're joshing me again. You're comparing apples to oranges. Obviously these two kinds of beach adventures are very different. Besides that, I'm now a happily married man looking forward to becoming a father in the near future, so I need to be more cautious about the kinds of adventure I get involved in."

"Are you sure you're not just getting soft with age?" Jerry asked.

"Those monsters we just observed are capable of causing anyone to lose his courage," responded Moose. "We have to respect their capabilities and use extreme caution when dealing with them."

Happy that her husband said all the right things, Dianne contentedly went back to work. She had a lab on the surface to play with.

Michelle reflected on the awesome display of brute power that she had just witnessed. The thought of living among these creatures caused her entire body to briefly shiver. She looked into her husband's eyes. "I remember a peaceful evening on the observation deck when you showed me the wondrous beauty of the universe and convinced me that we should leave the comfort and security of Earth to live on this planet."

"Are you having second thoughts?" Mike asked.

"The scene we just witnessed was rather frightening. On Earth, I never gave much thought to animal life while going about my daily activities. On this planet, I doubt that there'll ever be a routine day. All activities will have to be carefully planned to account for the possibility of encountering dangerous animals."

"That's definitely true. Everyday life on Alcent will be a constant challenge, but I welcome that challenge, and I'm glad we're here."

"So am I," responded Michelle. "Every day will be an exciting adventure filled with new discoveries."

"It's quite possible that we've just seen the largest herbivore and the largest carnivore that this planet has," commented Mike.

"They're so big that it's difficult to imagine finding animals that are even bigger. Even though, we had reason to believe that dinosaurs as large as these would be here, I wasn't prepared for what we just watched."

"That incredible display of brute power and ferocity would have been awe-inspiring no matter how well prepared we were. I wonder what Matthew thinks about those dinosaurs."

"He and Denise are with their tutor of the day," stated Michelle. "But her lesson plan was undoubtedly interrupted by the dinosaur scenes. I think I'll check on them and find out how they're doing. Also, I'll share what we just saw with Rex and Shannon. I will transmit the video with full sound effects. I'm sure they'll be fascinated by it."

As Michelle left the flight deck, Jerry said to those remaining, "I'm impressed with the intelligence shown by those sauropods. When faced with a threat from the T-Rexes, they reacted like a well-disciplined army. They demonstrated tactics, communication, discipline, and confidence. Also, they may have an understanding of simple numbers, as was shown by the fact that three sauropods charged three T-Rexes. If they are the biggest and most intelligent creatures on this planet, then, they might be the dominant species. And that means we should study them thoroughly."

"We can start by getting a blood specimen, a fecal sample, and a urine specimen and running them through the robot lab for analysis," Dianne said. "Our RPVs are so small relative to the sauropods that I doubt they'll even pay any attention to them." While she was speaking, Dianne launched an RPV from the robot lab and flew it toward the sauropods.

The robot lab was equipped with six small RPVs (Remotely Piloted Vehicles) that were designed for collecting samples and bringing them back to the lab for analysis. Each RPV was designed for a specific mission. The one launched by Dianne looked like a flying saucer. It was quite small, having a diameter of only 18 inches and a maximum thickness of only five inches. Its counter-rotating propellers were mounted in a 12-inch diameter opening through the middle of the RPV. The propellers were driven by electric motors powered by rechargeable batteries. The RPV was capable of taking off and landing vertically, hovering, and flying in any direction. Silent operation was one of the key features of the RPVs. The electric motors made a barely audible hum, and the propellers were specially shaped for quiet efficient operation.

The RPV launched by Dianne had a camouflage paint scheme made up of dull browns and greens. It mimicked a large, wind-blown leaf as it quietly soared around.

Using images returned by the little RPV's video cameras, Dianne guided it to a landing on the herd leader's back. With small pincers, the RPV anchored itself to the thin bristle-like hair on the giant sauropod's back. Dianne deployed a small arm equipped with a microphone at its end. She placed the microphone in contact with the sauropod's skin and slowly moved it around while listening for the sound of flowing blood. After a bit of exploration, she found a blood vein that was appropriate for her needs. Then, she deployed a second arm and used it to apply some antiseptic to the area and to insert a tiny needle into the vein. After withdrawing a small quantity of blood, she flew it back to the robot lab for analysis.

While Dianne monitored the robot lab's examination of the blood sample, Moose flew a second RPV to the area and patiently waited for the herd leader to relieve himself. Then, he collected a urine specimen and a fecal sample and returned them to the lab for analysis.

Speaking to Mike, Jerry said, "I think it would be interesting to follow these sauropods around for a few days to observe their day-to-day behavior and see their territory."

"After what we've seen today, I'm not about to volunteer for the job," responded Mike, rather quickly.

Jerry laughed. "I wasn't implying that you should. What I have in mind is using a modified RPV to attach a small instrument package to the herd leader. Three video cameras, two microphones, and a transmitter should be sufficient to gain some interesting information."

"Where do you want to attach the instrument package?"

"I think the ideal location would be near the base of that big horn on top of his head. Then, as he moves his head around to investigate things of importance to him, we'll be able to see and hear what he sees and hears. In effect, we'll learn about his world from his perspective."

"I like your idea. The video and sound should be fascinating."

"I think so. Over a period of time, the herd leader will show us his territory. Perhaps these creatures are migratory and wander over great distances. If so, we'll see lots of real estate and many of the plants and animals that live on it. We'll find out if predators are a serious problem for the sauropods, and we'll learn how the members of the herd intermingle on a day-to-day basis. By observing how the herd reacts to the different sounds that the leader makes, we'll begin to understand their communication and learn how extensive a vocabulary they have. That should help us determine how intelligent they are."

"So, in effect, what we're going to do is recruit the biggest creature we've ever seen to show us his world and teach us his language."

"That's exactly right. How long will it take you to put it together?"

"It shouldn't take more than a few days. Attaching the instrument package to that horn is going to be a bit tricky, but he has to sleep sometime, and that will be the best time to do it. Also, I think we should send this package down by special delivery, rather than wait for the next robot lab to take it down. This offers a quick way to gain some special information about the planet we plan to live on."

"I like the special delivery idea. Let's send it down as soon as you have it ready to go."

Mike turned to leave. "I'll get started right away."

TIME: 6 Years, 278 Days ALE.

Mike designed, constructed, and delivered to the surface an instrument package that he planned to attach to the base of the top horn on the sauropod herd leader's head. To accomplish this, he joined two RPVs with the instrument package secured between them.

Speaking to Jerry, Mike said, "For the last four days, that herd has shown up in the early evening to drink at the lake. After that, they lie down in an open area and sleep for the night, with one of the adults always awake and on guard. The other adults always surround the infants."

"Even while sleeping, all that bone and muscle makes a formidable protective enclosure for the infants," stated Jerry. "I continue to be impressed by the intelligence and discipline the adults demonstrate while protecting themselves and their young."

"But, is their behavior instinctive or the result of reasoning?"

"That instrument package you put together will enable us to monitor their activities, and that will help us determine how intelligent they are."

"I hope they return to the lake again this evening, so we can install our instruments."

"I don't expect them to leave the area as long as there's plenty of food and water for them. I wonder if they always drink from that same location because there's good solid footing there."

"Their feet are so large that they seem to be able to get around on any kind of ground, even though they are very heavy. I think they drink from that same area every night and morning because the large open meadow is a good place to sleep. Since there is no cover for predators, they only need to post one sentry."

"Your explanation for their behavior is too logical for it to be purely instinctive. I think it's the result of intelligent planning."

"It looks that way," agreed Mike. "On another subject, do I need to launch any additional satellites?"

"The three that we've deployed should be adequate to handle our needs for the time being."

The three satellites referred to by Jerry had been placed in geosynchronous orbit, and as a result, each would remain indefinitely over a point on Alcent's Equator. The three satellites were equally spaced around Alcent, with one of them placed over the equator directly south of the robot lab's landing site.

The satellites had two primary functions: communications and weather observation. The satellite in orbit above the robot lab was used to receive the lab's transmissions and relay them to the Challenger, either directly or through one of the other satellites. The three satellites allowed the

Challenger to be in continuous communication with ground experiments regardless of its orbital location.

The weather observation instruments on the satellites provided detailed global data about Alcent's weather systems. This information would be a consideration in the selection of a site at which to live and would help in understanding the planet's ecosystem.

TIME: 6 Years, 278 Days, 9 hours ALE.

It was nighttime over the meadow where the robot lab was located. The sky was relatively free of clouds, and the meadow was illuminated by light from two moons. The sauropods were sleeping under the watchful eyes of one of the females, currently the lone sentry.

Michelle joined her husband on the flight deck, because she wanted to watch his attempt to attach the instrument package to the sauropod herd leader. Mike was explaining to her that the task would be easy.

Pointing to an image on the computer screen, Mike said, "As you can see, I've joined two RPVs, and the instrument package is mounted on the platform that connects them. The wide-open C-clamp at the front of the instrument package will grasp the sauropod's top horn. There is a trigger at the base of the clamp. When that trigger crashes into the animal's horn, the clamp will snap shut. Then, the RPVs will detach from the instrument package and fly back to the lab."

"You are going to attach an instrument package to a 100-ton dinosaur, and you make it sound like a simple task," Michelle said.

"All I have to do is fly the RPVs to the vicinity of the animal's head, and then crash the base of the wide-open clamp into the horn a few inches above his head. Keep in mind that Dianne has already collected three blood samples from this creature, and she's also used ultrasound to take a look at the creature's internal anatomy. Installing this instrument package will be no more difficult than those tasks. Even though these RPVs are larger than the ones Dianne uses, they're still very quiet in flight and should not disturb the animal."

"It's the advanced technology that's been incorporated into our RPVs that makes these seemingly impossible tasks appear so easy," concluded Michelle. "They truly are amazing little machines."

Speaking to Michelle, Jerry said, "It's time for your husband to put his piloting skills to work before something disturbs that herd leader and wakes him up."

Since Mike already had everything checked out, he launched the connected RPVs and guided them to the giant sauropod. The linked RPVs quietly approached the sauropod head-on. After hovering for a few moments to verify the final approach parameters, the RPVs slowly soared forward and gently crashed into the horn as planned. The clamp snapped shut, and the RPVs detached and began their return flight. The procedure was so quiet and gentle that the giant sauropod never even stirred.

Mike turned away from the controls and smiled at his wife. "It was a simple task, and we now have a 100-ton tour guide, one of the many benefits available to those contemplating a move to Alcent."

"This is amazing!" Michelle exclaimed. "Think about it! As these gigantic creatures go about their normal everyday activities, we are most certainly going to get some priceless imagery and sound effects. I will select some of the more dramatic scenes and include them in my daily transmissions to Earth. I'm sure they'll find them fascinating."

"After they see that spectacular video of the incident between the sauropods and the T-Rexes, I'm sure they'll be prepared for anything," stated Mike. "In that video, the sound effects alone are spine-chilling."

"More than four years will go by before they get to see that. Even though I traveled and actually experienced the vast distance between here and Earth, it still boggles my mind to realize that my transmissions traveling at the speed of light require 4.35 years to reach Earth. By the time they see the sensational scene that we saw a few days ago, we'll have forgotten about it; yet for them, it will be the news event of the day."

"Our long journey has given all of us a new concept of space and time," Mike said. "And now that we're here and have seen some of the huge animals that we're planning to live among, the whole setting is almost surreal. It's almost as if we're characters in a science fiction movie rather than real people with real lives."

"So that's how you make all these difficult tasks look so easy. None of this is real; we're all just part of a movie."

"I sometimes feel that way," Mike admitted.

TIME: 6 Years, 291 Days A.L.E.

Michelle's latest mission update to Earth:

"It has been 17 days since we landed our first robot lab on Alcent. To determine as quickly as possible whether the human immune system is capable of defending against attack by Alcent's microorganisms, Dianne and her assistants have maintained an intense pace of research with the lab. Also, they are attempting to answer an equally important question: Will the immune systems of Alcent's animal life be able to defend against microbes from Earth?

"We cannot land until these questions are answered. We've come too far to risk being wiped out by alien diseases. Likewise, we cannot risk killing Alcent's life with diseases from Earth. While the risk from diseases cannot be eliminated, we do need to understand how serious the threat is.

"Using the robot lab's sophisticated equipment to analyze specimens delivered by our RPVs; we are identifying and cataloging Alcent's microbes. In the search for microorganisms, the RPVs have collected water samples from the lake, from streams, and from stagnant pools. Rainwater

156

has also been analyzed. A broad variety of soil samples have been investigated. The RPVs have also managed to locate and return fragments of decaying flesh missed by predators and scavengers. Numerous air samples have been investigated in the search for microbes. Samples of both living and decaying plant life have been investigated.

"As each new microorganism is discovered, its identifying features are fed into the Challenger's computer, which then searches its memory to determine if a similar microbe exists on Earth. Then, using a model of the human immune system, the computer determines the microbe's potential danger to humans.

"The other part of the project is to learn as much as possible about the immune systems of Alcent's animal life. To that end, the RPVs have collected blood, urine, and fecal specimens from twenty-three species of animal life. Locating antibodies in a creature's blood gives some insight into the capabilities of the creature's immune system, because specific antibodies are produced by a healthy immune system to attack and kill specific invading microbes. By isolating an antibody and doing a detailed description of it, the researcher can draw some conclusions about what the targeted invading microbe looks like. Also, the degree of sophistication of the antibody indicates how capable the immune system is. Immune systems that are able to design and produce complicated antibodies are capable of defending against a broad variety of germs.

"Preliminary conclusions from the research done to date indicate that microbes from Earth will not be a serious threat to Alcent's animal life and that Alcent's microbes will not be an insurmountable challenge to our immune systems. Needless to say, we are encouraged by these results.

"Dianne has decided that it's time to send down a second robot lab. This one will land on the large island in the middle of the lake."

TIME: 6 Years, 291 Days, 3 Hours ALE.

The second robot lab was in its final approach glide. Having continuously monitored flight parameters, Mike said, "Everything looks good for a perfect landing."

"This is exciting!" exclaimed Michelle. "We're about to take a close look at the island we hope to live on."

"That's true only if we achieve a safe landing. Even though everything looks good, we're still at the mercy of the wind. If the para-wing gets hit by a sudden change in wind speed or direction, the robot lab's landing could be fouled up, and it could be seriously damaged."

"You always express a note of caution, yet you always seem to accomplish the things you set out to do."

"Thanks for the compliment, but I'm not a miracle worker. I just try to anticipate all contingencies and plan for them as best I can."

A minute later, an enthusiastic cheer echoed throughout the Challenger as the robot lab made an excellent landing. Michelle beamed an admiring smile at her husband. "Nice work!"

The robot lab now rested on a plateau located near the south end of the island. The plateau was 300 yards wide by 700 yards long. It was located at the top of a nearly vertical rock formation that rose 150 feet above the surrounding land. Only the north face of the rock formation deviated from the vertical. It was a rockslide with a 45-degree slope.

Mike activated one of the lab's surveillance cameras. While he panned the area, everyone viewed the scenes from the plateau with utmost interest. These scenes were of the precise area where the people of the Challenger expected to build their homes. Even though all had already seen the detailed images provided by the Challenger's powerful optical instruments, the images originating from on-site equipment were of keen interest, because for the first time, the people of the Challenger were seeing the area as they would see it when they were living on it. After all, the robot lab had landed on a spot that could conceivably be in the middle of someone's front yard in the near future.

After Mike scanned the area around the lab, he raised the camera to view the distant lakeshore. Then, he did a 360-degree sweep to survey the island's picturesque surroundings. The spectacular scenic beauty and vast openness of the area fanned the flames of desire in the Challenger's inhabitants to leave the starship and live in traditional homes.

"What a dream location!" Michelle exclaimed.

"What do you like about it the most?" Mike asked.

"Everything!"

"It seems to me that a professional reporter could be more specific."

"I do like everything about it," declared Michelle with enthusiasm. "But if you want me to be specific, let's start with the view. To the east, there are eight miles of open water against a backdrop of meadows, forests, and snow-capped mountains. To the west, there are seven miles of open water against a backdrop of meadows, forests, and low-level mountains. North of the plateau, there is the rest of the island, which extends for three miles and is covered with dense forest. South of the island, there are twenty miles of water against a backdrop of meadows and forest land, which is so far away that it just blends into the skyline."

"It's definitely picturesque," agreed Mike. "But what I like about this island is that its shoreline provides twelve to fifteen miles of waterfront property. Plus, the four small islands lying just offshore from the main island are large enough to live on. In short, each family will have a choice location on which to build a home and more than one hundred acres of land to go with the home. That's what I call spacious living."

"That will be a refreshing change from the city living I knew back on Earth," stated Michelle. "I sure hope that we don't discover anything that prevents us from living here."

"Everyone is probably anxious about that possibility," commented

Mike. "But we must think positively and hold the expectation that this island will become our home."

"Of all the locations we've looked at, none is more ideal than this one," stated Jerry. "This island is large enough to give us plenty of living space, but too small and too isolated to provide enough prey to support large carnivores. Therefore, there shouldn't be any on the island."

"On Earth, some carnivores are good swimmers," commented Mike.

"We could live on the plateau," responded Jerry. "Then, any large carnivore that manages to swim to the island will be faced with the difficulty of climbing to the plateau. On three sides, there's a 150-foot rock cliff. On the north side, there is a steep rockslide. Some large carnivores might be able to climb that rockslide, but it should be easy to set up a warning system. It seems like we should be quite secure in homes on that plateau. It should be a place where we can relax and enjoy life."

"I agree," Mike said. "The plateau is the safest place to build our homes, but I hope that we'll discover that we can live anywhere on the island in comfort and safety."

"I believe that will prove to be the case, but I think we should live on the plateau until we find out if large carnivores ever visit the island."

"That sounds like a prudent approach," agreed Mike.

"I have an image in my mind of a spacious log cabin," stated Connie. "With all those tall trees growing on the island, it should be easy to build a comfortable cabin. The inside could be furnished with the best that our technology has to offer, but the outside would always remind me of those rugged, self-sufficient, early American pioneers."

Jerry gazed into his wife's eyes for a few moments and noted how sincere she was. Then, he said, "So you really have your heart set on living in a log cabin."

"Well, it does fit right in with what we are. In every sense of the word, we are pioneers. We'll be living in a heavily forested area, and we must be rugged and self-sufficient."

"A sturdily constructed log home would be symbolic of all that and would look like a natural part of the setting. It's also practical in terms of available construction materials. I like the idea. Let's plan on it."

Bubbling over with excitement at the prospect of soon having a real home to live in, Connie asked, "When can we go down and get started?"

"During the next two weeks, we're going to investigate the island. If we don't find anything that would prevent us from living there, we'll send Charlie down for a final look. If he wanders the island for a couple weeks without anything of consequence happening to him, then we'll carry out our first manned landing."

"I wish we could speed up that process," Connie said. "We've been in space for a long time, and I'm ready for something as simple as watching the clouds drift across the sky."

After a few moments of silent daydreaming by everyone on the flight deck, Connie said, "I think the crew for the first manned landing should definitely include a doctor in case a medical problem arises."

"I think the chief engineer should be part of the crew in the event there is an unforeseen equipment problem," Mike quickly asserted.

"I think an expert biologist should be present to do an on-site evaluation of the threat posed by the life forms that inhabit the area," stated Dianne with conviction.

"Since this will be an epic event in human history, it seems to me that there should be a reporter present to cover the news aspects of the occasion," stated Michelle.

Jerry looked at Moose and said, "I believe everyone on this ship is going to express an important reason to justify inclusion in the crew for the first landing. What's your excuse?"

"Well, I'm sure that everyone already realizes that my broad variety of skills and talents would come in handy to cope with whatever problems happen to arise," stated Moose with complete sincerity. "But the main reason I'd like to be part of the first landing is just simply for the pure excitement of it. This will be the first time that mankind will set foot on an alien planet filled with life. What an adventure. No matter how much research we do with the robot labs, there will still be an element of risk."

"Despite his lack of humility, he is being truthful," Dianne said.

"I wasn't trying to be boastful," retorted Moose. "I was merely pointing out that I'd be a valuable addition to the landing party."

"I already knew that," responded Dianne. "It was just your way of saying it that caught my attention."

"I haven't yet decided how many people are going down on the first landing, let alone who," stated Jerry. "Until we complete our research with the onsite robot lab, we won't be able to define all of our objectives for the first landing. Also, what happens to Charlie while he's wandering around on the island will help determine our personnel roster. I'm just as excited about going down there as all of you are, but we must be patient."

Pointing at the video screens, Jerry said, "Even though the island scenes look very peaceful, we must keep in mind that they are only of the plateau. The rest of the island could prove to be a very dangerous place. I suggest that we get stated exploring it."

Responding to Captain J.J.'s directive, Moose and Dianne each launched a small RPV. Both RPVs were equipped with video cameras and microphones. Moose planned to explore the island's east coast and south end while Dianne explored the island's west coast and north end. After this, they would begin exploring the island's interior.

Mike launched the lab's largest RPV. Its payload was a neatly packaged marine explorer consisting of a deflated pontoon equipped with underwater exploration instrumentation. He skillfully piloted the RPV out over the lake to a point about 100 yards off shore. There, he brought the RPV to a halt and had it hover motionlessly over the water. Using the RPV's winch, Mike lowered the deflated pontoon about ten feet below the RPV and about three feet above the water. Then, he inflated the pontoon and lowered it onto the water.

The marine explorer's battery pack, electric motor, and instrument package were attached to the bottom side of the pontoon. With the bulk of its weight attached to its underside, the pontoon was very stable and could not easily be tipped over. Except for two small video cameras and a transmitting antenna, the topside of the pontoon was covered with solar cells to recharge the batteries.

The marine explorer would be used to accomplish the critical objective of ensuring the safety of shuttle landings and takeoffs. Mike planned to search the underwater world around the island for hazards to shuttle operations. In addition, the marine explorer's underwater cameras and sonar would be used to search for fish and other marine life.

TIME: 6 Years, 298 Days ALE.

One week after landing a robot lab on the island's plateau, Captain Jerry Jerontis and his colleagues were discussing recent discoveries. "I've made RPV flights all over the island," stated Moose. "And I've been unable to find any large creatures. Apparently, this island is inhabited primarily by small mammals, reptiles, birds, and insects."

"Are any of them a threat to us?" questioned Jerry.

"None of them are large enough to be a physical threat; however, some of the reptiles could have a poisonous bite. Also, some of the insects appear to have stingers. We can evaluate the danger from these creatures when we send Charlie down."

"How long before Charlie will be ready to go?"

"We could send him down now, but there are some additional capabilities I'd like to give him that will expand his usefulness. Specifically, I'm attempting to give him the ability to run at speeds up to 20 mph. Also, I'm installing an infrared camera and radar to enhance his nighttime recon capability. I need three more days to finish Charlie."

"Those capabilities are worth the delay," agreed Jerry. "Have you learned anything new about those flying dinosaurs you discovered two days ago?"

"In some respects, they are the most remarkable creatures I've ever seen. I'm going to show you a video that I finished making an hour ago."

Moose opened his video file in the computer, and a movie showing the dinosaurs in flight appeared on a wall-sized video screen accompanied by full sound effects. Moose narrated, "I made this video by flying one of the RPVs with the creatures. In some ways, they resemble the pterodactyls that flew in Earth's atmosphere back in the dinosaur age. But there is one big difference, these creatures have feathers. Also, their feet are interesting. They're webbed like duck feet, but they have talons like an eagle. I think the most impressive thing about these creatures is their size. Two of them have 45-foot wing spans. The other two have 20-foot wing spans. I think we're looking at two adults and their offspring.

"It appears that the adults are teaching the youngsters how to feed themselves. One of the adults went into a high-speed dive, and I followed him down with the RPV. When he reached the lake's surface, he sank his talons into a large fish that was swimming too close to the surface. Then, he made a quick pull up from the dive.

"What happens next is most interesting. First, he transfers the fish from his talons to his teeth-lined jaws. Then, he taunts the juveniles with it by going from one to the other and acting like he's going to feed them, but then pulling away. Now that he has their attention, he closes his jaws tightly, biting a piece out of the middle of the fish. While he eats this, the tail end and the head end of the fish start falling towards the water. Apparently, the juveniles haven't yet mastered all their flying skills, because they're quite clumsily making their way down to the water in pursuit of the pieces of fish. Evidently, the adult has intentionally given the juveniles an incentive to learn diving techniques, which is what they'll need to eventually be able feed themselves."

"That's an amazing video you put together," commented Jerry. "I'm impressed with your skill in flying that RPV. You stayed with those pterodactyls through some rather fancy maneuvers."

"Thanks for the compliment, but our RPVs are highly maneuverable and easy to fly."

"Why didn't you include these pterodactyls among the creatures that you said inhabit the island?"

"I don't think they live there. I saw them fly in from the south. After that feeding scene we just watched, I saw them fly off to the north. It's possible they were just passing through on a migration flight."

"Whether they live on the island or were just passing through, they do pose a threat, and this island might not be the ideal place to live that we hoped it would be."

"They're definitely a threat. With talons and teeth like they possess, they could easily kill an adult human. I don't know what their maximum lifting capability is, but I believe the adults could carry away one of us. Our children would definitely be easy prey for them."

"We might be able to effectively deal with them by setting up a radar station to warn us when they're around," stated Jerry. "If they turn out to be the only detriment to living on this island, I'll have to vote in favor of living there. This island just has too many advantages to pass up."

"I agree with that. Plus, I've just discovered another advantage, lots of fish. That school of fish the pterodactyls feasted on is very large. Take a look at this video, and you'll see what I mean."

Moose replayed selected parts of the video they had just seen, and Jerry said, "There must be thousands of fish in that school. I wonder if they're ocean fish migrating to mountain streams to spawn."

"That's a possibility," responded Moose. "They sure are big. They look like their weight ranges from sixty to ninety pounds. I haven't been fishing for a long time, and the sight of all those fish is giving me the fishing fever. I hope they're still around when we arrive."

"Even if they aren't, a lake that large must have other fish in it. Something else revealed by your video is the exceptional clarity of the water in that lake. I don't know how far below the surface those fish are, but we aren't having any trouble seeing them."

"The clearness of the water caught my attention too," stated Mike. "While exploring the water around the island, I put together some spectacular video of underwater scenery and marine life. Thanks to the remarkable clarity of the water, I've discovered several species of fish."

Looking at Moose, Mike said, "I can assure you that you'll have lots of exciting sports fishing. If half the species of fish I've seen are edible, it'll be a long time before we'll be hurting for something to eat."

Turning to Jerry, Mike said, "In regard to shuttle operations, there's no reason why we can't land and take off on either side of the island. The water is deep, and there are no obstacles."

"That's great, but there's another possibility that we should consider, and that's the possible existence of large marine animals. If they exist and if they swim from place to place in groups, they could present an unpredictable hazard to shuttle operations."

"I will expand my underwater exploration to greater distances from the island in a search for large marine creatures," responded Mike.

"Also, because of the remarkable water clarity, we might be able to spot them with RPVs," added Moose, "assuming they exist and sometimes swim near the surface."

"I trust that you gentlemen will make a determined search," stated Jerry. Moose and Mike nodded while making eye contact with Jerry.

Turning to Dianne, Jerry asked, "Have you discovered any lethal microorganisms?"

"I haven't found any that would pose a greater danger than what our immune systems had to contend with back on Earth."

"I don't know if I should take comfort in that or not. Some of Earth's microorganisms can be lethal. Would you mind elaborating a bit?"

"The most dangerous microbe I've found so far is a strain of bacillus similar to the bacteria that produces botulin. Botulin is the toxin that causes botulism, a disease of the nervous system. Although it's potentially deadly, it'll be no more difficult to deal with here than it was back on Earth. Following basic sanitary procedures in the preparation and preservation of food should eliminate the danger posed by these bacteria."

"If that's the most dangerous microbe you've found so far, we don't have much of a problem. Have you found anything else that might cause medical problems?"

Dianne turned to Doctor Connie Nemard who said, "Specimens we took from a small squirrel-like mammal living on the island showed it to be carrying an influenza-type virus. Detailed information about the virus has been entered into the computer, and it's developing a vaccine to counteract the virus. It should be ready in a few days. As a precaution, I recommend that we vaccinate all who are going down."

"That sounds reasonable," agreed Jerry.

Glancing from person to person, Jerry asked, "Can anyone think of a reason that would prevent us from establishing our homes on this island?"

During the silence that followed the question, Jerry established eye contact with each of his colleagues and received no verbal response. Then, he said, "I am going to interpret your silence to mean that you have no reason to delay going down."

Jerry turned to Moose. "Send Charlie down as soon as you have him ready. I want him to visit every part of the island. If nothing of consequence happens to him, we'll make our first manned landing."

Moose nodded and left the flight deck, heading for the shop to assist the crew working on Charlie. He intended to expedite the improvements being made to Charlie.

Jerry addressed those remaining on the flight deck: "I've been thinking of a name for the island, and I'd like to call it Pioneer Island. I think this would be an appropriate name for our home. By any definition of the word that you choose to use, we are pioneers."

"That's most definitely true," stated Connie, "but there's another reason why we should name our home Pioneer Island and that's to honor the early American pioneers. I've studied the early history of the United States, especially the lives of the pioneers. For the most part, those people were rugged individuals. They were survivors. Most of them were self-reliant and proud of it. They didn't look to government or anyone else to do for them what they could do for themselves. They loved their freedom and independence too much to allow themselves to become dependent on others, especially government. Their freedom and determined can-do attitude were largely responsible for the United States becoming the greatest nation on Earth. If they hadn't laid the foundation for this great nation, we probably would not be here. In honor of them and what they achieved, I believe we should name our home Pioneer Island."

Several moments of thoughtful silence followed Connie's speech. Then, Jerry said, "If we surpass their strengths and avoid their mistakes, we should be able to build the foundation for an even greater nation. Pioneer Island is definitely a fitting name for our home."

164

"The thought of living in a large log cabin on Pioneer Island appeals to me," stated Connie. "It's even romantic!"

"Since we are on the subject of names, I propose that we name the lake Clear Lake," suggested Mike.

"That name fits," agreed Jerry.

"I believe the meadow where we landed our first robot lab should be named Sauropod Meadow," stated Dianne. "Since the sauropods sleep there every night, they apparently consider the meadow to be theirs."

"If they think that meadow is theirs, I don't think we should disagree with them," responded Jerry.

TIME: 6 Years, 301 Days ALE.

On the flight deck, Moose was watching a large video screen with a deeply felt personal interest. What he saw was a real-time motion picture of the final approach glide of a robot lab suspended from a para-wing. This lab was modified to deliver Charlie to the surface and support his activities. What made this video so filled with detail was that it originated from cameras on the robot lab already on Pioneer Island.

"I like this," Moose said. "I feel like I'm standing on the plateau watching Charlie arrive. I feel like he's heading directly toward me, which means he's heading directly toward the lab that's already on the plateau."

Turning to Mike, Moose said, "You aren't going to crash Charlie into the lab that's already there are you?"

"Don't worry," responded Mike. "We're only going to land near the lab. The flight control system is homing on a signal from the lab, but Charlie will land a short distance beyond it and a little to the right."

"I hope you're right. I don't want Charlie hurt in a crash landing."

"You remind me of an expectant father, who is nervously awaiting the birth of his first child. You have to relax and remember that Charlie isn't a real person; he's just a robot."

"Charlie is more than a robot. He's my creation, and I want him delivered safely."

Pointing at the video screen, Mike said. "As you can see, the para-wing has just veered slightly to the right. We should have touchdown in a few seconds."

As promised, the lab carrying Charlie made a gentle landing fifty yards away from the lab already on the plateau. After letting out a big sigh of relief, Moose said, "I guess I really didn't need to worry. Once again, you've achieved a soft landing that is right on-target."

"That almost sounded like a compliment. Thank you."

"You're welcome," replied Moose, who proceeded to get Charlie out of the lab. When Charlie was standing next to the lab, Moose turned on the video cameras that made up his eyes and the microphones that made up his ears. He instructed Charlie to slowly turn his head from side to side.

Moose observed the video and listened to the sounds coming from Charlie. "It's almost as if I'm standing on Pioneer Island!" he exclaimed. "I can see and hear exactly what I would be seeing and hearing if I were standing where Charlie's standing."

Moose instructed Charlie to walk toward the other lab. While he walked the fifty yards, Moose observed him from the front and back using the video cameras on the labs. "He sure walks smoothly. A casual observer could easily mistake him for a real person."

When Charlie reached the lab, Moose instructed him to walk around the lab and visually inspect it. Then, Moose had Charlie stand up straight and face the distant mountain range to the east. Turning on Charlie's speakers and speaking into a microphone, Moose exclaimed loudly, "Hello, Alcent! My name is Moose! I am from Earth!"

When Moose's voice boomed out of the speakers on Charlie's chest and back, the microphones on the labs picked it up and broadcast it back to the Challenger. This enabled the people on the Challenger to hear Moose's voice as it sounded on the plateau.

Jerry turned to Mike and said, "I think Moose is acting like a kid with a new toy."

"It sure looks that way," commented Mike with a chuckle.

"You guys shouldn't be making fun of me, just because I'm having fun making sure that Charlie's systems are functional. I am serious about what I'm doing."

"Don't be offended by my comment," responded Jerry. "I'm enjoying this as much as you are. And Charlie is exactly the right kind of new toy for us to have at the moment."

Acting more like a proud father than the inventor and builder of a robot, Moose went back to checking out Charlie. He turned on Charlie's radar and instructed him to use it to measure the distance to the lab that had delivered him. Charlie's quick response was: 50.4 yards.

Moose instructed Charlie to run back to the lab. "I like the smooth way he runs," commented Moose. "Those long, graceful strides give him the appearance of a long-distance runner."

Moose checked out Charlie's infrared vision and found it to be functioning properly. Turning to his Captain, Moose formally declared, "Charlie is ready for duty, sir."

Jerry chuckled at Moose's formality. "You've done an excellent job in the design and construction of Charlie. I am impressed by the way you've completed such a complicated project in such a short time."

Feeling great satisfaction in his achievement and happy with the recognition given to him by his closest friend, Moose displayed a broad beaming smile and said, "Thank you for the compliment. I hope that Charlie fulfills our expectations."

"We'll soon find out because we're going to put him to work and find out what he can do for us. For the next few hours, let's have Charlie explore the area within 100 yards of either lab. Within that distance, the cameras on the labs can easily show us any insects or other creatures that investigate Charlie. Then, we'll use his support lab to give him a thorough inspection for stings and bites."

As Moose started Charlie walking in the direction of a clump of bushes, he said, "There sure aren't very many trees on the plateau."

"The openness of the plateau is one of the reasons why it's such an attractive place to land our labs," stated Mike. "It's possible that the soil on most of the plateau isn't deep enough to support tall trees. The fact that some small areas are exposed rock tends to support my speculation. There are fewer than 100 tall trees on the plateau, and nearly all of them are grouped in three small areas. We'll probably find deep soil only in those areas. On the rest of the plateau, I believe that the soil is only deep enough to support shrubs, grass, and other kinds of small plants."

TIME: 6 Years, 301 Days, 3 Hours, 30 Minutes ALE.

"Charlie has been exploring the area around the labs for three hours," stated Moose, "and nothing of consequence has happened to him."

"Let's recharge his batteries and give him a thorough inspection," Jerry said.

Fifteen minutes later, Moose said, "The lab has examined Charlie and he hasn't received any bites or stings, not even from insects. Wouldn't it be nice if there's nothing dangerous on the plateau?"

"It seems like that would make it a boring place to live," Mike said.

"If you need danger to make your life exciting, you could always visit Sauropod Meadow and wait for the T-Rexes to arrive," suggested Moose.

"I don't need that much excitement," Mike quickly said.

"Let's have Charlie hike through the trees," Jerry said. "I want to find out if there's anything living in the forest that might attack him."

A few minutes later, Charlie reached the first group of trees. He stopped and looked up in a determined search of their branches for living creatures. There weren't any present, except for a few birds and insects.

"These trees remind me of pine trees and fir trees," Moose said.

Charlie walked into the grove and stopped to look around. Then, he looked up and searched the branches. Part way up the trunk of a dead tree, he spotted a small hole with insects entering and leaving. Moose used Charlie's zoom lens to get close-up imagery of the insects. "Those bugs look like honey bees. I wonder if that's what they are."

"It's springtime in this area," noted Jerry, "and there are flowering plants everywhere. When Charlie leaves this grove, let's have him search the nearest flowers for these insects. If they are Alcent's version of Earth's honey bees, it should be apparent from their behavior."

"I hope they aren't Alcent's version of Earth's killer bees," warned Mike. "They could make our lives miserable, maybe even kill someone."

"We need to find out how aggressive they are," stated Moose.

"That's one job I'm not volunteering for," exclaimed Mike. "I have no desire to become a target for a swarm of killer bees."

"You don't need to. That's why we have Charlie," stated Moose while marching Charlie to the tree. Charlie tilted his head back and looked up at the small hole, which was eleven feet up the tree. So far, the insects were entering and leaving without concern for Charlie's presence. Moose instructed Charlie to walk around the tree. There was still no reaction from the insects. Then, Moose had Charlie pick up a small stone and lightly tap on the tree several times. This resulted in several dozen of the insects exiting the nest and excitedly buzzing around the dead tree.

"If we were on Earth and these were killer bees, Charlie would've suffered hundreds of stings by now," asserted Mike. "It looks like it would take a direct assault on their nest to provoke them to attack."

"I think we should find out," Moose said, as he directed Charlie to pick up a stick and tap on the tree, starting at ground level and gradually moving up toward the nest entrance. As the tapping got closer to the entrance, more insects exited the nest. They buzzed around in a frenzy as if seeking direction. When the tapping stick came within two feet of the nest entrance, several of the insects attacked Charlie, stinging the arm with the stick, his neck, and his face.

When Charlie stopped tapping on the tree and backed away from it, a few more of the insects stung him. Then, Charlie turned and ran away with a small swarm of the insects in pursuit. Only two of the pursuing insects stung him. All broke off pursuit by the time he was twenty yards away.

"Apparently, these insects won't attack unless their nest is directly threatened," Mike concluded.

"Let's give them a half-hour to settle down," suggested Jerry. "Then, let's have Charlie return to their tree and walk around it a couple times without doing anything threatening. I want to find out if they now recognize Charlie as an enemy and attack him or if they'll ignore him when he isn't doing anything to provoke them. In the meantime, let's have Charlie investigate some nearby flowers. If we find some of these insects gathering nectar, then we should take a look inside that tree and find out if they're making honey. If they are, we should get a sample for analysis and call these insects honey bees."

"We can do that," replied Moose while marching Charlie to a flowering shrub. Several of the insects were buzzing around it, going from one blossom to the next. Using Charlie's close-up capability, Moose zoomed in on a flower and saw one of the insects gathering nectar. When it left the blossom, it flew off in the direction of the nest. After seeing several of the insects do the same thing, it was decided to have Charlie follow them to verify their destination. Charlie's ability to run at speeds up to 20 mph allowed him to easily keep up with the nectar-laden insects.

When Charlie reached the trees, he slowed down to a walk. He could now see that the dead tree with the nest in it was the insects' destination. Charlie approached the tree at a pace comparable to that of a human out for a relaxing walk. Five feet from the tree, Charlie stopped and looked up at the nest entrance. The insects were entering and exiting without showing any concern for his presence. Next, Charlie walked around the tree. Then, he stepped up to the tree, reached out, and gently put a hand on it. He leaned against the tree like a human stopping to rest. Throughout this activity, the insects paid no attention to him.

"Evidently, they're quite docile and won't attack unless directly threatened," Jerry concluded. "Let's march Charlie back to the lab, so we can analyze the venom from the stings he received earlier. Hopefully, it will prove to be non-lethal to humans."

Several hours later, it was nighttime on the plateau, and Charlie was wandering the plateau under the light of a full moon and a half moon. Dianne and Moose were the only individuals on the flight deck, and they were directing and monitoring Charlie's activities.

"The plateau sure is quiet and peaceful," noted Moose.

"The light from two moons adds a pleasant romantic touch to the scene," commented Dianne.

"Let's pretend we're down there going for a walk in the moonlight. Using Charlie's eyes and ears, we can do that quite realistically."

"Sounds like fun. Let's go to the south end of the plateau and look down at the lake and the moonlight reflecting off the water."

"Walking Charlie around in the moonlight should help us determine if there are any nighttime predators that have managed to stay hidden from us during the daytime."

"Are you trying to add an element of risk to our make-believe romantic walk in the moonlight?"

"Since it's make-believe, all the risk will be to Charlie," replied Moose. "But in the very near future, we may actually go for a romantic walk in the moonlight. In fact, we may be doing that in less than ten days. So let's use this make-believe journey to evaluate the risks."

"Finally, after all these years in space, we're about to achieve our goal of settling down on Alcent for what we hope will be a long, happy life filled with peaceful prosperity. It's a life-long dream that's about to come true; and the best part of it is, I'm here with you. Two months from now, I might be pregnant with our first child."

Moose gave his wife a warm, loving hug and said, "That would be wonderful. Pioneer Island appears to be an ideal place to raise a family."

"I'm happy that those nectar gathering insects aren't going to be a threat to our children. They turned out to be docile, and their venom is similar to what bees produce back on Earth. If it turns out that they're making honey, then I think we should try to increase their numbers by providing them with hives to live in. Perhaps, we could harvest part of the honey. Wouldn't it be a pleasure to eat some warm, honey-covered, freshly baked bread made from our very own homegrown grain?"

"Yes, it would! And I must admit that the way you're talking is filling me with conflicting desires. I don't know if we should be heading for the bedroom or for the cafeteria."

"If talking about living on Alcent in conjunction with a make-believe walk in the moonlight has that kind of effect on you, then I'm really going to enjoy living there," responded Dianne. Suddenly, Dianne exclaimed, "Stop Charlie and get a close-up to his left!"

Moose did as directed and near the center of the video screen was a small rodent running as fast as he could. Moose zoomed in on the creature for increased detail. Then, out of nowhere, a diving bird suddenly entered the scene. The bird's sharp talons instantly dug into the rodent's back and neck followed immediately by a crisp blow to the rodent's head delivered by the bird's sharp beak.

"Nothing like sudden death to take the romance out of a stroll in the moonlight," commented Moose, as he directed Charlie's sensors to follow the retreating bird. Since his video cameras were equipped with light intensifiers, Charlie's nighttime vision was excellent. This along with his radar and infrared vision made it very easy for Charlie to track the bird.

"It looks like the bird's destination might be that group of tall trees near the south end of the plateau," speculated Dianne. "Perhaps, it has a nest in one of the trees and the rodent will be fed to its chicks."

"I'm going to head Charlie in that direction and look for a nest."

"While you're doing that, I'll take a close look at that bird and the rodent," stated Dianne, as she entered instructions into the computer to recall the video of the attack. She picked up the video at the instant that Charlie had zoomed in on the rodent. Running the video in super slow motion and freezing selected images, Dianne was able to study the animal in detail. "This creature would fit into a family of animals called ground squirrels back on Earth," she said.

"It looks like a gray gopher," stated Moose.

Dianne continued running the video in slow motion, freezing key images of the bird's attack and of it carrying away its prey. "On Earth, this bird could be fit into the owl species," she said. "It has a broad head and large forward facing eyes. These are the distinctive features of owls. It probably has excellent night vision and is primarily a nocturnal hunter."

"And it's a very skilled hunter, if the attack we just witnessed is typical of what it can do."

"If this bird were on Earth, it would be one of the larger members of the owl family. From this video, I estimate its wingspan to be slightly more than three feet."

"Charlie has just arrived in the grove," stated Moose, as he directed Charlie to search for the bird and a possible nest.

After several minutes of searching individual trees, Charlie's infrared camera located a warm body above a branch. Even though the body was fairly well concealed by foliage, its temperature of approximately one hundred degrees made it easily detectable in the infrared.

"I think we've located our bird," stated Moose. "I'm going to simplify this image by having the computer subtract out everything with a temperature outside of the 99 to 101-degree range."

A few seconds later, Dianne said, "That image is rather sketchy. Too much is missing because of having been blocked out by foliage, but it does look like our bird. I'm entering a request for the computer to compare this sketchy image to the detailed images it has of the bird to find out if it can make a positive identification."

Several seconds later, the computer responded: "The probability is .973 that this is the same bird."

"I think we can assume that this is our bird," stated Moose. "Now let's look for a nest."

"I think I see it," Dianne said. "It's a few feet below the bird."

"It looks to me like the bird is guarding the nest while its mate is hunting," commented Moose. "It is my prediction that this bird will not leave until its mate returns."

"Let's watch for a while and find out."

Twenty minutes later, the bird's mate arrived with a small reptile firmly clutched in its talons. "I wonder where that came from?" questioned Moose.

"It looks like a lizard. Even though it's only about fifteen inches long, it could still be dangerous if it has a poisonous bite. That's something we'll need to find out."

"Not to change the subject, but have you noticed that the bird that had been standing guard has already left?" Moose asked. "Now, I am going to make another prediction, and that is that the bird that just arrived with the lizard will not leave until its mate returns."

"If that's the case, there must be predators around that these birds fear."

"That might be true, but it doesn't take much of a predator to kill and eat baby birds. A carnivorous mammal no larger than a squirrel could raid an unguarded nest."

A few minutes later, Dianne said, "It seems like our romantic walk in the moonlight has turned into a bird-watching expedition."

"That's true, but I think it was a worthwhile interruption. I think we should always take advantage of unexpected opportunities to learn about our environment. The more we know about it; the more able we'll be to live in harmony with it. And that will make our lives easier and more relaxing than the alternative of continuously clashing with nature."

"Dianne nodded in agreement. "Also, I think our long-term survival and prosperity depends on living in harmony with our environment."

"The rapid acquisition of knowledge about it is the key. One quick way to gain this knowledge is to observe predators like this family of owls. Keeping track of the prey they feed their young will quickly make us aware of many of the small creatures that live in this area."

"Speaking about the owls, the other parent has just returned with a fish," announced Dianne.

"These birds are certainly versatile predators. I wonder how he managed to catch a fish."

"Perhaps this fish was sick or injured and was floundering around on the surface, and the bird recognized it as a meal of opportunity."

"That's a possibility," agreed Moose.

"I think we should launch an RPV, fly it to the grove, and land it on the branch of a nearby tree. Observing these owls with its video cameras will allow us to use Charlie to continue our romantic stroll."

"I'm still in a romantic mood," responded Moose.

"Getting in touch with our future home has me excited too," stated Dianne while launching an RPV. "I think we are going to have a good night, but first we need to take care of business."

While smiling at his wife, Moose said, "You've got my attention."

"Good!"

Shortly, Dianne said, "I've secured the RPV to a branch in a good location to observe the nest and its vicinity. The video from it is good, so let's resume our romantic walk in the moonlight."

"I'm ready. Let's go."

A short time later, Charlie was standing near the southern edge of the plateau. Sounding concerned, Dianne said, "You've marched him almost to the edge. If he takes one more step, he'll fall 150 feet and crash into the sandy beach. Simply losing his balance could topple him over the edge."

"Don't worry about Charlie; he has a very good sense of balance."

"But his feet are less than a foot from the edge."

Moose decided to repeat what Mike had said earlier in the day: "You must keep in mind that Charlie isn't a real person; he's just a robot."

"But I'm starting to become attached to him. He may be just a robot, but he is your creation, and he's serving us very well. I'd feel sad if he fell to his destruction."

"Well, if it'll relax your worried mind, I'll have Charlie back up a couple steps."

"You're a good actor, but you're failing to convince me that you're unconcerned. I know that you're just as attached to him as I am."

Moose chuckled and said, "It's becoming increasingly difficult to fool you. It seems like every time I try to mislead you, purely in fun of course, you see right through it."

"We've been married five years, and I do know you very well."

Now that Charlie had stepped back from the edge of the plateau, Moose directed him to drop into a prone position and peer over the edge. Displaying the view from Charlie's video cameras on the largest screen on the flight deck gave Moose and Dianne a very realistic sensation of actually being on the edge of the cliff.

"What a beautiful scene," commented Dianne. "It's so peaceful and inviting, and it's all softly illuminated by the light from two moons."

"Even the sounds are soft and peaceful. All that I hear is the whispering sound of a gentle breeze flowing through the trees, the splashing sound of small waves lapping the beach, and the sounds made by small nocturnal creatures busily living their lives."

"It's truly amazing that such a peaceful place could exist on a planet inhabited by a multitude of creatures with awesome size and power."

"We may've found the best place on Alcent to build our homes. With intelligent planning and hard work, Pioneer Island might become our island paradise."

"I wish we were down there right now. I'd love to make love on that warm sandy beach and then go for a midnight swim in the moonlight."

"I would too," responded Moose while putting his arms around Dianne from behind her.

After a few moments of silence during which Dianne and Moose soaked up the view and the sounds from their future home, Moose said, "We can't go swimming in the moonlight tonight, but we can go to our apartment and make love with that view covering one entire wall. With the only sounds in our apartment coming from Pioneer Island, we should be able to pretend quite realistically that we are down there on that beach."

"What a wonderful conclusion to an imaginary romantic stroll in the moonlight," responded Dianne.

Upon hearing the desired response from his wife, Moose left a note on the control console stating that Charlie was doing an important extended period of observation of the bay and was not to be disturbed. Then, he and Dianne left the flight deck and went to their apartment.

An hour later, Moose and Dianne returned to the flight deck. They were greeted by Connie, who looked at them and said, "You two certainly seem to be in a buoyant mood. Have you made some discovery that I should know about?"

Moose and Dianne looked at each other and chuckled. "I think you've already discovered the procedure responsible for our uplifted moods," Dianne said.

Instantly realizing that she had innocently asked a personal question, Connie said, "I didn't mean to pry into your private life. I just thought you might have discovered something wonderful about Pioneer Island."

"Actually, we have," responded Moose. Pointing at the large video screen, he said, "When we viewed that scene from our bedroom, we discovered that it had a rather erotic effect on us. It was very stimulating, and the overall experience was exquisitely satisfying. Being a medical professional, perhaps you could explain how this exotic scene from an alien planet could have had such an amorous effect on us."

While considering what Moose had just said, Connie silently gazed at the scene and listened to the peaceful sounds coming from it. After a few moments, she asked, "How long has Charlie been transmitting the sights and sounds from this area?"

"For about an hour," replied Moose.

"Is the entire transmission stored in the computer?"

"Yes, it is."

Attempting to sound both sly and innocent, Connie said, "I'm going to ask Jerry to review it with me from our bedroom. Perhaps we'll make the same discovery that you and Dianne made. If we do, and if you really do need an expert evaluation of it, I'll analyze it and give you a professional explanation from a medical perspective."

"I appreciate your offer," responded Moose, "but since I'm already quite knowledgeable on the subject, I must decline."

"That's the response I expected from you," stated Connie, as she turned and left the flight deck.

"I wonder what's on her mind," commented Moose with a big grin.

"As if you don't know," replied Dianne, while displaying a naughty smile of self-satisfaction.

Moose returned the smile, and gave his wife an affectionate hug. "This sure has been a great night," he said. "We've learned a lot about the plateau and we've had a wonderful time doing it. Tomorrow, Charlie will leave the plateau and wander the rest of the island."

"How do you plan to get Charlie off the plateau, so he can explore the rest of the island?"

"He'll tie a rope to a tree, and while grasping the rope for support, he'll make his way down the rockslide at the north end of the plateau. After each exploration trip, he can use the same rope to climb back up to his support lab."

"How much longer are we going to leave Charlie stranded at the south end of the plateau?"

"I think it's time to return him to his support lab. Then, we'll have him lie down for the rest of the night to simulate a sleeping human. The lab's video cameras will be trained on him to record anything that might happen to him, such as an attack by pterodactyls. If nothing that tragic occurs, then tomorrow morning, we'll give him a thorough inspection for insect bites and stings, or bites and stings of any kind for that matter."

"Your idea of designing and building Charlie was sure a good one," stated Dianne with obvious pride in her husband. "By the time we land, we'll have a much better understanding of potential risks than we would've had without him."

"I am pleased with the way he turned out. I expect that he'll be a valuable asset long after we've landed and built our homes. For example, Charlie will probably lead the way whenever we explore new territory. Using him in conjunction with RPVs should help us avoid deadly confrontations with the dangerous animals that inhabit Alcent."

"That's a good example of a way to harmonize with our environment, rather than, clash with it."

After a bit of silence, Dianne noticed that her husband was deeply lost in thought. "In what far away place is your mind?" she asked.

"Actually, my mind was back on Earth. I was thinking about the environmental extremists who tried to kill us to prevent us from coming here. It just occurred to me that anyone who would honestly evaluate the facts would have to conclude that we are being responsible in regard to Alcent's environment. We are doing, and will continue to do, everything within reason to protect it."

"Yes, but our commitment to that policy wasn't good enough for them. They think the human species is a form of environmental pollution. According to them, our very presence on Alcent pollutes the environment. In their view, the human species does not have the same right to evolve and expand its territory that other species have."

"They are, of course, entitled to speak their point of view, but they do not have the right to force others to live in accordance with it."

TIME: 6 Years, 307 Days, 2 Hours ALE.

Captain Jerry Jerontis opened a meeting in the cafeteria, which was being attended by all off-duty personnel. "The event we've been waiting for and preparing for is now less than twenty-four hours away. Tomorrow, our first manned landing will occur. I will pilot the personnel shuttle to a landing on the east side of Pioneer Island. My crew for this mission will be Doctor Nemard, Moose, and Dianne.

"Our primary objective will be to conduct medical research. Doctor Nemard will do a daily medical examination of each of us. If we don't experience any medical problems of consequence for thirty days, additional personnel will be landed on Pioneer Island. A second objective will be accomplished by Dianne. She will be searching for dangerous microorganisms. Also, she will be investigating insects and other life forms to determine their potential to harm us. Moose will begin the project of finding local sources of food. It is my prediction that he'll begin by looking for tasty, nutritious fish."

Much to Moose's chagrin, a round of laughter greeted this matter-of-fact statement of the obvious. Then, Jerry said, "I plan to continue the exploration of the island that has been started by Charlie. Although we've

175

learned a great deal with the RPVs and with Charlie, there is still much to be done. Moose will now give us the results of Charlie's activities."

"During the past few days Charlie has wandered all over Pioneer Island," Moose reported. "Each night he slept in a different location. He has slept on the beach, in the forest, on the plateau, in open meadows, even in a tree. While simulating a sleeping human, he was not molested except by insects, and none of them injected any venom into him. The only insects to ever inject venom into him were bees, and their venom was no more dangerous than bee venom on Earth.

"On three occasions, Charlie dripped blood on his trail. On two of these occasions, he was trailed by a small mammal that looked very much like a big weasel. In both cases, these mammals stopped following Charlie when they got close enough to become aware of his size. Apparently, Pioneer Island is home to carnivorous mammals the size of a large weasel. But Charlie's experience and the lack of large prey strongly indicates that there aren't any large predators living on the island.

"The only large predators we've seen are the pterodactyls, and apparently, they don't live on Pioneer Island, but only stop there to rest while on their way to somewhere else. On two occasions, they were flying over the island while Charlie was wandering around in open areas. Both times, they ignored him. Either they weren't hungry, or they didn't recognize him as potential prey."

After Moose's concluding remark, Jerry thanked him for his report and said, "Our next report will be presented by Dianne."

Dianne moved to a position in front of the group and delivered her report: "As you know, we've been engaged in a very intense research program to learn as much as possible about the immune systems of the creatures living on Alcent. You are all familiar with the details of the research, so I am not going to expound on that. I am simply going to say that we've concluded that Alcent's animals have evolved immune systems that are capable of guarding against attack by any microbes from Earth that we inadvertently introduce into their environment.

"Part of our research involved an intense effort to find and identify as many of Alcent's microbes as possible. Doctor Nemard has evaluated them from a medical perspective and has concluded that the human immune system should be able to protect us from them. Of course, we cannot be certain of that until we go down and live on the planet for an extended time, and that is what we plan to begin doing tomorrow."

After pausing briefly, Dianne said, "On another subject, I propose that the site of our first homes be named Stellar Plateau. Since we are the first interstellar pioneers from Earth, I believe this is a suitable name."

Noting that nearly everyone was nodding in agreement, Jerry declared: "Stellar Plateau, it is."

After a brief pause, Jerry continued, "When we land on Alcent tomorrow, a new era will begin; an era in which a new civilization will be built. Tomorrow will be the reference point in time for all future generations. When they look back in time, tomorrow will be seen as their genesis day. Tomorrow will be Day One on a new calendar.

"There is, however, one key event that must be accomplished before tomorrow's landing can take place. This afternoon, Mike will land a large capsule on Stellar Plateau that contains everything that we'll need to survive and accomplish our objectives during the next thirty days."

Turning to Mike, Jerry said, "Your skill in landing capsules precisely on target has been demonstrated repeatedly. I am confident that you will not have any problem delivering this one on target."

"Thank you," replied Mike. "The capsule is ready to go. Its flight control program and equipment have been checked and rechecked."

The habitation capsule was very similar in design to the Apollo Capsules used in America's first manned lunar exploration program. However, with a maximum internal diameter of 22 feet, this capsule was much larger. It had two floors in it that would be used for living space and research. It was packed with food, research equipment, survival equipment, construction materials, basic tools, and Moose's fishing tackle. The capsule would make its final approach and landing suspended from a large parawing. If all went according to plan, Mike would land it within fifty yards of the two robot labs already on Stellar Plateau.

After nearly seven years in space, the eve of the first landing had finally arrived. And the meeting to discuss the event evolved into a party to celebrate the event. The celebration lasted well into the night.

MAP ONE

MAP TWO

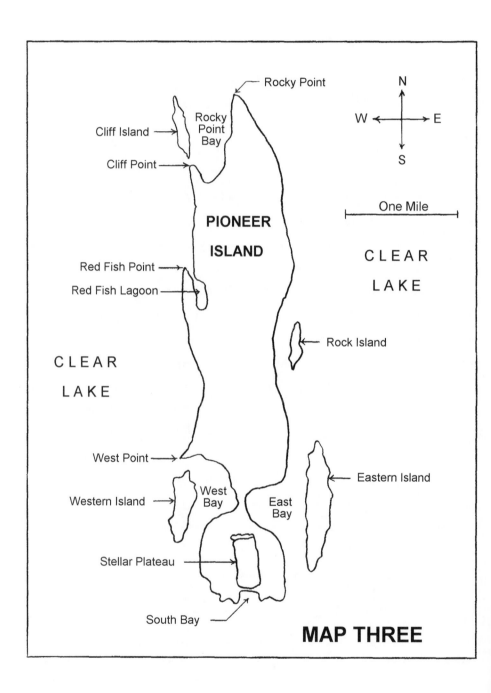

Rocky Point

Rocky Point Bay

Cliff Island →

Cliff Point →

PIONEER ISLAND

Red Fish Point →

Red Fish Lagoon →

CLEAR LAKE

Rock Island

West Point →

Western Island →

West Bay

East Bay

Eastern Island

Stellar Plateau

South Bay

N
W ← → E
S

One Mile

CLEAR LAKE

MAP THREE

180

SIX

The First Day of a New Era

TIME: 6 Years, 308 Days, 1 Hour ALE.

Captain Jerry Jerontis, Doctor Connie Nemard, Dianne, and Moose were in the personnel shuttle flying north one mile off the west coast of Pioneer Island. They were in a steep gliding descent and had just dropped below 35,000 feet.

While looking out a window, Connie said, "Pioneer Island sure looks small and drab."

"You don't sound very excited about going there," responded Dianne.

"What do you mean?"

"This is our big day! I'm so jacked up that I can hardly contain myself! But when you just described Pioneer Island, you sounded like you're down in the dumps this morning. What's that all about?"

"I don't know why I'm so down this morning. A dream that's driven my life since my early teens is about to come true, and I should be wildly excited, but I'm not. Maybe I'm worried that something might yet happen to prevent my dream from coming true."

"Anxiety isn't normal for you. Maybe fatigue is getting you down. You've been driving yourself pretty hard since we arrived here."

"That's true, and I didn't get much sleep last night. Our party lasted well into the night; then, when I finally went to bed, thinking about today kept me awake. And whenever I managed to fall asleep, wild dreams about today kept waking me up."

"The party was fun, but it looked to me like you weren't enjoying it all that much."

"I was worried about today."

"Well, today is here. You don't need to worry about it anymore. It's time for you to unwind! Relax! Enjoy yourself! This is our big day! We've waited a long time for this, and we'll remember it for the rest of our lives."

"That's quite a pep talk. I can see that you're really fired up."

"Yes! I am! And I suggest that you forget whatever it is that's been bothering you and get with the mood of the occasion."

Connie thought about Dianne's comments for a few moments. Then, she let out a deep breath and smiled. "Thank you. I needed that."

At that moment, the shuttle rolled 25 degrees and began a 180-degree right turn. While looking out her window, Connie said, "Take a look at this view. We've lost enough altitude so that I'm beginning to appreciate the immense size of Clear Lake. It totally dominates the scene."

"It's easy to see how well the lake isolates Pioneer Island from the surrounding countryside and the dinosaurs that live there."

"Maybe Pioneer Island really will be the safe secure home that we're hoping it'll be," Connie said, sounding hopeful.

"Our exploration and research indicates that it will be. Are you still worried about something?"

"The island has more than three square miles of thick forest that we've only partially explored. We really don't know for sure that it doesn't contain any serious dangers."

"That's true," agreed Dianne. "Exploring that forest is one of our top priority projects, and not knowing what we're going to discover makes that an exciting adventure, not something to be feared. We'll just have to be alert for dangers of any kind."

"If I'm going to be alert, I guess I'd better start getting more sleep."

"You might start with a short nap this afternoon."

"Good idea, maybe I'll have Jerry cover me with suntan lotion, so I can do some sunbathing while I nap. I haven't done that in years. But maybe I should call it Alpha Centauri bathing."

"I think most of us will continue to call it sunbathing; even though, the radiant heat will be coming from Alpha Centauri A. But I'm wondering how much of a nap you're going to get if you're planning to have Jerry massage your nearly nude body with suntan lotion."

"Well, I could always take a nap afterwards. Anyway, just a few moments ago, you said that I should relax and enjoy myself."

"That's true, but I wasn't thinking about sex when I made those suggestions."

"Well, I wasn't thinking about sex when I mentioned sunbathing. That was your idea."

"Yeah, I guess it was. But now that the subject has come up, it does seem like a good idea. Can you think of a better way to celebrate our arrival?"

"Not at the moment."

"I can't either, so some time today, I might just hand Moose a bottle of suntan lotion and ask him to cover me with it. I could probably seduce him and even make him think that it was all his idea."

"You sound rather cunning."

Dianne laughed. "Moose never seems to mind."

"It would be rather disappointing if he did."

Meanwhile, in the cockpit, Jerry said to Moose, "It won't be long now old buddy; we're almost there. You'll soon have an opportunity to enjoy an exotic beach with your lovely wife. I'm sure you'll find just as much excitement on Pioneer Island as you would've had on that vacation to the South Pacific that I interrupted nearly seven years ago."

"No doubt about that. I'm glad you found a way for me to be here."

"I am too."

A short time later, Moose confirmed, "Our hydrofoils are down and locked in position."

"We should have contact with the lake in less than thirty seconds," responded Jerry. "It's been a long time since I landed on hydrofoils, but our flight control computer makes the job easy."

"We're on course, and our speed is 195 mph, just as it should be."

A few seconds later, Jerry said, "Our stab-con-foils (small stability and control hydrofoils) have just entered the water."

A few moments later, Moose announced, "Our large hydrofoils are now in the water. What a soft landing! We've made an absolutely smooth transition from atmospheric flight to gliding on the water. We're here!"

As Moose finished his landing announcement, the hydro-drogues deployed, rapidly slowing the shuttle down. When its speed dropped under 40 mph, it settled into the water and floated on its hull. Jerry deployed the marine propeller, which was powered by a steam turbine using high pressure steam generated by the shuttle's nuclear reactor. Maintaining the shuttle's speed at ten mph, Jerry guided it into East Bay, where he brought it to a halt 50 yards offshore and dropped anchor in water 30 feet deep.

Finally, the excitement that she had been restraining reached the bursting point, and Connie exclaimed, "We're on Alcent! And there's someone standing on the beach waving to us!"

"That's Charlie!" stated Dianne. "I should've known that Moose would have him standing there to welcome us."

Moose opened a hatch and looked around East Bay for anything that might pose a danger. Not seeing anything threatening, he pushed out a plastic boat that quickly inflated. Then, Moose deployed a short ladder, picked up his rifle, climbed down the ladder, and stepped into the boat. Dianne and Connie joined Moose while Jerry handed him several guns before stepping out of the shuttle. After closing the hatch, the men picked up the oars and began rowing to the nearby shore.

Moose, Dianne, and Jerry were so preoccupied with the sights and sounds of Alcent that they did not see Connie quietly remove her hiking boots. Now wearing only snug fitting shorts and a halter top, she stood up and announced: "All of our research and underwater exploration indicates that this water is perfectly safe, so I'm going swimming." Before anyone could offer a word of caution, Connie took a deep breath and dove into the cool, clear, refreshing water.

Caught completely by surprise, Jerry exclaimed, "Why did she do that!" While quickly removing his shirt and boots, he said, "I wish she had

185

waited until we've had a chance to explore this lake more thoroughly before jumping into it."

"She obviously believes the water is safe and is eager to enjoy it," responded Dianne.

Grabbing one of the spear guns and strapping it to his back, Jerry said, "That may very well be true, but I'm concerned about her safety, and I wish she'd waited." Jerry dove into the water and swam fifteen feet straight down, where he searched for anything threatening. He quickly noted that the incredible cleanliness of the water allowed him to see for quite some distance in all directions. Much to his relief, he was unable to spot anything that looked dangerous. In fact, the water looked very peaceful with small schools of fish lazily swimming around. He noticed that he was behind his wife and that she was unaware of his presence.

A few seconds later, Connie surfaced twenty feet from the boat and exclaimed, "This is the most refreshing experience I've had in years! And it looks perfectly safe down there!"

Suddenly, Connie let out a terrifying scream, as she felt her ankles firmly grasped from behind. She felt herself being dragged down. Almost immediately, her ankles were released. Then, Connie noticed that her husband wasn't in the boat, and she realized what had just happened. A moment later, Jerry surfaced next to Connie, looked into her eyes, and waited for her to speak.

"I guess scaring me was your way of reminding me that we're on an alien planet."

Jerry smiled and asked innocently, "Did I use an effective method of communication?"

"Since you were underwater and didn't hear my scream, you have no idea how truly effective it was."

"I didn't hear your scream, but I felt you tremble."

Seeing that her husband was armed, and recognizing how quickly he had joined her in the water, Connie realized that she must have worried him greatly. "I'm sorry. I didn't mean to worry you, but based on our data, I really did think that swimming in this bay would be safe. Even so, I appreciate how quickly you entered the water to protect me."

"You are the best part of my life. If I lost you now, my life on this planet would be filled with sorrow. Today is the beginning of the future we've dreamed about, and I want to share with you the joys and excitement of that future."

"Thank you for making me feel so special on this very special day. And you're right, I was too quick to just blindly dive in, but since we didn't see anything dangerous down there, do you think we could go back down and take another look around?"

"It did look peaceful to me, so let's do it, but let's stay alert."

Connie and Jerry filled their lungs with air and swam fifteen feet straight down. After looking around and not seeing any danger, Jerry turned and swam toward his wife. Seeing her husband approach, Connie met him with open arms. Jerry embraced her tightly and gave her several intimate caresses. Passionately affected by her husband's erotic touch, Connie responded by caressing him. After a few moments of intimacy, they broke their embrace and headed to the surface for a breath of air.

As they broke the surface, Moose yelled, "What's it like down there?"

"Very stimulating," replied Jerry.

"That's a rather vague answer," responded Moose.

"To the contrary, it's right to the point," asserted Jerry. Then, he and Connie filled their lungs and went back into the alien underwater world to do some additional exploration.

Moose looked at Dianne and said, "There must be some exotic scenery down there in order for Jerry to describe it as very stimulating."

"Well, we are on an alien planet. Whatever they see down there could have a special air of excitement about it, especially when you factor in the possibility of grave danger unexpectedly showing up."

After looking around and digesting the sights and sounds of the immediate area, Moose said, "It seems rather calm and peaceful here. I wouldn't mind going for a good swim myself."

"That would be fun, but I don't think that more than two of us should be in the water at the same time until we know for sure that it's safe."

"You're right; two of us should be on guard."

About a minute after they had gone under, Moose said, "It seems like they've been down there a long time. I wonder if anything has happened to them. If it weren't for the light breeze and the ripple that it's putting on the lake, we might be able to see them."

Almost as if in answer to Moose's concern, Jerry and Connie surfaced just a few feet away from the boat. "You've been down there a long time," commented Moose. "I was starting to worry about you. What's down there that's so fascinating?"

Connie made eye contact with Dianne, displayed a sly expression, then turned to Moose and said, "The underwater scenery is enchanting, but what kept us down there is that we were warming up for sunbathing."

Before Moose could comment, Connie turned to Jerry and said, "Let's head for the shore."

"Okay, but let's make the swim in three or four underwater segments, so we can get better acquainted with the underwater world."

After Jerry and Connie went back underwater, Moose turned to Dianne and said, "I've done a lot of swimming and sunbathing in my life, but I fail to understand how swimming warms a person up for sunbathing. My experience has always been the exact opposite. Sunbathing always made me so hot that I usually went swimming to cool off."

"This sure is a mysterious planet," Dianne teased.

Moose looked at his wife and said, "Perhaps, there's something you could tell me that would clear up this mystery."

"What makes you say that?"

"I saw the sly expressions that you and Connie exchanged. Would you mind letting me in on the secret?"

Deciding not to tease her husband any longer, Dianne told him about the earlier conversation with Connie concerning suntan lotion and Jerry. Moose immediately understood what had been going on underwater and laughed at himself for not figuring it out sooner. In a hopeful tone, he asked, "By chance, did you pack some sunscreen in your travel bag?"

"I sure did," Dianne replied warmly.

"Maybe sometime this afternoon, we can take a break from work and find a comfortable secluded spot where we can relax and enjoy the radiant heat from Alpha Centauri A"

"What a wonderful idea."

As Moose resumed rowing, Dianne asked, "Have you noticed how clean this lake smells?"

"Yes, it reminds me of how fresh the air smells after a rain shower. I like that fresh, clean smell. We must never harm this lake's pristine state."

"We certainly have the technology to avoid polluting it."

A few minutes later, Moose and Dianne stepped into shallow water and pulled the boat onto the sandy beach. Shortly thereafter, Jerry and Connie joined them.

During the next few minutes, the four lone humans silently surveyed this small region of their new world. They gazed up and down the sandy beach, watching and listening to the water gently lapping the shore. They looked across East Bay to the one-mile long island that sheltered the bay from easterly winds. They looked at the forest and listened to the breeze whisper through the trees, and they wondered what dangers lay hidden in the forest. They gazed at the deep blue sky with its broadly scattered fluffy white cumulus clouds. To the north, they noticed four pterodactyls several thousand feet above Pioneer Island soaring beneath one of the clouds, apparently riding the thermal that supported the cloud.

"Evidently, these creatures sometimes fly purely for pleasure," Moose said. "Why else would they be at such great altitude? Surely, they aren't hunting for food way up there."

Fascinated by the pterodactyls, the people from Earth continued to admire the huge creatures. Watching them fly in large circles as they rode the thermal to greater altitudes led Moose to say, "Standing here and watching them gives me a very different feeling than watching video of them while onboard the Challenger."

"In what respect?" Jerry asked.

"Now that we are a part of their world, their size and killing capability makes me feel small and vulnerable. To use an analogy, I've seen fascinating movies about the Great White Shark, but I've never had the courage to go swimming with them."

"Are you suggesting that living here is like swimming with sharks?"

"No! I'm only saying that studying pterodactyls from the safety of the Challenger was like visiting the local library; whereas, studying them while living with them is dangerous. Even a small mistake could be life threatening. And what is particularly worrisome is that they might be quite intelligent. The more intelligent a predator is; the more dangerous it is."

"What leads you to think that they might be fairly intelligent?"

"Take a look at them," replied Moose. "It appears that they're flying purely for the joy of flying. They could just as well be sleeping somewhere. Apparently, they're intelligent enough to have made the choice between taking a nap for relaxation and flying for enjoyment. As further evidence of intelligence, they are flying in a manner that requires very little energy. Specifically, they're using their huge wings to ride a thermal. With their apparent intelligence, they could easily decide to dive upon us in a group attack. Their fifty-foot wingspans would make me feel like I was under attack by a squadron of fighter aircraft."

"That would be an alarming experience," commented Jerry.

"That's an understatement. I'd be more than alarmed. My adrenaline would be flowing, and my ability to shoot accurately would be tested."

"I think it's important to keep in mind that we don't have any evidence that they'll ever attack us," stated Jerry. "We've never seen them eat anything except fish, and they haven't paid any attention to Charlie, even when he's been out in the open."

"It's possible that they prefer fish and don't prey on land animals when fish are available," commented Dianne. "An obvious advantage is that fish are low risk prey in that they don't defend themselves the way many animals do. Why should these pterodactyls risk injury while obtaining food, if they don't need to."

"If what you're suggesting is true, do you think that's an intelligent choice on their part or purely instinctive?" Connie asked.

"I don't know," replied Dianne. "However, considering that this planet is approximately 500 million years older than Earth, these creatures have had ample time to have evolved intelligence."

"How intelligent they are is certainly an important question," noted Jerry, "but of more immediate concern is whether or not they'll ever try to eat us. We need to find that out as soon as we can."

"How do you propose to do that?" asked Moose.

"Very simple, we use ourselves as bait."

"That sounds dangerous," stated Connie.

"There will be an element of risk," admitted Jerry, "but with proper planning, the risk should be minimal. Anyway, whatever the risks are, we must not forget that we're here to evaluate the hazards of living here before we bring more people down. Defining the threat posed by pterodactyls seems to me to be of immediate concern."

"What do you have in mind?" Moose asked.

"Movement will usually attract the attention of predators, especially the kind of movement that indicates that the potential prey might be injured. So some time when there are pterodactyls above us, you and I will get into an open area and engage in vigorous activity designed to get their attention. When they've seen us, we'll move around as though we're crippled. Dianne and Connie will observe the pterodactyls and record their reactions to the things we do. We'll be armed, and we'll be near shelter that we can retreat to. Also, Charlie will be with us. If they approach, you and I will retreat to shelter while Charlie stays in the open. If and how they attack him will give us a great deal of information."

"If they attack Charlie, they'll learn something too," stated Moose.

"What's that?" Jerry asked.

"The ones that attack Charlie will learn that he isn't a very tasty meal, and hopefully, those particular creatures will leave us alone."

"That's a possibility," agreed Jerry. "But I don't think Charlie is durable enough to teach all the pterodactyls that pass through this area that we aren't good to eat."

"That's one thing that bothers me about your plan," stated Moose.

"What do you mean?"

"I put a lot of effort into designing and building Charlie, and I don't want to lose him by allowing these creatures to carry him away."

"It sounds like you've become quite attached to him. Need I remind you that he isn't a real person, that he's just a piece of equipment?"

"But he's a very valuable piece of equipment," countered Moose. "Before we conduct your experiment, I think we should equip Charlie with several canisters of highly irritating chemicals that we can release the instant he is attacked."

Turning to Dianne, Moose said, "It seems like our chief biologist should be able to formulate something that would be extremely irritating, but not do any lasting damage."

"I think I can do that," replied Dianne.

"Good idea," Jerry said. "If the chemicals work, we not only get to keep Charlie, but we can equip some of our RPVs with canisters of the chemicals and use them to chase away pterodactyls that get too close. Hopefully, we can avoid killing these magnificent creatures."

"Another thing to consider is that there may not be another species on this planet that looks like us," commented Dianne. "If that's the case, and if these pterodactyls have enough intelligence to recognize that we are something new in their environment, it's possible that they may be curious enough to want to investigate us. So if they approach us, we shouldn't assume that they're hungry; they might just be curious."

"You bring up an interesting point," responded Jerry. "If there isn't another species here that resembles us, then the creatures we encounter won't have any pre-learned ways to react to us. Some animals might be very tame, since they haven't learned to fear us. For the same reason, some predators might be fearlessly aggressive toward us."

"Finding out how each species reacts to us could be very dangerous," Dianne said.

"You're right," Jerry admitted. "We'll use reasonable caution, but it's impossible to eliminate all risk. During the next 30 days, we'll introduce ourselves to as many species as possible and learn what we can, but right now, it's time to go to Stellar Plateau. We have a capsule to unpack and a camp to set up."

After belting on her pistol and shouldering her rifle, Connie said, "Packing around all this artillery is going to take some getting use to."

"Having those big pterodactyls in sight makes getting use to it a lot easier," stated Dianne.

"Good point," responded Connie, while looking up at them.

With Charlie and Jerry in the lead, and Moose doing rear guard duty, the small group of humans began its trek to Stellar Plateau. After walking across twenty-five yards of sandy beach, they reached the forest, where they stopped and peered into its darkly shadowed interior, looking for signs of danger. Being on an alien planet, they weren't sure what form danger might take. Any insect, snake, mammal, or lizard-like creature could be capable of injecting deadly venom. Therefore, contact with any living creature would have to be avoided.

After intently searching for indications of danger, Jerry said, "I don't see anything threatening. Do any of you?"

"Even though we don't see anything threatening as far as animal life is concerned, let's not overlook the possibility of hazardous plant life," Dianne said. "Some plants protect themselves with toxic chemicals, and contact with them can be very painful. I realize that it's impossible to avoid all contact with plants, but let's avoid it as much as possible."

"This forest is quite thick, but I think we can pick our way through it with minimal contact with plants," responded Jerry. "In a little over a hundred yards, we'll be at the rockslide on the north face of the plateau, and there isn't much growing on it."

Jerry sent Charlie into the forest along the chosen path. Everyone intently observed Charlie and his surroundings. After Charlie walked ten yards without incident, Jerry entered the forest. Connie, Dianne, and Moose followed him at five-yard intervals.

A short time later, they arrived at the rockslide and climbed it using the same rope for support that Charlie had used. When all were on Stellar Plateau, they marched directly to the large capsule that would serve as their home. They put down their packs and took a few minutes to look around.

Slowly drifting around the capsule, they checked out the picturesque view in every direction.

As the stunning scenic beauty of the location fully gripped her, Connie exclaimed, "I am absolutely going to enjoy living here! Everywhere I look; I see a spectacular view! I am happy that there aren't enough trees on this plateau to block much of it."

Recalling Connie's earlier remark, while onboard the personnel shuttle, led Dianne to ask, "So, am I to assume that you no longer think this island is too small and too drab?"

"Yes! You can assume that, and I am thrilled to be here."

"My feelings exactly," agreed Dianne. "Would you like to do some exploring with me?"

"What do you have in mind?" Connie asked.

"Nothing too dramatic, I just want to look at the plant life. Also, I'd like to see what we can find by way of insects, birds, rodents, whatever."

"In other words, anything that's alive."

"That's right. Since this island is now our home, I want to become familiar with every living thing on it. So let's look around."

"We could start with those flowering bushes over there," suggested Connie, as she pointed at them.

"It sounds like there might be some happy birds in those shrubs."

"I wonder what they look like."

"I don't know, but they sure sound cheerful," noted Dianne. "All that chirping could be part of a mating ritual. It is springtime here."

"Let's go see what we can find out."

As Dianne and Connie started walking toward the bushes, Jerry yelled out, "Aren't you two forgetting something?"

"What do you mean?" Connie asked.

"Your rifles!" exclaimed Jerry.

"We aren't going very far," protested Connie. "We'll be close enough, so that you and Moose can protect us."

"Moose and I are going to be unpacking this capsule and won't be able to watch you all the time. Until we know that it's not necessary, I want all of us to be armed at all times."

Nodding in agreement, Dianne and Connie shouldered their rifles. Connie said, "It's so quiet and peaceful here that it's easy to get lulled into a false sense of security. At the moment, there aren't even any pterodactyls in sight, but I guess they can arrive unexpectedly at any time."

"Either them or some other creatures that we don't yet know about," stated Jerry.

Turning to Moose, Jerry said, "Let's open it up and get started. The first thing we need to do is set up our storage shed."

A short time later, Moose said, "These panels sure make the job quick and easy. We just snap them together, and they lock in place."

During the next hour, Jerry and Moose completed assembly of the storage shed. With a floor area measuring 12 X 24 feet, the shed had ample space to store the equipment and supplies still in the capsule. The shed had a single plane roof set at an angle of 30 degrees. Covered with solar cells and facing in the southerly direction, the roof would provide part of the electrical power needs of the small encampment.

Jerry and Moose walked a few yards away from the new shed and sat on outdoor chairs to drink a cup of coffee and admire their handiwork. They were joined by Dianne and Connie who had just returned from their exploration walk.

Connie looked at the shed and said, "That little shed makes me feel good. Even though it's just a simple little building, it's our first building, and it represents the beginning of turning this island into our home."

"That's true," agreed Dianne, "but the thing that we need to turn into our home is the capsule."

"Are you suggesting that we should transfer our supplies from it to the storage shed?" Connie asked.

"That would give us a comfortable, secure place to sleep tonight."

Turning to Moose, Jerry said, "I think our wives are in a homemaking mood."

Before Moose could respond, Dianne said, "Actually, I feel more like I'm on a camping trip. That capsule reminds me of a recreational vehicle. But it's full of supplies that we have to remove before we can camp in it."

"It's difficult to imagine being on a more exotic camping trip than this," commented Moose. "We're camped on an island in the middle of a huge lake that no one has ever fished in. The lake is surrounded by land inhabited by dinosaurs. We have creatures with fifty-foot wing spans soaring over our heads. We're on a planet that currently has two suns in its daytime sky and sometimes has two moons in its nighttime sky."

"I can't think of any camping trip I'd rather be on," stated Jerry. "This site is wilder, more isolated, and more pristine than any place I ever backpacked into back on Earth."

"It's simply amazing how far you have to travel these days to find good camping," stated Connie in a matter-of-fact tone.

Everyone chuckled at the innocence of Connie's remark. Then, Jerry said, "Camping here is going to be fun, so let's finish setting up our campsite. While the rest of you are transferring supplies to the shed, I will deploy the capsule's legs and adjust them to level it."

The capsule had landed on its heat shield, which was backed by shock absorbing material to cushion the landing impact. Since the capsule would almost always come to rest at an angle other than level, it was equipped with legs that could be deployed and adjusted to level it. The legs would be securely anchored to the ground and serve as a solid foundation to ensure that the capsule would be a sturdy home even during a wind storm.

After an hour of effort, the interstellar pioneers finished their jobs and sat down to eat lunch. "This is our first meal on Pioneer Island," Connie said. "And we have much to be thankful for. We are the first humans ever to complete an interstellar voyage. We've traveled a vast distance at fantastic speeds, and we've arrived here in good health. I think that's a very good reason for some joyful celebration."

"I do too," agreed Jerry.

"I have another big reason to be excited," Dianne said. "I am now living among a multitude of alien life-forms that I can study firsthand. This planet is a biologist's wonderland, and I intend to thoroughly explore the wonders of life."

"You'll have lots of help from the rest of us," stated Connie.

"I'm counting on that. It's a huge project that I can't do alone. Everything here is something new that we need to study."

"There is one big question that we need to answer for each life-form we encounter," stated Jerry. "And that is, does it pose any danger to us?"

"Except for our brief stay at B-2, that question hasn't concerned us in the last seven years," commented Dianne.

"Today marks the end of that part of our life," declared Moose. "Today is a turning point in our lives. It marks the end of the challenge of getting here and the beginning of the challenge of surviving and prospering now that we're here."

"One important aspect of that challenge is finding a way to provide ourselves with nutritious food," stated Dianne.

"That shouldn't be very difficult in view of all the plant and animal life that exists here," commented Jerry.

"Also, we have seeds for most of the basic food plants grown on Earth," stated Dianne. "I will analyze soil samples and experiment with growing some of them just as soon as I can."

"It'll be interesting to see how well Earth plants grow here, and how they react to alien diseases and parasites," Connie said.

"With a little genetic engineering, I should be able to give them defenses against most diseases and parasites," stated Dianne. "But they might not have any problems. We'll just have to grow them and find out."

"Speaking of food, I can't think of anything more wholesome or nutritious than delicious fresh fish," stated Moose. "With that indisputable fact in mind, I plan to begin my fish research tomorrow morning."

Being as obvious as she could, Dianne stared at Moose's fishing tackle neatly displayed in front of the shed and said, "I never would've guessed that you were planning to go fishing."

Moose smiled at his wife. "I admit it. I am eager to go fishing. Imagine the thrill of fishing where no one has ever fished before."

"That will be exciting," agreed Dianne.

"But I won't be doing it just for fun; it is a serious research project.

After all, fish are an immediate source of food. Unlike plants, we don't have to plant them and wait for them to grow up before we can eat them; they are already here. We just have to do some lab work on each species to make sure that they're nutritious and non-toxic."

"As far as time is concerned, your fish do have an advantage over my plants," admitted Dianne.

"Another thing that really excites me about my fish research is its immense potential because of the sheer size of Clear Lake. We're living in the middle 700 square miles of water! And it's connected to a huge ocean by a large river!"

"Your fish research might end up being far more exciting than you're expecting it to be," commented Jerry.

"Are you saying that because of something you saw underwater this morning?" questioned Moose.

"No, I was thinking about the pterodactyls. We've never seen them eat anything except fish. After you hook a fish, it might splash around on the surface while you're landing it. That will certainly get the attention of any pterodactyls that happen to see it. What happens next could be extremely exciting for you."

Looking a bit chagrined, Moose said, "Seeing a fish flopping around might be a bigger temptation than they can resist. One of them might try to grab it."

"And then, you might end up hooking a pterodactyl," stated Jerry. "That's one fish story you could take to your local tavern back on Earth and not be concerned about being outdone by anyone."

"Okay, I admit that your fish research could turn out to be a lot more exciting than my plant research," stated Dianne while laughing.

"You people are raising the possibility of a lot more excitement than I had in mind," Moose admitted. "I was just hoping to take the boat out tomorrow morning and enjoy catching a few fish. Then, if they check out in the lab, we can have fish for lunch."

"Whether we like it or not, the pterodactyls are part of our life," stated Jerry. "Sometimes they will inconvenience us, because their presence will force us to delay our plans. However, I think having the opportunity to study them is worth a little inconvenience."

After nodding in agreement, Moose suggested, "Why don't you come fishing with me tomorrow morning? When one of us is busy landing a fish, the other can be on alert."

"I was planning on asking myself along." Jerry smiled nonchalantly.

Sensing that Moose and Jerry were finished making their fishing plans, Connie said, "Sitting in this warm sunshine after a big meal is making me sleepy. I need a nap."

"As little as you slept last night, you should be sleepy," stated Jerry.

"You're right about that, and now, it's catching up to me."

"Well, the capsule is unpacked, and our bed is ready for use. If you're too tired to walk over there, I could carry you."

"I'm not disabled, just sleepy. Besides, I don't want to nap in our bed. I feel like enjoying the outdoors."

"What do you have in mind?" Jerry asked.

"I feel lazy, and I'd like to nap while sunbathing. The radiant heat coming from Alpha Centauri A really feels good, so does this gentle breeze. An outdoor nap would be most pleasant."

"Sounds like a recipe for a bad sunburn," commented Jerry.

"I have a bottle of sunscreen. Maybe you should take a break and give me a massage. I'll do the same for you. Let's enjoy some outdoor living."

Jerry briefly considered his work schedule. "I guess I have time to sit in the sun with you for a while." Pointing at Alpha Centauri A and Alpha Centauri B, Jerry said, "I've never been sunbathing with two suns."

"That alone will make this a novel experience," Connie said. Shifting her gaze to a huge boulder, she said, "There's a thick carpet of grass on the other side of that boulder. If we put down two air mattresses and cover them with beach towels, we should be comfortable and secluded."

Jerry looked at his watch. "I don't know if we'll be secluded. If I'm not mistaken, the Challenger should be passing overhead right about now, and they do have some very powerful optical equipment."

"By the time we get comfortable, they will have disappeared over the horizon and will no longer be able to watch us."

"True," agreed Jerry. "Let's get our rifles and the other things we need and go relax for a while."

Shortly after Connie and Jerry disappeared behind the gigantic boulder, Moose said, "Just in case they become preoccupied with each other and forget where they are, I think we should stay alert for danger."

Displaying a sly grin, Dianne said, "That's part of the plan."

"What plan are you talking about?"

"The one Connie and I put together when we were walking around."

"I thought you were out looking at the things that live in this area."

"We were, but we were also looking for a safe place to sunbathe. Safety is essential for one to be relaxed and carefree, so we included armed sentries in our sunbathing plans."

"When they return, are they going to stand guard for us?"

"What do you have in mind that will require armed guards?" teased Dianne.

Moose grinned. "I would love to be part of the erotic fantasy that you and Connie dreamed up."

"I'm happy we think alike."

After a few moments of silence in which Moose allowed his mind to drift into fantasyland, he asked, "How did you and Connie decide which couple would be the first to enjoy the pleasures of nude sunbathing?"

"We flipped a coin."

"How could you flip a coin? We don't have any coins."

"We had to improvise. We found a fairly flat pebble with distinctly different coloration on its two sides. I flipped it. Connie correctly called it and elected to be first."

"I wonder if Jerry knows that what he's doing at the moment was determined by the toss of a rock."

"It seems to me that you guys should be comfortable with that method of determining who makes the first play."

"What do you mean?"

"Back in your college football days, your games were always started with a coin toss."

"That's true, but at the moment, I don't think Captain J.J. is scrambling around trying to throw a touchdown pass."

"That's undoubtedly correct, but since he doesn't have to overcome any defense, I'm sure he'll score quite easily."

Moose smiled. "I'm glad you and Connie dreamed up this whole sunbathing thing. What a great way to enjoy this wild, scenic wonderland. Just thinking about it is getting me aroused."

"I can see that." Dianne smiled mischievously.

"You aren't supposed to be looking at my groin. After all, we are on guard duty."

"That's why I'm so alert to everything that's going on around me."

"You sure are quick-witted today. I can't seem to get ahead of you on anything."

"I'm in an elevated mood with my emotions running in several different directions all at once. I'm bubbling over with excitement. My happiness reservoir is filled to the brim and is overflowing every which way, obviously, because a lifelong dream has finally come true. Reasonable cause for being in a state of ecstasy, don't you think?"

"How could I possibly disagree? I'm also wildly excited."

"From what I can see, that's certainly true!"

"You're not going to miss an opportunity, are you?"

"No! I'm not! I'm happy, and I feel like having fun."

"So that's why you and Connie planned this erotic outdoor activity?"

"Well, can you think of a more delightful way to have fun and welcome ourselves to our new home?"

"Going fishing could be very exciting."

"Are you suggesting that we go fishing instead of nude sunbathing?" Dianne teased.

"No! I'm not!" Moose quickly exclaimed.

"I'm glad we cleared that up."

"Maybe we should try to conceive our first child in an outdoor setting, perhaps on a moonlit beach on a warm, pleasant evening."

"I like that idea. If nothing of consequence happens to us after living here for a couple months, I think we should do that."

"We've been waiting a long time to have children, but it was worth the wait. I think this island will prove to be an ideal place to raise a family. Two months should give us ample time to determine if it really is the safe place that we think it is."

During the next hour, Dianne and Moose continued discussing their new home and plans for the future. Their discussion was interrupted by the appearance of Jerry and Connie from behind the huge boulder. Eager for their turn, Moose and Dianne began walking toward them. When they met, Dianne looked at them and smiled. "You two sure look content."

Jerry and Connie looked into each other's eyes for a few moments and silently shared the deep love and happiness that was an integral part of their marriage. Then, Jerry said, "Thanks for standing guard and giving us the opportunity to relax and enjoy ourselves."

"It was just a flashback in time," responded Moose.

"What do you mean?" Jerry asked.

"Back in our football days, I was pretty good at protecting you."

"I can't argue that point, but I can return the favor by protecting you. So why don't you and Dianne relax and enjoy yourselves."

Faking formality, Moose turned to his wife and said, "You heard the Captain's orders!"

They faced Jerry, stood rigidly at attention, smartly saluted, and marched off in the direction of the large boulder. Jerry and Connie laughed at the sight of Dianne and Moose formally marching in unison.

"In view of that bit of clowning around, I believe they are in the perfect mood to enjoy themselves," commented Connie.

"I think so too," agreed Jerry.

While alertly looking for danger, Jerry and Connie walked back to the habitation capsule. When they arrived, Jerry did a panoramic scan of Stellar Plateau looking for anything threatening, but the plateau was peaceful. Jerry searched for pterodactyls in flight, but he found only a beautiful blue sky containing a few fluffy cumulus clouds. Feeling safe, he turned to Connie and feasted his eyes on her scantily clothed body. "You sure look good," he said.

"I feel good, I'm happy to be here, and I am still basking in the afterglow of the tender loving attention you just gave me. I think my pleasure was magnified because of where we are."

"We were sharing the joy we feel at finally arriving here after a very long journey, and the risk of unknown danger showing up added some extra excitement."

"That very real risk made me feel like we were engaging in forbidden sex," commented Connie.

"Now that you put it that way, I did feel like we were getting away with something." Jerry gave his wife an affectionate hug. "Speaking of risking danger and getting away with it; that was quite a stunt you pulled when you dove into the lake this morning."

"But it really wasn't an irresponsible act. Mike and his assistants did a thorough job exploring the water around this island with the marine explorer, and they didn't find anything that appeared threatening."

"Appeared is the key word in that statement," countered Jerry. "Piranha don't appear very threatening either when they're peacefully swimming around."

"Okay, you make a good point."

"However, now that the point has been made, I admit that it was fun."

"Are you suggesting that by diving into the lake, I put fun and excitement into your life by just being myself?"

"You sure got my attention in a hurry!"

"And you just admitted that it was fun."

Jerry recalled how happy and satisfying his marriage to Connie had been over the years. "You almost always make me happy by just being yourself. Pleasing me seems to be a natural talent of yours."

"All the love and respect you've given me over the years has made me feel so secure in our relationship that making you happy is something I like to do. Seeing you happy makes me feel good."

"Giving you love and respect is easy. You just seem to draw it out of me."

"That must be another one of my natural talents."

"You are a very talented woman. When you decided to knock me off my feet in the medical lab years ago, I was unable to resist your talents."

"As I recall, you didn't put up much of a struggle."

"I had no chance; I was already in love with you."

"I was in love with you too, and I'm glad I was able to knock you off your feet. We were meant for each other. We've had a wonderful life together, and now, we're here with a great future to enjoy."

"We're fortunate to have a special relationship on which to build our future. One of the things I really like about being married to you is that I can just be myself, and you are happy with me as I am. I don't have to try to be something that I'm not."

"That goes both ways. You also accept me as I am, and that's important, because being true to oneself, especially in a marriage, is essential to achieving personal happiness."

"Is that your professional opinion, Doctor?"

"I do sound rather formal at times, don't I?"

"Yes, you do."

"I don't mean to, but it's sometimes difficult to separate my professional life from my personal life."

"I wasn't suggesting that you should. I was just teasing you a bit."

"Despite your teasing, I do have some strong opinions on marriage and family."

"I would never have guessed that."

"You're teasing me again, but that's okay, because I know that your thoughts about marriage and family are compatible with mine. We have a great relationship, and our society will be off to a very good start if all the people on this mission end up in marriages as good as ours. Traditional families filled with the love, security, and mutual respect that we have will give our society a solid foundation to grow on."

"Is that another professional opinion, Doctor?"

"Most definitely! And it's valid too. You only have to look at the history of the U.S. to find out about the problems that can occur with the breakdown of the traditional family."

"I haven't done that, but there can be little doubt that children have a much easier time growing up and becoming responsible adults when their parents have a peaceful, loving relationship based on mutual respect."

"Children do thrive on security and happiness," stated Connie.

"Denise and our future children will get plenty of both."

"Speaking of our future children, I would like to have a fairly large family. And I see no reason why we can't, since I'm in excellent health and have at least a dozen child-bearing years left."

"You are the doctor in the family, so I'm assuming that's a valid professional opinion."

"It is."

"I wonder how Denise will react to having some brothers and sisters to contend with."

Thinking about Denise, Connie said, "She has been the center of our attention for a long time, but if we share the excitement of a baby with her, so that she feels included, I'm sure she'll do just fine."

"She might even be as thrilled about it as we'll be."

"Can you image how excited she'll be when we bring her down here in a couple months?" Connie asked.

"With her overly active curiosity, it's going to be a fulltime job just to follow her around and answer her questions. But before we bring the children down, we have to be certain that it's safe for them to be here. Big creatures, like the pterodactyls, are easy to see and can be dealt with by armed sentries. What worries me the most are small creatures that are able to inject painful or even lethal venom. How do we guard against them when we don't know what they are or if they even exist?"

"You make a good point. People on Earth have that knowledge because it was learned by the painful experience of thousands of generations. But we must gain this essential information quickly."

"That's a big job," stated Jerry. "We have to learn in two months what our ancestors learned in thousands of years."

"Basically, we have to capture every new organism we find, take it to the lab, and check it out. Even though this is a small island, there are probably hundreds, maybe even thousands of different species of bugs living here; plus all the small mammals, reptiles, and birds."

"Biological research is definitely our top priority."

"And we are part of that research by virtue of being here. During the next thirty days, I will give each one of us a daily medical evaluation, and to make my medical research meaningful, we need to experience this environment to the greatest degree possible."

"Is that why you dove into the lake this morning?"

"No! I just had the urge to go swimming, something I haven't done in a long time. But that is a good example of soaking up this environment. Microorganisms in the water were given an opportunity to enter our bodies. But in view of the kinds of microbes our robot lab tests have discovered in that water, I will be surprised if we suffer any ill-effects."

"That water seemed so fresh and clean. In fact, it even tasted good."

"You swallowed some of it!" exclaimed Connie, sounding shocked.

"I admit that it wasn't a wise thing to do, but I accidentally got some of it in my mouth, and it tasted so good that I decided to swallow it. I'm really not too worried about getting sick; after all, I am living with a competent doctor."

"But I think we should run more tests before we start drinking it."

"Perhaps more testing and exploration should've been done before we went swimming in it," suggested Jerry.

"I guess we were both a little too hasty, probably the result of suddenly being confronted by the great outdoors after being confined for a long time."

Jerry nodded.

"Now that Pioneer Island is our home, I'd like to enjoy lots of outdoor living, including going swimming every day."

"I would too, but we might be swimming with piranhas. We just don't know."

"I have an idea how we can discover if any of the fish in East Bay are voracious feeders."

"What do you have in mind?" Jerry asked.

"It seems reasonable to expect that voracious feeders would go into a frenzy if we present them with the scent of blood. I do have a supply of each of our blood types, and I think I can safely spare some of it for a potentially life-saving experiment. If you will design and build a blood dispenser that we can suspend 10 to 20 feet below our marine explorer, the rest will be easy. Whenever the marine explorer passes over a school of fish, we simply squirt out some blood and observe their behavior. If they become wildly excited and seek out and attack the source of the blood, then swimming in the lake could be dangerous. If the blood has no effect on them, I wouldn't expect them to attack us when we're swimming."

"Your reasoning seems valid, and the experiment will be easy to conduct. When would you like to do it?"

"As soon as we can, I enjoy swimming, and I've only been once in the last seven years."

"The device will be easy to make. It's essentially nothing more than a remotely operated squirt gun. I will improvise something after tomorrow morning's fishing trip; then, we can begin experimenting with it."

"It shouldn't take more than a few days to tempt every species of fish in the bay," stated Connie. "If we don't get any meaningful reaction from any of them, I will feel quite safe going swimming."

"It may not be totally safe, but I don't know of any risk-free way to discover all possible dangers. At some point, we simply have to dive in and take our chances. However, I don't want you to go swimming alone. I want to be with you. And until we know that it's not necessary, we will be armed when we're swimming."

"Carrying weapons while swimming will be a bit cumbersome and will take some of the fun out of it."

"That's true, but I don't see any way to avoid it. Clear Lake is large, deep, and connected to an ocean. It seems like large marine predators must exist somewhere in all that water. The question is: do any of them ever come near Pioneer Island?"

"It'll take at least a year to answer that question with any degree of certainty, especially, since many animals have seasonal migration cycles."

"Unfortunately, I think your time estimate is correct," agreed Jerry.

"It's not completely unfortunate. There is a benefit to this."

"What is it?"

"I'll have you with me when I go swimming, and that'll be a lot more fun than swimming alone."

"It'll be fun for both of us, and I'm sure Moose and Dianne will want to join us. For added safety, we can take ..."

Connie urgently interrupted Jerry. "Two pterodactyls are over East Bay!" she exclaimed while instantly getting her rifle ready to fire.

Jerry quickly turned to look at them while bringing his rifle to the ready position. Connie exclaimed, "They appeared above Eastern Island so suddenly that they must've approached it flying low and fast popping up at the last instant to get over it. Now they're gliding back down toward the water. Why are they flying so low and fast?"

"I don't know, but they're going to pass over our shuttle. With their size and strength, they could damage it if they choose to."

"I hope they don't decide to head directly at us!" exclaimed Connie. "As fast as they're flying, they could be on top of us in mere seconds."

"They are flying at least sixty mph, maybe even seventy."

As the two pterodactyls popped up to clear the narrow neck of land separating East Bay from West Bay, Connie said, "I guess they weren't the least bit interested in our shuttle."

Watching them fly over West Bay, Jerry said, "Apparently, they aren't interested in us either."

"You sound disappointed."

"We humans have become accustomed to thinking of ourselves as the dominant species, the center of everything. Being totally ignored by these creatures is a little deflating."

"I don't mind being a little deflated," stated Connie. "And I hope they continue to ignore us. I wonder if they would've ignored us if we'd been in the water. The suddenness with which they appeared is tending to dampen my desire to go swimming."

"Why? The possibility of them showing up just adds a little extra adventure to it."

"But I don't need all that adventure. I just want to enjoy a good swim now and then."

"I do too, but the possibility of being eaten by airborne creatures in addition to the possible existence of marine predators does turn swimming into a high-risk activity."

"It's a dramatic contrast to my childhood days when my mother used to warn me about the risk of drowning," commented Connie.

"The possibility of drowning seems to be the least of our worries."

"The fact that pterodactyls can appear so suddenly is frightening."

"The danger we face from them might be greater than we thought," stated Jerry. "Their low-level, high-speed flying ability combined with their ability to instantly pop up and over obstacles is impressive. A stealth approach based on these capabilities would allow them to attack prey on the far side of a hilltop with little or no warning."

"But how would they know there's prey on the far side of a hilltop?"

"They spot it while they appear to be innocently circling at high altitude. Then, they leave the area while mentally mapping the attack route to their prey. Within minutes of leaving, they could return and attack their prey with virtually no warning."

"Do you think they're intelligent enough to do all of that?"

"I don't know, but if they are, they present a deadly threat to us."

Connie looked worried. "I wonder if we'll ever be able to go swimming, or do anything for that matter, without the presence of alert armed guards."

"Until we've been here long enough to understand all the dangers we face, we don't have any choice. We have to always be armed and alert."

With her gaze intently fixed on the pterodactyls, Connie said, "Despite the possible risk they pose, I don't mind having them around. They are fascinating creatures to observe."

"They certainly are. What do you think this pair is up to?"

"Judging from the way they're circling Western Island, I think they're looking for a place to land."

"The obvious place would be at the top of that rock cliff near the island's north end. But why are they investigating it so carefully? What are they looking for?"

"There are two possibilities that come to mind," responded Connie. "Either they're hungry and are searching for prey, or they're preparing to land and are searching for enemies."

"It doesn't seem like they could be searching for enemies. These islands just don't have enough prey on them to support a predator that is large enough to be a serious threat to pterodactyls."

"That sounds reasonable, but they are inspecting that cliff top. If they're not searching for an enemy, what do you think they're doing?"

"The high-speed way they flew directly to Western Island raises another possibility," responded Jerry. "Maybe it's their home, and they've been gone for a while. Maybe they're inspecting it to see if anything has changed since they left. Maybe they're going to build a nest over there."

"If they nest over there, are we going to be comfortable having a family of pterodactyls that close to us?"

"That will depend entirely on their attitude toward us. Until we know what that is, their presence will require us to be alert."

"In other words, they'll do us a favor by forcing us to do what we should be doing anyway," commented Connie.

"It looks like they've completed their inspection of the island," Jerry said. "They're landing on the cliff top."

"If they do nest over there, then sooner or later, they'll discover us."

"When that happens, I wonder if they'll recognize that we're something new in their environment, and if they'll try to determine if we pose a threat to them."

"I hope the answer to that question is more important to them than whether or not we're good to eat," Connie quickly said.

At that moment, Moose and Dianne returned. Noticing that Connie and Jerry weren't paying much attention to them, Moose asked, "What are you two so preoccupied with?"

To answer the question, Connie handed Moose the binoculars she had been using and then pointed at the pair of pterodactyls perched on the Western Island cliff top. While Moose and Dianne took turns using the binoculars, Connie and Jerry briefed them on the activities of the pair.

After a short period of discussion, Jerry said, "I think it's time to finish making our home livable."

"In other words, it's time for us to hook up our water supply," responded Moose.

"Yes and our wives will accompany us and do guard duty."

Jerry and Moose removed two rolls of collapsed, lightweight hose from the shed. Even though the hose was light, it was tough and durable because it was made from high-tensile-strength fibers embedded in tough pliable plastic. Each roll contained 600 feet of hose.

Two water tanks were located above the capsule's second floor: one for hot water and one for cold water. The smaller of the two tanks had been used as a storage compartment for the capsule's high-speed parachute and would now be used for cold water storage. The larger of the two tanks had served as a storage compartment for the capsule's large para-wing and would now be used as a hot water tank.

After connecting one end to the capsule, Moose and Jerry laid the hose to the edge of the plateau, down the rockslide, through the forest, and across the sandy beach. They took great care to lay the hose in such a way as to minimize the risk of it being accidentally punctured.

Then, with Dianne and Connie standing guard, Moose and Jerry pushed the small inflated boat into the water and rowed out to the shuttle. They entered the shuttle and removed their water supply system's pump, its solar power plant, and its inlet filtration system. After rowing back to the beach, they set up this equipment.

Next, they turned on the pump's radio receiver, which would receive on/off signals from the habitation capsule. With a transmitter, Jerry sent a command to the capsule to turn on the water system. The capsule immediately sent a signal to the pump. The pump's electric motor hummed to life, and fresh, clear lake water entered the collapsed hose. The pioneers watched the collapsed hose swell to its full 1.25-inch diameter as the water progressed up it toward the capsule.

"Looks like we'll be able to take hot showers tonight," Dianne said.

"I don't know how hot they'll be," responded Jerry. "The hot water tank is fairly large and it will take time to heat that much water. It's getting so late in the day that the solar heat exchanger won't get much heat from Alpha Centauri A until tomorrow. Also, our solar cells won't produce much electricity until tomorrow."

"I guess we'll be taking lukewarm showers tonight," Dianne said.

"That's a reasonable guess," agreed Jerry.

"Right now, I'm more concerned about food than taking a shower," stated Moose. "All the activity since lunchtime has made me hungry."

"You're always hungry," responded Jerry.

"Lunch was more than four hours ago. I should be hungry."

Faking an air of disbelief, Jerry silently stared at Moose. After enduring the stare for a few moments, Moose said, "If you're trying to convince me that I shouldn't be hungry, it's not working."

Jerry grinned. "Actually, I'm hungry too, but there's one more thing I think we should do before we eat."

"What?" Moose asked.

"I think we should remove the few remaining things that we still have in the shuttle and send it back up to the Challenger."

"That will leave us stranded here with no quick way to leave, if we need to," Connie said.

"That's true," agreed Jerry. "But there are creatures on this planet that are large enough to wreck our shuttle, and I don't believe it would be wise to leave it anchored here and exposed to that risk. It is a critical piece of equipment."

Everyone considered Jerry's proposal, and all reluctantly nodded in agreement. Then, they entered the boat and rowed out to the shuttle.

While Moose and Jerry were in the cockpit preparing the shuttle for takeoff, Dianne and Connie transferred the few remaining supplies and personal items to the boat. After a half-hour, everyone returned to shore.

The shuttle rested low in the water, because its propellant tanks were now full of water. The water would be pumped through the shuttle's nuclear reactor where it would be instantly converted into extremely high-temperature, high-pressure water vapor that would expand out the shuttle's rocket nozzle. The shuttle's nuclear thermal rocket could accelerate it to orbital speed and altitude in less than ten minutes.

While the interstellar pioneers stood on the beach and watched, the personnel shuttle came to life under the direction of its flight control computer. Both anchors were lifted into the fuselage, and their hatches were closed. With a high-pitched whine and a muffled roar, the steam turbine came to life and its power fed into the shuttle's propeller, which began churning the water under the tail. At a speed of ten mph, the shuttle taxied out of East Bay and into open water. Then, with full power delivered to the propeller, the shuttle rapidly gained speed, rose up on its hydrofoils, and glided above the water at 45 mph. Suddenly, the powerful NTR boomed into action with a loud thundering roar quickly accelerating the shuttle to takeoff velocity. In less than a minute, it reached the cold upper atmosphere where the water vapor from the NTR condensed into a brilliant white vapor trail.

When the shuttle was out of sight, Connie said, "It's gone."

Noting that his wife sounded like she felt abandoned, Jerry said, "We can bring it back anytime."

"I know, but that's not the same as having it anchored right out there in the bay. Maybe it's just a psychological thing, but I feel like the umbilical cord has been cut and that we're now dependent on this planet. In other words, this is now our home!"

"Watching the shuttle leave certainly does reinforce that feeling," agreed Jerry.

"Food would reinforce my feeling that this is our home," Moose said.

Turning to Dianne, Connie said, "I think your husband is hungry, and it seems like we just had lunch."

Before Dianne could comment, Moose blurted out, "Lunch was five hours ago, and I'm starving!"

"Has it really been that long?" teased Dianne.

Looking at his wife, Moose said, "I suppose you're going to try to convince me that you're not hungry."

Dianne smiled. "Actually, it has been a long exciting afternoon, and my stomach is rumbling on empty at the moment."

"So what are we waiting for? Let's go eat," stated Jerry, as he began hiking in the direction of the plateau.

A short time later, the pioneers were seated at a table in front of their home. "What a pleasant evening for an outdoor dinner!" exclaimed Dianne who was wearing shorts and a sleeveless blouse.

"I could become addicted to outdoor living," Connie said.

"The kind of weather we're having today could cause me to join you in that addiction," stated Dianne.

"Yeah, I know what you mean. Our high temp was 83, and it's still 75. It doesn't get much better than that."

"The huge lake that surrounds us is going to have a moderating effect on temperature swings," Jerry said. "We're going to have warm summers that don't get unbearably hot, and mild winters that rarely ever have temperatures below freezing."

"Moderate climate is one of the big reasons we selected this area," stated Moose. "We should have lots of pleasant weather to enjoy."

When Jerry was finished eating, he stood up, looked to the west, and said, "We're about to experience a peculiar event relative to our past, but one that will be common place in our future."

After waiting a few moments for everyone to look to the west, Jerry continued, "This evening, we'll see our first double sunset. In a few minutes, Alpha Centauri A will disappear below the horizon. However, it's not going to get dark, because Alpha Centauri B won't set for nearly two hours."

"That's going to feel strange and take some getting use to," stated Connie. "Where we come from, it gets dark soon after sunset."

"It's going to seem weird for a while," agreed Jerry.

While the interstellar pioneers looked on in silence, Alpha Centauri A slowly slipped below the horizon. The brilliant yellow fireball that had dominated the sky and brightly lit the day was now out of sight. A much smaller appearing orange fireball, Alpha Centauri B, now dominated the sky. Even though it was currently about 25 times more distant from Alcent than Alpha Centauri A, its soft orange light was still many times brighter than the Full Moon in Earth's nighttime sky.

"It's been such a long time since I've enjoyed a beautiful sunset that I've almost forgotten the special aura that surrounds it," Connie said. "It is a time of transition. The harsh, brilliant glare of daylight is replaced by the soft glow of twilight. The heat of the day slowly surrenders to the coolness of the night. The sounds of the daytime creatures are gradually replaced by the sounds of the nocturnal creatures. Watching this brings back some fond memories from Earth, a planet that we'll never see again."

While the pioneers shared nostalgic memories from the distant planet Earth, Alpha Centauri A slipped so far below the horizon that the soft glow of twilight became so dim that it was no longer noticeable. And Alpha Centauri B became the only light source of consequence, and some very unearthly lighting effects became quite prominent.

"This is eerie," Dianne said. "All the colors of the landscape have taken on an orange tinge, giving everything a mysterious sense of unreality. I wonder how long it's going to take for this to feel normal."

Looking at her arms, Connie said, "Even my skin has taken on an orange hue, almost as if I've contracted some sort of skin disease."

"You should probably see a doctor about that," suggested Jerry.

"You seem to have developed the same condition," replied Connie. "Perhaps, we should see the same doctor."

"I've never had orange tinted skin before. Do you think it might be a serious allergic reaction to our new environment?"

"One thing I learned early on in medicine is that things aren't always as serious as they appear. Once we get used to this condition, I doubt that we'll even notice it."

"When you two are finished with your verbal trivia, perhaps we could go for a walk and explore this plateau," suggested Moose.

Jerry and Connie gave each other a puzzled look. "Apparently, Moose is in a serious frame of mind and isn't able to appreciate the fun we're able to have with silly small-talk," Connie said.

"He's always been rather serious and restrained when confronted by a strange new situation," noted Jerry. "It just seems like he's never really been able to relax and have fun with something new and unexpected."

"What do you mean?" objected Moose. "I've always been fun-loving and adventurous. That's why I would like to explore this plateau while we have this strange, weird kind of light. It'll be like an exotic stroll in the moonlight, only this light is much brighter than a Full Moon, but still so subdued that it has a romantic sense of unreality about it. That orange glow just makes everything look weird. Even the sky has an orange tint to it, and the clouds that have been white all day are now a creamy orange."

"Sounds like you're really emotional about this," Jerry said.

"I've waited a long time to arrive here, and now that I'm here, I plan to enjoy it to the fullest," declared Moose.

"Well, if you feel that strongly about something as simple as going for a walk, I suppose we could do it," responded Jerry.

"That nonchalant attitude that you're trying so hard to display doesn't fool me a bit," exclaimed Moose. "You're just as excited about being here as I am."

Having gotten all the expected reactions from Moose, Jerry chuckled with satisfaction and asked, "Do you have any objectives in mind for this exploratory walk?"

"On Charlie's first night here, Dianne and I used him to make an imaginary walk in the moonlight. I know that we don't have moonlight now, but I would like to retrace his steps."

"In other words, you'd like to turn an imaginary stroll in the moonlight into the real thing," Jerry said.

"That's what we want to do," stated Moose and Dianne in unison.

"So this is an experiment to find out if the real thing is more fun and exciting than your imaginary walk was," commented Jerry.

"Is there any doubt that the real thing will be better?" Moose asked.

"Sometimes, anticipation combined with imagination makes an imaginary experience better than the real thing," responded Jerry.

"Well, I guess it's up to us to make reality as good as the fantasy was," stated Dianne.

After picking up their rifles, the pioneers headed toward South Bay with Charlie in the lead. They walked at a relaxed pace, occasionally pausing to investigate a shrub, a wild flower, or a peculiar kind of grass. Birds and insects received similar attention. Even the texture and coloration of rocks were discussed in speculation of their mineral content.

"I like the openness of this plateau," commented Connie. "It doesn't give predators very many places to wait in ambush."

"As far as we know, there aren't any predators here that are big enough for us to worry about except for the pterodactyls," Dianne said.

"Until we've thoroughly explored this island, I don't think we should rule out the possible presence of dangerous animals," argued Connie. "For example, omnivorous creatures like the black bears that live on Earth could be quite content on the islands in this lake, particularly if they enjoy swimming and have some fishing skills."

"Good point," admitted Dianne. "Pregnant females might even swim to an isolated island to raise their young away from the huge T-Rexes."

"A bear-like creature probably wouldn't have any trouble climbing the rockslide at the north end of this plateau," stated Moose.

"Like I said a few moments ago, I'm glad this plateau is so open," reiterated Connie.

"Your point is legitimate," agreed Jerry.

"The three small groves on this plateau are the only hiding places of consequence," Moose said. "Perhaps this would be a good opportunity to explore them."

"I'd rather do that during the full light of day," stated Jerry. "This dim orange light is adequate in open areas, but I believe it's too dark in those groves to explore them safely."

"I think we should just walk to the south end of this plateau and enjoy the view," suggested Dianne.

"I like that idea," declared Connie.

A few minutes later, they arrived at their destination. Looking out over the water, Connie said, "The south end of the lake is so far away that it's indistinguishable from the land and sky. It all just seems to blend together."

"It's nearly 20 miles away," stated Jerry. "And this lighting is rather subdued. Also, the sky reflects off the water making it impossible to tell where the water ends and the sky begins."

"This viewpoint makes it obvious how large this lake really is and what an important part of our lives it's going to be," Connie said.

"I like the way it isolates us from the big predators," stated Jerry.

"But a bear-like creature that enjoys swimming could still reach us," argued Connie. "Swimming from one island to the next, it wouldn't have to swim more than three miles at a time. Give this animal fur consisting of hollow hair with sealed ends, and it would have the ability to float. That would make swimming very easy."

"Why are you so convinced that this kind of creature might exist?" questioned Jerry.

"I keep thinking about how carefully that pair of pterodactyls investigated Western Island before they landed. The existence of bear-like creatures would explain their caution."

"Such a creature would have to be fairly large to be a serious threat to pterodactyls," stated Jerry. "The adults would have to weigh at least 400 to 500 pounds."

"That would make them large enough for us to worry about," stated Moose. "And females with young could be very dangerous."

"Even though we don't have any direct evidence that such a creature exists, I think we should assume that it does until we prove otherwise," Dianne said. "Life does seek to be ubiquitous, and if given enough time, evolution will develop a life-form to fill every possible niche."

Speaking to Dianne, Jerry said, "I want you to have one of your assistants take a good look at the animals we've discovered so far to see if any of them might fit into the role we've been discussing."

Making eye contact with everyone in turn, Jerry continued, "If large animals have been visiting these islands regularly, we should be able to find clues to indicate that. Let's be alert for them."

"If pregnant females come to these islands to bear and raise their young, this might be the time of the year that they do that," speculated Connie. "It is springtime, and using Earth's animals as a guide, many do deliver their young during spring."

"In other words, we may soon meet these creatures, if they exist," commented Jerry.

"I think that's a reasonable assumption," responded Connie.

"Is it possible such a creature might already be here?" Jerry asked.

"Let's keep in mind that I marched Charlie the length and breadth of this island during the past week," stated Moose. "And he wasn't bothered by anything except insects."

"A female with babies probably would've avoided him unless he'd directly confronted her," argued Connie. "We need to look for them."

"Most large animals need water," Jerry said. "Unless pools or springs exist in the forest, they have to drink from the lake. If there are any large animals here, we should be able to find tracks on the beaches, since most of them are sandy. I think we should walk around the island tomorrow and see what we can find. We need to explore the place anyway."

"We might take some surveillance cameras with us and set them up at key points to monitor long stretches of open beach," suggested Connie.

"Good idea," agreed Jerry.

"I was planning to go fishing tomorrow," stated Moose.

"I think you could delay that for a day," responded Jerry. "The fish aren't going to go anywhere."

"But I'm hungry for fresh fish."

"I am too, but we need to inspect our beaches for tracks. If dangerous animals live here, we need to find them and see what they look like."

"I hope we don't get killed looking for them."

"We'll be on full alert."

After a pause in the conversation, Dianne and Connie wandered off to investigate a flowering bush. A gentle breeze had carried the blossoming bush's perfume to them. It reminded them of the rich pleasing fragrance of a lilac in full bloom.

Meanwhile, Jerry silently gazed out over the lake deeply lost in thought. Noticing the mood that had engulfed his best friend, Moose said, "It certainly does have an adventurous appeal to it."

"Yes, it does. I was just thinking about how much fun it would be to be out there in a sailboat when there's a good stiff breeze. It's been a long time since I've heard the pop of a sail and felt the wind whip through my hair with the sun beating down on my back."

Jerry's comments and the enchanting appeal of the huge lake brought memories of sailing adventures among the islands of the South Pacific to the forefront of Moose's mind. After a few moments of reveling in these fond memories from the distant planet Earth, Moose said, "I wish we could spend the next few days roaming around this lake in a sailboat."

"I do too, but unfortunately, we have higher priority things to do, and we don't have a sailboat."

"Our research submarine converts into a sailboat. We could have it put on the cargo shuttle and sent down."

"It's scheduled to be brought down in thirty days with the next group of people coming down. Are you proposing that we bring it down sooner, so we can start having fun with it?"

"There are other reasons to have it here besides having fun."

"Such as?"

"It would aid me in my fish research. I could go anywhere without

211

being exposed to the danger that I face in our small open boat. That little submarine is a rugged vessel. If pterodactyls were to show up, I could retreat to the sub's interior and close the hatch. Also, if we had the sub here, we could begin exploring the 700 square miles of underwater world that surrounds our island."

"You make a good case for bringing it down earlier than scheduled. But before we do that, we should explore this island thoroughly enough to convince ourselves that it doesn't have any hidden dangers."

"How long will that take?"

"Three square miles of thick forest will take some time to explore, but the only question we need to answer immediately is whether or not any dangerous animals live here."

"It shouldn't take more than a few days to do that," stated Moose.

"Then, we'll need a few days to finish setting up our equipment; the highest priority item being the wind-powered electrical generator."

"Assembling it shouldn't take more than a day."

"Also, we should work with our wives for a few days to help them with their medical and biological research."

"Adding it all up, it seems like we should be ready to bring that sub down in about two weeks," concluded Moose.

Sounding optimistic, Jerry said, "Perhaps, even a few days sooner than that."

"Wouldn't it be exciting to ride the sub over to Sauropod Meadow and watch those huge creatures come to the edge of the lake to drink?"

"That would be an awesome experience, like a scene out of a science fiction movie, only this will be real."

"I wonder how close to them we could get without alarming them."

After a little thought, Jerry replied, "A field mouse looks upon a house cat as a mortal enemy, but a deer totally ignores a house cat."

"Are you trying to say that a 200,000-pound creature would ignore a 250-pound creature no matter how close it got?" Moose asked.

"I think that's a pretty good possibility. On Earth, humans are the dominant species. Almost everything else fears us. Here on Alcent, that's not the case. I don't think those sauropods would be alarmed no matter how close we got to them. In fact, we could probably wander among them and they wouldn't bother us as long as we didn't act threatening."

"That sounds like a reasonable theory. When are you going to test it?"

Jerry grinned at Moose. "Not much over an hour ago, you adamantly claimed to be an adventurous person. So I thought you might eagerly jump right into this opportunity for some real adventure."

"I like adventure, but I haven't yet lost my mind," retorted Moose.

"But you just said that my theory sounds reasonable."

"Agreeing with your theory shouldn't be interpreted as volunteering to test it."

"But can you imagine what it would be like to be the first human to wander in the midst of 100-ton dinosaurs? What a trip that would be!"

"It would definitely be a thrilling trip," stated Moose. "But I don't think I could get the approval of my travel agent."

"What travel agent?"

"The one standing over there next to your wife."

"She seems to be a reasonable person," commented Jerry. "I think you could convince her, if you use the right approach."

"Why don't you show me how it's done by convincing your wife that it would be safe for us to wander among the sauropods, and then tell her that you're thinking about trying it."

"I think I'll wait until we're observing the sauropods from the submarine," replied Jerry. "Then, when our wives start exclaiming how huge those creatures are, I will throw out the suggestion that we go ashore to find out if we can wander among them and be ignored by them because we're so small compared to them."

"It'll be fun to see how they react to that proposal."

After chuckling in anticipation of the reaction they expected to get from their wives, Moose and Jerry returned to silently viewing various points of interest in their new world, each lost in thought. Shortly, their wives returned to their sides to enjoy with them the few remaining minutes of the strange, eerie light that preceded the second sunset of the day.

Alpha Centauri B now hung low over the western horizon casting a straight path of reflected orange light off the surface of the lake. This pathway of reflected light seemed to form a soft glowing avenue connecting the south end of Pioneer Island to the western shore of Clear Lake. To complete the exotic scene, the orange light of Alpha Centauri B also colored a large part of the western sky with a soft orange glow that reflected off the lake on either side of the radiant avenue of reflected light.

As if this eerie light weren't already enough to create an unearthly scene, a pair of pterodactyls arrived and began skillfully performing aerial maneuvers. Pulling out of steep dives at the last instant, performing vertical loops, barrel rolls, and banking into tight turns; the pterodactyls playfully demonstrated their skills. At times, their fifty-foot wingspans were fully silhouetted against the soft orange background light, readily revealing their immense size.

"What a wild primitive scene!" Connie exclaimed. "It's absolutely spectacular! And filled with danger! I feel small and vulnerable! Those pterodactyls could be on us in seconds, if they choose to attack." While speaking, Connie flicked off the safety switch on her rifle and held it firmly in a position that would allow her to respond quickly to an attack.

"Even though they're big and fast, we certainly have adequate firepower to defeat them if they attack," stated Jerry.

"Yes," agreed Connie. "But today is the first time in my life that I've had to face such awesome creatures, and it's a bit frightening."

"At the moment, they don't seem to be interested in us," observed Jerry. "So let's just stay alert and enjoy the show they're putting on."

"And what a show it is," commented Moose. "I'm almost convinced that they're engaged in some sort of stunt flying competition. But if they're smart enough to plan and carry out something that complicated, then we're dealing with some pretty intelligent creatures."

"It's possible that they're doing nothing more complicated than playing Follow-The-Leader, a simple game that young children play," Dianne said.

"You might be correct," responded Moose. "But I get the feeling that intelligent planning is behind the sequences of maneuvers they're executing. There seems to be a purpose to them."

"That's a possibility," admitted Dianne. "But it's also possible that it's nothing more than instinct. They might just be doing something that their ancestors have been doing for millions of years."

"In any case, I am amazed that such large creatures could have such remarkable flying agility," commented Moose.

"In order for them to do these complicated aerobatics with such skill and precision, they must have tremendous physical strength, an excellent sense of balance, and a superb flight control system," stated Jerry.

"In biological terms, that would be a highly capable brain and an excellent network of nerves that are able to rapidly carry messages between brain tissue and muscle tissue," stated Dianne.

Jerry grinned at Dianne. "I've never heard a flight control system described quite that way, but it definitely applies to these creatures."

"In an indirect way, you just agreed with me that these pterodactyls are intelligent," Moose said, while looking at Dianne with an air of smug satisfaction.

"What do you mean?" questioned Dianne.

"Saying that they have highly capable brains is nearly the same as saying that they're intelligent."

"Having brains that are able to control intricate muscle movements doesn't necessarily mean they're intelligent," argued Dianne.

"I am willing to bet that they are," retorted Moose. "Would you like to make a wager that they aren't?"

"Before I can accept that offer, you have to tell me what level of intelligence you think they have."

"I think they're capable of planning activities in advance," Moose responded. "I believe they're capable of elementary analytical thought to solve simple problems. And I think they can handle simple numbers. For example, if they saw seven animals enter a forest and five of them leave the forest, they would know that two remain in the forest."

"There's a reasonable chance that they do have that level of intelligence, so I'm not going to bet with you."

Moose smiled, silently feeling like he'd won the argument. "We don't have proof yet," Dianne said, while noticing his expression.

Observing that Moose and Dianne's debate had run its course, Jerry said, "If pterodactyls are intelligent enough to think and solve problems, then we face a very dangerous enemy if they decide that we are a menace to them and must be eliminated."

"If that's the case, then we'll have to use our weapons to teach them to respect us and leave us alone," declared Moose.

"But if they're intelligent, they might also prove to be good-natured and fun-loving," suggested Connie. "Every time I've seen them flying, they've appeared to be having fun."

"Creatures that enjoy living tend to be good-natured," stated Dianne. "If pterodactyls are good-natured, then the ones that get to know us should end up trusting us if we never give them a reason not to. To gain and keep their trust, we might even provide them with some valuable benefits."

"It would be wonderful to have them be allies who like us, rather than, enemies who respect us," Connie said. "Imagine how much easier it would be to raise children in this hostile environment if one of them decided to perform the role of guard dog."

"Having a flying guard dog with a fifty-foot wingspan would take some getting use to," responded Dianne. "But it would certainly be preferable to the alternative."

Making eye contact with Moose and chuckling a bit, Jerry said, "I think our wives have fantastic imaginations."

"It does sound like a wild fantasy," admitted Connie. "But you can't deny that it's possible."

Moose and Jerry looked at the huge creatures skillfully performing aerobatics; then, they looked at their wives, smiled and shook their heads in disbelief. Almost in unison they said, "It's definitely a wild fantasy."

"But it is possible," insisted Connie.

"If you really feel that way, why are holding your rifle so firmly?" Jerry asked his wife.

Connie quickly gave a serious response, "Because their capabilities are so awesome, and we don't yet know what their intentions are."

Then, upon seeing the smug grin displayed by her husband, Connie instantly realized that she had just fallen for his bantering remark. "You got me that time," she laughed.

"Even their endurance is almost unbelievable," declared Moose. "They're performing one high-energy maneuver after another. Aren't they ever going to get tired?"

"To have such remarkable endurance, they must have very strong, efficient cardiovascular systems and a high metabolic rate," Connie said.

"They are truly amazing creatures," commented Dianne.

"I don't mean to bring this discussion to a close," stated Jerry, "but that dim orange sun is about to slip below the horizon, and it's not going to take more than a few minutes to get very dark. Until we become familiar with this environment, I think we should avoid being out after dark."

After one last look at the exotic scene, the interstellar pioneers began the return trip to their campsite. Even though walking at a brisk pace, they stole occasional glances at their second sunset of the day and at the pterodactyls. By the time they reached their campsite, Alpha Centauri B had set, and the darkness of night was settling in on Pioneer Island. Also, the pterodactyls were circling Western island, preparing to land.

Tired from the day's activities, the pioneers entered their habitation capsule, anticipating a good night's sleep. Jerry and Connie would sleep on the capsule's first floor; Moose and Dianne on the second floor. They would sleep in relative security because the capsule had been constructed of durable material and was rugged enough to withstand considerable punishment. Also, using the capsule's night vision surveillance cameras, the crew in the Challenger would be on full alert for any dangerous creatures that might approach the capsule.

Having worked up quite a sweat with all the physical activities of the day, even cool showers would feel good. Afterward, the day's activities would have to be discussed with the people on the Challenger. With their elevated levels of excitement and curiosity, this discussion had the potential to last well into the night.

But there was one person who Jerry and Connie wanted to share the day with in a special way, and that was their daughter. However, Denise would not be alone; she would be with her close friend Matthew. And the children would be with Mike and Michelle. Both Jerry and Connie wanted to make sure that the children received some special attention on this special day.

After all of these activities had run their course, the two couples would retire for the night and share their aspirations with each other while drifting off into a deep sleep. The first day of a new era would finally come to a close.

SEVEN

Exploring Pioneer Island

TIME: Day Two.

After sleeping soundly for six hours, Jerry awoke feeling refreshed and happy that his first night of sleep on Alcent had not been disturbed by anything. He sat up and looked around the interior of the capsule, which was softly illuminated by the dim light of early dawn entering through a large eastward facing window. Noticing that Connie was still sleeping, and remembering how little she had slept the previous night, Jerry carefully avoided awakening her. He quietly slipped out of bed and got dressed.

Silently moving around on the capsule's first floor, Jerry looked through all six of its large, rugged, crystal-clear, plastic windows. After satisfying himself that there was nothing dangerous in the vicinity, he picked up his rifle and quietly went outside.

Jerry stood straight and tall and took a deep breath of the cool, fresh, early morning air. He was struck by its clean pristine scent and the invigorating feeling that came over him. Feeling fully alert, he intently looked around the area. Not seeing anything threatening, he started walking away from the capsule toward the large boulder that he and Connie had made love behind on the previous day.

Halfway to the boulder, Jerry stopped and looked at both robot labs and at the capsule where his fellow pioneers were still sound asleep. Seeing that two video cameras were tracking his progress and that other cameras were panning the area, Jerry appreciated that people on the Challenger were concerned for his safety. Facing the nearest of the cameras, he displayed a broad happy-to-be-here smile, gave a thumbs-up signal, and then continued walking toward the large boulder.

When he reached it, he climbed to its top. This put him a full 16 feet above the surrounding terrain. In the dim light of dawn, he again visually inspected the area. Then, facing the slowly brightening eastern sky, Jerry sat down to enjoy his first sunrise since leaving Earth.

Pioneer Island had an aura of quiet peacefulness about it. Most nocturnal creatures had already retired for the day, and most daytime creatures had not yet begun their activities. Even the air seemed still, as Jerry could not even feel a gentle breeze. He marveled that such quiet peacefulness could

217

exist on a planet so abundantly inhabited by large, dangerous creatures. He wondered if Pioneer Island would always be this peaceful. It seemed almost too much to hope for.

Deeply lost in thought, Jerry was startled by the sudden beeping of his communicator. Mike's voice came through with a sense of urgency: "The pterodactyls that slept on Western Island last night are flexing their wings. It looks like they might be getting ready to take off."

"Thanks Mike." Jerry turned to face Western Island. Using binoculars, he studied the pterodactyls. "With all the energetic flying they did last night, they're probably hungry for breakfast."

"I hope they don't have you in mind," Mike said.

"Don't worry; they seem to prefer fish to red meat."

Mike laughed. "I hope you're right."

A few minutes later, as Alpha Centauri A peaked over the eastern horizon, the pterodactyls launched themselves from their cliff top. Flying east, they passed over Pioneer Island a little to the north of Stellar Plateau. Over East Bay, they turned and flew to the southeast.

Three-fourths of a mile away from Jerry, they circled an area of the lake. Then, one of them folded its wings against its body and, straight as an arrow, dove into the lake with hardly a splash. In less than a minute, large fish were swimming near the surface, some of them leaping out of the water. The airborne pterodactyl swooped down and grabbed a fish with its talons. While pulling out of its dive, it transferred the fish to its beak. Then it circled back, swooped down, and seized another one.

The pterodactyl that was underwater broke the surface and made a running, wing-flapping takeoff. It joined its companion, who tossed it the fish it was carrying in its beak. Then, both pterodactyls returned to Western Island, where they landed and leisurely ate a seafood breakfast.

"Wow! What deadly efficient teamwork!" Mike exclaimed. "It sure didn't take them long to catch their breakfast."

In an incredulous tone, Jerry exclaimed, "Did you notice that creature's diving technique? It entered the water so cleanly that there was hardly even a splash. I'm amazed that such a huge creature could do that."

"That dive was definitely impressive, but the fact that it was even done came as a total surprise to me."

"It surprised me too. Yesterday, they impressed me with their flying skills. Now it appears that they're also at home in the water?"

"It looks that way," agreed Mike. "But they might not have enough speed and agility to catch fish underwater."

"Either that or they prefer to get under a school of fish and drive them to the surface where the airborne pterodactyl can easily seize them. Diving deep and approaching fish from below has several advantages. In the dim light of dawn, a dark predator coming up from the depths will not always be seen; whereas, the fish will be silhouetted against what little light there is. If the approaching pterodactyl isn't seen, it might catch one of the fish; if it is seen, the fish might panic, causing some of them to flee to the surface, where the airborne pterodactyl will make the kill."

"That strategy should work most of the time," stated Mike.

"This pair certainly executed the strategy with ease. They made it look like nothing more than just going for a walk in the park."

"How do you think they came up with such an effective strategy?"

"I don't know, but they sure don't need much time to get their food. That leaves them with the entire day to enjoy life and investigate things they're curious about. If they've had this much free time for thousands of generations, it's possible they may've developed significant intelligence."

"How smart do you think they are?" Mike asked.

"It looks like they have enough intelligence to fine-tune a fishing strategy that may've been passed from parents to offspring for many generations."

"For them to do that, they not only have to be able to recognize a problem and think it through to a solution, but they also have to be able to communicate that solution to each other, so that it can be included in the plan for the next fishing trip."

"Those are rather advanced thinking and communication skills," noted Jerry. "But it appears that they do have them."

"That makes them more advanced than most of Earth's animals."

"And far more dangerous," added Jerry. "If they decide that we are a threat to their way of life, it's possible that they could devise tactics to make our lives miserable, even though we are well armed."

"That's only possible, if they're smart enough to have formed a society in which members can call upon each other for help to achieve a common goal, such as preventing us from colonizing their planet."

"That would put us in a bad spot, because they could almost certainly overcome our weapons by overwhelming us with numbers. Especially, if they're cunning enough to cleverly use guerrilla warfare tactics. Even if we were able to achieve a hundred-to-one kill ratio over them, they would still win, albeit at a terrible price."

After a few moments of thoughtful silence, Jerry continued, "We haven't even been here twenty-four hours, and I've already seen pterodactyls four times. I'm starting to think that our life here will be greatly affected by what kind of relationship we have with them."

"That's a pretty good possibility," agreed Mike. "Even if it turns out that they aren't as intelligent as we think they are; their physical capabilities alone are an awesome force to be reckoned with."

"That's putting it mildly! They weigh more than most of Earth's most efficient carnivores, they can easily fly 70 mph, and they can swim fast enough to chase fish."

"But they might be mild-mannered rather than mean-tempered. If that's the case, they might even turn out to be fun to live with."

"That would be wonderful," stated Jerry. "But until we know that, we have no choice but to respect their capabilities."

"We need to learn more about them, as quickly as we can."

"I agree, so I want you to use the Challenger's instruments to search the area within 150 miles of Pioneer Island. Try to determine how many pterodactyls live in this area. If you find any large concentrations, you might land some RPVs near the largest group and study them up close. Attempt to determine if they're functioning as a closely knit social group or if they just happen to be living in the same place."

"I'll get that project started right away," responded Mike.

"You might also have someone observe the pair living on Western Island. They're the ones of most immediate concern, but we're going to be busy exploring Pioneer Island and won't have time to worry about them."

"I'll land a small RPV on that cliff top, so we can observe and listen to them. If they have an audio method of communication, I'd like to record it and decipher it."

"I like that idea. If they have a language that our computers are able to decipher, then listening to them will speed up our effort to understand them. But until we do understand them, our best policy is to avoid doing anything that might appear threatening. We certainly should not provoke them in any way that would cause them to become our enemies."

"That, in itself, might eventually produce some information about their intelligence and attitude," commented Mike.

"What do you mean?"

"If they start observing your daily activities on a regular basis when you haven't done anything to get their attention, I believe that would indicate that they have enough intelligence to have recognized that you are something new in their environment. It would also demonstrate that they have an inquisitive nature."

"But it wouldn't prove that they have the ability to think and solve problems."

"That's true, but being inquisitive about you would indicate a desire to acquire knowledge."

"Looking at us from their perspective, what do you think they would be most interested in learning?"

"Since they're predators, I think they would want to know if you're easy to kill and good to eat."

"That's not a very comforting thought, so if they start showing lots of interest in us, I will have to give them something to think about."

"What are you planning to do?"

"I will demonstrate the power of my rifle by firing an explosive bullet into a small dead tree. Hearing the explosion and seeing the tree fall down should convince them to leave us alone."

"It'll be interesting to see how they react to that."

"If they're able to think, they might conclude that it would be advantageous for them to be our allies."

"It almost sounds like you're admitting that your wife's idea about having a flying guard dog with a fifty-foot wingspan wasn't such a wild fantasy after all."

"How did you find out about that conversation?" Jerry asked.

"From my wife, who else? She and the children had an endless series of questions for Connie last night."

"Speaking of my wife, I think it's time I return to the capsule and awaken her and Moose and Dianne. I'm starving. It's time to eat breakfast and start exploring this island."

An hour-and-a-half later, the pioneers left their campsite carrying weapons and light packs. After climbing down the rockslide, they hiked through the forest to East Bay and headed north along the east coast of Pioneer Island.

"What a beautiful morning," noted Connie. "It's warm, the air smells fresh, and it's peaceful. The only sounds I hear are a few birds chirping in the forest and the gentle lapping of water on the beach. It also appears that there's nothing dangerous around. There aren't even any pterodactyls in sight."

"When they aren't present, this area doesn't look much different from the remote wilderness areas I hiked into back on Earth," stated Jerry.

"I'll bet those wilderness areas never had a lake as big as this one," responded Connie.

"No, but some of the lakes I hiked to were far enough into the wilderness to isolate them from crowds of people, and camping next to them was peaceful and relaxing. Being here reminds me of that."

"Well, we certainly are isolated from crowds of people."

"That's one of the things I like the most about being here."

"That doesn't surprise me, since getting away from people was one of the reasons you did so much backpack camping back on Earth."

"True, but besides that, I enjoyed the adventure of exploring remote wilderness areas. The more remote, the more I liked it."

"Little wonder you're so happy to be here. This island is as remote as it gets as far as humans are concerned."

"No doubt about that."

"And there's no doubt that we're going to find plenty of adventure here, and it will be more dangerous than your backpack trips on Earth."

"I can't argue that, but I did have three very dangerous bear encounters in Alaska."

"Maybe those encounters helped prepare you for some of the dangers we're sure to face here."

"They taught me to be aware of my surroundings when in the wilderness."

"I think you enjoy the natural high of a dangerous adventure."

"That's true, but for as far back as I can remember, I've always enjoyed exploring wilderness areas, even those that weren't dangerous."

"How far back can you remember?"

"I was only four years old when my parents took me on my first backpack trip. After that, we went backpacking so often that camping in wilderness areas was an integral part of my childhood. Sometimes, I feel like I grew up with a pack on my back."

"I'll bet your parents never dreamed that they were preparing you for life here on Alcent."

"They couldn't have, because when I was a kid, we didn't even know Alcent existed."

"Just the same, all that backpack camping you did must make you feel at home here on Pioneer Island."

"Glancing at the dense forest, Jerry said, "This is definitely a wilderness area, and yes, I do feel comfortable here."

A mile-and-a-half north of East Bay, the pioneers found a large log lying on the beach. They decided to sit on it and relax with a cup of coffee. Jerry faced the forest, alert for danger, while the others faced the lake and a small nearby island.

Gazing toward island, Moose said, "It looks like nothing more than a rock pile. I think Rock Island would be a suitable name."

"Other than one small grove of what look like palm trees, there isn't much large vegetation growing over there," noted Dianne. "A few bushes, grasses, and an assortment of other small plants are all that have managed to find a foothold among the rocks."

"It might be fun to go over there sometime and climb around on those rocks," stated Moose. "Who knows, we might find some useful minerals."

"If we had our boat here, we could go there right now," Dianne said. "And I could study the plants growing over there."

"It's only a couple hundred yards," stated Connie. "I could easily swim that far."

"I hope you're not planning to," responded Jerry. "We haven't yet found out if any of the fish have voracious feeding habits. Also, after what I saw those pterodactyls do this morning, I don't think swimming is a very good idea until we understand their feeding habits a lot better."

"What a quick response," Connie said. "I wasn't planning to go swimming. I only made that remark to find out if you were listening."

Jerry reached over and squeezed Connie's right leg playfully. "I'm glad you're happy with my reaction."

"If you two could get serious for a few moments, I want to point out that I've spotted something of interest on top of that island's cliff," stated Dianne, who was viewing it through binoculars.

While handing the binoculars to Connie, Dianne continued, "At first glance, it looks like a small brush pile. However, after inspecting it more closely, it's easy to see that it was carefully constructed from rocks, driftwood, and brush. I wish we could investigate it from up close and maybe determine its purpose."

"We can," responded Moose, who stood up and walked over to Charlie. Moose reached into Charlie's backpack and pulled out a small RPV and two video headsets. He handed the headsets to Dianne and Connie and gave the RPV's control unit to Dianne. "While you two are investigating that brush pile, I'll help Jerry stand guard."

The headsets were equipped with a separate video screen for each eye. Each screen showed the image detected by one of the RPV's two cameras. The RPV would aim the cameras at the same point in the same way that human eyes focus on a point. Thus, individuals wearing the headsets would see a three-dimensional view of whatever was in front of the RPV and have the illusion of riding in the RPV.

"It was nice of you to bring this equipment along," Dianne said. "Knowing how exercise stimulates your appetite, I thought that maybe you'd use Charlie's pack to stash some extra food."

"That thought did cross my mind, but I thought the RPV might come in handy."

After Connie and Dianne put on and adjusted their headsets, Dianne launched the RPV and flew it low and fast to Rock Island. Waiting until the last possible instant to pitch up and climb to the cliff top elicited a cry of alarm from Connie: "Pull up! We're going to crash!"

Hearing Dianne's loud laughter above the sounds from her earphones, Connie exclaimed, "You did that on purpose, just to startle me!"

"Thrilling, wasn't it?"

"It was so real! You shocked me right out of my laid-back frame of mind. Thanks to you, I now have a better appreciation for the thrill those pterodactyls must have felt yesterday when they flew low and fast, popping up and over Eastern Island at the last possible instant."

Basking in the afterglow of the adrenaline rush, Dianne piloted the RPV to the apparent structure, slowly circled it, and climbed above it for a top-down look. "At first, I thought it might be a pterodactyl nest, but it doesn't look like a nest. It looks more like a crudely built shelter."

"Yes, and it even has a rock foundation," noted Connie. "The rocks are more than a foot across and are arranged in a circle about eight feet in diameter. Pieces of driftwood have been carefully placed on the rocks to build a roughly circular wall. As the wall gets higher, each piece of driftwood is placed closer to the center of the circle gradually bringing the top to a close, shaping it roughly like a dome."

"It looks like the whole thing has been tied together with long, pliable branches and vines that have been woven into the structure," Dianne said. "This is amazing; some of the vines are even pinned under the rocks and used to tie the driftwood to the rock foundation."

"I wonder who or what built it and what is its purpose?"

"The most obvious answer to the first question would be that it was built by pterodactyls," replied Dianne. "For one thing, that cliff top is at least 40 feet above the surrounding rocks. Pterodactyls are the only creatures we know of that have the ability to carry those large rocks and pieces of driftwood up there."

"But why would they build it? It's obviously not a nest."

"There's a small opening on the north side. I'll try to fly the RPV through it, so we can see the interior. Maybe that will give us a clue."

A few moments later, Dianne said, "It sure is dark in here. They've done a good job of closing most open spaces in this dome. I feel like I'm inside of a den used by a wild animal to rear its young."

"Maybe that's the explanation. Maybe pterodactyls don't lay eggs. Maybe their young are born alive. Maybe a pair of pterodactyls built this dome to shelter their infants in."

"That's a possibility; however, this shelter would be quite leaky during a rainstorm."

"But if the rain were accompanied by wind and hail, an infant pterodactyl would be protected from the storm's worst effects."

"That's true," agreed Dianne. "Even though it's crude, it is stoutly built, and it would withstand a brisk wind and an intense hailstorm."

"That's one kind of extreme weather. Another kind is intense heat. On a hot day, that bare rock cliff top could become very uncomfortable."

"Are you suggesting that an infant would retreat to the shade in the shelter?"

"Either that or it could climb to the top of the shelter and roost there rather than on the hot rock."

"Both possibilities make sense. Also, this is a sturdy structure and that raises another possibility."

"What ?" questioned Connie.

"Pterodactyls could use it to protect an infant from predatory birds. If both parents wanted to leave for a while, they could push their infant into this shelter and shove a large rock against the entrance to close it. A bird comparable in size to the Golden Eagle would find an unguarded infant pterodactyl to be easy prey, but it would have a difficult time ripping this shelter apart to get to it."

Dianne piloted the RPV out of the shelter. Just outside the entrance and a little to one side, she found a large rock that appeared to be about the right size to block the shelter's entrance. Between the rock and the shelter's entrance, Dianne found numerous scratch marks in the rock surface of the cliff top. "It certainly looks like this rock has been pushed against the shelter's entrance many times."

After Connie agreed with her, Dianne landed the RPV and handed the control unit and her headset to Moose. Connie gave her headset to Jerry. While Dianne and Connie stood guard, Moose and Jerry inspected the shel-

224

ter. After examining it for a few minutes, they came to the same conclusions as their wives. While Moose flew the RPV back from Rock Island, Jerry removed his headset and watched the returning RPV. Speaking to Moose, he said, "Pass it to me."

As directed, Moose flew the RPV directly to Jerry, who reached out and caught it. "This RPV's close resemblance to a Frisbee reminds me of when we use to compete in Frisbee tournaments in college."

"Back then, I never imagined that I would someday use Frisbee-like RPVs to explore an alien planet," commented Moose.

"I don't think anyone in those tournaments had that in mind."

After returning the RPV and headsets to Charlie's backpack, the interstellar pioneers resumed hiking north along the water's edge. Walking at a leisurely pace and taking time to investigate things of interest, it was lunchtime when they arrived at Rocky Point.

"So far, we haven't found any evidence to support your theory that this island is periodically visited by animals large enough to be a threat to pterodactyls," Jerry said to his wife.

"We don't have any direct evidence, such as tracks on the beach," acknowledged Connie. "But we do have additional indirect evidence."

"What do you mean?"

"I'm referring to that shelter we found on the cliff top on Rock Island. Why haven't we found similar shelters on Stellar Plateau? After all, it is nothing more than a large cliff top. Perhaps it's because the cliff top on Rock Island is accessible only by air; whereas, Stellar Plateau can be reached by large predators able to climb a rockslide."

"Your conjecture might be correct, but it doesn't seem like enough to base a conclusion on. First, we don't know if the shelter on the Rock Island cliff top was built by pterodactyls. Second, even if it was, they may have built it there simply because they prefer small cliff tops."

Sounding genuinely worried about the possibilities, Connie said, "I can't refute what you're saying. However, I strongly feel that this island is visited regularly by large creatures that the pterodactyls are wary of, and if that's the case, we need to be wary of them too."

Jerry noted his wife's uneasiness. After thinking about how she rarely felt this way, he said, "I'm going to trust your feelings on this. So until we can prove otherwise, I'm going to assume that these creatures exist and that they pose a serious threat to us."

Connie appreciated the way her husband responded to her anxiety; then, she turned her mind back to the problem of identifying the creatures that she believed existed. "If these creatures swim from one island to the next, they could come to Pioneer Island either from the north or the south. Unfortunately, if they come here from the north, we aren't going to find any tracks on this rocky terrain. This point is larger than a football field, and it's nothing but rocks."

"Tracks on the beach are only good until the next rainstorm," Jerry said. "We might find some longer-lasting clues here in this field of rocks."

"Like what?"

"Take a look at this flowering bush. It's a lot like the wild rosebushes back on Earth. Not only are its blossoms delicate and fragrant, but its branches are covered with thorns. Since there are lots of them growing among these rocks, a creature passing through here might accidentally rub against some of the thorns and leave behind some hair or a bit of skin. Let's inspect them and try to find some."

Not wanting to interrupt them, Moose and Dianne had been silently listening to Jerry and Connie. But now that their conversation had reached a conclusion, Moose said, "Can we eat lunch first? I'm starving."

"That doesn't surprise me," commented Dianne.

"I don't think I can relax enough to eat lunch until after I've had a good close look at those bushes," stated Connie.

"I don't think I can put my mind into the investigation until after I satisfy my hunger," commented Moose.

"Why don't you and Dianne eat and stand guard, while Connie and I examine the bushes. When you're finished eating, we'll switch roles."

"That sounds good to me," responded Moose.

"Before you two start poking around in those bushes, you should let me test them for toxicity," advised Dianne.

"They don't look very dangerous to me," responded Connie.

"Poison Ivy looks harmless too, but contact with it causes severe skin irritation. Anyway, it'll only take me a few minutes to do the tests."

Dianne reached into her pack and removed a small kit. After putting on plastic gloves, she cut a small branch from one of the bushes. Then, she removed one of six bottles of chemicals from the kit, and placed a few drops of its contents on the stem, on a leaf, and on a blossom. Not seeing any reaction, she proceeded to the next bottle of chemicals. After testing with all six chemicals and not getting any reaction, she said, "It tests negative for all the surface toxins we think plants are able to produce."

Grinning at Dianne, Jerry asked, "Can I send you my medical bill, if I develop a severe reaction because of contact with these bushes?"

"Well, I don't know about paying the bill, but I could recommend a good doctor for you."

Connie smiled at Dianne and Jerry and said, "That sounds like a deal I can live with."

With Moose already sitting on a rock eating lunch, Connie and Jerry walked to the nearest clump of bushes and started examining them. After fruitlessly searching them for several minutes Jerry said, "This is taking too much time. There are so many bushes here that this is going to take all day. We need to narrow down the search."

Connie glanced at all the bushes and asked, "Do you have any ideas on how we can do that?"

Jerry considered the question for a few moments. "If a large creature swam to this island from the north, where would it most likely come ashore? What would be the first thing it would do after coming ashore? And what direction would it go when leaving the water's edge?"

"If we could answer those questions, we would know where to look for clues."

"And we could save some time. We still have the west side of this island to explore, and I'd like to be back at our campsite by first sunset."

"So would I. By then, I'm going to be tired and ready for a hot shower followed by dinner."

"Let's assume that an animal coming to this island from the north would either come ashore at its earliest opportunity or swim directly to its destination on some other part of the island."

"Its first opportunity would be the tip of Rocky Point."

"If you were this animal, what's the first thing you'd do after coming ashore?" Jerry asked.

"If I were a fur covered animal, I would vigorously shake myself to rid my fur of water, like dogs do when they come out of water."

"That vigorous shaking might cause your fur to lose any strands of hair that are loose. Perhaps we should search the rocks near the point."

Ten minutes after beginning a meticulous search among the rocks near the tip of Rocky Point, Connie exclaimed, "Look what I found!"

Jerry went to her side and looked where she was pointing. Stuck to the east face of a rock was a single strand of brown hair about four inches long. After looking at it for a few moments, Jerry said, "In order for that hair to be stuck to a nearly vertical surface like that, it would have to have been put there recently, or wind and rain would've removed it by now."

"The last rain was ten days ago. It was a fairly substantial storm, dropping about two inches in less than twelve hours."

"That would certainly have washed that hair off that rock. So whatever put it there passed through here since that rainstorm."

"If it was put here by an animal shaking water out of its fur, the animal must've been standing a little to the east of this rock for the hair to end up on the rock's east face," reasoned Connie. "Maybe a little bit farther east, we'll find some hair on the west faces of rocks."

After a few moments of searching, Jerry and Connie found four-inch long strands of brown hair on the west faces of two rocks. Noting that these rocks were about eight feet east of the rock with hair on its east face, Jerry said, "It looks like your mystery animal is small enough to stand between rocks that are eight feet apart."

"That's not a very comforting thought. A grizzly bear weighing 1200 pounds is small enough to walk between rocks eight feet apart."

"That's true, but our mystery creature doesn't have to be that big. An animal as small as 40 to 50 pounds vigorously shaking itself could easily have put that hair on those rocks."

"While that's possible, it seems to me that hair four inches long would come from an animal much larger than that."

"I think so too," agreed Jerry. "If you were this animal, what would you've done after shaking the water out of your fur?"

"That would depend on where I came from."

"Assume that you came from the next large island north of here."

"That island is more than three miles away. After swimming that far, I would be tired and looking for a place to lie down and rest for a while. Considering rocks to be uncomfortable to lie down on and wishing concealment while resting, I would find the forest very appealing and head directly to it along the path of least resistance."

After collecting the hair for laboratory analysis, Jerry and Connie started walking toward the forest following the easiest, most direct route. They were joined by Moose and Dianne, who had just finished their lunch. Jerry and Connie briefed them while they were walking.

Three-fourths of the way to the forest, the route they were following passed between two clusters of bushes. At the point where their route passed between the two clumps of bushes, there were two bushes separated by only 30 inches. Pointing at the opening between the groups of bushes, Jerry said, "Unless our mystery animal detoured around all these bushes, it had to pass through that opening. Let's inspect those bushes for clues."

After examining the bush to the right for a few moments, Connie said, "The thorns on this bush have snagged lots of hair, and it looks like what I've already collected."

"There's hair on this bush too," stated Dianne while investigating the other bush.

"Apparently, our mystery creature is considerably wider than the space between these bushes," noted Jerry. "Anyone have a tape measure?"

"I do," answered Dianne. "I brought one along in case I wanted to record the dimensions of interesting plants."

After locating two branches directly across from each other, Jerry measured the distance between the farthest points on which hair could be found. "Unless our mystery animal sways from side to side when it walks, the part of its body that left this hair is 42 inches across."

Next, Jerry measured the distance to the ground from the highest hair on any of the branches. "The part of the animal that left this hair was 54 inches above the ground. I don't know what this animal looks like, but these numbers indicate that it's fairly large."

"Definitely big enough to be very dangerous," stated Moose.

"Look at this leaf!" exclaimed Dianne.

"What about it?" Jerry asked.

"It's broken loose, and it's hanging from the branch by only a thin

228

thread of bark. I believe that it was broken away from the branch by the animal that left this hair and that this happened this morning. Even though this leaf is limp, it still contains a lot of moisture. It isn't dried out like it would be if it had been broken loose a few days ago. In fact, this leaf could've been torn loose as recently as an hour ago."

"How do you know that the hair was deposited here at the same time the leaf was torn loose?" Jerry asked. "How do you know that the hair wasn't left here several days ago, and then something else, a bird for example, tore the leaf loose this morning?"

"Look closely," directed Dianne. "As you can see, when the leaf was torn loose, a thin strip of bark was torn from the cane. The leaf is now hanging on the end of that thin strip of bark. But what is important here is that there's a strand of hair lying across the part of the cane where the bark was torn away. That hair could only have been put there after the bark was torn away. I believe that our mystery animal plowed through here rubbing this branch hard enough to tear this leaf loose. Then, this thorn snagged this strand of hair and left it draped across this injury."

"If you're correct, our mystery creature passed through here within the last couple hours," commented Jerry.

"And if he found a spot just inside the forest to lie down and take a nap, he might still be there," suggested Connie.

"If that's the case, I doubt that he would still be sleeping, in view of all the talking we've been doing," stated Jerry. "If he's still around, he's probably watching us very closely trying to figure out what we're up to and if we're good to eat."

Assuming he was still responsible for guard duty, Moose took a few steps toward the forest to position himself between his colleagues and the forest. Flipping off the safety switch, he held his rifle in a quick-response position and intently stared into the forest searching every shadow for movement, however slight.

Feeling confident in Moose's ability to protect them, Dianne and Connie collected additional hair for laboratory analysis. They also inspected thorns for traces of skin, flesh, and blood that could be collected for analysis.

While they were doing this, Jerry reached into Charlie's pack and retrieved the RPV, its control unit, and a headset. Speaking to Moose, he said, "I am going to look around in the forest. I'd like to find our mystery creature and see what he looks like, and I'd like to find out how he's reacting to us."

"If he's still here, he's well hidden," Moose said. "I can't see him."

After putting on the headset, Jerry launched the RPV and flew it 150 feet straight up. Then, he flew it 50 yards over the forest before dropping into the forest. Slowly flying the RPV among the trees, Jerry searched the forest directly ahead of Moose, to his right, and to his left. Sounding disappointed, he said, "Apparently, he's no longer here."

After landing the RPV, Jerry said to Moose, "In case I missed something, I'd like you to repeat the search while I stand guard."

Feeling a tap on his left shoulder, Jerry turned and saw Dianne who said, "Why don't you let me repeat the search, so you can eat lunch with your wife."

"Thanks! I am hungry."

After finding a couple rocks with fairly flat tops, Jerry and Connie sat down to enjoy their lunch. Connie asked, "When you think about our mystery creature, does an image form in your mind?"

"We don't know very much about it; other than, it's big, covered with brown fur, and can swim at least three miles. We can speculate that it probably walks on fairly large padded feet, since the gravel areas that it walked over weren't disturbed in any obvious way. A large animal walking on hooves, or small feet, would've left tracks in the gravel."

"But what do you think it looks like?"

"The image that keeps forming in my mind is that of a bear, and that worries me. Depending on the shape of its body, this creature could weigh a thousand pounds, or maybe even a lot more. Grizzly bears that big are very powerful animals and are sometimes mean-tempered. I wish we could've gotten a good look at this animal."

"Do you think it knows that we're here?" Connie asked.

"What little breeze we have is blowing from north to south, so if it has a good sense of smell, it knows we're here."

"Do you think we should follow it and try to get a look at it?"

"Only with the RPV, I don't want to follow it on foot with the breeze blowing in its direction. It would surely know that it's being tracked, and it could lie in ambush somewhere. I think we should fly the RPV into the forest a few hundred yards, searching from side to side, and then follow a different route on the return trip. If we don't find it, we should put off the search until tomorrow. I'd like to use this afternoon to explore the west side of this island."

"Knowing that creature's roaming around will give me something to think about tonight when I'm trying to sleep. Imagine waking up in the middle of the night with that thing staring in one of the windows."

"That would be a bit alarming," responded Jerry.

"*A bit alarming!* To me, it would be more like a nightmare."

"It might be frightening, but I doubt that we'd be in any danger. As strong as that creature probably is, I doubt that it could break into our capsule. It is a very rugged shelter designed to withstand severe physical punishment. It was designed and built with dinosaurs in mind. Even the plastic windows are thick, strong, and tough."

"I realize that, but it would still be scary to wake up to a large animal looking in the window wondering if we're good to eat."

"Our friends on the Challenger have our campsite under continuous surveillance, so when we go to bed tonight, I want you to forget about our mystery creature."

"Are those the Captain's orders?"

"Yes, they are!"

"Will the Captain be there to make sure I follow those orders?"

Displaying a naughty smile, Jerry said, "I think the Captain's looking forward to being there and to giving you something else to think about."

"That sounds promising," responded Connie, returning the smile.

After a few moments of daydreaming, Jerry said, "I think we should get our minds off tonight's pleasures and get back to the problem at hand."

"You're throwing cold water on the fantasy I was starting to get into."

"Sorry about that, but we have a dangerous animal to worry about."

"Making love with dangerous animals hanging around just makes the experience more exciting," commented Connie.

"I know, so if you'll keep your fantasy tucked away in a corner of your mind, maybe tonight, we can turn it into reality."

"I like that idea."

"Okay, let's get back to our mystery creature. While it's not going to be able to break into our capsule, it could sure make a shambles out of our supply shed. Also, it could probably seriously damage our robot labs."

"The pterodactyls could wreak the same havoc if they wanted to."

"That's true," agreed Jerry, "but I don't sense that they pose that threat because of the way they obtain their food and the ease with which they keep themselves well-fed. In comparison, our mystery creature might be a bear-like animal, and it might aggressively rip into anything that smells like it might contain food. Some of the scents emanating from our labs and supply shed might make it think there's food inside."

"We need a way to protect those facilities when we aren't there."

"An easy way to do that would be to ring each facility with an electric fence. A single wire thirty inches above ground and six feet out from the facility should work. We can make the voltage and amperage high enough to give the creature a painful jolt, but low enough so that it's not likely to be seriously injured."

"Also, we could put some of our skin oil and perspiration on those wires every night and morning," suggested Connie. "If our mystery creature has a keen sense of smell, it will detect the scent before it receives a painful electrical shock. Perhaps it will associate pain with the human scent and be motivated to leave us alone if it picks up our scent when we're out wandering around."

"That's a clever idea! In fact, we might carry that idea a step farther. So far, we've been following the same path up and down the rockslide. If this creature decides to stalk us by following our scent, it will climb the rockslide along the route we use. Near the top of the rockslide, we could install an electric wire across our route and cover it with our skin oil and perspiration. If the creature follows our scent, it will certainly sniff that wire. As a result, it will receive a painful electrical shock to its nose."

"That might cause it to quit stalking us."

"Or it might decide to bypass the fence to avoid the painful shock. If it does that, it will have a decision to make when it arrives at our campsite and finds wires with the same scent on them."

"Is it possible to set up these electric fences this evening?"

"We don't have the materials to do that, but Mike could put the things we need into a small capsule and send them down. Besides the electric fence materials, I'll ask him to equip two RPVs with spray canisters of irritating chemicals and send those down too."

"How long will it take him to send everything down?"

"Mike's able to get things done fast when it's important. I won't be surprised if he has these things in our campsite before we get back."

"We're sure going to great lengths to avoid killing this mystery creature," commented Connie.

"Do you disagree with that policy?"

"No, I like it, because we don't know if this animal is a threat to us. If we kill it to avoid possible risk, we lose the opportunity to learn about it and its species."

"I believe everyone on this mission shares those feelings," stated Jerry, as he reached for his communicator. He called Mike and told him about the mystery creature. Then, he gave him his shopping list.

"The requested items will be in your campsite waiting for you when you return this evening," Mike replied. "Would you like us to use the robot lab's RPVs to search the forest for your mystery creature?"

"Yes! In particular, I'd like you to search the forest along the waterfront on this island's west side, both ahead of us and behind us."

"We'll make sure that you aren't stalked or ambushed."

Before Mike could say another word, Connie grabbed Jerry's wrist and pulled it toward her. Then, she spoke into his communicator: "Thanks, Mike! I appreciate that."

At the conclusion of the conversation, Moose and Dianne approached Connie and Jerry. "I've searched the immediate area and failed to find the creature," Dianne reported. "Then, I flew the RPV farther into the forest and found some footprints in a wet area next to a small marsh."

"I'd like to see those footprints," Jerry said.

Dianne handed him the headset and said, "I have its memory recall set at the beginning of the footprint sequence."

Jerry put on the headset and viewed the footprint images. "They look like bear tracks," he said, after studying them for a few moments. Then, he took off the headset and handed it to Connie.

While she studied the tracks, Jerry briefed Moose and Dianne about the planned electric fence and his discussion with Mike. Then, he said, "I don't think there's anything more to be gained by searching this area for additional information about our mystery animal."

"There's one more thing I'd like to do before we move on," Dianne said, as she removed binoculars from her pack. "That little island over there looks a lot like Rock Island, except that it has a higher cliff. I am going to look at that cliff top and see if I can find another one of those rock and driftwood shelters."

While Dianne inspected the cliff top, Moose looked at the island. "I think we should name it Cliff Island, since that cliff is its most prominent feature."

"Okay," Jerry agreed.

"Large parts of the cliff top are sloping toward the west, and I can't see those areas from here," Dianne said.

"I'll fly the RPV over there and take a look," Jerry said, as he picked up the control unit and put on a headset. Jerry soon had the RPV flying low above the cliff top. Still wearing the other headset, Connie decided to join him and switched from memory recall to live action.

A few moments later, Jerry said, "I found one of those shelters."

After examining its exterior, Jerry flew the RPV through the small entrance and investigated the interior. Upon leaving the dome, he said, "This shelter very closely resembles the other one. There's even a large rock next to the entrance and scratch marks in the cliff top to indicate that it has been used to close the entrance."

Before returning, Jerry circled the cliff. "As we saw on Rock Island, there is no easy access to this cliff top except to fly there."

"When we get back, let's check the cliff top on Western Island," suggested Connie. "And let's find out if it's only accessible by flight."

"If there's a shelter there, it'll be interesting to see what our resident pterodactyls are doing with it," Jerry said.

A few minutes later, the pioneers began walking south on the western shore of Pioneer Island. Shortly, they saw a pair of RPVs circling them. They waved at the RPVs, which waggled return greetings before heading into the forest.

"I feel safer with our friends searching the forest," stated Connie.

"I do too," Jerry said. "But let's not allow their presence to reduce our alertness. We are on an alien planet, and there might be grave dangers here that our friends won't discover with the RPVs."

"The discoveries of the past hour have intensified my alertness. If we hadn't suspected the existence of the mystery creature and been looking for evidence to confirm its presence, we probably would've made a short lunch stop on Rocky Point and continued on our way without even knowing that it's here, which makes me wonder what we should be looking for the rest of the day."

"All we can do is carefully observe our surroundings and investigate everything that attracts our attention," responded Jerry.

"Right there, next to that rock, is something that interests me."

"Are you referring to those seashells?"

"Yes! Look how big they are! They're as big as large dinner plates! Evidently, something had a seafood dinner here. The question is what?"

After examining a few of the shells, Jerry said, "Apparently, the creature that feasted on these clams was fairly large."

"What leads you to that conclusion?"

"A small creature would've had to smash the shells with a rock, but the creature that ate these clams only broke away the edge of the shell. It apparently had enough strength to pry the shells open."

"A bear-like animal could do that," stated Moose. "Once it had the edge of the shell broken away, it could stick its front feet claws into the shell and pull it open."

"Perhaps these shellfish were eaten by our mystery creature on a previous trip to this island," suggested Connie.

"Or another member of its species," added Dianne.

"I like seafood," Moose said. "I wonder if these clams taste good."

"I can't think of any food that you don't like," responded Dianne.

"I can't deny that, but I especially like good fresh seafood."

"If these shellfish taste anything like abalone, I would consider them a delicacy," Connie said. "When we have time, we'll have to do some lab work on them and find out if we can safely eat them."

"I wonder if they live on the lake bottom or if they dig themselves into it," questioned Dianne. "If they live on it, rather than in it, they should be very easy to find and harvest."

"If they turn out to be a delicacy and are also plentiful, they will provide us with an abundant source of delicious food," noted Moose.

"It looks like we may be in competition with our mystery creature's species for them," suggested Jerry.

"If they're prolific, that shouldn't be a problem," commented Dianne.

"But they might not be all that abundant," Connie said. "I don't recall seeing any large shells along the east coast of this island."

"Maybe they live in those waters but are too deep for our mystery creature to reach," commented Jerry. "It's possible that our mystery creature lacks diving skills and can only harvest shellfish in water that is shallow enough so that it can reach the bottom."

"Maybe they prefer a rocky, gravely bottom," speculated Dianne. "If the lake bottom here in Rocky Point Bay is like the beach we're walking on, then it's definitely rocky and gravely."

"We have lots of underwater imagery taken with the marine explorer," stated Connie. "Someone on the Challenger could review it and find answers to some of our questions."

"That sounds like a good job for one of my assistants," Dianne said, as she entered a number into her communicator.

The pioneers resumed walking south along the waterfront of Rocky Point Bay. Upon reaching Cliff Point, Jerry said, "Judging from all the shells we've seen, it appears that there's an abundant supply of shellfish in this bay. Also, it's evident that lots of them are accessible to our mystery creature and his cohorts."

"You're assuming that those are the animals that have been eating them," Connie said to Jerry.

"They are the prime suspects. If there's an abundance of large shellfish living near the islands in this lake, it would give these animals an easy source of food and a reason to swim from island to island."

"If that's the case, they might be frequent visitors to this island and present us with a constant threat," Connie said, sounding concerned.

"As time goes on, we'll learn how serious a threat they are," responded Jerry. "The first thing we need to do is find out what they look like. I think we can do that by installing a surveillance camera right here on Cliff Point. The second thing we need to do is attach a radio transmitter to the back of each animal we locate, so we can track them."

Looking up the rocky slope of Cliff Point, Jerry said, "The top of that large boulder up there would be the ideal place to locate a camera. From there, it could scan nearly all of the shoreline of Rocky Point Bay."

"How do you plan to get to the top of that boulder?" Connie asked.

"I don't think I can. It looks like it's a little beyond my reach, but I can lift you high enough so that you can scramble the rest of the way to the top. After you set up the camera, I will help you climb down."

"I'm sure happy to hear the last part of your plan," Connie said.

"I like that part of the plan too. I couldn't possibly leave the most wonderful part of my life stranded here on top of a boulder," Jerry said, giving his wife a hug.

Connie began scrambling up the rock strewn slope with her colleagues following her. When they reached the large boulder, Moose and Dianne stood guard while Jerry boosted his wife up the side of the boulder, so she could climb to its top. There, she took a few moments to enjoy the view and said to Jerry, "You were right. This vantage point does provide an unobstructed view of Rocky Point Bay's entire waterfront."

Connie set up the camera's tripod and glued it to the boulder. Next, she installed the camera with its electric motors. Then, she deployed the camera's antenna and solar panels. After contacting Mike, she put the camera through a sequence of operations to verify that it was functioning properly. Mike confirmed that a strong signal, carrying clear images, was being received on the Challenger.

After taking a few moments to enjoy the scenic view again, Connie said, "I can't believe that we're finally living here. I feel like this is all part of a dream, and that I might yet wake up. The picturesque beauty that surrounds us is breathtaking."

"Since you're enjoying the scenery so much, does this mean that the last part of my plan is no longer important to you?" questioned Jerry.

"No!" Connie quickly said. "I'm not implying that I want to stay up here. You can help me down now."

Jerry reached up and helped his wife scramble down off the boulder. Then, the pioneers resumed their southward march.

"I think we should bring our research submarine down soon," Connie said. "I'd like to do an underwater cruise. It would not only be fun, but our future well-being depends to a great degree on what lives in this lake, and the sooner we start exploring it, the better off we'll be."

"Great idea," agreed Dianne. "The sub's transparent hull and this lake's clean water will allow us a great view of the underwater world."

"Exploring the lake is important," acknowledged Jerry. "But before we do that, we should explore the dense forest on this island."

"We explored the forest rather extensively with RPVs for more than two weeks before we landed here," noted Dianne. "What do you expect to discover that we haven't already found?"

"I don't know, but even though our RPVs are valuable exploration tools, there are still things that can best be accomplished by a human presence. For example, this morning, we located three strands of hair that put us on the trail of a large creature that may, or may not, prove to be dangerous, but at least we know it's here. If there are any serious dangers in this forest, I want to find them and study them, so we can account for them when planning our daily activities."

"In other words, you're hoping to make our lives safer."

"That's my primary goal, but I also want to become more familiar with this island's terrain. Walking on the land and feeling it underfoot gives me a different perspective than looking at it with an RPV."

"Studying plants and animals in person also has advantages over using an RPV," added Dianne.

"I agree with both of you," stated Connie. "That's why I think we should bring our submarine down. With it, we can spend long periods of time in the underwater world. This will allow us to gain knowledge more quickly than studying video from the marine explorer. Plus, it will be fun."

"What you're saying makes good sense," acknowledged Jerry.

"So when can we bring the sub down?" Connie asked.

"We should finish setting up our camp and do what we can to make it safe and secure before we bring our sub down. Two things we must do are set up our electric fence and assemble our wind-powered generator."

Speaking to Connie, Dianne said, "I think we can talk him into bringing it down in about five days."

"That sounds reasonable to me," responded Connie.

"I think our wives are getting pretty good at arm-twisting," Moose said to Jerry.

236

Connie and Dianne innocently smiled at each other. Then, Connie asked, "What do you think? Can we bring the sub down in five days?"

"That seems like an attainable schedule," responded Jerry.

Moose shrugged his shoulders, shook his head, and grinned. "It appears that our wives have much more influence over you than I do."

"What do you mean by that?"

"Last night, when I asked you about bringing the sub down, you didn't think we could do that for a couple weeks. When they talk to you about it, it can be done in five days."

Jerry glanced at Moose; then, he looked at Dianne and Connie. After a few moments, he said, "It seems quite obvious why they have more influence over me than you do."

"That's an unfair advantage," protested Moose.

"We can't help it that we're beautiful women," declared Connie. "God made us that way!"

Jerry stared at Moose and patiently waited for a reaction. Feeling like he was on the proverbial hot seat, Moose exclaimed, "If you think I'm going to disagree with that assertion, you're crazy!" Dianne and Connie looked at each other, silently expressing an air of smug satisfaction.

Several minutes later, the pioneers entered an open grove of trees growing right to the water's edge. "These trees look like palm trees," Connie said. "And broken nut shells are scattered all over the place."

"They look like coconut shells," noted Dianne.

"And there are husks laying around too," added Connie. "Apparently, these nuts were encased in husks when they grew high up in these trees."

"I wonder if our mystery creature and its peers ate these nuts," questioned Dianne.

"We don't have any other suspects," responded Jerry. "But whatever ate them was strong enough to remove the husks from the nuts and then crack open the shells."

"I'd like to find a nut that's still intact and take it home for analysis," Dianne said. "They may be a source of food for us."

After searching the grove for a few minutes, Moose found a nut still encased in its husk. He removed the husk and handed the six-inch diameter nut to his fellow pioneers for examination.

"I'm amazed at how closely it resembles a coconut," Connie said. "In fact, I'm amazed that so many of the plants here resemble earth plants."

"We are on an earthlike planet," stated Dianne. "When you consider the seemingly infinite variety of plants that nature has evolved on Earth, it seems reasonable to expect that many of the plants we find here will look like copies of earth plants."

"That might also be true for animal life," speculated Moose while placing the coconut in his backpack.

"It probably is," agreed Dianne. "There are many designs a creature can take, but inefficient designs usually become extinct as they are crowded out by designs that are better equipped to survive and prosper. The features that allow an animal to survive and prosper here probably aren't that much different than on Earth. In other words, the laws of evolution apply here as on Earth, and we end up with many plants and animals that look like copies of plants and animals from Earth."

As the interstellar pioneers resumed their southward march, Moose said, "The fish I looked at in video taken by the marine explorer didn't look much different from the fish on Earth."

"That doesn't surprise me," stated Dianne. "There's a limit to the number of variations in shape and color that fish can have. Evolution dictates that only the efficient designs will survive. It seems reasonable to expect that two earthlike planets would evolve many similar species of fish if the process of evolution is allowed to run for hundreds of millions of years like it has here and on Earth. However, it's also reasonable to expect that there will be many species that are unique to each planet to fill the special niches that exist on each planet."

"In any case, I am still eager to do some fishing," insisted Moose.

A few minutes later, the pioneers arrived at the lagoon they had named Red Fish Lagoon. Video from the marine explorer had revealed an abundance of fish in the lagoon shaped much like the freshwater bluegill, but with most of its body colored a vivid scarlet. The species was given the name redfish, hence the name: Red Fish Lagoon.

Moose feasted his eyes on the lagoon and said, "We need to do some fishing in this lagoon. There are plenty of redfish here. If they're as tasty as bluegills and as much fun to catch, we're going to have some great fishing here and some excellent seafood meals."

"Since our submarine is also a good surface vessel, we'll have a sturdy boat to fish from once we have it down here," Jerry said.

"In view of where we're living, it might turn out to be our most valuable piece of equipment," Moose said. "Consider its uses: a research submarine, a fishing boat, a sailboat, and a means of transportation."

"It's definitely a versatile piece of equipment," agreed Jerry, "but in time, it won't have to fill all those roles. After we've determined that it's medically safe to be here and our people have come down, we'll be able to build a variety of boats. Then, we'll use the sub primarily for research."

"And for underwater sightseeing trips," added Connie. "The sub does have a transparent hull, and the water in this lake is incredibly clear."

"Imagine how romantic it will be to go on an underwater cruise, alone with your favorite man," Dianne suggested to Connie.

Obviously excited by Dianne's comment, Connie smiled at Jerry. "It does have a romantic appeal to it, doesn't it?"

"The idea has potential," Jerry replied, calmly.

"I hope I'm the man in your fantasy," Moose said to his wife.

"Of course you are," responded Dianne. "I was just thinking about how unique it would be for us to conceive our first child on such a romantic voyage."

"That would be unique," agreed Moose. "But if our research submarine is going to be used for romantic voyages, we might have to start calling it the Love Boat."

After chuckling at Moose's suggestion, Jerry said, "I think our wives are getting really good at conniving. If they keep this kind of talk going, they'll have us bringing that submarine down tomorrow."

"That's a wonderful idea," stated Dianne and Connie in unison. "Whatever made you think of that?"

Jerry gave Connie a silent, admiring glance and a warm affectionate smile. "I would like to bring the sub down tomorrow, but there are some projects we should do first. If we put our minds into it and work hard, we should be able to finish them in three days. Then, we can bring the sub down."

"I think we can make that plan work," agreed Moose. Dianne and Connie also expressed their approval.

After completing their hike around Red Fish Lagoon, the pioneers resumed their southward journey. Late in the afternoon, they arrived at West Point.

"I don't know about you, but I'm hungry and tired," Connie said to her husband.

"That's understandable," responded Jerry. "We've been on our feet all day, and we've hiked about ten miles, much of it over sand and gravel. That's enough to tire most anyone."

"I still have some food left in my pack. Perhaps we could stop for a short rest and eat a snack."

"That's a good idea. We could sit on that log over there and enjoy the view out over the lake."

"I'm not all that hungry," Dianne said. "While you two are eating, I'll fly the RPV to Western Island and search for those dome structures."

"I'll stand guard," stated Moose.

A few minutes later, Dianne said, "The pterodactyls we watched yesterday aren't on the island at the moment, but I think I know why they made such a thorough search before landing. The wreckage of one of those dome structures is scattered around on the cliff top."

"I can understand how that would've gotten their attention," commented Connie, "especially, if they're the ones that built it and used it to shelter their young."

Dianne continued reporting her observations of the scene: "The west side of the cliff top is much lower than the east side. In fact, it's only about 40 feet high, and there's a large tree leaning against it that extends well above the cliff top. It's my guess that the tree was tipped against the cliff during a recent storm. Then, a large animal arrived, climbed the tipped tree to the cliff top, and tore apart the dome structure. Perhaps it was looking for

239

an easy meal, or maybe it just felt like being destructive. Evidently, the pterodactyls that arrived yesterday hadn't been here for a while, and when they saw the wreckage, they decided to investigate before landing."

"Maybe the storm that tipped the tree destroyed the shelter," suggested Moose.

"That's possible," acknowledged Dianne. "But the fact that the pterodactyls investigated the scene before landing implies that the devastation was done by a creature they fear."

"Good point. That means that the animal that caused the destruction is capable of seriously injuring or even killing adult pterodactyls. Also, it must be a good tree climber and very good at stealth."

"The tree leaning against the cliff is at an angle of about 45 degrees. An animal wouldn't have to be a good tree climber to scramble up it."

"Perhaps a member of our mystery creature's species is responsible for the devastation," suggested Moose.

"We think our mystery creature is a bear-like animal," Dianne said. "But the creature the pterodactyls fear could just as easily be a cat-like animal. A feline weighing as little as 200 pounds could kill a pterodactyl. It could silently climb the tipped tree, sneak up on a sleeping pterodactyl, leap on its back, and bury its fangs in the creature's neck. Give this feline feet that are larger than a cat would normally have, put webs between its toes, and you have an animal that would be a good swimmer."

"Almost sounds like a huge, overgrown sea otter," suggested Moose.

"That's also a possibility," agreed Dianne.

"Although a cat as small as 200 pounds could kill a pterodactyl, I don't think that it's likely to happen except to a lone pterodactyl. In the case of a mated pair, I doubt that the mate of the dead pterodactyl would allow the cat to feast on the kill unless it was much larger than 200 pounds. A pterodactyl could kill a 200-pound cat by burying its talons in the animal's body. To insure death, it could strike it in the head with its beak, or it could lift it to an altitude of a few hundred feet and drop it."

"The only point I'm trying to make is that once we've located our mystery creature, we should not assume that we've found the animal the pterodactyls fear," stated Dianne. "Whether they weigh 200 pounds or 600 pounds, dangerous cat-like creatures might be visiting Pioneer Island."

"We should investigate the scene and look for clues to indicate what kind of creature wrought the destruction," stated Jerry.

"What if the pterodactyls return while we're doing that?" Connie asked.

"I wasn't implying that we do the investigation in person. This could be done effectively with our mechanical bugs. We fly four of them over there with an RPV and have two of them crawl around among the pieces of wreckage. We use the other two to crawl around on the tree. Our friends on the Challenger could control the bugs and monitor their instruments."

"We may not find any clues," Dianne said. "We don't know if this destruction occurred a few days ago or several months ago. All clues could be washed away or blown away by now."

"That's true for hair, blood, and footprints," agreed Jerry. "But since it would require lots of force to rip apart one of these dome structures, we may find some claw marks in the driftwood. How far apart the claw marks are combined with the width and depth of individual marks would tell us something about the animal responsible for the destruction. Also, the creature may have left claw marks in the tree while climbing it."

Dianne nodded. "We shouldn't rule out the possibility of finding some hair. The tipped tree is still alive and growing. If it suffered any injuries during the storm that tipped it, sap oozing out of them would have been sticky enough to trap some hair if an animal rubbed against it before it dried."

"If we find any hair, do you have the right equipment down here to determine if it's from the same species as the hair we've already collected?" Jerry asked.

"With the equipment I have, I can not only determine if it's from the same species, I can also determine if it's from the same animal."

"I'd sure like to have that information," stated Jerry. "It would be nice to know if more than one species of large animals visit this island."

"If there's any hair there, I'm confident that our colleagues on the Challenger will find it," stated Dianne. "I believe they'll enjoy searching the scene with mechanical bugs. With 3-D headsets, they'll see what their bugs see and have the illusion of crawling around on Western island, and we know how eager they are to come down here. With four people running four bugs, they may even make a game out of it with a prize for the one who finds the most clues."

"I'd be surprised if they don't make a contest out of it," replied Jerry.

"I don't mean to change the subject," Connie said. "But look up there! It's still quite high, but if I'm not mistaken, that's a para-wing circling Stellar Plateau."

"It looks like Mike has kept his promise, and the materials for our electric fences will be waiting for us," Jerry said. "Unless something really grabs our attention, let's make a nonstop hike to our campsite. I'd like to set up part of that fence yet today."

Forty-five minutes later, the pioneers arrived at their campsite. They found the newly arrived capsule 100 yards from their habitation capsule. As they approached it, Connie's communicator started beeping. She answered it and received a cheerful, "Hi! How are you?" from Michelle.

"Other than being exhausted, I feel pretty good," replied Connie.

"That's good news!"

"You think it's good news that I'm exhausted?" Connie joked.

"I wasn't referring to your fatigue. I'm happy that you feel good, and haven't contracted any mysterious illness after two days on Alcent."

"I thought that was the case, but I couldn't resist teasing you. Medically speaking, it's much too soon to conclude that we aren't going to have any problems. However, it's encouraging that we feel good and haven't had any adverse reactions to anything. Tomorrow, I will give everyone a medical exam."

"Hopefully, you won't find any problems. I'm eager to join you. After seven years in space, I'm ready for some outdoor living. Something as simple as a backyard barbecue in a scenic setting would be fun."

"That does sound like fun, and this island certainly does have an abundance of scenic settings."

"I'm glad you like the idea. If you'll look inside the capsule we just sent down, you'll find some thick juicy steaks, a grill, and a bag of charcoal. I hope you're hungry, because we also packed several side dishes to go with your steaks."

"What a wonderful surprise!" exclaimed Connie. "I am famished, and a barbecue will be fun. Thank you for being so thoughtful."

"It was Mike's idea, but we worked out the menu together. Also, Denise let us know what kind of pie you like, and she insisted on helping our chef make it for you."

"That was thoughtful of her. I will be sure to thank her when I visit with her this evening."

"She'll appreciate hearing from you. Enjoy your dinner!"

"We will, and once again, thank you."

Turning to Dianne, Connie said, "I'd really like to take a shower and put some clean clothes on before we eat."

"I would too," stated Dianne.

Having overheard the conversation about steaks and charcoal, Moose could not resist the temptation to play the part of an expert. Using a boastful, high-spirited tone, he said, "I would like to point out that back on Earth, I was a respected gourmet chef when it came to outdoor cooking."

"I don't know if he's trying to impress us, or if he wants to volunteer to cook our steaks," Dianne said to Connie.

"I don't know either, but I think we should go take our showers and give him the opportunity to show us how skilled he is."

Dianne nodded; then, she and Connie silently stared at Moose and patiently waited for him to react. After enduring the combined stare for a few moments, Moose said, "It appears that I just volunteered to get the charcoal going and cook the steaks."

"How sweet of you to offer," responded Dianne, as she started walking toward the large habitation capsule.

Amused by the whole episode, Jerry quietly laughed and said, "I guess they have considerable influence over you too."

"What do you mean by that? I enjoy outdoor cooking. I just wanted them to think that they coerced me into doing the cooking."

Jerry shook his head in disbelief. "That's not how it looked to me. But whatever the case may be, you now have the opportunity to demonstrate your expertise. And I think the steaks had better turn out pretty good, or you'll never hear the end of it."

"You're right. Let's open up that capsule, so I can get the charcoal started. I don't know what they sent down to go with our steaks, but while I'm cooking them, I might as well prepare the entire meal."

A few minutes later, Jerry said, "They packed enough food for ten people, and that's great, because I'm starving."

"This is going to be fun," stated Moose, as he grabbed the grill and charcoal. "I love the aroma of sizzling steaks."

"I hope our mystery creature doesn't find it appealing. What little breeze we have is now coming from the south. The scent from our sizzling steaks is likely to drift out over the entire island to the north of us. If he has a good sense of smell, he may decide to investigate."

"We'll have to be extra alert this evening," declared Moose.

"Also, I'd like to set up our electric fence along the north end of this plateau yet today. It's only a thousand feet and shouldn't take more than two hours. All we have to do is drive a plastic stake into the ground every 15 feet, rollout and attach the wire, hook it up, and turn on the power."

"There isn't much soil in some places," commented Moose. "We may have to support some of the stakes with rocks."

"I'll get the project started while you're playing backyard chef."

A half-hour later, Dianne and Connie emerged from the habitation capsule looking refreshed. When they approached Moose, Dianne said, "Those steaks really smell good. How long before they're ready?"

"Just a few minutes."

"Is there anything we can do to help?" Dianne asked.

"Everything's on the table except the steaks and something to drink."

"I'll take care of the beverages," offered Dianne, as she turned and went back to the habitation capsule.

When she returned, the pioneers sat down at their outdoor table to enjoy their second dinner on Alcent. The mouthwatering aroma from the charbroiled steaks with their special sauce and spices served to intensify their ravenous hunger. Warm garlic toast, baked potatoes, steaming vegetables, and a mixed green salad made up the main part of the dinner. Dessert consisted of Denise's cherry pie topped with whipped cream.

A pleasant atmosphere for the feast was provided by mild temperatures, a gentle breeze, and a blue sky containing a few widely scattered cumulus clouds. The perfect weather seemed to enhance the effect of the panoramic view of Clear Lake with snow capped mountains in the background to the east.

Hanging low in the western sky, Alpha Centauri A blazed brilliantly. Higher up in the western sky was the much dimmer orange star, Alpha Centauri B. Appearing between the two stars were both of Alcent's moons, which looked like double crescents. The side of each moon that faced Alpha

Centauri B appeared as a dim orange crescent; whereas, the side of each moon that faced Alpha Centauri A appeared as a much brighter creamy-yellow crescent.

As they began eating their dinner, Connie exclaimed, "What a feast! This steak is twice as big as what I would've eaten when we were on the Challenger, but all that strenuous activity and outdoor living has made me so hungry that I will probably eat all of it."

Dianne tasted her steak and said, "This steak is so delicious that it's hard to believe that it's an imitation steak made by a food synthesizer."

Moose smiled in self-satisfaction and silently shifted his gaze back and forth between Connie and Dianne. After a few moments, Dianne said, "That almost looks like an 'I am a good cook' expression. But you deserve a compliment. My steak is cooked exactly the way I like it. You did an excellent job."

"My steak is also done to perfection," Connie added. "Thank you!"

"Perhaps Moose should be permanently in charge of our outdoor cooking," Jerry suggested.

"Outdoor cooking is fun," Connie said. "I think we'd all like to take a turn at it."

"This steak is good," stated Moose, "but I wonder what barbecued dinosaur steak would taste like."

"Which species of dinosaur do you have in mind?" Dianne asked.

"There are several species of small dinosaurs that resemble flightless birds that might taste really good if properly prepared. One species in particular has adults that weigh about 500 pounds. I've observed them a number of times. They are herbivores that roam around in small herds. Being fast runners, they use their speed to escape predators. As numerous as they appear to be, we should be able to take one for food occasionally without doing the species any harm."

"These imitation steaks are excellent," stated Dianne. "I don't see how dinosaur steak could be any better."

"We won't know until we've tried some," countered Moose.

"I can't argue that," replied Dianne. "But I'm wondering if you might just be eagerly anticipating the excitement of a hunting expedition."

"That would be an exciting challenge," admitted Moose. "But there is a consideration that I think is more important than the excitement of a hunting trip, and that is: we need to identify as many food sources as possible. Even though our food synthesizers have served us well during our long voyage, now that we're here, I think we should acquire the knowledge to be independent of them."

"Are you suggesting that we should develop the capability to survive and prosper without our technology?" questioned Jerry.

"Only in regard to such basic needs as food, shelter, and self-defense," replied Moose. "We especially need to become independent of our food synthesizers. Even though it's not very likely, it's still possible that we could lose them in some tragic accident. On a planet as filled with life as this one, we should not get into a position of not having anything to eat simply because we don't know what's edible and what isn't."

"I agree," responded Jerry. "Finding out what's edible is an important project that we need to begin as soon as we've done enough exploration to ensure our safety."

"It seems like food is never very far away from my husband's mind," Dianne said to Connie.

"I've noticed that about him," Connie said, "but he has made a good point."

"That's true, but I still like to tease him anyway. He loves the attention, and it makes him feel like I still love him."

The pioneers continued discussing things of concern to them while they leisurely enjoyed their dinner and the pristine scenery around them. Being the first to finish eating, Jerry resumed setting up the electric fence and was soon joined by Moose.

Dianne and Connie stayed in the campsite to wash dishes and put away leftover food. After a half-hour, they were satisfied that the campsite was tidy, so they joined their husbands to assist them. To ensure that the electric fence carried a strong human scent, all four made a special effort to rub the wire over their skin to deposit skin oil and perspiration on it.

Upon completing the fence across the north end of Stellar Plateau, the pioneers installed an electric fence around their supply shed. When this was complete, they turned on the electric power to both fences and verified that they were electrified.

"I feel good about this," Jerry said. "If our mystery creature decides to follow our scent up the rockslide tonight, it will receive a painful jolt if it sniffs the fence wire. Hopefully, it will remember the pain the next time it encounters our scent and stay away from us."

"That would be the best possible outcome," agreed Moose. "But another possibility is the pain could fill it with rage that might cause it to charge through the fence. Then, we'll have an animal filled with fury charging around here on the plateau."

"That's a possibility," agreed Jerry. "But if that happens, we have the means to deal with the problem. In the meantime, I'm tired, and I'm heading for the shower."

"I'll be in there as soon you're out," Moose called after him.

Two hours later, after discussing the day's activities with their friends on the Challenger, the pioneers went to bed in a happy state of exhaustion.

EIGHT

Neighbors Drop in for a Visit

TIME: Day Three.

It was early dawn on Pioneer Island with the eastern sky just beginning to brighten while the rest of the sky was still dark and filled with stars. A few low clouds floated over the north end of Clear Lake, and a gentle breeze was coming in from the south.

As on Day Two, Jerry quietly slipped out of the habitation capsule leaving his wife and friends behind, still sound asleep. Wearing night vision goggles, he carefully inspected his surroundings. Then, he walked to the large boulder he had sat on the previous morning. After climbing to its top, he made himself comfortable and prepared to enjoy some peaceful solitude during the dawn of a new day.

Jerry was thankful that once again, they had slept peacefully without being disturbed by anything. He wondered where the mystery creature was, what it was doing, and why it apparently hadn't tracked them to a painful encounter with the electric fence. Perhaps, today's RPV search of the island would locate it.

Even though Jerry was deeply lost in thought, he was still alert for activity around him and noticed the movement of a dark shape near the habitation capsule. Using his night vision binoculars, he saw that it was Moose. Staying motionless, Jerry silently observed him. It became apparent to Jerry that Moose's destination was the boulder he was sitting on and that Moose was unaware of his presence.

When Moose was 60 yards away, he stopped and slowly turned to search his surroundings. He resumed walking at a slow, cautious pace while alertly looking from side to side. When he was 25 yards away, he again stopped and slowly turned to inspect his immediate vicinity.

Jerry decided to make sure that Moose was truly awake, so he picked up a baseball-sized rock and threw it so that it landed about ten yards behind Moose. The rock struck the ground with a forceful thud and bounced into a shrub imitating the sound of an animal crashing into a bush. Moose instantly spun around with his rifle ready to fire. Then, Jerry lobbed another rock, which again, landed behind Moose with a resounding thud. As with the first rock, Moose quickly spun around, ready to fire his rifle.

247

Jerry waited several seconds to give Moose's imagination a chance to run wild. Then, he laughed in a loud boisterous way and yelled, "You remind me of a kitten chasing tossed pebbles."

Instantly realizing that he wasn't surrounded by predators, but was instead the butt of a joke, Moose felt greatly relieved and laughed too. "That's the best one anyone's ever pulled on me!" he exclaimed. "For a few seconds, you had me convinced that a couple wild animals had me in mind for their breakfast."

"Did you have a mild adrenaline rush?"

"*Mild* isn't the right description! I was instantly ready for action!"

"Well, you certainly impressed me. Your reaction time is pretty good for an old man."

"What do you mean *old man?* I'm only 48, same as you. If I'm an old man, so are you."

"Well, maybe you're not that old after all."

"I'll bet you could react pretty fast too, if you thought you were about to become a meal for some wild animals."

"You're right about that. Perhaps my reaction time will be tested when we get around to going on a dinosaur hunt."

"I'm sure that will be the case," agreed Moose. "But at the moment, I'd rather go fishing than dinosaur hunting."

"I have some free time. Maybe we should go fishing right now."

"What about the pterodactyls? Being out in that small boat will leave us exposed to attack."

"That's true, but I watched pterodactyls fish yesterday, and I was amazed by their skill. When they can catch fish so easily, I don't think they'd have much interest in contesting us for ours, if we catch any."

"What if they see us as an easy meal?"

"We've been out and about for two days now with pterodactyls frequently in sight, and they haven't paid any attention to us. But if they threaten us, we have enough firepower to deal with them."

"What about our wives? They might be alarmed if they wake up and find us gone?"

"As tired as they were last night, we'll probably be back before they wake up. But if we aren't, they can beep us on our communicators."

"It's still quite dark. Aren't you concerned about being ambushed by our mystery creature when we walk through the forest?"

"You have so many objections that I'm beginning to wonder if you're serious about wanting to go fishing," teased Jerry.

"Well, I wonder why that is! Just a few minutes ago, you had me convinced that I was about to be attacked and possibly eaten. You scared the hell out of me and drove home the fact that we are on an alien planet that we really don't know much about."

"Are you suggesting that those rocks I lobbed at you might end up keeping you alive because you're now going to be overly cautious?"

"Let's just say that it'll be a long time before I get lax about being cautious. Which brings me back to our fishing expedition, have you considered the possibility of being ambushed in the dark forest?"

"By the time we pick up our fishing gear and scramble down the rockslide, there should be enough light to safely walk through the forest. Charlie will lead the way, and we'll be alert for anything that might be trailing us. Plus, I do have these night vision goggles."

"Okay, let's go."

A short time later, Moose and Jerry were at the bottom of the rockslide and ready to enter the forest. "I think we should wait for more light," suggested Moose. "It's still dark in there."

"We only have to go through 150 yards of forest to get to the beach," argued Jerry. "If you'll stand guard, I'll put on a headset and scout our route by marching Charlie to the beach and back. If there's a dangerous creature present, maybe it'll reveal its presence by attacking Charlie."

"I'll stand guard."

Ten minutes later, Charlie emerged from the forest unscathed, and Jerry said, "It looks perfectly safe between here and the lake."

"I'm convinced. Let's go fishing."

Moose and Jerry cautiously followed Charlie through the forest. When they reached the sandy beach, they noted that sunrise was only minutes away. After searching the sky for pterodactyls, they placed their rifles and fishing gear in the boat and pushed it into the water. A few minutes later, they were well out into East Bay.

"It's been a long time since I've been fishing," stated Moose. "And now I'm fishing where no one has ever fished before."

"What kind of fish are you hoping to catch?"

"Before we landed here, I did some underwater exploring with the marine explorer. One species of fish that caught my attention looks like northern pike, except that its coloration resembles that of rainbow trout. So I named it rainbow pike. I would like to catch one of them because they look like they would put up a good fight and be good to eat."

"How do you plan to catch a pike to the exclusion of other fish?"

"Rainbow pike are fairly numerous around this island. On three occasions, I saw one strike another fish and eat it. I've made some lures that I'm hoping will excite their appetites enough to provoke a strike. I'm going to try this one first."

Moose showed Jerry a double-jointed lure with a small shiny metal spinner in front of its nose. It had an additional spinner that revolved around the shaft of the triple hook attached to its tail. The body of the lure was painted blue-green on the top and silver-gray on the bottom with a scarlet stripe running down the middle of each side. The lure was nine inches long counting the fore and aft spinners.

"That's a fairly large lure," commented Jerry.

"I am hoping to catch a fairly large fish. Anyway, this lure is about the size of the fish that I saw rainbow pike eat. I've given it the same body colors, and the small spinners are there to attract attention."

"Where would you like to try your luck?"

"I've seen rainbow pike here in East Bay, but they seem to be especially numerous in the channel between Eastern Island and Pioneer Island. I thought maybe you could row us east along the south shore of this bay. If we don't catch one by the time we get into the channel, we could pick up a northward drift from the southerly breeze. When we get to the north side of this bay, we should row back into the bay, so we don't end up having to row the boat against the wind."

"It seems like your plan has me doing all the work, and you doing all the fishing."

"After the way you scared the hell out of me this morning, I think you owe me something."

"That was all your fault."

"What do you mean by that?"

"Well, if you didn't have the habit of sleeping in, you would've been outside before I was."

"When I got up, it was still dark. How can you call that sleeping in?"

"I was outside before you were; so relative to me, you slept in."

"That's pretty weak, but I'll make a deal with you. If I don't catch a fish during the time we go out to the channel, fish the channel, and circle back into the bay; then, I'll take over the rowing, and you can fish while you tell me what course to follow."

"That sounds fair. Let's go."

With the lighthearted negotiations complete, Moose dropped the lure into the water and pulled it along at different speeds to check its action. Then, he tested it with abrupt stopping and starting movements, during which a small weight ahead of the lure caused it to make shallow dives from which it abruptly recovered when pulled forward.

"I like that lure's action," Jerry said. "It looks like a swimming fish, except that all its movements are exaggerated. And when you apply irregular motion, it looks like an injured fish. With the spinners, there's more than enough action to attract any fish looking for a meal."

"I hope that's the case," responded Moose, as he lifted the lure out of the water and cast it toward the center of the bay. After it splashed down 30 yards away, Moose began reeling it in and said, "Now, we'll find out how the fish react to it."

After Moose retrieved the lure without success, Jerry rowed the boat forward about 25 yards. Then, Moose again cast it toward the center of the bay. "You can't believe how excited I am," he exclaimed. "I feel like a kid with a new toy."

"You should feel that way! You're fishing in a huge lake where no one has ever fished before."

"When I was a kid, I used to dream about fishing in a remote wilderness lake that had never been fished in, but those kinds of lakes don't exist on Earth anymore."

"Relative to where you were living when you were a kid, this lake is definitely remote and in a wilderness area."

"Another one of my childhood dreams has come true," declared Moose while reeling in his lure without success.

Jerry rowed the little boat another 25 yards to the east. Then, Moose cast in the direction of Eastern Island and said, "I'll try reeling it in with nothing but erratic, stop-start, jerking motion."

While Moose patiently worked his lure, doing his best to make it look like a wounded fish, Jerry said, "I wonder how many sports fishermen back on Earth would love to trade places with you right now."

"Probably all of them, but what's especially exciting to me is that this lake is so large that it's going to take several years to explore it all."

"And if we want some additional adventure, we can go 60 miles upriver to the north and there's another huge lake to fish in and explore."

"And don't forget that there's a huge river south of us that flows to the ocean," added Moose.

Suddenly, Moose's casting rod bowed sharply as a fish struck the lure and began rapidly pulling out line. "Wow! I think I've hooked a whale!"

Moose quickly tightened the drag hoping to turn the fish around before it pulled all the line off his reel. Within seconds, the fish abruptly reversed direction, and Moose quickly reeled in the slack line in preparation for the fish's next run. But before Moose could reel in all the slack line, the fish started another speedy run directly away from the boat.

"This reminds me of a 25-pound albacore I caught back on Earth!" exclaimed Moose. "I don't know what I've hooked, but it's big."

At that moment, the fish leapt completely out of the water, shook itself vigorously, then dove back into the water and swam toward the boat. "It's a large rainbow pike!" yelled Moose as he rapidly reeled in slack line.

On its next run, the fish didn't go quite as far before it tired and changed directions. A few minutes later, Moose managed to pull the tired fish close enough to the boat so Jerry could capture it with a landing net.

"What a catch! It must weigh at least 20 pounds," stated Moose. "And to think, our wives slept through all the excitement."

"I don't think so. There's been an RPV circling us almost from the moment the fish struck. I didn't tell you, because I didn't want to distract you. Apparently, when our wives woke up, they looked outside for us and noticed that your fishing gear was gone, and they decided to investigate. Anyway, I think we've been on candid camera."

"When Mike and the boys see that video, they'll be ready to come down right away!" Moose proudly exclaimed.

"They're already eager to come down, but I'm sure this will add a little fuel to the fire."

At that moment, the RPV swooped down and hovered close to the boat with its cameras focused on Moose's trophy. Then, via a speaker on the RPV, Dianne said, "That's quite a catch. It was thrilling to watch you guys bring it in. In fact, it was so exciting that I'm ready to go fishing too."

"All the excitement has made me hungry!" Moose declared. "If I knew it would be safe, I'd have fish filets for breakfast."

"When you bring it home, Connie and I will begin our research on it. If all goes well, we can have fish for lunch."

"Great!" Moose exclaimed.

While looking at the RPV, Jerry said, "Since you're here, would you mind scouting the forest around our trail. If our mystery creature's in the area, it might be tempted by the scent of fish."

"Can do," responded Dianne. With that, the RPV sailed off in the direction of the forest, and Jerry started rowing the boat toward the beach.

A short time later, Moose and Jerry arrived in camp without incident and put their fish into an ice chest with a generous covering of ice. Then, they sat down at their outdoor table to enjoy breakfast with their wives.

After breakfast, Dianne and Connie carried the ice chest into the habitation capsule. Except for the small area that Jerry and Connie used for sleeping, the capsule's entire first floor was devoted to research equipment. The facilities and appliances needed for comfortable living were located on the capsule's second floor.

"Let's start by dissecting this fish and examining its internal organs and the contents of its digestive tract," Dianne said.

"When we're finished with that, let's identify the chemicals and biological structures present in its body fluids and tissues and compare them to earth fish," suggested Connie.

"That information should give us a pretty good idea whether or not this fish is safe to eat."

"I think we can get all this done by lunch time. What do you think?"

"I think you're ready for some fresh fish."

"Is it that obvious?" Connie asked.

"Between you and my husband, I'm not sure who is the most eager for a seafood meal," commented Dianne.

"I'm just ready for a change in our menu. And why shouldn't I be, we've been eating food produced by our food synthesizers for seven years. If it's safe to eat, this fish will be our first meal that is from Alcent. That's a big step toward making Alcent our home."

"While that's all true, I still think you just want to eat fish."

"Okay! I admit it! But you haven't answered my original question."

"Getting back to that, yes, I think we can get our research done fast enough to find out if this fish is safe to eat for lunch, especially, if we use the robot lab for part of our research."

"That's a time saving idea," agreed Connie.

Meanwhile, out by the supply shed, Moose and Jerry were busy attaching mechanical bugs to an RPV while listening to Mike. "As soon as you playboys get those bugs attached, we can start investigating the destruction scene on Western Island."

While displaying an air of contentment, Moose asked Jerry, "What do you think he's referring to when he uses the term playboys?"

"I don't know," Jerry said, sounding puzzled. "We've been working hard ever since we arrived here. Why just this morning, we got up when it was still dark, so we could begin our research into native food sources."

"I watched the video of that research," stated Mike. "It looked like the only searching you guys did was for a good spot to catch fish. I just don't know how you can handle all the stress you're subjecting yourselves to."

"It's not easy," responded Moose. "But we're in such good physical condition that we can endure constant strenuous activity without any debilitating fatigue. Also, we have such rock-solid emotional control that we can be continuously alert for danger without getting stressed out."

"Moose's degree of alertness is so fine-tuned that earlier this morning, he was spooked by bouncing pebbles," commented Jerry.

Mike laughed. "Spooked by bouncing pebbles? That doesn't sound like rock-solid emotional control to me."

"It was dark out, and I couldn't see a thing," Moose quickly retorted. He gave Mike the details of what happened, concluding with, "I'm willing to bet you would've reacted the same way I did."

"You're right," Mike said. "But I think it was hilarious just the same. This may go down in our history as the Bouncing Pebbles Incident."

After a brief pause in the conversation, Jerry said, "The bugs are attached and ready for operation. I hope your team can figure out what sort of animal destroyed that dome structure."

"If there are any clues there, we'll find them and identify the culprit," stated Mike. "Since the pterodactyls aren't there anymore, we can do a meticulous search without being interrupted by them."

"When did they leave?"

"Yesterday morning."

"Tell me what you saw."

"Early yesterday, I flew an RPV to Western Island to observe them and listen to them. I'd hoped to start learning their language, if they have one, but they left shortly after I arrived. Before leaving, they surveyed the wreckage and examined the tree leaning against the west side of the cliff. They even tugged at it in an attempt to dislodge it, but they quickly discovered this to be futile and gave up. They took off, circled the area twice, and left. It looked like they were reluctant to leave."

"I wonder if they'll be back anytime soon?" questioned Moose.

"If they're a mated pair looking for a place to raise their young, then whether or not they return will depend on how successful they are at finding another suitable location," responded Jerry. "If they were just passing through, then we probably won't see them again."

"I don't think they were just passing through," commented Mike. "When they tried to dislodge that fallen tree, it looked like they were trying to reclaim their home."

"I wonder if pterodactyls are possessive about their nesting sites and keep reusing the same one," questioned Moose.

"That's something we can only speculate about," commented Mike. "But I can say with certainty that this pair was very reluctant to leave Western Island. They seemed quite attached to it, and it wouldn't surprise me to see them return."

"There is a personal consideration in this that none of us has mentioned," Jerry said. "And that is that we're planning to live in log cabins. It seems reasonable to ask two questions. Is the creature that tore apart the dome structure strong enough to tear apart a log cabin? If so, how sturdy do our homes need to be so that we'll be secure inside of them?"

"Getting answers to those questions and building accordingly will have a direct influence on how soundly I sleep at night," stated Moose.

"You're not the only one with those feelings," Jerry said.

"Maybe our investigation on Western Island will answer the questions you raised," Mike said. "Also, we're going to do an RPV search of Pioneer Island today. Maybe we'll find your mystery creature."

"Good luck on both projects," Jerry said, sounding hopeful.

Then, he and Moose removed the components of the wind powered electrical generator from the supply shed. "Where do you think we should set it up?" Moose asked.

Jerry pointed at the top of the huge boulder he had thrown rocks from. "We need height, so let's put it up there. The telescoping pole that supports the turbine is 36 feet long when fully extended. The big rock will add 16 feet to that."

"That's a good location," agreed Moose. "Including the height of this plateau, our turbine will be more than 200 feet above the lake. Most of the time, there should be more wind up there than down here."

"Not only that, but that rock is as large as a two-story house and will provide a solid foundation on which to bolt the turbine's support pole."

"I'm glad we have this wind powered generator," stated Moose. "It will provide us with backup power in case we get an extended period of rainy weather that reduces our solar power to very low levels."

"Hopefully, that kind of weather system will have enough wind with it to keep our turbine spinning."

"It won't take much wind to get three to five kilowatts out of this generator, and on a windy day, we'll get several times that."

Working intently, Moose and Jerry assembled the windmill in only three hours. After scrambling down off the boulder and walking a short distance away, they looked up at the windmill to admire their handiwork.

"I feel good about this," Jerry said. "It's only the second structure we've built here, but it's another significant step in the long process of turning this island into our home."

"It's so firmly anchored to that boulder that it has a sense of permanence about it. It seems to say that we're here to stay."

"I wish we had more wind, so we could give it a good test."

"Let's turn it on anyway," suggested Moose. "Then, we can find out what it'll do with the little breeze we do have."

Jerry turned on the windmill, and its wind direction vane swung the turbine, so that it faced directly into the wind, and it immediately started rotating. "Apparently, the wind is blowing a little harder up there than here on the ground," he said.

"This is great!" exclaimed Moose. "Even though we don't have much wind, we're still generating two-and-a-half kilowatts. On windy days, we're going to have more power than we know what to do with."

"We'll find a way to use it. Also, don't forget that more people are coming down in four weeks, and everyone is coming down 30 days after that."

"That's only if we don't encounter any serious medical problems."

"My intuition tells me that we won't," commented Jerry. "This is only our third day here, but I'm already starting to feel at home. I just don't sense that we're going to encounter any problems we can't solve."

"I'm starting to feel at home too. I like it here. If our wives determine that the fish I caught is safe to eat, I'm going to feel even more at home."

"Let's find out how they're doing with their research."

As they approached the habitation capsule, Moose sniffed the air a couple times and smiled in satisfaction. "It smells like we're going to have fresh fish for lunch."

"I smell it too, and it smells good. Apparently, they decided to pan-fry it, rather than charcoal-broil it."

"Maybe they're fixing a special lunch for us, and they want it to be a surprise," commented Moose. "If they'd cooked the fish outdoors, we would've immediately known that it passed all their tests."

When Moose and Jerry entered the capsule, they were greeted by the sizzling sound and mouth watering aroma of frying fish. They ascended the stairs to the second floor, and found their wives setting the table and putting the finishing touches on a gourmet seafood lunch. Both looked up from their work and cheerfully greeted their husbands.

"I hope you guys are hungry, because we've prepared a feast," Connie said.

"I am hungry," responded Jerry. "But even if I weren't, this meal smells so good that it would make me hungry. All I need to do is wash my hands, and I'll be ready to eat."

"It's been a long time since I last enjoyed home-cooked fish," commented Moose. "The sizzling sound and pleasant spicy aroma are bringing back childhood memories of my mother's home-cooking."

"I hope our cooking measures up to what you remember of your mother's cooking," responded Dianne.

"I have no doubt that it will," stated Moose.

A few minutes later, all were comfortably seated at their small dining table. Connie looked at the feast laid out before them and was so moved by it that she said a special prayer of thanksgiving. She was especially thankful that the meal's main course was from Alcent. Since this was their first such meal, it represented a special occasion.

After tasting the fish, Moose said, "This is delicious."

"I don't recall ever eating fish this good," stated Jerry.

Speaking to Connie, Dianne said, "I think they're complementing us on our cooking."

"We sure are," stated Moose.

"The flavor is excellent," Jerry said. "What did you do to make it taste so good?"

"We really didn't do all that much," replied Dianne. "When cooking seafood, it helps to start out with something that's really fresh. Cooking fish a few hours after it's caught is about as fresh as it gets."

"All we did was fry it in butter-flavored oil and give it a light sprinkling of Cajun spices," explained Connie.

"They not only did a superb job on the fish," Moose said to Jerry. "But they also came up with some great side dishes. This is a real feast."

"Even better than the dinner you fixed for us last night?" Dianne asked.

After pondering the question for a few moments, Moose decided to subdue his ego and give a safe answer. "Even though I cooked an excellent meal last night, I think this one is even better."

Realizing what had just transpired in Moose's mind; Dianne gave him a look of loving appreciation.

Speaking to Dianne and Connie, Jerry said, "Since we're enjoying delicious fish filets, I assume that your research found this fish safe to eat."

"Chemical analysis of its tissues and fluids didn't reveal any significant differences from Earth's fish," responded Connie.

"Also, the anatomy of this species is nearly identical to that of Earth's fish," added Dianne.

"Did that surprise either of you?" questioned Jerry.

"No," replied Dianne. "Keep in mind that Earth and Alcent are similar planets and that evolution has been going on for hundreds of millions of

256

years on both planets. Evolution allows only the most efficient creatures to survive. Inefficient creatures must evolve, or they become extinct. As on Earth, the fish that exist here are the end result of eons of evolution. Since Earth and Alcent are similar, it's reasonable to expect evolution to produce similar fish."

"If your reasoning is valid, then many of the creatures we find here should be similar to creatures that exist or have existed on Earth," commented Jerry.

"As time goes on, I believe we'll find that to be the case. But I also expect to find creatures here that are different from any that have ever existed on Earth, because Alcent is older than Earth and has had a different history. Both of these factors can affect the evolution process."

"For whatever reason, I'm glad evolution has given us fish to eat," stated Moose. "There's something about a delicious home-cooked meal that makes me feel at home."

"Makes me feel at home too," agreed Jerry.

Dianne and Connie established eye contact, and for a few moments, seemed to be reading each other's thoughts. "We're glad you men feel at home with our cooking," commented Dianne.

"Yeah, we wouldn't want you to run off with other women simply because they cook better than we do," Connie said with a smug grin.

Both men laughed. "Do I sense a feeling of smugness because you are the only women on the entire planet?" Jerry asked.

"There are some advantages to that," replied Connie.

After a bit of silence, Connie said, "I'd love to go swimming sometime this afternoon. It's a beautiful day, and it's warm."

"That does sound like fun," agreed Jerry. "But before we do that, we need to run the blood experiment on the fish in East Bay to find out if any of them are voracious feeders, like piranha. I don't want to become a meal for fish right after we've had a meal of fish."

"That would be a bad turnabout of events," commented Connie.

"I had Mike make a blood dispenser," Jerry said. "He sent it down with the fencing materials yesterday. After lunch, Moose and I'll install it under the marine explorer. Then, while we explore the south lobe of this island, you and Dianne can expose the fish in East Bay to human blood. Hopefully, it won't provoke any frenzied reactions from any of them, and when Moose and I return, we can go swimming."

"That sounds like fun," responded Dianne. "I haven't been swimming since we left Earth."

"We'll take turns swimming and standing guard," stated Jerry.

A few minutes later, everyone finished lunch. While Dianne and Connie put away the leftover food and washed the dishes, Moose and Jerry went to East Bay to install the blood dispenser under the marine explorer.

An hour later, Jerry called and said, "Your blood dispenser is installed and ready for action."

"Good!" responded Connie. "We'll begin exposing fish to human blood right away."

"We'll check in later and find out how the experiment's going. Right now, we're going to take a look at the south end of this island."

"Be careful. I don't want anything to happen to you guys."

"Don't worry; we're not about to become a meal for anything."

"I sure hope not," responded Connie. Then, she turned to Dianne. "Let's find out how our local fish react to human blood."

"Let's start close to shore in the area where we plan to swim and then move out into the bay," Dianne suggested.

A few minutes later, Dianne and Connie were seated and wearing video headsets to view imagery from the marine explorer's underwater cameras, which covered the complete field of view beneath the marine explorer. The images from the cameras were smoothly joined by a powerful computer, making them look like a single continuous image. The video headsets worn by Dianne and Connie were equipped with motion sensors to detect their head movements. These motion detectors told the computer which direction the wearer of a headset was looking. The computer then showed the wearer the scene in that direction. This gave the wearer of a headset the illusion of sitting inside a transparent capsule suspended beneath the marine explorer.

Since Connie was piloting the marine explorer, she was viewing forward-downward imagery, while Dianne was viewing rearward-downward imagery. Connie switched on the explorer's electric motor and slowly headed out into the bay. About 20 yards offshore, in water 15 feet deep, she spotted a school of sunfish. They were shaped like small dinner plates equipped with heads, tails, and fins. The fish were multicolored, but the dominant color was golden yellow. Since these fish looked like Earth's freshwater sunfish, they had been given that name.

Connie lowered the blood dispenser into the midst of the fish and ejected a small quantity of blood. Dianne and Connie observed the blood as it slowly dispersed into the water. As it spread out into a larger and larger volume of water, some of the fish came into contact with it.

After observing the fish for a short time, Connie said, "They seem to be oblivious to the fresh blood in their environment."

"Either they can't taste or smell it, or they aren't flesh eaters and don't recognize it as an indication that food might be close by," commented Dianne. "Also, their mouths don't seem to have the right shape for attacking large prey like us."

As the peaceful afternoon wore on, Dianne and Connie became ever more engrossed in their experiment. The panoramic imagery developed by the marine explorer's video system made them feel like they were actually in the alien underwater world with the fish they were exposing to human blood. Even though it was just an illusion, the feeling that they were underwater was so real that it added excitement and a sense of danger to their experiment. It gave them a very real feeling of what it would be like to be underwater and bleeding from a small cut with fish around picking up the scent of blood. Each time they exposed fish to blood, they felt anxiety while wondering if the fish would attack the source of the blood. Each time they exposed fish to blood without getting a reaction made them more confident that swimming in Clear Lake would be safe.

Suddenly, they were jolted out of their underwater world by the beeping of a communicator. While Connie continued to observe the fish she had just exposed to human blood, Dianne answered the call.

It was Michelle. "Don't go outside!" she warned. "Two pterodactyls have just landed north of your capsule, and they are approaching you."

"Thanks for the warning," responded Dianne.

"I need to observe these fish a bit longer," Connie said. "Maybe you can check out those pterodactyls."

"Okay," replied Dianne, as she removed her headset and turned to look out the north window. Dianne's pulse suddenly quickened at the sight of the slowly approaching pterodactyls that were now only fifteen yards away. Their obvious size and power sent a chilling tingle up and down Dianne's spine. This was her first meeting with any of the fierce wild creatures that lived on Alcent. That they could just drop in without warning made Dianne realize just how vulnerable she was on this planet. Why are they here? She wondered.

Ten yards away, the pterodactyls stopped, peered intently at the capsule, and then made some squawking sounds back and forth. This activity led Dianne to say, "It looks like they're having a discussion about what to do next."

While observing the scene with the video camera on top the capsule, Michelle said, "It appears that it has dawned upon them that there are some alien structures in their world that they need to investigate."

"In spite of their size and strength, they sure are wary," noted Dianne.

"I can't fault them for that," stated Michelle. "They're investigating something that is different from anything they've ever seen. The fact that they're even doing this demonstrates intelligence, curiosity, and courage on their part."

Without coming any closer than about ten yards, the pterodactyls slowly circled the habitation capsule and storage shed. While they were doing this, Dianne went from window to window to observe them. "They're staring at this capsule from top to bottom. I wonder what there is about it that they find so interesting."

"Since they've never seen one before, they might be trying to figure out what it is," responded Michelle. "Specifically, they may be trying to determine if it poses any danger to them."

"Or they might be trying to find out if this capsule contains anything they can eat."

"Obtaining food doesn't seem to be much of a problem for them, so I don't think that's the case."

"If you're convinced of that, I guess I could safely step outside and introduce myself to them."

"I don't recommend that you do that," Michelle quickly replied. "I was just stating an opinion."

By this time, Connie finished observing the fish that she had exposed to blood, so she joined Dianne and said, "I wonder if these are the same pterodactyls we saw on Western Island."

"I was wondering about that too," Michelle said. "So I had the computer make an image comparison, and it confirmed that they are the same creatures."

"It's possible that they're thinking about rebuilding the wrecked shelter on Western Island in preparation for a baby and have decided to investigate us first," Dianne suggested.

"We don't know if they're capable of that kind of advanced thinking," argued Connie.

"While that's true, it certainly looks like they're thinking and communicating," responded Dianne. "As you can see, they've returned to their starting point, and they're standing there squawking back and forth while looking at this capsule."

"How close to the windows did you stand when you followed them around this capsule?" Connie asked. "Were you close enough so they could see you?"

"I think so. These windows are large, and there's lots of light in here, so they must be aware that this capsule is inhabited."

"Let's stand very close to the north window, wave at them, and see how they react," suggested Connie.

Dianne stepped forward to within a few inches of the window and waved at the pterodactyls. Then, Connie joined her and did the same thing. The pterodactyls intently stared at them for a few moments; then, they resumed their squawking.

"I don't think there's any doubt that they know this capsule's inhabited," Connie said.

"Let's move from window to window and find out if they'll follow us around the capsule," suggested Dianne.

Connie moved to the next window to the west. Then, while standing very close to the north window, Dianne pointed at Connie. After Dianne saw that the pterodactyls had shifted their gaze to Connie, she joined her. Following a few moments of back and forth squawking, the pterodactyls also moved to the west, apparently in response to Dianne's actions. By repeating this procedure, Dianne and Connie moved the pterodactyls from window to window until they were on the south side of the capsule.

"It looks like you've established communication with them," noted Michelle. "It appears that they interpreted your hand signals to mean that you wanted them to follow you around the capsule. But why have they so willingly followed you from window to window?"

"Apparently, they decided that we aren't any threat to them, and they couldn't think of any reason to not follow us," responded Dianne.

"But what do they hope to gain?" questioned Michelle.

"Perhaps, it's a matter of curiosity," replied Dianne. "They might be inquisitive creatures who are hoping to learn something about us. Maybe they think that we're trying to tell them something and are following us hoping to gain that information. Maybe they want to meet us."

"The window we're standing by is next to our front door," Connie said. "I think I'll slowly open the door and step out onto the front porch."

"That could be dangerous," warned Michelle.

"I thought it was your opinion that they're not interested in eating us," replied Connie.

"I did say that, but I wasn't implying that you should put my opinion to the test."

"Eventually, we have to find out how these creatures are going to react to us in a face-to-face meeting," argued Connie. "Right now, we have a perfect opportunity to do that."

"Admittedly, there is some risk, but Connie is right," Dianne said to Michelle.

"I think the risk is minimal," argued Connie, as she picked up her 10.5-mm pistol and selected a ten-round clip containing ammunition with explosive bullets. "They've maintained a distance of about ten yards, and if they decide to attack from there, I'll have ample time to deal with it."

"It would be a shame to have to kill these magnificent creatures," commented Dianne.

"I won't unless I have to," stated Connie. "I plan to stay very close to the front door, so I can quickly jump back inside and slam the door shut. The gun is only my last resort."

"In case you need assistance, I'm ready," stated Dianne, as she picked up her handgun, which was similar to Connie's.

With Dianne standing against the window observing the pterodactyls, Connie unlatched the front door and slowly began opening it. "You have their attention," stated Dianne. "They're staring at the door."

Connie continued to slowly push the door open with her left hand while she held her gun in her right hand ready for instant use. When the door was wide open, she stood straight and tall in the doorway and faced the pterodactyls. Since they seemed to be a bit nervous and uncertain about what to do, Connie did not make any sudden movements that might be seen as threatening. Instead, she stood still and shifted her gaze back and forth between the large wild creatures. In a soft, soothing voice, she said, "I don't know what you guys are so nervous about. Both of you are so much bigger than I am, and you can leave anytime you want to."

The largest most colorful of the two pterodactyls made some squawking sounds, and the smaller, plainer colored pterodactyl stepped backwards a few yards. Then, the larger one also stepped backwards and the two began squawking back and forth while keeping an eye on Connie.

"I think they're talking about you," commented Dianne.

"It sure looks that way," agreed Connie.

A minute later, Dianne said, "I don't know what all that squawking means, but they seem to be losing some of their nervousness."

"Now that they appear to be more relaxed, I'll give them a better view of me," stated Connie, as she slowly stepped onto the front porch while grasping the door with her left hand and her gun with her right hand.

The larger of the two pterodactyls noticed this, and as if to mimic Connie, he slowly stepped forward a couple yards. Then, he stopped, stood in what appeared to be a relaxed posture, and gazed at Connie with eyes that seemed to be searching for information.

Observing this, Connie said, "You sure look like a wise old bird. If I could squawk in a way that you could understand, I would answer your questions, but I can't. So, how do I go about telling you that we would like to be friends with you and your mate?"

Meanwhile, Moose and Jerry were sitting on the sandy beach at the foot of South Bay discussing the construction of an elevator to get on and off the south end of Stellar Plateau. This discussion was prompted by the fact that when they arrived at South Bay, the temperature was 80 degrees and the water looked so inviting that both removed their hiking boots and waded out a few yards. After discovering how warm the sheltered water in the south-facing bay was, they decided that it was better for swimming than the cooler water in East Bay and that some sort of simple elevator was needed. Being practical minded engineers, they soon became preoccupied with how best to build one.

Both men were so relaxed in their pleasant surroundings that when Jerry's communicator beeped, it was almost an unwanted intrusion. "Are you going to answer that or just let it beep?" Moose asked.

"I'd better answer it. It's probably Connie calling to check on our progress. She and Dianne do have their hearts set on going swimming this afternoon."

"That's true, and they might also be worried about our safety. After all, we're out here in the open exposed to possible danger."

"I'm glad our wives are inside the capsule, and we don't have to worry about their safety," commented Jerry.

"Me too," stated Moose.

When Jerry finally answered the call and discovered that it was Mike, he said, "Hi Mike. I'm surprised it's you. I thought my wife was calling."

"She's rather busy at the moment," Mike said. "She's standing on the front porch having a conversation with a pair of pterodactyls."

"SHE'S DOING WHAT!"

"She's standing on the front porch having a conversation with a pair of pterodactyls," repeated Mike.

After a bit of silence, Mike asked, "Do you have a hearing problem?"

"No! I heard you, but you're so matter-of-fact about it that I'm trying to decide whether you're serious or just kidding."

"I'm not kidding."

"I wish that she weren't exposing herself to so much risk."

"She seems to have the situation under control. If you'll put on your video headset, I'll beam you the imagery that we're watching. Everyone here on the Challenger who isn't doing a pressing job is watching this drama unfold, wondering how it will end."

A few moments later, Jerry was wearing his headset. He watched Dianne join Connie on the front porch and heard her say, "Since we can't squawk in a way that these creatures will understand, maybe we should indicate our desire to be friends by offering them a gift."

"That might work," agreed Connie. "But what can we give them that they would appreciate receiving?"

"We have raw and cooked fish, and we know they like fish."

"But they can easily get all the fish they want. I think we should offer them something that they've never had before."

"Those cinnamon rolls you baked this morning were delicious, and we still have about a dozen left."

"Why don't you get some of them? We'll each eat one, and depending on how they react, we might throw them one or more."

The pterodactyls watched with interest as Dianne disappeared into the capsule and then reappeared a few moments later. Dianne handed Connie a cinnamon roll, and both ate their rolls with the pterodactyls watching.

"It's encouraging that they haven't made any menacing moves toward us," commented Connie.

"Maybe they're trying to lull us into lowering our guard in preparation for an attack."

"I don't get that feeling, but they sure are observing us closely. I think they've figured out that these rolls are good to eat, so would you like to toss one to the big guy in front?"

Dianne held up a roll and stepped forward two steps. Then, she extended her arm out as far she could reach. The pterodactyl looked at it and stepped forward two steps and stopped. Now only five yards away, he looked at Connie, then at Dianne, then at the roll.

"He seems reluctant to come any closer," Connie said.

"He's not as reluctant about that as I am," Dianne quickly said.

"Well, you have his attention, so toss him the roll."

Dianne tossed the cinnamon roll to the huge pterodactyl. With a quick head movement, he easily caught it with his beak. However, he did not immediately eat it; instead, he held it in his mouth for several seconds.

Noticing this, Connie said, "I don't know if he's trying to prolong the enjoyment of an unfamiliar flavor or if he's trying to determine if the roll is safe to eat."

"He just ate it, so it didn't take him long to make up his mind."

"He must've liked it," noted Connie, "because he's looking at you like he's hoping you'll toss him another one."

"If he wants more rolls, what's keeping him from attacking me and taking them? He can't possibly know anything about guns, but he does know that he's much bigger than we are, so why is he treating us with so much respect?"

"We can debate that later," responded Connie. "I'm not sure this is the right time to test his patience."

"Perhaps not, but while I have his attention, I want to try more sign language and see how he responds." Dianne held up a cinnamon roll for the large pterodactyl to look at. Then, she pointed at his mate.

In response, the large pterodactyl made some soft squawking sounds, and his mate stepped forward. Dianne tossed the roll to her, which she easily caught. After briefly checking out its flavor, she ate it. Dianne then tossed each pterodactyl one of the two remaining rolls.

After they ate them, Dianne asked, "Well, what do we do now?"

"I think we should go back to our fish research. I don't know that there's much more we can accomplish with these creatures at the moment. We've had our first face-to-face meeting, and they now know who we are. I think you should step into the capsule while I watch them. Then, I'll back into the capsule and close the door. That should indicate to them that the meeting is over. We'll find out how they react."

With the pterodactyls alertly watching, Dianne and Connie entered the capsule and shut the door. Feeling drained from the intense encounter, Connie sat down. "Wow! I can't believe what we just did."

"It was incredibly exciting," stated Dianne.

"It was also very dangerous, and if we'd thought about it a little longer, we might not have faced them outside."

"Despite the danger, we had to do it. We were presented with an opportunity to increase our knowledge about these creatures, and we had to take advantage of it."

"That's true," Connie agreed. "But I'm wondering why they gave us that opportunity. What motivated them to drop in and investigate us?"

"We can only speculate, but one possibility is that they're planning to rebuild the wrecked shelter on Western Island in preparation for an infant, and they decided to investigate us first."

"Are you suggesting that they have enough intelligence to not only think and plan, but to also recognize and investigate possible hazards to their plans?"

"Again, we can only speculate, but my impression of them is that they are quite intelligent."

"Apparently, they've concluded that their meeting with us is over," noted Connie. "They seem to be leaving."

Looking out the south window, Dianne and Connie observed the pterodactyls walking south. Then, the large male in the lead started running. Spreading his wings to their full 52-foot span, he took off. The smaller female immediately followed.

"What an amazing sight," stated Connie.

"It's hard to believe that we just had a meeting with those magnificent creatures," commented Dianne.

"It might be difficult to believe, but I have a feeling that we'll be meeting with them again. In fact, it's possible that we might even play a crucial role in each other's lives."

Dianne wondered how that might happen, but she didn't say anything. She just silently watched the huge creatures fly away.

When the pterodactyls were out of sight, Connie said, "Let's finish our fish research. I'd still like to go swimming this afternoon."

Meanwhile, down at South Bay, Jerry said, "Our wives are back in the capsule, and the pterodactyls are flying this way."

"Are they going to land here to meet us?" Moose asked.

"I hope not. We're out in the open with no place to retreat to, and we'd have to kill them if they made any threatening moves."

Moose pointed up. "They're directly overhead, and they're turning west. Apparently, they aren't interested in us."

"Whatever they learned from our wives must've satisfied their curiosity about humans for the time being."

"It looks that way."

"I think we should resume our hike and get back home before our wives find some other dangerous activity to get involved in."

"What they just did caused us some anxiety, but we do have to admire them for their courage."

"That's true," agreed Jerry. "But I hope their courage never gets them into situations where there's too much risk, and they end up suffering the consequences."

"I don't think we need to worry about that; they do have pretty good judgment. For example, in their meeting with the pterodactyls, they did have their handguns ready for action, and they are very quick and accurate with those weapons. I think they concluded that their risk was minimal, and I agree with that conclusion."

"Nevertheless, I'm glad the encounter had a successful outcome, and I am more comfortable with us taking the risks, instead of our wives."

"Me too," stated Moose.

A few minutes later, Moose and Jerry rounded the southwestern tip of Pioneer Island and headed north. Shortly thereafter, Jerry's communicator beeped. It was Mike. "Stop right where you are!" he exclaimed. "We've located an animal that might be your mystery creature. He's in the forest 150 yards in front of you. You are upwind from him, and I believe he's picked up your scent, because he's sniffing the breeze with great interest."

"What does he look like?" Jerry asked.

"He's big, at least 1,000 pounds. If he had white fur instead of brown, he could easily pass for a polar bear."

Turning to Moose, Jerry asked, "Would you like to calmly stroll up the beach and find out if we can pass by him without being attacked?"

"Are you crazy?"

"No! I just wanted to find out where your thinking is at?"

"Well, I think we should turn around and go back the way we came. If this animal is mean-tempered or hungry, he'll most certainly attack. Then, we'll have no choice except to kill him. As a consequence, we'll lose the opportunity to observe his daily living habits."

"I do agree with you," responded Jerry, as he turned around and started rapidly hiking away from the area.

Moose and Jerry heard laughter come through the communicator. "Sounds like you guys aren't as adventuresome as your wives," Mike said.

"They do have courage," admitted Jerry. "But in this situation, we must avoid killing this animal, so we can learn about it. A radio transmitter to track its movements would be helpful."

"I'm ahead of you on that," responded Mike. "We already have a small RPV approaching the animal from behind, and we should have a transmitter attached shortly."

A few seconds later, Mike announced, "A tiny radio has been entangled in the animal's fur on its back between its shoulders, and it's transmitting a strong signal. We also grabbed a few strands of hair for comparison to what you found yesterday and to what we found on Western Island earlier today."

"I wasn't aware that you found any hair on Western Island," responded Jerry.

"We just completed the search a half-hour ago, and I haven't had an opportunity to talk to you about it until now. We did find some hair stuck to sticky sap on the tipped tree. We also found some claw marks in the driftwood from the wrecked shelter. We've returned the mechanical bugs and the hair specimens to the robot lab."

"It'll be interesting to see if all of our hair samples are from the same animal," Jerry said.

"I think you guys should pick up the pace," stated Mike. "The animal we just tagged has stepped out of the forest and is heading south."

As Moose, Jerry, and Charlie broke into a slow run, Jerry asked, "Are you sure he's after us? Maybe he's just going somewhere."

"He just stopped to sniff the air, and he's now heading south again. I don't think there's any doubt that he has your scent and has decided to investigate. I don't know if he's just curious or if he's hungry, but he does look determined."

"We can't outrun a bear!" Jerry exclaimed. "Unless you can persuade him to stop following us, we will have to shoot him. This might be a good time to test those modified RPVs that you sent down yesterday."

"We've already launched them," replied Mike. "Also, the bear has not yet broken into a run; he's just trotting along."

"But once he catches sight of us, he's probably going to charge," stated Moose.

"Especially, if he's hungry," commented Jerry.

A few minutes later, Moose, Jerry, and Charlie were approaching the foot of South Bay. "The bear will come around the point shortly," Mike said. "If he sees you running, you might look like escaping quarry, and that could provoke a charge. So you might want to stop and face him."

"Let's hide behind that pile of driftwood," directed Jerry. "We'll have our backs against the cliff, and we'll be able to watch the bear while being almost completely hidden."

When they were behind the logs, Jerry supported his rifle on top of them and aimed at the point. He chambered a cartridge, turned on the laser spotter, and focused the telescopic sight.

When the bear came lumbering around the point, Jerry said, "He's huge, well over 1,000 pounds. And he's definitely following our trail."

"I'd hate to be walking on the beach and have him come charging out of the forest with no warning," stated Moose.

As the huge animal steadily came closer, Moose and Jerry's adrenaline started flowing causing their hearts to beat faster and their excitement to become intense. Finally, Jerry said to Mike, "The bear is close enough. I suggest you start discouraging him."

"I've been waiting for your command. I didn't want to spoil your fun. When your wives tell you their pterodactyl story, you'll need to have a good story of your own."

"Our story's exciting enough! Start discouraging this brute before we have no choice except to kill it."

"Yes sir!"

At that moment, a piercing high-pitched scream filled the air as a pair of 40-inch-diameter RPVs came swooping down with their electronic sirens wailing with deafening intensity. The bear instantly stopped its advance and looked up at the diving RPVs. The first RPV pulled out of its dive and hovered ten feet in front of the bear at an altitude of 12 feet. The second RPV hovered 20 feet ahead of the bear at an altitude of six feet.

The bear stared at the RPVs, but because of their small size, he was not intimidated by their screaming sirens. After a brief pause, he resumed his advance, so a smoke bomb was released from the nearest RPV. It landed three feet in front of the bear and burst open releasing a cloud of irritating fumes that enveloped the bear's head. Some of it got into his eyes and nose causing him to roar with rage at the painful irritation. He quickly backed out of the cloud and charged into the water of South Bay. After washing his eyes and nose for nearly a minute, he came out of the water, shook himself vigorously, and resumed pursuing Moose and Jerry.

"It looks like he doesn't want give up," noted Mike. "Since he's not willing to respect our warning, we'll have to drop a larger bomb."

Again the RPVs came swooping down with their electronic sirens screeching. Both RPVs stopped and hovered side by side ten yards in front of the bear at an altitude of ten feet. The bear stopped and looked at them and then let out a loud terrifying roar.

"It looks like he did learn something from our warning bomb," commented Mike.

"It also looks like he's trying to scare away the RPVs with that loud roar of his," stated Jerry.

As Jerry finished speaking, the bear stood up on his hind legs, pounded his chest, and repeated the bloodcurdling roar. Then, he took three steps forward, stopped, and again repeated the horrifying roar while pounding his chest.

"Instead of dropping a larger more-potent chemical bomb, I will try a different tactic," stated Mike. "I will drop several of the small smoke bombs; each one will be a few yards closer to the bear. We'll find out if he's smart enough to get the message."

"Good plan," responded Jerry.

Mike dropped the first smoke bomb. When it exploded, the bear roared defiantly. Then, the second smoke bomb exploded three yards closer, and again, the bear roared defiantly. When the third smoke bomb exploded, it was close enough so that the bear got a faint whiff of the irritating fumes. This caused just enough pain to remind him of his previous painful experience, and he turned, dropped down on all four feet, and took off running with a pair of screaming RPVs in pursuit. After running 50 yards, the bear turned to the right and headed into the forest crashing through bushes as though they didn't exist. Pursuit with the RPVs was discontinued 50 yards into the forest.

"I don't think he'll bother us for a while," commented Moose.

"I hope so, but I don't trust him," stated Jerry. "I am glad we have a transmitter on him, so we can keep track of where he is."

"I wonder if that's the creature that came to this island yesterday," questioned Moose.

"I've just been handed the lab report on the hair analysis," responded Mike. "This bear is not the animal that came to your island yesterday, but his hair does match the hair we found on Western Island. Analysis of hair from the animal that came ashore yesterday indicates that it belongs to the same species as the bear that just added a little excitement to your day."

"That means there are at least two of these brutes on this island," stated Jerry, "one we know the location of and one we don't."

"Considering what we just experienced, I'd sure like to know where the other one is," stated Moose.

"Our personnel are searching the forest with all available RPVs, and we haven't yet found him," stated Mike. "But we have several hours of daylight left, and we may still find him today."

"I don't think we should explore the forest in person until we've located the other bear," Jerry said. "There are just too many hiding places that a hungry bear could ambush us from. So I want you to continue a systematic search with RPVs until the missing bear and any others that might be here have been located and tagged."

"Whatever it takes, we'll find them," stated Mike.

"While you're doing that, we could begin our underwater exploration, if we had our submarine down here."

"We've already loaded it on the cargo shuttle. We can send it down this evening or tomorrow morning."

"Tomorrow morning will be just fine."

"Good! We'll use this evening to give it one final checkout, so that it will be ready for immediate use. Also, if there's anything else you want sent down, let me know."

"We could use our portable sawmill, a chainsaw, some basic wood working tools, and 300 yards of rope able to support at least 3000 pounds," responded Moose.

"Are you planning to lasso one of those bears and build a corral to put him in?" Mike asked.

After taking a few moments to visualize doing what Mike had suggested, Moose said, "I've carefully considered your question, and I'm not able to envision a desirable conclusion to such a project."

"Once you have him in the corral, you would have an opportunity to study him up close," suggested Mike.

"You're not convincing me! I've already been as close as I care to get. The project we have in mind is to build an elevator to get on and off the south end of the plateau."

"And when we're finished with that, we'll try our skill at building a small log cabin," added Jerry.

"Those projects don't sound as exciting as the one I just suggested," teased Mike.

"That's true," responded Moose, "but they need to get done. We'll save your brainchild for you, so you can have some exciting adventure when you get here."

"No thanks, just being down there will be exciting enough for me."

"I think it's time for us to return to our campsite," stated Jerry. "We're planning to take our wives swimming yet this afternoon."

"That sounds like fun! I wish I could join you."

"In just a few weeks, you'll be down here," Jerry assured Mike.

"I can hardly wait, but as busy as you guys are keeping me, the time will go by fast."

"There is something that you might do for us during the next couple hours," stated Jerry.

"What?"

"You might concentrate your RPV search in the forest that borders East Bay. We don't need any bad surprises while we're swimming."

"Good idea," responded Mike. "Also, we'll keep the marine explorer between you and the open water and watch the underwater world."

"Thanks! Also, we could use more surveillance cameras. If large bears occasionally visit this island, it would be nice to see them arrive, so we can attach transmitters to them."

"I'll take a look at a map of the island, determine how many cameras you need, and send them down in the morning."

Moose and Jerry made the return journey to their campsite without incident. Upon entering the capsule, they found their wives fully engrossed in their fish experiment. Wearing a sly grin, Jerry looked at Moose and said, "I wonder if their afternoon was as exciting as ours."

"We had a lot more excitement than we were expecting," Connie exclaimed.

She and Dianne removed their headsets and eagerly told their husbands about their sensational pterodactyl encounter. Listening to their story, it became obvious to Moose and Jerry that their wives felt tremendous satisfaction with what they had done. They were glowing with pride. They had calmly faced wild, fierce creatures and had confidently remained in control throughout the encounter, despite the danger. They have every right to be proud of themselves thought Jerry.

When they finished their story, Jerry asked, "Did either of you sense any hostility in the pterodactyls?"

"We were alert, and we had our guns ready, but they never made any threatening moves," Connie replied.

"I never felt threatened either," commented Dianne. "Now that I've had a chance to think about it, I could almost believe that they made a conscious effort to make sure that we felt comfortable in their presence."

"Why would they do that?" questioned Jerry.

"Maybe they have enough intelligence to recognize that the structures we have here could only have been made by beings far more intelligent than they are," Connie speculated. "Maybe they've decided that it would be better to be friends with such creatures than enemies."

"What do you think we should do next to continue our communication with them?"

"I think we should avoid doing anything that they might interpret as threatening and wait for them to come to us."

"That's my feeling too," commented Dianne. "As mobile as they are, they can meet with us anytime they want to."

"That's true," agreed Jerry. "But let's not lower our guard until we're sure that they are friendly."

Everyone nodded in agreement. Then, Moose turned to his wife. "I'd like to go swimming. Did your fish experiment find any man-eaters in East Bay?"

Dianne shot her husband a naughty glance and wondered if she should make a sexy comment in response to the easy opening that he had just given her. However, before she could say anything, Moose noticed the way she was looking at him and quickly rephrased his question: "I'd like to know if you discovered any fish with feeding habits like the piranha?"

While still wearing a naughty grin, Dianne said, "If there are, we haven't identified them. In fact, we didn't get any frenzied reactions from any of the fish we exposed to blood."

"We didn't even see anything that looked threatening," added Connie. "Everything looked so peaceful that I'm ready to go swimming."

"What are we waiting for!" exclaimed Moose. "Let's go!"

On the way to East Bay, Dianne asked, "Did you guys enjoy your stroll on the beach?"

"It was fun," replied Moose. "We even had an unexpected encounter on the sandy beach of South Bay.

"It sounds like you met some erotic sunbathing mermaids, and that dashes my assumption that Connie and I are the only women on the planet."

"Our encounter wasn't quite that exotic, but it was intense."

"Was it more intense than our pterodactyl encounter?"

"Comparable."

"You guys had that much excitement, and you haven't told us about it yet!" exclaimed Dianne.

"You never asked," countered Moose.

"Now that you've baited my curiosity, I'm dying to know what happened."

"We were stalked by a huge bear that wanted to eat us for lunch, but Mike managed to convince him that following us wasn't a good idea."

"That must've been wild. Stop stringing me along and tell me what happened," Dianne demanded.

By the time they reached the forest, Moose and Jerry finished their bear story, and Dianne reacted by saying, "I don't feel all that comfortable about entering the forest."

"I don't think we have much to worry about," responded Moose. "This area is buzzing with RPVs. Our friends on the Challenger are determined to

271

find anything that might be a threat to us."

"Just the same, I intend to be ready," stated Dianne, as she took her rifle off her shoulder and held it in a ready-to-fire position.

"I wasn't implying that we shouldn't be on guard. I was only saying that we aren't likely to be ambushed on our way to the beach."

Moose proved to be correct. The hike through the forest was peaceful.

On the beach, Connie said to Dianne, "Since Jerry and I have already been swimming; you and Moose can go first, while we stand guard."

"Thanks," responded Dianne, as she stripped down to her swim suit. "Race you into the water," she said to Moose.

Dianne ran into the water with Moose in hot pursuit. After wading out to a depth of about four feet, she started swimming. Thirty yards from the beach, she did a surface dive and headed for the bottom with Moose only a couple yards behind her.

A minute later, they surfaced, took several deep breaths, and again, headed down into the underwater world. When they surfaced again, they were 15 yards farther out.

"It's only 60 yards out to the marine explorer," stated Moose. "Let's swim out to it. When we get there, we can swim around underwater within view of its cameras and put on a show for our friends on the Challenger."

"Sounds like fun; let's do it."

Moose and Dianne leisurely swam out to the marine explorer and lazily circled it in view of its above water cameras. Then, they swam down to a depth of about 15 feet, faced the nearest camera, smiled, and waved. After swimming around under the marine explorer for about a minute, they headed for the surface.

"This is the cleanest lake I've ever swam in," stated Moose. "I'm amazed at how clearly we could see the bottom from the depth we were at. It had to be at least 30 feet below us."

"It's incredibly clean, but I wish it were a little warmer."

"I don't think it's really all that cold," commented Moose.

"It's not cold enough to be uncomfortable, but it's not as warm as I'd like it to be either."

"It's only early spring. Even though this is a deep lake, it should be warmer by the end of the summer. In the meantime, we should be swimming in South Bay; it's warmer than this. To make it more convenient, Jerry and I are going to build an elevator to get on and off the south end of the plateau."

"That sounds good to me. Let's do one more underwater swim for the cameras, and then let's head for the beach and let Jerry and Connie have their turn."

After their second underwater performance for their friends on the Challenger, Moose and Dianne spent ten minutes playfully frolicking around in the water as they swam to the beach. Then, while Moose stood guard, Dianne stretched out on a beach towel to soak up some of the radiant energy pouring out of the twin stars, Alpha Centauri A and B.

Connie noted that Moose seemed to be standing guard with a special air of alertness about him. On the way to the water, she turned to Jerry. "That bear seems to have had quite an effect on Moose."

"He had quite an effect on me too. It's going to be a long time before either one of us falls asleep on guard duty."

"That means we can enjoy our swim, since Moose is on full alert."

For the next 20 minutes, Jerry and Connie enjoyed the pleasures of a refreshing dip in Clear Lake. Then, they laid out beach towels and joined Dianne in some lazy sunbathing while Moose continued to stand guard. During the next half-hour, they spoke very little, each content to be lost in thought. The setting was so peaceful that Connie and Dianne fell asleep.

Jerry got up, and speaking not much louder than a whisper, said to Moose, "I think it's my turn to pull guard duty."

"Okay, but rather than sunbathe, I'm going in for another swim."

Ten minutes after entering the water, Moose returned and said, "I'm hungry. It must be almost dinner time."

Both Connie and Dianne were now awake. "I'd like to take another quick dip in the bay before we eat," Dianne said. While Moose stood guard, Jerry and Connie entered the water with her.

A short time later, they returned feeling refreshed. "I'm ready to go home," Connie said. "And when we get back, I'm going to put some fish in the frying pan. My stomach is growling."

"You mean I'm not the only one who is hungry?" Moose asked.

"I think we're all ready for dinner," responded Dianne.

"Let my vote make that unanimous," stated Jerry.

Twenty minutes later, they were back in their campsite. Their plan for the rest of the day was to just have a peaceful, relaxing evening.

At 10:00 P.M., all were ready for bed, but they decided to go outside and do some stargazing first. The sky was dominated by Alcent's two moons. The nearest moon, which journeyed around Alcent once every ten days, was high in the southern sky and appeared as a half moon. The more distant moon, which required 17 days to travel around Alcent, was 45 degrees above the western horizon and appeared as a crescent moon. Since the more distant moon was considerably larger than the nearer moon, it appeared to be about the same size, despite its greater distance. Even though both moons were smaller than Earth's moon, they appeared to be about the same size because of their proximity.

Because of their familiarity with Earth's time keeping, it was decided to keep the same time system as existed on Earth. The fact that Alcent's day was 24 minutes longer than Earth's day was accounted for by having 61 minutes in each hour. One year on Alcent, the time required to make one journey around Alpha Centauri A, was 364 Alcent days.

"What an enjoyable evening this has been," commented Connie.

"It has been peaceful and relaxing," agreed Dianne. "I'm really starting to like it here."

"I like the great weather," stated Moose.

"We have had good weather," acknowledged Jerry, "but that might soon change. Mike told me there's a large low pressure system building out over the ocean that's heading our way. He's predicting a windy rainstorm in a day or two."

"We do need the rain," Dianne said. "The last rain was eleven days ago, and some of the plants here are thirsty."

"I haven't experienced a windy rainstorm in seven years," stated Moose. "I think I just might enjoy being out in that."

"I enjoy having two moons in the sky," Connie said, "but it seems so unreal. I wonder how long it's going to take to get used to it."

"I think it's romantic," commented Dianne. "Several times each year, we'll be treated to having two full moons. If Alpha Centauri B is also in the nighttime sky, it just simply isn't going to get dark. Two full moons, plus a dim orange sun, won't that be exotic?"

"All the vacations I took to exotic places in the South Pacific can't begin to compete with what we have here," stated Moose.

"We should name those moons," suggested Jerry.

"I think we should give them romantic names," responded Connie.

"Do you have any suggestions?" Jerry asked.

"A full moon is romantic only because it occurs during the nighttime. Romance that occurs during the night can be called nocturnal romance, so why don't we name one of these moons Nocturne?"

"When you put it that way, the name does have a romantic twist," agreed Dianne. "I like it."

"We have two moons to name," Jerry reminded everyone.

"I have a suggestion that sticks with the romantic theme," Dianne said. "Going back to ancient Greek Mythology, there was a goddess of love and beauty named Aphrodite. I think we should name one of our moons Aphrodite."

"Good idea," agreed Connie.

"It seems we have our names," Jerry said. "Now the question is which moon gets which name?"

"That's an easy question," declared Moose. "Since it's desirable to be as close as possible to a love goddess, we need to name the nearest moon Aphrodite and the more distant moon Nocturne."

"That kind of logic is hard to disagree with," responded Jerry.

"Don't you just love the way our husbands think?" Connie asked Dianne.

Displaying a naughty grin, Dianne said, "There are some advantages to the way they think."

"Who was it that made the love goddess suggestion?" Moose quickly asked.

Dianne snuggled up to Moose. "I plead guilty."

Moose wrapped his arms around her. "It's great that we think alike."

"That does have its advantages," she responded.

"I'm starting to lose interest in stargazing. Maybe we should retire for the night," suggested Moose.

"I don't seem to be all that tired just yet," Dianne teased.

"Good, I'm not ready to go to sleep either," responded Moose, as he led Dianne toward the habitation capsule. Looking over her left shoulder, Dianne said, "See you two in the morning. Don't disturb us."

Jerry and Connie smiled at Dianne. Then, they also went indoors.

At 11:50 PM, Jerry was startled out of a sound sleep by the urgent beeping of his communicator. He answered it with a sleepy-sounding voice, and Mike responded, "Hello Jerry, I'm sorry to wake you like this, but that bear you encountered this afternoon started tracking you 45 minutes ago. He's now climbing the rockslide."

Instantly, Jerry became fully awake. "I hope the shock from our electric fence will be painful enough to keep him off this plateau."

"I have my doubts about that," replied Mike. "The impression I got earlier today is that this is a very strong-willed animal who does not easily give up on what he sets out to do."

"Whatever it takes, we cannot allow that bear to roam around here on our plateau," stated Jerry. "He's too large and powerful. I'm going to turn up the power on the fence. I hope the shock will be strong enough to knock him on his butt."

"It'll be interesting to see how he reacts to that. We've been following him with a small RPV, so you can watch him if you turn on one of your video screens. He is only about ten yards away from your fence."

Jerry turned on a screen and watched the bear approach the fence. It stopped, sniffed the wire, and detected the human scent. In response, the bear let out a menacing growl, as if to protest the presence of the fence.

"Come a little closer and touch the wire," coaxed Jerry.

As Jerry spoke, the bear continued sniffing the wire without contacting it. Each time the bear sniffed the fence, he voiced a menacing growl.

"Apparently, these animals use scent to mark territorial boundaries," Mike said. "This guy sounds like he's upset that you've marked a territory. It looks like he's trying to decide if he should respect it."

"If he touches that wire with his nose, it might help him make up his mind." Jerry barely finished speaking when the bear did exactly that. The intense electrical shock that entered his tender nose tissue caught him completely by surprise. The excruciating pain caused him to jump back several feet and to let out an extremely loud horrifying roar that split the quiet peaceful night with a bloodcurdling effect.

So loud was the roar that it instantly jolted Moose and Dianne out of a sound sleep. Thinking the bear was outside the capsule and about to break in; Moose practically flew out of bed, grabbed his rifle, and ran down the stairs to the first floor. Dianne quickly joined him with her rifle in hand.

The pain of the electrical shock passed, but the bear continued to roar defiantly as he walked along the fence sniffing it from a distance of a couple feet. Watching and listening to the bear, Jerry said, "I wonder if he's going to challenge the fence again."

"I don't know, but he seems very determined," noted Mike.

"He has just had his second painful experience while following the human scent," stated Jerry. "I wonder if he's smart enough to accept the warning, or if he'll need additional convincing."

"A couple screaming RPVs would remind him of what happened this afternoon and might be all the convincing he needs," suggested Moose.

"We're ready to launch them on a moment's notice," Mike said.

"Let's give him a chance to respect our territory before we do that," suggested Jerry.

When the bear reached the west end of the fence and found that it went to the very edge of the plateau, he turned around and followed it to its east end. But he could not get around it there either, so he roared in defiant protest. Then, he turned around and walked along the fence in a westerly direction, occasionally stopping to sniff it from a distance of a few inches. Each time he stopped to sniff the wire, he let out an angry growl before continuing on his way.

"I think it's starting to sink into his brain that he cannot roam around here on the plateau unless he solves the fence problem," stated Jerry.

"It looks that way," agreed Mike, "and it appears that he isn't very happy about it."

"I don't think his objective is to roam around here on the plateau," commented Moose.

"I don't think so either," Jerry said. "I think our scent has convinced him that we might be good to eat. Why else would he track us at nighttime unless he's hoping to catch us sleeping and get an easy meal?"

"Maybe he's just curious about us," suggested Dianne.

"That's a possibility," conceded Jerry. "You were visited by curious pterodactyls."

"I've been watching this bear," stated Mike. "And I'm convinced this is a hunter seeking prey."

"I wonder what he's up to now," questioned Jerry.

All looked at the video screen and saw that the bear had backed away from the fence a few yards and was facing it. He began growling and pawing the ground.

"He reminds me of a bull trying to gather up enough courage to charge," stated Moose. "If he does charge, he will get a painful shock when he hits the fence, but his momentum will carry him through it."

"I believe it's time to call in our Air Force," Jerry said.

At that moment, Mike's assistants launched the chemical-bomb-carrying RPVs and turned on their sirens. However, rather than hit the bear with full volume sound effects, a subtle psychological strategy was used. The sirens were turned on just barely loud enough for the bear to hear with the objective of making him think that enemies were sneaking up on him.

The purpose of this strategy was to give the bear a chance to recall his previous painful experience at the hands of the RPVs and to retreat before having to face them. With the steep rockslide behind him, the bear could not quickly retreat, and a sudden confrontation with loudly screaming RPVs might have made him feel cornered. Since cornered animals sometimes charge out of desperation, and since the goal was to keep the bear off the plateau to avoid killing it, the slow approach was judged to be the strategy most likely to succeed.

At the first faint sound of the sirens, the bear stopped pawing the ground. He became very still and his ears perked up as he attempted to pinpoint the direction the sound was coming from.

Observing that he had captured the bear's attention, Mike directed the RPV pilots to separate their aircraft by a hundred yards. After this was done, the pilots flew their RPVs slowly toward the bear while gradually turning up the volume of the sirens.

The bear stared in the direction of each approaching RPV. Then, he intently listened to the RPV approaching from the left. Next, he sniffed the air in an attempt to identify a scent. After this, he gave the same attention to the RPV approaching from the right. Then, he slowly crept backwards. After backing over the edge of the plateau onto the rockslide, he stopped his retreat. With his eyes, ears, and nose protruding above the edge of the plateau, the bear tracked the advance of the RPVs.

"It looks like he doesn't want to face two enemies along with the electric fence," observed Mike.

"Apparently, he has no desire to repeat his experience with the burning pain caused by our chemical bombs," commented Jerry. "Maybe he did learn something from that experience."

"That might be, but it also looks like he's not yet ready to quit tracking us," stated Moose. "He has only retreated far enough to conceal himself from the approaching RPVs."

"Are you suggesting that he's hoping the RPVs won't find him and go away, so that he can continue tracking us?"

"That's a possibility, or he might be hoping the RPVs will go away, so he doesn't have to confront them while climbing down the rockslide."

"Let's bring back the RPVs and find out what he does," Jerry said.

A few minutes after the RPVs were returned; the bear cautiously raised his head, looked around, sniffed the breeze, and intently listened. Then, he climbed over the edge of the plateau and cautiously approached the electric fence. After sniffing it from a distance of a few inches, he stood still for a few moments, apparently considering what to do next.

"Should we turn on the sirens to help him decide?" Mike asked.

"No!" replied Jerry. "I think he's going to leave. But if he doesn't, turn on the sirens to full volume and approach him at high speed. Hover a few yards away from him and drop some chemical bombs."

Second by second, time ticked away, and Jerry proved to be correct. The bear turned and walked toward the rockslide, which he proceeded to scramble down slowly and cautiously.

"I think he decided that he's up against a force that he's not equipped to defeat," commented Dianne.

"That might be," replied Jerry, "but I believe this is a strong-willed animal with a dogged determination to get what he wants. With his obvious size and strength and apparent cunning intelligence, he has the potential to be very dangerous. Living here is going to require continuous vigilance, especially if these bears are frequent visitors to this island."

"It would be helpful to always know where they are," stated Connie.

"That's exactly what we're going to do," responded Jerry. "When our submarine arrives tomorrow, we'll cruise around this island and install surveillance cameras at key locations, so we can monitor our entire waterfront. We can attach a radio to every animal that comes here and track its movements. In time, we'll learn how serious this problem is. But for right now, I am tired, and I'm going back to bed."

NINE

Feeling at Home

TIME: Day Four.

A half-hour after first sunrise, the interstellar pioneers were enjoying breakfast when they received a call from Michelle. After the usual greetings, she said, "Your favorite bear is eating a shellfish breakfast. If you would turn on one of your video screens, you could watch him."

"Thanks for letting us know," replied Jerry, as he turned on the capsule's largest video screen just in time to see the bear break the edge off a clam the size of a large dinner plate. After inserting his front claws into the shell, he pulled it open and completely ate the contents, even to the point of licking the shell clean.

The bear, which had been sitting, got up, wandered into the water, and swam out a short distance. With only his back legs sticking out of the water, he reached down to the bottom of Rocky Point Bay and grabbed a shellfish. With the big clam in his mouth, he returned to the beach.

"That surveillance camera you set up on Cliff Point sure gives us an excellent view of what he's doing," Jerry said to Connie.

"And since he doesn't know he's being watched, we get to see his natural behavior," commented Connie.

"It looks like he might not have any diving skills and can only eat what he can reach," noted Jerry.

"I think that's true," agreed Dianne. "His hair is hollow with closed ends, so he might have too much buoyancy to be a good diver."

"Even so, he's big enough to reach the bottom in water at least eight feet deep," commented Jerry. "That should give him access to more than enough shellfish to keep him supplied with food for a long time."

"Apparently, he decided to have a seafood breakfast after he figured out that he couldn't have us for a midnight dinner," stated Moose.

"When shellfish are so easy for him to get, I'm wondering why he was stalking us," questioned Jerry.

"Some foods smell better than others," Connie replied. "Your scent probably made him think that you guys would taste better than shellfish."

"That's not a very comforting thought," stated Jerry. "Some foods smell so good that they make me feel like eating, even when I'm not hungry. If the human scent affects these bears that way, then, they'll be a serious problem for us."

"That's a possibility," agreed Connie. "But it's also possible that the human scent only affects this bear that way. We need to expose more of them to our scent before we'll know how serious the risk is."

"When we get all of our surveillance cameras set up, we'll be able to monitor our entire waterfront and attach a radio to all bears that come here," stated Jerry. "Knowing where they are and staying armed and alert should reduce our risk of becoming a meal for a bear to almost zero."

Pointing at the video screen, Moose said, "I wonder how many shellfish he's going to eat. I see eight empty shells next to him."

"Nine, counting the one he's eating," Dianne said.

"I wonder how big those shellfish get at depths beyond what the bears are able to harvest," questioned Moose.

"When we sail through Rocky Point Bay later today, we should check that out and pick up a few of them," suggested Dianne. "If they pass the lab tests, we can have them for dinner."

"Great idea," stated Connie. Turning to her husband, she asked, "What time are we expecting our sub to arrive?"

Jerry looked at his watch. "It should be here in 40 minutes."

"Sailing is going to be fun," exclaimed Connie.

A half-hour later, everyone walked to the northeast corner of Stellar Plateau to await the arrival of the large cargo shuttle. In just a few minutes, they spotted it high in the western sky heading north. Thirty seconds later, the stillness of the early morning was shattered by a loud sonic boom. By this time, the shuttle was already several miles north of Pioneer Island, flying at subsonic speeds, and well into its 180-degree turn that would put it on the final leg of its landing approach.

"It's been a few years since I heard a sonic boom," stated Moose.

Viewing the shuttle with binoculars, Jerry said, "Its flight is a thing of beauty. The turn looks very graceful, and it looks like it's on course."

A short time later, the shuttle's small stability and control hydrofoils entered the water followed immediately by its large hydrofoils. Its hydrodrogues deployed, rapidly slowing it down to the speed where its hull settled into the water. The shuttle cruised into East Bay at ten mph and came to a stop 150 yards offshore.

"Even though it's unmanned, I feel like we have a visitor," Connie said.

"That's the kind of comment I'd expect to hear from someone living out in the boondocks who rarely has company," Dianne said. "Surely, we haven't been here so long that you're already craving visitors."

"I guess I'm starting to feel at home, and I'm ready for some friends to stop by for a visit."

"We don't know if they're friends, but we did have a couple creatures drop in yesterday afternoon."

"That was definitely the high point in my day. I've never had an unexpected visit from humans that was as exciting as the visit from those pterodactyls. I wonder if they'll stop by again sometime."

"It wouldn't surprise me if they do," replied Dianne. "They've started rebuilding that shelter on Western Island, even though the bear that destroyed it is still right here on Pioneer Island. Evidently, they believe they can defend that site against this bear."

"I wonder why they're so attached to that site. Why don't they just use one of the abandoned shelters we discovered two days ago?"

"Maybe they aren't abandoned, but just temporarily not in use," speculated Dianne. "Maybe these creatures have a sense of private property and respect each other's property rights."

"Until we know the answer to that question, I think we should respect their property too," stated Jerry.

While looking at each of his colleagues, Moose said, "As soon as you people resolve the issue of pterodactyl property rights, I think we should unload our submarine, so we can take it on a cruise."

"Let's do it," stated Jerry.

Twenty minutes later, the pioneers tied their boat to the shuttle and entered it. Moose and Jerry went to the flight deck where they checked instrumentation readouts to verify that the shuttle's essential systems were healthy. Then, Jerry opened the large clamshell type doors on the bottom of the shuttle's cargo bay and lowered the submarine three feet to provide additional space between it and the top of the cargo bay. Standing up, he said, "I'm going to the submarine to give it a brief checkout."

Appearing eager for adventure, Connie said, "I'd like to go with you." Jerry nodded, and he and Connie headed for the cargo bay.

A few minutes later, they were inside the submarine with the hatch closed. Jerry sat at the sub's control console and turned on its systems. Speaking to Moose, he said, "I'm ready. You can lower us into the bay."

Moose turned on the winches that were supporting the submarine. As they fed out cable, the submarine slowly dropped out of the shuttle's cargo bay into the water. When the top of the submarine was ten feet below the bottom of the shuttle's fuselage, Jerry released the support cables, allowing the sub to fall away from the shuttle. He turned on the sub's electric motor and headed toward the mouth of the bay.

With an overall length of 36 feet and a maximum internal diameter of seven feet six inches, the little submarine could accommodate four people on an extended voyage of exploration. Additional people could be carried on shorter voyages.

Most of the submarine's batteries and ballast were contained in its keel, which had a maximum width of 54 inches and a depth of 46 inches. The electric motor, essential equipment, facilities, and instrumentation occupied about half the space inside the main hull leaving the other half for human occupants.

The most appealing feature for users of the submarine was its transparent plastic hull. Advanced plastics technology made it possible to have a strong, tough hull that was as clear as high quality window glass.

Sitting next to her husband in the submarine's nose, Connie exclaimed, "Wow! What a view! This hull is so clear that it's almost like there's nothing between us and the water."

"It's amazing that such a strong material can be so transparent," Jerry said.

"I'm also amazed by how quiet this sub is. I don't hear anything, except the underwater sounds of the lake."

"The capability to cruise silently was designed into this sub, so that we could move among the creatures we want to study without alarming them with lots of noise."

"That feature is also going to make underwater sightseeing trips very peaceful and relaxing," commented Connie.

"Until we become totally familiar with this lake, there's not going to be much difference between an exploration trip and a sightseeing trip."

"Whatever we call them, they are going to be fun."

"They're probably going to be so much fun for everybody that this submarine is going to be the most popular piece of equipment we have."

"I have no doubt about that," agreed Connie.

After testing the submarine's controls and equipment, Jerry and Connie stayed in the underwater world for an extra 15 minutes to enjoy the fascinating sights and sounds. Then, they surfaced near the shuttle.

When Connie emerged from the submarine, she was greeted by Dianne who was standing on one of the shuttle's wings. Seeing Connie's beaming smile, Dianne said, "It looks like you had fun. What was it like?"

"I felt like I was inside a glass bubble submersed in a huge aquarium filled with exotic life-forms, and I was amazed by the remarkable clarity of the water. I could see the underwater landscape for great distances, and I loved its unique, scenic beauty. I felt like I was visiting an alien world."

"We are on an alien world."

"But, I felt like I was visiting a separate alien world."

"You mean exploring the depths of this lake is going to be an exotic, scenic adventure," declared Dianne.

Connie nodded. "It's a project that I'm eager to begin."

"I am too!" exclaimed Jerry. "Let's get our wood working equipment unloaded. Then, we'll pack the equipment up to our camp and have an early lunch. That will leave us the rest of the day to explore the underwater world around our island and set up some of our surveillance cameras."

Two hours later, the interstellar pioneers were on the plateau looking down on the cargo shuttle, which now rested low in the water because its propellant tanks were filled with water. Moose and Jerry had prepared the shuttle for takeoff, and now, the flight control computer would do the rest.

Like a giant that had just awoken, the shuttle came to life and slowly cruised out of East Bay looking for enough open space to flex its muscles and demonstrate its immense power. Upon reaching the vast openness of Clear Lake, the shuttle's nuclear reactor flooded its marine propulsion system with an abundance of power. Very quickly, the shuttle accelerated to 45 mph and rose up out of the water to ride on its hydrofoils. Then, the powerful NTR thundered to life with an ear-shattering roar, and in a matter of seconds, the large cargo shuttle became airborne and began a steep climb toward space. While climbing through the cold upper atmosphere, the extremely hot water vapor pouring out of the NTR's exhaust nozzle condensed into a brilliant white vapor trail dramatically contrasted against the deep blue sky.

"What a spectacular sight," exclaimed Connie. "It's an awesome display of technology and power."

"And the best thing about it is that it's clean power," stated Jerry. "We are living in a pristine environment, and I'm happy that we have the technology to keep it that way."

"Let's eat a quick lunch and go for a submarine ride," Moose said.

"That's the first time I've ever heard you suggest that we have a quick meal," commented Dianne.

Moose grinned. "I do like to take my time at the dinner table, but I'm excited about taking the sub out for a cruise."

"I am too," stated Dianne.

"It won't take long to fry some fish filets," Connie said. "I'll do that, and you can fix the side dishes."

"It's a deal," replied Dianne.

"We should take some food with us," suggested Moose. "It might be late by the time we get back."

"That's quite likely," agreed Jerry.

Eighty minutes later, the pioneers were in their boat rowing out to the submarine. "We need to build a dock to tie it up to, so we don't have to row out to it whenever we want to use it," Moose said, admiring it.

"With the power saws and tools that came down today, that shouldn't be all that difficult," commented Jerry.

Speaking to Moose and Jerry, Dianne suggested, "Before we build a dock, I think we should build a trail up the rockslide to make it easier to get on and off the plateau."

"Good idea," agreed Connie.

"It appears that the trail has a higher priority than the submarine dock," Jerry said to Moose.

"A trail would be convenient," agreed Moose.

While they were tying up to the submarine, Jerry said, "Since we have a new toy to play with, I think we should indulge ourselves for a few days before we build the trail and the dock. If the weather stays nice for one more day, we can sail over to Sauropod Meadow. I'd like to be there when the big sauropods arrive in the late afternoon to drink water."

Dianne and Connie looked at Jerry with anxiety written on their faces. Jerry immediately added, "We will, of course, be anchored a safe distance offshore. I just think it'll be a blast to see those huge animals up close."

"Maybe we should go over there today and set up our surveillance cameras tomorrow," suggested Moose.

"We could do that," conceded Jerry, "but our submarine is rather cramped for space at the moment. We have 20 camera packs onboard. If we deploy as many of them as we can today, then we should be able to finish the job tomorrow morning. That will leave the afternoon free for a trip to Sauropod Meadow."

"That is the best plan," admitted Moose.

"We need to tow this boat along for transportation to and from shore."

"That's going to put a limit on how deep we can dive."

"How deep do you want to dive?" Jerry asked.

After thinking about it for a few moments, Moose said, "I guess we shouldn't have to dive more than fifty to sixty feet to see lots of scenery, since we'll be staying in shallow water close to the island."

"If we tow the boat at the end of a rope 200 feet long, it won't interfere with us diving to those depths."

"How much rope did you bring along?" Moose asked.

"Eighty yards," replied Jerry.

A few minutes later, the interstellar pioneers were inside their submarine heading out of East Bay to the first camera installation site. They immediately put the little submarine into a shallow dive, so as to cruise about eight to ten feet above the bottom of the bay.

"This is fantastic!" Dianne exclaimed to Connie. "You could not have described it better when you said you felt like you were in a glass bubble submersed in a huge aquarium. There are colorful fish everywhere, and it's so quiet and peaceful."

"Based on our research with the marine explorer, we knew that it would be like this," commented Connie. "But actually being here is much more exciting than the illusion of being here."

The pioneers enjoyed the underwater scene for ten minutes while cruising to their first camera installation site, where they surfaced, retrieved their small boat, and rowed to shore. While Moose and Dianne stood guard, Jerry and Connie set up the camera and tested it. Then, they went back to the submarine, took it down, and proceeded northward along the east coast of Pioneer Island to the next site.

By mid-afternoon, they arrived at Rocky Point. Since island-hopping bears coming from the north would most likely land there, two cameras were set up to continuously cover every foot of the waterfront.

Then, the pioneers took the little submarine into the depths of Rocky Point Bay. While exploring it, Moose said, "There sure are lots of large clams all over the bottom of this bay. I wonder why so many of them live here and so few on the rest of the lake bottom we looked at today."

"There must be some special conditions here that they like," responded Dianne. "The question is: what are they?"

"Perhaps, we'll find other clam beds in this lake," stated Moose. Then, we can determine what they all have in common."

"Do you still want to take a couple of them home with us?" Jerry asked Dianne.

"As late as it's going to be when we get back to our camp, we aren't going to be able to have them for dinner. However, I could do the lab work this evening, and if they check out, we could have them for breakfast. If they turn out to be like abalone steak, they're going to be a delicacy."

"I think she's trying to say that we should take a couple of them home with us," stated Moose. "How do you plan to capture them?"

"We could surface directly above a couple choice specimens. Then, I'll dive in, swim to the bottom, and grab them."

"You're not going to have any problem finding choice clams," noted Moose. "Some of these guys are huge, easily two feet wide."

"The water here is 40 feet deep, and apparently, the bears aren't able to reach them. Forty feet is also a little deeper than I care to go without diving equipment. Let's see what we can find in 15 to 20 feet of water."

A minute later, in water 19 feet deep, Jerry said, "I'm amazed at how numerous these shellfish are. On average, they're no more than three to four feet apart."

"I think this proves that the bears are unable to dive and can only harvest what they can reach from the surface," commented Moose.

"I'm able to dive," stated Jerry, as he brought the sub to the surface.

"Do you think it's safe to swim in this water?" Connie asked.

"I've been observing the fish, and I haven't seen any species that aren't in East Bay. Have you?"

"No, I haven't, but I've noticed that the water's not as clear here as what we've explored so far today. I don't know if that's a risk factor; it's just something that I've noticed."

"Maybe that's why the clams are here," suggested Dianne. "The water in this bay might be rich in the organisms they feed on."

"I'm going to go down and get a claim," stated Jerry. "If those tiny organisms make me sick, I will have to see a doctor."

Connie smiled. "I know where you can find a good one."

"Let's take back a bottle of this water, so we can study these organisms," stated Dianne. "Then, if there's a problem, the doctor will be better able to treat it."

"That's a good idea," agreed Connie.

Jerry climbed through the hatch onto the submarine's deck. Then, he pulled the small boat part way in and retied it, freeing up about 50 feet of rope. Turning to Moose, who had joined him on deck, he said, "Those clams are going to be easier to bring up with this rope than for me to hold onto with one hand while swimming with the other."

After attaching the end of the rope to his waist, Jerry stepped to the edge of the submarine and dove into the water. Still inside the submarine, Connie watched her husband swim straight down to the bottom, select a large clam, and tie the rope around it. Then, Jerry immediately swam back to the surface for air, while Moose hauled up the large shellfish.

"I am amazed at how big this clam is," stated Moose, as he pulled a tape measure off his belt to measure it. "It's 27 inches long, 22 inches wide, and has a maximum thickness of nearly eight inches."

"I don't know how big the edible parts are," Jerry said, "but my guess is that there's more than enough to make a feast for us. So let's not take any more until we find out if they're safe to eat and taste good."

"If they are, we'll have another abundant food source," stated Moose.

After securing the clam to the submarine's exterior, the pioneers went to their next destination and installed another surveillance camera. During the balance of the afternoon, they installed three additional cameras. Then, they returned to East Bay, arriving just as Alpha Centauri A set in the west. Twenty minutes later, they were back at their campsite.

After dinner, Connie, Dianne, and Moose proceeded to do the lab work on the clam and to take a look at the organisms in the water from Rocky Point Bay. Meanwhile, Jerry had a meeting with Mike to discuss the day's events and future plans.

"We still haven't located your mystery bear," Mike said.

"Maybe that bear has already left Pioneer Island," suggested Jerry.

"It's also possible that it's a female that has crawled into a well concealed den and has given birth to one or more cubs. We don't know anything about these animal's reproductive methods, but it's certainly possible that she might stay with her cubs for a few days."

"Eventually, she'll need to come out for food and water. If she goes to the beach to drink, one of our cameras will spot her. After we attach a radio to her, we'll find her den. Then, we can send in a small mechanical bug to investigate."

"If she does have cubs, the bug will give us some interesting video."

"In the meantime, we're going to delay exploring the forest. We certainly don't want to stumble onto a female with cubs. She would probably attack; then, we'd have to kill her. I'd rather study her and learn how these animals raise their young."

"That's definitely preferable to killing her," agreed Mike. "By the way, your problem bear spent most of the day sleeping after having clams for breakfast. But he's now awake and wandering south on the west coast of your island."

"It'll be interesting to see how he reacts when he discovers the tracks we made crossing the beach to install cameras."

"If he has any memory at all, your tracks and scent will remind him of the painful experiences he had yesterday."

"With that memory in mind, I expect that he'll try to avoid contact with us and retreat from our spoor. But if he stays put and issues defiant challenging roars when he stumbles upon our spoor, then I will have to conclude that he is a fearless animal and extremely dangerous."

"If he continues on his present course, we'll soon know his reaction," stated Mike.

After a few moments of silence, Mike asked, "What are your plans for tomorrow?"

"In the morning, we're going to set up as many cameras as we can and hopefully, complete our surveillance network. Then, we're going to eat lunch and sail over to Sauropod Meadow for a close look at those huge animals. Are we going to have nice weather for one more day?"

"The storm system that's moving in is a big one. It's going to be with you for a few days. You are going to get several inches of rain and some wind, perhaps gusting up to 50 mph. We don't think the rain will arrive before tomorrow night, but the wind is going to pick up sooner than that."

"At lunchtime tomorrow, I'll need your latest reading on this system."

"We'll have it ready for you," assured Mike.

"What have our pterodactyl neighbors been doing today?"

"They've been busy rebuilding the wrecked shelter. Watching them has been fascinating. They are fast, efficient builders. They know exactly what to do, and their teamwork is excellent."

"How much of it did they rebuild today?"

"They're almost finished; a couple hours in the morning ought to wrap it up. Dianne's colleagues have concluded that these creatures' young are born alive and that this female is nearly ready to give birth."

"That would explain their urgency in rebuilding the shelter."

"I wonder how they plan to defend that site if your problem bear returns to destroy the shelter again."

"I think they're intelligent enough to have developed a strategy for defending the site, or they would not be rebuilding the shelter."

"That bear tested you twice yesterday. I think he's very strong-willed. It wouldn't surprise me if he were to return to Western Island in search of a baby pterodactyl to eat."

"If he does, it's going to be interesting to see what the defense strategy is," commented Jerry.

At that moment, Michelle appeared on the video screen next to Mike and said, "Your daughter would like to ask you some questions."

Denise stepped in front of Michelle, "Hi Daddy! Is our new home fun? Is it safe? When can I come down?"

For the next half-hour, Jerry visited with his daughter, patiently answering all of her questions. Then, Matthew joined Denise and repeated many of the same questions, which Jerry also patiently answered.

After concluding his visit with the children, Jerry stepped outside to enjoy the cool, fresh evening. Looking to the west, he noted the dim orange sun Alpha Centauri B hanging low above the horizon. To the east was Aphrodite, which would be in a full moon phase in one more day. High in the southern sky was Nocturne, currently in a half moon phase. "What a bizarre scene," Jerry said to himself.

For the next half-hour, Jerry wandered around the campsite looking at things and pondering the future. Deeply lost in thought, his communicator startled him when it started beeping. It was Mike. "Your problem bear is about to wander upon your spoor. We have the surveillance camera at that location trained on him."

"I'd like to see his reaction," stated Jerry, as he headed for the capsule. Once inside the capsule, Jerry turned on the largest video screen and tuned in to the signal from the surveillance camera. The screen was filled by the image of a large bear wandering down the beach.

When the bear reached the fresh human tracks, the scent immediately caught his attention. Instantly, he came to full alert. His ears perked up, he intently stared at his surroundings, and he sniffed the breeze. Satisfied that he was alone, the bear followed the spoor to the water's edge. Then, he turned and followed it to the large boulder on which the surveillance camera was mounted. Upon reaching the boulder, he stood up to his full height sniffing the scent trail up the side of the boulder. With his head just clearing the top of the boulder, he stared directly at the camera.

After a few moments, he circled the boulder looking for a continuation of the trail. Unable to find it, he followed the spoor back to the water's edge. After staring out over the water for a few moments, the bear resumed his southward journey along the waterfront.

"What are your thoughts?" Jerry asked.

"I think he remembers his painful experiences of yesterday," Mike said. "But I don't think he's intimidated by them."

"The way he investigated our spoor seems to support those conclusions. This bear appears to be a strong-willed creature that is every bit as intelligent as the smartest animals back on Earth."

"It wouldn't surprise me if these bears prove to be more intelligent than Earth's smartest animals," commented Mike.

"I wonder if he's going to revisit out electric fence and try to find a way to overcome it."

"I don't know about that, but he is heading in your direction."

"I'm glad we have a radio on him. In fact, it might be a good idea to attach a second radio to him. Since these radios are only glued to the bear's fur, they could be lost if a little fur were shed in that area."

"I'll take care of that the next time he takes a nap," stated Mike.

At that moment, Moose joined the conversation. "I have some good news on the shellfish. They're safe to eat, and I'm going to sauté some right now and find out what it tastes like."

"I hope you people don't get fat with all the good things you're finding to eat down there," commented Mike.

"Are you kidding?" Moose retorted. "With all the physical work we've been doing, it's a struggle just to keep from losing weight."

"That must be difficult for you to deal with," stated Mike.

"What do you mean?" questioned Moose.

"The fact that you can eat all you want and not worry about gaining weight must be putting a real strain on you."

"Yeah, it's a tough situation, but I'm flexible enough to deal with it."

A short time later, the interstellar pioneers sat down at their dining table to enjoy a bedtime snack of shellfish filets. After tasting it, Dianne said, "This reminds me of abalone steak."

"I think it tastes better than abalone," commented Connie.

"Since it's been a long time since any of us have had abalone steak, you must have a very good memory to make that claim," noted Dianne.

"Back on Earth, abalone was a delicacy for me. It was a rare treat that I enjoyed very much, but I think this is better."

"You're probably right," responded Dianne after savoring another piece of the shellfish steak.

"I think it's time we give these creatures a name," declared Moose.

"Why don't we just call them abalone," suggested Dianne, "since that's what they taste like."

While enjoying the delicate flavor and tender texture, everyone nodded in agreement to Dianne's suggestion. "We seem to have unanimous agreement that these shellfish be called abalone," noted Jerry.

"Considering how tasty they are, we're very fortunate to have such an abundant supply of them," commented Connie.

"I agree," stated Jerry, "and I think we should do a thorough study of the conditions that exist in Rocky Point Bay and determine exactly what it is that allows these abalone to thrive there. Then, we need to make sure that we never do anything to jeopardize their environment."

"We've already started that research," responded Dianne. "This abalone's stomach contained the same kinds of organisms that we found in the water we took from the bay. If we can determine why these organisms are so abundant in that bay, then we'll know why the abalone thrive there."

"I wonder how many years it takes them to reach the size of the one that we harvested today," questioned Moose. "How fast they grow will determine the rate at which we can harvest them."

"That's an important question for the long-term," Jerry agreed. "But from what we saw today, I don't think it's possible for us to deplete this resource in the near-term, if we take only what we need."

"I think you're right," stated Moose. "Even after all of our people are here, we just won't be able to eat that much. We'll get at least three meals out of the one we brought home today."

"I like the last part of what you just said," stated Dianne.

"What do you mean?"

"You spontaneously referred to this campsite as home."

"It really is starting to feel like this is our home," stated Moose. "I guess I'm surprised that I feel like that after only four days."

"It's the food that makes you feel that way," commented Jerry in a jovial way.

"I think that's part of it," acknowledged Moose, while savoring a bite of abalone steak. "But as exciting as these four days have been, they are only the beginning. I can spend the rest of my life exploring, fishing, and hunting; and there will be no letup in the excitement. Danger will always be present, and the unknown will never be very far away."

"So, in other words, living in an area that fills your life with risk and adventure makes you feel at home," commented Jerry.

"That sums it up quite well."

"I like lots of adventure too," stated Connie. "But I really don't need very much risk."

"After that stunt you pulled with the pterodactyls yesterday, I believe that you also like taking risks," commented Jerry.

"You're right. That experience did give me an adrenaline rush, but I don't think I was in much danger. Those pterodactyls never did anything threatening, and I did have my trusty handgun ready for action."

"I think we all thrive on risky adventure," noted Dianne. "There isn't a single person on the Challenger who isn't aching to come down here."

"There's no doubt about that," stated Jerry.

As the evening wore on, the interstellar pioneers continued their light-hearted conversation, deeply enjoying the cozy relaxing atmosphere in their new home. Eventually, fatigue from the day's activities caught up with them, and they reluctantly ended their party and went to bed. Feeling comfortable and secure in their home and optimistic about the future, they settled into a deep peaceful sleep.

TEN

Face-To-Face With Death

TIME: Day Five.

It was late dawn, and the eastern sky was bright in anticipation of Alpha Centauri A peeping over the horizon to begin a new day. Jerry and Connie stepped outside to enjoy the sunrise and the refreshing early morning air, while Moose and Dianne prepared breakfast. With binoculars in hand, Connie surveyed the vicinity looking for anything of interest. With rifle in hand, Jerry looked for anything of a threatening nature.

Suddenly, the early morning stillness was pierced by loud shrieks coming from the northwest. Looking in that direction, Jerry and Connie saw a pair of pterodactyls diving on and screeching at something in the water off the north end of Western Island.

Focusing on the scene with her binoculars, Connie said, "There's a bear swimming toward the island, and the pterodactyls are extremely upset by this. They're trying to intimidate the bear into staying off the island."

"If that's the bear that's been after us, I don't think he's going to be intimidated. The pterodactyls will need to use force, and I don't think they can fight the bear and win, unless they have some clever strategy in mind."

"I'll bet they do. I faced them two days ago, and when I looked into their eyes, I sensed intelligence. I also got the feeling that they aren't wanton killers. At the moment, I think they're trying to persuade the bear to stay off Western Island, before they resort to force."

"If persuasion doesn't work, do you think they can defeat this bear?"

"I doubt they would've rebuilt the shelter without an effective defense strategy."

"If they're as wise as you think they are, then it makes sense that they would try intimidation before putting themselves at risk in a battle with a large powerful opponent."

At that moment, Jerry's communicator beeped. It was Mike. "Good morning, how do you like the action so far?" he asked.

"It could turn into a savage battle," replied Jerry.

"I think that's a certainty if your problem bear continues on his present course. We're getting a good view of the action from the surveillance camera on West Point."

While Mike was talking, Dianne and Moose stepped out of the capsule. "If there's a battle, I'm betting on the pterodactyls," Moose said.

"You might be right," responded Jerry. "But the pterodactyls have a big size difference to overcome. They weigh less than 400 pounds and the bear weighs well over 1,000 pounds."

"I think they can defeat the bear," stated Moose. "And we'll soon know how, because it looks like the pterodactyls are about to attack."

The words were barely out of Moose's mouth when the male pterodactyl swooped down and glided low over the water approaching the bear from the rear. When he reached the bear, he pitched up into a stall stopping his forward motion. Then, as he dropped down, he dug his sharp talons into the bear's rump. Very quickly, the pterodactyl removed his talons and retreated as the bear howled with rage, rolled over, and attempted to grab him.

Undeterred by the painful attack, the bear continued swimming toward Western Island. In a well coordinated double attack, the female pterodactyl dove into the water behind the bear, swam beneath him, and quickly jabbed him in the back with her sharp beak when he rolled over to fend off a second attack from the airborne male pterodactyl. Again, the bear howled with rage, but continued on course.

The female pterodactyl surfaced for air a short distance behind the bear. Upon seeing her mate bank into a tight diving turn, she dipped back underwater to swim beneath the bear. Again, she jabbed the bear in the back with her beak when he rolled over to defend against the airborne attack. Again, the bear howled with rage, but continued on course.

"That bear sure doesn't like to be told where he can't go," stated Moose.

"He's definitely very strong-willed," commented Jerry.

"Apparently, the pterodactyls have decided that their tactics aren't going to work, because they've returned to the cliff top," noted Dianne.

"I don't think they've given up," stated Mike. "They're squawking back and forth like they're discussing a new strategy."

"I wonder what they're considering," questioned Jerry.

"Whatever it is, we'll know shortly, because that bear is only a minute or two away from their island," replied Mike.

Since the Western Island cliff top sloped to the west, the pioneers could not see the pterodactyls, so they went into the capsule to watch video from a camera that had been placed on the cliff top with an RPV. What they saw amazed them. The two pterodactyls were hopping around looking at rocks. When they found rocks of the right size, each pterodactyl picked up two rocks, took off, and flew toward the bear.

The bear was now wading ashore. Once completely out of the water, he stopped on the rocky beach to shake water out of his fur. The pterodactyls circled the bear at an altitude of 300 feet.

"Those rocks must weigh 30 to 40 pounds each," stated Jerry. "I don't know how accurately they can drop them, but if they hit the bear in the head, he is going to have a severely fractured skull. It seems like that would kill him."

"We'll soon know," responded Moose. "The female is ready to begin her bomb run."

Swooping into a shallow dive, the female pitched up into a stall directly over the bear. Satisfied with her position, she released both rocks. They missed the bear by only a few feet, but one of them struck a large rock on the beach with such a hard impact that it shattered. A jagged softball-sized fragment hit the bear squarely in the side of the head, opening a gash, and momentarily stunning him.

Within seconds, the pair of rocks dropped by the male pterodactyl came crashing down. One of them grazed the bear's ribs on his right side causing a painful abrasion. The other rock hit the gravel beach a few feet in front of the bear kicking sand and gravel into his face.

Unable to retaliate against his tormentors, the bear stood up on his hind legs, looked up at the circling male pterodactyl, and issued a loud defiant roar. The male pterodactyl screamed loudly in return.

Meanwhile, the female pterodactyl had quickly returned to the cliff top. There, she picked up a 100-pound piece of driftwood leftover from the shelter-building project. With a sense of urgency, she carried it over the roaring bear and released it.

Upon seeing the log falling toward him, the bear grudgingly accepted the precariousness of his position, dropped to all four legs, and charged into the forest. Pushing his way into a thick clump of trees, he sought protection from the aerial bombardment. The male pterodactyl circled low over the thicket screeching loudly at the bear.

Already feeling early contractions indicating the onset of labor, the female returned to the cliff top. There, she made herself comfortable next to the nearly completed shelter and waited for nature to take its course.

Fascinated by the encounter, the interstellar pioneers discussed what they had just seen. "I'm impressed by the way the pterodactyls warded off the bear without putting themselves in jeopardy," commented Moose.

"They aren't out of danger yet," stated Jerry. "The tree that allows the bear access to the cliff top is still there, and the bear is on Western Island."

"Also, it looks like the female may be in labor," Connie said. "If she gives birth shortly, and the bear picks up the scent, he may sense the vulnerability of the situation and attempt to take advantage of it."

"He still has the male to contend with," Jerry said. "While climbing the tipped tree to the cliff top, he will be exposed to attack. The male could allow the bear to climb most of the way to the cliff top and then attempt to knock him off the tree. The fall would either kill or cripple him."

"And the bear would have to endure a bombardment of rocks while in route to the tree," stated Moose.

"If he's running fast and uses the forest for cover, he will be difficult to hit," countered Jerry.

"We could eliminate the problem by dropping that tree," suggested Connie. "These pterodactyls did stop by to investigate us two days ago. We can only speculate on their motives, but it's possible they'd like to have a cordial relationship with us."

"Dropping that tree would solve an urgent problem for them and show them that they should be friendly toward us," stated Dianne.

"After what we've just seen, there's no doubt in my mind that it would be to our advantage to have them as friends," declared Moose. "Despite our weapons and technology, they could make our lives miserable through intelligent use of their capabilities."

"Also, it's obvious that they are able to think and communicate," stated Connie. "With millions of them living on this planet, they could jeopardize our efforts to begin a new civilization if they decide that we are a threat to their way of life. I think we should demonstrate our desire to be friends with them by dropping that tree. Then, we should go about our normal daily activities and wait for them to make the next move."

"We could do it with an explosive charge delivered with an RPV," suggested Moose.

"The blast might be very nerve-wracking to the female currently giving birth," Dianne said.

"To convince them that we want to be friends, they have to know that we're the ones who brought the tree down," stated Jerry. "That means we need to go over there and cut it down with a chainsaw."

"That will be risky," Moose warned. "If the male decides to drop rocks on us, we'll have to shoot the creature we're trying to help."

"If Dianne and I take the lead when we get to Western Island, I don't think that will happen," argued Connie. "We did have a friendly encounter with them just two days ago. Also, both pterodactyls are preoccupied. One is busy giving birth, and the other is watching a known enemy."

"We haven't yet explored Western Island," cautioned Moose. "We don't know what we're going to run into on the way to the cliff."

"There are risks involved," admitted Jerry. "But we do have an opportunity to demonstrate to these pterodactyls that it will be to their advantage to be friends with us. Despite the risks, I believe we must go to Western Island and drop that tree."

"How they react to us helping them will give us some insight into how their minds work," commented Connie. "Will they be appreciative and find a way to show their appreciation, or will they completely ignore the fact that we did them a big favor?"

"The answer to those questions will indicate to us if there's any potential for achieving a good relationship with them," stated Jerry.

The interstellar pioneers quickly gobbled down their breakfast. Then, they picked up their electric chainsaw, its battery pack, and their weapons, and headed for the submarine. Once onboard, they cruised around the south end of Pioneer Island and went to the west side of Western Island. While in route, Jerry put on a headset, launched an RPV, and investigated the forest between the tipped tree and their anticipated landing point.

Upon reaching their objective, they anchored the sub, stepped into their boat, and rowed to shore. The male pterodactyl, still circling above the bear, noticed this and flew over to investigate. Connie and Dianne stepped out of the boat onto the beach. Standing straight and tall they looked up at the circling pterodactyl and tried to appear friendly. After circling them only once, the pterodactyl returned to the bear.

"Apparently, he recognizes us as friendly," noted Connie with a big sigh of relief.

"With a known enemy to watch, I don't think he'll bother us," commented Jerry.

After strapping the chainsaw onto his back, Jerry picked up his rifle and led the small group into the forest along the route he had just explored. With the battery pack strapped to his back and rifle in hand, Moose performed rear guard duty. After cautiously making their way through 150 yards of forest, they arrived at the tipped tree, which was the only tree growing in a rock strewn clearing at the base of the cliff.

When they looked up the tree to determine how to drop it, they saw the male pterodactyl perched on the edge of the cliff looking down at them. "Apparently, he doesn't completely trust us," commented Dianne.

"Maybe he's just being cautious," suggested Connie. "His mate is giving birth, and he's only had one encounter with us on which to base his judgment of us."

"That's true, but we gave him no reason to believe we are anything other than friendly," argued Dianne. "He should trust us."

"That may be," Jerry said, "but he doesn't know what our intentions are. The sooner we start sawing, the sooner he'll know why we're here."

"Unless we climb halfway up this tree, it's going to take several cuts to bring it down," stated Moose. "If we cut it off at the bottom, it will still be leaning against the cliff. If we cut it off halfway up, I think it'll dislodge itself from the cliff when it falls."

Looking up at the alert pterodactyl perched on the edge of the cliff, Jerry grinned at Moose and asked, "Are you brave enough to climb halfway up this tree?"

After a quick glance at the big male, Moose said, "I wasn't volunteering to climb this tree."

"It sounded to me like you were."

"Well, I wasn't."

"If you're going to chicken out on me, I guess I'd better start sawing," stated Jerry while still grinning from ear to ear. "While I'm sawing, I want you to be alert for that bear. He's less than 200 yards north of here."

While Moose moved into position to guard approaches from the north, Jerry spoke to Dianne, "I'd like you to guard us from the south." To Connie, Jerry said, "That leaves the west for you to watch."

"Who's going to keep an eye on the pterodactyl?" Connie asked, sounding concerned.

"When I turn this saw on, I think he'll figure out what's happening."

Jerry selected a point six feet up the tree and started sawing. When the saw started biting into the tree spewing out copious amounts of sawdust, the pterodactyl came to full attention and watched with keen interest. In a matter of seconds, the saw sliced through the tree, and Jerry quickly stepped back as the tree slid down the cliff a few feet when its bottom end dropped to the rocky terrain.

The pterodactyl nimbly hopped backwards a few feet in surprised reaction to the tree's movement. Then, Jerry made a second cut six feet up the tree and quickly stepped back when the tree again slid down a few feet. Now, it dawned on the pterodactyl what was happening, and he excitedly started hopping around the top end of the tree in anticipation of its disappearance from the cliff top.

After three more cuts, Jerry decided that what was left of the tree was in a very unstable position and that one more cut would bring it down. After determining where it would fall and warning the others, Jerry made the final cut and quickly stepped out of the way while the remainder of the tree came crashing down.

The big male looked down at the fallen tree and the man with the chainsaw. Then, he hopped around making some squawking sounds.

"It sure looks like he's dancing around in celebration of this tree being gone," observed Connie.

"This is a joyful time for him," declared Dianne. "The bear no longer has access to the cliff top, and his mate is giving birth."

"Now, he's looking at us and clapping his wings against his sides, and that sure looks like applause," noted Connie.

"He might be trying to thank us," suggested Jerry.

"It looks like these creatures might be emotional as well as intelligent," commented Connie.

"One thing is certain," stated Dianne, "and that is, we have a lot to learn about them."

After watching the excited pterodactyl for a few moments, Jerry said, "With a young one being born and with a rainstorm due to arrive tonight, I'll bet they could use some pine boughs to finish up their baby's shelter. So I'm going to cut a bunch of the smaller branches off the top end of this tree. Then, we'll find out if they make use of them. This clearing looks big enough for them to land and take off in."

While the big male pterodactyl watched with interest, Jerry cut the branches off the upper part of the tree. When he finished the job, he looked up at the big pterodactyl. The creature stared directly at Jerry establishing eye contact. After a few moments in which he seemed to be searching for a way to communicate, he again clapped his wings against his sides.

Not knowing how to respond, Jerry simply smiled broadly, raised his right hand, and waved. Seeming to sense that Jerry was saying goodbye, the big male nodded his head as if to say he understood.

After picking up their equipment, the pioneers returned to their submarine. "We accomplished our mission with flying colors," stated Jerry. "Now, let's go install some cameras."

As the morning progressed, Jerry and his colleagues installed surveillance cameras at key locations on the south end of Pioneer Island. Then, they returned to their campsite for lunch.

It was an improvised lunch. Everyone just helped themselves to whatever they could find in the refrigerator and sat down at the kitchen table to eat.

"We sure had a great morning," stated Moose with a sense of satisfaction. "What are we going to do this afternoon?"

"We could sail over to Sauropod Meadow," suggested Dianne, sounding hopeful.

"That would be fun," acknowledged Jerry, "but we still have four cameras to set up."

"Do we have to set them up today?" inquired Connie, while facing her husband.

Jerry quietly read the facial expressions of his colleagues. "If I say yes to that question, it looks like I might have a mutiny on my hands."

Everyone laughed at Jerry's comment; then, Moose said, "According to Mike, this afternoon is the last good weather we're going to have for several days. If need be, we can set up those remaining cameras between showers, but rain would sure take the fun out of a sailing trip."

"I could not have said that any better myself," stated Jerry. "So let's finish our lunch and go sailing."

"I wonder how long it will be before the pterodactyls visit us again," questioned Connie.

"I think they're going to be busy with their infant for a while," responded Dianne, while she turned on the largest video screen and tuned in to the camera on the Western Island cliff top. As Dianne panned the area, images appeared that showed the female resting in the sun with her infant snuggled against her. The male was busy finishing the shelter, meticulously weaving pine boughs into it from the bottom to the top.

"It didn't take him long to figure out what to do with all those branches you cut off that tree," Dianne said to Jerry.

"The way he's overlapping them, it looks like he's had roofing experience," noted Jerry. "There's no way that it's going to be leak proof, but he sure is making an effort to have it shed water. I wonder if he can sense the drop in atmospheric pressure and know that rain is on the way."

"That's possible," replied Dianne, "but he may be doing this because the infant has already arrived and you provided him with the materials."

"They sure look content," observed Connie.

"They should," stated Dianne. "They have what appears to be a healthy infant, and the bear is no longer a threat."

"I wonder what that bear is up to now," questioned Jerry.

"I checked on him a short time ago," responded Moose. "He was still in the thicket nursing his wounds."

"The bears worry me," stated Connie. "I'm starting to think they might be permanent residents of the islands here in Clear Lake."

"The islands do provide them with food and security from T-Rexes," stated Moose.

"I think the adult bears have enough speed and intelligence to elude the T-Rexes," commented Jerry.

"But on these islands, they don't have to worry about T-Rexes," argued Moose.

"That makes these islands prime sites for females with cubs and for bears too old to run from the T-Rexes," commented Dianne.

"Does that mean that Pioneer Island might be both a retirement home and a maternity ward for bears?" Connie asked.

"That's a possibility," replied Jerry.

Facing Jerry, Connie said, "When we were still in space, I had assumed that raising our children here would require constant vigilance. But when we discovered Pioneer Island, I hoped we would be isolated from all the large dangerous animals and our children could grow up in a safe secure setting. A constant bear problem sure dashes that hope."

"I understand your disappointment," replied Jerry. "But we can deal with the bears. To start with, we can keep them off this plateau. That will give our children a large area on which to run around in safety."

"We can certainly keep bears off the plateau," agreed Moose. "But I'm concerned that pterodactyls might be a threat to our children."

"It looks like we may be able to develop a friendly relationship with the ones we assisted this morning," stated Jerry.

"That may be, but we don't know if all pterodactyls are like them," argued Moose. "Take a look at humans; most are kindhearted, but some are evil predators. Pterodactyls might be the same way. The ones on Western Island might be good to us, but others might try to eat us."

"Your reasoning is hard to argue with," stated Jerry. "But make no mistake about it; we will make this plateau safe for our children."

Connie gave her husband a big hug. "Thanks, I appreciate that." Then, she turned to Dianne. "Let's pack some food and beverages for our sailing trip."

A short time later, all were onboard the submarine expecting a fun afternoon sailing on the surface. One feature that helped make sailing on the surface enjoyable was the little submarine's spacious deck. Mounted just above the hull, the deck was eight feet wide by 28 feet long.

Just below the deck, on each side of the submarine, there were two plastic tubes that extended nearly its entire length. Each tube contained a deflated pontoon. These pontoons were attached to telescoping booms that could be extended 21 feet out from the submarine's hull. When the pontoons were inflated, the submarine's telescoping mast could be extended upward and its main sail deployed, thereby converting the submarine into an outrigger sailboat.

However, if there was inadequate wind to operate a sailboat and if the sky was clear and sunny, then the submarine's solar sails could be used. These were rolled up inside tubes mounted on each side of the submarine. Deploying the solar sails was easy. They were just unrolled and laid out horizontally on top of the booms supporting the outrigger pontoons. During midday, the energy radiating down on the solar sails from Alpha Centauri A would produce 40 to 45 kilowatts of electrical power.

Moose and Jerry deployed the outrigger pontoons and inflated them. There was very little wind, so they deployed the solar sails. With a nearly clear sky and Alpha Centauri A almost directly overhead, the solar sails generated 43.6 kilowatts of electrical power.

"We have enough power to make a quick trip out of this," declared Moose. "But I think a slow voyage would be more enjoyable."

"Let's cruise at four mph," stated Jerry. "That will give us a couple hours to be lazy while en route, and we can use the surplus electrical power to bring our batteries back to a full charge."

"A leisurely cruise on a large pristine lake; what a pleasant way to have a relaxing afternoon," commented Connie.

"It sounds like you approve of my plan to cruise slowly."

"How could I possibly disapprove? I'm ready to kick back and relax for a few hours, and I'm going to begin the afternoon with some serious sunbathing. When I've had my fill of that, I'll go below deck and enjoy viewing the underwater world for a while."

"All that strenuous activity seems like too much of a burden for one person," commented Dianne. "I'll join you, in case you need help."

While Dianne and Connie made themselves comfortable on air mattresses, Jerry piloted the vessel out of East Bay. Moose went below deck and entertained himself by observing the underwater world and devising strategies to catch some of the fish he was seeing.

When they were out of East Bay, Jerry turned control of the boat over to its navigation computer. Then, he made himself comfortable on an air mattress next to his wife and basked in the warm radiant energy pouring down from Alpha Centauri A. He listened to the gentle lapping of small waves against the boat. The soft splashing sound had a relaxing hypnotic effect on Jerry that nearly put him to sleep. But the sudden screeching cries of a passing gull-like seabird snapped him out of it. Jerry looked up at the bird and watched it soar out of sight; then, he turned his attention to his boat. He listened intently in an attempt to hear the boat's electric motor and propeller, but no matter how hard he strained his hearing, he was unable to hear either one. Jerry deeply appreciated the sensation of just silently drifting along.

In the laziness of the afternoon warmth, Jerry became aware of a gentle breeze that was kicking up, and he enjoyed its pleasant caress. Reveling in this pleasure, Jerry gazed upward and noted that the sky had a beautiful deep blue color. Against this deep blue backdrop, there were a few fluffy cumulus clouds floating around.

He closed his eyes and let his mind wander. The first thought that entered his mind was that he was deeply enjoying the pleasures of sailing. He thought about the fact that he was on a huge lake with 700 square miles of water. He noted that he and his colleagues were the only people on the lake, on the entire planet for that matter. He recalled sailing outings when he felt like he was hemmed in by too many boats. What a contrast this was! Jerry loved the vastness of the lake, but for a few moments, the thought of being one of only four humans on the entire planet made him feel lonely.

Jerry lazily rolled over onto his right side. He lifted his upper body and supported it by leaning on his right elbow. Facing his wife, he said, "I am glad you're here."

Connie looked at Jerry, puzzled, "What prompted that comment?"

"Look around you. What do you see?"

Connie sat up and looked at the lake. "I see mile after mile of open water."

"That's what prompted my comment. We are four lone humans. We are isolated. There is no one else here."

"You sound troubled by that."

"I'm not troubled by it. I was just thinking about how crowded Earth is. Billions of people live there. By contrast, there are only four people on this planet, which is about the same size as Earth."

"What motivated you to think about that?"

"I was thinking about past sailing outings and how little space there was to maneuver on some of them. Those memories make me appreciate the vastness of this lake and that we have it completely to ourselves. We don't have to compete with anyone for a share of a limited space."

"How did that prompt you to say that you're glad I'm here?"

"The downside of being the only people here hit me hard for a few moments."

"Are you going to tell me what you were feeling during those few moments?" Connie asked.

Jerry looked into his wife's eyes. "I was lying here thinking about how much fun it is to have this whole place to ourselves, but then, I was struck by a scary thought: What if I were the only person here? The thought of not having anyone to share this with made me feel lonely. That is when I turned to you and said, 'I am glad you're here'."

Connie gazed out over the vast wide-open lake and tried to imagine being the only human on the planet. "Being here by myself would be a very lonely life. I'm not sure I could handle that."

"I'm here, so you don't have to," responded Jerry, as he leaned over and gave Connie an affectionate kiss.

"Since sailing makes you appreciate me so much, I think we should spend a few days on the lake."

"I always appreciate you, but that's a great idea, and your presence would definitely be appreciated on such a voyage."

Up to this point, Dianne had politely remained silent, but now, she sat up and looked at Jerry. "That sounds like fun. I hope I'm included."

"I think we could find a spot on the crew for you," responded Jerry.

"Good! I would enjoy a few days on the lake, but I'd like to do a much longer voyage."

"What do you have in mind?" Jerry asked.

"I'd like to sail completely around this lake staying close to shore. That would give us an opportunity to see the many plants and animals that live in this area."

Jerry thought about the possibilities. "Such a voyage would be interesting. It would be almost like a journey back in time to Earth's dinosaur age."

"This area might be a fairly accurate replica of a scene from ancient Earth," commented Connie.

"I've often wondered what it would be like to explore Earth when the dinosaurs ruled the planet," stated Jerry.

"An extended cruise around this lake just might make you feel like you're visiting Earth's dinosaur age," suggested Dianne.

"In a couple hours, we'll get a preview of that cruise," added Connie.

"Why do I feel like the arm twisting has already begun?" Jerry asked.

"As if you needed any arm twisting," argued Connie. "You want to do this voyage as much as we do."

Jerry smiled in acknowledgment of Connie's accusation. "Unfortunately, it might be several weeks before we have time to make such a voyage."

Looking hopeful, Connie said, "I think we can do it sooner than that. Later this afternoon, we're going to approach animals that are many times larger than any that humans have ever seen. That will wet your appetite for doing the cruise sooner."

"That's possible," admitted Jerry.

"How close to the big dinosaurs are we going to get?" Dianne asked.

"That will depend on how they react to us," replied Jerry. "If they aren't alarmed by our presence, we might sail quite close to shore, so that we can really appreciate their immense size."

"I'd like to appreciate their size from a safe distance," stated Connie.

"That's a thought I can relate to," echoed Dianne.

"After the fearless way both of you faced those pterodactyls two days ago, I wouldn't think that you'd be afraid to get close to the sauropods," bantered Jerry.

"I don't think you should assume that we were without fear," responded Dianne.

"Don't forget, we had a safe place to retreat to," added Connie. "Those sauropods are so big that you'd need a well-built concrete bunker as a safe shelter to retreat to if they decided to attack"

"As small as we are relative to them, they'll probably think us to be insignificant and not a threat," commented Jerry.

"Being viewed as insignificant by animals could very well be a new experience for members of the human species," Connie said.

"That would not be very flattering to my ego," stated Dianne.

"It wouldn't be very flattering," agreed Jerry. "But the practical consequences might be significant. If the sauropods think we're too small to be a threat to them, they might ignore us. Then, we might be able to move around the area in relative safety by simply staying in their midst."

"That would take some getting use to," stated Dianne.

"I'm not sure I'm ready to go hiking with creatures that weigh up to 100 tons," Connie said.

"But what an adventure it would be," stated Jerry.

"Observing the countryside from the safety of this boat would be adventuresome enough for me," Connie said.

"An around-the-lake voyage would also give us an opportunity to study aquatic life," commented Dianne. "If the water in the rest of this lake is as clean as it is around Pioneer Island, then our transparent hull will make aquatic research easy."

In a serious, matter-of-fact tone, Jerry said, "It sounds like both of you prefer the sailing voyage over a hiking trip with the sauropods, but I think we should do the hike first. It would be more exciting than sailing."

Dianne and Connie looked at each other in shocked disbelief. "I can't believe he's serious about the hiking trip," Dianne said.

"Whether I'm serious or not, you'll have to admit that it's possible we could make such a trip."

"It'll be easy to test your theory," stated Dianne. "When we arrive at Sauropod Meadow, we can send Charlie ashore and have him wander into the herd and watch how they react to his presence."

"I'm planning to do that," replied Jerry.

"However that turns out, I still prefer sailing," Connie said.

"There's no doubt that exploring this lake's coastal regions would be a super adventure," acknowledged Jerry.

"And it would be a quick way to survey the countryside around our lake and the life that populates it," added Connie.

"I don't know how quick it will be," commented Jerry. "This is a big lake with several hundred miles of coastline. An around-the-lake voyage could easily take a week, especially if we conduct the voyage in a leisurely way so that we have plenty of time to relax and enjoy it."

Connie smiled at Jerry. "I like the last part of what you just said."

"I do too," agreed Dianne. "A slow, leisurely voyage is not only the best way to have the most fun, but it's also the best way to learn the most about the countryside and the life that inhabits it."

"From the way you two are talking, I think this voyage could easily take much longer than a week," Jerry said.

"What's wrong with that?" Connie asked.

"It seems like too long to be away. What I mean is: we are trying to turn the plateau into our home."

"That's true," acknowledged Connie. "But I think we should make the voyage anyway."

Jerry smiled at Connie. "You seem to have your heart set on this."

"Yes! I do! It would be fun, and it could aid our medical research."

"How?"

"Our main reason for being here is to find out if our immune systems can defeat Alcent's germs. The more of this area we're exposed to, the more germs our immune systems will be exposed to. The more exposure we have, the more meaningful our medical research will be."

"You make it sound like we're lab animals taking part in a research project," commented Jerry.

"That is what we're doing," stated Connie.

"Also, in addition to direct exposure, we can search for dangerous microbes by collecting specimens for later analysis," added Dianne.

"You're putting a lot of work into my pleasure trip," Connie said.

"Not really. The RPVs make sample collection easy. Besides, the opportunity to gain information will be too good to pass up."

Connie turned to Jerry. "I'm ready to sail around the lake, but Dianne's trying to take the fun out of it by filling it up with work."

"I'm not trying to fill the voyage with work," objected Dianne. "I'm just trying to sell your husband on the idea of making the voyage."

"I don't think it's a tough sell. I think he wants to go too."

"That's true, but he has a prioritized list, and we have to motivate him to put the sailing trip near the top of the list." As Dianne finished speaking, she and Connie turned to Jerry and smiled at him expectantly.

Jerry switched his gaze back and forth between them as they silently waited for his reaction. "If Mike's weather forecast is correct, we're going to have stormy weather for a few days. After that, let's plan on cruising around the lake."

Dianne and Connie turned to each other glowing with expressions of satisfaction. They smiled at Jerry.

Jerry thought about the planned sailing trip. "To add to the adventure, Moose and I might find some safe looking areas where we can go ashore and explore."

Dianne was suddenly filled with anxiety. "That sounds too dangerous. I really don't want my husband going ashore. I could end up losing him."

Connie looked worried. "I share Dianne's concern. The countryside is a dangerous place. Do you and Moose need to take that much risk?"

"We would be cautious. Besides, we would only be doing this to aid your medical research."

Connie reacted with disbelief. "In what way?" she asked.

"Correct me if I'm wrong, but I think you said the more of this area we're exposed to, the more meaningful your medical research will be."

Connie smiled at how easily her husband had used her words to make a point. She turned to Dianne. "He's right about that."

However, Dianne was unconvinced. "I still don't like the idea of Moose going ashore. The very thought scares me."

Noticing how worried Dianne looked, Jerry said, "I know Moose very well, and he's not going to do anything stupid that could get him killed."

"You don't know him as well as I do. With his driving spirit of adventure, it wouldn't surprise me if he found a way to stumble into an unarmed confrontation with a T-Rex."

"Before going ashore, we would scout the area with RPVs. T-Rexes are very big animals. I don't see how we could miss their presence."

"What you're saying is true, but I think Moose could unintentionally find a way to have a confrontation with one of those brutes."

"I think you worry too much," commented Connie.

"That might be, but we've waited a long time to build a home and have children. And I don't want to risk losing him."

"So that's it," Connie said. "You're on the verge of realizing a dream, and you fear that something might happen to prevent that."

Dianne nodded silently.

Connie put her right hand on Dianne's left shoulder. "I understand how you feel. We live on a dangerous planet, but we must live our lives fully. We must not take foolish risks, but neither should we avoid all adventure because it might be dangerous. We must carefully evaluate the risks, plan for them, and then go forward."

Dianne thought about Connie's comments. "You are, of course, correct, but I will still be worried if Moose goes ashore."

Jerry looked into Dianne's eyes. "I don't think Moose has any plans to go ashore today, so let's set our worries aside and enjoy the lake."

Dianne nodded and looked at Jerry and Connie. "Thanks for your understanding."

Jerry stood up and wandered around on deck, gazing out over the lake in all directions. The northern and southern shores were 20 miles away and could not be seen. This gave Jerry an appreciation for the vastness of Clear Lake and the knowledge that might be gained by exploring its waterfront.

As Jerry's gaze shifted eastward to Sauropod Meadow, he thought about the huge creatures that lived there. Realizing that a lifelong fantasy of seeing dinosaurs up-close was about to come true, Jerry's pulse quickened with excitement, and he wondered about the possibility of spending a day wandering around with the huge sauropods. He went to his supply pack and removed a video headset. After stretching out on an air mattress, he put on the headset and tuned in to the signals coming from the camera pack mounted on the primary horn of the sauropod herd leader. Jerry soon became engrossed in the sights and sounds coming from the vicinity of the sauropods and imagined himself being with them. The fantasy seemed very real, because the sights and sounds coming into Jerry's headset gave him the illusion of sitting on the herd leader's head.

Dianne and Connie were basking in the radiant heat pouring down from Alpha Centauri A. The warmth had a sensual effect, which was magnified by the gentle breeze caressing them. Taking advantage of the pure laziness of the situation, Dianne allowed her mind to wander through fantasies that seemed appropriate for the occasion. When she reached the point where her fantasies were no longer satisfying, she turned to Connie. "I'm going below deck to help my husband enjoy the underwater scenery." Dianne winked at Connie. "Don't disturb us for a while."

Connie grinned. "I think we'll stay here on deck until one of you returns. We wouldn't want to interrupt a deeply penetrating research project at a critical moment."

"That would be a bit frustrating," replied Dianne, as she disappeared below deck.

Having grown tired of lying down, Connie decided to wander around on deck and gaze out over the lake. She marveled at the quiet peacefulness that seemed to be everywhere. Starting with the vessel she was riding, she noted that it seemed to be just quietly drifting along. Try as she might, she could not sense even the slightest sound or vibration. So well designed and insulated for sound was the vessel's electric motor that its operation could not be detected by the human ear. Likewise, its large low-speed propeller was meticulously sculpted for silent operation.

Gazing out over the lake, Connie thought, what a contrast to lakes on Earth where on a beautiful day like this, the water would be crowded with boats of all types, thereby destroying the peacefulness of the day. Here, there are only sea birds, and occasionally, a fish jumping out of the water.

Surveying the sky, Connie noted three widely separated pairs of pterodactyls at high altitude. Judging from the seemingly effortless way they were soaring around like sailplanes, Connie concluded they were flying purely for the pleasure of it.

I love the peaceful solitude of this area, thought Connie. We are very fortunate to have such a wonderful place to build our home. We must make every effort to maintain this area in its pristine condition. With our technology, we should be able to live a prosperous life and harmonize with our environment, so that we preserve all of its wondrous beauty.

For the next half-hour, Connie soaked up the peaceful serene beauty of her surroundings. While lost in thought, she was abruptly jarred out of her meditative mental state by Jerry who had removed his video headset, sneaked up behind her, and placed his hands on her waist.

Quickly recovering, she turned to him and gave him a big hug. "It's absolutely wonderful out here! Our new home is turning out to be everything that I'd hoped it would be. How is everything in the world of the sauropods?"

"When I removed my headset, they were peacefully eating every kind of plant life that could possibly be edible. I wonder how much food a 100-ton animal needs to consume in a day to sustain itself."

"I don't have an answer to that question, but it's possible that an adult sauropod might eat as much in a day as 100 head of cattle."

"Whatever the amount, as healthy as they look, they apparently aren't having any problem keeping themselves well-fed," noted Jerry.

"This area is filled with lush vegetation, and the climate is conducive to rapid growth of plant life. The plants they munch on probably generate new growth and restore themselves rather quickly."

At that moment, Dianne appeared from below deck glowing with a broad smile of contentment. She winked at Connie. "I managed to take Moose's mind off of fish for a while." Connie returned the wink, nodded, and smiled.

Moose climbed through the hatch from below deck. "What a fascinating lake this is."

"What do you mean?" Jerry asked.

"I'm amazed that so many different kinds of fish live here. I would like to be responsible for figuring out how to catch fish in each species."

"I really don't think it's fair to expect you to do that entire project by yourself," responded Jerry.

"I don't think so either," agreed Dianne. "That's just too much work for one person."

"What you're trying to say is that it would be too much fun for one person," countered Moose.

Jerry looked at Dianne. "Your husband sure has good insight into what other people are thinking."

"He's always been very good at recognizing the obvious," Dianne said, good-naturedly.

"You people can tease me all you want," retorted Moose, "but sports' fishing is one of my areas of expertise. And out of the goodness of my heart, I'm willing to share some of my fishing skills with the rest of you."

"That's certainly a generous offer on your part," replied Jerry. "Sign me up for some lessons."

"As numerous as these fish are, it shouldn't take very much fishing skill to catch all we can eat," noted Dianne.

"We could have a contest to find out whose technique is the best for catching a particular species," suggested Moose.

"I accept that challenge," Jerry quickly responded.

"Dianne and I will be the impartial judges in this contest," offered Connie. "But what will be the prize for the winner?"

"I think ego gratification should be the winner's prize," suggested Dianne. "And the loser should clean the fish, cook the meal, and clean up afterward."

Jerry looked at Moose. "Well, what do you think of that?"

"Sounds good to me," Moose confidently replied.

After a few moments of silence that seemed to indicate an end to the fish conversation, Jerry said, "I'm starting to feel hot and sweaty, and I'd like to dive in for a cool refreshing swim."

"I would too," stated Connie. "Do you think it's safe to swim in this part of the lake?"

"Let's go below and look around," suggested Jerry. "If we don't see anything that looks threatening, let's dive in."

Jerry and Connie went below and observed the underwater world for a few minutes. "Most of these fish look like the various species we exposed to human blood in East Bay," commented Connie. "The few strange ones look like the type that would prey on smaller fish rather than make a massive group attack on large prey."

"But you can't be sure about a fish's feeding habits just by considering its appearance."

"That's true, but pterodactyls dive into this lake every day to catch fish without themselves being devoured. Also, the bears seem to be able to safely swim from island to island. Those two facts alone seem to indicate that piranha-type fish don't exist here."

"That sounds reasonable. However, it's also possible that piranha-type fish are here, and that there's something about pterodactyls and bears that they don't like, and consequently, don't feed on them."

"Unfortunately, that's possible," admitted Connie. "But the water looks so clean and inviting. I just think it would be fun to dive in. Isn't there some way we can be sure that it's safe to swim here?"

"We can't be 100 percent sure, but if there are piranha-type fish in this lake that feed on animals, it seems that they would live close to shore in areas that thirsty animals frequently visit. If one of them happens to get bumped into the lake, it would become a prime target for a feeding frenzy. It doesn't make sense for this kind of fish to be present out here, miles away from the nearest animals."

"Unless they feed on other fish in massive group attacks."

"Well, we certainly don't look like fish," stated Jerry.

"It sounds like you're about to conclude that it would be safe for us to go swimming."

"We don't have any evidence that it isn't safe, even our sonar data looks good, so let's cut power and let this boat drift while we go have some fun in the water."

Jerry and Connie went topside, walked to the front of the deck, and dove into the cool, clear, water. They were joined by Moose and Dianne. After frolicking around for a while, the pioneers returned to their boat feeling refreshed and ready to lazily enjoy the warmth of the afternoon.

It didn't take long for the radiant heat from Alpha Centauri A to dry them off and warm them up. Being relaxed and carefree, all were content to let their minds wander into that marvelous fantasyland that the imaginative human mind is so capable of producing. Apparently, Jerry and Connie were mentally experiencing similar landscapes, for when Connie turned to Jerry and made eye contact with him, he seemed to know what was going on in her mind. When she quietly stood up and went below deck, he eagerly followed her.

Noticing this, Dianne said to Moose, "I don't think we should go below deck for a while."

Moose grinned. "I think I'll trust your insight on this one."

Not quite a half-hour later, still below deck, Jerry and Connie were basking in the afterglow of successfully bringing a fantasy into reality. Casually looking at a small school of unusually colorful fish, Connie said, "Is it just me, or do you feel it too?"

"Feel what?"

"It seems like our lovemaking has had an added air of excitement to it ever since we arrived here. It's just so satisfying."

"I think it's because we're on an alien planet that's just about as exotic as it could possibly be. Every day brings exciting new discoveries, and the element of danger is always present. Being here has put us into a heightened state of awareness that carries over into our love life."

"It's been so exciting that I feel like we're on our second honeymoon."

"I do too," responded Jerry.

"We had our first honeymoon on a starship in interstellar space, and now, we're having our second honeymoon on an alien planet. Where do you suggest we go for our third honeymoon?"

"We really don't have much choice in that matter, but even if we did, I would choose to stay here. Every day is a fantastic adventure. This morning, we befriended a pair of pterodactyls. In less than an hour, we'll become the first humans to ever come face to face with huge dinosaurs, perhaps, the largest that have ever lived here or on Earth."

At that moment, the computer called Jerry's attention to a significant change in the sonar data, which he immediately looked at. "We've just had an abrupt increase in depth. For the last two miles, the lake has averaged about 300 feet deep, but now, we're over an area that is 1600 feet deep."

"That's a big drop-off."

"I wonder if this is just a deep hole, or if it's an underwater canyon that runs the length of the lake."

"If it does, that would make it a large, deep-water ecosystem that might contain life forms very different from the shallower parts of the lake. To fully understand this lake, we'll have to explore those depths."

"One more job for our little submarine," stated Jerry in a tone that denoted pride in the vessel.

"Can we safely dive 1600 feet?"

"We can safely dive 5000 feet."

"I wonder if there are places in this lake that are that deep."

"I'd be surprised if there are, but then, I didn't expect to find water as deep as it is right here either."

Fifteen minutes later, Jerry said, "The depth has abruptly decreased to 250 feet. If we have a lake bottom canyon, it's a mile wide at this point."

"If it turns out to be an underwater crater, it's still large enough to have its own ecosystem."

"We're going to arrive at the east coast about two miles south of Sauropod Meadow. On the return voyage, we'll sail two miles north of there before we turn west. If this deep hole exists four miles north of here, then it will begin to look like a canyon."

"We must be getting close to the coast," commented Connie.

"We're only a mile away. We'll be there in fifteen minutes."

"I'm going up on deck to scan the coast and countryside with binoculars. If I find something interesting, I'll call you."

"I'll continue observing the underwater world. Perhaps, I'll discover fish and other creatures that we don't have around Pioneer Island."

When Connie appeared on deck, Dianne looked at her and said, "You sure look cheerful and content."

"Is my mood that obvious?"

"Yes, it is. It looks like your mood might be the result of doing some of that deeply penetrating research that Moose and I engaged in earlier."

Connie gave Dianne a sly grin. "We were able to probe to totally unexpected depths, and Jerry has assured me that we'll look for the same depth during our return voyage."

Not expecting what appeared to be a very candid response, Dianne's mouth dropped open, but no words came out, as she stared at Connie in complete surprise. Obviously pleased with the effect of her comment, Connie said, "I wouldn't have answered your question if I'd realized that you'd lose your voice as a result."

"It isn't that I've lost my voice. It's just that your comment has raised so many questions that I don't know which to ask first, or even if I should ask any, since they are rather personal."

"I don't see anything personal about doing research that probes to unexpected depths. My husband assures me that such research is perfectly safe and should lead to the discovery of new life. In fact, you might want to join us; you could find it interesting."

"What! I can't believe that you're suggesting that I watch you."

Pleased that Dianne still hadn't caught on, Connie maintained her composure and said, "You might even help us if you feel up to it; after all, you are very well qualified."

Having overheard the conversation, Moose was beginning to suspect that Dianne was being misled and decided to join the ruse. "I can vouch for the fact that she's definitely very well qualified."

Pleased by her husband's comment, but shocked by its implication, Dianne silently stared at him, then at Connie.

"If you're going to keep losing your voice like this, you should probably see a doctor," suggested Connie.

"It's the doctor who's causing me to be speechless, and I'm starting to wonder exactly what it is that she's up to."

Realizing that the gag had run its course, Connie let out a burst of laughter.

"Now, I know I've been had!" Dianne exclaimed. "Would you mind telling me exactly what you've been talking about, and please use words that don't have double meanings."

"I was very specific in everything I said. It's just that you've had sex on your mind all afternoon, and you chose to interpret my comments in that context."

"You certainly didn't do anything to discourage that interpretation."

"I couldn't do that; I was having too much fun."

"If I interpret your comments literally, I must conclude that you and Jerry found a deep hole in the lake bottom, and that you used sonar to probe those unexpected depths. Furthermore, you want to explore those depths to see what lives there, and you want me to help."

"You've just proven that I'm easy to understand when you choose to listen to what I say instead of jumping to erroneous conclusions based on what's going on in your mind."

"Well, we are on vacation this afternoon, and Moose and I did have a delightful erotic experience, so I just assumed that you and Jerry did too, and that this was responsible for your vibrant mood."

"We did, and it was, but you gave me an opening I couldn't pass up."

"I appreciate that, and just to prove that I'm a good sport, I'm going to put my imagination to work and find a clever way to get back at you."

Connie displayed a smug smile. "I have no doubt that you will, but I'll bet it won't be as good as the way I just got you."

"That's a challenge I can't pass up. Now, I'm determined to make it even better."

Connie grinned at Dianne in a way that seemed to say: I don't think you can outdo me on this one. Then, she turned, walked to the front of the boat, and started scanning the east coast with binoculars.

In just a few moments, she spotted a herd of dinosaurs similar in appearance to the Styracosaurs that lived on Earth during the late Cretaceous. As near as she could tell, the herd had 30 members, some of which had waded into the lake. She focused her gaze on what appeared to be the largest member of the herd, a big male pacing back and forth along the waterfront, occasionally stopping to look inland and smell the air.

While Connie studied the large bull, Dianne joined her with binoculars in hand and immediately focused on the styracosaurus herd. The restive pacing of the big bull also caught Dianne's attention. "That animal sure looks nervous about something."

"Maybe these creatures are nervous by nature," commented Connie.

"The rest of the herd seems quite relaxed," noted Dianne. Then, she handed her binoculars to Moose.

After observing the overall scene, and then, the large bull, Moose said, "Perhaps there are other large bulls in the area who want to take over his herd, and he's anxious about an impending battle."

"That would explain why he's the only member in the herd who is restless," stated Connie. "If there were T-Rexes prowling the vicinity, it seems like the whole herd would be anxiously on alert."

"Maybe the rest of the herd is confident in that big bull's ability to defend them against a T-Rex," commented Moose. "I'm guessing that he's about 30 feet long, including his stout tail, and he must weigh at least eight or nine tons, maybe even as much as ten tons."

"He definitely looks big and powerful," agreed Connie.

"But that's only part of the story," stated Moose. "Take a look at his fighting assets. He has a big rhino-type horn on his head, plus he has six large horns growing out of that large bony neck shield. Also, he's not totally defenseless when attacked from the rear. That stout muscular tail has a bony structure near its end. If that tail is as strong as it looks, that large bony blob makes it a lethal club."

"It looks like he's the only animal on guard duty," noted Connie.

"I think he's capable of doing the job," declared Moose.

"Perhaps we were too quick to conclude that he's nervous about something," suggested Connie. "He might be wary because he's taking guard duty seriously."

"With T-Rexes living in this area, it's hard to fault him for that," stated Dianne.

"That such large animals, so well equipped for fighting, must maintain such a keen vigilance really demonstrates that we are surrounded by a savage world," commented Connie. "Can you imagine what it would be like to build a home among those creatures?"

"Survival would definitely be a daily challenge," stated Moose. "It would be a kill or be killed situation."

"I would rather live on Pioneer Island and just occasionally visit the wild countryside," Dianne said.

Moose handed his binoculars back to Dianne. "I'm going below to take over fish watching, so Jerry can look at this herd."

Shortly, Jerry arrived on deck, and Connie handed him her binoculars. While Jerry observed the styracosaurus herd, Connie and Dianne related their observations and thoughts to him.

"This is exciting!" Jerry exclaimed, with his pulse picking up speed. "I feel like I've just journeyed 70 million years into Earth's past."

"Studying them should give us a special insight into Earth's dinosaur age," stated Dianne.

"We can start by getting a close look at those brutes and finding out how they react to us," responded Jerry. "Our present course puts us on a direct approach to them, but I don't think approaching them head-on is a good idea. They might think we're challenging them for their space, and I sure don't want them to see us as a threat."

Jerry continued speaking while changing course. "After we've gone south for several hundred yards, we'll turn toward shore. When we're about 200 feet from shore, we'll head north and maintain that distance. To them, it should look like we're just passing by and not a threat."

Jerry belted on his pistol and shouldered his rifle. "Have either of you spotted any predators that might be good swimmers?"

Dianne and Connie said no, but both armed themselves in reaction to Jerry's question. Then, Dianne said, "You make a good point. Considering all the animals that come to this lake to drink, it seems like there should be predators that are proficient at pursuing prey that has been spooked into the water. Such a predator might think we look good to eat."

"Let's also be alert for pterodactyls," warned Jerry. "We don't know that they prey only on fish, and we could look like an easy meal for pterodactyls that prey on animals."

Connie searched the sky, and Dianne searched for swimming predators, while Jerry piloted the boat. At that moment, Moose joined them on deck to help with the sentry duty.

The four lone humans were so filled with wild anticipation of their first encounter with dinosaurs that time seemed to drag by slowly. But eventually, the sailboat was headed north along the waterfront.

As they approached the styracosaurus herd, Jerry reduced speed to less than two mph, and the boat appeared to be silently drifting along. One of the adults in the water, the one closest to the humans, noticed the slowly approaching boat and sounded a warning. All herd members heard the warning and looked in that direction. Discovering the boat, they intently stared at it and sniffed the air.

We might be the first humans to have ever gained the attention of a herd of dinosaurs," Jerry exclaimed, while throbbing with excitement. "They're checking us out, but they sure don't seem to be alarmed by us."

"Apparently, we don't look like any of their enemies," stated Moose. "The big bull that's been pacing the beach is more concerned about threats coming from the land and has returned his attention to that direction."

"The rest of them sure are curious about us though," observed Jerry.

"Maybe that's why the big bull has wisely gone back to watching the land," suggested Dianne. "He knows the rest of the herd is alert to anything we might do."

"I wonder if they're aware of us, or if they only see our boat?" questioned Jerry. "We're still a hundred yards away from them, and it may be that all they're able to see is our boat, which should look to them like an inanimate object slowly drifting by and not cause for alarm."

"Even if they're able to see us, we're so small compared to them that there's still no reason for them to be alarmed," Moose said. "Also, they've never had any bad experience with humans, or any experience at all for that matter, so they have no reason to view us as enemies."

"But wild animals survive by being wary of things they've never seen before," argued Dianne.

"We're now as close as we're going to get, and they still don't seem to be alarmed by our presence," Jerry said. "Some of them have even lost interest in us."

"It might be that we're far enough away from them, so that we haven't infringed on their space," speculated Dianne.

"That theory is easy to test," Jerry said. "After we've passed by them, we'll turn around, come back, and go by them at a distance of 100 feet."

"To make the experiment realistic, we need to walk around on deck," suggested Dianne. "Then, there'll be no doubt in their minds that living creatures are approaching them."

"That's a good experiment to do," stated Moose. "Someday, we might want to do an overland hike, and we'll need to know which creatures will tolerate our presence."

A few minutes later, the pioneers completed their 180-degree turn and headed south. When they were 100 feet from the nearest styracosaurus, Dianne said, "All they're doing is just occasionally glancing at us."

"We now know that they aren't bothered by us being only 100 feet away from them," stated Moose.

"Let's briskly move around and find out if that stimulates any interest," suggested Connie.

While everyone followed Connie's suggestion, Jerry said, "It looks like they're not impressed."

After passing by, the pioneers turned around and cruised by the herd at a distance of only 50 feet. While all engaged in physical activity, Dianne said, "Other than occasional glances, they still aren't interested in us."

"Apparently, they really do think that we're too small to be a threat to them," stated Connie. "Humans have dominated the animal world for so many centuries that this is going to take some getting use to."

"Does that mean they will ignore us no matter how close we get to them?" questioned Moose.

"Unless we go closer, we won't know the answer to that question," responded Jerry. "And the lake bottom here is only a couple feet below the bottom of our hull, so we really can't go any closer."

Moose looked at Jerry. "We can't go any closer with this boat, but we can go closer; in fact, we can go right into their midst. How adventuresome do you feel at the moment?"

"I've always been willing to take reasonable risks when justified, but I'm not sure that what you're about to propose is justified."

"You haven't heard my proposal yet."

"I know you well enough to guess what it is. You're either going to suggest that we swim among those animals or that we get into our little inflated boat and row into their midst."

"We did bring it along in case we need it," declared Moose.

"We brought it along in case we find a safe place to go ashore," stated Dianne. "But I don't believe this is a safe place to do that."

"If these animals consider us to be irrelevant because of our small size, there shouldn't be any problem," argued Moose. "Anyway, I wasn't considering going ashore in the middle of the herd; I just want to slowly approach those that are in the water to see how they react. On land, they could charge and kill me, but those that are 95 percent submersed in water can't charge, and they don't look like they can swim either. If I stay away from their tails, I should be safe."

"Your reasoning sure sounds good," stated Jerry, sounding skeptical.

"I'm not convinced either," stated Dianne. "But if you insist on doing this, I am going with you."

"Would you like to swim, or should we use the boat?" Moose asked.

"I can see advantages to either approach; you decide.

"I think we should use the boat. Then, if the styracosaurus that we approach decides to attack, we can dive in and swim for it, while he destroys our boat."

"That makes sense," agreed Dianne. "And it looks like there aren't any piranha-type fish here for us to worry about."

"If there are, they certainly aren't hungry at the moment," stated Moose, while looking at all the dinosaurs in the water.

Several minutes later, Jerry brought the boat to a halt 100 feet offshore and dropped anchor. Then, Moose hauled in the inflated boat that had been in tow. He and Dianne entered it and began slowly rowing toward the nearest styracosaurus.

With rifle in hand, Jerry was on full alert for danger from any source. With video camera in hand, Connie sent a steady stream of imagery up to the Challenger, so all could observe the historic event as it unfolded.

When Moose and Dianne were 20 feet away from the styracosaurus, he started acting uneasy. He raised his head and bellowed out what sounded like a warning.

"I don't think he wants us to come any closer," stated Moose, as he brought the boat to a stop.

"I'm surprised we got this close," commented Dianne.

"As small as we are compared to him, I thought we'd get much closer. I wonder if he can differentiate between us and the boat, or if he thinks that we and the boat make up a single, fairly large, living organism. If so, that might explain the warning bellow."

"An animal that has never seen equipment could think that."

Moose backed the boat away from the styracosaurus a few yards. "Watch for a reaction. I'm going to show him that we aren't one organism."

Moose quietly entered the water without a splash and slowly swam away from the boat under the watchful eye of the styracosaurus. Then, Moose stopped, looked back at the animal, and then, at Dianne.

"I don't know what he's thinking," Dianne said. "But whatever it is, he apparently doesn't feel in any danger from us, because he isn't making any move to leave the water."

"If you were as big as he is, would you feel any danger from creatures as small as we are?"

"Absolutely not!"

"Why don't you join me in the water? It's warmer than it was out in the middle of the lake. It's actually quite pleasant."

Dianne looked at the large styracosaurus, which was less than 40 feet away. She thought about its awesome strength and fighting capability, but with 95 percent of the animal submersed, it certainly could not run or move very fast in any direction by whatever means. Then, she thought about the novelty of being one of the first humans ever to swim in the immediate vicinity of dinosaurs, and she quietly slipped over the side of the boat and slowly swam toward Moose.

"Now that we're no longer in the boat, and he can see how small we really are, I wonder how close we can get," Moose said.

"How close do you want to get?"

"I'd like to become the first human ever to touch a living dinosaur."

"Are you crazy?" exclaimed Dianne.

"No! It's just something I'd like to do. I wouldn't try this on land, but here in the water, I don't think I'm in that much danger, especially if I approach him slowly and back off if he sounds another warning."

"I think what you're planning to attempt is foolish, but I sense that you're going to do it anyway."

"Whether or not I can pull it off depends on these animals. If they're mild-mannered when dealing with small, non-threatening creatures, I'll be successful. If they're mean-tempered, I won't."

"By the time you find out what their attitude is, you could be dead or crippled for life."

Determined to convince his wife, and perhaps himself, that it wasn't that dangerous, Moose pointed at a pair of waterfowl that looked like Canadian geese. "They're swimming right next to a styracosaurus, and they're being ignored. Over there, a pair of birds that look like seagulls are perched on the back of one of these brutes, and they're being ignored."

"I hope you're not planning to do that."

"Do what?"

"Climb onto the back of one of these animals."

Moose stared at the nearest styracosaurus while he considered Dianne's comment. Then, he turned to Dianne as if to say something, but did not. Instead, he returned to looking at the large dinosaur.

"I shouldn't have mentioned sitting on his back, because I can see that you're considering the possibility. And you're daring enough to try it."

"You'll have to admit that it's an intriguing idea. Imagine being the first human to not only touch a dinosaur, but to also sit on one. When the video reaches Earth, it'll be the most sensational news event of the day, and I'll become an instant celebrity."

"There's no doubt about that, but these are wild animals, and the idea of sitting on one is just too dangerous. Besides that, I don't think they're going to allow you to do that anyway."

Pointing at them, Moose said, "Those seagulls are being allowed to. I realize that I don't look like a seagull, but if these animals prove to be mild-mannered, and don't see me as a threat, then sitting on one should be perfectly safe."

"I think you'll be taking too much risk to gain nonessential information. Remember, all that we're trying to find out is if they'll tolerate us being close to them. Knowing which dinosaurs we can safely be close to does have practical value."

Moose displayed a mischievous grin. "I wasn't serious, but when you mentioned the idea, it did sound like an exciting challenge, something worth exploring."

"You sure enjoy leading me on, and I thought you were serious."

Moose laughed. "Trying to get close enough to touch one of them is all the risk I care to take."

"I'm relieved to hear that."

Moose began slowly swimming toward the big styracosaurus. When he was ten feet away, he stopped and looked at the dinosaur's head. The first feature that caught his attention was the big horn located on his face a few inches below his eyes. With a length of about five feet, the horn would be a very formidable weapon. Moose looked at the dinosaur's neck shield. Of the six horns growing out of it, the two at the top were the largest and appeared to be about four feet long. Those protruding to either side were only about three feet long.

Studying the dinosaur's massive head, neck shield, and horns, Moose noticed a large L-shaped scar on the right half of the neck shield. Moose looked into the dinosaur's eyes and in a soft voice said, "I wonder what kind of battle you were in when you got that scar. It's rather wicked-looking, but since you're here, you must have won the fight. Despite that scar, you seem peaceful, but you look so frightening that I'm not sure I want to get any closer."

While Moose was speaking, the styracosaurus pointed his nose at him and sniffed. Using the same soft tone, Moose said, "Do I smell like a friend or like an enemy? Not having smelled a human before, I guess you probably don't know what to think."

Moose cautiously moved a yard closer and slowly reached out with his right arm placing his hand only a few feet from the dinosaur's nose. In response, the styracosaurus flared his nostrils and sniffed several times.

"You're going to have a difficult time identifying my scent; we're newcomers to your world. But we plan to be here for a long time, so why don't you get my scent firmly impressed into your brain, so you can remember me."

Looking at the dinosaur's big nose horn, Moose decided he didn't want to get close enough to touch the animal. The horn just looked too deadly, and he did not want to be within its range. However, Moose's decision turned out to be meaningless, because the big styracosaurus stepped forward and touched his nose to Moose's hand to get a stronger impression of his scent.

Moose was surprised by the big dinosaur's move, and now that he had achieved his goal of becoming the first human to touch a dinosaur, he wasn't sure that he wanted that distinction. He wondered how to get out of the situation he was now in. He quickly decided that his best move was to not make any sudden moves but to remain perfectly still. So even though his heart was pounding, he did his best to not panic and to appraise his situation in a calm, relaxed way. He took a good look at the big dinosaur's head and softly said, "Despite your fearsome weaponry, your touch is as gentle as that of a milk cow. Even so, I'm now within the range of your nose horn, and I feel vulnerable. Maybe I was crazy to have put myself into this position, but I'm here now, so what do I do next?"

After Moose pondered the question for a few moments, the big styracosaurus moved his head up and down a few inches to rub some of its soft nose tissue against Moose's fingertips leading Moose to say, "So you have an itch that you need scratched. You're too big to argue with, so I guess I'd better start scratching."

Moose proceeded to gently scratch the area, and the styracosaurus reacted by moving his head in small amounts to place the annoying itch precisely under Moose's fingertips. Fully aware of the dinosaur's big horns, Moose said, "I sure hope you find this satisfying, because this is one time I don't want to face an unhappy customer."

When the big dinosaur's itch had been alleviated, he moved his head away from Moose's hand and made some soft mooing sounds. Looking into the creature's eyes, Moose said, "I wonder if you're expressing appreciation."

After a few moments, during which the styracosaurus seemed to be thinking, it slowly turned to the right, leaving its left side exposed to Moose. "If you're going to turn your weapons away from me like this, I guess you must have decided that I'm harmless. I wonder what your intentions are."

Behind the dinosaur's left shoulder, a few inches above the water line, Moose noticed that he was twitching his hide. "Are you trying to tell me that you have another itch you want scratched? I don't think it would be wise to disappoint you, so I guess I'd better scratch it."

When Moose moved closer to scratch the itch, he noticed a peculiar looking bug, about an inch long and a half-inch wide, sitting on the dinosaur's skin. "I wonder if that bug is causing your irritating itch."

Moose reached out, grasped the bug between his thumb and forefinger and tried to remove it, but found that it was firmly attached. "This must be some sort of parasite, but as big as you are, I can't see that it's causing you much of a problem."

However, the styracosaurus continued to twitch its hide at the site of the parasite. "I guess I should try to remove it," stated Moose, as he reached down to his belt to get his hunting knife. Moose gently slide the knife's sharp point under the parasite and with a prying motion caused it to release its pincers. Upon turning the bug over, Moose noticed that it was equipped with a suction tube that appeared to be about a half-inch long. After studying the bug for a few moments, Moose dropped it into the lake. It was then that he noticed other similar bugs floating in the water next to the styracosaurus.

Speaking to Dianne, who was anxiously watching from 20 feet away, Moose said, "I wonder if these parasites need to breathe and can easily be drowned. If so, entering the water would be an easy way for these dinosaurs to get rid of them."

"Except for the ones on their backs, that would work," replied Dianne. "And it's possible that those seagulls are removing those. I see that they've moved to another animal, and they appear to be inspecting its back and occasionally pecking at something."

"This dinosaur must think I'm related to those seagulls, because he's twitching another part of his hide, and I see that there's another one of these parasites there."

Moose moved a little to his right, reached up with his knife, and gingerly removed the parasite. He spotted another one just beyond his reach. Noticing that the styracosaurus was completely tolerating his presence, Moose decided to crawl partially onto his back, so that he could remove the parasite. After this, he spotted one between the dinosaur's shoulders. Moose positioned himself to remove it, and then realized that he had placed himself completely astride the dinosaur's back without having given it any thought. He sat upright and looked at Dianne. "Sorry honey, I guess I've ended up doing what I was only kidding about."

"Well, that big brute doesn't seem to have any objections to your presence."

Moose looked at Jerry and Connie, and knowing that he was on camera, waved and smiled. However, the smile was short-lived, because a loud bellowing roar erupted from the throat of the big styracosaurus doing guard duty. The loud roar brought an instantaneous reaction from the styracosaurus that Moose was sitting on. It reared up on its hind legs and twisted its huge body toward shore. To keep from falling off, Moose instinctively grabbed a mane of hair growing along the dinosaur's backbone. When the dinosaur came down from its reared up position, it began a mad galloping rush toward shore, and Moose was now getting the wildest ride of his life. He quickly thought about slipping into the water and swimming to safety, but discarded the idea out of a fear of being trampled to death.

Wondering what the wild rush was all about, Moose looked toward shore and saw five T-Rexes rapidly approaching. A surge of adrenaline hit Moose, his heart started racing, and his mind instantly presented him with an image of being caught in the middle of a battle between dinosaurs. Now the possibility of being trampled didn't seem all that risky, and Moose decided to swim for it, but it was too late. There was a styracosaurus on either side of him, and there wasn't any clear water to dive into. Quickly looking over his shoulder, Moose saw that there was even one behind him.

In just a few seconds, the styracosaurus Moose was riding reached shore. It quickly bellowed out orders that caused the largest members of the herd to form a defensive line. With water no longer concealing its true size, Moose saw that he was riding the largest member of the herd, apparently the herd leader, for he confidently marched to the center of the defensive line.

"How did I get into this mess?" Moose asked himself. "I have five hungry T-Rexes in front of me, and a styracosaurus herd nervously primed for battle to either side and behind me."

Moose looked straight ahead at the nearest T-Rex, which was only ten yards away, and wondered: How did I ever get so close to one of those bloodthirsty killing machines armed with only a knife?

Moose's gaze was drawn to the T-Rex's massive jaws and teeth. Noting the abundant slobber falling from its lower jaw, Moose thought: With saliva flowing that freely, that animal is convinced that he's about to eat. Those teeth lining his jaws are as long as my hunting knife and look like daggers. It looks like he could eat me in two or three bites. What a monster, a ten-ton killer.

At that moment, the T-Rex's eyes focused on Moose for a few seconds, and it recognized that Moose was something different than it had ever seen on the back of a styracosaurus. Apparently, it considered him too small to be relevant, because it went back to inspecting the styracosaurus defensive line.

Nevertheless, during those few seconds, Moose felt the cold determination of a huge predator that was determined to eat. He felt like he had stared into the face of instant death, and he was filled with a cold, spine-numbing fear. But with an intense mental effort, Moose tuned out that fear, because he could not afford the luxury of entertaining it. To survive, he needed to keep his mind functioning freely.

Moose watched the big T-Rex look to the right and then to the left, apparently seeking a weak point in the styracosaurus defensive line, which was made up of adult males. Behind the line were the females and the juveniles. While the females had large nose horns, they were not equipped with neck shields and the additional horns growing out of them, but they appeared ready to defend their calves to the death if necessary.

Attempting to determine his chance for survival, Moose looked to the right and saw five males pawing the ground with their front feet and nervously moving their heads around while snorting. To the left, he also saw five males ready for battle.

The dominant T-Rex turned to the left and moved down the line looking for the weakest male. He occasionally sounded a challenging roar hoping to panic one of the styracosaurs, but they did not panic. They bellowed return challenges and pawed the ground with even more determination.

The remaining four T-Rexes followed their leader while looking at and roaring at the styracosaurs. The noise was deafening as the T-Rexes looked for a weak point in the styracosaurus defensive line. Not finding one, they increased the intensity of their roared out challenges hoping to spook a nervous young styracosaurus into making a panic run from behind the line. Without the protection of the herd, it would become easy prey.

Adding to the deafening sound, the styracosaurus herd leader loudly bellowed out some orders, and three of the males to his right moved forward, turned left, and followed the T-Rexes. Then, the herd leader and the other two males from the right side defensive line dropped back and moved to the left behind the left-side defensive line.

Observing what was happening, Moose thought, I like this strategy. We now have a five-man defensive front with three roving line backers, and the rest of the defensive line is pursuing the offense in the offensive backfield.

Unable to find a weak point in the defensive line and seeing additional defenders behind the line, the T-Rex leader was forced to conclude that he and his pack could not reach the cows and calves without fighting a fierce, costly battle. He looked behind him with the idea of trying the other end of the defensive line, but he found that his pack was being pursued. The T-Rex leader roared out in protest at having to go hungry. Then, he and his pack turned inland and quietly left the area in search of weaker prey.

With his ears numb and ringing, Moose thought, boy am I glad this ended peacefully. The herd and I have escaped death and injury, but I still have a big problem: how do I get out of here?

Moose looked toward the lake and estimated it to be 80 yards away, straight through the middle of the herd. He thought about some of the long touchdown runs he had made back during his college football days and recalled: I was very good at evading defenders on the way to the goal line, but they weren't big and lethal like these brutes. I wonder if I could zigzag my way through this herd. Would I be better off to run for it or to walk slowly? If I walk slowly and stay as far away from individual animals as I can, will they ignore me?

This herd leader seems to be totally unconcerned about having me on his back, or has he forgotten that I'm here? He couldn't possibly have thought about me during the T-Rex encounter. Maybe he has forgotten me, and he can't see me, because I'm sitting behind his neck shield. If I sit still, he should remain unaware of my presence.

It seems like I should be safe as long as I sit still, but sitting still doesn't get me back to the boat. I wonder how he'd react if I were to slide off his back and head for the water. What if he attacks, am I quick enough to evade him? I used to be very good at evasive running. Should I slide off and make a run for it, or should I play it safe and stay put?

My problem would be solved if this big guy would go back into the lake, but he seems to have decided to do guard duty. Is it possible that I am trapped on the back of a ten-ton dinosaur?

I never dreamed I'd ever be in a situation where staying on the back of a dinosaur would be my safest course of action. But that does seem to be the case, so I might as well relax and enjoy this unique experience while I watch for an opportunity to escape.

Meanwhile, Dianne had returned to the sailboat. With binoculars in hand, she anxiously observed Moose doing what he had joked about doing. "Now that the T-Rexes have left, my husband doesn't appear to be in imminent danger, but how do I get him back?"

"I think all we can do is wait," responded Jerry. "Eventually, that herd leader will put another animal on guard duty. Then, if we're lucky, he'll come to the lake to drink. It is a warm afternoon, and he is active; hopefully, he'll get thirsty soon."

"Also, those animals seem to enjoy being in the water," added Connie. "Some of them have already gone back into the lake. The herd leader may do that too."

"I hope you're both right," stated Dianne.

"There's always the possibility that Moose will make a run for the lake," Jerry said.

"But that would expose him to possible attack," Connie said.

"We'll have to be alert for that possibility and shoot any animal that attacks," stated Jerry.

"But as big as those dinosaurs are, even if we inflict lethal wounds, they still might be able to kill Moose while they're dying," Connie said.

"While that's a possibility, I believe the explosive bullets in our rifles have enough destructive power to immediately drop any animal we shoot."

"I think my husband has considered his options and has decided to stay put."

"That seems to be his wisest choice at the moment," stated Jerry.

"He sure looks relaxed," observed Dianne. "How can he be so relaxed when he's in such grave danger?"

"I don't think he's in grave danger as long as he stays right where he is," commented Jerry. "The beast he's riding seems to have accepted him and will also protect him from predators. The danger will occur when he dismounts to return to us."

"I'd sure like to talk to him," Dianne said. "Maybe we could deliver a communicator to him with an RPV."

"I think we can do that without disturbing the styracosaurus," Jerry said. "But a conversation might call his attention to Moose's presence."

"Moose talked to that beast while they were in the water, and the sound of his voice didn't seem to bother him," argued Dianne. "As far as my voice is concerned, we can turn the speaker down, and Moose can hold it close to one of his ears."

"You might be right," Jerry agreed. "Let's attach a communicator to an RPV and send it to him; then, we can plan his escape together."

"I'll take care of that," volunteered Connie.

"It's unfortunate we don't have one of the big RPVs with us," Dianne said. "Then, we could deliver some weapons to Moose."

"Had we known that your adventurous husband was going to ride a dinosaur into a confrontation with T-Rexes, we would've been better prepared," commented Jerry.

"How do you plan for something as unexpected as that?" Dianne asked. "That wild ride is the biggest surprise he's ever had. I wonder what thoughts raced through his mind when he realized what was happening."

"I don't know," Jerry said. "But he came to this planet looking for exotic adventure, and it doesn't get much more exotic than riding a dinosaur that's preparing to battle T-Rexes."

"I've attached a communicator to this RPV," stated Connie.

"Fly it to him, and then, let's wait until he contacts us," directed Jerry.

A minute later, Moose saw the RPV circling him. It came up from behind him, passing slowly over his left shoulder. Moose reached up and caught it. He removed the communicator and released the RPV.

Moose brought the communicator up to his mouth, but changed his mind and did not speak. Instead, he thought: If I speak, will this dinosaur associate my voice with the me that he saw in the lake? Will he figure out where the voice is coming from and realize that I am still on his back? If he does, will he even care?

Moose surveyed the herd and noticed that there were seagulls on the backs of some of the animals. Some of the gulls were actively looking for parasites; others were just perched and doing nothing. Then, he noticed some of the birds squawking at other gulls.

The gulls are accepted with a total lack of concern, Moose thought. Although I am much bigger than a gull, my weight is still only about one percent that of this styracosaurus. If these animals aren't worried about gulls sitting on them, why would they be worried about me? They've never had any bad experiences with humans to cause them to be wary of us. But I think I'll be quiet anyway and just wait for a good opportunity.

During the next half-hour, the big styracosaurus paced back and forth along the inland side of his herd alertly surveying the countryside for signs of danger. Moose sat still on the big dinosaur's back and did some surveying of his own.

Then, what Moose had waited for and hoped would happen, finally did; the herd leader turned to one of the other adult males and bellowed out an order. The male got up from his resting position and took over guard duty while the herd leader calmly walked into the midst of the herd where he stopped and looked around.

Now, I'm only 40 yards from the lake, thought Moose. I wonder why this big guy has stopped. What's he looking for?

While Moose pondered the question, the herd leader turned to his left and walked toward a female and calf resting near the edge of the herd. When he arrived, he made a soft mooing sound and the female answered in kind. Then, the herd leader gently rubbed his nose against the sleeping calf. He folded his legs under him and rested with the calf between him and the female.

This is my chance, thought Moose. I'm only 20 yards from the lake, and there's only one dinosaur between me and the water. Moose looked at the styracosaurus blocking his direct route to the lake and noted: he's lying down with his eyes closed. He appears to be sleeping. I'll try gently sliding off this big guy and calmly walking toward the lake. With a little luck, I won't disturb any of these dinosaurs, but if any of them are upset by my presence, I believe I can dash into the lake before they can attack me.

I guess I should consider the possibility of predators lurking in the bushes that are too small to concern these dinosaurs, but big enough to kill me. Moose carefully searched the vegetation near the herd, but was unable to spot any movement that might reveal the presence of a hidden predator. Still not wanting to use his communicator, Moose looked out at the sailboat and saw his wife and friends alertly watching him. I only have a knife, but they have rifles, and they know what I'm about to do.

Moving gingerly, Moose slid off the big styracosaurus without incident. Noting that the big dinosaur was undisturbed by his presence, Moose stood within a yard of him and again, searched the area for evidence of hidden predators. Not seeing any, Moose calmly walked to the lake, while watching the nearest dinosaurs and staying alert for predators.

Shortly, Moose reached the water's edge, waded in, and began leisurely swimming toward the sailboat. Seeing her husband in the water, Dianne dove in and swam out to meet him. When she reached him, she gave him a big hug. "Boy am I happy to have you back! The thought of losing you really made me feel empty. We're just beginning the most exciting phase of our lives, and I want you here to share it with."

"What happened this past hour is part of what makes our lives so exciting," responded Moose.

"I know, but I wish it weren't so dangerous. I want you around, so we can enjoy building a home and raising a family."

"That's my dream too. I didn't plan what happened. I was a victim of circumstances. One thing just led to another, and I got carried away."

Dianne laughed. "You certainly did put some new meaning into that centuries-old cliché."

Before Dianne and Moose could say anything more, Jerry yelled, "If you two don't mind returning to the boat, we could still see those giant sauropods today."

"That's a good idea," agreed Moose. "I'm ready to lie down on deck and relax for a while."

"Why do you need to lie down?" Jerry asked. "You've been sitting for most of the last hour."

"What choice did I have?"

A few moments later, Dianne and Moose were on deck, and Jerry said, "The sauropods should be at their favorite drinking spot in 15 minutes. By cruising at 12 mph, we'll be there waiting for them."

Looking at Moose, Jerry continued, "Since you're the most experienced person we have at contacting dinosaurs, you might want to go ashore and greet them when they arrive."

"No thanks! I've had enough excitement to last me for a few days."

Moose laid out an air mattress. But before he could lie down, Dianne grabbed him. "You have one of those parasites on your back."

"Now that you've mentioned it, I do feel a biting-kind of an itch below my left shoulder blade. Is that where it is?"

"That's exactly where it is."

"I hope it isn't poisonous."

324

"I don't know if it has injected any venom," responded Dianne. "But its suction tube has penetrated your body and may have placed some of Alcent's germs beneath your skin."

"Let's try to remove this thing without killing it," Dianne said to Connie. "When we get back tonight, we need to do some lab work and find out what microbes it's carrying. Also, we should dissect it and look for poison glands."

"And when we get back, I'll draw a blood specimen from Moose and examine it to see if his immune system is developing the appropriate antibodies," stated Connie.

Speaking to Moose, Connie said, "Judging from those scratches and abrasions on your legs, you just might have been exposed to a multitude of Alcent's microorganisms."

"My immune system's tough enough to fight off anything this planet has to throw at it."

"That may be true, but I'm going to do some medical work on you anyway," asserted Connie.

Dianne and Connie carefully removed the parasite and placed it in a specimen container. Dianne said, "Since this appears to be a bloodsucking insect, let's call it a tick."

"Since I discovered them on the herd leader, I think we should call them styracosaurus ticks, which we can simplify to sty-ticks," Moose said.

Observing a couple droplets of blood oozing out of the tiny puncture wound in Moose's back, Connie opened her medical bag and retrieved a suction device to pick up the blood and suction the wound to obtain a bit more for later analysis. "Some of the microbes that sty-tick was carrying should be present in this specimen," she said. "And if it injected any venom, some of that should also be present."

"It's a bit ironic to think that organisms too small to be seen without a microscope might end up doing me more harm than the ten-ton brute I sat on," commented Moose.

"That's a possibility," agreed Connie. "But I'm confident I can treat anything that your immune system has trouble with."

"It sure is nice to have a competent doctor onboard," stated Moose.

Jerry grinned at Moose. "I sure enjoy having her along."

Moose slapped Jerry on the back. "I think you're talking about something other than her medical skills."

"He's trying to say that I find lots of ways to fill his life with joy and happiness," Connie quickly said.

Moose looked at Dianne with an obvious expression of fondness. "I am happy to say that I also find myself in that situation."

A few minutes later, the interstellar pioneers arrived at the sauropods' favorite drinking spot. Dropping anchor 50 yards offshore, they awaited the arrival of the giant dinosaurs, which were still a quarter of a mile away.

"Even at this distance, it's obvious that they are huge," stated Dianne.

"They must be thirsty, because they sure aren't wasting any time getting here," observed Connie.

"They are marching along at a pretty good pace," agreed Dianne. "And their marching has a distinct majestic style to it."

"That style seems to indicate that they think they own this place and that all other creatures should step aside or be trampled," noted Connie.

"There's no doubt in my mind that they are the dominant species as far as land animals are concerned," stated Jerry. "And apparently, there's no doubt in their minds either."

"As long as they're alert and avoid being ambushed, they certainly don't have to worry much about predators," Moose said.

"You're willing to make that claim after staring into the eyes of a T-Rex?" questioned Jerry.

"The T-Rex I made eye contact with probably weighed ten tons, and he was the biggest in the pack. This sauropod herd leader probably weighs 100 tons. He has three large horns on his head and three smaller horns on his tail. In my judgment, being ten times bigger, and well armed, makes him extremely difficult prey, even for the fierce T-Rex."

"That's probably true, but as big as these sauropods are, eventually, even they must become weak because of old age or serious illness. Then, they can be preyed on by the T-Rexes. Can you image what a feast a creature weighing 80 to 100 tons would be for them?"

"That does provide an incentive for a T-Rex pack to occasionally challenge a sauropod herd to find out if there's a weak member."

When the sauropods reached the lake, they lined up along the water's edge to drink, except for one male who faced the open meadow watching for predators. "What an impressive slight!" exclaimed Connie.

"We may be looking at the largest land animals that have ever lived, here or on Earth," commented Dianne.

Jerry grinned at Moose. "Sitting on the herd leader's back would put you higher than the peak of the roof on a two-story house."

"You seem to be implying that I should try it," responded Moose.

"You did come to this planet looking for adventure, and you are an experienced dinosaur rider."

Before Moose could respond, Dianne said, "My husband's had enough adventure for one day, and I'd like him to stay alive for a while."

"It appears that your idea has been vetoed," Moose said to Jerry.

"Attempting to climb his tail to get onto his back would be risky," admitted Jerry. "As big as he is, you could fall off and break your neck."

"You're right about that," agreed Moose. "It's hard to imagine an animal so big that one could be killed by just falling off it, but here we are looking at animals that are that big."

"Probably, the safest way to experience their size would be to walk through underneath one of them," commented Jerry. "I think we could do that without even ducking."

"We could try it," responded Moose. "I don't think it would be as dangerous as climbing onto one's back."

"I'll bet if we walked under the herd leader, he would ignore us," speculated Jerry. "We don't weigh much over a tenth of a percent of what he weighs, and that should make us extremely small in his mind. Relative to him, we would be like a pair of one-pound kittens wandering up to a 1,000-pound bull moose. Why would that big sauropod even pay any attention to us? We would have to look totally irrelevant to him."

"You aren't serious about trying this, are you?" questioned Connie.

"It would be exciting," responded Jerry. "Imagine standing under a dinosaur that might be the largest animal that has ever lived."

"I'll grant you that it would be exciting, but I think it's an unnecessary risk. We're finally in a position where we can start fulfilling our dreams, and it seems like we should avoid unnecessary risk taking."

"I don't think there's any risk of being attacked, but there is the possibility of being stepped on and squashed."

"It's not very comforting to know that the possibility of being crushed is the only risk that you would face," stated Connie in a cool tone.

"I understand your concern, but in my younger days, I was the fastest quarterback in college football, and I'm still pretty quick on my feet. By being alert and ready to react instantly, I think I could get quite close to one of those animals with very little risk of being stepped on."

"I am confident in your ability, but the possibility of losing you is real. Is the novelty of being near one of those giants worth the risk?"

"This wouldn't be just a daredevil stunt. Since we're planning to live here for the rest of our lives, we need to find out how the animals living here react when they see humans approaching. Some day, we'll make exploration trips into the countryside. Should the need arise; retreating into the midst of a herd of large well-armed herbivores that tolerate our presence might be a possible way to gain protection from some predators. This strategy might be an effective alternative to killing them. Also, it's even possible that this self-protection strategy could become a necessity. Suppose one or more humans were stranded in the countryside without firearms or were simply out of ammunition."

"There's no doubt that the more knowledge we have about the creatures that live here, the better off we'll be, if we stay alive while we're gaining that knowledge."

Displaying a gleaming smile, Jerry gazed into Connie's eyes. "You sound so different than the person who earlier this afternoon said that we must not avoid adventure because it might be dangerous. I think you said that we must evaluate the risks, plan for them, and then go forward. I think you also said that we must live our lives fully."

Connie thought about Jerry's comments for a few moments. "You're right. I did say all of that."

"Have you changed your mind, or do you still feel that way?"

"I still feel that way, but we've just had a rather harrowing experience. It started out in an innocent way, and all of a sudden, Moose's life was on the line. Going ashore is very dangerous. We don't know all the risks, and we can't evaluate risks that we don't know about."

"That's true, but risk-taking is now part of our lives. If my theory is correct, the risk should be minimal in this case."

"Even though I sense great danger, you may be correct, and if you insist on going ashore, I want to go with you. I've never played football, but I can move just about as quickly as you can."

"I'm not going to dispute that, and you're welcome to come with me. We'll take Charlie along and send him in first to find out how the sauropods react."

Turning to Moose, Jerry said, "You and Dianne can watch our back-sides while we're preoccupied with those big dinosaurs."

A few minutes later, Jerry and Connie beached the small inflated boat 70 yards south of the sauropods. After carefully scanning the immediate area for signs of hidden predators, they sent Charlie walking toward the sauropod herd. The closest sauropod was the giant herd leader, who was still standing at the water's edge and drinking occasionally.

When Charlie approached to within 20 yards, the big dinosaur turned his head toward him, briefly looked at him, and then went back to drinking. Charlie continued walking straight toward the dinosaur's mid-section. A few seconds later, he walked underneath the big sauropod and then turned around and passed under him again.

"It looks like my theory is correct," commented Jerry. "Apparently, that big brute decided after only a casual glance that Charlie's just too small to be any kind of threat."

"So, are you now ready to do what Charlie just did?"

"I think so, but before I do that, let's take another careful look around to make sure that we aren't being stalked by predators."

After an intensive visual search of the vicinity, Jerry said, "Let's station Charlie a few yards behind you and a little to your right and keep him slowly pacing back and forth. If there are any predators hidden in that thick brush over there, Charlie will be between you and them."

With Charlie in position, Jerry began walking toward the big sauropod in as relaxed a manner as possible. Connie stood with her back to the lake, so she could easily make frequent glances inland while she observed Jerry. She held her rifle in the ready-to-use position with a cartridge in the chamber and the safety off.

When Jerry was 15 yards from the big sauropod, he stopped and studied the creature from head to tail for a few moments. Totally awed by the dinosaur's immense size, Jerry thought, it's difficult to believe that an animal could grow so huge. He's easily 100 feet long.

Jerry studied the dinosaur's legs and marveled at the enormous bones and tremendous muscle power required to support and move such a huge animal. Just one of those massive legs must weigh more than any land animal on Earth, except for maybe a full-grown elephant. They must be eight to ten feet in diameter with feet that are 12 to 14 feet across.

I wonder how old this guy is. It must take several decades to grow up and become a full-sized adult. In much of the animal world, adulthood can last three to ten times as long as the growing-up time period. That means this guy could easily be well over 100 years old.

At that moment, the big sauropod looked in Jerry's direction, and after glancing at Jerry for a few seconds, returned to sipping water out of the lake. He sure doesn't have much interest in me, but why should he be concerned about me when I'm so tiny compared to him?

Encouraged by the sauropod's seeming lack of interest, Jerry decided to move closer, and a few seconds later, he was beneath the dinosaur's stomach. He stopped, tilted his head back, and looked up at the huge creature's underside, which was about a foot above him. I can't believe I'm actually doing this. I am actually standing under a dinosaur that probably weighs 100 tons. But, I should get out of here; I've already proven my theory. But first, I have to touch this guy, so I can say that I've done it. I hope he isn't ticklish.

Jerry reached up and gently touched the sauropod's stomach. He smiled in satisfaction and began walking back to his wife. Even at a distance 70 yards, Jerry noticed that she seemed to breathe a sigh of relief.

About 20 yards away from the giant dinosaur, Jerry stopped to look back at him, and thought: It may be a while before I …

At that instant, Jerry's thoughts were abruptly interrupted by the sudden sharp report of a rifle followed instantly by an explosion. Jerry quickly spun around to the sight of a saber-tooth cat-like creature knocking Connie to the ground. The sight of a large cat pinning his wife to the ground horrified Jerry. Loud, ripping snarls added to the horror.

Jerry instantly decided not to fire his rifle at the cat, because it was armed with explosive bullets powerful enough to kill his wife when fired into the cat on top of her. So he dropped his rifle and broke into an all-out sprint toward Connie. Before he reached her, he saw that a second cat had knocked Charlie down and was violently shaking him and snarling.

The massive charge of adrenaline flooding Jerry's body added speed to his sprint and caused his brain to race so fast that it seemed like everything around him was moving in slow motion. The cat shaking Charlie seemed to be doing it very slowly. The cat pinning Connie seemed to be motionless.

Even though looking directly at the cat on top of his wife, Jerry's peripheral vision saw that the cat shaking Charlie had dropped him and was also bounding toward his wife. Instantly, Jerry thought, I guess he didn't taste any blood in Charlie, so now, he's heading toward Connie. Simultaneously with that thought, he drew his 10.5-mm pistol and quickly fired three explosive bullets into the cat without even slowing his sprint.

Jerry holstered his pistol, drew his hunting knife, and dove at the cat on top of Connie. He quickly plunged his knife into the animal's chest behind its right shoulder. In that instant, Jerry also wrapped his left arm under the cat's neck. He stood up, jerked the heavy cat off his wife, and rapidly rammed his knife into it three more times before realizing that the animal was already dead.

Fearing the worst, Jerry looked down at his blood-drenched wife lying in a pool of blood. Then he dropped to his knees at her side.

Before Jerry could say anything, Connie struggled to sit up. She smiled weakly. "Thanks for getting that thing off me."

Reaching toward Jerry, she said, "Would you mind helping me up?"

The flood of adrenaline that had surged through Jerry's body was now replaced by an abundant flow of tears streaming down his face. Seeing this, Connie said, "If seeing me drenched with cat blood is going to make you cry, I guess I should get cleaned up."

"It was horrible! I thought I'd lost you! I'm overjoyed that I haven't!"

"I feel weak and banged up, but you haven't lost me."

Jerry gently helped her up and put his hands on her shoulders. "I hope I never again see you lying in a pool of blood with a carnivore on top of you. Are you all right?"

"I think so, but I did suffer some bruises when that cat knocked me down and fell on top of me. He slammed me into the ground pretty hard."

"This attack sure happened fast."

"It was very fast! I was watching you stop to look back at the dinosaur, when out of the comer of my eye, I saw a rapid movement. I quickly turned in that direction to see a cat knock Charlie down and a second cat spring toward me. Instinctively, I instantly raised the end of my rifle and fired, from the hip so to speak. The last thing I remember seeing was the bullet exploding and ripping open the left side of the cat's chest. He must've been killed instantly, but he had already sprung and was only a couple yards away from me when the bullet exploded. Even though already dead, his momentum carried him forward, knocking me down. My head must have struck a rock, and I must have lost consciousness, because the next thing I was aware of was you lifting the dead cat off of me."

"You're bleeding from your left shoulder. It looks like one of that cat's saber teeth punched a hole in you when he crashed into you."

Connie looked at the wound, then at the dead saber-tooth lying next to her feet. As her gaze focused on the cat's open mouth and its prominent fangs, a cold shudder passed through her body. "It's frightening to think that those daggers were headed for my neck. Except for a quick, lucky shot, I would've been killed almost instantly."

"It wasn't just luck. You were trained to react instantly and decisively to surprise attack. But what about this puncture wound?"

"It doesn't appear to be very serious, but I'm glad it's in my shoulder and not in my neck."

"Just the same, I want to get you back to the boat, so Dianne can examine you. All the medical training you gave her during our long voyage can now be put to good use."

"I'd like to get out of these bloody clothes and wash this cat blood off me."

"But not in the lake. All that blood could certainly attract marine predators, if there are any. I'll help you bathe when we get back on deck. Right now, I'm going to help you into the boat. Then, I'm going to pick up our rifles and Charlie and get us out of here."

"Okay."

A short time later, when they were back on the sailboat, Dianne exclaimed, "You sure are a bloody mess! I hope that's not all your blood."

"Most of it is from the cat I killed." Beaming with pride, Connie said, "I was pretty quick with my rifle, wasn't I?"

"It's fortunate that you were," stated Moose. "We weren't able to shoot at the cats, because you were directly between us and them."

"That grueling survival training we went through sure paid off," commented Dianne.

"That's the reason I'm still alive, and I now feel like I've been combat tested."

"You have, and you passed in a colorful way, mostly red. Let's get you cleaned up, so I can examine and treat your injuries."

"Let's save some of this cat blood for analysis," suggested Connie.

Dianne collected cat blood samples from Connie. Then, she bathed her and examined her injuries. "This puncture wound could cause you some problems. Since that saber-tooth never brushed his teeth, you could have some nasty microbes in your body. I need to suction this wound and save the fluid for analysis."

"If you'll give the wound a good cleaning, I think my immune system can handle the rest."

"Your immune system is definitely being tested. You and my husband will give us our first good look at how the human immune system handles the alien microbes that gained entry via your open wounds."

"The next several days are critical. What a confidence builder it'll be if Moose and I don't develop any pathology."

"Listening to our wives talk makes me feel like a medical research animal," Moose said to Jerry.

"One of our objectives is to evaluate human reaction to Alcent's environment," stated Jerry. "So your feeling is soundly based in reality."

"I know, but in my younger days, I never dreamed that I'd someday play the role of a medical research animal on an alien planet."

"You probably never dreamed you'd ride a dinosaur either."

"That's true, and I'll bet none of your fantasies ever included standing under a 100-ton sauropod and reaching up to touch him."

"You're right, but now that we're here, I had to prove a point; namely, that animals as big as these would consider creatures as small as us to be irrelevant. I believe that we'll never be attacked by these giants and that the only danger we face from them is that of being stepped on if we're ever standing between them and wherever it is they want to go."

"That would yield the same result as a human stepping on a beetle: Squish!"

"That sums it up very well," stated Jerry.

While looking at Jerry, Connie asked, "Do I look better now?"

"Definitely! Red never was a good color on you. How do you feel now that your injuries have been treated?"

"My head aches, my left shoulder hurts, and I have several bruises. But I feel very fortunate that I'm still alive. My aches and pains will pass. The pain killer I took should kick in shortly, and that will help."

Jerry gave his wife a gentle hug. "You handled yourself very well in the face of such an ordeal. I am proud of you."

Connie smiled. "Thank you."

After a few moments of thought, she continued, "What just happened is a sobering lesson on just how dangerous the countryside is. As vigilant as I was, I still came within a split second of death. I am amazed by how quickly those saber-toothed cats just seemed to appear out of nowhere."

"They've convinced me that they are masters of stealth," Jerry said. "And their stealth ability is greatly aided by their camouflage color schemes, allowing them to be nearly invisible when they are in the right vegetation and under the right lighting conditions."

"Their stealth capability and size relative to us makes them extremely dangerous predators," stated Moose.

"I am guessing they might weigh 350 to 400 pounds," commented Jerry. "And you're right, our size should make us look small enough to be an easy kill, but big enough to be a pretty good meal."

"I could use a good meal myself," stated Connie. "I'm starving!"

"Me too," Jerry said. "Let's eat dinner and head for home."

"There's a heavy cloud front moving in from the west," Moose said. "In a few minutes, Alpha Centauri A will be behind those clouds, and we're not going to get much power out of our solar sails."

"But the wind is starting to pick up," stated Jerry. "This might be a good time to try out our wind sails."

"It looks like the stormy weather Mike's been predicting is going to hit us in an hour or two," commented Moose.

"If the system contains some strong wind, our sailing could become wildly exciting," Jerry said. "Let's get these solar sails rolled up and put away. Then, let's deploy our wind sails."

A short time later, Moose and Jerry had the solar sails put away and the tall telescoping mast and main sail deployed. "I love the sound of a sail flapping in the breeze and then snapping taut when it's properly oriented to the wind," stated Jerry. "It's been a long, long time since I've enjoyed hearing those sounds."

"This does bring back memories," commented Moose. "But the last time I went sailing, there were too many other boats. This time, we have a huge lake all to ourselves, and that really appeals to me."

"I hope the wind gets a lot stronger in front of the incoming storm, so we can have some real fun," stated Jerry.

"Let's talk to Mike and find out what his forecast is," Moose said.

While Moose was talking to Mike, Dianne and Connie appeared from below deck with dinner in hand. The sight and scent of food motivated Moose to cut short his conversation with Mike and head for the picnic table set up on deck. Soon, all were seated and enjoying a delicious meal of abalone steak and rainbow pike. With the navigation computer in control, Jerry was free to relax and enjoy dinner with his wife and friends.

"Mike said the wind will be much stronger before we get home," Moose reported. "He said he wished he could be here with us. From the sound of his voice, I think he's counting the days until he can join us."

"Everyone up there has been following our day-to-day adventures," stated Connie. "They're all eager to come down, and I can't blame them. They've been inside the Challenger for a long time. Even Denise wants to come down, and she doesn't even know what it's like to be on a planet. She just knows how exciting our lives are and wants to be with us."

"On her first day here, I think we should plan on spending lots of time with her," stated Jerry. "As active as her curiosity is, showing her around and answering her questions is going to keep us busy for a while."

"But it will be fun," Connie said. "Watching her wide-eyed reactions to the simple things that children born and raised on Earth take for granted will give us some precious moments to remember for a long time."

"We should put much of her first day on video, so she can enjoy it when she's older," suggested Jerry.

"That will also provide us with some priceless future enjoyment," added Connie.

While Jerry and Connie talked about Denise, Moose and Dianne made silent eye contact. They read each other's minds as surely as if they had spoken to each other. "Would you mind sharing those thoughts with us?" Connie asked them.

"We're thinking about getting pregnant when our 30-day quarantine is over," replied Dianne.

"We've been waiting for a long time," added Moose.

"Promise me that you'll let me give both of you a thorough physical before you do that," requested Connie.

"I think we could submit to that," responded Dianne.

"This whole month is one continuous medical exam," stated Moose. "By the end of it, there won't be much about us that you won't know, but I guess one final checkup won't hurt anything."

Connie grinned. "I assure you that it won't hurt."

"I've been thinking about our 30-day quarantine," Jerry said. "If we get through it without any significant medical problems, I wonder if we really need a second 30-day quarantine involving a few additional people. Maybe we can safely skip that and just bring everyone down."

"I think we should keep that option open," replied Connie. "But let me make a thorough evaluation of our medical situation at that time."

Looking at Jerry, Moose said, "Looks like you got the same answer we got in regard to getting pregnant."

"Now and then, there comes a time when the doctor should have the final word," commented Connie.

"I don't know about the final word, but at least a strong recommendation," responded Jerry.

Realizing that she may have claimed a little too much authority for herself, Connie said, "That is a better way of saying what I meant."

Jerry smiled at his wife; then, his communicator beeped. It was Mike. "I have a weather update for you."

"Is it good news or bad news?" Jerry asked.

"That depends on what you're looking for. Your pleasant weather will soon come to an end. The storm front is about ten miles west of Clear Lake. There are heavy rain squalls over there with sustained southerly winds in the 25 to 30 mph range and gusts up to 40. If you want some wild sailing, you're going to get all the excitement you can handle. The storm is moving toward you at ten mph, so you should experience a gradual increase in wind speed. Enjoy your sailing."

"Thanks Mike," replied Jerry.

Connie looked worried. "Can this boat handle that much wind?"

"It sure can," replied Jerry. "If the wind gets too strong, we'll partially retract the telescoping mast and roll up the bottom of the sail. The stronger the wind gets; the less sail we'll need to move this boat."

"But this is a big lake," argued Connie. "And winds up to 40 mph can generate some huge waves."

"If the situation gets too rough, we'll completely retract the mast and sail," Jerry replied. "Then, we'll retract, deflate, and stow the outriggers. Our boat will again be a submarine, and we can dive to a depth that isn't affected by the surface storm. No matter how stormy things are on the surface, the depths are always peaceful and quiet."

"In other words, I have nothing to worry about?"

"Not a thing," assured Jerry. "Just relax and enjoy the ride."

"We need to clear the deck," stated Moose. "Strong winds could blow away some of this stuff."

Jerry nodded. "While you're doing that, I'm going below to check the sonar data. I'm curious about whether this side of the lake has a deep underwater canyon."

"I'll join you," Connie said.

When they were below deck, Jerry asked, "How are you feeling?"

"I feel pretty good. The pain killer I took has taken effect."

"I'm glad you feel well enough to enjoy our sailing adventure."

Jerry put his arms around his wife. "Seeing that saber-tooth on top of you put a real scare in me. It makes me shudder to think what a close call you had."

In response to Jerry's embrace, Connie snuggled up against him and enjoyed the love and security that she always felt with his strong arms around her. She closed her eyes and mentally blocked out everything except Jerry's love, which seemed to flow into her very being. After relishing in the feeling for several moments, she said, "My brush with death really makes me appreciate the special relationship we've enjoyed for so many years. This is a very dangerous planet, and each day we have is precious, so let's enjoy them to the fullest."

"By their very nature, some of our most exciting and enjoyable adventures will be fraught with danger."

Backing away from her husband, Connie looked into his eyes. "I hope I didn't sound like I was implying that we should avoid adventure because it might be dangerous. I only meant that we should appreciate the time we have and make sure we enjoy everything we do."

"A close call with death does tend to enhance one's appreciation for just being alive."

"I also have a new appreciation for Pioneer Island. Can you imagine trying to build a home in the countryside among the fierce creatures that live there?"

"That would be challenging, but I prefer the lesser challenge of making a safe home on Pioneer Island."

"I wonder if there are any life-threatening hazards hidden in its dense forest," questioned Connie.

"A few days of exploration should help answer that question."

"As isolated as the island is from the countryside, I wonder if any dangerous animals besides bears are able to swim to it."

"I don't know, but our lives depend on being prepared for any possibility."

"In view of my near-death experience, I think it'll be a long time before anyone gets careless about being alert for danger."

Jerry smiled and nodded. "Let's take a look at our sonar data."

A few moments later, Jerry said, "It looks like we might have a deep underwater canyon. We're about two miles north of where we were when we first detected deep water, and it's also deep here, about 1800 feet. The drop-off occurred about where I thought it might. And again, it was very abrupt, indicating a nearly vertical underwater cliff."

While Jerry studied the sonar data, Connie observed the fish that came within viewing range. After ten minutes had gone by, Jerry said, "We've reached the west side of the deep water, and it abruptly ends with a nearly vertical underwater cliff. Present depth is about 280 feet."

"If it is a canyon, I wonder if it extends the length of the lake."

"I think it probably does. I sent sonar pulses to the north and to the south, and I was unable to find the underwater cliffs that would be there if this were just a deep crater-like hole. On another day, we'll take this boat down and investigate this canyon. Today, we're going to enjoy sailing."

A few moments later, Connie and Jerry joined Moose and Dianne on deck. "It's beginning to look like Mike's forecast might be right," commented Moose. "The wind is getting stronger, and that heavy cloud bank in the west is now much closer."

"He did predict rain," stated Connie. "And it sure looks like we're going to get drenched before we get home."

"I haven't been rained on in so many years that it just might be fun to get drenched," commented Moose.

Jerry scanned the huge lake and noticed how rough the water was getting. Then, he looked at the approaching storm west of Pioneer Island. His gaze shifted to the large sail stretched tight by the force of the wind. "It's us and one small boat against the elements," he exclaimed.

"And what a contrast those elements are to the controlled environment onboard the Challenger," added Connie.

"After living in that pleasant climate for such a long time, some stormy weather will be exciting," stated Dianne.

Turning to Moose, Jerry said, "Let's deploy our jib to increase our speed a bit."

"Good idea," agreed Moose.

A short time later, with both the main sail and jib deployed, and with the wind steadily gaining in strength, Moose said, "This boat is a marvelous piece of equipment. After using solar power all afternoon, we're now zipping along at a pretty good clip with nothing but the wind for power, and if Mike's right, the wind's going to get much stronger, further increasing our speed."

"If it gets strong enough, we'll have an opportunity to test this boat's capabilities," stated Jerry.

"And an opportunity to test some sailing skills you haven't used since leaving Earth," Connie said.

"I might be a little rusty, but I haven't forgotten. I did have extensive training on this boat and one of its sister ships."

With the boat racing along and cutting through big waves, Connie enthusiastically said, "This is wild. Maybe you could teach us the fundamentals of sailing."

"Be more than happy to."

With the wind whipping her hair around and spray from big waves splattering her body, Dianne gleefully exclaimed, "This is fun! I'm ready for some sailing lessons!"

During the next hour, Jerry explained the basics of sailing and the particulars of operating the boat they were on. Having had a great deal of sailing experience on a variety of boats, Moose easily grasped the details Jerry presented. Even though Dianne and Connie had never been sailing, they were eager students and learned quickly. With a little practice, they too would become skilled sailors.

Noting their location, Jerry said, "We're only two miles from Pioneer Island, and it looks like the storm has already arrived on its west coast."

Suddenly, the dark storm clouds were brilliantly lit by a powerful lightning bolt that appeared to strike Pioneer Island. "It's time to convert this boat into a submarine," stated Jerry. "I don't want to be caught on the surface in a sailboat during an electrical storm."

"Mike didn't tell us this system contained thunder and lightning," commented Moose.

"Weather forecasting still isn't a perfect science," responded Jerry.

The pioneers rolled up and stowed their sails. They retracted the tall telescoping mast. Last, they retracted, deflated, and stowed the outriggers.

With the lake now very rough and the little boat pitching and rolling with the waves, the pioneers paused to take a final look at the rapidly approaching electrical storm. They watched a powerful lightning bolt strike a tree on Eastern Island, instantly exploding it into a flaming torch. Three seconds after the explosive flash, they were jolted by a crack of thunder so loud that it sounded like the entire sky had been split open.

"I'm glad that one didn't hit us!" shouted Jerry. "Let's dive!"

Jerry dropped through the hatch into the sub's interior and headed for the controls. With the image of the exploding tree vividly in their minds, Dianne and Connie needed no urging to quickly follow Jerry. Being the last one through the hatch, Moose closed it tightly while Jerry initiated the diving sequence. Within seconds, the little submarine disappeared from the surface of Clear Lake and headed for a depth of 60 feet.

"That was an awesome display of the raw power of nature," stated Connie. "What would be left of us had one of those lightning bolts struck our boat?"

"That's something I'd rather not find out," responded Jerry.

"I can't believe how quiet and peaceful it is down here even though there's a powerful storm raging on the surface," commented Connie.

"It's also quite dark," noted Dianne. "Everything has a sense of unreality about it, but even though there isn't much light, the water's so clear that

I can still see for quite some distance. In its own way, the low light level adds a special kind of beauty to the depths, kind of like the countryside on a moonlit night."

"It does have a romantic appeal to it," Connie said.

"Especially, when you consider that there's a violent storm raging only 20 yards above us," added Dianne.

While his colleagues relaxed and enjoyed the quiet peacefulness of the depths, Jerry navigated the little submarine around Eastern Island and into the wind protected water of East Bay. "Judging from the increased lighting, I think the thundershower has passed," noted Jerry. "Let's surface and go home before the next one arrives."

A few minutes later, everyone was standing on deck appreciating a break in the storm system. "I love the fresh air smell after a heavy shower," Connie said.

"And look at that beautiful rainbow in the east," stated Dianne.

Connie turned and stared at the rainbow for a few moments. "Its elegant beauty makes it easy to understand why it became the Biblical symbol of hope after the great flood. Even though it has a simple scientific explanation, its does make me feel elated and hopeful."

"A display of nature's awesome firepower immediately followed by a colorful display of beauty, what a contrast," commented Dianne.

"Based on what I see in the West, the next display of firepower isn't very far away," stated Jerry.

"I think he's suggesting that we head for home," Connie said.

A few minutes later, the pioneers stood on the beach and watched the little submarine slip below the surface. Jerry had decided to anchor it a few yards off the bottom, so it would be protected from lightning strikes and whatever else the storm might throw at it. A small orange buoy with a radio antenna marked the sub's location.

After a short hike through dripping rain-drenched forest and a climb up a slippery wet rockslide, the weary pioneers hiked to their habitation capsule, arriving only moments before the next thundershower hit. When all were inside with the door closed, Dianne said, "I'm glad this capsule is rugged and well built."

After watching the electrical storm through one of the large windows for a few moments, Moose said, "I'm glad it's equipped with a well grounded lightning rod."

"All things considered, this is a safe comfortable home," Dianne said.

"I feel tired enough to sleep until noon tomorrow," stated Connie.

"You should be tired," responded Jerry. "We've had a very busy day, and you had a near-death encounter with those saber-toothed cats. That, all by itself, could leave you physically and emotionally drained."

"I could use a few days off to just relax and do a few easy things close to home," stated Connie.

"I think that's a good idea," agreed Dianne.

"I think we can find enough interesting things to do around here to entertain ourselves for a few days," Moose said to Jerry.

"We could probably do that without even leaving Stellar Plateau," commented Jerry. "Depending on how long this storm hangs around and how long the breaks are between showers, we may not have any good opportunities to travel very far, so let's rest for a few days."

ELEVEN

Life Starts to Become Routine

TIME: Day Six, Late Morning.

Worn out from five very active days with not quite enough sleep, the interstellar pioneers were still in bed, even though Alpha Centauri A had long since risen. Nature had obligingly accommodated their need for extra rest by concealing Alpha Centauri A with heavily overcast skies, making it quite dark inside the capsule. However, dark overcast skies sometimes have another side to them, and the quiet peacefulness inside the capsule was suddenly shattered by a loud, sky-splitting crack of thunder. The deafening boom from a nearby lightning strike instantly jarred everyone awake.

Jolted out of a sound sleep, Connie and Jerry abruptly sat up. "Nature's alarm clock calls," Jerry said.

While looking out the large window near their bed, Connie said, "What a cloudburst!"

"The driving wind magnifies the force of the rain and makes it seem heavier than it actually is," commented Jerry.

"That may be, but wind or no wind, this is a deluge." Connie hardly finished speaking when the noise generated by the storm dramatically increased.

Walking across the capsule to a downwind window, Jerry said, "Look at this. There are hailstones bouncing all over the place."

"Wow! That's awesome! I wonder how often hailstorms come through here."

"I hope they're not very frequent. Growing fruit trees and vegetable gardens will be impossible if hailstorms are a frequent occurrence."

"The plant life is definitely taking a beating. The ground is already white with ice, and it's still coming down."

For the next two minutes, Jerry and Connie were fascinated by the bouncing hailstones. Then, just as suddenly as it started, it abruptly stopped. Within minutes, Alpha Centauri A and B flooded the plateau with the brilliant light of day, which had a special eerie brilliance to it as it reflected off a landscape covered with bright white hailstones.

"What a weird scene!" Connie exclaimed.

"Once again, the destructive power of nature has been demonstrated to us," commented Jerry. "And it sure is a dramatic contrast to the tame environment we took for granted onboard the Challenger."

A worried look spread across Connie's face. "What are you thinking about?" Jerry asked.

"I'm wondering if the infant pterodactyl on Western Island survived all of this."

"We can easily find out. Using an RPV, Mike installed a camera inside the infant's shelter. Let's take a look."

First, Jerry tuned in to the signal from a camera on the Western Island cliff top. Panning the area, Jerry and Connie saw that the shelter had survived the storm and that the cliff top was covered with hailstones.

On another screen, Jerry tuned in to the camera inside the shelter. At first, the shelter looked deserted. Then, there was movement in a pile of leaves and grass, and shortly, the baby pterodactyl's head poked out of it.

"Thanks to a sturdy shelter and a pile of bedding, that chick looks quite comfortable," commented Connie.

"That shelter is definitely well built," stated Jerry. "It withstood the full force of this storm, and I'm amazed by how little rain leaked into it."

"The male did a good job with those pine branches you cut yesterday. He's woven them and tough vines into the driftwood to tie the whole thing together."

"It's good for the infant that I cut them. If the male had to hunt for material, he would never have completed the shelter before the storm hit."

"I wonder where the adults went during the hailstorm."

"They probably took shelter in the forest on the downwind side of that cliff." Turning his attention to Connie, Jerry asked, "How do you feel this morning?"

"Except for some aching bruises and a sore shoulder, I feel great."

"Any indication that the puncture wound might be infected?"

"No, I feel fine, but after breakfast, I'll have Dianne draw a blood sample, which we'll analyze to see if there are any alien microbes circulating in my system. If we find any, we'll check to see if my immune system is producing the appropriate antibodies."

"You've really gotten personally involved in our medical research."

"Believe me, I didn't plan this injury. But if my body is able to effectively deal with whatever nasty microbes were present in that carnivore's mouth, it'll sure help build confidence that our immune systems can protect us here on Alcent."

"I wouldn't expect the mouth of a meat eater who never uses dental floss to be a very sterile place, so I can't argue with you on that point."

"Dianne took the fluid she suctioned out of my shoulder wound and put it into the robot lab last night to have it analyzed. That analysis should have been completed hours ago, so we should have a good reading on what kinds of microbes lived in that cat's mouth and how much risk I might be facing. Likewise for the fluid I suctioned out of Moose's sty-tick wound."

Jerry affectionately embraced his wife. "I admire the courageous way you're facing a situation so filled with potential danger."

Connie beamed a happy smile at Jerry. "I have confidence in my immune system and in our medical technology."

After a few moments of silence, Jerry said, "I'm going outside to look around. I want to see how much damage this hailstorm caused."

"I'm coming with you."

"Let's collect some hailstones and put them in the freezer for later analysis. As violent as this storm was, these hailstones may've formed high in the stratosphere and contain dust and microbes from some other part of this planet."

"What do you expect to learn from them?" Connie asked.

"I don't know. I just think we should do the analysis."

Jerry and Connie collected several dozen hailstones ranging in size from 1/4 to 1/2-inch in diameter and put them in the freezer. Then, they went back outside to explore the eerie scene.

Shortly thereafter, Moose and Dianne joined them. "This is unreal," stated Moose.

"Even though the air feels warm, all this ice laying around makes me feel chilly," Dianne said.

"You've just gotten soft from all those years of comfort on the Challenger," teased Connie.

"There might be some truth to that," admitted Dianne.

"Let's walk to the south end of the plateau," suggested Connie.

Everyone agreed, and with the crunching sound of ice pellets crushing under their feet, they set out to soak up the sights and sounds of their ice covered plateau and inspect damaged plant life. In about an hour, with most of the hailstones already melted, they returned to the capsule hungry for a hearty breakfast. After breakfast, Dianne and Connie anxiously plunged into their medical research hoping for a good outcome.

Facing Jerry, Moose said, "I think we should go down to the submarine and retrieve Charlie. I want to inspect him and see how difficult it'll be to repair the damage inflicted by the saber-tooth."

Agreeing to Moose's suggestion, Jerry accompanied him to East Bay. After bringing the submarine to the surface, they entered it and examined Charlie.

In less than an hour, Moose found and repaired a severed control line between Charlie's right leg and his inertial guidance system. With the line repaired, Charlie was able to stand up and walk around.

"It appears that most of the remaining damage is bent structure and ripped skin," Moose said. "But now that he can walk, let's take him home and do a more thorough checkout of his circuitry."

"I'm amazed that Charlie suffered so little critical damage during the attack by the saber-tooth," commented Jerry.

"Making him durable was one of my goals when I designed him."

"It's possible that my wife is alive only because your brainchild was between her and the attacking cats. I'm very grateful to you for coming up with the idea for building Charlie. My life would be empty if I'd lost Connie yesterday."

Moose looked into Jerry's eyes, and for a few moments, there was silent communication and understanding. "Losing Connie would've been a tragedy for all of us. I'm happy Charlie was there, and everything turned out okay."

After returning to the capsule, Moose and Jerry spent the rest of the day working on Charlie while Dianne and Connie diligently pursued their medical research.

Late that evening, after they were in bed, Jerry said, "I'm thankful that your shoulder wound hasn't developed any complications."

"I am too," replied Connie. "But it's too soon to say that there won't be any. Some germs can lie dormant for a long time before they attack. As deep as my puncture wound is, there may be germs in it that weren't present in the fluid Dianne removed from it. However, I am encouraged by the way my immune system is reacting to the ones we did isolate."

"Hopefully, the wound will heal properly, and you'll be left with nothing but a small scar to use as a conversation piece in the distant future when you'll be telling our grandchildren stories about the early days."

"I like that scenario, and I promise I'll do everything I can to make it happen."

"More restful days like today might help you keep that promise."

"Today was rather uneventful. Except for that hailstorm this morning and an occasional passing thundershower, not much happened. What a contrast to yesterday."

"A few more days like today and life here might start to feel just as routine as living back on Earth," commented Jerry.

"I'll grant you that we might be able to establish a routine here on the plateau, but wild adventure will never be very far away. And you and I are both anticipating more days like yesterday, despite the hazards."

TIME: Day Seven.

At the breakfast table, Jerry said to Moose, "Let's build a trail up the rockslide. Even working between showers, it shouldn't take us more than two or three days to get it roughed out."

"Good idea," Connie said, before Moose could respond. "Using a rope to scramble up and down that steep slope is just too cumbersome."

"I like the idea too," agreed Dianne.

"I guess it's unanimous," stated Moose. "But I think you're being too optimistic on how quickly we can build it."

"How much time it'll take depends on how fancy we get and how steep

344

we make the grade. If we follow the path of least resistance, I think we should be able to rough out a functional trail in just a few days. It won't be perfect, but we can improve it later."

"A trail with a grade as steep as 15 to 20 percent would be a big improvement over what we have now," commented Moose.

"With that kind of grade, we'll have 800 to 1000 feet of trail to build," Jerry said. "If we follow the route I've been considering, the trail will have six switchbacks. We can make most of the trail by removing selected rocks and rolling them down the rockslide. Starting an avalanche is the biggest risk we'll face, so we'll have to be careful not to remove rocks that are supporting rocks that are above us."

"If we have to, we can always shore up some areas with small logs. There are plenty of trees between the bottom of the cliff and East Bay that we need to cut down anyway to thin out the forest along our path to the water. That will give us better distance vision to spot bears and other predators that might want to ambush us."

"Thinning out that stretch of forest is an important job," agreed Jerry.

"Cutting down the trees we need for the trail is a practical way to begin that project," commented Moose.

"When you're finished eating, we can start moving rocks."

"I've had some experience working with rocks, and it's hard work. I need to eat a little more; I will need the energy."

Several minutes later, Moose and Jerry picked up their tools and weapons and headed for the rockslide. Dianne and Connie decided to do biological research on some of the plants and other organisms living on the plateau, along with continuing their medical research.

TIME: Day Nine, Mid-Afternoon.

Moose and Jerry were standing at the bottom of the rockslide looking up at the trail they had just completed. Feeling a sense of accomplishment, Jerry said, "I think it looks pretty good, considering that we did it in less than three days. As I recall, you didn't think we could do it that fast."

"Well, we did work hard, and we put in some long days. Also, we did get some help from the weather. We didn't get any rain all day yesterday or today. That storm system moved through faster than predicted."

"But more important than any of that, we used our intelligence," commented Jerry. "We routed the trail in a way that required minimal movement of rocks, and we made some key stretches by muscling in some logs and anchoring them in place."

"You're right; we did lay it out for the easiest possible construction, but we still worked hard, and I'm ready for some fun. Let's go swimming, and then, let's see if we can catch another one of those rainbow pike. We're out of seafood, and I'm hungry for a big dinner."

"That sounds good to me. Let's give our wives a call and see if they'd like to join us."

"I think they will, and you know they'll want to try out our new trail."

Jerry reached for his communicator and beeped Connie. After telling her what he and Moose had in mind, she said, "We'll be right there."

While waiting for Dianne and Connie, Moose said, "I'm hungry for some gourmet smoked fish."

"That does sound good, but there aren't any seafood markets around here, so I guess we'll have to smoke the fish on our own."

"Smoking fish was one of my hobbies back on Earth. I developed some special flavors."

"I remember that you had quite a talent for that. Are you going to resume the hobby here?"

"It would be easy to do. We have an unlimited supply of fish, and it wouldn't be very difficult to build a small smokehouse. We also have quite a variety of trees and shrubs here on the island. Burning green wood with not quite enough oxygen will produce lots of smoke. The question is which tree or shrub will produce the most flavorful smoke?"

"Also, there's another important question: do any of the trees or shrubs produce smoke that will make the smoked fish poisonous?"

"Maybe tomorrow we should cut samples from different trees and shrubs and test the smoke for toxins and fragrance," suggested Moose.

"Besides building a small smokehouse, that'll keep us busy all day."

"But it'll be fun. As hard as we've worked building this trail, I think we deserve a day of recreation."

A few minutes later, Dianne and Connie appeared at the edge of the plateau and proudly marched down the new trail carrying Moose's fishing tackle and a snack for their husbands. "I like it," Dianne said. "It sure beats scrambling down the rockslide while hanging onto a rope."

"In time, we'll make it wider and add some guard rails," stated Jerry. "But this is functional, and by being careful, it's also quite safe."

"Let's head for the beach," suggested Moose. "I'm hot and sweaty, and I need a good swim."

"Me too," agreed Connie. "I've been doing research all day, and I'm ready to be lazy on the beach and go swimming."

"Aren't you worried about infecting your shoulder?" Jerry asked. "It's not healed yet."

"I covered the wound with a waterproof bandage. It should be okay."

When they reached the beach, Jerry said, "Let's bring the submarine to the surface and use it as a diving platform." Using his communicator, Jerry commanded the sub to rise to the surface. While it surfaced, the pioneers placed their fishing gear and snacks in the inflated boat and rowed out to the sub.

When all had their fill of diving and swimming, Moose and Jerry entered the inflated boat and headed for the same spot where Moose had previously caught a large rainbow pike. Dianne and Connie sprawled out on the sub's deck to do some serious sunbathing.

With Moose manning the oars, Jerry selected the same lure from Moose's tackle box that had been successful for Moose. As they approached their destination, Moose stopped rowing and let the boat drift.

"It's time to show you how it's done," Jerry said, while casting out the lure. He waited briefly to give the lure a chance to sink a few feet, then, began reeling it in with a stop-start jerking motion to simulate an injured fish. In a few seconds, Jerry received a massive strike, sharply bending his fishing rod and quickly removing line from the reel. Worried that all the line would be removed and broken, Jerry tightened the drag causing the fish to change direction. He quickly reeled in the slack line. When the line became tight, the fish leapt out of the water, briefly standing on its flapping tail.

"That's a beauty!" exclaimed Moose.

The fish headed for the bottom, rapidly stripping line off the reel. Upon reaching the bottom, it headed away from Jerry. However, the tightened drag again forced the fish to change directions, and Jerry quickly reeled in the slack line.

A few minutes later, Jerry managed to reel the now exhausted fish up to the boat where Moose netted it and hauled it in. "It's big!" exclaimed Moose. "But it doesn't look quite as big as the one I caught."

"But I didn't have to make a whole bunch of casts to catch it. With just the right touch, it's possible to catch dinner on the first cast. With a little practice, you might be able to do that too."

Moose stared at the fish. "I don't think there's any doubt that the one I caught was bigger, but that doesn't surprise me, catching the big ones does require a special kind of talent."

"This one's big enough to give us a few meals. I'm guessing that it weighs at least fifteen pounds, maybe even twenty."

"The one I caught was over twenty."

"You'd best enjoy that record while you can. I don't think it's going to hold up."

"Now that's a statement I can agree with, because I plan to break that record myself."

TIME: Day Ten, Late Afternoon.

Moose and Jerry collected and tested samples of seventeen kinds of young, tender, sap-rich wood. Testing consisted of burning them individually and channeling the smoke into the robot lab's spectrographic gas analyzer. Computer analysis of the data provided Moose and Jerry with a list of the chemicals contained in the smoke. Also, unburned samples of wood, sap, and bark were analyzed by the lab, and their component chemical compounds were identified.

347

They were discussing the test results when Dianne and Connie joined them. Connie leaned over Jerry's right shoulder in a way that was intended to get his attention. "Does any of that wood contain anything toxic enough to cause medical problems?" she asked.

Jerry briefly entertained the promise implied in the unexpected physical distraction and decided to pursue it later. "Only one shrub contains toxins," he said. "But in its natural state, it doesn't appear to be strong enough to be a problem, but I think you should look at the data. Some additional testing might be needed."

Jerry showed Connie and Dianne the video of Moose cutting the sample from the shrub in question. Then, he showed them the results of the chemical analysis of its sap and smoke.

Dianne and Connie briefly reviewed the data. "I agree with your analysis and your suggestion that we do more testing," Connie said.

Moving on, Jerry presented video of a tree. "The sap from this tree has a very high sugar content and a good flavor. When reduced, it should be as good as maple syrup. I've tapped a few trees, and I'm hoping to collect a few gallons of sap to reduce to syrup. If I'm successful, let's plan on having pancakes for breakfast tomorrow."

"When I was a kid, pancakes soaked with butter and drowned with maple syrup was a favorite breakfast of mine," Connie said, with her mouth watering.

"We also found two trees and three shrubs that produce fragrant, flavorful smoke," stated Moose. "And I believe there's enough difference in the smoke to produce smoked fish with five distinctly different flavors. Along with marinating the fish in special spice solutions, I guarantee that we'll have some tasty eating."

"As enthusiastic as you are, it looks like you're ready to back up your words with action," Dianne said.

"First, we need to build a smokehouse. And there's a tree over there that was knocked down by the storm. I'll cut some small logs out of it with a chainsaw and cut them into boards with our sawmill. Then, I'll nail them together. It shouldn't take me more than a few hours to build a crude, but functional, smokehouse. Then, we'll need to catch more fish."

"I can help you with both of those tasks," offered Dianne.

Speaking to Jerry, Connie said, "Let's go check those trees you tapped. And while we're there, let's tap a few more just to make sure we have enough sap to make lots of syrup."

Remembering how Connie had distracted him only a few minutes earlier, Jerry smiled at her. "This could turn out to be an enjoyable outing."

Acting like she didn't know what he was talking about, Connie said, "I've never tapped maple trees, so I don't know how enjoyable it will be."

"Tapping maple trees is an art, but with a little forethought, I'm sure we'll use the right technique for the best results."

"Perhaps, you'll take a little extra time to demonstrate this technique for me, so that I'll be able to fully appreciate the artwork involved."

"I'll be more than happy to do that for you."

"I think we should get started. Where are the maple trees?" Connie asked, with a subtle, but noticeable, degree of eagerness in her voice.

While pointing at the nearest grove, Jerry said, "There are several of them in that grove."

"I'm glad they're right here on the plateau. That makes them conveniently close. If your technique fulfills expectations, we could do some more trees tomorrow."

"That favorite breakfast of yours that you were talking about earlier is starting to sound like a special dessert."

"I've sometimes thought of it that way."

Jerry and Connie looked at each other and silently decided that there had been enough conversation. So they picked up the things they thought they would need and started walking toward the nearby grove.

TIME: Day Eleven, Early Dawn.

Dianne awoke early and quietly slipped out of bed. Looking out the east window, she gazed at the soft red bottoms of distant clouds and listened to chirping birds anticipating a new day. She noticed the red color of the sky reflecting off the lake, giving it the appearance of a sea of fire.

Consumed by the exotic beauty of the scene, she failed to notice that Moose had gotten up and was standing behind her. She was startled when he exclaimed, "What a spectacular sunrise! We're fortunate to have the opportunity to build a home in the presence of such natural beauty."

"How long have you been standing behind me?"

"Just a couple minutes."

"I really must've been mesmerized. I didn't even notice you."

"You were definitely preoccupied."

"This kind of natural beauty can easily put me in a trance."

For a couple minutes, Dianne and Moose silently enjoyed the magnificent beauty of the sunrise. Then, Dianne asked, "Would you like to go down to the bay with me? I want to try my hand at fishing."

"Not much doubt about my response to that question. We did finish the smokehouse last night, and I'd like to fire it up."

An hour later, when Connie and Jerry were finishing their breakfast, they looked outside and saw Dianne and Moose returning with a large rainbow pike. Stepping outside to greet them, Jerry said, "That looks like the largest fish we've caught so far."

Bubbling over with excitement, Dianne said, "It took me ten minutes to tire him out enough, so Moose could net him and lift him into the boat."

"Are you saying that you caught this giant?" questioned Jerry.

"Yes! And it was a battle! My arms are still aching!"

"That really surprises me," responded Jerry.

"You're surprised that my arms ache?"

"No, I'm surprised that you caught that fish."

"Why is that?"

"Just two days ago, your husband told me that catching the big ones requires a special kind of talent. There was no doubt in my mind that he was implying that only he has this talent. And now, you show up with a fish much bigger than the one he caught."

Jerry's remark caused everyone to stare at Moose, who immediately blurted out, "Well, she did have a good coach."

Everyone continued to stare at Moose; then, Dianne rescued him by saying, "I must admit that Moose did give me some helpful tips."

Moose bowed slightly. "Thank you."

"It really was a team effort," Dianne continued. "I would've had a difficult time landing this monster by myself. Let's weigh him and see just how heavy he is."

A few moments later, Dianne proudly exclaimed, "Thirty-three and one-half pounds!" She looked at Moose. "That should be enough fish to test your smokehouse."

"It sure is," agreed Moose, enthusiastically.

"Are you going to marinate the fillets first?" Jerry asked.

"I plan to start out by trying the natural flavor of the fish combined with the natural flavor of the smoke."

"Which smoke?"

"One of the shrubs we tested yesterday produced a smoke with a really spicy aroma. For lack of a better name, let's call it the spice bush. Anyway, I want to try it first. I think smoke from it will give the fish a spicy flavor not too different from Cajun spices, but perhaps milder."

"You're making my mouth water. When will it be ready?"

"This afternoon, and my mouth is watering too, but I haven't had breakfast yet. Maybe I should eat before I start smoking fish."

"There's a half bowl of pancake batter and a pitcher of syrup on the counter," Connie said. "The syrup was made from the sap we collected. It is excellent; every bit as sweet as Earth's maple syrup, but the flavor is stronger. To me, it tastes like maple syrup accented with a bit of butterscotch flavor."

"Sounds delicious," Dianne said.

"I can't wait to try it," Moose said.

"I'll fix the pancakes," volunteered Connie.

"While you're eating breakfast, I'll cut some spice bush for the smokehouse fire," Jerry said to Moose.

"We are going to have a delicious smoked fish dinner tonight!" declared Moose.

After breakfast, Moose cut the fish into fillets, placed them on racks in the smokehouse, and got the fire going. As the day wore on, Moose and Jerry busied themselves tending the smoky fire, exercising special care to avoid making it too hot inside the smokehouse.

While doing this, they made detailed plans to build an elevator for the cliff at the south end of the plateau. They decided to have the pulleys and axles made on the Challenger and to make the car and support structure out of wood. The elevator would be powered by an electric motor sent down by Mike with the pulleys, axles, brackets, bolts, and cable.

Dianne and Connie spent the day doing medical and biological research. They also started exploring South Bay with the marine explorer. With the water in South Bay being about five degrees warmer than East Bay, it would become the choice swimming area.

By mid-afternoon, Moose could no longer resist the temptation and announced, "I think it's time to do a taste test." He removed a fillet and put it on a plate to cool off. "It certainly looks good," he said. "And it smells pretty good too."

Moose began picking the fillet apart to see if it was completely baked. "It looks done as far as the cooking is concerned, but if we lower the heat a bit, we can leave the fillets in a little longer to dry them out some. I like smoked fish on the dry side."

Moose tasted it. "This is delicious, but another hour in the smoke would make the flavor a bit stronger."

After tasting the fish, Jerry said, "You're right. This is good."

"But I think another hour in the smoke will make it even better," stated Moose.

Jerry savored another mouthful of the freshly smoked fish. "This is already so delicious that I'm not sure it can be made better."

"I think it can, but to give your opinion some weight, I'll take half the fish out and smoke the rest for another hour."

"While you're doing that, I'm going to talk to Mike about our elevator design, so he can make the things we need and send them down."

Jerry called Mike, and they discussed the design. "I'll make sure you have the things you need by noon tomorrow," Mike promised. Then, he said, "On another subject, I've been tracking your favorite bear, and early this morning, he left your island and headed south. He's now taking a nap on the next big island."

"Good riddance!" exclaimed Jerry. "I'm not going to miss him. However, somewhere on this island, we still have the mystery bear. I am surprised that one of our surveillance cameras hasn't spotted her on the beach by now. But with all the rain we just had, there are probably lots of small pools and streams all over this island to drink out of."

"You're assuming it's a female."

"I think it's a female with cubs in a well-hidden den. You've done a thorough search of the forest with RPVs and haven't found her, so that's the best explanation I can come up with. But I suppose it's also possible that she left before we had all of our surveillance cameras in place."

"A female with cubs can be very dangerous, and as time goes on, the situation might become even more dangerous for you guys."

"What do you mean by that?"

"I've noticed that you guys are having a difficult time at the dinner table, that is to say, a difficult time getting away from the table. With all that good alien food you're discovering, you're bound to get fat, and you know how that can slow you down."

"As physically active as we are, you don't need to worry about us getting fat."

Having overheard the last few remarks, Connie said, "Speaking of physical activity and food, Dianne and I have located a couple areas where we would like to start experimental gardens. We would appreciate it if you and Moose would work the soil for us."

"It's a little over two hours until dinner time," responded Jerry. "Spading that soil over will give us an opportunity to work up an appetite, so we can feast on some delicious smoked fish."

"Why do I feel like that comment was made for my benefit?" questioned Mike.

"I was merely taking advantage of an opportunity to assure you that we're working hard and won't get fat and slow."

"I think you made that statement to make me hungry for smoked fish," retorted Mike.

"That possibility might have been a little side thought back in some recessed corner of my mind."

"Baloney! Making me hungry was your main objective."

"I want to make sure you're ready for a seafood feast when you come down in a few weeks. We plan to prepare a banquet for the next group that comes down, and I'm assuming that you'll be part of that group."

"That's an assumption I can live with."

Speaking to Jerry, Dianne said, "Let me know when you and Moose are ready to start working the soil for our experimental gardens. I want to be there. I need to watch for bugs and worms living in the soil, so I can collect some for lab work."

"I'm ready to start right now. Moose can join us when he's done smoking fish."

"I'll pick up some specimen containers," replied Dianne.

"This is going to be slow, difficult work," stated Jerry. "Soil that has never been tilled is usually root-bound and difficult to break up."

"Fortunately, these are small experimental gardens. If you and Moose will do the hard work, Connie and I can do some additional soil preparation tomorrow when we plant the gardens."

"That's a good plan. I'll get some tools."

Jerry picked up a shovel, a spading fork, and a grub hoe. "I'm ready to start digging," he said to Dianne.

Dianne showed Jerry the selected garden areas, and he vigorously began the backbreaking project of hand tilling the soil. Dianne alertly watched for and collected some of the little critters living in the soil.

A half-hour later, Moose applied his muscle power to the project. After a few minutes, he said, "This is hard work."

"I'm not going to disagree with you," Jerry said, drenched in sweat. "Using muscle power is fine for these small gardens, but before we do any large gardens, we need to bring down some power equipment."

"That's true, but I am enjoying this, even though, it is tough." After a few moments of thought, Moose said, "Maybe I misstated that. Maybe I'm enjoying this because it is hard work. Strenuous activity always gives me a healthy feeling that I don't seem to be able to get any other way."

"I can relate to that. Hard work always makes me feel good too."

"If I'd known you guys were going to enjoy this so much, I would've selected much larger areas," Dianne said.

"These areas are big enough," Moose instantly responded. "By the time we're done, I'll be ready for a hot shower, a big dinner, and a good night's sleep."

Dianne smiled at Moose. "I really appreciate the help you're giving me, and I believe you'll sleep well tonight."

Two hours later, both experimental gardens were ready for planting, and the tired, hungry gardeners headed for the shower. They had sore aching muscles and felt like basking in the hot shower. However, they took quick showers. They knew that Connie was putting the finishing touches on a large feast featuring freshly smoked fish.

TIME: Day Twelve, Late Morning.

Dianne and Connie were planting their experimental gardens. They put seeds directly into the ground and transplanted an assortment of plants brought down from the Challenger.

"It'll be interesting to see how these plants do here," Connie said.

"I wonder how they're going to react to Alcent's insects and diseases," Dianne said.

"If they encounter problems they're unable to cope with, our resident plant doctor will have to make some house calls."

"This is the first time I've ever been called a plant doctor, but I might very well become one. The defenses these plants developed back on Earth might not be adequate here."

"In that event, your skills will be tested."

"I should be able to develop a treatment for any problems they encounter, and we should have a nice variety of salad greens to eat in as little as a month or two."

"Maybe some ripe tomatoes too; these plants are loaded with green ones."

"Throw in a few pea pods and some grated sweet onion, and we'll have some great salads."

"And not too long after that, we should have string beans, carrots, potatoes and sweet corn," added Connie.

"Home grown foods are always wholesome and delicious. I'm really looking forward to them."

"Me too! Our food synthesizers served us well over the years, but I'm ready for garden-grown foods that contended with the forces of nature."

Meanwhile, on the south end of the plateau, Moose and Jerry were cutting and shaping wood for the elevator car and its support structure. Suddenly, their activities were interrupted by a beeping communicator. It was Mike who said, "If you guys will move out of the way, I think I can land the items you requested very close to where you're working."

Looking up and searching the sky, Moose and Jerry saw a circling, descending para-wing. They noticed that two pterodactyls were flying close to it. When the para-wing turned into its final approach glide, the pterodactyls took up positions a little behind it and to either side.

"I wonder if they're the birds from Western Island?" questioned Jerry.

"When they get closer, we'll be able to tell, but right now, I think we should get out of the way. That thing is headed directly at us."

The capsule full of supplies landed where Moose and Jerry had been standing, but the pterodactyls did not land. They circled and watched with interest as the para-wing collapsed on the ground.

Jerry warily observed the circling pterodactyls. "They sure look like the birds from Western Island."

"I think you're right, and they're very interested in that para-wing."

"Pterodactyls are the largest fliers on this planet. Since we arrived, they've seen things in flight that are larger than they are. If they're as intelligent as we think they are, I would expect them to be curious about these large flying objects."

"If we fold up the para-wing and put it away while they're watching, I wonder if they'll figure out that it's an inanimate object and not some new flying creature that they need to be concerned about."

"They do have an infant on Western Island," stated Jerry. "Maybe they're trying to figure out if this is a flying creature that could be a threat. Perhaps, folding it up and putting it away will put their minds at ease."

"That's possible, but I don't think we've been around them long enough to know if we can trust them not to attack while we're folding up something that they might see as a threat."

"Let's stay alert and be prepared."

Moose and Jerry checked their 10.5-mm pistols to make sure they were ready for use. Then, while watching the circling pterodactyls, they walked over to the para-wing, unhooked it from the capsule, folded it up, and packed it into its storage compartment in the upper part of the capsule. When this task was finished, the pterodactyls headed toward Western Island, and Moose and Jerry went back to elevator construction.

TIME: Day Fifteen, Lunch Time.

The interstellar pioneers were at the south end of Stellar Plateau admiring their new elevator. "It certainly looks rugged," stated Dianne. "But is it safe to ride?"

"We loaded 2,500 pounds of rocks onto it and hauled them up and down several times," responded Moose.

"Then, it should certainly be safe for the four of us," stated Connie. "Let's go down to the beach and enjoy a picnic lunch."

A few moments later, all were in the elevator and slowly descending along the south face of Stellar Plateau. "This isn't very fast," Connie said.

"That's true," agreed Jerry, "but it's convenient. As slow as it is, it still only takes a couple minutes, and that's much faster than hiking down the trail we built on the rockslide. Not to mention that you'd still have to walk the beach to get to South Bay."

"This open-air cage sure makes for a thrilling ride," commented Connie while leaning over the guard rail and looking down."

"Almost too thrilling," stated Dianne. "What will happen to us if the support cable breaks? It's a 150-foot drop to the beach."

Moose showed Dianne and Connie the guide cable located at each corner of the car. "Each of these cables passes through a friction brake that will automatically engage if the main support cable breaks."

"Then, we'd be stranded at whatever height the support cable broke," commented Connie.

"No, the friction brakes can be used to maintain a controlled descent," responded Moose.

A few seconds later, the elevator came to a stop at the base of the cliff, and Connie said, "I like it. You guys did a good job."

Shortly, all were seated at a table located on the sandy beach a few feet from the water. Dianne considered the table's location and said, "A table on the beach, and an elevator to get to it, what a convenient setup."

"And it's a rugged outdoor table," added Connie.

"We didn't spend much time on it," Jerry said. "It's just a few slabs of wood bolted to some legs."

"It definitely has a crude backwoods appearance," noted Moose. "But it's perfect for our needs, and it makes me feel like I'm on a camping trip."

"If you guys keep building things, this island will soon feel like home rather than a camp-out," commented Dianne.

"I'm not sure if that's a complaint or a compliment," Moose said to Jerry.

"I'm not sure either. But they've been busy planting and tending gardens, and a garden filled with fresh vegetables can sure make a campsite look and feel like home."

"My remark was intended to be a compliment," Dianne said. "But even after we've been here for a few years, and have all the conveniences of home, I think I'll still feel like we're camping out, because we'll still be a lone human outpost on a hostile planet very far from Earth."

"As if we need a reminder that we're on an alien planet, there's a pair of pterodactyls circling," Connie said. "And they seem to be studying us."

Jerry looked up at them. "They aren't the pair from Western Island, and they're closer to us than I feel comfortable with."

Jerry got up from the table, picked up his rifle, and prepared for defensive action. Moose, Dianne, and Connie followed his example.

"Even though they're uncomfortably close, they aren't doing anything threatening," commented Connie.

"No, they aren't," agreed Jerry. "They may be doing nothing more than wondering if we'd be a good alternative to eating fish all the time."

"That's not a comforting thought," responded Connie.

At that moment, the male pterodactyl from Western Island arrived on the scene and made some loud squawking sounds that got the immediate attention of the circling pterodactyls. They turned to meet him and made some squawking sounds in return.

With giant raptors apparently conversing directly above them, the humans watched in spellbound amazement. After two minutes of back and forth squawking, the new arrivals left, flying toward the northeast. The male from Western Island circled once and let out a squawking sound that seemed to have a reassuring tone to it; then, he left.

While looking at his fellow pioneers, Jerry asked, "What do you think of that?"

"I think the new arrivals were told to leave us alone," replied Connie.

"But was it a warning, or was he telling them that we are friends?" questioned Jerry.

"Either way, it looks like removing that tree from his cliff top home has made him feel indebted to us," responded Connie.

"That's probably true," agreed Jerry. "But there are some other possibilities we need to consider. Is it possible that the pair on Western Island has observed us long enough to know that we are far superior to them and that we are capable of defending ourselves with lethal force? Is it possible that the new arrivals are friends of the Western Island pterodactyls and that the big male told them about our capabilities?"

"If we say yes to those questions, then we're saying that pterodactyls are smart enough to do deductive reasoning," responded Dianne.

"And we're also saying that they're capable of communicating on a fairly advanced level," declared Moose.

While continuing to speculate on how intelligent the pterodactyls might be, the pioneers enjoyed their picnic lunch. When Jerry finished eating, he changed into his swimming trunks and stretched out on the sand next to the water's edge. Shortly, Connie joined him.

"You removed your bandage and stitches this morning," observed Jerry. "And it looks like your puncture wound is completely healed."

"It is, and my shoulder feels good too. So except for this small scar, I seem to be fully recovered from my brush with death."

"Does that mean that you're ready to return to the countryside for some additional adventure?"

"No way! I will be content to put on a video headset and explore the countryside with an RPV."

"When we sail around the lake, we should see some interesting sights and learn a lot using that approach."

"And we can enjoy the adventure from the safety of our submarine. The next time I'm attacked by a carnivore, I might not be so lucky."

"I hope there won't be a next time," Jerry said softly.

"Considering where we are, that might be unrealistic."

"Unfortunately, I think you're right."

"I'm really looking forward to our exploratory voyage around the lake," Jerry said. "It'll not only be fun, but we'll also discover lots of plants and animals, greatly adding to our knowledge about our new home."

"We'll also gain a great deal of knowledge about the underwater world," stated Moose. "There might be many different kinds of edible fish living in other parts of the lake."

"My husband's mind never seems to be very far away from food," commented Dianne.

Moose looked at his wife. "Don't tell me you've already forgotten how excited you were when you caught that big rainbow pike a few days ago?"

"That was pretty exciting."

"And haven't you been enjoying the smoked fillets?"

"They are delicious," admitted Dianne while nibbling on one.

"I have nothing more to say in my defense," stated Moose.

Watching Dianne munch on the smoked fish fillet, Connie said, "As a member of the jury, I must say that I think the defense won this one."

Dianne made fleeting eye contact with Connie. She continued to enjoy her smoked rainbow pike. Moose smiled in satisfaction.

"When do you think we can go on our voyage of discovery?" Connie asked Jerry.

"There are some things we should do here on the island before we take off on a week-long sailing trip. We've been here more than two weeks, and we still haven't explored this island's forest. I'd like to spend a few days poking around in the bushes before we leave for a week."

357

"While you're doing that, Dianne and I can continue our research on the things we found living in the soil in our gardens."

"We also need to observe the insects that visit our gardens and determine if they're beneficial or detrimental," Dianne said.

"Since we're talking about food, we need to find out if some of the other species of fish that live around this island are edible," Jerry said.

"Now that's a project I wouldn't mind devoting some time and energy to," stated Moose. "Being the devoted husband that I am, I've noticed that my wife seems to have developed a real taste for smoked seafood."

Everyone stared at Dianne waiting for a response. "I admit it. It is delicious," she said, shrugging her shoulders.

Moose gave Dianne a loving smile.

"I like the idea of going sailing for a few days," Dianne said to Jerry. "What a fun way to get acquainted with our little corner of this planet. I think I could be ready to go in three days."

"Unless something unforeseen develops in the next few days, let's plan on going," stated Jerry.

"I'll be ready," declared Connie. "But right now, I'm ready to go swimming. It's time we check out the water in South Bay."

"I'll go with you," stated Jerry.

"I'll stand guard," declared Moose.

"I'll help you," offered Dianne. "And when they return, maybe we can go swimming."

"That sounds good to me."

TWELVE

A Shocking Discovery
Makes Life More Complicated

TIME: Day Sixteen.

The interstellar pioneers were eating breakfast when they received a call from Mike. After the usual greetings, he said, "I have some video that I think you'll find interesting."

Before anyone could respond, Mike's image disappeared from the screen and was replaced by an image of the Rocky Point Bay waterfront. A large bear stepped out of the forest onto the beach followed by two small cubs that looked like playful fur balls. The bear family walked along the waterfront until they came to a tree that the mother liked. After sending her cubs up the tree, she entered the bay and swam out a short distance. Then, she submerged her head and body. With only her hind legs sticking out of the water, she reached down and grabbed a large abalone.

Once back on shore, she called her cubs, and they scrambled down the tree and bounded up to her. When she presented them with the abalone, they smelled it and pawed it. They circled it, wondering what to do with it. Having aroused their curiosity, she opened the shell and gave each cub a piece of abalone to chew on.

"Looks like our mystery creature has finally appeared," Jerry said.

"If you'd like to collect a hair sample for analysis, she and her cubs are still on the beach," stated Mike, as he turned off the video and switched to live coverage from the surveillance camera on Cliff Point.

"While we're doing that, let's attach a transmitter to her, so we can track her movements," Jerry said.

"It'll be interesting to see if the hair matches what we found in the thorn bush at the north end of the island," commented Moose.

"I'm betting it will," stated Jerry.

Connie pointed at the cubs. "They sure are cute."

"I'm amazed by how small they are," noted Dianne.

"Those playful little fuzz balls remind me of teddy bears," commented Connie. "They would make cuddly little pets."

"Your cuddly little pets could turn into 1500-pound pets in a few years,"

359

commented Jerry. "Anyway, I think their mother might take exception to your idea."

"If she's anything like the bears back on Earth, she would probably fight to the death in defense of her cubs," stated Connie.

"It'll be good to have a radio on her, so we can keep our distance when we explore the forest," stated Moose.

"If she's using this island as a safe haven on which to raise her cubs, she's probably going to be here for a few years," Dianne said.

"That won't be a problem if we know where she is," Jerry said.

While the pioneers continued observing the bear family, Mike said, "On another subject, the pterodactyls that arrived yesterday are repairing the shelter on Rock Island, so it looks like you have some new neighbors."

"Some new neighbors who are apparently expecting to give birth," added Connie.

Dianne grinned. "It's a good thing they don't know you're a doctor, or they might expect you to make a house call."

"You're letting your imagination run away with you," stated Connie.

"Am I? Let's suppose that they're intelligent enough to recognize us as vastly superior beings based on what they see us do. Think about it! When they see us do things that are incomprehensible to them, isn't it possible that they might think us capable of doing just about anything?"

"Are you suggesting that at some point, they might look upon us as gods who can treat any medical problem they might have, or any other problem for that matter?"

"That's a possibility," stated Dianne. "Ancient humans had a tendency to make gods out of forces they were unable to understand. Suppose these pterodactyls have the intelligence of prehistoric humans, isn't it possible that they could see us as gods? After all, we did descend out of the heavens, and we routinely bring down supplies."

Connie considered Dianne's comments. "If they eventually conclude that we are benevolent, all powerful creatures, they might look for ways to pay us homage or even worship us. I don't think I'd be comfortable with that. What would happen the first time we disappoint them?"

"And what would happen among them if they were to start competing for our favors?" questioned Dianne.

"I don't want to be worshipped either," stated Jerry. "And I certainly don't want them to frequently and aggressively seek favors from us. The ideal situation would be for them to just respect our capabilities, be our friends, and otherwise leave us alone."

"That seems to be exactly what the pterodactyls on Western Island are doing," noted Moose.

"Hopefully, the new arrivals will do the same," stated Jerry as he got up from the table. "I'm going to outfit an RPV, tag that bear, and collect some hair before she disappears into the forest."

"I'll do the hair analysis," volunteered Dianne.

"Thank you," responded Jerry. Turning to Moose, he said, "After I tag her, let's start exploring our forest."

Moose followed Jerry out the door. "What part of the forest do you want to look at today?"

"Let's hike north from the bottom of the rockslide and follow the island's crest to Rocky Point."

"What do you expect to discover? This island has been thoroughly explored with RPVs."

"We may not discover anything of consequence, but I need to gain the familiarity that comes from setting foot on the soil, scrambling over logs, and poking around in the bushes. I can study RPV video all day, but until I set foot on the soil, I won't have the feeling that this land is ours."

TIME: Day Sixteen, Late Afternoon.

Moose and Jerry arrived at Rocky Point after a strenuous hike through dense forest. Even though the straight-line distance was only three-and-one-half miles, the hike took all day. Progress was slow because they used extreme caution and had to work their way through or detour around dense underbrush. Also, they investigated things of interest. Happy to be at their destination, and tired and hungry, Moose and Jerry sat on a large boulder to eat a snack and enjoy the view of Clear Lake.

Shortly before arriving at Rocky Point, Moose and Jerry decided that they had done enough hiking and called their wives to ask them for a ride home. Connie and Dianne were now on the way with the submarine.

"On the way home, why don't we sail into Red Fish Lagoon and catch a couple redfish," suggested Moose. "I'd like to find out if they're edible and taste good."

"Good idea, but I'd like some abalone steak."

"Me too! Why don't we pick up a couple large ones? I could smoke some of it, and we could find out how it tastes."

"Do you have any doubt about how it will taste?" Jerry asked.

"No! It will be good! However, it does take a little experimenting to create the perfect smoking technique. That's a good project for tomorrow, unless you're planning for us to do more forest exploration."

"We do have more exploration to do, and it's such slow going that it will probably take a few days to finish the job."

"It seems like we should be able to safely delay completion of that project. We didn't discover anything of consequence today, and if tomorrow's going to be more of the same; then, I'd rather spend it smoking abalone."

"I can count on you to always be thinking about food."

"When you taste my smoked abalone, you're going to appreciate my talent with smoked delicacies."

"I already appreciate your talent in that area, especially after hiking through the forest all day," Jerry said, enjoying a piece of smoked fish.

"What does hiking have to do with how tasty my smoked fish is?"

"To start with, I've worked up quite an appetite. Besides that, this fish has a flavor that just seems to make it a natural part of outdoor activity, especially hiking and camping."

"I agree," stated Moose, reaching for another piece of smoked fish. "I am surprised by your assertion that we didn't discover anything of consequence today."

"What do you mean? All we saw were birds and small mammals, and they didn't look much different than similar creatures back on Earth."

"But that is significant!" stated Jerry. "We hiked the entire length of the island without encountering any dangerous creatures. Except for the bears, Pioneer Island might be a very safe place to live. But just to make sure, I will explore around the base of the plateau."

"Alone?"

"Why not?"

"There is safety in numbers, and we don't know for sure that this island is safe."

"But just a few minutes ago, you said you didn't want to do any forest exploration tomorrow. You said that we would just see more of what we saw today and that we wouldn't discover anything of consequence."

"Just because I said that doesn't mean that I think it's a wise idea for you to wander around in the forest by yourself," argued Moose. "We are on an alien planet, and we just don't know what dangers might exist."

"It sounds to me like you're having a flashback to our football days when protecting me was one of your responsibilities."

"That's possible." For a few moments, Moose thought about his college football days and all the times he had saved Jerry from being sacked. "I did take that responsibility very seriously, and I did a good job at it too, I might add."

"I can't dispute that, and to put your mind at ease, I have no intention of exploring the forest alone. I think my wife might like to go with me."

"She would be excellent backup in case of trouble. She has proven to be very quick with her rifle, and she can provide medical assistance if the need arises."

"You've convinced me. You can stay home and smoke your abalone. We'll expect a feast tomorrow night when we return."

"No problem."

"Getting back to today's exploration, I'm surprised that we didn't see any predators," commented Jerry. "With the abundance of small mammals and game birds living on this island, it seems like a feline predator about the size of a house cat should be able to thrive here."

"Before we landed, we had Charlie walk through the forest leaving a trail of blood droplets, and he was tracked by a small animal that looked like a cross between a large weasel and a small mink. So we know there are small predators here. Perhaps, we didn't see any because they did not want to be seen."

"That might be the case," agreed Jerry. "Out of necessity, hunters are masters of stealth, and they could've easily hidden from us. But even though we didn't see any, they must be a fairly numerous."

"Why do you think that?" Moose asked.

"Because we saw numerous species of small mammals, and if they're anything like similar species on Earth, they're capable of rapid reproduction. To keep their populations in check, hunters must also be fairly numerous."

"As far as keeping the mammal population in check, the land hunters are undoubtedly getting help from predatory birds. We saw several of them today, and there's an owl nest right on Stellar Plateau."

"And those owls are large enough to prey on the kind of small predator that tracked Charlie," commented Jerry.

"We need a name for the hunter that tracked Charlie. Since it looked like a cross between a weasel and a mink, let's call it a weamink."

"I suppose that name is as good as any."

While gazing at the panoramic scenery, a sparkling glitter caught Jerry's attention. Pointing to the west, he said, "Some of those rocks sparkle like gem stones."

Moose turned toward Alpha Centauri A to view the glittering rocks. After a few moments, he said, "There's a reflection over there that's especially bright, almost what you'd expect from a small mirror."

"That is brilliant. Let's take a look at it. Who knows, we may be living on a treasure island loaded with gem stones."

"Who would we sell them to? There's no market here, and we can't ship them back to Earth."

"It would be frustrating to discover a vast supply of gems and not have a market for them," stated Jerry.

Moose and Jerry walked over to the source of the reflection, and right there in front of their feet, they saw a small piece of shiny metal wedged between two rocks. Astounded by the implication of what they were looking at, Moose and Jerry were speechless for a few moments, while their minds raced through possible explanations for the origin of the metal.

"Is this discovery consequential enough to make your day of exploration worthwhile?" Jerry asked Moose.

"Consequential? I'm shocked by the implication of what we're looking at! We might not be alone!"

"That's a definite possibility," agreed Jerry.

"It sure is! Where did that metal come from? How did it get here?"

"There is a remote possibility that it broke loose from one of the vehicles we landed here."

"I doubt that," argued Moose. "Our equipment is very well built."

"Then, it either came from another planet, or there are intelligent creatures living somewhere on this planet with the technology to work with metals. But it seems like our reconnaissance would've spotted some indication of their presence."

"If it came from another planet, the most likely candidate is B-2."

"If it came from there, I wonder which side in the Great War sent a spacecraft here, how long ago, and was it manned or unmanned?"

"If the spacecraft was manned, it may've been heading for one of the islands in this lake for the same reasons that brought us here."

"This is a choice area, so that is possible," agreed Jerry.

"I wonder if there are any survivors."

"Why wouldn't there be survivors?" Jerry asked.

"A piece of metal that small indicates that the spacecraft might've disintegrated. Maybe no one survived."

"That's possible if the metal came from a spacecraft."

"What else could it have come from?" Moose asked.

"What if intelligent beings safely landed here, explored for a few weeks, and then left. Isn't it possible that this piece of metal could be the remains of a food container or beverage can?" Jerry asked.

"That's possible, but what if they landed and were unable to leave. There could be intelligent beings living on one of the islands in this lake, or on one of the islands in the big lake up the river to the north. If they're somewhere in this area, they've certainly seen our shuttle flights, and consequently, they know that we're here. In fact, they would know exactly where we are! But we have no clue where they are."

"It seems that our lives are a bit more complicated now than they were a few minutes ago," Jerry said, calmly.

"That's definitely the understatement of the century!"

Jerry reached down and picked up the piece of metal. Holding it so that he and Moose could see it closely, he said, "The first thing we need to do is analyze this alloy to see what elements it contains. That information, along with its physical properties, should give us a pretty good idea what it may've been used for."

"We also need to search for more pieces of metal and items that may've been brought here by intelligent beings," stated Moose.

"Unfortunately, they're going to be difficult to find. If this is part of a spacecraft that broke up, and if this happened several years ago, any pieces that came down in the forest would've been buried by falling leaves long ago. Our best bet might be to search the lake bottom with the submarine."

"Pieces on the lake bottom could also be buried by sediment."

"While that's true, it wouldn't happen as quickly as in the forest. Falling leaves from just one season could easily bury a small piece of metal, and searching with metal detectors would be very time consuming."

"Much of Stellar Plateau is open. I could search it tomorrow while I'm tending my smokehouse. Also, the rockslide would be easy to search."

"After what we just discovered, you're still planning to smoke abalone tomorrow?"

"Of course, I don't think we should stop living our lives just because we might not be alone. We should live the way we want to, while being alert to the possibility of attack by aliens. Your question implies that you feel otherwise."

"No, I don't. I agree with you, but we do need to find out as quickly as possible where this piece of metal came from. If there are aliens living here, we need to find them and determine if they pose any danger to us."

"If there are advanced beings living on this planet, there numbers must be small," suggested Moose. "Our orbital reconnaissance would've easily found a large society."

"That sounds reasonable, but since we don't know what kind of beings we're looking for, I don't think we should make that assumption. We need to use the Challenger's instruments to search this planet for anything that cannot be explained as a natural occurrence."

Jerry reached for his communicator and entered Mike's number. After discussing the situation with him, Jerry asked, "How much progress have Michelle and Shannon made at understanding each other's language?"

"They're fluent enough to have regular gossip sessions."

"I heard that remark!" exclaimed Michelle. "And I would like to point out that all of our conversations have been very informative."

"Does that answer your question?" Mike asked.

Jerry chuckled a bit. "I would say they're fluent."

"We're fluent enough, so I can find out if Rex and Shannon know if any spacecraft were ever sent here," stated Michelle.

"I would also like to know which side sent them, how long ago, and were they manned or unmanned?"

"I will send the information request right away, but because of the distance involved, it will be a few hours before I receive a response."

"That time delay must make conversation a bit cumbersome."

"It does, but we've adjusted to it quite well."

"I concluded that from Mike's comment."

"Just because Shannon is interested in social customs back on Earth, Mike likes to tease us that we spend a lot of time gossiping; when in reality, we're learning about each other's culture."

"Maybe Mike needs more projects to occupy his mind."

"Life has been getting a bit routine," admitted Mike. "But now, I can help you solve the mystery of that piece of metal."

"I would like you to start by doing a meticulous reconnaissance of all the islands within 200 miles of Pioneer Island. Search for any evidence that technologically advanced beings might be living here."

"How about the countryside around Clear Lake?"

"Do the islands first. From what I've seen of the countryside, aliens would have a difficult time surviving there. Even if they came here well armed, they would've eventually run out of ammunition, and they would've found a way to move to an island before that happened."

"We'll start the search right away."

"I am going to analyze this alloy. When I find out what it is, we can compare it to the alloys used in the spacecraft we captured."

"That might tell us if that piece of metal came from B-2," Mike said.

Moose tapped Jerry on the shoulder and pointed at the lake. "There's a submarine surfacing over there, and it looks like ours."

"Until a few minutes ago, I would've made that assumption without a second glance. But our lives are now a bit more complicated."

TIME: Day Seventeen, Early Morning.

Over breakfast, the pioneers discussed the previous day's discovery. Mike and Michelle joined the discussion via the communications system.

Holding it up for all to see, Jerry said, "I am convinced that this piece of metal originated on B-2. It is identical to the alloy used in some parts of the derelict satellite we captured. The question is: which side in the Great War sent a spacecraft here?"

"We sent Rex pictures of the inscriptions on some of the parts in that satellite," responded Michelle. "He said that they are in the language of their enemies in the Great War."

"Since we destroyed their biological warfare complexes, I think we should assume that they're also our enemies," added Mike.

"I'm glad they're too far away to bother us," stated Moose.

"Are you sure about that?" Jerry asked. "Keep in mind that they may've already demonstrated their ability to come here."

"But the Great War has left their country in a shambles, and I can't imagine that they could come here now," argued Moose.

"Earth's history is filled with examples of very determined nations recovering from the devastation of war in just a few years," stated Jerry.

"That's true," agreed Moose, "but would this nation's recovery effort be directed toward rebuilding their society or toward seeking revenge against us?"

"That would depend on the ambitions of the political system that's in power," responded Jerry.

"According to Shannon, that country was run by a brutal dictator during the Great War," stated Michelle. "As the war dragged on and turned into a stalemate, she thinks the military killed him and took over."

"If they're in charge, they may be more interested in revenge against us than in rebuilding their country," stated Jerry, as he turned to Connie and asked, "Would you care to speculate on how their minds work?"

"Based on what we've seen, it's difficult to find adequate words to

366

describe their psyche. Such terms as cruel, sadistic, and malicious don't begin to describe their lust for inflicting death and destruction. After all, they were conducting a campaign of genocide against half of their planet until we shut them down."

"During one of our early orbits over their territory, I sensed intense hatred and a foreboding feeling of evil," Dianne added. "I felt in grave danger. I sensed that they would've killed me if they could have."

"Are you suggesting that they'll use any manufacturing capability they have left to make armed spacecraft to attack us; rather than, make products to improve the lives of their people?" Mike asked.

"They are extremely evil," Dianne replied. "They were attempting to kill all warm-blooded life on half of their planet; rather than, let the war be over and devote their energy to rebuilding their country. We stopped them, and I think we should assume that they'll seek revenge. Their attacks on us might even be carried out by suicidal fanatics."

"But can they get here?" questioned Moose.

"We don't know," replied Jerry," but apparently, they've come here before."

"According to Rex, both sides moved critical manufacturing facilities underground before the Great War," Michelle said. "Much of this was attacked with nuclear weapons, but some facilities did survive."

"If they have a fanatical determination to get revenge, they'll find a way to attack us," stated Jerry.

Moose reluctantly nodded in agreement; then, he said, "There's little doubt that they know where we are. All they had to do was track us when we left and monitor our daily communication with Rex and Shannon."

"I think we're in agreement that they could get a spacecraft here and that they may be possessed with a fanatical determination to get revenge," Mike said. "However, even fanatics respect overwhelming military power. They've seen firsthand what we can do with our antimatter particle-beam gun. I'm not sure that they would want to have another encounter with its destructive firepower. They may decide to just rebuild their military and not do anything to risk bringing us back to attack them again."

"Or they might try to figure out a way to destroy the Challenger," suggested Jerry, "and if that's successful, then attack us."

"If they have the intelligence to get here, they should also realize that in the vacuum of space, our antimatter particle-beam gun could destroy them at a range of several million miles," argued Mike. "They should realize that an attempt to attack us would be an exercise in futility."

"We can only destroy them if we're able to detect them," countered Jerry. "What if stealth technology is incorporated into the design and construction of their spacecraft?"

"We do have recon satellites orbiting B-2," stated Mike. "So we will get adequate warning of an impending attack. Since their rockets still rely on chemical propulsion, a vehicle able to reach us with a meaningful payload would be large and easy to detect during launch. Its speed would be low enough, so that it would take a few years to get here, giving us plenty of time to find it and destroy it."

"You sound very confident," commented Jerry.

"With their level of technology, I don't think they can build a spacecraft that I can't find when I have a few years to work the problem."

"We haven't yet presented you with a problem you weren't able to solve," stated Jerry.

Mike smiled in satisfaction. "Thanks for the compliment."

After a bit of silence, Jerry said, "Our mission plan calls for stripping the Challenger of everything useful and bringing it down here, but now that we have a potential external threat, that plan is no longer viable. Specifically, we must keep our shuttles and the Challenger functional for as far into the future as we possibly can."

"It's good that we made our long journey at .73c rather than .77c," commented Mike. "Because of that key decision, we still have an ample supply of antimatter. We can even return to B-2 and cripple the war making ability of an enemy, if we have to."

"Let's hope it doesn't come to that," stated Jerry. "But in case it does, let's be prepared."

"I'll get some people working on the development of operational procedures and maintenance plans to keep our shuttles and the Challenger operational far beyond their design life spans," stated Mike.

"Good!" replied Jerry. "Now, let's get back to the more immediate problem: are there humanoids from B-2 living here on Alcent?"

"Rex doesn't know for sure," Michelle said. "But he thinks their opponents in the Great War sent a manned spacecraft to Alcent about 30 years ago, shortly before the war started. He does not know what the mission's objectives were, but he said that the brutal dictator in charge at that time had a fanatical desire to expand his empire. He used a form of religion to control his subjects. He even had religious police who would persecute and sometimes kill individuals who refused to bow to his religious dictates. He maintained that he was God's representative and that he had divine powers. Rex speculates that the evil dictator may've been trying to expand his empire to other planets to satisfy his ego and bolster his claim to divine powers."

"If Rex's speculation is correct, we might have some evil fanatics living here on Alcent," suggested Jerry.

"If they arrived 25 to 30 years ago, there may not be any of them alive anymore," Connie said. "I was almost killed less than a week after our arrival."

"And on that day, I could easily have been killed," added Moose.

"While it's possible that none of them are alive anymore, we must assume that they came here prepared to survive and multiply," stated Jerry.

"And that means they were well armed and the crew included both males and females."

"But Rex does not know for sure that a manned mission was sent here," argued Moose. "All we have to go on is a small piece of metal, which could just as easily have come from an unmanned spacecraft that broke apart in the right place for a piece to fall on Pioneer Island."

"That's true enough," agreed Jerry. "But our security requires that we assume that a manned mission came here and that there are survivors. Even though they might be living thousands of miles from here, we need to be alert to the possibility that they could be living nearby."

"Wherever they are, they may be preoccupied with surviving and building their own society," Connie suggested. "Accomplishing those objectives may have caused them to drop their fanatical religion and extremist political system. They may not be a threat to us."

"That's a possibility," acknowledged Jerry. "But I will need to see proof of that before I can accept it."

"Me too!" exclaimed Dianne.

"If there are intelligent humanoids living on Alcent, it shouldn't be all that difficult to find indications of their presence," commented Mike.

"Let's start with what we know," stated Jerry, "namely that their best chance to survive and prosper would be to live on an isolated island like we are. Also, we've explored Pioneer Island thoroughly enough to know that they aren't living here. All of our beaches are constantly being scanned by surveillance cameras, so they cannot come here without us knowing about it. But for our own peace of mind, we need to take a look at the other islands in this lake. The best way to do that is with RPVs."

"There are people up here who would like to fly those RPVs and help you with the search," stated Mike. "But there is one small problem: the RPVs don't have the endurance to do an extensive search after flying to the islands and still have enough juice to return."

"We have a choice," Jerry said. "We'll either have to park them in the sunshine to recharge their batteries for the return flight, or we can land them on the deck of the submarine and use it to ferry them to the islands."

"Sounds like our multipurpose boat is about to become an aircraft carrier," commented Moose.

Being a student of naval history, Jerry formed some mental images of some of the giant flattops that the U.S. Navy had operated in the past. "It requires a real stretch of the imagination to call our boat an aircraft carrier," he said to Moose.

"But if we discover hostile aliens living in our vicinity, we could spy on them as well as attack them with RPVs launched from our boat, so in effect, it could function much like an aircraft carrier."

Jerry nodded. "In a limited sense, that's true. But today, it's going to be used to complement reconnaissance done by the Challenger. If intelligent

369

humanoids came here 25 to 30 years ago, we will either find them or evidence that they've been here."

"Sounds like a perfect job for a little aircraft carrier loaded with reconnaissance aircraft," stated Moose.

Convinced that Moose was determined to win the semantics argument, Jerry nodded in agreement. Then, he gave his attention to Connie, who asked, "Which island are we going to search first?"

"We'll start with the next island to the north. It's the second biggest in this lake and is just as isolated from the countryside as Pioneer Island."

"I'd like to go with you," stated Connie.

"I'd enjoy having you with me," replied Jerry.

"I'll stay here and search the rockslide and this plateau for spacecraft parts," Moose said. "Also, I can tend my smokehouse while I search."

"I'll stay here and help Moose," Dianne said.

Jerry turned to Moose. "Before you fire up your smokehouse, I need you to help me check out the RPVs and get them onto our boat."

Moose nodded in acknowledgment of Jerry's request. Then, Jerry turned to Connie. "I should be ready to leave in about an hour."

"I'll pack our supplies."

"Pack enough for a long day, because we might look at all four of the northern islands."

"Okay."

"Don't eat too much while you're gone," Moose said. "I will have some delicious smoked abalone fillets waiting for you when you return."

Connie did her best to show Moose a naughty grin. "Don't worry, we'll be hungry. After all, we do have all day to work up an appetite."

Moose grinned and said to Jerry, "Your day might be a bit more involved than just looking for aliens."

"I am capable of dealing with any opportunities that come up," responded Jerry.

"So am I," stated Connie.

"You people are sure having a tough life down there," commented Mike. "Every day just seems to be filled with fun and excitement, and you have an abundance of delicious real food to enjoy."

"Making sure it's safe here for the rest of you has put quite a strain on us," Jerry said. "But we're shouldering the burden as best we can."

"Yeah, and it looks like a real struggle too," Mike chuckled. "I sure hope that creating an abalone delicacy doesn't burden Moose with an overwhelming amount of stress."

Determined not to have his project belittled even in a joking way, Moose asserted, "Discovering and developing local food sources is absolutely essential to our future health and prosperity."

Mike laughed. "Yeah, that's true. I just hope meeting that important responsibility isn't so stressful that you end up with high blood pressure."

"You don't need to worry, because I have so much talent in this field of human endeavor that it's actually a recreational activity for me."

"I think those last four words do a pretty good job of describing your life down there to date," bantered Mike.

"There might be some truth to that, but remember our lives have gotten a bit more complicated recently."

TIME: Day Seventeen, Late Morning

Jerry and Connie approached the first island to the north of Pioneer Island. While scanning the south end of the island with binoculars, Connie said, "It sure doesn't look inhabited."

"I doubt that it is," Jerry said. "If it were, it seems like our orbital recon would've spotted boats of some sort in the water around the island."

"That should apply to all the islands. I can't imagine people living on an island in a big lake and not having boats for fishing and transportation."

"I can't either, but the only way we can be certain that these islands are deserted is to investigate them."

"I hope we don't find any aliens here, because if we do, and they're hostile, we'll have to kill them before they kill us. The idea of genocide is repugnant to me."

"Killing them wouldn't be our only option," stated Jerry. "We could leave Pioneer Island and live somewhere else."

"But I'm starting to think of Pioneer Island as home, and I really don't want to leave. During our long voyage from Earth, I had assumed that this planet would be kind of like the way Earth was during its dinosaur age. It never occurred to me that we might also find humans here."

"You may be jumping to conclusions too quickly. All we've found is one small piece of metal."

"That's true, but that small piece of metal has enormous implications. The need to be constantly on guard for potentially hostile aliens adds a dangerous complication to our lives, kind of like a lurking storm cloud casting a shadow over what could otherwise be a simple, peaceful life."

"But if they're here and living thousands of miles away from us, we'll still have the kind of life that you want. This is a large planet, and the probability that they came to the same place we came to is very small."

"That's true," agreed Connie.

"And it's possible that the piece of metal came from an unmanned probe and that there never was a manned mission. Even if there was, there might not be any survivors."

"I would be content with any of those possibilities."

"We'll soon know if the islands in this lake are uninhabited," stated Jerry, as he picked up his communicator and called Mike. "Your eager pilots can start launching their RPVs."

Mike acknowledged, and almost immediately, the first RPV took off and headed for the island. As the small makeshift aircraft carrier slowly cruised northward along the island's east coast, the remaining RPVs took off at regular intervals until all eight were airborne. When each RPV completed the search of its area of responsibility, it returned to the boat for a recharge. When the eighth RPV was recovered, the carrier headed northwest to the second island in the chain.

"We've searched the eastern half of the island, and there's no indication that humanoids have ever lived there," Mike reported.

"The search went so smoothly, that I think we might be able to look at the rest of the northern islands today," responded Jerry. "That will leave the two southern islands for tomorrow."

Stifling a chuckle, Mike said, "But if we do all of the northern islands today, you might get home too late for Moose's smoked abalone dinner."

"If it's as good as his smoked fish, we'll be able to feast on it no matter what time we get home," retorted Connie.

"I wouldn't mind showing up for that feast," Mike offered.

"Hang on for two more weeks, and I think you'll be free to come down," responded Jerry.

"I hope so. I am definitely ready to bask in the outdoor living that you've been enjoying."

Twenty minutes later, the little aircraft carrier arrived at the second island. RPVs were launched at regular intervals while sailing northward along the island's eastern shore. After 45 minutes, the carrier reached the north end of the island. Satisfied that there weren't any aliens living on the eastern half of the island, Jerry decided to go to the third island.

Connie looked at her watch. "It's 12:30 and I'm hungry. Let's eat lunch."

"Good idea, I'm hungry too."

"We couldn't ask for a more pristine setting in which to enjoy our lunch," commented Connie.

Jerry smelled the fresh air and gazed across the pollution-free water to the distant, snowcapped mountains. He enjoyed the quiet peacefulness that surrounded him. "One of the things that adds a special air to this setting is that we're alone; at least, I think we are."

"I like being alone. For me, the presence of aliens would detract from the pristine nature of this area, spoiling it to some degree."

"In what way?" questioned Jerry.

"It's a matter of attitude. We came here with the idea of living in harmony with our environment, doing what we can to preserve its pristine nature. The aliens we're looking for came from a society so barbaric that it was conducting genocide against half a planet until we stopped them."

"But that was in the context of a 30-year war. The ones that came here might not be barbarians. If they're still alive, they may've developed a benign life style, killing only what they need for food or in self-defense."

372

"That's possible, but based on what we saw on B-2, I think they're more likely to be plunderers. Anyway, after traveling across four light-years of interstellar space, I'd hoped we'd have a pristine planet all to ourselves, and that we could build a society that would take good care of the environment. Aliens from B-2 might not respect the environment."

"That's a legitimate concern; especially, if they're living close enough to have an effect on us."

"Their possible presence is already affecting us. Instead of enjoying the romantic aspects of this beautiful setting, we're discussing aliens."

"That's a good point," conceded Jerry.

Jerry and Connie continued their discussion and arrived at the third island while finishing their lunch. After searching its eastern half and finding nothing of concern, they went to the fourth island and searched it. Much to Connie's liking, Mike reported, "We've completed the search of this island, and there's no evidence that aliens have ever lived on it."

"That's great news," Connie said. "And it's only 3:30. If our return trip takes the same time as it took to get here, we'll be home by 10:00."

"I think we can be home by 9:00," stated Jerry. "We should be able to make pretty good speed. Our batteries are fully charged, and we have a favorable wind, so let's deploy our sails. I'd like to be back well before second sunset, so we don't have to hike through the forest in the dark."

"Are you worried about safety in the forest?" Mike asked. "Or is it possible that you're able to smell smoked abalone, even though you're 20 miles from home?"

"My nose isn't quite that good, but I did talk to Moose a few minutes ago, and he said the smoked abalone is delicious."

"With a dinner like that waiting for me, I could get enough speed out of that boat to get home before 8:30," declared Mike.

"It isn't just a matter of speed," responded Jerry. "We still have a lot more recon to do, and we need to be reasonably thorough."

"Our RPV pilots are getting quite efficient, and I believe we'll finish the recon sooner than you think."

"Okay, show me how good they are. Then, when we've finished that project, I'll push this boat to the limit and find out how much speed I can get out of it."

"It's about six miles from the first island to East Bay, so you'll have a pretty good run on which to play with the speed."

"Keep in mind that this boat wasn't designed to win any races. It's able to do a lot of different things, but going fast isn't one of them."

"True enough, but it's not an old barge either."

"I have enough charge on the batteries to run the motors at full power. The only question is whether there'll be enough wind to use the sails."

Mike displayed the latest weather information on his video screen and studied it. "I predict you'll have westerly winds of 12 to 20 mph."

"The high end of that range would sure make playing around with the sails worthwhile. With that much wind power added to the battery power, I should be able to get at least 20 mph out of this boat."

"So it will take you less than 20 minutes to get home after we've finished the recon."

"That's true if the wind's in the high end of your predicted range."

"Discussing sailing makes me wish I could be there. I've been in this starship for so many years that I'm ready for exposure to the elements."

"Be patient for two more weeks. If all goes well, you'll be free to come down."

"I think I'll make the time go faster by occupying my leisure time with a challenging project."

"What are you thinking about doing?"

"I would enjoy designing and building a water glider."

"That kind of boat could take many different shapes. Do you have a basic concept in mind?"

"A modified two-person kayak equipped with a large sail, outriggers, and hydrofoils might be a good starting point. Speed will be my main objective. I want to be able to easily ride the hydrofoils even when the wind isn't real strong, so minimizing weight will be a key consideration."

"To easily achieve stability and control, you might consider adding some motion sensing vanes with a direct link to control vanes. That would leave the pilot free to play with the sail to achieve maximum speed without having to worry about flipping the boat over."

"That's a good idea, but I might go high-tech and use a modified inertial guidance system to assist with the stability and control, or I might use a combination of the two approaches. The goal will be to make this water glider as safe and as easy to operate as possible, while making it as fast as possible. On a windy day, I want it to be fast enough to make your adrenaline flow."

"Streaking around on this lake with that kind of toy would get me high. Of course, when you bring it down, it will have to be tested for safety, and you'll probably need a test pilot for that."

"That job just might be reserved for the project's chief engineer. However, the boat will seat two people, and the chief engineer might need an assistant in case unforeseen problems come up."

"That's good sound reasoning. Sign me up for the copilot position."

"Consider it done."

"How long do you think it will take to complete the project?"

"This toy will be so much fun to play with that I have a feeling that most off duty personnel are going to volunteer to work on it. I see no reason why we can't have it ready to bring down with us in two weeks."

"That sounds a bit ambitious, but proper motivation will always get a job done quickly."

TIME: Day Seventeen, 8:20 P.M.

Jerry and Connie arrived in East Bay, tired but happy. They were tired from a long day of sailing and searching for aliens, but they were happy that they found no evidence to indicate their presence.

While Jerry and Connie put their weapons and gear into the inflated boat for the short trip to shore, Mike's RPV pilots launched their aircraft and flew them into the forest to search for danger.

When the last RPV disappeared into the forest, Connie said, "I've been looking at this lake all day and haven't had an opportunity to go swimming, and I think a good swim would be refreshing."

Jerry checked the position of Alpha Centauri B. "We're certainly back early enough to squeeze in a quick dip before it gets dark."

While Connie was undressing, she stole a quick glance at Jerry to see if he was watching her. Noting with satisfaction that he was, she completed the removal of her clothing and dove into the cool water followed immediately by Jerry.

They swam under and around their multipurpose boat enjoying the pleasant evening and the peaceful solitude of East Bay. As the minutes ticked away, their swimming evolved into a playful game with the rules being invented as the game progressed. Eventually, the game came to a satisfying conclusion that left both contestants feeling like winners. They climbed out of the water onto the deck, toweled off, and dressed.

"You were right, that was refreshing," Jerry said with a warm smile.

Looking around at the scene lit by the soft orange glow from Alpha Centauri B, now low on the western horizon, Connie said, "That orange light seems to have a warm romantic tone to it."

Jerry gazed across the water of East Bay to Eastern Island and noted the warming effect of the soft orange hue on its pristine beauty. He turned his gaze in the opposite direction and noted that much of East Bay's shoreline was deeply shadowed. "I think we should head for home before it's completely dark in the forest."

Jerry and Connie rowed ashore. Then, they followed Charlie through the forest without incident. A short time later, they arrived in the capsule to the aroma of freshly baked bread and smoked abalone. "Dinner smells really good," stated Jerry.

"After being out all day, it's a real pleasure to find a good dinner waiting for us," added Connie.

Pleased by their comments, Dianne said, "I'm glad both of you are hungry. We've already eaten, so we'll play the roles of cook and waitress. You can pretend you're dining out at your favorite restaurant."

"We don't have any money," declared Connie.

"Then, I guess you'll have to wash dishes," suggested Dianne.

"That's certainly a bargain price for a good dinner," replied Connie.

"Now that the negotiations are out of the way, it's time for you to sit down, relax, and enjoy some exquisite dining pleasure," stated Moose.

"That's an invitation I can't refuse," responded Jerry.

Jerry and Connie sat down, and Dianne placed a salad in front of each of them. "This salad is a first," she said. "It's made entirely from native greens, tubers, and herbs."

"Is it safe to eat?" Jerry asked Dianne.

"I checked out each ingredient in the lab, and I've also eaten them."

"You look healthy to me. How long ago did you eat them?"

"I ate all of them yesterday, and I haven't suffered any ill-effects."

Noting that the salad looked good, Jerry tasted it. "It's delicious!" he exclaimed. "Where did you find all the ingredients?"

"The clumps of vines we see growing in some places here on the plateau are fed by tuberous roots. The tubers not only have a delicious mild flavor, but they're also highly nutritious. The brownish-orange ingredient in your salad is from shredding some of the tubers. They also taste good cooked, so I diced and steamed some of them."

"What about these crisp dark green leaves?"

"They're from an aquatic plant that grows about six feet tall in shallow water. The leaves are from the part of the plant that is above the water. The greens in your salad are from plants growing in shallow water near the mouth of South Bay."

"I love the flavor of the dressing," commented Connie.

"That flavor comes from two plants that I've classified as herbs. Each has a flavor that seems to complement the other. The dressing was easy to make. I just put some stems and leaves in a blender with some water and a little starch. Next, I cooked it for a few minutes, and then, I chilled it."

"For being that simple to make, it sure tastes great," stated Connie.

"Thank you," replied Dianne.

When Connie and Jerry finished their salads, Dianne served them smoked abalone, smoked fish, a special imitation rice dish, the diced root vegetable dish, and freshly baked bread. After he had tasted everything, Jerry exclaimed, "This is excellent! If I'm going to get this kind of dinner when I go out searching for aliens, I'll have to do that more often."

"It's a great way to celebrate that you didn't find any," noted Dianne.

"It might be too early to celebrate," commented Jerry. "We still have lots of searching to do."

"That's true, but each day we don't find any aliens is worth celebrating," stated Dianne.

THIRTEEN

Condition Critical
A Grave Medical Challenge

TIME: Day Eighteen, Mid-Morning.

The pioneers searched the small island two miles south of Pioneer Island and found no evidence that it had ever been visited by aliens. So they headed south toward the southernmost island in Clear Lake.

Twenty minutes later, they neared the island. "It sure looks peaceful," commented Connie.

"And mysterious," added Dianne.

"That's what you said about the last one."

"It did look mysterious. That island and this one are covered with deep dark forests. Why shouldn't they look mysterious to me?"

"That's a good point, but this is the sixth island that I've looked at since yesterday morning, and we haven't found anything mysterious on any of them. And I'm happy that we haven't found any aliens."

"I'm happy about that too," replied Dianne.

"As quiet as this island looks, I doubt that there are any here either."

"I don't know about that. This island is too mysterious. It's hiding something; I feel it."

With her binoculars, Connie searched the island for anything unnatural that might support Dianne's uneasiness. "I sure don't see anything unusual."

Dianne reached for the binoculars. "Let me take a look."

Handing them to Dianne, Connie said, "Maybe you'll spot something I missed."

Dianne closely scrutinized the island while they cruised slowly southward. She watched one of the RPVs repeatedly sail into and out of the forest as its pilot searched the island's waterfront from the safety of the Challenger. After a few minutes, Dianne handed the binoculars back to Connie. "I didn't see anything that looked suspicious, but there's something mysterious about this island. I can just feel it."

"Perhaps that's because you're a biologist, and you have a strong desire to study the plants and creatures that live there. Once you become familiar with them, the island won't seem so mysterious."

"I've been doing research on this planet's living organisms since our arrival, but I haven't felt a sense of mysteriousness about it."

"From the sound of your voice, I sense that you really are worried about this, and that's not like you. Do you think we're in danger from something on this island?"

"I don't know, but I do feel some anxiety."

"Are your feelings like what you felt when we were orbiting B-2?"

"The sensation I have now isn't as strong, but I believe it's real. I feel like something or someone is trying to probe my thoughts, but isn't quite able to make contact."

"Does it feel like a hostile probe or a friendly probe?"

"I can't tell; it's just too feeble."

"The last time your thoughts were probed, we ended up getting involved in the final phase of a 30-year war."

"But the mental probe from the beings we ended up attacking was very intense and filled with hatred. Even though this probe isn't like that, it could still be from the aliens that we're looking for; and even though this island looks deserted, they could be living here."

"I think we should tell our husbands what you're sensing."

"Moose is flying one of the RPVs, and I don't think we should distract him, or he might crash it into a tree."

"That would embarrass him, and we don't want to do that," Connie said with a bit of laughter. "I think Jerry's talking to Mike about the exploration of this island, so let's talk to them."

Dianne and Connie approached Jerry, but before they could say anything, they heard Mike exclaim, "We've just found something that you need to see!"

"Show me!" Jerry said, putting on a video headset.

When the image appeared, Jerry's attention immediately focused on an old rotted stump that was almost completely concealed by vines, but the vines did not conceal the shape of the stump's top. Surprised by its appearance, Jerry stared at it for a few moments before he said, "A stump with a flat top is a curious thing to find on a planet where dinosaurs are the dominant species."

"Are you saying that you haven't seen any dinosaurs running around with saws?" Mike asked in a joking way.

"Some of the dinosaurs we've seen don't need chainsaws to knock trees down," replied Jerry. "The obvious implication here is that this tree was cut down by the aliens we're looking for, but let's not rule out other possibilities, however remote they may be."

"It appears that there's a factual basis for what you've been sensing," Connie said to Dianne.

Having overheard the remark, Jerry asked, "Would you mind explaining that comment to me?"

While Dianne and Connie reported to Jerry, the search continued, and more old stumps with flat tops were found, all in the same small area. "What's puzzling about this is that we aren't finding an old log cabin," noted Mike. "With so many trees cut down in such a small area, it seems like there should be a log structure of some sort within the area."

"The logs could've been used for some other purpose, such as building a boat or raft," commented Jerry.

"Are you suggesting that the aliens were here, built a boat, and left?" Connie asked.

"That's a possibility."

"But why would they leave a location that has so many pluses and so few minuses?"

"What's attractive to us might not have been to them, but we don't know they left; it's only a possibility."

"Maybe they did build a log cabin, and it was destroyed by fire," suggested Moose. "As prolific as the vegetation is here, the site would've been quickly overgrown."

"But why wouldn't they have built a new one?" Dianne asked.

"One of our big concerns is whether or not our immune systems can handle the microbes on this planet," responded Moose. "Perhaps theirs didn't, and they were killed by disease. Then, maybe their cabin was struck by lightning and set on fire. Within a few years, the site would've been overgrown, making it look to us like they moved on."

"That scenario is certainly possible," acknowledged Jerry. "But how likely is it that a lightning strike would've occurred at precisely the right place to destroy the evidence that aliens had once lived here?"

"I don't know," replied Moose, "but it is possible."

"I think we need to go ashore and poke around in the bushes and see what we can find," stated Jerry.

"Before you do that, there is another possibility you should consider," Mike suggested, "and that is that they may've tunneled into the hillside and used the logs for internal support. They might still be living on the island and waiting to ambush you, but I must admit that it does look deserted."

"I'm counting on you and your RPV pilots to make sure that it is deserted before we go ashore."

"We'll do an exhaustive search."

"While you're doing that, we'll circle the island and inspect the waterfront."

"I have a theory for you to consider," Connie said. "Let's assume that their immune systems weren't able to handle the microorganisms here and that they were killed by them. If they went to bed when they got sick, they could've died in their homes. If they lived in underground homes and those homes had small entrances, they could now be overgrown with brush and be difficult to find. To us, the island would look like it had been deserted by the aliens; when in fact, they lived here and died here."

"While that's possible," acknowledged Jerry, "it seems to me that it would take quite some time to build an underground home. If they were killed by microbes, wouldn't they have died before completing such a home, and wouldn't we see some unused logs lying around?"

"Not necessarily, while some diseases kill quickly, others take a long time to develop."

During the next two hours, the interstellar pioneers slowly circled the island and searched its waterfront while the RPV pilots searched its interior. Mike summed up the results by saying, "It looks like no one has lived on this island for a long time. So the question remains: what happened to the trees that were cut down?"

"I am convinced that they were used to build a raft or boat of some sort," responded Jerry.

"Why do you think that rather than the scenario that Connie proposed?" Mike asked.

"Something that I noticed about the stumps, all the big ones are close to the water, and you can tell from the saw-cuts that these trees were dropped into the water. The logs from these trees would've been too heavy for use in building a log cabin or to shore up an underground home, but they could've been used to make a raft. I think the logs from the smaller trees were used as cross members to hold the big ones together, to build a shelter on the raft, and perhaps to make masts for sails."

"But where did they go?" Connie asked.

"I don't know, but we're going to try to find out," replied Jerry, as he noticed that Dianne was staring at the island so intently that she seemed to be in a trance. All turned their attention to her, but no one did anything to disturb her.

After a minute had gone by, Dianne came out of her state of intense concentration. "I just experienced what I think was another attempt to establish mental contact with me."

"Are you sure?" Connie asked. "We've taken a pretty good look at this island, and it does look deserted."

"I agree that it looks deserted, but I have a strong feeling that it isn't, at least not completely."

"Are you suggesting that all the aliens are gone except for one or two?" questioned Jerry.

"I have a feeling that there's only one on the island."

"Is there a basis for that feeling?" Jerry asked.

"During the attempted contact I just experienced, I felt like there was an aura of intense loneliness hovering around my mind."

"Was that aura of loneliness continuous?" Connie asked. "Or was it interrupted by moments of excitement or hope?"

Dianne closed her eyes and tuned out her surroundings while she focused her mind on the recent experience. After a few moments she said,

"I think there were some fleeting moments of hope and excitement."

"An intelligent humanoid living in isolation for a long period of time could exhibit that kind of aura," commented Connie. "Suppose this individual has been alone for many years, he might be so hungry for companionship that he would even attempt to contact an alien species that could turn out to be hostile to him. Particularly, if he is old or ill and doesn't think he has much time left anyway."

Dianne shuddered. "I would become horribly lonely if I had to live alone on one of these islands for the rest of my life."

"If there is an alien living alone on this island, is he alone because the others died, or is he alone because he was deserted by his colleagues?" Connie asked.

"The evidence we have indicates that a large raft was built, and that they left," replied Jerry.

"But why would his colleagues have left without him?" questioned Connie. "It doesn't seem likely there would've been enough of them, so they could afford to discard one of their members."

"It sounds like you're arguing in favor of the premise that they never left this area," Jerry said.

"This is a huge lake," stated Connie. "And a large raft could've been built simply to navigate it. If we can prove that they never left this area, and that they're all dead except for the one attempting to contact Dianne, then we can stop searching the planet for them."

"It's important to keep in mind that we have no evidence that they lived here, only that they were here long enough to cut down trees that appear to have been used to build a raft," Jerry said.

"If we could find the being that's attempting to contact Dianne, maybe we could get answers to some of our questions," suggested Moose. "Right now, we don't even know for sure if this being is one of the humanoids from B-2. It could be some other kind of entity that's native to this planet."

"That's possible," conceded Dianne, "but I sense that it's one of the aliens we're looking for."

"Do you have any idea where this alien might be?" Jerry asked.

Dianne considered Jerry's question for a few moments. "I sensed the attempted mind probe most strongly after we passed around the island's south end and started heading north."

"Let's go there and search that part of the island," stated Jerry.

When the pioneers arrived at the island's south end, they surveyed the overall lay of the land and noted that the rocky beach was quite similar to that at the north end of Pioneer Island. But set back 50 yards from the water was a steep cliff that rose 200 feet. The top of the cliff sloped gently downward toward the north, so that there was no inaccessible plateau on the cliff's top. This feature led Jerry to say, "An alien living here would not find safety from large animals by living up there." Looking at each of his colleagues, Jerry asked, "If you were living here and were out of ammunition, where would you want to live?"

Moose was first to respond. "I would try to find a cavern with an entrance barely big enough for me to squeeze through."

"Such a cavern would be convenient," stated Jerry. "But where would you live if one didn't exist?"

For a few moments, Moose thought about the problem of surviving; then, he said, "The bears that visit these islands are huge, up in the 1,500-pound range. They are strong, ferocious animals. I doubt that a lone human lacking construction equipment could build a structure that would withstand assault by one of these bears. Without weapons, I don't think I could survive here without a secure refuge, such as a cavern with a small entrance."

"If we assume that such a cavern exists, we must also assume that its entrance is well concealed, or we would've found it," commented Jerry.

"There are lots of trees and bushes growing against the base of that cliff," observed Connie. "I'll look behind them with one of the RPVs."

Before Connie could begin searching, Dianne said, "That won't be necessary. The alien has decided that he wants to be found. An image of a tall tree has just appeared in my mind, and it looks just like that one over there. I now see an image of a cave entrance at the end of a large branch 25 to 30 feet up the tree."

"I wonder why he's decided to show us where he is," Jerry said.

"He might be looking for companionship," suggested Connie.

"I don't think that's a big enough reason for him to assume the risk that we might be hostile," argued Jerry.

"I don't know what this alien's normal life expectancy is," Dianne said. "But if he was middle age when he came here, he'd now be quite old. Perhaps he's ill and is hoping that we're friendly and able to help him."

"We don't know that this is an alien from B-2," stated Moose. "It could be an entity that is native to this planet that is trying to play on our sympathies and lead us into an ambush."

"That's possible," agreed Jerry. "So I will investigate and find out. I'll fly a small RPV inside that tree's foliage. If I find a cave entrance, I'll inspect it and investigate the cavern."

Turning to Dianne, Jerry said, "I want you to put on a headset and clearly hold the images from the RPV in your mind while staying open to communication from the alien."

To Connie and Moose, Jerry said, "In case this is a trap of some sort, I want you two to be alert to everything going on around us."

Jerry looked at the tree and noted that it stretched nearly to the cliff top, making it almost 200 feet tall. While all tingled with excitement; Jerry put on a headset, launched an RPV, and flew it to the big tree. Flying in under the tree's foliage, Jerry circled and inspected the tree's trunk noting that it was at least 12 feet in diameter and that its bark was rough enough to provide hand and foot holds for a humanoid wanting to climb it. Jerry quickly found a well-worn path up the tree where deeper cavities had been carved into the bark. Jerry judged the spacing to be about right for easy climbing for a humanoid about six feet tall.

Jerry flew the RPV upward following the improvised ladder. At a height of 30 feet, the carved out ladder came to a branch that was about three feet in diameter at its base. Jerry noted that the top of the branch showed some wear as though it had been walked on for many years.

He flew the RPV along the top of the branch following it for about 35 feet before coming to the solid rock wall of the cliff. Here, unable to grow outward any farther, the branch split and grew to both the left and the right, hugging the rock wall. Noting that the wear pattern turned to the right, Jerry followed this fork of the branch for about 20 feet before finding a cave entrance a few feet above the branch.

For the benefit of Moose and Connie, Jerry said, "I've found an opening in the cliff, and as we suspected, it's big enough for one of us to crawl through, but much too small for the big bears."

"I'd sure like to see what's inside," Connie said.

"I would too," stated Jerry, as he flew the small RPV slowly into the cave. In just a few feet, the tunnel started to broaden. In a few yards, it turned gently to the left and sloped upward. About 50 feet from the entrance, Jerry found a fairly large cavern.

Immediately catching Jerry's attention was a bright patch of sunlight on the cavern floor. Looking upward, he noted that the cavern extended all the way to the cliff top. Even though it narrowed considerably, there was still a fairly large hole at the top letting in an ample amount of sunlight.

Jerry surveyed the cavern and noted that it was about 30 feet wide and perhaps 50 feet long. Near one end, Jerry found a pile of firewood and a fire pit made out of stones. Next to the fire pit were some scorched abalone shells that had apparently been used as cooking pots.

A short distance from the fire pit, Jerry found a table and chair made from artistically carved wood and tied together with fiber that appeared to be from vines. On a rock ledge a few feet behind and above the table, Jerry saw water seeping out of a small crack in the rock wall. An abalone shell placed tightly against the wall to catch the water was full and overflowing with the overflow disappearing into a crack in the ledge.

Jerry slowly rotated the RPV to view the rest of the cavern. At the end of the cavern opposite the fire pit, Jerry found the cavern's occupant and exclaimed, "I've found him, and he looks very much like the humanoids that inhabit B-2!"

"What is he doing?" Connie asked.

"He's in bed, either asleep or in a trance."

"It's probably the state he needs to be in to achieve telepathic communication," suggested Dianne.

"Are there any weapons next to the bed?" Moose asked.

"I see a spear with a neatly crafted rock point and a bow with a quiver full of arrows. I also see a hunting knife with a metal blade that looks like it is 12 to 15 inches long."

"Unless we provoke him, I don't think we need to worry about those weapons," stated Dianne.

"Those might be primitive weapons, but when skillfully used, they are deadly," asserted Jerry. "The fact that this man is alive proves that he is skillful in their use."

"He looks old, and I don't think he is as capable as he once was," commented Dianne.

"He may be old, but he looks lean and muscular," stated Jerry.

"But I think he has a serious injury and needs help," Dianne said.

"Why do you think that?" Connie asked.

"He is suffering great pain. I can feel it."

"Any idea what's causing the pain?" Connie asked.

Jerry focused the RPV's cameras on the alien's head, and then slowly moved down his body.

"His head and upper body look healthy," noted Dianne. "But his lower body is covered with what looks like a hand woven blanket. It's impossible to tell where the pain is coming from."

"If he has a medical problem, his situation must be desperate, or he wouldn't have led us to his home," commented Jerry.

"But if he brought us here because of a life-threatening medical problem, it seems like he'd find a way to tell us what it is," Dianne said.

"It's possible that his situation has deteriorated to the point that he has used his last ounce of energy just to bring us here," suggested Connie.

"You may be right, because I'm no longer sensing anything," stated Dianne. "I think he has passed out."

"Has he passed out, or has he died?" questioned Connie.

Hoping to answer Connie's question, Jerry flew the RPV close to the alien and focused on his chest. "He's breathing, but not very strongly," he said, after a few moments.

"He is trembling weakly," Dianne noted.

Checking data from the RPV's infrared detector, Jerry said, "His body temperature is 104.7 degrees."

Instantly alarmed, Connie urgently said, "If we're going to save him, we need to get to him soon."

Deciding to tease his wife a bit, Jerry said, "Yesterday, you said you hoped we wouldn't find any aliens, because they would make our lives more complicated. Now, you want to save this one's life."

"But he's sick and suffering. He needs our help."

Jerry smiled at getting the reaction he expected. "I'm glad you feel that way. If we can save him and learn to communicate with him, there is much we can learn from him. After all, he has lived here for a long time."

"You're assuming that he'll be friendly and willing to give us information," argued Moose. "If we allow him to die, we won't have to live with the risk of having an alien with unknown intentions in our midst."

"I think the potential for gaining useful, perhaps even critical, information is worth the risk," countered Jerry. "If he turns out to be a nasty individual, we can always deal with him."

"That's true, but if we save him and he turns out to be a nasty individual who is very cunning in his ways, he might do us great harm before we discover his true nature."

"That's possible," admitted Jerry. "We'll have to be on guard until we get to know him very well."

"These alien humanoids are similar to us," Connie said. "I think it's important to keep this one alive and study his physiological processes, especially his immune system. If he's different from us in some crucial way that has allowed him to survive here, I would like to discover that. Also, I would like to find out if he's had any illnesses of consequence."

"You make him sound like a lab animal," commented Moose.

"The medical tests I will do on him won't be any different than the ones I do on us, just more intensive."

"All things considered, I am convinced that the potential benefits of keeping him alive far outweigh the risks," asserted Jerry.

Jerry took several minutes to inspect the cavern looking for possible hazards, such as traps rigged to kill an intruding carnivore. When he satisfied himself that there weren't any, he handed the RPV control unit to Dianne. "Keep an eye on him. Connie and I are going in."

Jerry and Connie checked their pistols and strapped them on. Then, they checked their rifles and shouldered them. Connie handed her medical cases to Jerry, who placed them in the inflated boat. With Moose alertly on guard and Mike's RPV pilots surveying the vicinity, Connie and Jerry headed for shore.

Once there, Jerry climbed the tree to the large branch and stepped onto it. With a piece of rope he hauled up Connie's medical cases. Then, she climbed the tree and followed him to the cave entrance.

Jerry beamed a bright light into the cave and carefully inspected it to where it curved out of sight. Not seeing anything suspicious, he strapped the light to his head and cautiously entered. Very slowly, Jerry crawled down the tunnel as it curved to the left and upward. Pushing her medical bags in front of her, Connie followed him.

Noticing how smooth the tunnel floor was, Jerry wondered how many times the alien had pushed or dragged objects into and out of his refuge. He must have countless stories to tell, thought Jerry, and after living in isolation for all these years, he might be eager to tell them, if he's been able to maintain his sanity and memory.

When Jerry and Connie reached the cavern, they stopped and looked around. After a few moments, Jerry said, "It looks safe, let's go in."

While warily approaching the alien, Connie inspected the cavern and noted, "It looks like he was able to make himself reasonably comfortable considering his situation."

"If he's lived here for 30 years, he's had plenty of time to fashion some comforts."

"He's also kept his home clean and orderly. If he has taken care of himself as well as he has maintained his home, that might help explain how he has survived for so many years without medical help."

"Let's see if we can keep him alive for a few more years."

"I'll do my best, but first, I have to find out what's wrong with him."

Not seeing any problem on the alien's upper body, Connie removed the blanket covering his lower body. The appearance of his right leg made two problems immediately obvious. The calf had a deep four-inch long gash in it and was swollen and horribly discolored. Also, the ankle was swollen and the foot was turned out at very unnatural angle.

"There's little doubt that he has multiple fractures in that ankle," stated Connie. "However, the injury to his calf is the one that might be life-threatening. Apparently, it has become infected by a microbe that his immune system is having difficulty coping with."

Connie checked the alien's vital signs. "His condition is critical. To save him, I'll have to kill the invading microbe, and I don't even know what it is. There may even be more than one kind. All I can do is inject him with every antibiotic I have and hope that at least one of them will be effective and that none of them kill him. His system may be different from ours in some way that will make our antibiotics toxic to him. But by the time I do the lab work to find out which antibiotic will be effective and whether it will be toxic to him, he will probably be dead. So I have no choice but to use the shotgun approach."

Connie had six distinctly different broad spectrum antibiotics in her medical bags. First she drew a blood specimen for lab analysis; then, she injected the alien with what she judged to be the maximum safe dose of five of the antibiotics.

Turning to Jerry, she said, "I have one more antibiotic to give him, but it's most effective when administered intravenously. Also, he looks like he's suffering from severe dehydration. It's possible that he hasn't had anything to eat or drink for several days, so I need to get some water and nutrients into him. If you would tie down his right arm and rig a support for the I.V., I would appreciate it."

Jerry cut a short piece of rope and gently secured the alien's forearm to the bed structure. Then, he tied the alien's spear to the small bedside table and attached the I.V. bottle to it with a short piece of cord.

Connie looked at the setup with approval. "What a unique way to use a man's spear to save his life."

386

"You're right about that. This just might be the first time that a spear has ever been used this way." Jerry looked at the unconscious alien. "What do we do next?"

"We have to wait for the antibiotics to work and hope that they do. While we wait, we'll monitor his vital signs and do what we can to keep him alive if they start deteriorating."

"How long do you think we'll be here?"

"It may take a day or two before he recovers to the point where we can move him."

"Move him?"

"If we're successful in curing his infection, I'll repair his ankle. If it's a multiple fracture that's as serious as it looks, I'll have to open it up to fix it. There might be some delicate microsurgery involved, and that would be a lot easier to do at home than here in this cave."

Not wanting to miss an opportunity to tease his wife, Jerry said, "Yesterday, you hoped we wouldn't find any aliens; now, you want to bring one into our home."

"Finding a lone individual desperately in need of help is different than finding a large, powerful group living nearby."

"But if we take him home, and you're able to cure him, he might not want to leave."

Connie smiled. "If he turns out to be a warmhearted individual, he could be a real benefit to us."

"What if he turns out to be cold-hearted to the point of being evil?"

"Then, I would consider him to be no different than a malignant tumor that needs to be either removed or neutralized."

"Judging from the appearance of that leg and ankle, he's not going to be a threat to us for quite some time. We should use that time to learn how to communicate with him and try to gain some insight into how he might behave when he's back to normal."

Connie nodded. "That might be possible. Michelle has made great progress learning Rex's language. Perhaps she could do the same with this alien."

"There's a possibility that this guy might understand Rex's language; even though, he apparently is from the other side in the Great War."

"That might be true, but I'm not sure that it would be wise to speak to him in Rex's language."

Jerry looked at his wife curiously. "What bothers you about that?"

"What if the Great War was the final war between ethnic groups who've hated each other for centuries? This alien could see Rex's language as the language of a hated enemy and associate us with that enemy simply because we used the language."

"Perhaps it would be best to just teach him English. If he decides he wants to join our society and become an effective part of it, he'll have to learn English anyway."

"That's true, but first, he has to survive the battle that's raging inside him, and I think we'll know the outcome of that in the next few days."

"If we're staying here for a few days, we're going to need some camping supplies, including some pretty good lights. Unless this cavern has luminescent walls, it's going to be very dark in here tonight. If our patient regains consciousness, I think it's important that we have enough light, so he can see the medical set up and realize that he's being helped."

Having watched and listened to everything that was going on via the RPV, Dianne decided that it was time to join in. "Moose and I can go home and get everything we need to camp here for a couple days."

"I need some lab work done on the blood specimen I took from this alien," Connie said.

"If you'll attach it to my RPV, I'll take it home and do the lab work while Moose puts our supplies on the boat."

"It would be helpful if you could identify the microbes I'm trying to defeat. Then, I'd have some guidance on what to attack them with."

"If they're present in your specimen, I'll find them and get you some pictures."

"To make sure that we find them, I'll give you an additional specimen to examine," Connie replied. While Jerry directed a beam of light on the gash in the alien's leg, Connie collected a sample of the fluid oozing out of it. She attached it to the RPV along with the blood specimen.

"Also, you might bring along an extra air mattress and some extra blankets," requested Connie. "We need to give this alien something clean to sleep on, after we give him a bath."

"Good idea. Anything else we need?"

"No, but I'll call you if I think of something."

Four hours later, Connie received a call from Dianne. "I've identified the microbe that's causing our patient's problems, and the antibiotic that you're administering with the I.V. is effective against it. However, there is a possible complication in that this appears to be a very nasty little bug that is capable of severely damaging any fleshy tissue that it chooses to invade. I think it could easily be fatal if it were to establish a colony in a vital organ."

"So even though we're killing the bug, we might lose our patient anyway, because he may've already suffered life-threatening damage to a vital organ."

"That's the way I see it. Has he gotten any better since you started treatment?"

"His vital signs are stable; in fact, I'm even seeing some modest improvements."

"Maybe you got to him soon enough to prevent critical damage. Perhaps he's lucky that we found him when we did."

388

"It wasn't just luck; he revealed his location to you. Apparently, he had reached the conclusion that he was dying and that we were his only chance for survival."

After a brief pause, Connie asked, "When are you coming back? All of our food is on the boat, and I'm starving."

Moose has our supplies loaded, so we'll be there in about 45 minutes. Have you thought of anything else you want us to bring?"

"Bring extra food, including some that's ready to eat."

"Knowing my husband, that's probably the first thing he put on the boat."

When Dianne and Connie finished their conversation, Jerry said, "It's starting to get dark in here; I think it's time to build a campfire."

"That would add a warm, cozy atmosphere to this place."

Checking the alien's firewood supply, Jerry found some dried grasses, kindling wood, and a large supply of firewood. After placing some of each in the fire pit, he lit it and soon had a brightly burning campfire.

When Moose and Dianne returned, Jerry went out to help bring in the supplies while Connie stayed with the alien. The first items brought in were the lights and the evening meal. Dianne and Connie set up the lights, put the finishing touches on dinner, and laid out the meal on the alien's table. While they were doing these tasks, Jerry and Moose completed the laborious job of hauling the rest of the camping supplies up the tree and dragging them through the tunnel into the cavern.

Then, the interstellar pioneers filled their plates and sat on the cavern floor next to the blazing campfire to enjoy a hearty dinner. Being famished, they ate in silence for a few minutes; then, while gazing around the cavern, Connie said, "Camping in here makes me feel like I'm visiting the home of one of Earth's prehistoric cave dwellers."

"From the appearance of this cavern, I think this guy has been living more comfortably than Earth's cave dwellers ever lived," stated Jerry.

"That might be because he has enjoyed one big advantage over Earth's cave dwellers, and that's knowledge," commented Moose. "To me, it's inconceivable that he would've been allowed on an interstellar mission unless he was very intelligent and excelled in the training for the mission."

Dianne looked at Moose. "You became a part of this mission without any training for it."

"That's because my best friend was in a position of authority and was fully aware of my knowledge and capabilities."

As he finished speaking, Moose shifted his gaze from Dianne to Jerry, who looked at Dianne. "Are you implying that I made a mistake by sneaking Moose onto this mission?"

Now feeling the combined stares of Moose and Jerry, Dianne quickly replied, "No! I'm not implying that at all. I am very happy that you thought highly enough of Moose to give him the opportunity to be with us. I was only pointing out that this alien didn't necessarily have to excel in a training program to be part of an interstellar mission."

"Are you implying that I'm only here because of friendship and that I didn't excel in my profession?" Moose teased her.

Shifting her gaze back and forth between Moose and Jerry, Dianne said, "This seems to be pick-on-Dianne night, and I think my easiest way out is to just simply admit that this alien wouldn't be here unless he was very intelligent and extremely capable at the time the mission departed."

Moose and Jerry exchanged smiles of satisfaction. Jerry said, "It's also quite likely that this alien was rigorously trained in survival techniques, including the manufacture of lethal weapons from available materials. I am impressed with the quality of his stone-tipped weapons."

"But even as well-made as they are, they seem inadequate as a defense against the big bears that visit these islands," commented Moose.

"Apparently, he has been quite adept at avoiding the bears, and these weapons were only a last resort," Jerry said.

"I suspect they were used primarily to hunt small game for food," suggested Moose. "Some of the waterfowl we've seen look like they might be a good source of food and an easy target for someone skilled in the use of a bow and arrow."

"As interested as you always are in good food, I'm surprised you haven't yet treated us to some barbecued waterfowl," Jerry said.

"I've been focused on seafood, but the birds are next on my list. Also, I'd like to bag one of those ostrich-like dinosaurs that we've seen in large numbers. However, that would require a trip to the countryside, and that's not a very friendly place, so I'm not eager to shoot one of them. The scent of fresh blood might attract every nearby predator."

"Aw you're just a chicken," teased Jerry.

"Not too long ago, I rode a ten-ton styracosaurus into a face-off with a pack of ten-ton T-Rexes. I haven't seen you do that yet."

"No, but I did walk under a 100-ton sauropod. Also, I reached up and touched him."

"I think you both have enough courage to get yourselves killed," stated Dianne.

"I came close to being killed by a saber-tooth during that little adventure," stated Connie. "For the time being, I think I will be content to explore the countryside with an RPV from the safety of our boat."

"I wonder if this alien ever made any trips to the countryside?" questioned Jerry.

"He would've needed a boat to do that, and we haven't seen one," responded Moose. "Besides that, armed with only stone-age weapons, I doubt that he would've survived such a trip."

"There are lots of bushes on the waterfront, and he could easily have a small boat hidden away," stated Jerry.

"But if he's living alone here, why would he bother hiding his boat?"

questioned Dianne.

"If he saw one of our robot labs land, he may have been hiding from us," replied Jerry. "Those para-wings are big and would've been easy to spot. If he missed all the robot labs, he would certainly have heard and seen our personnel shuttle take off on the day we arrived."

"That was an awesome sight," commented Connie. "He could easily have reacted to it with a mixture of joy and fear."

"Whatever his feelings were, he did choose caution as the wisest course of action, and he kept himself hidden from us," stated Jerry. "Speaking of feelings, I wonder how he would react to seeing us sitting around this camp-fire if he were to regain consciousness right now."

"If he's as intelligent as we're giving him credit for, he should recognize from the medical setup that he's being helped," responded Connie. "Unless he's totally cold-blooded, he should be appreciative of our presence and think of us as friends."

"Or he could be suspicious of our motives," Jerry warned.

"What do you mean?" Connie asked.

"He might think that we're cold-blooded and that we're only keeping him alive because we're hoping to pump some information out of him, and once we have that, we'll dispose of him."

"That possibility is a good reason to never speak to him in Rex's language," stated Connie.

"Let's keep in mind that we're here by invitation," noted Dianne.

"How do you figure that?" inquired Moose.

"He invited us into his home by revealing his location to me."

"But that invitation was actually an act of desperation," argued Moose. "It doesn't mean that he'll be sympathetic toward our goals after he has regained health."

"Even if he isn't sympathetic toward our goals, he has already helped us a great deal," Jerry said. "The fact that he has survived here for many years with nothing more than Stone Age weapons at his disposal bodes well for our future."

"Whether he wants to or not, he can help us a lot more than that," stated Dianne.

"In what way?" Jerry asked.

"We can take a tissue sample from him and send it up to the Challenger for DNA analysis. Once we have a complete DNA profile on him, we can compare the genetic blueprint for his immune system to the genetic blueprint for the human immune system. If we can establish that the design and function of his immune system is essentially the same as ours, then we can confidently bring down all of our people."

Speaking to his wife, Jerry asked, "Would the doctor care to comment on that?"

"All the evidence we have indicates that he has lived here for a long time, perhaps 30 years. It also looks like he has lived here alone, which means he has not had any medical help, which means that his immune system has served him well. If his immune system is basically the same as ours, then I will vote in favor of bringing everyone down."

"Are you saying that you would have no problem bringing our daughter down?"

"As far as diseases and infections are concerned, I would have no problem bringing her down."

"What about the bug infecting this alien?" Jerry asked. "Why is his immune system having trouble with it, and is it a threat to us?"

"It might be that his immune system is starting to break down because of his age, or the bug may've gained entry to his body at a time when he was in a weakened condition because of some other factor. As far as the threat to us is concerned, I believe that our immune systems can handle this bug; if not, we have an antibiotic that is effective against it."

Turning to Dianne, Jerry asked, "How long will it take to do a DNA profile on this alien and a genetic code comparison of immune systems?"

"My assistants are tired of being confined to a spaceship, and they're eager to come down. With that kind of motivation, they'll probably work day and night on the project. My guess is that it won't take them more than a few days, certainly less than a week."

"This DNA project does pose some risk for the people on the Challenger," Connie warned. "Sending up a specimen for analysis creates the possibility of accidentally putting some of Alcent's microbes into the Challenger's environment. Some of these might be lethal to humans, and we might not be able to develop a cure quickly enough to save the lives of those infected. This DNA project could take away from the people on the Challenger the option of living out their lives in space, should it prove to be impossible to live here."

"Both of our shuttles have been down here and have returned to orbit," commented Moose.

"But they haven't entered the Challenger," argued Connie. "They're orbiting near the Challenger, and no one has entered either of them."

"That's true," acknowledged Moose.

"It appears that we have a dilemma here," Jerry said. "We now have a possible way to prove that the human immune system can deal with the microbes that exist here, but an accident could doom the people on the Challenger if it turns out that our immune systems aren't up to the job."

"I believe we need to do this DNA project," asserted Dianne. "And we should be able to set up procedures that reduce the risk to almost zero."

"But we cannot reduce it to zero," stated Connie.

"No, but we can get pretty close," argued Dianne.

"We've been here for nearly three weeks and none of us have gotten sick," stated Moose, sounding very confident.

"That's true," admitted Connie. "But there are diseases that take much longer than three weeks to develop."

"And that's the reason we need to do this DNA project," stated Jerry. "If it turns out that our immune systems are essentially the same as this alien's, then we won't have to be anymore concerned about illnesses here than we were on Earth. We could freely travel back and forth between Pioneer Island and the Challenger. We could bring down materials and equipment and start building our homes. We could have children and start building the new civilization we came here to create."

Dianne turned to Connie. "I think it's time to work out a fail-safe procedure for doing the project."

"We can bring the personnel shuttle down tomorrow to pick up your specimens," stated Jerry.

"We'll have the procedure worked out by then," declared Dianne.

Connie reluctantly nodded in agreement.

Noticing this, Jerry said, "You seem to be troubled by the need to do this project."

"I realize how important the project is, but finding this alien on the verge of death because of a horrible infection clearly illustrates that microorganisms might be the greatest danger we face here. I'd hoped that we could define that danger quite well before exposing our daughter to possible risk. No matter how good a procedure we set up, the possibility of human error or having an accident will still exist."

"But if our immune systems are essentially the same as this alien's, then we should be able to assume that the risk from microbes is no greater here than on Earth."

"That's true, but I wish we could prove that without exposing our daughter to possible risk."

"Like us, our daughter is a pioneer. Being a pioneer often involves risk taking. We must do everything we can to minimize the risk, but then, we must go forward. In this case, it is necessary to take a risk in order to minimize a risk."

Connie again nodded in agreement; then, she looked at her wrist monitor and said, "This alien just might pull through; his vital signs are continuing to slowly improve."

"Any guess when he might regain consciousness?" Dianne asked.

"I don't know, but I'd like him to be clean and comfortable when he does. So when we finish dinner, let's give him a bath and some clean bedding. Also, let's put an air mattress under him."

"Okay," responded Dianne. "Being clean and comfortable when he wakes up should help convince him that we care about him and that we're not just trying to keep him alive for our needs."

An hour later, while bathing the alien, Dianne asked, "How long ago do you think this guy injured himself?"

"Judging from his condition, he had the accident at least a week ago, maybe two," Connie replied. "Considering the mess he's made, I don't think he's been out of this bed for several days."

"He definitely needs a bath and clean bedding."

"Being clean and having an air mattress under him should make him feel a lot better when he regains consciousness."

"But that leg infection and fractured ankle are going to be agonizingly painful for him. Have you added any analgesic to the I.V.?"

"I haven't because of the possibility of an allergic reaction."

"He could've reacted to one of the antibiotics you gave him."

"That's true, but I had no choice except to hit him with everything. Now that he seems to be recovering, I'll add a small amount of analgesic to the I.V. If he doesn't react, I'll increase the dose. If there's no adverse effect from that, I'll add a drug to reduce the swelling and see if he tolerates it. If he does, I'll increase the dose."

"If this guy's lucky, he won't regain consciousness until sometime tomorrow. By then, all of our drugs will have had a chance to work, and he should wake up feeling fairly good."

"That's only possible if he hasn't already suffered critical damage to one or more vital organs," commented Connie.

"We can only hope for the best. I wonder if we'll be able to move him by tomorrow afternoon."

"If he continues his slow steady improvement, I think we should take him home tomorrow even if he hasn't regained consciousness. The immediate danger of death will have passed, and I need to give him the kind of exam that's possible with the equipment we have at home."

"It's going to be a difficult job taking him out that narrow tunnel and lowering him 30 feet down the tree without aggravating his condition."

"I think we should dump that problem on our husbands and let them apply their engineering talents to it," stated Connie.

"They'll probably figure out an easy way to do the job."

A short time later, Connie and Dianne finished making the alien comfortable and joined Jerry and Moose who had just finished exploring the cavern and were again seated next to the campfire.

"How is your patient doing?" Jerry asked Connie.

"I think he's going to make it."

"I don't think there's any doubt that he's very strong willed in his determination to live," noted Jerry.

"That's an important factor in surviving any serious illness," stated Connie.

"I'm amazed at how well this man has lived without any guns or modern equipment," Jerry noted. "The only thing in this cavern to connect him to an advanced society is a hunting knife with a stainless steel blade."

"He is definitely very well-equipped with ingenuity and survival skills," commented Moose.

"I think the fact that he has nothing modern except for his knife indicates that he was deserted by his colleagues," noted Jerry. "If they'd died here of disease, then he would have the tools, weapons, and equipment that they brought with them."

"But why did they desert him with nothing but a knife for defense?" questioned Dianne.

"Apparently, he was left here to die," replied Jerry. "Perhaps, their intention was to take all of his weapons, and the knife was overlooked."

"So what crime did he commit that was deserving of the death penalty?" Connie asked. "Is it possible that I'm trying to save the life of a psychopathic killer?"

"If that's why he was deserted, we certainly don't need him to get well and live with us," stated Moose.

"There is another possibility to consider," Jerry suggested. "And that is that he may've been staunchly opposed to something the group was doing or was planning to do, and they deserted him simply to get him out of the way."

"If that's the case, it would be helpful to know what sort of evil activity this man was trying to prevent," stated Dianne. "If the group has survived and prospered, we might have a tribe of evil people living somewhere in this vicinity that we'll have to deal with sometime."

"It looks to me like we have a potential problem either way," Moose said. "Either we're trying to save the life of a dangerous man, or we're going to have a group of evil beings to contend with."

Jerry grinned at Moose. "It seems like our lives are a bit more complicated than they were a few days ago."

"How can you joke about something as potentially dangerous as this?" retorted Moose.

"I'm not trying to belittle the problem, but we do have the tools to deal with it, so long as we stay alert to all possibilities."

"And there's something else to consider," commented Connie. "Let's suppose this alien was abandoned 30 years ago because of a criminal act. Thirty years is a long time, and people sometimes change drastically with time. After living in isolation with nature for 30 years, he could easily have undergone some drastic changes in his thinking."

"But those changes could just as easily be for the worse as for the better," argued Moose.

"That's true," admitted Connie. "We'll just have to watch him until we know him very well. For that reason and to monitor his medical condition, we'll have to sleep in shifts tonight. I can watch him until around 3:00 to 4:00 A.M., and then, I'll need to be relieved."

"I'll stay up with you and help you stay alert," Jerry said. "Even though the alien has found security in here for a long time, I think we need to be on guard anyway."

Speaking to Connie, Dianne said, "Wake me up when you need to be relieved. Moose and I will take over."

FOURTEEN

Saved By a Savage Attack

TIME: Day Nineteen, Late Morning.

After a long, uneventful night in the alien's cave home, the interstellar pioneers were sitting around a campfire enjoying breakfast when they were interrupted by a creaking sound. They turned toward the sound and discovered that it was coming from the alien's bed. He had just regained consciousness and was struggling to sit up, but he succeeded only in raising his head and turning toward the humans.

The alien looked at the humans for a few seconds; then, he shifted his gaze to the medical setup. After scrutinizing the I.V. for a few moments, he looked at his clean, comfortable bedding. Noticeably satisfied with his greatly improved situation, he shifted his gaze back to the pioneers. An expression of gratitude seemed to pervade his facial features. Then, weakness overcame him, and his head slumped down on the pillow provided by the pioneers.

"He certainly doesn't seem to be alarmed by our presence," commented Jerry. "In fact, he seems to be quite comfortable with the idea of having us here."

"And it looks like he's grateful to us for what we've done for him," Connie said.

"He should be," stated Moose. "We saved his life."

"It'll be a few days before we'll know that for sure," Connie said.

"But if he thinks we saved his life, he should trust us and be happy that we're here," argued Moose.

"That's true," Dianne said, "but there might be more to it than that."

"What do you mean?" Jerry asked.

"He may've concluded that we'd help him before he revealed his presence to us."

"How could he have known that?" questioned Jerry.

"Don't forget that he contacted us using his telepathic powers. It's possible that he may've first used those powers to probe our minds. Even though there is a language barrier, he may've been able to detect whether we are kindhearted or cold-blooded."

An expression of concern appeared on Jerry's face as he considered the

397

implications of what Dianne had just said. "If he can probe our minds, is it possible that he might be able to get into our minds and control us?"

"The ability to mentally transmit information directly into our minds is a form of communication," responded Connie. "Having the ability to communicate is not the same as having the ability to control."

"But he is a member of an intelligent alien species that we know very little about," argued Jerry. "I don't think it would be wise to assume that his telepathic powers are limited to communication."

"I'm not advocating that we make that assumption, but if he is able to control the activities of those around him telepathically, then his colleagues could not have deserted him unless he allowed them to."

"What if his colleagues had telepathic powers greater than his?" argued Jerry.

"Then he would not have been able to prevent them from deserting him," replied Connie.

"You're saying that there might be a colony of humanoids somewhere on this planet that might have a telepathic ability to control us," Moose blurted. "If we ever have to fight them, our superior weapons won't give us any advantage if they can prevent us from using them."

"That's a sobering thought," commented Jerry.

"I think it would be difficult to control another person with telepathic powers unless the targeted person allows it to happen," argued Connie.

"That might be true," agreed Dianne, "but telepathically planted suggestions could certainly influence the activities of a person who is unaware that the suggestions are being planted. Hypnotists do quite well with verbally planted suggestions."

"But hypnotists can only hypnotize those who are willing to surrender control," countered Connie.

"Both of you might be correct," stated Jerry. "So I think our best defense is to be aware that suggestions might be planted and to be stubbornly determined to remain in control of our own actions."

"That's a good policy for each of us to follow," agreed Connie. "Especially, now that it appears likely that there might be a colony of telepathically capable aliens living somewhere on this planet."

"And there's also this alien whose life we're trying to save," added Moose. "Even if it turns out that he cannot control us telepathically, I don't know if I like the idea of having someone around who can read my mind."

Displaying a mischievous grin, Dianne asked, "Is there something you're trying to hide?"

Moose squirmed. "Of course not, it just seems rather spooky to have to constantly guard my thoughts."

"This alien might turn out to be a considerate individual who would always respect the privacy of our thoughts," Connie said.

"I still don't like the idea that my thoughts might be open to him any time he decides to look at them," stated Moose.

"I think we should be alert to that possibility without jumping to conclusions until we get to know him and the extent of his powers," argued Connie.

"There is another possibility to consider," suggested Jerry. "And that is this alien could turn out to be a vital ally if there is a colony of aliens nearby that have telepathic powers. If he is grateful to us for saving his life and mad at those who deserted him, he might choose to assist us. He might be able to sense when the others are attempting to use their telepathic powers against us."

"I understand the importance of saving his life and caring for him while he recovers," Moose reluctantly admitted. "But I don't like the idea that my thoughts might be open to him any time he cares to look at them."

"I don't think that'll be a problem until he understands our language," commented Dianne. "If your thoughts are in English, and he tunes in to them; what good will it do him? I think that until he understands English, he'll only be able to pick up your mood, or see images that are in your mind, or transmit images into your mind."

"That means he cannot plant suggestions in our minds until he learns English," stated Jerry. "If he attempts to plant suggestions using images, it should be obvious that something unusual is happening."

"Are you suggesting that we delay teaching him English until we learn more about him?" Connie asked.

"I think that would be the prudent thing to do."

"We communicated very well with Rex using only images," Dianne reminded everyone.

"Let's learn as much as we can about this alien and those that came with him by communicating with images," stated Jerry. "If we eventually decide that we can trust him, then, let's teach him English."

"I like that approach," declared Moose.

"I think it's time to remove the I.V.," Connie said. "I've pumped enough drugs and nutrients into him to last for a while. He's no longer dehydrated, and it appears that we've killed the microbes that were ravaging his body."

"How long before we can take him home?" Jerry asked Connie.

"I think he has recovered enough, so we can safely move him, if you and Moose can devise a way to do that without aggravating his condition."

"All we have to do is immobilize his injured leg and strap him to a sturdy stretcher. We can easily carry him. I doubt that he weighs more than 180 pounds. We can use ropes to lower him down the tree."

"It might be beneficial to show him what we're planning to do before we start moving him," suggested Connie. "If he knows what the plan is and approves, then he won't do anything to resist. In his weakened state, I don't want him to get alarmed and do something foolish."

"If he's still awake, let's introduce him to one of our video headsets,"

Jerry said. "With it, we can show him our boat, a map of this lake, and which island we're taking him to. We can show him some video of our camp. Then, we can show him the stretcher and indicate to him that we're going to put him on it."

"After all of that, he should be smart enough to figure out what our intentions are," stated Connie.

"And by using his telepathic powers, he should be able to tell us if he has any objections," added Dianne.

Facing Dianne, Jerry said, "So far, all telepathic communication has been with you. I don't know why, but I'm going to assume that if he wants to communicate with us, it'll be through you. So while I show him what we're planning to do, I want you to keep your mind open."

After Dianne acknowledged the request, Jerry picked up two video headsets and calmly approached the alien, followed by his fellow pioneers. The alien watched them with utmost interest but did not appear alarmed. Jerry showed him the headsets. Then, he handed one to Moose who put it on. Using gestures, Jerry indicated to the alien that he wanted him to wear the other headset.

After a few moments, Dianne said, "An image of the alien wearing a headset has just appeared in my mind."

"That was quick," commented Jerry.

As Jerry leaned over the alien to put the headset on him, the alien lifted his head to make the task easier. When the headset was comfortably in place, Moose launched the little RPV that the pioneers had brought into the cavern and flew it down the tunnel and out of the cave. Moose flew the RPV out to the boat and slowly circled it to give the alien a good view. While Moose was doing this, Connie removed the I.V., and Jerry accessed the Challenger's computer to call up images to show the alien.

After landing the RPV on the boat, Moose took off his headset and gave it to Jerry who put it on, so he could view the images he planned to show the alien. First, Jerry used the computer to create an image of the boat with the pioneers and the alien on it. Then, he showed the alien an image of Clear Lake. Next, he slowly zoomed in on an area that included Pioneer Island and the alien's home Island. He used computer graphics to show the boat moving from the alien's home island to Pioneer Island. Next, Jerry used the video cameras on Stellar Plateau to present images of their camp. Finally, he used the computer to create an image of the alien lying on a table with Connie working on his broken ankle.

A few moments after Jerry turned off the video, Dianne said, "I have an image in my mind of us and the alien on our boat. Now I have a new image of the alien standing on one leg while being supported between Moose and Jerry. Now I have a new image of the alien with a glass of water in one hand and some food in the other."

"It appears that our therapy has knocked out his infection and made him feel much better," noted Connie. "He's hungry, and he thinks he's strong enough to hobble his way to our boat with a little assistance."

"I'll get him some water and breakfast," Dianne said.

"While you're doing that, I'll bandage his leg and immobilize his broken ankle," stated Connie.

Turning to Moose, Jerry said, "Let's break camp and put our equipment on the boat."

An hour and a half later, all were onboard the boat and sailing toward Pioneer Island. Deeply interested in the boat, the alien looked at the solar sails. Then, he noted that Alpha Centauri A was almost directly overhead in the midday sky. Having determined that the boat must be electrically powered, the alien looked at the stern and listened intently for the sound of an electric motor, but he was unable to hear even a faint hum. He was deeply impressed that these strangers had seen fit to use their advanced technology to create a propulsion system that would silently propel this boat. A pleasant smile of approval appeared on his face.

Comfortably seated in a portable lounge chair, the alien relaxed in the warm sunshine with a gentle breeze caressing his body. Hearing only the sound of small waves lapping against the boat and pleasant conversation among his new-found friends, the alien became drowsy and fell asleep.

A half-hour later, he felt a gentle prod on his right shoulder and awoke to find Dianne next to him, pointing up at something in the western sky. He looked upward and saw the personnel shuttle heading north. Dianne handed him a pair of binoculars, which he eagerly accepted and immediately focused on the shuttle. He watched it turn to the east and then to the south as it glided into the last leg of its landing approach. After landing, it turned and headed toward South Bay.

Arriving at the south end of Pioneer Island at the same time as the shuttle, Jerry decided to follow it into South Bay. The shuttle dropped anchor 30 yards offshore, and Jerry dropped anchor between it and the shore. He turned to Moose and said, "Let's unload it and send it back up."

"We have 4,000 pounds to unload," commented Moose. "It's going to take a couple hours to haul all that to shore."

Stepping into the inflated boat, Jerry said, "The sooner we get started; the sooner we'll get done. Anyway, I think we can get the job done in less than two hours. If we swim rather than ride in the boat, we can put more in it. When we're ashore, we can haul the boat in with a piece of rope."

Ninety minutes later, Moose and Jerry moved the last boatload of cargo ashore. Dianne and Connie had already carried the items they could lift to the elevator and hauled them up to Stellar Plateau. With two additional trips on the elevator, Moose and Jerry lifted the remaining cargo up to the plateau. Then, they returned to the sailboat to pick up the alien.

When they were all on the plateau, Jerry said, "Let's launch the shuttle, so our colleagues on the Challenger can start the DNA project."

Dianne glanced at the alien. "I wonder how he would react if he knew that his DNA might be the final piece of evidence that we need to prove that it's safe for humans to live here."

"I don't see how he could possibly object to helping us that way," commented Connie. "After all, we saved his life. In my opinion, he was no more than a day or two away from death when we found him."

"You would never know that by looking at him now," noted Dianne. "He seems to be making an amazing recovery."

"Well, we did give him some very effective medical help, but even so, I am surprised by his speedy recovery."

"Me too," Dianne said. "It's only been 24 hours, and he not only seems to be feeling pretty good, but he also seems to be mentally sharp and alert. He has been very interested in everything that we've done."

"That's understandable," noted Connie. "He's been alone for a very long time. Now, he finally has some visitors, and the visitors are from another planet. He should be interested in us and our technology."

"Since he's so eager to learn about us, let's give him a good vantage point to watch our shuttle take off," Jerry said. "It's not only an impressive display of advanced technology; it's also a spectacular sight."

A few minutes later, all were at the southeast corner of Stellar Plateau observing the shuttle taxi out of South Bay. Upon reaching open water, the shuttle quickly accelerated to hydrofoil speed; then, its powerful NTR burst into action with a thundering roar. Seeming to have a mind of its own that yearned for a speedy return to orbit, the shuttle leapt off the lake and pitched into a steep climb. Rapidly reaching the cold stratosphere, the shuttle left a brilliant white vapor trail and was soon out of sight.

Jerry stole some brief glances at the alien to observe his reaction to the shuttle's departure. "It looks like our guest is deeply impressed with our technology," noted Jerry. "I also sense a desire on his part to ride our shuttle into orbit."

"That seems like a reasonable reaction," stated Moose. "After all, he is an interstellar astronaut."

"But that gleam I saw in his eyes is a gleam that I've seen only in the eyes of test pilots about to go up in a hot new aircraft. I think it's quite likely that he was the mission pilot, and once they arrived here, that skill was no longer essential, making it easy for his colleagues to desert him in response to whatever conflict they had."

"That concerns me," stated Moose.

"What concerns you?" Jerry asked.

"The possibility that he was the mission pilot concerns me, because we don't know why he was abandoned by his colleagues. It may've been because of ruthless criminal behavior on his part. If he was an excellent pilot, it won't take him long to figure out how to fly our shuttles once he learns our language. Then, he could steal one if given the opportunity."

"And what would he do with it?" questioned Jerry.

"He might use it to punish those who deserted him, if he knows where they are."

"I think you're letting your imagination get the best of you."

"That may be, but what I'm suggesting is possible."

"While that's true, you have to consider the fact that this alien isn't a young man anymore. He might just want to live out the rest of his life in a peaceful, relaxing way. He might even want to become a member of our society for social reasons and to enjoy the benefits of our technology."

"Well, I don't think we should trust him until we know a lot more about him. Right now, it's possible that he's being friendly only because he needs us."

"Because of his needs, he's not going to be in any kind of physical condition to steal a shuttle for at least six weeks," stated Connie. "It's going to take at least that long for his ankle to heal, after I do the surgery."

"During that time, I think we should assume the best and treat him as an honored guest while we learn about him and his past," Jerry said. "If we determine that he'll be a threat to our well-being, we can always take appropriate action."

"That self-propelled wheelchair he's sitting in seems to be making him feel like an honored guest all by itself," noted Dianne.

"He's definitely pleased that we've provided him with an easy way to move around," observed Connie.

"It was thoughtful of you to have it sent down," commented Jerry.

"Just taking care of my patient."

"It's actually more than that," stated Jerry.

"What do you mean?" Connie asked.

"Giving him the means to easily move around should indicate a degree of trust on our part. Now, the burden is on him to show that our trust is justified. Also, if he thinks that he's being treated the same as we would treat one of our own, he might conclude that we're trying to tell him that he's welcome to join our society. Again, the burden is on him to avoid doing anything that would cause us to revoke the invitation."

"I really didn't have all of that in mind when I requested a wheelchair. I was just trying to be a good doctor. However, I agree with your thinking."

Speaking to Jerry, Moose said, "Giving him as much freedom as possible is sort-of-like giving him enough rope to hang himself."

"You're sure in a distrustful mood today," stated Jerry. "But you're right. If he abuses his freedom, he will face undesirable consequences."

"That's a rather mild way of saying what I just said."

Speaking to Moose, Connie said, "Whether or not we trust him, there can be little doubt that we'll learn more about him by giving him as much freedom as possible than what we would learn by restricting him and directing his every activity. The implications behind the free choices he makes in day-to-day life should reveal much about him."

"That's probably true, but if he's clever, he can conduct himself in ways that are designed to deceive us," argued Moose.

"If he does, I think you'll see right through his deceptive activity as suspicious as you are," responded Connie.

"I don't think I'm being overly suspicious just by considering possibilities. After all, our shuttles are essential pieces of equipment."

"Until this alien learns English, he'll have a difficult time learning how to operate our shuttles," stated Jerry. "While the flight control computers make shuttle operation quite easy, it's impossible for him to learn how to operate those computers until he learns English. Also, if he was deserted 30 years ago and wants revenge, wouldn't it be simpler for him to make friends with us and ask for help?"

"If he does, and we refuse to help, then, I think theft of a shuttle becomes a real possibility," stated Moose.

"For that to happen, those who deserted him have to still be alive, he has to know where they are, and he has to have a desire for revenge," argued Connie.

"If they're still alive, his telepathic ability might enable him to find them," stated Dianne. "If he considers us to be his friends, he might be willing to tell us where they are, saving us the job of searching for them."

"By the time his ankle heals, we need to have answers to all pertinent questions about him and those who came here with him," Jerry said.

"Dianne and I are planning to do the ankle surgery tomorrow morning," stated Connie.

"After he's had time to recover from the stress of surgery, I'll begin getting information from him," Dianne said. "Hopefully, it won't take long to get enough answers to put my husband's mind at ease. I don't want him to get high blood pressure from worrying about this alien's intentions."

Connie quickly assured Dianne, "Don't worry, if he gets high blood pressure, I can treat him for that."

"Would you use drugs, or would use psychological therapy to help him deal with the stress caused by excessive worrying?"

"I'd have to do a careful diagnosis to determine which treatment would be most effective."

Moose looked at Jerry. "I think I'm being picked on for doing nothing more than expressing concern about a potential problem."

Jerry chuckled. "Why do I get the feeling that you're enjoying the attention?"

"That question should be easy for him to answer," Dianne said.

"Our guest seems to have picked up the mood of our conversation," commented Connie. "He seems to be softly laughing too."

"So, even the alien that I'm concerned about gets a good laugh at my expense," Moose said.

"I still get the feeling that you're enjoying the attention," Jerry said to Moose. In response, Moose grinned at Jerry.

"I think we should forget the alien for a while and take care of the cargo we just unloaded," suggested Jerry. "Let's start by putting together the ATV (all-terrain-vehicle). Then, we can use it to haul the rest of the items home."

"It shouldn't take us more than an hour or two to put it together," stated Moose.

"I think you're right," agreed Jerry. "All the small parts have already been assembled into major components. All we have to do is put them together, so let's get started."

As Moose and Jerry went to work on the task at hand, Dianne asked, "Do you guys need any help?"

"Thanks for asking," responded Jerry, "but this ATV was designed for quick easy assembly. We should be fine."

"Maybe you could fix us some dinner," suggested Moose. "By the time we're finished here, I'm going to be starving."

"That doesn't surprise me," commented Dianne in a playful tone. "Do you have any particular kind of dinner in mind?"

Moose ignored Dianne's teasing remark and smiled at her. "I'd love to sit down to a large spicy pizza with a salad on the side."

"You just might be in luck," replied Dianne. "Some of these boxes contain groceries. I believe pizza-making ingredients are included."

Dianne looked through the supplies, found the box she was looking for, picked it up, and handed it to Charlie. While she was doing this, Connie asked Jerry, "Would you like us to take the alien with us or leave him here?"

"He has the controls to his wheelchair. Let him decide."

"What do you hope to learn by presenting him with that choice?"

Jerry looked into his wife's eyes and displayed a sly grin. "We might find out whether he prefers to be with men or with women."

"I don't know if I like giving him that choice. I might feel rejected if he chooses to stay here with you guys, especially when you consider that he probably hasn't seen a woman in thirty years."

Making some subtly suggestive movements, Dianne added, "We could end up feeling unattractive."

Moose noticed Dianne's body language, and his face lit up with a broad smile as he recognized the opportunity that the women had just presented him. In a compassionate tone, Moose said, "If the alien decides to stay here with us, I could arrange for counseling to help you deal with your bruised egos, but this would occur only after a careful diagnosis of your traumatized emotions."

Caught off-guard by Moose's remark, Dianne and Connie looked at each other with wide-eyed expressions of surprise. "I think my husband's been studying elementary psychology," Dianne said.

"That may be," noted Connie. "But I don't think we're going to have damaged egos for him to repair, because it looks like the alien has taken quite an interest in the parts to the ATV. Evidently, he's mechanically minded and has already started mentally assembling it. I think he'll stay here and watch our husbands put it together."

Connie proved to be correct. When she, Dianne, and Charlie started walking toward home, the alien glanced at them briefly; then, he returned to watching Moose and Jerry.

Two hours later, with a bowl of salad on the table and a pizza in the oven, Dianne and Connie stepped out onto the front porch to watch Moose, Jerry, and the alien drive up in the new ATV. Apparently, Jerry had claimed captain's privileges, because he was seated in the driver's seat.

The ATV had two front seats and a truck bed able to accommodate 1000 pounds of cargo, or a seat for two people could be installed in the bed leaving room for 500 to 600 pounds of cargo. The vehicle was four-wheel drive with each wheel having its own electric motor. Its fairly large low-pressure tires were equipped with lugs, giving them excellent traction. This feature made it possible for the ATV to be used as a light tractor to pull soil-working equipment.

Acting like children with a new toy, all admired the ATV. "I think Dianne and I should take it for a test-drive after dinner," Connie said.

"Good idea," agreed Dianne, "and we can pick up some of the supplies that came down today."

"I'm hungry," stated Moose. "And I smell something good."

"Dinner does smell good," Jerry said. "And it's such a pleasant evening that I think we should eat outdoors."

A few minutes later, all were seated at the picnic table. Before they started eating, Jerry said, "It's time to introduce ourselves to our guest."

One by one, the pioneers pointed to themselves and announced their names. The alien repeated each name. Then, he pointed at himself and said, "Zebronyrick."

Each pioneer struggled with the name attempting to correctly pronounce it, so the alien slowly said, "Zeb-ron-y-rick."

After each pioneer correctly pronounced his name, the alien smiled in satisfaction. Then, he pointed at himself and said, "Zeb."

"Why didn't he just say Zeb in the first place?" Moose mumbled.

"I think our guest found some amusement with our struggle to pronounce his full name," noted Jerry. "Perhaps, he has a sense of humor."

Zeb was the last to begin eating. He watched each pioneer for a few moments; then, he imitated their manners. First, he tasted the salad. After a few moments, he looked at Dianne and Connie and smiled in approval. Then, he tasted the pizza; again, he smiled in approval.

"Apparently, our dinner is a big hit with our guest," Dianne said to Connie.

"This might be the first time he's been out to eat in thirty years," commented Connie.

"That would make this a special occasion for him," noted Dianne. "Especially, when you consider that he's eating a meal prepared by beings from another planet."

"He's definitely enjoying the occasion," stated Connie.

A half-hour later, Connie asked Dianne, "Are you ready to go for a ride?"

"Yeah, let's go. We can do these dishes later."

"Why don't you just enjoy yourselves," suggested Moose. "I'll take care of the cleanup duties."

Dianne smiled at Moose. "Thank you." She turned to Connie and said, "I love it when my husband is well-fed. It always puts him in such a good mood."

"What do you mean? I'm always in a good mood," stated Moose.

Dianne looked at Moose affectionately for a few moments. "Well, I suppose that's true."

A couple minutes later, Dianne and Connie were in the ATV heading south. "This is great!" exclaimed Connie. "We'll no longer have to walk everywhere we go."

"And we won't have to carry everything that we want to move around," added Dianne.

"Life here on the plateau will be easier. I wish we had one of these down on the beach."

"Maybe you could talk your husband into having another one sent down."

"That shouldn't be too difficult," responded Connie.

While watching Dianne and Connie drive off in the new ATV, Moose said, "They're acting like they just took delivery on a new car."

"In other words, they're as excited as we are," commented Jerry.

Zeb picked up the mood of the occasion and seemed pleased that everyone was enjoying the new vehicle. Noticing this, Jerry said, "I think our guest is starting to realize that it would be very beneficial to him to join our society."

"That may be, but he still has to prove himself trustworthy."

"If I were a gambler, I would bet that he will."

"Time will tell," stated Moose. "But your comment did have a word in it that I like."

"What word is that?"

"Beneficial," replied Moose. "I think it would be very beneficial to us to bring down another ATV. We could use it for getting around on this island. Most of the waterfront is passable to an ATV. The few places that aren't could easily be made passable by moving a few rocks or clearing some brush or cutting down some trees."

"In other words, you want to build a road around the island."

"A rough trail that's passable to an ATV could hardly be thought of as a road."

407

"That's true, but whether we call it a trail or a road, once we start driving around instead of walking around, we will have taken a significant step in the creation of a modern society."

"I'm ready for that step," declared Moose.

"Are you saying that your legs aren't as young as they used to be?"

"I believe I could still keep up with you in a foot-race, but I'm ready for the convenience of having some wheels to get around with."

"I'm not sure that's a good idea,"

"What do you mean?"

"As much as you eat all the time, you're probably going to get fat if you start driving instead of walking."

"With all the work that we have to do to turn this island into a comfortable home, I think I'll get more than enough exercise to burn off the excess calories. Besides that, I don't eat much more than you eat."

"I don't know about that; it seems like you're always hungry."

"Why shouldn't I be? Look at the active outdoor life we live. Good clean living is supposed to make me hungry."

"Are you sensitive about your voracious appetite?" Jerry joked.

"I'm not sensitive about it, but you seem to be implying that there's something wrong with me because I've been blessed with a highly developed sense of taste that enables me to enjoy the delicate flavors of choice foods. In addition to my highly refined sense of taste, I live an energetic life style that stimulates my appetite. Also, I'm constantly being tempted by an abundant supply of delicious delicacies."

"You sure use lots of big words to explain something you're not sensitive about."

"Being able to express myself fluently is one of the benefits of my extensive education. And I might add that I've found that this is a valuable asset. On more than one occasion, my expert ability to communicate has allowed me to present my point of view in a way that allowed me to prevail over others with differing points of view."

"Are you telling me that you rarely lose an argument?"

"I am exceedingly articulate, and I can't remember the last time I failed to persuade others to accept my opinion."

"Aren't you too young for that?"

Puzzled by Jerry's question, Moose asked, "Too young for what?"

"It seems to me that you're too young for your memory to be going bad."

"There's nothing wrong with my memory! In fact, it has just occurred to me that I promised our wives I'd do the dishes, so before I do anything else, I suppose I should do that, or they might be looking for an explanation as to why I didn't keep my promise."

"That shouldn't be difficult for one who has an expert ability to prevail over others with a differing point of view."

"But wives can sometimes be quite emotional and unwilling to consid-

408

er a well thought out explanation."

"So your enhanced ability to express yourself does have some limitations."

Moose considered Jerry's remark for a few moments. Then, he said, "I think I'll start by putting away the leftover food."

Jerry chuckled. "I'm surprised that there is any leftover food."

"Zeb and I did justice to the meal, but we could've used a bit more help from you."

"I ate my share, but I never could keep up with you. I think Zeb kept up with you only because he hasn't eaten much during the past week, and now, he has some catching up to do."

Jerry noticed that Zeb became quite attentive when he heard his name mentioned, but he did not seem alarmed. Apparently, the mood of the conversation put Zeb's mind at ease, thought Jerry, as he turned to Moose and said, "I'm going to take Zeb inside and use the video screen to give him some general information about us, like where we're from, how we got here, and some scenes from Earth.

"Well, don't give him anything he might use against us. He is an alien, and we don't know if we can ..."

Moose's comment was interrupted by a loud cry of alarm from Zeb who was urgently pointing skyward. Moose and Jerry quickly turned to see what Zeb was alarmed by. What they saw filled them with terror. There was a huge pterodactyl in the midst of an attack dive with their wives as the target. Instantly, Moose and Jerry leapt from their chairs and grabbed their rifles, but before they could aim and shoot, the calm, quiet air of the evening was shattered by a savage blood-curdling scream. The diving pterodactyl broke off its attack to answer the challenge, but it was too late. As he spread his wings to pull out of his dive, the big male pterodactyl from Western Island struck him, quickly burying his talons into his back. He finished the job by grabbing his victim's neck with his powerful beak and clamping tight with a bone crushing crunch. The big male released his mortally wounded victim, which fell from the sky crashing onto the plateau with a dull thud a mere three yards from Connie and Dianne.

Sitting in the driver's seat, Connie quickly sped away from the fallen pterodactyl, because she didn't know if it was dead or just wounded. In the passenger's seat, Dianne drew her 10.5 millimeter pistol and turned to face the fallen creature. She also made quick wary glances skyward looking for other attackers, but she saw only the big male from Western Island, circling the scene looking very much like an alert sentry.

Meanwhile, Moose and Jerry were running toward their wives with rifles ready to fire, closely followed by Zeb in his self-propelled wheelchair. When they arrived, a noticeably shaken Dianne stepped out of the ATV and turned to her husband for support. After receiving a reassuring hug, she silently gazed at the fallen pterodactyl for a few moments. She turned to Connie and shuddered. "One of us was only a few seconds away from becoming a meal for that creature."

"We haven't even been here three weeks, and this is my second brush with death," Connie commented, soberly. "In both cases, I would've been torn apart and eaten by a predator."

"That's a chilling thought," stated Jerry, as he wrapped an arm around his wife to comfort her.

Dianne pointed skyward. "We're fortunate that the big guy circling up there came to our rescue."

"I wonder why he did that," questioned Connie. "Was it out of loyalty to us for having helped him, or was he just killing an enemy?"

"I don't know if we'll ever know the answer," Jerry replied. "But whatever the reason, I'm glad that the big guy was in position to protect you and that he did the job so effectively. Zeb yelled out a warning, but it all happened so quickly that I don't know if we could've shot the attacker in time to save you."

Moose pointed at the fallen pterodactyl. "I think we should find out if it's dead; if it isn't, we need to finish the job."

The pioneers cautiously approached the pterodactyl with their guns ready for action. However, when they got close to it, it was obvious that the creature was dead.

Having recovered from the shock of their sudden brush with death, Dianne and Connie proceeded to inspect the wounds inflicted by the big male from Western Island. The severity of the neck injuries caught their attention immediately. "I am amazed at how much force these pterodactyls can exert when they close their beaks," Connie said. "This one's neck isn't just broken in two spots; the bone is completely crushed."

"The bones of a flying creature are usually hollow and very light, making them easier to crush than those of a land animal," stated Dianne. "But even so, I'm surprised at the amount strength that has been shown, and I wouldn't want that beak clamped onto any part of me."

Connie examined the talon-inflicted wounds. "Judging from the amount of blood on this creature's back, I would guess that one of the big guy's talons ripped a large hole in a main artery."

Dianne stared at the dead pterodactyl's talons. "Those are awesome weapons. They look like curved daggers, and we were only seconds away from an agonizing death inflicted by them." Dianne trembled at the thought.

"We're lucky that the big guy used his deadly weapons to save us," stated Connie. "I wish I knew if he was killing an enemy, or if we actually do have a loyal 400-pound flying guard dog."

"It's difficult to believe that a fierce, wild creature who doesn't need us for anything would voluntarily decide to be our protector, but it's starting to look like that might be the case," Dianne said.

"But why would he do that?" questioned Connie.

"We can only speculate," replied Dianne. "But it's possible that ptero-

410

dactyls are intelligent enough to think about the future. Considering what the big guy has seen us do, he may have concluded that we'd be valuable friends to have in case he ever needs our help."

"This dead pterodactyl gives us an opportunity to gain some direct information about their intelligence," stated Connie. "We can open the skull, remove the brain, and study it in the lab. While we won't be able to determine how intelligent these creatures are, we should be able to determine their potential."

"It's an opportunity that we need to take advantage of," Dianne said. "In fact, we should study all of its organs."

"If we're going to do that, we need to get started soon," stated Connie. "Once the postmortem processes have had a chance to do their damage, it'll be more difficult to get the information we want."

"And there's also the possibility that nocturnal scavengers could eat most of this carcass by morning," commented Dianne. "There are lots of birds here, and I suspect that even those that aren't scavengers will have a difficult time passing up an easy meal."

"That's a good point," agreed Connie. "I am tired, but if we get started right away, we should still get a good night's sleep. It shouldn't take more than a few hours to remove and preserve tissue samples and organs for future study."

"I think we should also open up its digestive tract and attempt to determine what kinds of creatures it has preyed on in recent days," suggested Dianne.

A rather squeamish looking Moose said, "You're going to open up this creature's guts after the meal we just ate?"

Surprised by Moose's comment, Dianne said, "Why not? We are scientists, and one of the reasons we're here is to study alien life."

"But the sight and smell of partially digested prey might be enough to cause me to lose my dinner."

"You don't have to watch us, but it would be nice if you would help us get set up," Dianne said. "We are going to need some lights, because it's going to be dark before we finish. Also, you could stand guard in case some overly aggressive scavengers show up."

Before Moose could respond, Jerry said, "I think we can do that."

Turning to Moose, Jerry said, "We don't have much of a breeze, but we can take advantage of what little there is by doing guard duty upwind from the carcass. Then, your highly refined sense of taste won't overreact to the odors and cause you to lose your dinner."

Moose grinned. "This is one of those rare occasions when my ability to appreciate delicate flavors is a burden that I have to endure."

"The next couple hours will put you to the test," Jerry said.

"What test is that?"

"I'm going to find out if you'll make a good hunting partner for me?"

411

"What does being a connoisseur of fine foods have to do with being a good hunting partner?"

"Nothing, but being easily nauseated could be a problem. When we make a kill, we'll most likely have to butcher it quickly and make a hasty retreat with whatever we can carry. There won't be time to nurse nausea problems caused by the odors involved in the butchering process."

Jerry noticed that a blank expression appeared on Moose's face while his eyes were staring off in the distance as if he was trying to see the distant countryside. After a few moments, Jerry said, "It looks to me like you're trying to visualize a successful hunt."

"I was, and you're right; there won't be time to contend with nausea. So I'm going to find out just how serious this problem might be."

"How do you plan to do that?"

"If you'll do the guard duty, I'll assist our wives with the dissection of this pterodactyl."

"That will be a realistic test."

Looking up, Jerry said, "I need to stay here and guard the carcass while you help our wives get the things they need. All these birds that are beginning to show up look hungry. You need to bring me a shotgun."

Moose looked at the birds. "They remind me of sea gulls, and if they're like sea gulls, they'll eat just about anything that's edible."

A short time later, Connie, Dianne, and Moose started dissecting the pterodactyl. At first, Moose had a difficult time controlling his queasy stomach. However, as time progressed, his determination to maintain control allowed his mind to make steady progress in gaining dominance over the nausea, which was a deep-seated reaction to blood and guts that dated back to a bad childhood experience. By the time three hours had gone by, Moose gained complete control over his nausea problem, and the trio finished removing and preserving organs and specimens of interest.

From the beginning, one of Dianne's assistants onboard the Challenger used Charlie's video capabilities to record every aspect of the procedure. But now that the operation was finished, Charlie was marched a short distance away from the carcass, so that his cameras could be used to record the expected feeding frenzy of the flying scavengers that were getting increasingly more bold and impatient. Leaving the scene, Connie said to Dianne, "I am exhausted, and I feel like collapsing into bed for about ten hours. If I had a coin, I'd flip it with you for the first shower."

"Why don't you go first; I want to check our specimens to make sure they're properly preserved."

By the time the pioneers traveled 25 yards, the scavengers had already begun fighting over the choice parts of what remained of the dead pterodactyl. An almost deafening noise was created by the loud squawking of challenges and counter challenges, occasional shrieks of pain issued by fighting competitors, and the sound of hundreds of flapping wings.

The pioneers stopped to look back at the tumultuous scene, but were unable to see anything because neither Aphrodite nor Nocturne was in the night sky, and they had only starlight to see with. Noting the sounds of combat, Moose said, "Those birds must have excellent night vision if they can see well enough to fight."

"Nocturnal hunters and scavengers do have excellent night vision," stated Dianne.

"I know, but I'm still amazed by it," Moose said. "They're carrying on like it's daylight out here, and I can't see a thing."

Besides its headlights, the ATV was equipped with a brilliant searchlight. Currently seated in the driver's seat, Jerry said, "I'd like to see what's going on back there."

Jerry turned the ATV around and pointed the headlights at the scene. He used the searchlight to pan the area above the remains of the pterodactyl. Moose immediately said, "They remind me of a school of piranhas in the midst of a feeding frenzy. There must be hundreds of them. Where did they all come from?"

"They arrived one and two at a time while you were working on the pterodactyl," replied Jerry.

"That's a terrifying scene!" exclaimed Connie, as a cold chill ran up and down her spine. "If we'd been caught in the middle of that, we could easily have been overwhelmed, and then, we might have become part of the meal."

"We would've been very busy with our pistols," remarked Moose, "but there are hundreds of them."

"The barrel of my shotgun would've gotten hot," stated Jerry. "But I would not have been able to kill those that were close to you."

"The loud banging of rapidly firing guns is unfamiliar to them and may've scared away those that we didn't kill," commented Moose.

"That's a comforting theory," stated Connie. "But I'm sure glad we didn't have to test it."

"I wonder if these birds ever make a massive group attack on a large living creature in an attempt to overwhelm it with the force of numbers," questioned Jerry. "If they do, they could pose a serious danger to us, especially to our children."

"I haven't seen them prey on anything except marine life along the waterfront and small creatures of opportunity," responded Dianne. "I can only speculate, but I don't think they have the intelligence to form a large group for the purpose of bringing down a large animal. I believe this group formed in response to the scent of blood and the possibility of an easy meal. Rather than work together to attack a large animal, I think they're more likely to fight each other for a share of an already dead animal."

"But what if a small child became injured in a way that caused bleeding, and the scent of the blood attracted a large number of these birds?"

Jerry asked. "Would the child look vulnerable enough so that they would attack? I'm concerned that the more aggressive members of the flock might attack the child while he's still alive in order to gain advantage over their competitors. Then, the rest would join in, and the child would quickly be overwhelmed and devoured."

"That's a scene out of a horror movie," responded Dianne with a cold shudder. "We need to find out if our children really do face that risk."

"I know how we can do that," stated Moose.

"What do you have in mind?" Jerry asked.

"Charlie has been invaluable to us. We could make a child-sized version of him, march him into an area frequented by these birds, have him fall in a fake accident, and then have him stumble along with blood oozing from a fake injury. Then, we watch the birds to see how they react."

"I like the idea," Jerry said. "When can you get the project started?"

"I'll put in a call to the Challenger yet tonight. Some of the people who helped me make Charlie will still be up. They can start the project in the morning."

"How long do you think it will take them to finish it?"

"By working in shifts around the clock, they should be able to do it in less than a week."

"Good! When they're done, we'll bring it down and run the experiment. And whatever response we get from these birds, we'll verify by repeating the experiment several times with variations to see if we always get the same reaction."

The pioneers watched the feeding frenzy until they had seen enough. Then, they headed toward home, looking forward to a night of peaceful sleep inside their rugged habitation capsule. Zeb would be given a thick air mattress to sleep on.

FIFTEEN

An Unexpected Erotic Response

TIME: Day Twenty, Early Evening.

It was a pleasant evening, and the interstellar pioneers were enjoying dinner at their outdoor table. Looking to the south, Connie said, "It's amazing how peaceful this plateau is compared to the wild savagery that went on here last night."

"Last night's dinner was equally peaceful," noted Jerry.

"Maybe that's why I was almost killed," commented Connie. "For the most part, our life here on the plateau has been peaceful, so peaceful that we've become complacent."

Feeling apprehensive, Connie stood up and searched the sky and landscape. Then, she sat down and said, "There doesn't appear to be anything dangerous in our little corner of this planet. The pterodactyls from Western Island are the only big creatures in the area, and they seem to be soaring around purely for the pleasure of flying."

"Maybe they're looking for threats to us," suggested Dianne.

"After the way the big guy saved our lives last night, I'm inclined to agree with you. In fact, I'm starting to think that we just might have a pair of flying guard dogs."

"Time will tell, but in any case, it does look like they'll play a role in our daily life, so I think we should name them."

"Speaking of names, I think we've been using the name *pterodactyl* rather loosely. These creatures look more like giant golden eagles."

"And their talons protrude from webbed feet that look like they belong on a giant goose," stated Moose.

"I've never seen a goose with long, sharp talons," argued Dianne.

"You know what I mean," retorted Moose. "If you cut off the talons, the feet would look like they belong on a giant goose."

Noticing that Dianne was quietly laughing, Moose said, "You're developing quite a talent for making me think you're serious when you're not, and I fell for it again."

"Somehow, I get the feeling you enjoy the attention," responded Dianne while affectionately smiling at Moose, who returned the smile.

After a few moments, Dianne turned to Connie. "You're right. These creatures are significantly different than Earth's extinct pterodactyls, but we have good reason to believe that these creatures have had an additional 500 million years to evolve."

"Evolution is a slow process," noted Connie, "but with that much time, even a slow process can produce marvelous results."

"These pterodactyls are an outstanding example of that," stated Jerry. "They not only dominate the sky, but they're also able to dive deep and catch fish. As if that's not enough, they can also prey on land animals."

"Apparently, the one we dissected last night preferred land animals," Dianne said. "I wasn't able to find any fish parts in its digestive system."

"And it had every intention of eating one of us," added Connie.

"But the local king of the sky put a stop to that," stated Moose.

"That's the name we're looking for," Connie said.

"What is?" Moose asked.

"King," responded Connie.

"I was just making a comment," Moose said. "But I think the big guy just might be the boss in this area as far as pterodactyls are concerned. He's the biggest one I've studied so far. His wing span exceeds 52 feet, and the computer estimates his weight to be nearly 400 pounds."

"When I was a kid, we had a dog named King," Dianne said. "He was a big German shepherd, and he was intelligent, loyal, and protective. I like the idea of naming the big guy King."

"If we name him King, then Queen is the obvious name for his mate," suggested Connie.

The pioneers looked at each other and nodded in agreement. "Okay, it's official," Jerry said. "Their names are King and Queen."

After a few moments of silence, Jerry asked Connie, "How did the ankle surgery go?"

"I don't know how Zeb broke that ankle, but it was a nasty multiple fracture with torn ligaments. It took us three hours to repair everything."

"How long will it take for it to heal?"

"He's an alien, and I don't know how quickly his body can heal an injury as serious as this one. However, if I had a similar injury, it would probably take two months before I could begin to gingerly walk on it and an additional two months to fully recover."

"So it's possible he'll be dependent on us for at least two months."

"I think that's a reasonable guess."

"So if he has any common sense at all, he'll avoid doing anything to alienate us for at least two months."

"That's what I would expect of him," agreed Connie. "In fact, he might even look for ways to be helpful in an attempt to convince us that it's to our advantage to care for him."

"Even to the extent of being cooperative with our objectives?"

"I think so. Why? What do you have in mind?"

"Zeb has lived here for a long time, and there's lots of information he could give us. We don't know what he'll do when he no longer needs us, but while he's dependent on us, he should be cooperative. So I think we should begin teaching him English. If he's willing to work with us, I think we can teach him enough in just a few weeks so he can carry on a conversation with us. Before he's back to normal, I'd like to know how and why he became separated from his colleagues and where he thinks they are. On a more casual note, I'd like to sit down next to a campfire and listen to him tell stories about his life on this planet."

"My only concern with your plan is that if he becomes fluent in our language, he might be able to learn how to get into our computers and operate some of our key pieces of equipment," Moose warned. "If that were to happen, and if he turns out to be a bad individual; then, when he no longer needs us, he could do serious damage to us."

"But that possibility is two to four months away. If everything goes according to plan, everyone will be down here by then, and there'll be enough of us to keep an eye on him. If we have any reason to be suspicious, we can always take appropriate action."

"But teaching him English before we know him does expose us to additional risk," argued Moose.

"That's true," admitted Jerry, "but teaching him English will help us get to know him sooner. Besides that, it's not just him that we need to worry about. We must find out what happened to his colleagues. If they're still alive, have they multiplied and prospered? Where are they? How strong are they? Are they a threat to us?"

Moose thought about it for a few moments; then, he said, "Despite my concern, it looks like we have to increase our present risk to gain knowledge that might reduce our future risk."

"That's how I see it," stated Jerry. "However, I don't think the risks involved in teaching him English will be all that great, if we're careful to teach him nothing more than simple conversational English. To get into our computers and steal a key piece of equipment, he would need a good understanding of the sophisticated technical language involved. And we aren't going to teach him that."

"Let's not forget his telepathic abilities," cautioned Dianne. "Once he understands even simple English, he may be able to read our thoughts and probe our memories, and that could lead to all sorts of problems."

"But could he do that to an individual without the individual being aware of what's happening?" Jerry asked.

"That question is impossible to answer," replied Dianne. "We simply don't know enough about telepathic powers."

"Maybe Rex could tell us if it's possible to telepathically probe someone's mind without the person being aware of it," Jerry said.

"I'm sure he knows as far as his species is concerned," commented

Dianne. "But his knowledge of the human mind is limited."

"But there was an extensive exchange of information between your mind and his mind through the use of telepathic images," stated Jerry. "He may have learned enough about your mind to at least have an opinion."

"Michelle is in contact with Rex and Shannon every day. She could explain our situation to them and see what the response is. However, what they say might only apply to my mind. For whatever reason, both Rex and Zeb communicated telepathically only with me."

"Are you implying that there might be something unique about your mind that allows telepathic communication?" Connie asked.

"That's a possibility."

"If that's the case, then it's possible that only your mind would be open to covert telepathic probing by Zeb once he understands English," Connie suggested.

"That's possible, but again, we don't know."

"We seem to have more questions than answers," commented Jerry.

"Unfortunately, that's true," agreed Dianne. "But humans have never before had to face the possibility of having their minds covertly probed by a being with telepathic powers. We don't know much about this, but eventually, we'll find answers to our questions. Until then, we need to do what we can to protect ourselves."

After a bit of silence, Jerry said, "The possibility of having our minds covertly probed is another reason to teach him only basic conversational English until we know him better. We have extensive vocabularies, and much of what's in our minds is in the form of technical terms that Zeb won't be able to understand, even if he is able to probe our minds covertly. So let's begin teaching him English, but let's keep it simple."

"That should protect the technical knowledge in our minds," Dianne agreed. "However, thoughts and memories of life's everyday experiences will not be protected."

"I think that's a risk we'll have to take," stated Jerry. "He has lived here for a long time and has knowledge that we need."

"Simple English combined with the images he's able to project into my mind should enable me to gain a wealth of information from him," Dianne said.

At that moment, everyone noticed that Moose was smiling broadly. Then, the smile turned into soft laughter. Everyone stared at Moose, patiently waiting for an explanation. When none was given, Dianne said, "All right! I give up! What's so funny?"

"I was just thinking about all the fun Zeb is going to have if he's able to get into my mind and tune in to the memories that I have from the years when I was young and carefree."

Dianne stared at Moose for a few moments. She decided to put her husband on the hot seat. "Why have you mentioned memories from those years rather than memories of the experiences we've had together? Are you implying that the girlfriends you had during your playboy days were more exciting than I am?"

"Whoops! I think I just said the wrong thing," Moose said to Jerry.

"I believe your thinking is correct," Jerry responded, after catching Dianne's expression.

"Well, how do I get out of this one?"

"You're on your own old buddy."

Moose turned to his wife and racked his brain for the right thing to say. After a half-minute of steadily building tension, he said, "I wasn't implying that our life together hasn't been exciting and fulfilling, but when I was single, I lived a recklessly wild lifestyle at times."

Now, it was Dianne's turn. "We had our honeymoon on a starship in interstellar space. We're now living on a wild alien planet inhabited by dinosaurs. And you recently rode a ten-ton styracosaurus into a face-off with a pack of ten-ton T-Rexes. Have you ever had a lifestyle more recklessly wild than ours?"

Moose smiled and gave Dianne a big hug. "You win this one."

While displaying a contented smile of satisfaction, Dianne turned to Jerry. "I think we need to teach Zeb simple English, so he can entertain himself by telepathically exploring my husband's memories."

"Having an alien poking around in my subconscious mind seems rather spooky," commented Moose. "However, I have nothing to hide."

"We don't know if he has the ability to do that," stated Dianne. "But teaching him our language might be the best first step toward finding an answer to that question. We'll just have to stay alert to the possibility that a covert mental probe might be happening."

Facing Dianne, Jerry said, "I agree, and since Zeb has communicated only with you via telepathic images, I think you're in the best position to take the lead in teaching him English."

"I will enjoy doing that," replied Dianne. "But I will need some help, or I won't have much time for research."

"We'll all be available to assist you," responded Jerry.

Dianne nodded. "That still leaves the question of whether or not we should talk to Rex about the possibility that Zeb will be able to covertly probe our minds once he understands English."

"The answer to that question boils down to whether or not we want the people on B-2 to know that one of their kind is living here," Jerry replied.

"What concerns you about that?" Dianne asked.

"In view of the attack we carried out, we undoubtedly have a hate-filled enemy on B-2 with a burning desire for revenge. If they were to find out that one or more of their kind are living here, they might find a way to make contact. At the very least, they could then gain some knowledge that would help them plan an attack."

"But Rex would never tell anyone that one of their people is living here, if he thought that would put us at risk."

"That's true," agreed Jerry, "but Rex has friends and colleagues who know about us. Some of them might have access to the messages we transmit and see them before Rex has had an opportunity to keep them confidential."

Nodding in agreement, Dianne said, "Not only that, but the very question we need an answer to might come into play; and that is, if these humanoids have the ability to covertly probe each other's minds, then it would be impossible for Rex to keep the information confidential."

"That's exactly what concerns me," stated Jerry. "In a war that has gone on for 30 years, we have to assume that each side managed to plant numerous spies. Some of them might be so deeply entrenched that they're still around. Eventually, one of them would find out that one or more of their kind are living here, and that could lead to trouble for us."

"So you're saying that we must not tell Rex about Zeb."

"Not until we know for sure that Zeb is trustworthy."

"That means we need to find out ourselves whether or not Zeb can covertly probe our minds," stated Dianne.

"I don't see any alternative," stated Jerry. "Eventually, we'll have the answer to that question. But until then, we must stay alert for any clues that indicate that our minds are being probed."

Everyone quietly thought about the situation for a short time; then, Moose nonchalantly said, "It seems like our lives have become a bit more complicated ever since we found that shiny piece of metal among the rocks at the north end of this island."

Jerry laughed at the innocent way that Moose intentionally understated the current problem. "That was a rather shocking surprise, but something unexpected can happen at any time, and that's what makes our life such an exciting adventure."

"We haven't had very many dull moments," responded Moose.

"Years ago, when I invited you along on this mission, I did promise you an adventure beyond your wildest dreams."

"You've certainly fulfilled that promise!"

"I have an adventure in mind for tomorrow that I think will continue the fulfillment of that promise," Jerry said calmly.

Before Moose could comment, Connie said, "It's probably something dangerous that has the potential to get someone killed."

Jerry made eye contact with his wife. He nodded in agreement, but his body language seemed to say that he respected the dangers and would be triumphant over them. When he saw that Connie would say nothing more for the time being, he turned to Moose.

"What adventure do you have in mind?" Moose asked in a way that implied that he wasn't sure he really wanted to know.

"First, I want to say that the seafood we've been eating has been excellent, but we've been eating seafood almost every day, and I'm ready for a change in the menu."

"Sounds like we're going hunting," commented Moose.

"I'm hungry for barbecued steak, and I don't mean steak from our food synthesizers. I haven't had a real steak since we left Earth."

"Real steak comes from beef, and there aren't any cattle running around here," noted Moose.

"But there is an abundant supply of dinosaurs ranging in size from very small to the 100-ton sauropods," stated Jerry. "The species I think might be a good source of steaks reminds me of the ostrich in some respects. In fact, I think ostri-dino would be a good name for them."

"I think they're bigger than ostriches," noted Dianne. "However, if their hides were covered with feathers, they would resemble ostriches."

"There are plenty of them roaming the countryside," stated Moose. "In fact, ostri-dinos just might be the most numerous of all the dinosaurs."

"That will make them easy to hunt," stated Jerry. "And if they turn out to be good to eat, killing one occasionally certainly won't hurt the species. They're so numerous that they're probably a prime source of food for many of the predators."

"So what's your plan?" Moose asked.

"There are hundreds of them living in Sauropod Meadow. Some of them drink water out of the lake. If we cruise slowly along the waterfront, it shouldn't take long to find a choice specimen. We simply shoot it, go ashore and quickly carve out some chunks of flesh to make into steaks. Then, we leave before dangerous predators show up. I would like to avoid killing other animals in defense of our kill."

"The one time I went ashore over there, I came within a fraction of a second of being killed," stated Connie.

Dianne looked at Moose. "The only time you went ashore, you could easily have been killed in a fight between T-Rexes and styracosaurs."

Moose turned to Jerry. "I'm not sure our wives approve of your plan."

"It will be dangerous," argued Connie.

All eyes were on Jerry as he thought about how to sell the plan to his wife. After a few moments, he said, "It will be dangerous, but I have an idea how to take some of the danger out of the hunt."

While looking into the eyes of his colleagues, Jerry asked, "Do you remember the day that we landed our first robot lab on top the big boulder in Sauropod Meadow?"

All nodded, then Jerry continued. "We were watching and listening to herds of dinosaurs peacefully grazing in the meadow when all of a sudden a spin-chilling roar reverberated throughout the Challenger. It was the defiant challenge issued by the leader of a group of T-Rexes that boldly marched into the meadow. All creatures except for the giant sauropods ran in response to the challenge."

Dianne shuddered. "Those T-Rexes are part of the danger that you'll face over there."

"That's true," agreed Jerry. "But those T-Rexes can protect us."

Sounding incredulous, Connie asked, "How are you going to get them to do that?"

"That defiant challenge is stored in the Challenger's data banks. If we take a powerful amplifier and a couple large speakers with us, we can sound out that challenge just before we go ashore to butcher our kill. I'd guess that we'll then be alone with our kill for several minutes, and that's all the time we'll need."

Moose grinned broadly. "I think that idea will work, but there's only one problem: we don't have a powerful amplifier or large speakers down here."

"No, we don't, but our personnel shuttle could deliver them to us tomorrow morning. I want to bring down another ATV anyway. I'm sure that each of you has something you'd like brought down. It shouldn't be that hard to fill up the personnel shuttle."

"In view of what happened last night, I think we should bring down a radar unit to monitor pterodactyl activity in this area," Connie suggested.

"I agree," Dianne said.

Jerry thought about the request. "The radar could be monitored by a computer that would send out a warning signal whenever a pterodactyl gets too close. Our communicators could be programmed to receive the signal and sound an alarm."

"I really like that idea," declared Connie.

"Me too," echoed Dianne.

"We could also program our communicators to keep the computer informed where each of us is located," Moose suggested. "As long as we are within the radar's range, the computer could monitor pterodactyl activity in each person's vicinity and send out individual warnings."

"That's a great idea," stated Dianne. "The next time some pterodactyl decides to attack, King and Queen might not be around to defend us."

"Not only that, but when all of us are down here, there will be too many of us for them to defend," added Connie.

"Also, we don't know if King was defending us, or if he was killing an enemy," noted Dianne.

Jerry picked up his communicator, called Mike, and relayed his shopping list. Then, each of the pioneers talked to Mike in turn with their shopping lists.

When they were finished, Dianne and Jerry took Zeb into the habitation capsule to begin teaching him English and to give him some information. Jerry used the largest video screen and the computer library to present a star map and show Zeb where they were from. Next, Jerry showed Zeb the Solar System. After showing Zeb Earth as seen from space, Jerry took him on a brief scenic tour of the planet. Obviously deeply interested, Zeb watched in

422

spellbound fascination. When Jerry decided that he had shown Zeb enough, he turned off the video and turned to face Zeb and did his best to present Zeb with an expectant expression that seemed to say, "Okay, now it's your turn."

Zeb responded by heading his wheelchair toward the door. Once outside, he pointed at Alpha Centauri B located just above the horizon in the western sky. Alpha Centauri A had already set.

Jerry turned to Dianne. "I think he just told us where he's from. Let's take him back inside and show him B-2 from space and see if he'll show us which continent he's from."

When they were back inside, Moose and Connie joined them, and Jerry displayed a slowly rotating image of B-2 on the large video screen. Zeb perked up immediately and watched with deep interest. Then, a distant expression appeared on his face that slowly changed to sadness, causing Dianne to say, "I think he's homesick."

While pointing at the slowly rotating image of B-2, Zeb said, "Zebron."

"I think he just told us the name of his home planet," Jerry said. "What we've been calling B-2 is called Zebron by the people who live there."

Zeb moved closer to the video screen, pointed at himself, and then at the continent currently visible on the screen. This caused Dianne and Jerry to look at each other with puzzled expressions. "He just pointed at Rex's home continent," stated Jerry. "But Rex said the manned mission to here came from the other side in the Great War."

"It would appear that someone's not telling the truth," Dianne said.

"Or Zeb might be one of those deeply entrenched spies I mentioned earlier," suggested Jerry.

"That would be incredible!" exclaimed Dianne.

"What do you mean?"

"I think it would be incredible to the point of being unbelievable that a spy could rise high enough in the enemy's air force to be selected to be part of the first manned mission to another star."

"If he pulled that off, he is a very capable individual," stated Jerry.

"This would be a possible explanation for why he was deserted by his colleagues," speculated Moose. "Imagine their reaction if they found out after arriving here that Zeb was a spy."

"We could have Michelle speak to him in Rex's language and see how he reacts," suggested Connie.

While Zeb continued viewing the slowly rotating image of B-2 with a distant, forlorn expression on his face, Jerry thought about Connie's suggestion. After a few moments, he said, "If we do that and find that Zeb is fluent in Rex's language; then, we can delay teaching him English until we find out if we can trust him. Using that approach, only Michelle will be at risk of having her mind covertly probed in a telepathic way. And she doesn't know how to operate either of our shuttles, or the Challenger, or any of the Challenger's essential systems."

"That would limit the amount of damage Zeb could do to us if he turns out to be an enemy," commented Moose.

"But do we want to expose Michelle to the risk?" Connie asked.

"I will discuss the situation with her and Mike and let them decide," stated Jerry.

"I don't think there's much risk to her as long as she's onboard the Challenger and stays off the observation deck," Dianne said. "Rex was only able to telepathically communicate with me when I was on the observation deck. It seems that the energy field generated by Rex's mind was blocked by the metal in the Challenger's hull, but the plastic hull on the observation deck allowed it to pass through."

"If Zeb is fluent in Rex's language, Michelle might not be able to come down here when everyone else does," stated Jerry. "She might have to stay on the Challenger until she feels that she can trust Zeb to stay out of her mind."

"How do you ever trust a professional spy?" Moose asked.

"We don't know if he was a spy," replied Jerry. "We're only speculating."

"But if he was a spy and rose high enough in the enemy's air force to become part of an interstellar mission, then, he is an absolute master of deceit," Moose argued.

"If he was a spy, he may have been chosen for that career because of his telepathic ability," Dianne added. "What I'm trying to say is that his telepathic ability might be far greater than that of others in the society he came from. He may even have received special training in how to use his telepathic ability in covert ways."

"We may be nursing an extremely dangerous individual back to health," warned Moose.

"Because of that possibility, it is imperative that we get answers to all of our questions before he has fully recovered," stated Jerry. "Also, it's imperative that we change our earlier decision and avoid teaching him English until we have good reason to trust him. If Zeb is from the continent he claims to be from, he should understand Rex's language, and it won't be necessary to teach him English if Michelle will agree to talk with him. When I explain the situation to her and Mike, I am confident that she will agree to accept the risk, which should be minimal as long as she stays on the Challenger and off the observation deck."

Speaking to Dianne, Jerry said, "Also, we can supplement Michelle's dialog with Zeb if you'll keep your mind open to telepathically transmitted images from him, and we'll use video to present him with images."

"I don't have any problem with that," responded Dianne. "And if Michelle agrees to talk to Zeb, he'll have ample opportunity to answer our questions and convince us that he is trustworthy."

"One thing I don't understand is that with a full scale war pending, why would a nation want one of its spies on an interstellar mission?" Connie asked. "Wouldn't he have been more valuable in the enemy's air force?"

"To answer that question, I think we have to ask why a nation would launch an interstellar mission when they were planning a full-scale war," responded Jerry. "Maybe they were hoping to find a technologically advanced society on this planet and that there would be technology here that would give them a decisive advantage in the pending war. If Rex's country had no interstellar mission in the works, the only way that they could've protected themselves from such a technological bonanza would've been to place a spy on the mission."

"That sounds reasonable," Connie said. "If you're correct, and Zeb's true role was discovered after arriving here, he's lucky that he was only deserted, he could've been shot."

"Perhaps, his colleagues planned to shoot him, but he stopped them," commented Dianne.

"How?" Connie asked.

"Maybe in a covert way, he telepathically planted suggestions in their minds that deserting him without weapons would be a worse fate than shooting him."

"That would be a unique method of self-defense," stated Jerry. "The possibility that he may be able to do that supports our decision to avoid teaching him English until we've determined that we can trust him to stay out of our minds."

"How soon we can trust him might depend on how soon he feels he can completely trust us," stated Connie. "Right now, he could think that we're only keeping him alive because we want information from him. Likewise, we have to consider the possibility that he's trying to be helpful because he needs us. However, if it turns out that he is from Rex's country, we might be able to completely win his trust by telling him about the horrible war that took place and our part in putting a stop to the final phase of it. If he still has patriotic feelings toward his homeland, he might be motivated to ally himself with us."

"It seems like that would be a normal reaction to what we've done," agreed Jerry. "If our speculations are correct, his knowledge and capabilities will make him a valuable asset to our society, especially when you consider that he may've lived here for 30 years."

"The key test will occur when Michelle appears on the video screen and addresses him in Rex's language," Connie said. "How he reacts might be more important than what he says."

"We might try that tomorrow after breakfast," stated Jerry. "I will discuss it with Mike and Michelle shortly, and if they agree, we'll do it then. In the meantime, you might show him additional scenes from Earth."

Turning to Dianne, Jerry said, "Keep your mind open for telepathic images in case he wants to tell us anything."

Dianne and Connie nodded in acknowledgment of Jerry's request. Then, Jerry contacted Mike and Michelle.

TIME: Day Twenty-One, Shortly After Breakfast.

The pioneers and Zeb were seated in the habitation capsule facing the main video screen. Zeb expected to see more video from Earth, but instead, Michelle appeared on the screen wearing a broad friendly smile. She paused briefly; then, she said, "Hello Zeb! My name is Michelle. Do you understand this language?"

When Michelle spoke, the effect on Zeb was electrifying. He became so excited that he forgot his broken ankle and started to jump up out of his wheelchair, but a jolt of pain from the ankle caused him to sit back down. "Yes, I understand!" he exclaimed. "But how do you know my language?"

"Before we came here, we visited your home planet. We have friends there who are teaching me their language."

"I'm happy they are. I haven't had anyone to visit with in a very long time."

"How long have you been alone?"

A distant expression appeared on Zeb's face as he appeared deeply lost in thought. "It's been so long that I've lost track of time, but I think it might be 30 years."

"I'm amazed that you were able to survive alone on such a hostile planet."

"I've had many close calls, but I've been lucky."

"I suspect that you've had more than luck on your side."

"I had survival training before coming here, but I'm lucky that I never had any injuries like the one I have now. If you people hadn't treated me, I would be dead by now. Please say thank you to your friends for helping me, and tell them that I will find ways to repay them."

Michelle interrupted her dialog with Zeb and told her colleagues what he had just said. Connie felt warmly appreciated upon hearing Zeb's heartfelt expression of thanks for saving his life and repairing his injuries. She smiled at Zeb to let him know that she was happy to hear his expression of appreciation.

Zeb nodded and smiled warmly to indicate that he understood. Then, he noticed that Moose was eager to say something, so he turned his full attention to him.

Moose turned away from Zeb and faced Michelle on the video screen. "Tell Zeb that I'd like to know what he has found that is good to eat."

"It doesn't surprise me that that would be the first thing my husband would want to know," commented Dianne.

After a bit of laughter at Dianne's remark, Moose exclaimed, "Well, it is an important question!"

Wondering what the laughter was about, Zeb asked Michelle for an explanation. After receiving one, Zeb said, "When I was a young man, my

426

friends used to tease me that I had an insatiable appetite for fine foods. Tell Moose that I understand his keen sense of taste."

While Michelle did this, Zeb faced Moose waiting for a reaction. Pleased with Zeb's comment, Moose smiled. "Maybe Zeb and I have a mutual interest to pursue."

After hearing the translation of Moose's comment, Zeb said, "Tell Moose that if he'll take me on a tour of this island, I'll show him which plants produce edible parts and which are especially delicious. The warm moist climate here has produced an abundance of plant life. There are quite a variety of trees and bushes that produce fruit, berries, and nuts. Other plants produce edible seeds. Some plants have stems and leaves that are quite tasty. Some have edible roots."

After Michelle told Moose what Zeb had said, Moose became animated with excitement. He turned to Jerry and exclaimed, "We should skip today's dinosaur hunt and take Zeb on a tour of the island."

"I understand your excitement, but I am hungry for some charbroiled steak. You can tour the island tomorrow."

Reluctantly, Moose said, "Okay, I guess you did have the hunt planned first, but let's not make any other plans for tomorrow. We now have an opportunity to gain a tremendous amount of information in just a few hours that would've taken us months, if not years, to learn."

"The ATV that's coming down today will make it easier to take Zeb on a tour of the island," Jerry said.

"I can't argue with that. We can assemble it tomorrow morning. In the interest of safety, I think we should set up our radar today."

"I can live with that plan," responded Jerry.

Speaking to Michelle, Connie said, "Tell Zeb that I'd like to know about any illnesses, injuries, and infections he's had while living here."

Michelle relayed the request to Zeb, who responded, "I will discuss my medical history with Connie whenever she wants to. I don't think I'll have a very demanding schedule during the next few weeks."

After Michelle relayed the response to Connie, Jerry said, "I'm going to display a slowly rotating image of B-2 on another screen. Ask him to show us the launch site of his interstellar mission."

When Zeb heard the question, he put his finger on a point that Jerry judged to be about 50 miles from one of the mountain fortresses that he had attacked. Knowing that Mike was watching, Jerry said, "Mike, please check our recon data to see if the ruins of a space center are at that location."

When Mike acknowledged the request, Jerry said to Michelle, "I think we may as well be candid. Ask him how he became part of an interstellar mission launched by a country with hostile intentions toward his homeland?"

Michelle relayed the question to Zeb. Then, she continued the conversation with Zeb while translating his responses to her colleagues.

"An uneasy peace existed between our nations during the many years it took to design and build the hardware needed for the interstellar mission. Our politicians felt that a joint historic space mission would promote peace, but our enemy just used us to help pay for the mission. War broke out a few days before we arrived here. I was accused of being a spy, and I was deserted by my colleagues."

"Were you a spy?"

"With a war in progress, I would've been alert for anything that would help my country."

"How many were on your mission?"

"There were eight of us, four from each nation."

"What happened to the other three from your country?"

"Two of them turned out to be spies for the other side. The third was to become my wife, but they forced her to go with them for reproductive reasons. Her name was Zonya."

"Do you know where they went?"

"They built a large raft and incorporated our landing capsule into its structure. I believe they followed the river to the ocean and then used the prevailing winds to sail far to the south."

"Do you know if they're still alive?"

"With my telepathic powers, I stayed in contact with Zonya for as long as I could. However, they sailed beyond the range of my telepathic ability, and I don't know if any of them are still alive."

"Your life must've been filled with terrible emotional pain having to live with the knowledge that your loved one was being held captive."

"My life was filled with great sadness for a long time. I felt helpless, because there was nothing I could do. In effect, my island was my prison. I could not follow them by land, because I did not have adequate weapons. I could not follow them by sea, because I did not have tools to build an ocean going vessel by myself."

"If Zonya is still alive, would you like to see her?"

"Yes!"

"Do you want us to help you find them?"

"I'd like that, but you've done so much for me already that I really cannot ask more of you."

"We need to find them for our own reasons. Maybe you can help us."

"If I were onboard your starship, I could telepathically search for them."

"If we haven't located them by the time our quarantine is over, we may enlist your help."

Mike interrupted the discussion with Zeb with the announcement: "The personnel shuttle is on its way down and should arrive in South Bay in 15 minutes."

"Let's watch the shuttle come in," Jerry said. "I want to unload it right away, so we can head for the countryside for our dinosaur hunt."

"What about our discussion with Zeb?" Michelle asked Jerry.

"I'm going to give him a communicator and take him with us. As much as possible, I want to include him in our everyday life. If he has a communicator, he can stay in contact with you. The kinds of questions he asks and the comments he makes should give us an insight into his personality and character much more quickly than if we don't include him. Besides that, I want him to feel like he's part of our society. That will give him an incentive to be loyal to us if a situation ever comes up where he'll have to make a choice between us and those who deserted him. I don't want there to be any doubt in his mind that he should ally himself with us."

"I agree with you," stated Connie.

A few minutes later, all were in the ATV headed for South Bay. Suddenly, they were jolted by a sonic boom. They stopped, looked up in the northwestern sky, and saw the shuttle begin a 180-degree right turn that would put it into the final leg of its landing approach.

"I love to watch our shuttles land and take off," stated Jerry. "Even though they're rugged and powerful, they always look graceful because their control systems are so finely tuned."

"I also enjoy the smooth graceful way they operate," Connie said. "But I especially appreciate how rugged and dependable they are."

"Are you talking about me or about our shuttles?" Jerry asked.

Connie snuggled up to her husband. "I've never really compared you to our shuttles, but I guess you do have some things in common." Jerry smiled and affectionately put his right arm around his wife while they observed the incoming shuttle.

After the shuttle landed and began taxiing toward South Bay, the pioneers resumed their drive to the south end of the plateau, where they rode their elevator down to the sandy beach. While awaiting the shuttle's arrival, they gazed out over the pristine water and enjoyed the scent of clean air lightly perfumed by flowering plants.

When the shuttle arrived and dropped anchor, the pioneers unloaded it. Then, they returned to the plateau where they watched the shuttle taxi out of South Bay and begin its takeoff run. Upon reaching hydrofoil speed, its powerful NTR roared to life, and in just a few seconds, it leapt off the water and pitched into a steep climb. Deeply impressed by the performance of the powerful vehicle as it rapidly climbed out of sight, Zeb said to Michelle, "That is a marvelous piece of equipment. What is it powered by?"

"It has a nuclear reactor," responded Michelle.

"I suspected that might be the case," commented Zeb. "We had to use chemical rockets on our interstellar voyage, and that greatly limited the scope of our mission. Nuclear rockets were still in an experimental stage when our mission was launched."

"Because of the distance involved, our interstellar voyage would've been impossible with chemical rockets or even nuclear rockets. We used an antimatter propulsion system."

"On my planet, the idea of using antimatter was only a wild theory."

"Well, it does work," declared Michelle.

"I was the pilot on our mission," stated Zeb. "I enjoy flying, but I haven't been flying in a long time, and I'd like a ride on your shuttle."

"You may have an opportunity after our quarantine is over, but that will be Captain J.J.'s decision."

TIME: Day Twenty-One, Early Afternoon.

The pioneers, including Zeb, sailed toward the eastern shore of Clear Lake. With a mostly clear sky and very little wind, they deployed their solar sails and cruised at 12 mph.

Pointing skyward toward the northwest, Connie said, "It looks like we'll soon have an operational test of our new radar warning system."

Suspecting that Connie was pointing at approaching pterodactyls, everyone looked up to see them. "I think they're about a half-mile away," Jerry said. "If they keep coming toward us, we'll get our first warning at 500 yards. At 300 yards, we'll get a second warning. At 100 yards, our communicators will sound off with loud, urgent sounding screeches that will be impossible to ignore."

The pterodactyls kept coming, and as programmed, everyone's communicator sounded an alarm at 500 yards and a second alert at 300 yards. The pterodactyls passed directly over the pioneers, but the urgent 100-yard alarm did not occur because they were flying above 300 feet.

"I like it!" exclaimed Connie. "It might save one of our lives someday."

"I'm glad we have it," Jerry said. "We should've installed it sooner."

"What does the third warning sound like?" Connie asked.

In answer to the question, Jerry contacted the radar control computer and directed it to send out the 100-yard alarm, and everyone's communicator began shrilly shrieking. Even though she expected it, Connie was so startled by the sudden sharp sounds that she flinched and exclaimed, "You're right! That sound is impossible to ignore!"

About a half-mile beyond the boat, the pterodactyls started circling. Noticing this, Moose said, "It looks like it's time for a seafood lunch."

Moose hardly finished speaking when one of the creatures dove into the lake. Moose picked up a pair of binoculars for a better view of the action. Less than 20 seconds after the pterodactyl dove in, large fish were frantically leaping out of the water. The airborne pterodactyl quickly grabbed one of these with its talons. Within seconds, the other pterodactyl emerged from the lake with a fish securely clamped in its beak.

"I've seen them do this several times," Moose said. "But I'm still amazed at how deadly efficient they are."

Shortly, the pterodactyls again flew over the pioneers on their way

430

home. Watching them closely, Moose said, "The fish captured by the one that was in flight is really huge. I'll bet it weighs a hundred pounds. I'd like to catch one of those."

"This isn't a fishing trip," responded Jerry. "It's a hunting trip."

"I know, but if we changed course a little bit, we could sail right through the area where those fish are. And if we slowed down, I could put a lure in the water and troll on our way through. It wouldn't delay us that much, and I might catch one of the big ones."

Intervening on Moose's behalf, Connie said, "From a medical perspective, I think Moose has caught a severe case of fishing fever. I recommend that you honor his request, so that we don't have to watch him suffer for the rest of the day."

"That's the best medical advice I've heard in a long time," declared Moose, grinning broadly.

Jerry looked at Moose, then at his wife, then at Dianne, who said, "I don't want to listen to him snivel about the big one that he might've caught. So I think we should do some fishing while we're here. Besides, if we catch one, we'll have a chance to check out one more species of fish."

"I think I've been out-voted," stated Jerry. "Get your gear ready," he said to Moose. "I'm going below to use the sonar to locate those fish. I'll take you through the thickest part of the school."

"That's the kind of talk I like to hear," declared Moose.

A short time later, as they approached the large school of fish, Moose said, "I think we should pull in our solar sails and outriggers. If I manage to hook a big one, he's going to be all over the place before I tire him out and land him. I don't want to risk tangling the line on the outriggers or damaging the solar sails."

"Good idea," agreed Jerry.

A few minutes later, with the boat in a clean configuration and running on battery power, they headed into the school of fish towing a large triple-jointed lure designed to act like a crippled fish. In just a few minutes, Moose's fishing pole bent almost in half when the lure was savagely struck by a hungry fish.

Moose fought the wildly active fish until his arms and shoulders ached with pain and cried out for rest, but the battle continued. In its struggle for freedom, the fish swam with speed and power, abruptly reversing direction numerous times. It alternated between heading for the bottom and leaping out of the water, but all to no avail, for it was securely hooked. After a half-hour had gone by, Moose and Jerry landed the fish.

"That's the biggest fish I've ever caught in a lake!" Moose exclaimed. "I'll bet it weighs over a hundred pounds."

"Easily over a hundred," agreed Jerry.

"Aren't you glad we talked you into this?" Moose asked.

431

"Yes, but I still want charbroiled steak."

"Let's go get some," stated Moose. "If this fish is good to eat, I'll freeze part of it and smoke part of it. It'll be part of the feast that we're planning for our colleagues when they come down in about ten days."

"If everything goes as planned, we'll start bringing them down sooner than that," commented Jerry.

"At this time, I have no medical reason to prevent that," Connie said.

"In four to six days, we'll have the genetic blueprint for Zeb's immune system," added Dianne. "And we'll know how closely it compares to our immune systems."

"I'm betting that the comparison will be favorable," stated Jerry. "If it is, and the four of us pass our medical exams, then, everyone will be free to come down. I think charbroiled steak would be a delicious addition to the welcoming feast."

The pioneers deployed their solar sails and resumed their voyage to the countryside. A half-hour later, they arrived at the location of Moose's styra-cosaurus/T-Rex encounter. Here, they launched two RPVs. Jerry flew one to the north and Moose flew one to the south.

A few minutes later, Jerry announced, "I've found a herd of ostri-dinos grazing in Sauropod Meadow, and some of them are only a hundred yards from the lake."

Jerry returned his RPV and put the boat on a course toward the herd. Fifteen minutes later, they arrived and dropped anchor 100 yards offshore.

After inspecting the herd, Jerry said, "They don't seem to be thirsty; they're just peacefully grazing."

"How far inland are you prepared to go for a steak dinner?" Moose asked.

"I'd like to stay close to the water."

"I like that plan," agreed Connie.

"I do too," stated Jerry. "But the fact that they're peacefully grazing indicates that they're not concerned about predators, so there probably aren't any around at the moment."

"The saber-toothed cats that almost killed me were so well hidden that we didn't know they were there," Connie argued. "These ostri-dinos are about the right size to be good prey for those cats. If some of them are downwind and concealed, the herd won't be aware of them."

"That's a good point," agreed Jerry. "So I want you and Dianne to launch two RPVs and thoroughly search this area for predators."

Turning to Moose, Jerry said, "Check the amplifier and speakers. Make sure they're ready to blast out the T-Rex challenge."

A half-hour passed by, and none of the ostri-dinos came to the lake to drink. "I don't think they're thirsty," Jerry said. "And the herd seems to be slowly drifting away from the lake, so we have to go inland a bit."

"I wish you wouldn't," stated Connie.

"Looking into Connie's eyes, Jerry asked, "Have you found any predators?"

432

"No!" she responded. Dianne also said, "No."

"We'll be careful," Jerry said. "Let's move closer to shore."

After moving in to about 25 yards offshore and dropping anchor, Jerry turned to Moose and said, "Grab your rifle. Let's go hunting."

Jerry turned to Dianne and Connie. "Have your rifles ready in case we need help, and be ready to blast out the T-Rex challenge."

Moose and Jerry stepped into the small boat and rowed to shore. After beaching the boat, they looked around warily. Unable to discover anything of a threatening nature, they began stealthily moving closer to the herd.

At about 50 yards, Jerry selected an animal on the edge of the herd that he thought might be a source of some choice cuts. Jerry raised his rifle and took aim, but the animal moved a few steps with its head bobbing around. Jerry waited patiently, because he wanted a good clean head shot. When the animal stopped moving and returned to grazing, its head was fairly stable for a few seconds, which was all the time Jerry needed. His rifle boomed, and the animal dropped right where it stood, never knowing what hit it.

The sound of the rifle shot was followed immediately by the loud T-Rex roar from the speakers on the boat. Instantly, the ostri-dino herd stampeded inland, and the entire area became quiet in response to the deafening roar.

Jerry and Moose ran up to the fallen ostri-dino, which was still kicking even though its brain was fatally injured. Jerry circled the animal and approached from its back. Then, he drew his long sharp hunting knife and cut into the animal's neck searching for a major artery. Almost instantly, his knife found a main artery, and the fallen animal's still beating heart sent hot blood gushing out, which formed a small pool.

"You're really a bloodthirsty cutthroat!" Moose exclaimed.

"It might look that way, but this is an essential part of the job. By bleeding the animal, we'll get much better steaks, and this will quickly complete the dying process."

Moose accepted Jerry's response without comment while warily searching the surrounding area for danger. He looked at the still bleeding ostri-dino. "What a strange looking creature. Why would an animal have wings if it can't fly?"

"The wings aren't large enough to allow flight," responded Jerry. "But they're large enough to help the animal make abrupt turns when running at high speeds. A closely pursuing predator without wings might have a larger turning radius, allowing the ostri-dino to gain distance on the predator."

"That sounds reasonable," commented Moose, as he studied the ostri-dino for a few moments. "Apparently, they use their wings a lot, because they have very well developed breast muscles, much like birds that fly."

Jerry nodded in agreement; then, noting that the bleeding had slowed to a small trickle, he said, "It's time to get our meat and leave."

Jerry knelt down next to the animal and expertly peeled back a section of hide to reveal breast muscle. He cut away several pieces of flesh and put

433

them in tough plastic bags that he zip-locked shut.

Jerry contacted Connie. "Blast out the T-Rex challenge again."

Almost immediately, Moose and Jerry were hit by the deafening T-Rex roar. Moose trembled. "That roar sends shivers up and down my spine; even though I know it's only coming from the speakers on our boat."

"I have more butchering to do," stated Jerry. "If there are any predators in the area, I want to keep them away from us."

Jerry moved to the upper part of the legs, peeled back the skin, and cut several pieces of thigh meat, which he stuffed into plastic bags. He stood up and looked at all the meat bags. "Not a bad hunt. I think we have about 150 pounds of fresh meat."

"I hope it's edible and tastes good," Moose said.

Looking skyward, Jerry said, "I think we should get out of here. The sea birds that showed up in large numbers on the plateau the other night are arriving. Other scavengers can't be too far behind."

Once again, Jerry asked for the T-Rex roar. Then, he loaded the bags of meat onto two backpack frames. Jerry shouldered his pack while Moose stood guard. Then, Moose strapped on his pack while Jerry stood guard.

They took one last look around, before beginning the 150-yard hike back to the lake. They had taken only a few steps when a medium sized T-Rex stepped out of the forest to the south and rapidly marched northward on the beach.

"We got trouble!" exclaimed Moose, as he moved his rifle into a quick fire position. Jerry did the same, but neither man fired; they just closely observed the T-Rex.

After a few moments, Jerry said, "I don't think it has seen us. I'd like to avoid killing it, if possible."

A few moments later, Moose said, "It doesn't seem interested in us or the scent of blood coming from our kill, and what little breeze we have is carrying the scent in that direction. Apparently, it isn't hungry."

"It's not as big as some of the T-Rexes we've seen."

"It looks huge to me!" exclaimed Moose.

"But it's not as big as they get. Maybe we can scare it away with the T-Rex challenge if we turn up the volume to the maximum. If that doesn't work, we can wait a few minutes for it to move on. And if it doesn't, we'll have to kill it. We can't hang around here too long. I don't want to get caught in the middle of a scavenger feeding frenzy."

Jerry contacted Connie who did as requested. When the now even louder T-Rex roar blasted out, the T-Rex on the beach stopped, listened, and headed directly toward the boat at increased speed.

Puzzled by the reaction, but quick to take advantage of it, Jerry said to Connie, "Move farther off shore and head north. Keep blasting out the T-Rex roar. Maybe you can lead this one away from us, so we can get to our boat and out onto the lake."

Dianne and Connie did as directed, and the T-Rex followed even to the point of entering the water. However, it could not swim, so it stayed close to shore.

Seeing that the T-Rex was preoccupied, Jerry said, "Let's run for it, but let's watch our backs. I don't want to be killed by something else while being distracted by a T-Rex."

With haste tempered by caution, Jerry and Moose made their way to the small boat without incident. They pushed off, got in, and rowed straight out into the lake. When they were a safe distance from shore, Dianne and Connie changed course to pick them up.

When they were safely on the sailboat, Moose and Jerry stared at the T-Rex pacing the beach. Its size and obvious killing capability made their spines tingle when they thought about the fact that they had been close enough for it to have charged them.

"That's an awesome killing machine," declared Moose.

"I get the feeling that flirting with danger really gets you high," commented Dianne.

Acting very cool, Moose calmly said, "Well, I'll have to admit that being close to a T-Rex does cause a bit of an adrenaline rush."

"That sounds to me like *a bit of an* understatement," Dianne said.

Moose smiled at his wife in a way that acknowledged the validity of her comment.

"I wonder why that brute ignored the smell of fresh blood and responded to the roar from our speakers with such determination," questioned Jerry.

"I don't know," replied Moose, "but I'm glad it did. If it had charged us, we would've had to kill it. Even lethal hits with explosive bullets might not have prevented it from killing us in its death throes."

Since Zeb was confined to his wheelchair, he wasn't able to participate in the action, but he was a wildly excited spectator and obviously pleased with the outcome of the whole episode. Noticing that his newfound friends seemed to be puzzled by the T-Rex's behavior, Zeb contacted Michelle and said, "Could you please ask Jerry why he called the female T-Rex."

Michelle was puzzled by the inquiry, because she wasn't aware that Jerry had called a female T-Rex. Curious about why the question was asked, she eagerly relayed it to Jerry.

Jerry was also puzzled by the question, but his face lit up with amusement as it began to dawn upon him what he might have unintentionally done. "Tell Zeb that I used the T-Rex challenge to scare away predators. Ask him why he thinks I was calling female T-Rexes."

Michelle relayed the message and question. Then, she translated Zeb's reply. "That wasn't a T-Rex challenge. That was the male T-Rex's mating call. They try to sound as loud and ferocious as possible in an attempt to impress females that are in heat."

Realizing what they had done, the pioneers laughed about it. "Whose idea was that anyway?" Dianne asked.

"It was Jerry's," replied Connie.

Dianne's face lit up with a broad, naughty grin. "Your husband must have some pretty big balls if he feels the need to proposition female T-Rexes. How do you satisfy such a man?" she asked Connie.

Connie flashed Dianne a smile of smug satisfaction. "He usually sleeps pretty good by the time I get done with him; and I might add, I do too."

After making the remark, Connie turned to Jerry and gazed at him affectionately. Jerry responded by saying, "I have no complaints."

Jerry noticed that Moose was chuckling. "What's on your mind that's so funny?"

"I was just thinking about how I'd thought that your idea was a very clever way to scare away predators. Had I realized that we were trying to impress female T-Rexes, I might've been a lot less comfortable when we went ashore."

"I still think it was a clever idea. What creature would want to get caught between a pair of ten-ton T-Rexes with the mating urge?"

"Not me!" exclaimed Moose.

"I wonder how long that T-Rex is going to pace the beach," Connie said.

"She looks very frustrated," commented Dianne.

"She'll get over it," stated Jerry.

"That's my buddy," Moose said. "First, raise their hopes, then, leave'em frustrated, really insensitive."

"But it worked," stated Jerry. "We went ashore and had a successful hunt without killing anything except the animal we took for food. If the meat is good, we can eat steak every day and still have more than enough for our welcoming feast."

Proud of the results of the hunt and wanting to retain the freshness, Jerry put the bags of meat into several ice chests and covered them with ice. While he was doing this, his colleagues set sail for home.

Even though it was late afternoon, Alpha Centauri A was still high enough in the sky to provide considerable energy to the solar sails. In addition, there was now a steady breeze blowing out of the north, so the wind sails were also deployed. The combination of solar energy and wind power enabled them to make the return voyage in less than an hour without using any battery power.

After arriving home, the first thing Jerry did was enter two samples of thigh meat and two samples of breast meat into the robot lab for analysis. All four tested negative for toxins, so Jerry fired up the barbecue pit.

Twenty minutes later, the aroma of sizzling steaks pervaded the air of the campsite. "I don't know what they're going to taste like," commented Moose, "but they smell so good that my stomach is growling."

"Mine is too," echoed Jerry.

"I think the aroma is getting to our wives. They're preparing the rest of the dinner more quickly than usual."

"Well, the steaks do smell pretty good, and we've had a long day. They're probably as hungry as we are."

Soon, all were seated around the outdoor table. Jerry was first to sample the steak. Everyone watched him and waited for his reaction. In just a few moments, he said, "It's tender and juicy, and it tastes every bit as delicious as any steak I ever ate back home."

Now, everyone cut a small piece from their steaks and critically tasted it. "This is good," stated Moose. "I think I'll experiment with smoking some of this in various ways to see what I can come up with."

"When it comes to food, my husband's imagination can be quite creative," Dianne said. "I'll bet it won't be long and we'll have ham, sausage, and jerky."

Moose took the comment as a compliment. He smiled at his wife and nodded in agreement.

"If we grind up some of it, I'll bet I could make a delicious meat loaf," Connie said.

"The challenge would be to do that using nothing but local ingredients," suggested Dianne.

"Zeb wants to take us on a tour of the island to show us what's good to eat," Connie reminded everyone. "Maybe, after we've done that, I'll be able to meet that challenge."

"Let's do that tour tomorrow," suggested Jerry.

SIXTEEN

Grocery Shopping in the Wilderness

TIME: Day Twenty-Two, Mid-Morning.

Jerry and Moose were on the beach of South Bay putting the finishing touches on their second ATV. When they were done, they stepped back a few paces to admire it. "It's not a race car," noted Jerry, "but it's going to make getting around the island a lot quicker and easier."

"And we can haul things instead of carrying them," added Moose.

"I'm definitely ready for the convenience," Jerry said.

"Let's take it for a test drive," suggested Moose.

"Great idea," responded Jerry, who hopped into the driver's seat.

After a five-minute drive up and down the beach, Jerry said, "Everything works; we're ready to go."

"It's going to be fun blazing a trail around the island with this rig."

"Why is that?" Jerry asked.

"It's a rugged, well-designed vehicle that's able to handle rough terrain, and I'm eager to find out just how good it is."

"Most of our trip is just going to be an easy drive on the beach."

"That's right, but there are places where the forest extends to the water's edge, and it's littered with fallen trees. In other areas, the land is rough and rocky. I'm sure we'll find enough challenges to have some fun."

"Not much doubt about that," agreed Jerry.

"I don't know which I'm more excited about: the challenge of driving this rig around the island, or learning about the plants that kept Zeb alive and healthy."

"It'll be an interesting day. I'd like to get started."

"They must've heard you," commented Moose, as he pointed to the cliff top where Zeb, Connie, and Dianne were getting on the elevator.

A few minutes later, all were in the ATV. With an ice chest full of food and beverages and two large thermos bottles full of hot drinks, the pioneers set out to explore the island. They planned to drive north along the west shore and then return home along the east shore.

However, before they had even left South Bay, Zeb stopped them to show them several patches of cane-like plants growing along the edge of the forest. He pointed out that the pulpy core of the canes could be eaten raw and that it had a sweet, mild flavor. He said that the canes grew all year and were a mainstay of his diet. He noted that harvesting the canes seemed to stimulate the plant's root system to send up new shoots.

Under Zeb's direction, Moose cut a choice cane and handed it to Zeb who opened it and started eating the white core. He offered a sample to Moose who was tempted to try it, but Dianne stopped him and said, "Even though Zeb has eaten this for a long time, we won't know for sure that it's safe for us to eat until we test it. There may be some basic differences between Zeb's digestive system and ours. In a few days, we'll have his genetic blueprint, and we'll compare his system to ours."

Moose nodded.

Dianne noted that the most mature plants were about nine feet tall with canes about two inches in diameter at the base. Then, she collected a cane sample, and the pioneers moved on.

They stopped numerous times to examine plants at Zeb's direction. He showed them vines and shrubs that produced edible berries, as well as, other shrubs that produced edible nuts. He also showed them fruit and nut trees. Zeb also identified plants whose berries had made him sick.

To gain as much knowledge from Zeb as possible, Jerry showed him how to fly an RPV. The ease with which he learned how to do this made it obvious that he had been a pilot at one time.

Zeb flew the RPV on short trips into the forest. In some places, he found small areas where trees were almost nonexistent for various reasons. It was in these small open areas that enough sunlight reached the ground for the low-lying berry and nut producing vines and shrubs to flourish.

In one of these areas, Zeb pointed out a plant with foliage much like a horseradish. "The leaves are crisp with a mildly tart flavor," he explained. "And the tan carrot-shaped roots are delicious with a mildly sweet flavor. Best of all, these plants are numerous and prosper year around."

"I've seen some of them on Stellar Plateau," commented Connie. "From the way Zeb has described the flavor, shredded roots and leaves might work very well in a meatloaf."

"Steamed roots might also make a great side dish," added Moose.

Even in the dense parts of the forest, Zeb identified food sources. In some locations, conditions were right for mushrooms to flourish. Zeb pointed out three species that he had eaten frequently. He also identified numerous poisonous varieties.

"Sliced mushrooms can work wonders in a meatloaf," stated Connie.

So many stops were made to collect samples that the pioneers did not reach Redfish Lagoon until mid-afternoon. Here, Zeb showed them a rice-like plant growing in the shallow marshy water along the shoreline. He explained that the island he lived on had several marshy areas along its shoreline where this plant grew abundantly. Its seeds were ripe by late spring with a second crop in early fall. Cooking a mixture of this grain and

440

the pulp from the canes made a sweet hot cereal with a mild flavor.

It was at Redfish Lagoon that Moose and Jerry met their first serious trail blazing challenge. The lagoon had very little sandy or rocky beach. For the most part, swampy marshland separated the lagoon's open water from the solid land of the forest.

To get around the lagoon, they had to rough out a half-mile of trail through the forest. It took several hours to cut through enough fallen trees to make a trail for the ATV. When they finally arrived on the north side of the entrance to the lagoon, it was early evening and Jerry said, "I think we should go home and finish our tour tomorrow."

Dianne thought about all the specimens already collected and said, "I have a great deal of research to do tomorrow. I want to find out if all the things Zeb showed us are safe to eat."

"I can help with that," Connie offered. "Plus, I'd like to make a meatloaf for tomorrow night's dinner using only ingredients from here."

Moose said to Jerry, "I guess that leaves it up to us and Zeb."

"And Michelle," added Jerry. "We can't do this without her until Zeb learns English."

"Maybe we should start teaching him," suggested Moose. "I'm starting to get a feeling that we can trust him. His helpfulness seems to be coming from the heart. It's just too real to be faked."

"I am inclined to agree with you," Jerry said. "But before we teach him English, I'd like to know if he can telepathically probe our minds in a covert way. If he can, then not teaching him English is the best way we have to prevent him from tuning in to our thoughts and memories."

Moose nodded. "I guess the language barrier isn't that much of an inconvenience as long as Michelle is available to be a translator."

"I think she's enjoying the job," commented Connie. "It keeps her involved in our daily adventures."

"Speaking of adventure, I think we should drive up to Rocky Point before we go home," suggested Dianne. "It's less than two miles, and I believe the drive is all open beach."

"Do you have any particular objective in mind for wanting to make this drive?" Jerry asked.

"No, I just think it would be fun. We've worked hard all day, and we've learned a lot. Now, it's time to enjoy ourselves. It's a pleasant evening, and a scenic drive along the waterfront just might be fun."

"You've twisted my arm just enough to convince me," replied Jerry. "But I'm hot, sweaty, and covered with sawdust. Before we make the drive, I'm going for a quick swim as soon as we find some choice beach."

"That shouldn't be difficult," Dianne said.

In just 200 yards, Jerry stopped the ATV and said, "This is some good looking sand, and the water looks very inviting. I'm going in."

"I'm coming with," declared Connie. "I thought we might go swimming at the end of the day, so I brought along some clean clothes for us on the return trip."

Connie opened her travel bag and removed the clean clothes and two towels. "Uh-oh, it looks like I forgot our swimsuits."

Jerry looked around. "The beach seems to be deserted. I think we can get along without swimsuits. I'll race you into the water."

Jerry was quick, but not quick enough to win the race. Connie beat him by one full step.

Both charged into the water until it was too deep to run. Then, they swam with power and speed. By the time they were 150 yards offshore, Connie was three yards ahead of Jerry. She stopped and said, "It looks like I'm still faster than you in the water."

"That's okay; as long as you stop and let me catch you."

"I've never minded being caught by you."

After an affectionate embrace, Jerry and Connie took several deep breaths and dove into the underwater world to check it out. The water was so clear that distance vision was great. Even though they only went down about fifteen feet, they were easily able to see the bottom, which was thirty-five feet below them.

After looking around for about a minute, they surfaced for air and playfully splashed around on the surface. "I rather enjoy swimming in the nude," commented Connie. "It gives me a sense of freedom."

"It does have some advantages," added Jerry.

"It makes me feel rather sensual."

"I know what you mean."

Jerry and Connie took several deep breaths, and then disappeared beneath the surface.

Meanwhile, back on shore, Moose said, "I hope they come in pretty soon. I need a good swim too."

"Be patient; we'll get our turn."

"They've sure been underwater for a long time. I hope nothing has happened to them."

"You don't need to worry. They're both excellent swimmers with good breath endurance."

"I know; I just hope nothing has happened to them."

"I think they're just enjoying the underwater world."

At that moment, Jerry and Connie broke the surface and headed for shore. When they arrived, Connie beamed a glowing smile at Dianne and said, "That was refreshing. I feel great."

Dianne turned to Moose. "It's our turn, and it seems as though I also forgot our swimsuits. It never occurred to me that we might go swimming today."

Noticing that Dianne had packed some towels and clean clothes, Moose wondered if she really did forget the swimsuits. But Moose didn't bother to search the travel bag because he saw that Dianne was already strolling toward the water, discarding her clothing item by item along the way. Moose quickly removed his work boots; then, he added the rest of his clothing to the trail left by Dianne.

A few minutes later, they were 100 yards offshore playfully engaging in delightful carefree activity that seemed to them to be a well-deserved reward for a productive day of hard work. As the minutes ticked by, their improvised game gradually worked its way to a satisfying conclusion.

"That was a pleasurable way to add a pleasing touch to a fruitful day," Dianne said in Moose's embrace.

"You might call it the best part of the day, maybe even the climax of the day."

"Whatever caused you to make a comment like that?" Dianne asked, glowing with satisfaction.

"I thought it was appropriate."

"In a few days, we're going to have a decision to make," Dianne said.

"What's that?"

"I'll be capable of getting pregnant. I think it would be nice if our first child could be the first baby conceived here on Alcent. Matthew is the only child conceived on Earth and born in space. Denise is the only child conceived in space and born in space. I'd like our first child to be the first conceived here, and hopefully, the first born here."

"I like the idea" stated Moose. "It'll definitely be an historic event when the first child is born here."

"In a few days, we'll have Zeb's genetic blueprint. If his body is nearly identical to the human body in its biological processes, and if we can pass a medical exam, then, there'll be no reason to delay getting pregnant."

"We've waited a long time to start a family, and I'm ready."

A few minutes later, Dianne and Moose were back on shore. Dianne beamed a smile at Connie. "You're right, that was refreshing!"

"Now that everyone's feeling refreshed, I think it's time for an evening pleasure drive," Moose said.

"Let's go!" Jerry yelled boisterously. "We still have a full hour before first sunset. That should give us plenty of time to drive to Rocky Point and then back home before dark."

Five minutes later, the pioneers rounded Cliff Point and headed toward the foot of Rocky Point Bay. When they rounded the foot of the bay and started heading north, everyone's communicator started beeping. Then, the early warning computer on Stellar Plateau announced: "You are now within 200 yards of the bear with cubs."

Jerry stopped the ATV, turned on its video screen, and called up a map of the island's north end. A blinking red dot indicated the bear's position. "The radio tag we put on her is working well," Jerry said. "If we continue up the coast, we'll pass within a hundred yards of her. With the breeze coming out of the northwest, she won't smell us until we're 50 to 100 yards past our closest approach."

"Are we going to continue on our way?" Connie asked.

"Yes, we need to find out how she reacts to the human scent."

Jerry turned to Moose. "Launch an RPV and find them, so we can watch them."

"That won't be difficult. I'll just home in on the radio signal."

A few minutes later, Moose located the mother bear and her cubs. He approached them from downwind, found a suitable rock, and landed the RPV on it. He aimed the RPV's cameras at the bears, and they appeared on the ATV's video screen. The RPV's microphones picked up and relayed the sounds of the forest, which seemed calm and peaceful.

"They sure look relaxed," noted Connie.

"But they are heading toward the beach," stated Jerry.

"Maybe an abalone dinner is on her menu," suggested Dianne.

Jerry resumed driving northward. "It'll be interesting to see if she changes her mind when she picks up our scent."

A minute later, Jerry judged that they were directly upwind from the bears, so he stopped the ATV. "It'll take a minute or two for this breeze to carry our scent to them."

The pioneers anxiously watched the bears on the video screen. When their scent reached the mother bear, she sniffed the air intently.

"She's making quite an effort to identify our scent," noted Dianne.

"Has she ever seen any of us?" Connie asked.

"I don't think so," replied Jerry.

The pioneers heard a low, menacing growl emanate from the ATV's speakers. The growl sent the cubs scrambling up the nearest trees, and the forest in the vicinity of the bears became ominously silent. The mother checked her cubs' positions and seemed satisfied that they were safe. After issuing another low growl, which was apparently a command for the cubs to stay in the trees, she cautiously moved forward.

"It looks like she's going to investigate us," stated Jerry.

"What do we do now?" Connie asked.

"I think we should stay put and give her a chance to see us. I'd like to find out how she reacts to us."

Turning to Moose, Jerry said, "Follow her with that RPV, so we can watch her every move."

"What if she decides to attack when she sees us?" Connie asked.

"I don't think she will. She has her cubs high up in the trees 150 yards from us. She shouldn't see us as a threat to them. If she attacks anyway, then we have another problem bear on our hands, and the assumption that we can peacefully coexist with these animals might not be valid. If she attacks, it might be because she sees us as prey. We need to know."

"But what do we do if she does attack?" questioned Connie. "Are we going to kill her in self-defense? If we do, what happens to those cute little cubs? They're such innocent looking little fur balls."

"We're thirty yards from the forest, and we have a half-mile of open beach in front of us. Moose will keep her in sight with the RPV. If it looks like she's going to charge, we can quickly accelerate to fifty mph. I doubt the bear can run that fast; she's just too bulky. As a last resort, we do have our guns."

"I would hate to have to kill a mother with cubs," stated Connie.

"I don't want to either," Jerry said. "But we have an opportunity to learn more about the risk these animals pose, and we have to take advantage of that opportunity." Realizing that Jerry was right, Connie checked her rifle and pistol to make sure they were ready to fire.

Everyone stared at the video screen as the mother bear cautiously moved toward them. When she approached the edge of the forest, she flattened out and slowly crawled forward. She stopped behind a couple bushes; then, she silently wiggled into position between them. There, she intently stared at the ATV and its occupants.

Connie looked at the forest and located the two bushes. "She's extremely good at stealth. Even though I know exactly where she is, I can't see her. She blends right into the shadows. If it weren't for our technology, we wouldn't even know she's there."

"Something to think about next time we go for a walk on the beach," commented Dianne.

Connie's inner being responded to Dianne's suggestion, and an involuntary chill ran up and down her spine. Within moments, the chill passed and she said, "A walk on the beach definitely has more potential for adventure here than it did back on Earth."

"No question about that," agreed Dianne. "And that's one of the reasons why I'm glad we're here."

"It looks to me like she has no intention of attacking us," noted Moose. "In fact, I think she's wary of us."

"She has cubs to care for," stated Dianne. "And she can't do that unless she stays alive. It seems reasonable that she would try to determine what danger we pose without placing herself at risk."

"But this is quite a contrast to the bear we encountered shortly after we arrived here," commented Moose. "That bear doggedly stalked us. I believe it wanted to eat us."

"That was a male," Dianne said. "It didn't have cubs to worry about."

"Or he may've just been a mean-tempered animal," suggested Connie. "Perhaps, most animals in this species aren't that way."

"There might be another factor involved," commented Jerry.

"What?" Dianne asked.

"The male saw Moose and me as individuals much smaller than itself. This bear sees an ATV with five occupants. To it, we might look like one

445

large, strange creature. Since it has never seen any kind of vehicle, it can't possibly know that this ATV is a machine containing individuals."

"That means we aren't going to find out how this bear will react to us as individuals unless we get out of this ATV," Dianne said.

"I could get out and walk around," offered Connie.

"I don't like that idea," objected Jerry. "That could put you in serious danger. I would prefer to do that myself."

"I am just as fast on my feet as you are," argued Connie. "Besides that, you're behind the wheel, and you are more of a daredevil driver than I am. That's important in case we need to leave in a hurry."

"Moose is flying the RPV, so that leaves it up to me and Connie," added Dianne.

"Too bad we didn't bring Charlie along," commented Jerry. "We could've used him for this."

"We couldn't," stated Moose. "There's a malfunction in the repairs we did on him after the incident with the saber-toothed cats."

Jerry looked at the video screen. "That bear sure is staring at us intently, and she's still doing her best to stay hidden. I don't get the feeling that she's going to attack any time soon."

Jerry thought about it for a few moments and decided that he would like to be the driver if the bear charged. He turned to Connie. "I agree with your plan, but I want you to stay in front of the ATV and be prepared to jump back in on the run."

"I'll leave my rifle behind. I can jump in more quickly without it."

Connie checked her 10.5-millimeter pistol to make sure it was loaded with explosive bullets. "This ought to be lethal enough to stop a bear, if I have to shoot."

Connie set the gun to automatically fire three rounds with each pull of the trigger. Then, she stepped out of the ATV and walked away from it at a leisurely pace. The bear instantly lifted its head a little bit and stared at Connie, apparently puzzled by what had just happened.

When Connie was about fifty feet in front of the ATV, she stopped, and Dianne stepped out and leisurely strolled toward Connie. The bear raised her head a little bit more and inquisitively stared at the puzzling scene. "Our wives have really gotten her attention," stated Moose. "But she still doesn't appear to be interested in attacking."

"She might be too confused to attack," Jerry suggested. "When she first saw us, she might have concluded that a strange new creature now inhabits this island. Then, she saw the new creature break up into individual creatures. She might have enough intelligence to be aware that something peculiar is happening, but not enough to figure out what."

"In other words, we aren't going to find out how she'll react to us as individuals until one of us encounters her alone," commented Moose.

"I think you're right, so let's really confuse her by putting the strange new creature back together."

Speaking to Dianne and Connie, Jerry said, "She's watching you close-ly, but I don't think she's going to attack. Come on back, and let's move on. I want to find out what she does at the sight of us leaving."

Dianne and Connie returned to the ATV, and the pioneers resumed their drive to Rocky Point. The bear watched attentively, but remained concealed. She waited until they were well on their way; then, she ambled onto the beach. After sniffing the tire tracks and the footprints, she stood up on her back legs, stretched to her full height, and looked northward. Assuring her-self that the strange new creatures had left, she returned to the forest and headed in the direction of her cubs.

The pioneers drove northward with ease, but the sandy, gravely beach gave way to an impassable rocky beach when they reached the vicinity of Rocky Point. After stopping the ATV, Jerry grabbed the roll bar above him and stood up. He briefly surveyed the area. "Making a trail through this rock pile is going to be a challenge."

"But it's a challenge we can handle," declared Moose.

"Let's take a look at it and map out the path of least resistance. Then, we'll know just how big of a job it's going to be."

"After that, I think we should experiment with our winch and find out how good it is at moving rocks."

"Haven't you two done enough for one day?" Dianne asked.

"Seems like you guys should be able to just relax," stated Connie.

"This ATV is still a new toy," responded Jerry. "And it's still fun to check out its capabilities. It was designed to handle rough terrain. It's pos-sible that by pulling a few key rocks out of the way, we might be able to drive across this rock pile yet tonight."

"It's also possible that the job might be too big for the winch," com-mented Moose. "We may have to bring along some explosives when we come back tomorrow."

"This ATV might be a new toy, but your plan sounds like work to me," commented Connie. "I'm glad I'm not included, because I'd like to be lazy for the rest of the evening."

While Jerry and Moose scrambled over the rocks looking for the easi-est way through; Zeb, Connie, and Dianne found a spot from which to enjoy the scenic views. Once settled, they helped themselves to food and bever-age, and engaged in casual conversation.

"If all the things that Zeb showed us today pass our lab tests, we're going to have quite a menu of local foods to select from," Dianne said, enjoying a sandwich. "You shouldn't have any problem making a yummy meatloaf for tomorrow night's dinner using only local ingredients."

"Spices and fillers won't be a problem, but I wish I had some eggs to put in it."

"There are lots of waterfowl around here. Maybe Zeb knows which ones produce edible eggs."

Connie picked up her communicator, called Michelle, and explained the question to her.

After Michelle discussed it with Zeb, she reported: "Zeb said that eggs have been part of his diet. He has eaten the eggs of several species, but he prefers the eggs from the large waterfowl that resemble Canadian geese. These birds weigh about fifteen pounds, and their eggs are fairly large. He only needed one egg along with side dishes to make a good meal. Winters here are very mild, allowing these birds to nest year-round. Different birds nest at various times on a random basis making the eggs constantly available. When they nest, they usually lay about a dozen eggs over a ten-day period before starting the incubation of them. They nest in the forest near the water and protect their eggs by finding very well concealed nest sites. Until incubation starts, the nests are unattended for several hours each day. Using care to not disturb the nest, taking a couple eggs never attracted the birds' attention. He also said the birds taste good."

"Ask him if he can find me some eggs tomorrow morning."

A few moments later, Michelle replied, "Zeb said the nests are so well concealed that they're difficult to find, but if you'll let him use an RPV, he'll try to locate one. Back on his island it would be easier because these birds usually reuse their nest sites, and he knows where several are."

"How serious are you about putting eggs in your meatloaf?" Dianne asked.

"They're not essential, but they would give it a better texture. Why did you ask that question?"

"I was just wondering if the eggs are important enough to make them worth a boat trip to Zeb's island. It would be kind of like going shopping."

"I like the texture that eggs give a meatloaf, but I don't know that it's worth a special trip to Zeb's island."

"The round-trip wouldn't take more than a couple hours. That allows for a half-hour of travel time in each direction, and with an RPV, Zeb could quickly check all known nesting sites."

"The most dangerous part of the trip would be going ashore to get the eggs," noted Connie.

"Zeb should be able to warn us of any dangers; after all, he has lived there for thirty years."

"But we don't know if we can trust him to do that," argued Connie.

"I think we can. He still needs our medical help, and that gives him a personal interest in keeping us alive."

"I don't think our husbands will like the idea of us doing this."

"Tomorrow, they'll be busy completing the trail around the island and won't have time for a trip like this. Besides that, I don't think we need their permission to go shopping."

"I don't think so either," agreed Connie. "But this isn't exactly a trip to the grocery store. We should at least talk to them about it. I'm sure they'll be concerned about our safety."

"Safety is a legitimate concern, but if they can be out all day without us, we should be able to go on a two-hour trip without them. After all, you and I did extremely well in survival training. We were near the top of the class, and we are experts with our weapons."

"That's all true, but a short time ago, I was unable to see a bear, even though I knew exactly where she was. Bears do frequent these islands. Also, I was nearly killed by a pair of saber-tooth cats that we were unaware of. It looks to me like the predators on this planet are very good at what they do. It's possible that our survival training didn't fully prepare us for the dangers we face here."

"You're starting to make me think that eggs aren't all that important to your meatloaf."

"You're starting to make me think that you'd like to go on an exciting adventure without our husbands."

"There might be some truth to that," admitted Dianne. "Not to mention the fact that we would be in the company of a strange man."

"Who happens to be crippled at the moment and uses either a wheel-chair or crutches to get around."

"But he did see both of us nude today, and I noticed that he did look."

"Can you blame him? He hasn't seen a woman in thirty years. Besides that, to him, we are aliens, and he should be curious about us."

While conversing and eating, Dianne and Connie gazed out over the lake, appreciating its serene beauty. The most dominant sounds, in their otherwise quiet evening, were the occasional drone of the ATV's electrically powered winch and the crashing noise of the rock that it was moving. After a while, these sounds were replaced by the hum of the ATV's electric motors as it made its way over the rocks working its way toward them.

Soon, the ATV stopped near them, and Jerry announced, "The challenge wasn't as great as we thought it might be. Thanks to this rig's ability to handle rocky terrain, we only had to move five rocks. It's a slow bumpy ride, but we can now drive across the point."

When Moose stepped out of the ATV, Jerry asked Connie, "Would you like to enjoy the thrill of a rough ride over a rock pile?"

"Sounds like fun," replied Connie, eagerly stepping into the ATV.

A few minutes later, when they returned, Connie was driving and Jerry was sitting in the passenger seat. Connie exclaimed to Dianne, "That was fun! Now, it's your turn!"

Moose got into the driver's seat to demonstrate the trail that he and Jerry had made. But, a few minutes later, when they returned, it was Dianne who was driving. "Climbing around on a rocky slope with this machine could easily be made into a real sport," she said, looking excited.

After briefly gazing at the western sky, Jerry said, "I don't want to bring this party to an end, but first sunset is only minutes away, and I think we should head for home."

To Dianne, who was still in the driver's seat, Jerry said, "Turn on the video and check the location of the bear family."

Dianne did as requested. "They're on the beach a half-mile south of us," she said.

"Looks like we have a problem," commented Connie.

"I think it's an opportunity," stated Jerry. "We can drive south at a leisurely pace, occasionally honking the horn to let her know we're approaching. I expect that an early alert to our approach will cause her to take her cubs into the forest, but she could defiantly stand her ground. I want to find out which alternative she chooses."

The pioneers headed south. When they were 300 yards from the bear family, they started honking the ATV's horn and flashing its headlights. This instantly got the mother bear's attention. She stood up on her hind legs for a better view. For a few seconds, she observed the steady approach of the strange new creature that had entered her life. Then, she uttered a low pitched growl that sent her cubs scurrying into the forest. She watched for a few more seconds; then, she dropped down to all four feet, picked up the remains of an abalone, and followed her cubs.

By watching the blinking red dot on the ATV's video screen, the pioneers monitored the bear's retreat. "Apparently, there's no panic on her part," noted Jerry. "She's just leisurely moving out of our way."

"She seems to have no desire to subject her cubs to unknown danger," commented Connie.

"This might be a bear that we can coexist with," stated Jerry. "But we need to find out how she'll react to the approach of one of us on foot, and we need Charlie for that job."

Moose thought about Charlie's malfunction and said, "I can repair him the day after tomorrow."

"But if she looks upon Charlie as prey, she could destroy him," protested Connie.

"Not if we rig Charlie with the right equipment," stated Jerry.

"What do you mean?" Connie asked.

"We don't want this bear to see us as prey, so if she attacks Charlie, we need to teach her a lesson that she'll remember for a long time."

"How?" questioned Connie.

"We need to rig Charlie with some electrical equipment that will put out a strong shock every second or two while he's under attack."

"I like the idea," stated Connie. "All dangerous animals that come here should be introduced to the human race by an electrified Charlie."

Dianne nodded. "That would be a good way to teach them to leave us alone."

"As long as they aren't smart enough to tell the difference between

Charlie and real people, it should work," commented Jerry.

"Charlie looks like a real human," stated Moose. "He walks, runs, and talks like a real human. And we can certainly make sure that he carries the human scent."

"Scent is another good way to teach dangerous animals to leave us alone," suggested Dianne. "Many predators have an extremely sensitive sense of smell, so why don't we also equip Charlie with a number of small canisters of highly irritating aerosols."

"Good idea," agreed Jerry. "Back on Earth, the lowly skunk does a pretty good job protecting itself with a noxious spray. Many predators simply leave it alone."

Speaking to Moose, Jerry said, "Contact Mike and ask him to work out the details for electrifying Charlie and equipping him with irritating chemicals."

Moose picked up his communicator, called Mike, and discussed the project with him. Mike concluded the conversation by saying, "I'll send down the things you need in a day or two."

The pioneers leisurely completed their drive home, arriving after first sunset but before second sunset. After discussing their day, they retired to bed feeling good about their accomplishments. Shortly, they dropped off into a deep, well-deserved night of sleep.

TIME: Day Twenty-Three, After Breakfast.

Jerry and Moose were preparing to leave the habitation capsule to continue working on the ATV trail around the island. "I don't think we'll have any problem completing the trail today," commented Jerry. "In fact, we might even be done by mid-afternoon."

"I don't know about that," argued Moose. "It's going to take a while just to get from South Bay to East Bay. There are lots of trees growing right to the water's edge on more than half of that coastline."

"But if we can make it to East Bay by lunchtime, it should be easy to get to Rocky Point by mid-afternoon."

"I can't argue with that. Most of the east coast is sandy beach. There are only two small stretches of waterfront where the forest extends to the water, and there aren't any rock piles before Rocky Point."

"I'd like to finish at least by late afternoon, so let's get started."

"Aren't we taking some food along?" questioned Moose.

"If we don't get past East Bay by noon, we'll be close enough to home to eat lunch right here."

"I think I'll take something along anyway. We'll be working hard, and I'll probably need a midmorning snack."

"That doesn't surprise me," teased Dianne. Jerry and Connie grinned at Dianne's comment while Moose ignored it and packed some food.

A few minutes later, as they were leaving, Jerry turned to Connie and

451

Dianne. "We'll see you later. Don't work too hard."

"We won't," responded Connie. "We're just going to check out the specimens we collected yesterday and make dinner."

"Well, don't push it too hard. Just relax and enjoy the day."

"Is that the Captain's direct order?" Dianne asked.

Jerry smiled at Dianne's formality. "No, it's just a suggestion."

"It's a good suggestion," agreed Dianne. "Maybe we'll take the boat out for a couple hours."

"That's one way to relax and have fun," commented Jerry, as he turned and left.

"See how difficult it was to get the Captain's approval for our shopping trip," Dianne said to Connie, smugly.

"You didn't exactly tell him the whole story, like the fact that we might be sneaking around in the forest on Zeb's island."

"He didn't ask where we're going."

"And you didn't volunteer any information either."

"Neither did you."

Connie thought about the truth of Dianne's remark. "Maybe I have a subconscious desire to make this trip even while my conscious mind is telling me not to."

"You are a psychiatrist. You should be able to figure out what's going on in your head that would cause that kind of mental conflict."

Connie considered some possibilities. "Maybe I need to prove to myself that we can travel and successfully face possible danger without the support of our husbands. Maybe I need to do that to feel at home here."

"Being able to move about freely is part of feeling at home."

"Back on Earth, I took the freedom to go places for granted, but here, every little trip, no matter how short, can bring one face-to-face with death." Connie paused briefly. "Perhaps, there's another factor coming to the surface."

"Want to tell me about it?"

"Do you remember how at the end of our survival training each one of us had to live alone for two weeks in a remote tropical jungle?"

"I'll never forget that experience! Why are you bringing that up?"

"During those two weeks, I had a vivid dream every night that I would be killed by an animal on this planet."

"That must have been scary when you were alone in the jungle."

"It was a real nightmare." Connie briefly trembled at the memory.

"But you didn't put out a call to be picked up, like some people did."

"I didn't want to be washed out."

"Did you talk to anyone about those dreams?"

"No! And it was for the same reason. I was afraid that I'd be labeled as someone with a deep-seated abnormal fear and be washed out."

"I think you should be proud of yourself. By maintaining a tough mental attitude, you passed the final test of survival training despite having to

452

endure terrifying dreams every night. But now that you're here, I hope that you don't seek out dangerous situations to be triumphant over just to prove that those bad dreams were meaningless."

"That is something I'll have to think about and guard against."

"If I were your patient and told you what you just told me, what would you do?"

"I would try to discover the origin of those horrifying dreams and help you understand them. While doing that, I would caution you to avoid looking for dangerous situations to overcome, so that you wouldn't end up turning those dreams into a self-fulfilling prophecy."

"That sounds like a good approach. Want me to repeat those words of caution to you?"

"That won't be necessary. I can follow my own advice. However, if we go to Zeb's island to get some eggs, I want to be the one who goes ashore to get them."

"I think we should both go ashore. Two people looking for danger should be safer than one."

"We may not be going to Zeb's island. He might find some eggs here. Let's give him an RPV, so he can start the search."

During the next two hours, Zeb searched for eggs. Although he located several nests, they were all deserted except one, and this one was occupied by a hen that was already incubating her eggs.

Speaking through Michelle, Zeb said, "On my island, I know the locations of 19 nests. Do you want me to keep searching here, or do you want to take me there, so I can check those nests?"

"Do you have any idea what the probability is of finding eggs that aren't yet being incubated?" Dianne asked.

Zeb considered the question for a few moments. "I think the odds are better than even. Over the years, I've gained some familiarity with the nesting habits of the birds that use those nests. There are three pairs that seem to prefer nesting at about this time of the year. There's a pretty good chance one of those nests will have eggs we can take."

Turning to Connie, Dianne said, "I think we should go check them out. If one of those nests has eggs, this could end up being a quick easy trip, a joy ride on a pleasant day."

Connie nodded, and a short time later, they were sailing out of South Bay on their way to Zeb's island. Since it was a mostly clear day with very little wind, they deployed the boat's solar sails.

The little boat moved silently at ten mph. Zeb was below deck taking advantage of the boat's transparent hull and Clear Lake's amazingly clear water. Dianne and Connie were on deck enjoying the pleasant late morning air. With the boat under the control of its navigation computer, they were free to be lazy and just enjoy the cruise.

Connie surveyed the deep blue sky with its widely scattered cumulus clouds and soaring sea birds. Then, she slowly scanned the lake in all directions. Her gaze eventually settled on the south end of the receding Pioneer Island. She thought about all the things they had already done to turn it into a secure home on a hostile planet. So far, everything had gone very well: no deaths, no crippling injuries, and no serious illnesses. Also, an abundant supply of nutritious food from a big variety of sources had been discovered. If everything continued to go so well, all of the Challenger's personnel could come down in about a week.

Cruising on this lake sure is quiet and peaceful, thought Connie. Wondering why Dianne hadn't said anything to interrupt her thoughts, Connie turned to see what she was doing and found her stretched out on an air mattress sound asleep. Wearing only short shorts and a halter top, Connie became aware of the radiant heat of Alpha Centauri A and the gentle caress of the pleasant late morning air and concluded: if I were sun bathing, I would fall asleep too.

Connie wondered if the current peacefulness was lulling them into a false sense of security. What dangers should I be concerned about? She asked herself. Our radar will warn us of approaching pterodactyls, and our sonar will warn us if a large marine creature approaches. Connie scanned the lake and the sky and saw only sea birds. Then, she recalled the savage feeding frenzy of the sea birds on the dead pterodactyl and wondered: what provokes them into a feeding frenzy like that one? What if Dianne and I were both sound asleep? Would they attack because we look defenseless or would we have to be dead and lying in a pool of blood? Maybe they respond to the pterodactyl battle cry knowing that something is going to die. With more questions than answers, Connie decided to stay alert for dangers, but she also decided to enjoy the cruise while being alert.

When Zeb's island was only a few hundred yards away, Connie woke Dianne and summoned Zeb from below deck. Using gestures and telepathic images, Zeb informed Dianne where he wanted to begin the search for eggs. While Dianne piloted the boat, Connie and Zeb put on headsets. Connie wanted to see how well the nests were hidden and what difficulties she would encounter while robbing one of a couple eggs.

Zeb launched a small RPV and flew it toward the first of three nests. A minute later, he reported that the nest was occupied by a hen and that he didn't know if she was already incubating her eggs or if she was there to lay an egg. After checking three more nests and finding nothing, Zeb returned the RPV to the boat.

Under Zeb's direction, Dianne piloted the boat to the next nesting area. Speaking through Michelle, Zeb explained, "There are five nests here. Two of the three that I think might be in use are here."

Wanting to see what the nests looked like and how well hidden they were, Dianne asked Connie to stand guard while she wore the second headset. Dianne then directed Zeb to show her all five nests. Even though nine eggs were discovered at the second nest, Dianne insisted on seeing the remaining three to gain information on the bird's nesting habits.

While Zeb returned the RPV, Dianne handed the headset to Connie, so she could replay the video of the nest with eggs. After looking at it, Connie said, "That nest is in the middle of a patch of thorn bushes. How does that bird get to it without being scratched up?"

"Replay the video and look at the small opening that Zeb flew the RPV through," suggested Dianne.

Connie did as directed and said, "I don't know if I can fit through that opening. I'll have to stretch out on my stomach and inch my way along. If that bush has dropped any twigs, I could end up with thorns stuck in me."

"I thought you wanted some eggs for your meatloaf."

"I do, but I don't want to get seriously injured while getting them."

"Getting poked by a thorn isn't exactly a serious injury," teased Dianne. "It really wouldn't be any different than getting a shot at the doctor's office. And don't you doctors usually tell your patients that it won't hurt all that much."

Connie stared at Dianne. "I think you're punching below the belt, but you do make a good point." After a moment's thought, Connie said, "I think there's something more serious than being scratched by thorns that we need to think about."

"What?"

"While I'm slowly inching my way through a small opening through thorn bushes, I will be vulnerable to attack. With my upper body encased by thorn bushes, I will not be able to quickly respond to an animal that attacks my lower body."

"I'll be there to protect you."

"We could just cut a larger opening through the thorn bushes."

"The hen might notice that and desert the nest," objected Dianne.

"That would probably be the case," Connie agreed.

"If Zeb could successfully steal eggs over the years without disturbing that nest, then we should also be able to."

Connie looked at Zeb, then at herself. "I think I can slip through a smaller hole than he can. Let's go ashore and try it. After coming this far, I don't want to go home empty-handed."

Speaking through Michelle, Connie explained the plan to Zeb.

"I've taken eggs from that nest a number of times over the years," Zeb replied.

Michelle said to Connie, "You sure are determined to have some eggs to put in your meatloaf. Why don't you just play it safe and make the meatloaf without eggs?"

"It's a matter of principle," replied Connie. "When I set out to do something, I like to be successful, no matter what the task is. I like to overcome any obstacles that show up."

Dianne and Connie checked their pistols to make sure they were loaded with explosive bullets. Then, they checked their rifles and were about to step into the small boat to go ashore when they noticed that Zeb appeared to be in a trance. They looked closely at him wondering what was happening, but they did not disturb him because he appeared to be breathing normally and not in any medical trouble.

When Zeb came out of the trance, he spoke through Michelle. "There's a bear downwind from the nest, and he's in a bad mood."

With a bit of laughter in her voice, Dianne said, "Speaking about obstacles that show up, how do you plan to overcome this one?"

"Forget the bear and the eggs for a moment! We just learned something about Zeb: his telepathic ability is able to detect the presence of bears and what mood they're in."

"That explains how he was able to avoid being killed by a bear during the thirty years he lived on this island."

"If he can detect the energy field generated by a bear's brain, maybe he can detect the presence of any large animal and the mood it's in," suggested Connie.

"He didn't give us an early warning when a pterodactyl had one of us in mind for its dinner."

"Maybe his telepathic ability only works when he shuts out all distractions and totally focuses his mental energy."

"Either that's the case, or his telepathic ability doesn't work with pterodactyls," commented Dianne.

While looking into Diane's eyes, Connie said, "You're ignoring a third possibility."

"Not really, I just don't believe he would've avoided warning us if he had known we were about to be attacked."

"I don't think so either, but I'd sure like to find out how extensive his telepathic abilities are. In regard to our bear problem, can he pinpoint the bear's location or does he just know approximately where it is?" Speaking through Michelle, Connie asked Zeb if he knew the bear's location well enough to approach him with an RPV from downwind. Zeb said he did, and Connie directed him to do so.

When the RPV was in place with its cameras aimed at the bear, Connie said, "Let's find out if this bear is interested in the human scent."

Connie picked up a small RPV and smeared some of her skin oil and perspiration on it. As an after thought, she added her female scent to it. Then, she handed the RPV to Dianne, who added her scent to it.

Connie put on a headset and slowly flew the RPV toward the bear approaching him from upwind while Dianne watched video of the bear. The bear picked up the scent when the RPV was still more than 200 yards away. He flared his nostrils and sniffed the air several times. Then, as if annoyed by the scent, he growled and set off to investigate it.

456

"It looks like Zeb was right," stated Dianne. "This bear is in a bad mood. He's making no attempt at stealth in his effort to find the source of our scent. There's no doubt in my mind that he would attack us if we were there, and we'd have to kill him."

"I'll keep the RPV out of sight, so he won't know where the scent is coming from. If he continues to follow it, maybe I can lead him at least a half-mile upwind from the eggs we want."

Determined to find the source of the scent, the agitated bear aggressively pursued it, occasionally letting out a menacing growl. "I wonder why this bear is in such a bad mood," questioned Dianne.

"I don't know, but I wouldn't want to be on that island with nothing more than the weapons Zeb had at his disposal for the last thirty years."

A few minutes later, Connie found a large boulder at the north end of the island and landed the RPV on it. "I think this rock is big enough so that the RPV will be out of reach," she said. "Hopefully, the bear will circle it several times trying to figure out how to get to our scent. By the time he loses interest, we should have our eggs and be on our way home."

"That's a good theory, but I'd like Zeb to keep an eye on him and let us know if he starts coming back."

With the bear temporarily preoccupied, Connie and Dianne stepped into the small inflated boat and rowed ashore. They beached the boat and cautiously entered the forest. Slowly and quietly, they made their way toward the nest. Frequently, they stopped and listened to the sounds of the forest while intently scanning their surroundings for signs of danger. Even though the nest was only 150 yards from the edge of the forest, it took Dianne and Connie nearly ten minutes to reach it.

When they arrived at the small clump of thorn bushes, they slowly circled it looking for danger. Not finding any, Connie said, "I'm going in."

She put her rifle down, stretched out flat on her stomach, and slowly inched her way through the small opening into the clump of thorn bushes. When she reached the nest, she selected three eggs and put them in a small bag. Then, she began inching her way backwards out of the thorn bushes.

When Connie was free of the bushes, she stood up and brushed the dirt off herself. "I could use a quick swim."

"You do look like you've been rolling around in the dirt."

"A little swimming will clean me up. Then, I'm going to do some sunbathing on the way home, while you stand guard."

"I guess it is my turn," agreed Dianne.

At that moment, an image appeared in Dianne's mind with a mood of urgency attached to it. The image clearly depicted a bear heading south along the waterfront. "I think we should get out of here," stated Dianne. "That grumpy bear is returning."

Not wanting to kill the bear, Dianne and Connie hastily made their way to the beach. But they did not throw away caution. They moved as fast they could while staying alert to their surroundings.

In less than two minutes, they were on the beach. As they began pushing their little boat into the lake, the bear rounded a bend about 200 yards away and immediately broke into a charge. However, less than 100 yards into the charge; he skidded to a dead stop and flattened out on the sandy beach as if trying to make himself invisible. Several seconds later, as Dianne and Connie reached the submarine; the bear got up and resumed his charge, quickly covering the remaining distance. He then rushed into the lake and swam in pursuit of his quarry. By the time the bear was half way to the submarine, Dianne and Connie had it on the move and heading toward Pioneer Island. As the submarine steadily pulled away, the bear decided that he could not catch it and returned to Zeb's island.

"I wonder what caused that bear to skid to a dead stop right after breaking into a full charge," questioned Connie.

"I suspect Zeb had something to do with that," responded Dianne with a bit of laughter.

"Are you saying that he's able to project images into a bear's mind?"

"At the moment, that's the best explanation we have for what the bear did. Imagine a bear charging what looks like an easy meal, and then, the image of us fades from his brain and is replaced by the image of an angry T-Rex. Wouldn't that cause him to do what he did?"

"If I were that bear, I certainly would've skidded to a halt and tried to look invisible, but I don't think I would've resumed the charge as soon as he did. Unless, the T-Rex image faded out and our image reappeared."

"That might be what happened, and I have a possible explanation. When the bear began its charge, it seems reasonable to assume that his brain was intently focused on making a kill. That intense concentration may've made his brain resistant to a telepathically projected image. Placing a T-Rex image in the bear's brain may've required so much mental energy that Zeb was unable to maintain it for more than a few seconds."

"That ten to fifteen seconds was all the time we needed to escape and avoid killing the bear," stated Connie.

"Maybe Zeb realized that and broke contact when he saw that we were safe."

"That's possible," agreed Connie, "and he does look tired. He can hardly keep his eyes open, and that supports your theory about the mental energy required to place a T-Rex image in the bear's brain."

"We don't know if that's what he did. We're only speculating."

"When he wakes up, let's discuss it with him. Right now, I'd like to take a look at our eggs."

Connie reached into her egg bag and took out the eggs. "These are three times bigger than the eggs I used to buy at the grocery store back on Earth. I won't need more than one in my meatloaf."

"I'll use the other two to make an omelet," Dianne said.

"I don't think there's a problem, but we should do the lab tests anyway just to make sure that they're safe to eat."

Dianne nodded in agreement.

"I need to get cleaned up," stated Connie while bringing the boat to a stop. "Perhaps, you could stand guard while I go swimming."

"Okay, and when you're done, I want to go for a quick swim too."

After 15 minutes of playful, slow-paced swimming, both underwater and on the surface, Connie climbed out of the water. She looked at Dianne and asked, "Do I still look like I've been rolling around in the dirt?"

"You look like you just stepped out of the tub, and now, it's my turn," stated Dianne, as she stepped to the edge of the deck and dove in.

Ten minutes later, Dianne climbed out of the water. "That was great! I feel rejuvenated and filled with energy."

"Good, because I feel like taking a nap."

"I can't believe that a little grocery shopping would tire you out so much that you need a nap. Maybe you and Jerry should've spent more time sleeping last night."

"It doesn't take us all night. Anyway, I always sleep well afterwards."

"Since you're tired now, that means you didn't sleep well last night, and that means you didn't ..."

"Thank you for your concern! But I slept very well last night! I'm only sleepy now because it's such a warm, pleasant day, and I feel like being lazy for a while."

Dianne smiled in satisfaction at Connie's reaction. Then, she got the boat underway while Connie stretched out on an air mattress. With the radiant heat of Alpha Centauri A pouring down on her, Connie felt pleasantly warm and relaxed. She listened to the soft peaceful sound of small waves splashing against the boat. She felt the sensual caress of the gentle breeze flowing over her almost nude body. Thank God we can have such peaceful relaxation on this planet that is so filled with danger, she thought as she became drowsy and fell asleep.

Meanwhile, Dianne noted that Zeb had recovered from his earlier drowsiness. Speaking through Michelle, Dianne questioned him about his telepathic ability with animals, bears in particular. Dianne found Zeb in a talkative mood, and their conversation lasted all the way home.

TIME: Day 23, Dinnertime.

Since it was a warm pleasant evening, the pioneers decided to eat dinner at their outdoor table. Before sitting down, Moose said, "This looks like a real feast, and it smells so good, it's making my mouth water."

Jerry gazed at the various dishes; then, he gave Dianne and Connie a smile of approval. "You've prepared a bigger variety of foods than at any meal we've had here so far."

Obviously pleased, Dianne proudly proclaimed, "Everything that went

459

into these dishes was obtained locally."

"Even the spices are from local plants," added Connie who was pleased that they had prepared the meal from native foods.

"I guess we don't need our food synthesizers anymore," Jerry said.

"That might be true," agreed Moose. "But I don't think we should throw them away just yet. After all, it is possible to create some rather unique delicacies with that technology."

"I wasn't implying that we should throw them away. What I am suggesting is that as far as food is concerned, we could bring everyone down right now and show them a broad variety of native foods to eat. In other words, we've accomplished one of our major objectives."

Jerry established eye contact with his wife. She sensed the question in his mind and said, "From a medical perspective, I haven't discovered anything that would prevent us from bringing everyone down."

Jerry turned to Dianne, who said, "The DNA analysis on Zeb is proceeding smoothly. In three days, we should have his genetic blueprint and be able to compare his immune system to our immune systems. If the comparison is favorable, we'll be able to bring everyone down with a lot more confidence than would have been possible without him."

"Zeb has turned out to be a big help in many ways," stated Connie. "All the samples we collected yesterday under his direction turned out to be safe to eat."

"There's no doubt that he has been a big help," commented Jerry.

"That's true," admitted Moose, "but I don't think we should totally trust him just yet."

Dianne made eye contact with Connie, and even though no words were spoken, they seemed to understand each other's thinking. Then, Dianne turned to Moose. "You might not be ready to trust him, but he did keep us out of trouble today by twice warning us of the presence of a bear when we were on his island."

Jerry stared at Dianne and Connie. "You were on Zeb's Island today! What were you doing there?"

"We needed some eggs for our meatloaf," responded Connie. "And Zeb said he knew where we could find some."

"It seems like you subjected yourselves to considerable risk just for a few eggs."

"We didn't take any more risk getting the eggs than you and Moose took getting the meat," responded Connie. "Also, we didn't add to our risk by calling a female T-Rex to the scene."

Jerry couldn't help feeling pride at his wife's quick wit. He smiled at her affectionately. "I get the feeling that it's going to be a while before I live that one down, but even though I didn't know that's what I was doing, it did work. All other animals did leave the scene."

"We only had one animal to contend with," stated Connie. "And we managed to lure him away from the area."

"How did you do that?" Jerry asked.

While Jerry and Moose listened attentively, Connie gave them a detailed account of the egg gathering expedition. When she finished, Dianne said, "If we're going to make eggs a regular part of our diet, we need to domesticate some birds to provide us with them. It would be a bit inconvenient to go tramping through the bushes every time we need eggs."

"But that would take away the adventure," teased Connie.

"Living here is all the adventure I need," declared Dianne.

"Jerry chuckled at the exchange between Dianne and Connie. "Then, he asked Dianne, "How do you plan to get birds that nest two or three times a year to produce eggs all the time."

"That won't be difficult. I can stimulate egg production with hormones, or I can alter the birds genetically."

"I think we should start the poultry project as soon as we have time to do it," Jerry said. "We can start by incubating some eggs."

Munching on a piece of meatloaf, Jerry said, "This is the first time in my life that I've eaten meatloaf made entirely from things grown in the wild, and it's excellent. Thinking about the effort that went into obtaining each of its ingredients really makes me appreciate how good it is."

Speaking to Dianne, Jerry asked, "Were you able to find out from Zeb how effective his telepathic ability is with animals?"

"He said he can't contact any of the dinosaurs or pterodactyls, but he can get into the minds of some mammals, especially the big predators."

"That's convenient," commented Jerry.

"He told me some stories about how he has used this ability to avoid being killed by bears. His favorite trick is to place an image of an angry T-Rex in the bear's mind."

Jerry laughed. "I see some humor in that."

"In what way?" Connie asked.

"I can picture a bear aggressively pursuing Zeb, fully intent on eating him; when all of a sudden, Zeb's image disappears from the bear's mind and is replaced by the image of a T-Rex. Instead of seeking a meal, the bear would have to instantly figure out how to avoid becoming a meal. Seeing a large predator make that kind of an abrupt change in plans purely because of an illusion would get a laugh out of me."

"Some magicians make a good living using illusions," noted Connie.

"That's true," agreed Jerry, "but Zeb has used illusions not to make a good living but to stay living. I am impressed with the concept. I wonder how effective he is with that technique."

"He's very effective," stated Dianne. "Earlier today, we watched him bring a charging bear to a screeching halt."

Dianne recalled the scene and visualized what had happen. "Now that I think about it, it was very amusing that Zeb could so completely fool such a large animal using nothing more than a special mental power."

"I wish I could do that," Moose said.

"That would be a useful skill," commented Jerry, "especially, if we could get into the minds of all predators."

"When we have Zeb's complete DNA profile, we might be able to determine how his brain does that," commented Dianne.

"That could be dangerous knowledge to have," argued Connie.

"Why?" questioned Dianne.

"You are a competent genetic engineer. You might be tempted to genetically alter the human species, so that some of our offspring will have the same telepathic ability that Zeb has. Can you imagine raising children who could read your mind, but you could not read theirs?"

"That could make a rebellious teen-ager extremely difficult to deal with," admitted Dianne.

"But it would be a useful survival skill," argued Jerry.

"I was a rebellious teenager" stated Moose. "My parents and those in authority had enough trouble with me as it was. Had I been able to read their minds, I might've been impossible to deal with."

"For having been a juvenile delinquent, you turned out pretty good," stated Dianne.

"Thanks to my high school science teacher, I managed to get my life turned around."

"I'm glad he straightened you out. If he hadn't, you wouldn't be here, and I wouldn't have such a wonderful husband. But what really impresses me is the simple way he influenced you to mend your ways."

"I agree," responded Moose. "The profound changes he effected in my life clearly show that constant exposure to a simple message can be very persuasive. As I've told you many times, he had a sign on his desk that said, MY FUTURE DEPENDS ON THE CHOICES THAT I MAKE TODAY. That message didn't mean much to me at first, but it was so prominently displayed that I couldn't help seeing it every day. Over a period of time, it got me thinking about my future. I decided what things I wanted to do and started making choices that supported my goals."

"If you'd had the ability to read people's minds, do you think that message would've still gotten through to you?" Connie asked.

"I think it would've, but I don't know that I'd enjoy raising a child who could read my mind. Even if he were a perfect child, I'd still have to guard my thoughts. Raising children is difficult enough without having that added burden."

"But there would be benefits to shouldering that burden," argued Jerry. "For example, when your children become teenagers, they might decide to explore the wilderness without your permission. It seems to me that you would be far less worried about them if you knew that they could mentally sense the presence of predators and avoid them."

462

"That's true," admitted Moose. "But with our technology and weapons, I'm not sure we need additional survival skills, especially one that could cause problems for parents. Besides that, Zeb's telepathic ability only works with mammals, and most of the predators are dinosaurs."

"I suspect that when Dianne figures out how Zeb's telepathic ability works, she'll also figure out why it doesn't work with dinosaurs," Jerry said. "Then with her genetic engineering skills, she'll figure out how to alter the human species, so our offspring can communicate telepathically with dinosaurs and mammals."

"You're giving me tremendous credit that I haven't yet earned," stated Dianne. "You may be expecting me to do the impossible. Dinosaur brains may be so incompatible with the brains of mammals that it'll be impossible to achieve telepathic communication with them."

"I guess I am getting out in front of the research results," admitted Jerry. "However, if it becomes possible to give our offspring the ability to mentally detect predators and influence their behavior, we will have a very big decision to make. The problems that this ability would cause in our everyday lives will have to be weighed against the increased probability that our new civilization will survive and prosper. We are few in number, and this is a hostile planet. As I see it, an effective survival skill should not be lightly discarded."

"What you're saying makes sense," agreed Moose. "But I'm not comfortable with the idea of raising children who would always know what I'm thinking. It seems like that would put me at a severe disadvantage. It might even put my sanity in jeopardy."

Dianne turned to Connie. "I agree with what you said earlier: understanding how Zeb's telepathic ability works might be dangerous knowledge to have."

"It sure took a lot of discussion for you to reach that conclusion," replied Connie.

"It wasn't the discussion as a whole; rather, it was my husband's concluding remark. I certainly don't want to be the one responsible for jeopardizing his sanity."

Connie laughed at Dianne's comment; then, she looked at Moose who said, "I'm serious! Kids who could read my mind would drive me crazy."

Amused by Moose's excited emotional state, Jerry laughed softly. "You're taking this rather seriously in view of the fact that a possible threat to your sanity is still years away, if it ever happens at all."

"Just thinking about it seems to be threatening his sanity," commented Dianne.

Speaking to Dianne, Connie said, "What's puzzling about this is that this conversation started when Moose said he wished he had the ability to do what Zeb does. Now, he seems to be troubled by the possibility."

"You people are twisting things around. I stand by my earlier statement.

I do wish I had Zeb's ability. It would be a real advantage here on this hostile planet, and it would be a real advantage for parents to be able to read the minds of their children. But children having that advantage over their parents could lead to disaster. Anyway, I don't see how you can make fun of me over something so serious. Think about it; you're talking about genetically altering the human race."

"Only the small part of it that lives on this planet," stated Jerry. "But you're right, it is a serious matter, and when the time comes, we'll have a big decision to make."

"Actually, we'll have two decisions to make," commented Dianne.

"What do you mean?" Jerry asked.

"If we learn how to genetically alter the human species to give it a telepathic ability, do we transmit that information to Earth, or do we keep it to ourselves?"

"I think we should keep it to ourselves," declared Jerry. "I believe that the trouble this knowledge would cause back on Earth would outweigh any possible benefits."

"I agree," stated Moose. "But now that I've said that, I will have to admit that back when we were playing football, it would've been very helpful to have always known what the defense was planning to do."

"That would've made us look real good, but during our last two years, we won all of our games anyway."

"But it would've been fun to have always had the best offensive scheme to take advantage of the defense."

"If we learn how to give the human species a mind-reading ability, we must never transmit that knowledge to Earth," Jerry said to Dianne. "Application of that knowledge could be very disruptive to their society. For example, competitive sports would be forever changed in that deceptive plays would no longer be possible."

Connie giggled. "What would happen to slick politicians if deception were no longer possible?"

"What would happen to the legal profession if members of the jury could see through the deceptive maneuvers of trial lawyers?" Dianne asked.

Moose and Jerry grinned from ear to ear considering the possibilities suggested by the two questions. "Maybe you should reconsider your decision," Moose said to Jerry. "Maybe we could shake up Earth's society in some very beneficial ways."

"Perhaps the benefits would outweigh the problems," Jerry said.

Dianne and Connie looked at each other, and Dianne asked, "Isn't it amazing how asking the right questions can cause someone to reconsider a decision that seemed irrevocable?"

Connie nodded; then, she and Dianne watched Jerry for a reaction.

"I haven't yet made the decision. I was merely stating what was in my mind at the moment."

"It sure sounded like a decision," commented Connie.

"When I think out loud, I sometimes do sound unyielding. But as all of you know, I am flexible in my thinking, and I'm always open to ideas."

"I can't deny that," replied Connie. "And I do like that about you."

"It will be a revolutionary discovery if I'm able to figure out how Zeb's telepathic ability works and what genetic alterations I need to make to give our offspring that ability," stated Dianne. "Discovering new knowledge is one of the objectives of our mission. However, I never thought I'd learn how to give the human species a telepathic ability. We'll be able to advance the human species to a new level. But will we want to do that? Will we transmit the knowledge to Earth?"

"Our situation is far different from what exists on Earth," responded Connie. "Society on Earth has been evolving for tens of thousands of years, and application of this knowledge could be very disruptive. But here on Alcent, we are a tiny group of people. We are the beginning of a new society. It's possible that we could have a telepathic ability and agree to laws governing its use. It's possible that our society could evolve in ways that incorporate this ability to full advantage."

"When the time comes, we'll have some big decisions to make," stated Jerry. "But all of us are here because we made the right choices throughout our lives, and we'll make the right choice this time too."

Jerry turned to Dianne. "I'd like to learn more about how Zeb has used this special ability over the years. Perhaps, you could tell us the stories that he told you about his bear encounters."

Dianne narrated the stories Zeb had told her. When she finished, Moose and Jerry had a new respect for Zeb and his survival skills.

Moose looked at Dianne and Connie. "Your day was far more exciting than ours. All we did was work."

"Our day might not have been very exciting," commented Jerry, "but we did finish another project."

"Are you saying that we can now drive all the way around the island?" Connie asked.

"That's right."

"Did you run into any unexpected difficulties?"

"Cutting a trail through the forest from South Bay to East Bay took more time than I expected. The forest is so dense and tangled with undergrowth that it was mid-afternoon before we finished that stretch. It took no time at all to get to Rocky Point."

"It sounds like you worked hard today. You must be tired."

Moose cut in, "We worked our butts off. I think we should take a couple days off and save some of the hard work for the people coming down in a few days."

"You must be getting old," commented Jerry. "I remember a time when hard work didn't seem to bother you all that much."

465

"I can still do more than my share," retorted Moose. "I just think we should take a few days off and enjoy the solitude we have. In a few days, everyone will probably be free to come down. Then, it'll be a lot more crowded here, and our peace and quiet will be gone."

"You make it sound like we're about to be hit with a population explosion," commented Jerry. "There'll only be twenty-nine of us, and we have an entire planet at our disposal."

"That's true," admitted Moose. "But we'll all be living right here on the plateau, and it won't be as quiet and peaceful as it is now."

"I sense that the prospect of everyone coming down is a bit upsetting to you," commented Connie.

"Not really. I've just enjoyed having the whole place to ourselves. I feel like we've been camping in some remote wilderness area, and now, it's time to return to civilization. Only, in this case, it's coming to us."

"I've also enjoyed our solitude," stated Jerry. "Maybe we should take the next couple days off. After we bring everyone down, we're going to be busy building homes and getting everyone settled in. It's going to be a very different life. A few days vacation would be good for us."

"I could use the time to play around with my smokehouse."

"Do you think you could come up with something comparable to ham?" Jerry asked.

"I'm going to try. I'm also going to try to create something similar to beef jerky, and I'm going to experiment with making sausage."

"I thought you were going to take some time off," commented Connie. "It sounds like you're going to be quite busy."

"My husband never gets tired when he's creating good things to eat. In fact, that seems to be his favorite leisure time activity."

Moose looked at Dianne suggestively. "Let's just say that creating tasty food is my second most favorite leisure time activity."

"I'm happy to hear that I'm still ranked above smoked sausage on your priority list," responded Dianne with a smile.

Connie gained Jerry's attention. "Why don't you and I take the boat out tomorrow? Perhaps we could explore part of the western shore of this lake. We haven't been over there yet."

"That would be fun, but the weather might not cooperate. Mike said a small storm system is coming our way. He's predicting that we'll have rainy weather tomorrow."

"If it's a small system and moves through here in just one day, we can sail over there the day after tomorrow."

"Maybe on the day after that, Moose and I can take the boat out," suggested Dianne.

"Good idea," agreed Moose. "After everyone comes down, we'll have to get on a waiting list to use the boat."

"It will be a popular piece of equipment for a while," agreed Dianne.

466

"After we get our homes built, we'll make some boats, so that our submarine can be used primarily for research," Jerry said. "I want to thoroughly explore the depths of this lake. If there are any dangerous creatures living in it, I want to find them. Also, I want full knowledge of what resources it contains. In other words, I want to know everything that there is to know about it."

His colleagues nodded in agreement and Jerry continued, "If tomorrow's weather isn't good for sailing, I'll get together with Michelle and spend a major part of the day talking with Zeb. I haven't had time to have a lengthy conversation with him, and it's time I do that."

"That should be interesting," commented Connie. "I might join you for part of that, but first, I should do a medical evaluation of each of us."

"I thought we were going to take a few days off," objected Dianne.

"Can you think of a better way for me to relax than to leisurely do something that I enjoy?" asked Connie.

"I've never thought of a medical exam as a recreational activity," replied Dianne.

"I don't know about that," commented Jerry. "I still remember that medical exam she gave me right after we left Earth. I can honestly say that it put a smile on my face."

Connie grinned and turned to Dianne. "As far as I can tell, he's been a well satisfied patient ever since."

"After those comments, you expect me to trust you to give my husband a physical tomorrow morning. Maybe I should assist you."

"I knew I could count on you," stated Connie. "With your help, we'll get the medical work done early; then, we can take the rest of the day off."

"Somehow, I get the feeling that I've been finagled into helping you with your work on my first day off in quite some time."

Connie smiled. "Even with the lab work, it won't take us more than an hour or two. We'll have the rest of the day off."

"That sounds good to me," responded Dianne.

"What are you going to do tomorrow?" Connie asked Dianne.

"I'd like to wander around here on the plateau looking for interesting plants and creatures to study."

"That sounds like work. You just told me that tomorrow's your first day off in a long time."

"But I enjoy my profession, especially, when I can work at a leisurely pace. Learning about the things that live here is fun for me, but it's a big job. It's going to take a long time to catalog all the life that lives here on the plateau; then, there's the rest of the island, the marine life in the lake, and the life in the countryside."

"How can you talk about leisure time in the same breath that you outline a lifelong project?" Connie asked.

"I'm not going to do the whole project tomorrow; I'm just going to

467

wander around looking for things that grab my attention."

"That might be interesting. Maybe I'll join you when we're done with the medical work."

"I thought you were going to join your husband's visit with Zeb."

"If it's raining, I'll do that; if we're between showers, I'll join you."

"You'd never make it as a biologist," commented Dianne.

"Why is that?" asked Connie in a surprised tone.

"We need to understand how various life forms behave in the rain as well as in the sunshine. And there are creatures that stay out of sight during sunny weather and come out only when it's raining. But I guess you could always be a fair weather biologist."

"Okay! Rain or shine, I'll join you."

"That's a plan I can live with. Especially, after the way you finagled me into helping you."

TIME: Day Twenty-Four, Early Afternoon.

Dianne and Connie were enjoying the great outdoors while exploring the plateau. "I love the way the air smells after it rains," Dianne said.

"I do too. It just has such a fresh, clean feel to it."

"We did need the rain. It was starting to get dry around here."

"As usual, Mike's forecast was right on," stated Connie. "We've had several showers since midnight, but now it looks almost over, and this warm sunshine really feels good."

"We aren't necessarily done with the rain yet; there are still a few showers hanging around the area."

Connie pointed to the northeast. "I see what you mean. That one is really big. It could certainly take the fun out of a sailing trip."

"But it's producing a beautiful rainbow, one of the most colorful I've ever seen."

Suddenly, the heavy cloud formation was split from end to end by a powerful lightning bolt. Ten seconds later, a sharp booming crack of thunder reached the plateau, jolting Dianne and Connie with its power.

"How spectacular can it get?" exclaimed Connie. "We're being treated to the beauty and violence of nature all at once." Dianne and Connie gazed in silence at the magnificent rainbow and occasional lightning bolt; then, they resumed wandering the plateau.

"There sure are lots of wildflowers here," stated Connie. "Have they always been so numerous? Why haven't I noticed them?"

"Many of these plants have blossomed since our arrival."

"They're beautiful, and I haven't paid much attention to them. Maybe I need to take more breaks to enjoy the beauty we have here."

"I am studying these plants. That's a big job, and you're welcome to help me. Then, you can learn about them while appreciating their beauty."

"That's a good idea," responded Connie, while pointing at a small shrub covered with pink blossoms. "That bush is exceptionally beautiful."

"And it smells good too," noted Dianne.

"It's little wonder that the air smells so good. It has not only been washed by rain, but it's also being perfumed by lots of wildflowers."

"This bush is buzzing with bees, and they look like the ones nesting in the dead tree we discovered a few weeks ago. Seeing them reminds me that we never did investigate that tree to find out if they're making honey."

"Why don't we do that now? We have the time."

"I don't know that I feel like being stung," replied Dianne.

"We should be able to figure out a way to investigate the inside of that tree without getting stung or even unduly disturbing the bees."

"If the bees don't agree with your plan, we could end up with numerous painful stings."

"I don't think these bees are overly aggressive," stated Connie. "When we used Charlie to check them out, they didn't bother him until he pounded on the tree."

"So how do you plan to investigate their nest without provoking an attack on us?"

"I have cameras that are so small I can snake them through a blood vein in search of trouble. It seems like we could use that instrument to investigate the bee nest. A couple hours of video should give us some pretty good insight into what their normal activity is. And if they're making honey, we can find out how much is in the tree. If they have a surplus, we can figure out how to get some of it."

"And you guarantee that we're going to do this without being stung."

"I can't guarantee that, but why are you so concerned about being stung? It's no more painful than getting a shot at the doctor's office, and we know that isn't very painful."

"That's what you doctors always say, but I know better. Besides that, we don't know for sure how toxic their venom is."

"Charlie was stung several times, and we analyzed the venom. Even though it's somewhat different than bee venom back on Earth, it's still in the same class of poisons. I believe the human body can handle the tiny amount that these bees are able to inject."

"What if we can't? What if one of us is stung and has an allergic reaction?"

"When we identified the chemicals in the venom, I had one of my assistants develop an antidote for it. I have an adequate amount of it in our medical supplies."

"I seem to have run out of objections, and you seem to be quite determined to investigate those bees."

"It is something that we need to do. If there is lots of honey in that tree, it would be nice to get some of it. But even more important than that, we need to find out how well the human body handles their venom."

"It almost sounds like you're hoping to be stung."

469

"I don't relish the idea of suffering one or more painful bee stings, but my daughter may be coming down in a few days. As active and curious as she is, sooner or later, she will suffer a bee sting. I need to find out if that's going to be a serious problem, and getting stung is one way to do that."

"It looks to me like a mother's protective instinct is at work here."

"That's true, but setting aside concern for my daughter, if all goes according to plan, there'll soon be twenty-nine of us living here. It's only a matter of time and someone will be stung. I need to know if that's going to be a medical emergency or just a painful annoyance."

"Okay, I'm convinced! Let's investigate the nest."

"Let's take a look at our equipment options and work out a plan. The hole in that tree is higher than we can reach, and I don't think it would be a good idea to climb the tree."

"But I thought that you wanted to be stung."

"Two or three stings are fine, but I don't want them to make a pincushion out of me."

"So how do you plan to get into that tree without becoming a pincushion?"

"One thing that might work is a thin rod to reach the nest entrance. The thinner it is; the less threatening it'll look to the bees."

"My husband's fishing rod might work," Dianne suggested.

"That's an idea. If it had a ninety-degree bend near the end, we could reach the hole and enter it, and by simply feeding out line, we could lower our camera into the nest."

My husband is very possessive about that fishing pole. I'm not sure that he'll be comfortable with us modifying it in any way."

"Let's talk to him. He's an engineer. Let's get him to modify it in a way that he's comfortable with that also meets our needs. Anyway, the possibility of adding honey to our menu will be a good incentive for him."

"That's true. His mind is never very far away from food."

A few minutes later, Dianne and Connie found Moose putting wood chips on the smoldering fire in his smoke house. Jerry was busy telling Moose some of the things he had learned from Zeb.

When Jerry finished his narration, Dianne and Connie explained their plan. Moose and Jerry listened attentively; their practical engineering minds were already at work.

When they finished, Jerry said, "Your plan should work and will be easy to implement."

"I can easily modify my fishing pole," Moose said. "All I need to do is take a piece of stiff wire, bend a small loop at one end for the line to pass through, put a ninety-degree bend in the middle, and then tape it on the end of the fishing rod."

"And I can make you a camera pack," stated Jerry. "The tiny cameras in our mechanical bugs will do a good job, and they are easy to remove from the bugs. Those cameras have a 120-degree field of view. By stacking three of them, I can make you a camera pack with a 360-degree field of view. That will eliminate the problem of trying to aim a camera hanging on the end of a fishing line."

"How long will it take?" Connie asked.

"Less than an hour," responded Jerry.

"It won't take me more than a few minutes," replied Moose.

"There is one possible problem," commented Jerry, "and that is we don't know if the nest extends downward from the entrance. If the nest extends upward, your plan to lower the cameras into it won't work."

"If the dead tree is hollow because of decay and the action of bugs, insects, larvae, whatever; then, the nest probably extends up and down from the entrance," Moose said. "Why don't we attach an upward looking camera to the wire I'm adding to my fishing pole."

"Good idea," agreed Jerry. "And I will add a downward looking camera to the camera pack."

"I knew these guys could put it together for us," stated Connie.

"You did present us with a simple problem," Jerry said.

"This might be the first time in history that a fishing pole was used to look for honey," Moose said. "But if you find some, I will find a way to use it on some of the smoked meat delicacies I'm creating."

Connie and Dianne looked at each other and smiled. "I guess we were right," Connie said.

"What was that all about?" questioned Moose.

"Just something Connie said earlier that I agreed with."

"That's an evasive answer."

"I know, but we can't tell you everything. We need to be a bit mysterious at times."

Realizing that he wasn't going to get a straight answer from his wife, Moose went back to nursing the smoldering fire in his smokehouse. When he was satisfied that it didn't need any attention for a while, he set out to modify his fishing pole.

Just over an hour later, Connie and Dianne arrived in the grove containing the bee nest. They stopped several yards from the nest and observed a steady stream of bees entering and leaving.

"They're sure active," commented Connie.

"With all the rain we've had, plants aren't hurting for water, so their blossoms should be rich with nectar. The bees are probably harvesting it as fast as they can."

"In other words, they're getting it while the getting is good."

"That's one way to put it. What I think is happening is they don't have to visit very many blossoms to pick up as much as they can carry, so it doesn't take them very long to fly out, fill up, and return."

"They don't seem to be paying any attention to us," noted Connie.

"Let's move a little closer and find out what happens."

Dianne and Connie moved toward the tree, stopping ten feet away. After a brief pause, Connie said, "Still no reaction. I'm going in."

Walking slowly, Connie reached the tree without incident. Then, she cautiously lifted the fishing pole up toward the nest entrance. When the end of the pole reached the opening, she said, "Still no reaction. I guess the end of the pole doesn't look or smell like any of their enemies."

"Let's take a look inside," suggested Dianne. "I'll put on a headset, monitor the images from the cameras, and give you direction." A few seconds later, Dianne said, "Okay, I'm ready."

Connie slowly moved the modified end of the rod through the nest entrance and into the tree until Dianne said, "Stop."

Dianne looked at the imagery. "This is a very big nest. I see what look like honeycombs as far up and down as I can see. If these combs actually do contain honey, there is a huge supply here. Try lowering the camera pack."

Connie slowly reeled out line lowering the cameras into the lower part of the nest. "What an amazing sight," commented Dianne. "These bees are hard at work. They aren't stopping what they're doing when approached by our camera pack. They're just totally ignoring it."

"Maybe they don't have any enemies that look or smell like our camera pack," suggested Connie.

"That must be the case," agreed Dianne.

"Too bad we can't get a sample of what they're making to find out if it is similar to honey," Connie said.

"I think we can. I can see the bottom of the nest, and they're making honeycombs down there. If you'll release the brake on the reel, the camera pack will crash into those honeycombs. The downward pointing camera should end up being coated with what they're making."

"Let me know when you've seen enough, and I'll do that."

"As long as we're here we should probably watch them for a few more minutes. Besides that, you haven't been stung yet, and that's something you wanted to investigate."

"Crashing our camera pack into the bottom of their nest might provoke them," commented Connie.

"But if they see it as an enemy and try to sting it, that still won't get you stung."

"Let me know when you're ready, and I'll drop it. Then, we'll find out what they do."

"Before we do that, let's get more imagery of their nest activity. I want you to slowly raise the cameras, stopping when I tell you to."

For 15 minutes, Connie moved the cameras around under Dianne's direction, occasionally stopping to watch individual bees at work. Finally, Dianne said, "I have enough video to study, so I can get a pretty good idea what goes on inside their nest. Let's drop the camera pack."

Connie released the reel's brake, and the small camera pack fell six feet crashing into the honeycomb at the bottom of the nest. Then, she reeled it up to the nest entrance and removed it. Angered by the damage it had just caused, several bees followed the camera pack. They were determined to chase it out of their nest.

Seeing an opportunity to get stung, Connie set the stock end of the pole on the ground and held the other end at arms length. With her other hand she reached toward the camera pack. The bees that had escorted the camera pack out of the nest continued to buzz around it and Connie's hand, but they did not sting her. Eventually, they returned to their nest.

"I guess I'm just not going to get stung today," stated Connie.

"You don't have to sound so disappointed. After all, it is painful."

"I don't need the pain, but I do need to find out how the human body reacts to their venom."

"As docile as these bees are, getting stung might be a rare occurrence, something that only happens with some very blatant provocation or in defense against known enemies."

Connie and Dianne looked closely at the thick sticky syrup coating the bottom of the camera pack. "It sure looks like honey," Dianne said.

Connie sniffed it. "It also smells like honey. Let's take it to the lab. I want to find out how sweet it is and if it contains any toxins."

"If it's sweet and safe, I know someone who will eagerly volunteer to taste it."

"If it tastes good, how long do you think it'll take him to figure out how to get some of it out of that tree?" Connie asked.

"By the time he's finished smoking meat, he'll have a plan."

"Actually, harvesting some of that honey shouldn't be all that difficult. I think we should figure out how to do it."

"Dianne nodded. "The trick will be to do it without causing the bees to abandon their nest. The video I watched shows that the back side of the tree is what's loaded with honey. All we should have to do is drill some holes into it and dig out some honey. When we're done, we plug the holes and use them again at some future time."

"Are you volunteering to drill the holes?" Connie asked.

"You're the one who wants to be stung, and drilling holes in the tree might provoke an attack."

"The problem is it might provoke a massive attack."

"That's possible, but if we quietly approach the back of the tree and drill the holes without a lot of noise or vibration, they might not bother us at all. If we avoid breaking through the surface of the honeycomb, they might not be aware of what's going on beneath the surface."

"That's a good possibility," agreed Connie. "Let's analyze this stuff and then talk to our husbands about it."

A short time later, with the lab results in hand, Connie and Dianne met with Moose and Jerry. "It's very sweet, it's not toxic, and it tastes good," stated Connie.

"I'd like a taste," Moose requested.

Connie handed him the small camera pack and a toothpick, which Moose used to scrape off a bit of honey. After tasting it, he said, "This is delicious. How much is in that tree?"

"The tree is nearly three feet in diameter," responded Dianne. "The hollow inside varies from about 1.5 to about 2 feet in diameter. It appears that about three-fourths of the interior is filled with honey."

"Wow!" exclaimed Moose. "There could be fifty gallons in there. Why would they make so much?"

"It's food for them to eat during hard times," responded Dianne. "Evidently, they haven't had any hard times in recent years because it has probably taken them a few years to build up such a large supply."

"What would cause them to have a tough time?" Moose asked.

"An extended period of dry weather could cause many plants to not blossom very abundantly," replied Dianne. "In their struggle for survival, some plants might not flower at all. If the bees can't find enough nectar to live on, they would have to eat some of their stored honey."

"Evidently, the opposite has been the case," commented Connie. "Apparently, the flowering plants here on the island have seen ideal weather for the last few years, and the resulting abundance of flowers has resulted in the bees producing an abundance of honey."

"That does seem to be the case," agreed Dianne.

Moose tasted another bit of honey. "Whatever the reason for the abundance, we need to get some of it. This is really delicious. I wouldn't mind having some of this to put on some hot cinnamon rolls."

"You get the honey, and I'll make the rolls," Dianne said.

"That's an offer I can't refuse. But am I going to suffer multiple bee stings in the process?"

"I invaded their nest with a camera pack and didn't get stung," Connie said.

"But you didn't break into their food supply and attempt to steal a half-gallon of it," commented Moose.

"You need to use stealth," suggested Connie. "Steal it without them knowing what you're doing."

"Do you have a plan in mind?" Moose asked.

"Most of the honey is stored on the side of the tree opposite the entrance. If we could quietly drill a hole into the back of the tree, we should be able to take some honey without them being aware of it."

"How large a hole do you have in mind?" questioned Moose.

"I have medical instruments that allow me to do internal surgery through very small openings. You drill me a half-inch hole, and I'll get some honey."

"Wouldn't it be easier if the hole were larger, like maybe three inches in diameter?" Jerry asked.

"Definitely! Then, we could just dig it out with a large spoon."

"In our tool chest, we have a drill bit with an adjustable head. I could drill a three-inch hole, and I could do it quietly with very little vibration."

"If you're volunteering to do that, I'll stay here and finish smoking this meat," Moose said.

"Sounds like a convenient excuse to avoid the possibility of being stung," commented Jerry.

"It might sound that way, but I do have some real delicacies in my smoke oven. Being the master that I am, I just can't leave before they're done. There might be some loss in quality if someone else were to finish this job."

Speaking to Connie and Jerry, Dianne said, "That's just one more demonstration of the ego that I have to contend with every day."

"You don't seem to mind," commented Connie. "In fact, you seem to be quite content in your relationship."

"Moose does have a point," Jerry said. "He is quite good at making delicious foods."

"Aw, the master finally gets some well deserved recognition," stated Moose.

"I'll find out at dinnertime if the praise was premature," replied Jerry.

"You won't be disappointed," declared Moose.

"Let's go get some honey," Jerry said to Connie. "Just to play it safe, I am going to wear some protective clothing. I wouldn't mind one or two stings, but there's always the possibility of a mass attack."

"I'll skip the protective clothing and watch you from a safe distance."

Jerry and Connie picked up the things they needed and headed for the bee tree. In less than an hour, they returned with two gallons of raw honey.

"How did it go?" Dianne asked.

"It went smoothly," replied Connie. "Jerry drilled three holes. Then, he scooped out all the honey he could reach. Before plugging each hole, he broke through the surface of the honey comb into the open space in the nest, so the bees would be aware of the cavities we left. Hopefully, they'll fill those cavities. At some later date, we can pull the plugs and remove the fresh honey."

"It'll be interesting to find out how long it'll take them to replace the honey you and Jerry took," Dianne said.

"In a couple weeks, we'll drop the cameras in there and see how they're doing," Connie said.

While looking at Connie, Dianne said, "You seem to have a fresh red welt on your forehead."

Connie held up her left arm. "I also have one right here on my wrist and another one on my hand."

"How painful are they?"

"About the same as a bee sting back on Earth."

"Three stings should be enough to find out how the human body responds to their venom."

"It'll tell us how my body reacts. I'd like you to draw a blood specimen, so we can find out if this venom is affecting my blood chemistry in any significant way."

"I think we should treat you as a possible poison victim and check out all of your vital signs."

"Even though I feel just fine, I do agree with you." Turning to Jerry, Connie asked, "While we're checking me out, would you mind separating this honey from the wax?"

"I can do that," replied Jerry.

Speaking to Jerry, Moose said, "I'm done smoking meat, so I'll join you, and you can give me the details of the honey collecting expedition."

An hour and a half later, the pioneers sat down to enjoy their evening meal. The featured items were Moose's version of ham, sausage, and jerky along with hot cinnamon rolls smothered with raw honey. Steamed vegetables and a salad rounded out the meal. All items were locally obtained except for the ingredients used to make the cinnamon rolls.

After dinner, Jerry noted that Alpha Centauri A had already slipped below the western horizon and that Alpha Centauri B would set in less than a half-hour. Looking to the south and southeast, he saw Aphrodite and Nocturne high in the sky and noted that both would be in the full moon phase in two days. Two full moons will be a unique sight that we haven't yet seen, thought Jerry.

He looked out over the plateau softly lit by the dim orange glow from Alpha Centauri B and the light of two moons approaching their full phase. The romantic aura of the scene gradually pervaded his mind, and he turned to Connie, "I feel like going for a moonlight swim in South Bay. Would you care to join me?"

"I'd be delighted to. Let's go."

SEVENTEEN

Vacation Sailing

TIME: Day Twenty-Five, Several Minutes before First Sunrise.

Jerry and Connie were onboard the submarine, cruising on the surface with battery power. They left South Bay and were rounding the southwestern tip of Pioneer Island en route to the west coast of Clear Lake. Jerry was at mid-deck piloting the boat while Connie was standing near the bow enjoying the sensual caress of the mild breeze. She took a deep breath while stretching straight and tall. She slowly exhaled and shook her arms and shoulders to rid herself of the last bit of early morning sleepiness. Now feeling fully awake and relaxed, she gazed out across the vast open water of Clear Lake and anticipated a fun-filled, carefree day. She turned and wandered from the boat's bow to its stern thinking, if Mike's forecast is correct, we're going to have perfect weather for a day on the lake.

When Connie reached the stern, she grasped the handrail and surveyed the sky. She noted a few widely scattered clouds, but it was the cloud bank in the eastern sky that caught her attention. Its elegant, natural beauty seemed to fill her with a profound sense of peacefulness that grew into a joyful sense of warmth and well-being. As she continued to gaze at the soft billowing clouds, she became aware of their delicate curves and was struck by their sensual, almost erotic, appeal. She noted that the cloud bottoms were awash with a soft pink glow that added a buoyant warm aura to the scene. As Connie continued to feast her eyes on the delicate artistic beauty provided by nature, her sense of warmth and personal well-being became so strong that she was unable to contain it. She felt an overpowering desire to share her joyful mood with the man she loved, so she turned to Jerry and exclaimed, "It's wonderful to be living here! Please stop whatever you're doing and enjoy this beautiful sunrise with me!"

Surprised by the passion in Connie's voice, Jerry turned away from piloting the boat and looked at her. He saw his wife silhouetted against the pre-sunrise glow of the eastern sky. Her golden blonde hair flowing in the breeze took on a reddish-blond tint. He noticed that her skin also reflected the warm glow. As he continued to gaze at Connie, he was struck by the way the pre-sunrise glow seemed to cause her to radiate a special angelic beauty. Jerry responded the only way he could. He slowed the boat to three mph

477

and put it on auto-pilot. Then, he stepped into position behind Connie and put his arms around her in a warm, loving embrace. While closely bound together, Connie and Jerry enjoyed the warm pre-sunrise glow that filled the eastern sky and reflected off the lake.

A few minutes later, Alpha Centauri A peaked over the eastern horizon and its brilliant glare signaled the beginning of a new day. Connie turned in her husband's embrace, looked up into his eyes, and kissed him warmly. "Thanks for enjoying that with me. Our day is off to a great start, and I feel like having fun today."

Jerry loosened his embrace of Connie, so he could back away from her one small step. With his hands warmly planted against her sides, he said, "You're sure fired up this morning."

"I feel like a big load has been taken off our backs."

"What do you mean?"

"We've accomplished most of our objectives for our first 30 days, and we've only been here 25 days. I believe we have a wonderful future here, so today, I want to celebrate. I want to relax and have fun."

"I like your objectives. You can expect full cooperation from me."

"As much as you enjoy sailing, I never had any doubt about that."

"Sailing is fun, and today promises to be a great day for it. We should have enough wind to use the sails effectively, but not enough to make the lake too rough."

"And we have the entire lake to ourselves," added Connie.

"Back on Earth, I could only dream about the freedom that comes from being the only boat on the lake."

"Privacy does have some advantages. As warm as it already is, I think it'll be hot enough this afternoon, so we can do some nude sunbathing."

"Now, you're getting me excited."

Connie smiled, stepped forward, and gave her husband a warm hug. "I like the romantic mood you're in," Jerry whispered.

"Perhaps my mood is the result of that romantic moonlight swim you took me on last night. I might still be basking in the afterglow."

"I don't think swimming has ever left me with an afterglow that I could get wrapped up in," Jerry teased.

"Do I need to be specific?"

Desiring to hear what she would say, Jerry gave her a naughty grin and nodded.

"It wasn't the moonlight swim," Connie responded. "It was that passionate episode on the beach that has left me with an afterglow."

For a few moments, Jerry pretended to be lost in thought. Then, he said, "Now that you've tweaked my memory, I vaguely recall that we did have some fun on the beach last night."

"You might be a good actor, but you're not fooling me. You were a bundle of passion last night."

Jerry smiled warmly. "You're right; I was, and so were you."

"I haven't yet gotten used to having two moons in the sky and that had a romantic effect on me. Plus, we're on a savage planet. The element of danger was present, and that added a degree of excitement. But most of all, I'm happy with our new home and the great relationship we have."

"Our marriage is special. I hope it continues to be as warm and loving as it has always been."

"Our life together will be what we choose to make it. If we continue to be faithful to each other, treat each other with love and respect, and look for ways to make each other happy, then, we'll not only continue to have a wonderful relationship, but it'll get even better."

"That's a prescription I can live with."

"Did I sound like a doctor writing a prescription?"

"No, but you are a doctor, and I couldn't help saying that."

"Well, right now, the doctor is hungry and about ready to write a prescription for breakfast."

"I'm hungry too, but let's deploy the sails before we eat breakfast."

Twenty minutes later, with the sails and outriggers deployed, Jerry again put the boat on auto-pilot. "Okay, I'm ready for breakfast," he said. "In fact, I'm starving."

Connie went below deck to prepare a hot breakfast while Jerry set up a portable table and chairs. In less than ten minutes, they were seated at the table, silently enjoying breakfast while surrounded by the pristine beauty of Clear Lake.

Connie broke the silence. "You seem to be deeply lost in thought. Would you mind sharing it with me?"

"I was thinking about some of the things I did back on Earth."

"Do you miss Earth?"

"Sometimes, I wish I could go back there for a few days to visit friends and family, but I'd rather live here."

"What got you started thinking about Earth this morning?"

"The sunrise we just enjoyed reminded me of some that I enjoyed on backpack trips into wilderness areas. As you know, backpacking was one of my favorite activities. I enjoyed the quiet peacefulness of the forest."

"That quiet peacefulness can be very beneficial. It can enable a person to get into a relaxed state of mind, allowing one to think on a higher level than what's possible during normal everyday living."

"It definitely did that for me. In fact, being in the wilderness seemed to stimulate my imagination. I would find a rapids in a mountain river and then scramble out to a rock in the midst of the rapids. While sitting on the rock, I'd let my mind wander. Sometimes, I tried to imagine what it would be like to go back in time and visit Earth during the dinosaur age. Living here isn't the same thing, but in a sense, it does fulfill that dream."

"Coming here is much more than a fulfillment of that dream. We're not just visiting a dinosaur planet; we're also building a home here."

"That's true, and living here is more wildly exciting than my daydreams ever were. I never imagined that I'd stand under a 100-ton sauropod, reach up, and touch him."

"You also probably never imagined that we'd befriend a pterodactyl who would then save my life by killing one of its kind."

"And I also never expected to see my best friend stranded on the back of a styracosaurus during a face-off with a pack of T-Rexes."

"Can you imagine what it would be like to put a pack on your back, hike into the wilderness, and do some overnight camping with those brutes lurking in the bushes?"

"I don't think that would be very relaxing. I'd be too busy just trying to stay alive to find time to relax."

"But think about the advantages. To start with, you wouldn't have to make a daydream trip into fantasyland to wonder what it would be like to have dinosaurs around."

"You're not convincing me."

"But I thought you liked the sense of adventure that's always present on a backpack trip."

"There is such a thing as too much adventure. This isn't twenty-first century Earth; this is Alcent, a wild, primitive planet. Just living here is a full-time adventure."

"But spending a few days in the countryside would be a challenging test of your survival skills."

"Someday, we'll probably make such a trip, but we'll probably do it with ATVs, so that we can be well-supplied and well-armed. We'll use RPV's to scout our vicinity. During the night, we'll have two guards equipped with night vision goggles. It would be a dangerous adventure, but I think we could do it without suffering any casualties."

"There's no way to know that for sure. I was almost killed by a saber-tooth when we went ashore for just a few minutes."

"That's true, and with that in mind, I don't think we'll be making any extended trips into the countryside anytime soon, unless we have a very important reason to."

"I don't feel the need for such a trip. Living on Pioneer Island has been a lot like camping out and has given me all the adventure I need."

"In a few days, that's probably going to change, because I'll most like-ly be giving the okay for everyone to come down and join us."

"Judging from the way you said that, I sense that you feel some reluctance about bringing everyone down."

"There are only four of us here, five counting Zeb. We've had a vast wilderness area completely to ourselves, and I've enjoyed more adventure and solitude than I ever had on any camping trip."

"I have too," admitted Connie. "But even after we bring everyone down, adventure and solitude will never be very far away."

"That's true, but Stellar Plateau has been a quiet, secluded place, and I've enjoyed that peaceful seclusion. After we bring everyone down, the plateau will be buzzing with activity, and building shelters will be the first thing on the list."

"How are we going to decide where to put them? Each couple will have their own idea about where they want to live."

"Probably the easiest way to avoid conflict will be to divide the plateau into public and private land. Then, we divide the private land into equally sized lots. The fairest way to decide which family gets which lot will be to simply draw numbers out of a hat."

"What about Zeb?"

"If he chooses to stay with us, he'll also receive a lot, and we'll build him a house on it."

"For thirty years, his life has been the ultimate in quiet seclusion."

"I wouldn't like to have that much seclusion," stated Jerry.

"Does that mean you now feel better about everyone coming down?"

"Let's just say I have mixed emotions. I've liked having the whole place to ourselves, but I'm also looking forward to the challenge of building a new civilization."

"If Zeb chooses to live with us, then in return for building him a home, he could make his cave dwelling available for people to camp out in. Anyone who feels the need for some isolation could live on Zeb's island for a few days. They could explore the island during the day and have a secure place to sleep at night."

"Good idea," stated Jerry. "In fact, all the islands should be fairly safe places to camp and explore, except for the bear problem. In time, we'll know just how much of a problem the bears are going to be. But that's okay; it's going to be a while before anyone is interested in going camping anyway. They've all been in space so long that living on the plateau is going to feel like camping out, especially until we get our homes built."

"When they're all built, the plateau is going to look like a village."

"But it won't be crowded. Even if we retain half of the land as public land, each family will still have a lot roughly three times bigger than a football field. And that should provide plenty of space to grow vegetables, fruits, berries, nuts, cereal grains, flowers, whatever."

"As readily available as food is in the wild, I don't think each family will face much of a challenge to grow enough additional things, so they can eat very well," Connie said.

"Speaking about food available in the wild, that honey we collected yesterday is delicious. I think it would be in everyone's best interest to make sure those bees have a good year every year. One way to do that would be to beautify our homes with flower gardens."

"Harvesting the honey would be much easier if we could get them out of that tree and into a beehive. It would be even better if we could divide the colony and get several beehives going."

"Our library should have the information we need to care for bees."

"But that information applies to Earth's bees," stated Connie. "We don't know how these bees reproduce. We don't know what keeps them together in a colony. We don't know what would motivate them to leave a nesting site and search for a new one. And we don't know how to divide them into several colonies."

"That's all true, but while we're getting answers to those questions, it would be easy to make some boxes similar to what bee keepers on Earth make for their honey bees and locate them near the honey tree. Maybe a few conveniently located nesting sites would cause them to move out of the tree or divide into colonies."

"It's worth a try," agreed Connie.

"I'll make the boxes tomorrow morning; then, I'll have the rest of the day to be lazy."

"I'll join you for that. It might be our last chance to be lazy in quite some time. Moose and Dianne are going sailing, so except for Zeb, we'll be home alone."

"I don't think Zeb will bother us much," commented Jerry. "He's been spending most of his time conversing with Michelle."

"He hasn't had anyone to talk to in 30 years, and ever since she decided to write his biography, he's been eagerly sharing his life with her at every opportunity."

"I'm glad she's doing that and that he's excited about it. Depending on how good his memory is, we should learn a great deal about our home, and we might even find out what life was like on B-2 before the long war."

"When we left Earth, I never dreamed that we'd discover an alien civilization or that we'd have an alien living with us."

"Zeb is an interesting addition to our lives," stated Jerry.

"Yes, he is, and he makes me wonder how many interesting alien civilizations live in our galaxy."

"That's something we can only speculate about, but I believe the Milky Way contains an abundance of life."

"Why?" Connie asked.

All three of the earthlike planets we know about are teeming with life, and the Milky Way contains eight billion Sun-like stars. If only one or two percent of them have earthlike planets, you could still have a hundred million planets teeming with life."

"That's an exciting possibility that's almost beyond imagination."

"The possibilities fire up my imagination, but I will soon have a big decision to make concerning life on this planet."

"My intuition is telling me that you'll make that decision tomorrow night and that you'll decide to bring everyone down the next day."

"If I don't bring them down pretty soon, I might have a mutiny on my hands. They might decide to take the risk and come down anyway."

"I don't think they'd do that. They're too professional."

"While I believe that to be true, they've been in space for a long time. They're so excited about the possibility of coming down soon that they can hardly contain themselves. Mike told me last night that everyone is packed. They even have the cargo shuttle packed and ready to go."

"Besides all of that, Dianne tells me that her assistants are working around the clock to discover the details of Zeb's immune system."

"It's amazing to me that you can learn so much about Zeb just by studying his DNA"

"As soon as we have his genetic blueprint, all we have to do is feed that information into the computer, and it will create 3-D imagery of any part of his body that we choose to study. If we ask the computer to display his cardiovascular system, it will do that. If we want to study his skeleton, we can call up a display of it from any angle we care to view it from. We can call up an image of his brain. Hopefully, that will give us some clues as to where his telepathic ability comes from. But that will come later. The first thing we'll do is display his immune system and make a detailed comparison to the human immune system."

"When will this information be available?"

Dianne's assistants are promising sometime tomorrow night. If they find that Zeb's immune system is comparable to ours or inferior to ours, then the fact that he has survived here for 30 years would indicate that we can safely bring everyone down as far as germs are concerned."

"What if Zeb's immune system is vastly superior to ours?"

"I sense that you're thinking about bringing everyone down anyway."

"That is what I'm considering. Keep in mind that he has lived here for 30 years without medical attention. To have survived that long without medical help might require a superior immune system. Our situation is different; we have superior medical technology and a competent doctor with very well trained assistants."

"I appreciate the compliment, but if we discover that Zeb's immune system has some unique capability that we don't have, then, I think we should try to understand that capability before we bring everyone down. That way, I will be able to determine if our medical technology can do for us what his immune system does for him."

"How long would it take to determine that?"

"That depends on what we discover."

"That's a safe answer, but I guess it's the only one you can give me."

"We could speculate on various possibilities, but that might take all day, and I'd rather relax and enjoy this day on the lake with you."

"I can live with that," responded Jerry with a big smile.

"The wind seems to be picking up a bit," commented Connie.

"Let's clear the deck."

"I'll put away the dishes."

"And I'll put away the table and chairs."

Five minutes later, Connie emerged from below deck, and she and Jerry got down to the serious business of enjoying a day of recreational sailing on a pristine lake with 700 square miles of water, a huge lake by any standard. Best of all, in their minds, it was a huge lake with no one on it except them. There was the unpolluted water teeming with fish that they could observe through the boat's transparent hull. There were sea birds soaring around, and there were soaring pterodactyls with their fifty-foot wing spans. The flying creatures were seen against the background of a deep blue sky sprinkled with a few fluffy cumulus clouds. All of this combined with warm temperatures would make it a very enjoyable day.

TIME: Day Twenty-Six, Mid-Afternoon.

Having spent the previous day enjoying the pleasures of sailing, Jerry and Connie were spending this day leisurely enjoying Pioneer Island. Expecting that everyone would soon be coming down, they were taking advantage of their opportunity to enjoy the peaceful solitude.

Meanwhile, Moose and Dianne were 20 miles from Pioneer Island sailing eastward along the north shore of Clear Lake. While cruising along the edge of a shallow bay, Moose exclaimed, "Look over there! If I'm not mistaken, that bay is filled with the same kind of wild rice that's growing in a shallow bay at Zeb's island."

Because of the shallow water, they could not sail into the bay, so Dianne studied the plants with binoculars. "I think you're right," she said, "And those plants are loaded with grain, but it's still green."

"When do you think it'll be ripe?"

"In two weeks, maybe three."

"I'd like to come back and harvest some of it. If it tastes good, it might become a key part of our diet."

"It's been a key part of Zeb's diet over the years. He said these plants produce a crop twice a year, one in late spring and one in early fall."

"Jerry and Connie found several patches of wild rice growing in shallow areas along the west shore of the lake yesterday, and there's some in Red Fish Lagoon. As abundant as this grain seems to be, it could become a major part of our diet too. I wonder what it tastes like."

"It must taste good, or Zeb would've found something else to eat."

"That might be," responded Moose, "but I'd like to cook some of it and be my own judge on its flavor."

"Unless Zeb has some stored in his cave, you'll have to wait a couple weeks."

"I'll be checking it often. As soon as it's ripe, I'll harvest some."

"When you check on it, you'll need to spend a day on the lake."

"That'll be a side benefit to my dedicated effort to make sure that our new civilization has enough to eat."

"Being a dedicated biologist, I'll have to accompany you, so I can study the ripening process of this potentially important plant."

"If more of these plants were growing around Pioneer Island, we wouldn't be forced to spend a day on the lake."

"Darn the bad luck!" exclaimed Dianne.

"I wonder why it isn't more prolific around Pioneer Island."

"I don't know, but my guess is that, in addition to shallow water, you have to have the right conditions on the lake bottom. Around Pioneer Island, the bottom is mostly sandy, gravely, and rocky. Maybe this plant likes a bottom covered with decaying vegetation."

"It would be easy to find out if your theory is correct, but I don't feel like doing that today. In a couple weeks, when we harvest some of it, I'll get some bottom samples."

"Good plan," agreed Dianne, "I feel lazy today too."

"If we were to grind some of the grain into flour, I wonder if we could use it to make bread."

"That's going to depend on how much gluten it contains."

"What's gluten?"

"My husband who claims to be a master chef doesn't know what gluten is. I am surprised."

"I can't be expected to know everything. Anyway, baking bread has never been one of my specialties."

"Gluten is a tough elastic protein that is abundant in wheat but is missing in most other grains. Because of gluten's tough elastic quality, it's able to hold the little bubbles of gas produced by growing yeast. This allows bread to rise."

"So gluten is essential to the bread baking process."

"Yes, it is."

"I'm excited about this grain," declared Moose. "If it contains gluten, is nutritious, tastes good, and is safe to eat; it could become the most common part of our diet."

"As abundant as it seems to be, we won't have to grow much grain."

"I think we should experiment with growing other grains anyway. They'll add variety to our diet."

"I've already started those experiments," replied Dianne. "I need to find out how well the grains we brought with us handle this planet's diseases and parasites."

"I know, but what I had in mind was to experiment with growing them in large enough quantities to be a meaningful addition to our diets."

"That will be next. First, we have to find out if grains from Earth do well here. If they don't, I'll have to make some genetic alterations to them, so that they can deal with the problems they encounter here."

"So those that do well, we can grow in quantity next year. Those that have problems, we can't grow until you make the alterations and test them by growing them through a complete season. And if they still don't do well, you'll have to make more genetic alterations and grow them through another season. That means that it could take years before we can grow in quantity some of the grains we brought with us."

"That sums it up quite well," replied Dianne.

"I sure hope this wild rice checks out well."

"Zeb's been eating it for years, so there's a good chance it will."

Dianne's gaze shifted to the meadows and trees. "I'd like to explore the countryside for a while."

"I don't think going ashore is a very good idea."

"I don't know about that; it looks safe to me. Anyway, I just want to look around for a while. I'm not planning to ride a dinosaur into combat."

"I didn't do that on purpose. It just happened unexpectedly."

"That's true, but you shouldn't be trying to sound so innocent."

"Why?"

"Because you're glad that it happened. You did something that no one else has ever done. It was the thrill of a lifetime, it was dangerous, and you came through it with hardly a scratch."

"That's a long-winded way of saying that it was a male macho thing."

"Well, you certainly did earn bragging rights."

"Yeah, I did, but whenever I think about that wild ride, there's one image that appears in my mind so vividly that it's still terrifying."

"Want to tell me about it?"

"It was that moment in time when I looked into the eyes of a ten-ton T-Rex with a wide open mouth lined with foot-long daggers. Those teeth sent a terrifying chill up and down my spine. At that instant, I knew what it would be like to be only seconds away from being eaten by a predator that could gulp me down in just a couple bone-crunching bites."

"That must have been terrifying."

"It made me appreciate the effective defense set up by the styracosaurus herd. They are large powerful animals and are very well equipped to defend themselves. Because of them, I am still alive and have an incredible story to tell, one that I can tell our children someday."

"First, we have to have some."

"Sounds like fun. When would you like to get pregnant?"

"How about tonight under the light of a double full moon?"

"I like the idea, but shouldn't we wait until the decision has been made that we've passed our quarantine?"

"That decision will be based on recommendations made by me and Connie, and I already know what we are going to say."

"So if we attempt to get pregnant tonight, our actions will be based on insider information."

"That's one way to put it."

"You could share the recommendations with me. I won't tell anyone."

"Since I'm suggesting that we get pregnant tonight, you already know what they're going to be, so I won't be telling you any secrets."

"I'm listening."

"Today is our 26th day here, and we haven't experienced any serious infections or illnesses. You could argue that 26 days isn't very long, but we've certainly exposed ourselves to the environment here. We've breathed the air, and we've all swallowed untreated lake water while swimming. We've all suffered scratches and abrasions. You were punctured by a sty-tick. Connie suffered a serious puncture wound from a saber-tooth. We've all suffered insect bites. Connie's bee stings healed without complication. Also, we've eaten raw food from here."

"I'm convinced, let's get pregnant."

"I'm not done yet. In addition to everything I just said, my assistants are going to announce tonight that Zeb's immune system is basically similar to the human immune system but may be somewhat more capable."

"You already know that."

"I've known since early this morning."

"Why are they withholding this information until tonight?"

"Because I told them to."

"Why?"

"Because everyone may have decided to come down today, and I wanted to have this day alone with you. They've all been in space for nearly seven years, and one more day isn't going to matter that much."

"But they're so eager to come down. How could you get away with telling them to withhold the information until tonight?"

"I didn't directly tell them. I just questioned part of their work and gave them a short list of additional things to check for, just enough to keep them busy for today."

"That was a bit devious."

"Yes it was, but I have another motive in mind."

"What?"

"I want our first child to be the first child conceived here, and hopefully, the first child born here. I checked my calendar yesterday, and it indicated that I could get pregnant today."

"So you dreamed up some additional work to keep your assistants busy for another day."

"It was a challenge, but the work I requested is worth doing, and they weren't able to voice any legitimate objections. But it's very likely that everyone will be coming down tomorrow."

"So that gives us today to get you pregnant."

"I tested myself a few hours ago, and the test was positive. I should be ovulating today. So whether or not I get pregnant is up to you."

"I will certainly do my part," declared Moose with a broad smile.

"I was fairly certain I could count on you."

"I'm ready any time you are."

"I think we should wait until this evening. We're going to have a double full moon, and that will be an exotic, romantic setting in which to conceive our first child."

"Okay, so what would you like to do with the rest of the afternoon?"

"We've never been to this part of the lake before, so I'd like to explore the countryside." Moose looked worried. "Don't worry," Dianne quickly said. "I'm not planning to go ashore. I'll use an RPV to look around."

"That's the safest way to do it, and I think we should live our lives as safely as we can until we've had a chance to have a few children."

"I'll remind you of that remark the next time you ride a dinosaur into combat."

"There's not going to be a next time! Once is enough!"

"It sounds like you're losing your spirit of adventure."

"No! That's not it at all. I'm just ready to begin the adventure of raising a family, and to do that, I need to stay alive."

"I'm glad you feel that way. We've waited a long time to have children, and I don't want to lose you now."

"We could store some of my sperm; in case, I die an untimely death."

"We need to do that for all of our men, but I sincerely hope we don't lose anybody. I for one have no desire to raise children without a husband. I will if there's no other way, but please do me a big favor and stay alive."

Moose looked into his wife's eyes. "I assure you that I will do everything I can to stay alive. It just isn't necessary to pull off anymore daredevil stunts. Once is enough. Now I'm ready for a peaceful life involving activities like building a comfortable home to raise a family in."

"Having a happy, secure family life is very important to me. I'm glad you feel the same way."

"It is a deep-seated feeling for me. I believe that how successful we are at building a new society is dependent on how successful we are at building stable secure families."

"True, but I'd like to know why you think that way."

"The future of our society is dependent on our children. To properly develop, children need stability and security. A stable, secure family life isn't the only way to provide that, but I believe that it is the best way."

"You speak with such conviction. I didn't know that you've studied child psychology."

"I haven't, but I was once a kid, and I remember what was sometimes missing in the lives of some of my friends. I hope you're not disagreeing with me on this."

"Rest assured, I do agree with you."

"Good, maybe you could tell me what you think is most important in raising children?"

Dianne considered the question for a few moments. "If we are to have a smoothly functioning society, all of our children need to have a good sense of values instilled into them. They need to have a good sense of what's right and what's wrong."

"Right on," stated Moose. "When I was a kid, I was on the wrong path for a few years. If I hadn't changed my ways, I might have become a career criminal. Instead of being here with you, I might now be in jail, or maybe even dead."

For a few moments, Dianne thought about what might have been. She tried to imagine Moose in jail. Then, she tried to imagine her life without him, and she was overcome by sadness. "I can't imagine being here without you. I am so very thankful that you changed your ways and that you're here with me. Working together, we must make sure that our children never get on the wrong path."

Moose gave his wife a reassuring hug. "Our children will receive plenty of love and guidance from me, but I just simply will not tolerate any of them getting into the kind of trouble I got into. I almost ruined my life, and I am not going to let that happen to our children."

"With me providing the gentle love and you providing the tough love, we should be successful."

"My tough love will be gentle most of the time. It will only be tough when necessary."

"We're going to be a good team. Maybe we should start now instead of waiting for the double full moon."

"I'm as eager as you are," replied Moose. "But before we left Earth, Jerry promised me some exotic adventure."

"What does that have to do with getting me pregnant?"

"I think getting you pregnant on a sailboat on a huge pristine lake under a double full moon fulfills part of that promise. A couple pterodactyls soaring around would make the setting even more exotic."

"But I seem to be in the mood now."

Moose stared at his scantily clad wife and noted that she seemed to be on the verge of removing what little she was wearing. Her seductive manner aroused him, but he made a halfhearted effort to resist and in an unconvincing way said, "I think we should wait until tonight."

"I don't feel like waiting. I really do want to get pregnant."

Dianne seductively removed her top. "Let's compromise. Let's do it now and again tonight."

"That's a great compromise."

"Only if you're still man enough to make it twice in the same day."

"Try me!"

"I intend to," stated Dianne, as she removed the rest of her clothing. She looked at Moose. "Well, what are you waiting for?"

Moose stared at his naked wife. "I just want to admire your beauty in this setting for a few moments. Would you mind doing some suggestive poses for me?"

"Turn on some music and I'll do an exotic dance for you."

"What kind of music do you want?"

"Punch *Music Erotic Dance* into the computer."

Moose did as instructed and some very enchanting music began pouring out of the boat's sound system. For the next five minutes, Dianne performed a seductive dance routine that was so perfectly choreographed that her body movements became one with the music.

It was good that the boat was on auto-pilot because Moose was so captivated by the performance that he was oblivious to the course being followed by the little boat. It could easily have run aground in the shallow water along the shoreline, but the boat's auto-navigation system kept it in deep water at a safe distance from shore.

At the end of the performance, Moose said, "WOW! Where did you learn how to dance like that?"

"We were in space for a long time, and I had some free time on my hands. I worked up this routine in secret and saved it for a special occasion. Was my performance exotic enough for you?"

"It was out of this world. Something I would expect to see at the palace of an ancient Roman emperor prior to an orgy."

"Judging from that bulge in your trunks, you could've performed quite well at that orgy. Do you still want to wait until tonight?"

"Are you kidding? That sexy performance of yours almost caused me to go off in my pants."

"How would that get me pregnant?"

"I guess that would've been wasteful on my part."

"It sure would have. Anyway, why are you still wearing your trunks? What are we waiting for?"

One second later, Moose said, "I'm not wearing any trunks, and we're not waiting any longer. Now, it's my turn to show you a little routine that I worked out that I've been saving for this special occasion."

For several minutes, Moose teased and stimulated his wife with erotic caresses until she became so aroused that she cried out, "I can't wait any longer! I need you now!"

Moose immediately gave Dianne what she wanted. So thoroughly aroused were both of them that they quickly reached satisfaction.

Lying next to each other on an air mattress, they rested while soaking up the warm radiant energy pouring down on them from Alpha Centauri A and to a lesser extent from Alpha Centauri B. If nature took the desired course, theirs would be the first child conceived on the new world. So complete was their satisfaction, and so comforting was the warm radiant energy striking them, that the hypnotic sound of small waves washing against

490

the boat caused Moose and Dianne to doze off into dreamland.

However, after just a few minutes of sleep, they were instantly awakened by the urgent chirping of their communicators. Recognizing the sound as the pterodactyl warning, Moose and Dianne searched the sky and found a pair of pterodactyls approaching from the north. They grabbed their rifles and warily watched the big creatures. Their communicators chirped out a second warning. A few seconds later, the pterodactyls spotted the little boat and began circling it at an altitude of 500 feet.

"They seem to be keeping their distance," commented Dianne.

"But with their diving speed, they could be on us in a few seconds," warned Moose.

"I want to take a closer look," Dianne said, as she put down her rifle and picked up the binoculars. She studied the huge creatures looking for the distinctive markings of King and Queen, but it was obvious that these birds were strangers. "They aren't King and Queen," she said. "In fact, they're an entirely different species of pterodactyl. What concerns me is they don't have webbed feet, which means they can't swim, which means they're not fish eaters unless they're able to grab them near the surface."

"Are you trying to say that this species preys on land animals and that they're wondering if we're good to eat?"

"I think that's the case, and it looks like they're investigating us."

"Then, we have a choice to make: Do we kill them now when they're easy targets, or do we wait until they attack? If they attack, they'll still be big targets, but we'll only have a few seconds to nail them?"

"I don't like the idea of killing these magnificent creatures unless we have to," replied Dianne. "I think we can safely wait. We're both crack shots, even against small moving targets, and these guys are big. Hitting them should be easy, and our rifles are armed with explosive bullets, so any hit should be lethal."

"I am comfortable with that, but I wanted to be sure that you are too."

"In a few seconds, we might have to shoot them or quickly go below deck. I get the feeling that they're about ready to attack."

"I don't want to retreat below deck, because these creatures could destroy our solar sails. I have another idea. Pick up your rifle and stand guard while I give them something to think about."

Dianne did as directed, and Moose quickly put his rifle down. Then, he opened the watertight hatch on a compartment containing emergency supplies. Very quickly, Moose located, removed, and loaded a flare gun. He looked up and noted that the larger of the two pterodactyls was preparing to dive. Moose aimed and fired at the exact instant the large predator entered its dive. At a range of 100 yards, the flare exploded creating a large smoke cloud directly in front of the diving pterodactyl. The smoke cloud and the loud boom from the explosion caused the diving pterodactyl to screech loudly in surprise and to break off its dive. It veered off to the side while

Moose quickly reloaded the flare gun.

"Very good!" exclaimed Dianne.

"The other one is still circling us."

"But he's circling at a greater distance. He seems to be wary of us. I doubt that he's going to attack."

"His partner is heading for the hills, perhaps in search of familiar prey."

"Maybe this one will join him." Dianne had barely finished speaking when the still circling pterodactyl turned and headed northward in pursuit of its partner.

"Either they aren't very hungry, or their usual prey is readily available, and they didn't want to make an issue out of attacking us."

"They've never seen humans before, and even though we are unknown to them, we must've looked like easy prey."

"But the flare I fired gave them some second thoughts."

"Are you saying that they're able to think?"

"I was using a figure of speech, but it should not have been difficult for the attacker to associate the exploding flare with us."

"Predatory birds have very keen eyesight. It's possible that the attacker actually saw the flare traveling from you toward him."

"If he didn't see the projectile, he certainly did see the smoke trail extend from me toward him. With even a minor amount of intelligence, he would have to have associated the exploding flare with us."

"That exploding flare must've been quite a shocking surprise considering that they've never before been shot at by their prey."

"They were scared away," stated Moose, "but they weren't injured in any way. So will that shocking surprise deter these two from attacking humans again? If it doesn't, and they do attack humans again, will firing a flare at them cause them to break off the attack, or will they remember that they weren't hurt this time and continue their attack?"

"There's no way we can answer those questions. Firing the flare was a clever idea that worked well this time, but it might not work every time. The safest thing for us to do is to always respond with lethal force when our lives are threatened."

"That's true, but I wanted to find out if I could scare them away."

"I'm glad you did that. It was an exciting experiment, and I was ready with the lethal force, just in case the flare didn't work. Now that I might be pregnant, I have to be extra careful to stay alive."

"You can't possibly be pregnant yet. I realize that I have some very ambitious sperm, but I don't think they could possibly have done their job already."

"Well, just in case they don't do their job by tonight, I am going to hold you to our plan to try again under the light of a double full moon."

Moose gave his still nude wife and admiring glance. "You don't seriously think I would try to get out of that, do you?"

492

Dianne took a few moments to appreciate Moose's admiring gaze. "I think you'll do your part."

For a few moments, Dianne thought about how many years she had waited to become pregnant. She fervently hoped that their efforts would be successful. Noticing that she and Moose were still nude, she said, "Maybe we should put some clothes on."

"Why? There's no one here except us, and I enjoy being naked."

Dianne felt the warm breeze caress her nude body. "I like it too."

Moose left the boat on auto-pilot but slowed it way down, so that it was barely moving. "I'm going swimming," he said as he dove in.

Dianne scanned the sky and saw nothing of a threatening nature, so she dove in too.

After leisurely swimming around for fifteen minutes, they climbed onto the boat. While drying off, Moose said, "I checked Mike's weather forecast earlier, and he's predicting a pleasant clear night with a gentle breeze and balmy temperatures."

"That's beautiful weather for what we're planning to do this evening."

"Maybe we shouldn't go home afterwards. With pleasant weather and a double full moon, I think it would be fun to camp on the boat all night."

"I don't know if that's a good idea," commented Dianne.

"Why?"

"After what those pterodactyls tried to do, how are you going to feel comfortable sleeping on the boat?"

"Our radar will warn us if pterodactyls approach. What else are you worried about?"

"We've only been here 26 days. I don't think that's enough time to discover all the dangers that might be here. There might be some dangerous nocturnal predators around that we're unaware of."

"That's a good reason to spend the night on the lake. Maybe we can discover them, if they exist."

"I don't want to discover nocturnal predators when I'm sound asleep on the deck of this boat."

"Well, I think it would be fun to sail under the light of a double full moon. It would definitely be exotic and would include an element of danger. We can enjoy it until we're tired; then, we can go below deck and sleep for a while. After that, we can get up early and enjoy sailing in the pre-sunrise glow of early dawn. Shortly after sunrise, we can sail into South Bay and await the arrival of our friends from the Challenger."

"But I didn't pack enough food for us to spend the night."

"I can't believe that you're worried about food. You usually accuse me of being overly concerned about food."

"Well, I didn't think we'd be out all night, and for some reason, we've both been eating more than I thought we would."

"I'm starting to think you've lost your spirit of adventure. I've never heard so many objections to something as simple as camping on a boat."

"Well, we are on a dangerous planet, and we are low on food."

"I can't eliminate the danger, but I can take care of the food problem," commented Moose, as he pointed at his fishing pole.

"There's something else to consider. If everyone comes down in the morning, tomorrow is going to be an active day. If we stay out all night, we aren't going to get much sleep, and being tired will take some of the fun out of the day."

"That's true, but sailing in the moonlight with beautiful weather is just too good an opportunity to pass up. It'll be so much fun that it'll be well worth being tired tomorrow."

"I guess if I'm tired, I can always find a little time to take a nap."

"It sounds like you've just agreed with me."

"Yeah, I guess I have, but tonight won't be much fun, if we're too hungry to enjoy it, so you'd better catch something for us to eat."

"No problem," stated Moose, as he reached for his fishing gear.

"I'm going to try my rainbow pike lure. But before I start fishing, we need to roll up the solar sails and pull in the outriggers. If I hook a big one, I want to move around the boat without getting my line tangled."

After putting the boat in a clean configuration, Moose said, "During all of our recent activity, I haven't paid much attention to our location. I'm surprised at how far we've traveled"

"I haven't paid much attention either. Where are we?"

Moose had a portable video screen on deck. With this, he accessed the boat's navigation computer, and a map of the lake appeared on the screen. A blinking red dot indicated their position.

In answer to Dianne's question, Moose said, "We're moving northeast along the northwest shore of the big bay in the northeast corner of the lake."

"Isn't there a big river flowing into this bay?"

"Yeah, there is, and 60 miles up that river, there's another big lake. Someday, I'd like to sail up that river and explore that lake. Wouldn't it be fun to take a couple weeks to make a trip like that?"

"Now that's something I'd like to do."

"I'm glad to hear that you aren't completely hopeless."

"You shouldn't interpret my concern about being out all night as an indication that I may've lost my adventurous spirit."

"Well, you sure voiced lots of objections."

"I know I did, but I really do want to sail in the moonlight and camp out on the boat. It's just that I expect tomorrow to be an exciting festive day, and I just don't want to be too tired to enjoy it."

"I can understand that, so you sleep as much as you want. I'll stay awake and enjoy sailing until I'm too tired to enjoy it; then, I'll put the boat on auto-pilot and get some sleep."

"It sounds like you're not planning to sleep all that much."

"I've never needed much sleep when there's a party going on, and as far as I'm concerned, the party has already started for us."

"Today has been more fun than I've ever had at any party, and partying always makes me hungry, so when are you going to catch us some food? I'm starving."

"It seems like we just had lunch a couple hours ago," teased Moose.

"I know, but we've had lots of activity in the last couple hours. Plus, the anticipation of fresh fish in the frying pan is making my mouth water."

"I think you really are hungry and aren't just teasing me about food."

"Yes, I really am."

Moose picked up his fishing pole and offered it to Dianne. "Would you like the pleasure of catching our dinner?"

"I know how much you enjoy fishing, so you catch one, and I'll cook as much as we need for dinner."

Moose adjusted the boat's speed to what he thought would be a good trolling speed. Then, he dropped the lure into the water and observed its action for a few moments before feeding out about thirty yards of line.

In just a few minutes, Moose's fishing rod bent sharply, and he exclaimed, "I've hooked something big!"

As the minutes went by, Moose patiently played the fish until he was able to bring it near the boat. Dianne reached into the water with a landing net and captured it.

When the fish was on deck, Moose said, "This is the smallest rainbow pike we've caught so far. I doubt that it even weighs fifteen pounds."

"You're referring to this fish as small? How does it compare to what you caught back on Earth?"

"My favorite fresh water fish was the northern pike. Most of the ones I caught weighed between two and seven pounds. The biggest one I caught weighed eleven pounds."

"It sounds like fishing is probably better here."

"Are you trying to tell me that I shouldn't refer to this fish as small?"

"In a roundabout way, I'm trying to say that as far as fishing is concerned, you must feel like you're in a dream world."

"No doubt about that. Back on Earth, I never imagined that someday I'd look at a fifteen-pound fish and say that it's the smallest I've caught so far, but then, I never imagined that I'd move to another planet either."

"I'm very happy that you're here with me, so let's celebrate with a fresh fish dinner."

"It doesn't get any fresher than this."

Within minutes, Moose had the fish cleaned and filleted. Dianne selected some choice fillets for the frying pan, and Moose put the rest of the fish in the refrigerator.

After enjoying a delicious meal, Dianne put on a video headset and launched an RPV to explore the countryside. Moose stood guard and studied the slowly passing shoreline that was only 60 yards away.

Finding interesting plants and creatures to study, Dianne continued her exploration of the countryside until Alpha Centauri A hung low on the western horizon. Then, she returned the RPV, took off the headset, and prepared to enjoy first sunset.

While turning the boat away from the waterfront, Moose said, "We need to be farther away from shore, so we don't tempt any nocturnal predators to try to swim out to us."

He called up a map of the lake and did a position check. "We've moved several miles northeast, and we're not very far from the mouth of the river. We're 30 miles from South Bay, and I think it's time to start heading back."

Moose laid out the desired course on the video screen and instructed the boat's auto-pilot to follow it. Then, he programmed in the desired arrival time and said, "There's nothing left for us to do now except enjoy the voyage. Since we're only going to be drifting along at 2.5 mph, it will be a silent, peaceful cruise on a beautiful, moonlit night."

"Let's enjoy first sunset, a double moonrise, and then second sunset."

"Is that exotic or what?" questioned Moose.

"It is compared to what we were accustomed to back on Earth," replied Dianne. Looking to the east, she said, "It looks like I got the order of events mixed up. Aphrodite has already risen, and Alpha Centauri A hasn't yet set."

Moose entered a question into the computer and received an immediate answer. "The double full moon will occur at 10:47 P.M., so both Aphrodite and Nocturne will rise shortly before first sunset."

Gazing at Aphrodite, Dianne said, "It's just as large and beautiful as the full moon back on Earth."

"Even though it's much smaller than Earth's moon, it looks just as big because it's so much closer," commented Moose.

Dianne picked up the binoculars for a closer look at Aphrodite's surface detail. "This is eerie," she said. "I feel like there's life there."

"You're just moonstruck. Aphrodite has no atmosphere. How can there be life there?"

"I don't know. I just have a mysterious feeling that there is, and that it's crying out for help."

"The last time you had that feeling, we got involved in a planet-wide war."

"I know, and I don't feel like going to war at the moment."

"Jerry's planning to investigate those moons after we get everyone settled down on Pioneer Island, so we'll find out then if there's any basis for your mysterious feeling."

Dianne continued starring at Aphrodite. She wondered what kind of life could possibly be on a moon that had no atmosphere.

A few minutes later, Nocturne began to appear on the eastern horizon, slightly to the right of Aphrodite. With the binoculars, Dianne watched it slowly move above the horizon. "It appears slightly smaller than Aphrodite," she said.

"Nocturne is actually much bigger than Aphrodite, but it's much farther away and consequently, looks smaller. Do you also sense that there's life there?"

"No, but it sure is beautiful to look at."

Dianne and Moose turned to the west and noted that Alpha Centauri A was lying on the horizon and beginning to slip below it. "This is really wild," stated Dianne. "We have two full moons and two suns in the sky."

Moose and Dianne enjoyed the exotic spectacle while Alpha Centauri A gradually disappeared below the western horizon. This left Alpha Centauri B alone in the western sky. It lay low above the horizon. Although not very bright when compared to Alpha Centauri A, it was many times brighter than the double full moon, and its dim orange glow colored the lake with a strange orange hue.

Moose and Dianne silently scanned the lake in every direction to soak up the effect of the peculiar lighting. "This is eerie," Dianne said.

"It's bizarre. It really drives home the fact that we're not on Earth."

"How many times will we have to experience this before it feels normal?" Dianne asked.

"I don't know if it'll ever feel normal for me. In just a few weeks, Alpha Centauri A and B will rise and set together. Six months after that, Alcent will be exactly between Alpha Centauri A and B. What will happen then will really seem bizarre. Alpha Centauri B will rise in the east at exactly the same time that Alpha Centauri A sets in the west. We simply won't have any dark nights. This weird orange glow will light up our world all night long. How can something that eerie feel normal?"

"It'll really be bizarre if we have a double full moon at about that time. Then, we'll have Aphrodite, Nocturne, and Alpha Centauri B moving through the nighttime sky together in a tightly knit little group."

"That will be a weird sight."

"With two moons and two suns, we might come to look upon a clear dark night with a sky full of stars as an unusual event."

"Since arriving here, we've only had one night that was clear and moonless," stated Dianne. "And the sky full of stars was spectacular."

"Clear, dark nights aren't going to happen very often for us, but this is the time of the year when that can happen. Six months from now, we'll be well into a two to three month time period when dark nights will be impossible."

"That is going to take some getting use to."

Noting that Alpha Centauri B was about to slip below the western horizon, Moose and Dianne stopped conversing and watched their second sunset of the evening. In silence, they observed and appreciated the natural beauty of one of nature's wonders. Lost in peaceful thought, they continued to gaze across the open water at the western sky for a few minutes after Alpha Centauri B set.

Suddenly, Dianne's communicator started chirping, instantly pulling her out of her thoughtful mental state. She answered the call and found that it was one of her assistants calling from the Challenger.

Dianne was informed that they had finished the additional research she had requested. As expected, the extra work confirmed previous results, which showed that Zeb's immune system was basically the same as the human immune system, although more sophisticated in some respects.

Before discussing the results in detail with her assistants, Dianne called Connie and Jerry, so they could be included in the discussion. After nearly an hour of discussing Zeb's immune system relative to the human immune system, it was decided that shortcomings in the human immune system relative to Zeb's immune system could be easily compensated for with medical technology.

Consequently, Jerry accessed the Challenger's public address system and loudly announced: "WE HAVE JUST DECIDED THAT HUMANS CAN LIVE AND PROSPER ON ALCENT. ALL OF YOU ARE FREE TO COME DOWN. WE EXPECT TO SEE YOU SHORTLY AFTER SUNRISE TOMORROW."

Moose and Dianne listened to the Captain's announcement as picked up by a microphone onboard the Challenger. Jerry had barely finished speaking when loud cheering resounded throughout the starship.

Moose turned to Dianne. "You were worried about being tired tomorrow. How much sleep do you think our friends on the Challenger are going to get tonight?"

"Not much."

"Do you think they'll have any trouble staying awake and enjoying themselves tomorrow?"

"They'll be pumped up from now until bedtime tomorrow night."

"I think they'll be so wildly excited tomorrow that some of their enthusiasm will rub off on you and keep you wide awake, so let's enjoy our moonlight cruise and not worry too much about sleep."

"That sounds like a good plan," stated Dianne.

EIGHTEEN

The Beginning of the Future

TIME: Day Twenty-Seven, Early Morning.

With the last vestiges of nighttime darkness lingering overhead, the eastern sky was awash with the glow of early dawn, while the western sky was brightened by Nocturne and Aphrodite. Even though Alpha Centauri A was more than a half-hour away from rising, the air over Clear Lake was pleasantly warm. The region had been in the grip of unusually warm weather since the last rainstorm.

After sailing all night, Moose and Dianne were approaching the south end of Pioneer Island. "What a beautiful morning," commented Dianne.

"Aren't you glad we spent the night on the lake?"

"It was fun," admitted Dianne, glowing with contentment.

"Even though we didn't get much sleep, you don't seem to be tired."

Dianne lazily stretched her sleep-deprived body. "I feel tired in a pleasant, laid-back sort of way."

"But you don't seem to be very sleepy."

"I'm not; there's too much excitement in the air."

Moose slowly took a deep breath. "I don't know what you're talking about; it seems to be ordinary air to me."

Moose had hardly finished speaking when the quiet early morning atmosphere was suddenly shattered by a sonic boom. "See what I mean; there's excitement in the air," Dianne said. Looking high in the western sky, Dianne spotted, and pointed at what appeared to be a bright moving star. "That must be one of our shuttles."

"But its shockwave cannot have reached us yet," stated Moose, as he turned to search the northern sky where he quickly spotted a second bright moving object. "That's the shuttle that jolted our senses."

"They sure didn't waste any time coming down," commented Dianne. "If they were any earlier, they would be landing in the dark."

"As it is, they're going to be on the water before sunrise."

"Maybe they want to arrive early enough to enjoy their first sunrise in a long, long time and have lots of time to enjoy their first day here."

"I can't blame them for that. I wonder if I should try to catch a rainbow pike and welcome them with a fish feast for breakfast."

"They might appreciate that, but we do have some fish left over from last night."

"That won't be enough."

"You're probably right, but I think we should get out of their way before you start fishing."

"They won't land this close to the island, so we're safe in that regard. And we're moving at about the right speed for trolling, so I'm going to drop my favorite lure into the water and see what happens. At this speed, it'll be seven or eight minutes before we arrive in South Bay and that should be enough time to snag a big pike."

"If we weren't trolling on the way in, we could go faster. I'd like to be there to greet them when they arrive."

"I know we're going slowly, but we should still be there when they arrive," stated Moose, as he dropped his favorite lure into the water.

Just then, Moose and Dianne were jolted by a second sonic boom, and Dianne picked up the binoculars for a better look at the shuttles. "It looks like the cargo shuttle will arrive first," she said.

"Half of them are on that shuttle."

"Splitting them up was a good idea. In case of a tragic accident, we would only lose half of our friends instead of all of them."

"Losing all of them would strike a hard blow at our prime objective. It would be difficult for us to start a new civilization with only four people."

"That's true. It would be difficult, but it wouldn't be impossible. However, I'd have to use genetic engineering to expand our gene pool."

"I think it would be much better if most of us would survive long enough to have several children."

"I definitely agree, because I don't want to be put into a position where I'd have to play God by deciding what our future population should look like and then start altering genes to make it happen."

"I wouldn't want that responsibility either," agreed Moose, as he worked his fishing pole to put some erratic action on the lure.

Dianne followed the big shuttle with binoculars and watched it land on its hydrofoils. It ended its landing run about a mile from the south end of Pioneer Island. Dianne felt a growing excitement as she watched the cargo shuttle turn toward South Bay.

Then, Dianne trained her binoculars on the personnel shuttle and watched it make a perfect landing along a course considerably closer to Pioneer Island than that followed by the cargo shuttle. When it finished its landing run, it took up a position 100 yards behind the big shuttle.

After just a few minutes, the shuttles were less than 200 yards from Moose and Dianne. On their present course, they would pass by at a distance of 50 yards. Watching the shuttles approach fired up Dianne and Moose. Their excitement rose to an even higher level when Moose's communicator started chirping with a call from Mike Johnson, who boisterously said: "Good morning, Moose and Dianne!"

"Good morning to you, and welcome to Alcent!" Moose exclaimed.

"Very happy to be here! I have a million activities planned for today, most of which I haven't been able to do in years. You must have a busy day planned too; you're up awfully early."

"Actually, we've been up most of the night. We've been sailing since yesterday morning."

"That's something I haven't done in years. Maybe I can go sailing later today. How is the fishing this morning?"

"Fishing's always good. Right now, I'm trying to catch breakfast for everyone."

"We'll be in South Bay in just a few minutes. If you haven't caught one by then, I'll be more than happy to show you how it's done."

Just then, Moose's pole bent sharply as he received a massive strike. "That won't be necessary; I have one on."

The fish swam rapidly toward the cargo shuttle, which was now less than 100 yards away. Moose tightened the drag to slow the fish down. It responded by leaping completely out of the water less than ten yards from the shuttle and then swimming rapidly toward Moose, who quickly reeled in the slack line.

"What a beauty!" exclaimed Mike. "Good luck landing him. I wasn't able to eat much this morning, but I'm starving now, and I haven't had fresh fish since leaving Earth."

"So far, I haven't lost any," stated Moose, as he skillfully played the fish. Soon, he had the fish next to the boat, and Dianne captured it with a landing net. While lifting it out of the water, she said, "This one is heavy."

Moose ran a knife through the fish's head, hung it on a scale, and proudly announced, "Thirty-seven pounds."

"More than enough for breakfast," commented Mike.

While Moose secured the fish and put away his fishing gear, Dianne piloted the boat toward South Bay. Wanting to greet the arriving guests, she ran the boat at full power. Since Mike and the pilot of the personnel shuttle had slowed down considerably upon approaching South Bay, Dianne was able to catch up with them, and all three vehicles dropped anchor at about the same time.

Almost immediately, a large door in the side of the cargo shuttle's fuselage was opened and a rolled up deflated pontoon barge was dropped into the water, where its pontoons began to inflate. As the pontoons inflated, the barge unrolled and its deck planks automatically snapped into place. In less than a minute, the barge was ready for use. Measuring 14 by 28 feet, it could haul 8,000 pounds and would find many uses besides hauling cargo ashore from the shuttle.

Jerry had parked one of the ATVs on the beach and was now swimming out to the barge towing the plastic cable from the ATV's winch. When Jerry reached the barge, he attached the cable to it. Then, he looked up into the smiling eyes of his daughter, who was very happy to see him.

"Hi Daddy! Is this our new home?" Denise asked.

"Yes, it is."

"It sure has lots of water. Where did it all come from?"

"Rain clouds bring water in from the ocean."

"I watched you swim to this boat. Is swimming fun?"

"It sure is."

"Will you teach me how to swim?"

"Later today, I'll give you your first lesson."

"I want to learn how to swim too," declared Matthew, who was now standing next to Denise.

"If you need another instructor, I'm available," volunteered Michelle.

Mike appeared next to Michelle wearing only a swim suit. "I need to find out if I still know how to swim," stated Mike, as he dove in. After swimming under water for several yards, he surfaced and yelled, "It sure feels good to be here."

Meanwhile, six people from the personnel shuttle were rowing ashore in a small inflated boat they had just deployed. Upon seeing Mike and Jerry having fun in the water, the people still on the personnel shuttle quickly changed into swimwear and dove in to join them.

While all of this was going on, Moose and Dianne were standing on the deck of the submarine shouting greetings to everyone. Then, Moose proudly held his catch high for all to see and yelled, "Fried fish will be ready shortly for anyone interested in breakfast."

After several people shouted that they were hungry, Moose and Dianne stepped into their small inflated boat and rowed to shore, where Moose picked up his fish and headed for the elevator. Accompanying him, Dianne said, "I'll drive you home; then, I'll return and pick up those who are hungry for breakfast. I have a feeling that I'm going to be a busy taxi driver for a while."

"Judging from the way everyone hungrily stared at my fish, I think I'll be a busy cook for quite some time."

"You can't blame them for that. They haven't eaten real fish in years. But some of them are so excited about being here that they're not going to be able to settle down long enough to eat anything for a while. So it'll probably be an hour or two before everyone wanders by for breakfast."

"And not too long after that, some of them will be looking for lunch. I could end up spending the whole day cooking."

"You'll have some help."

"I hope so. Maybe the best way to handle lunch would be to prepare a picnic table banquet with all the smoked delicacies I've made in recent days. Then, people could wander by and eat at their convenience."

"In a couple hours, I'll turn the taxi-driver job over to someone else and help you. I can make some salads and vegetable dishes to add to your lunch banquet."

"Starting at lunch time, I'll keep a bed of charcoal going in case anyone wants charbroiled steak or fish."

"Some fresh rolls would add a nice touch. Maybe I can talk Connie into making some."

"Cinnamon rolls with honey would be especially good," Moose said.

"I'll suggest that to her."

"Maybe we should get some help from the Challenger's chef. He served us very well during our long voyage."

"He is very talented," agreed Dianne. "But this feast will be made almost entirely with local foods he's not familiar with. I think this has to be our show."

"Okay, but if he hangs around and asks questions about the foods we're serving, I will find a way to put him to work."

"I have no doubt about that."

When Dianne brought the ATV to a stop at the campsite, Moose said, "I'm going to create the most delicious fish breakfast these people have ever had. It will be second to none."

Driving away from the camp, Dianne yelled, "I'll have your first customers here shortly."

"I'll be ready."

When Dianne arrived back at the elevator, she looked down on a scene bustling with activity. South Bay was now far different from the quiet, deserted place she had become accustomed to.

She felt the joy of the newcomers as she watched them find simple ways to celebrate their arrival. She watched them experience great pleasure doing ordinary everyday things that they weren't able to do during their long voyage through interstellar space. Some were swimming vigorously, while others were just playfully splashing around in the water. Some were running barefoot on the beach, enjoying the open space and the feel of the sand beneath their feet, while others simply stood still and silently gazed across the water in appreciation of the vastness of Clear Lake. A few were wandering around looking at plants, birds, and insects.

Then, there were those who had chosen to celebrate later and busied themselves with unloading the cargo shuttle. Dianne noted that several boxes, bags, crates, and suitcases had been loaded onto the barge, and that Connie was slowly pulling it toward shore with the ATV's winch.

When the barge ran aground a few feet offshore, a wide plank was set in place, and the barge's passengers stepped onto the beach. Denise ran to her mother, closely followed by Matthew and Michelle. Connie dropped to her knees and gave her daughter and Matthew a big hug. Then, she stood up and welcomed Michelle to Pioneer Island.

After visiting with Connie for a couple minutes, Michelle turned to Zeb and spoke to him in his language. Obviously excited by Michelle's presence, Zeb stood up on one leg and warmly greeted her.

Hungry for breakfast, four individuals grabbed their luggage and stepped onto the elevator. Dianne watched their ascent and greeted them when they reached the plateau. Bubbling over with excitement, the new arrivals surveyed the surrounding area, drinking up the panoramic view. When they satisfied their initial thirst, Dianne gave them a ride to the campsite, where Moose served them breakfast while she returned to the south end of the plateau.

Meanwhile, down on the beach, Connie and Michelle were walking barefoot with their children. When they approached a bush, they heard a bird chirping out a cheerful song, which was immediately answered by another bird in a nearby bush.

Denise turned to her mother. "Are songbirds making those pretty sounds?"

"Yes."

"I want to see them! Where are they?"

Connie pointed at the nearest shrub. "One of them is in that bush. He's hiding behind some leaves near the top. If you look closely, you can see him. He's green with red stripes on his wings."

Both Matthew and Denise stared intently where Connie was pointing. Then, the bird fluttered into a new position and again chirped out its song.

"I see him!" they both exclaimed.

"He's really pretty!" Denise said.

She headed toward the bush for a closer look. Spooked by her rapid approach, the bird flew away, and Denise asked, "Did I scare him?"

"Yes, you did."

Then, a couple sea gulls flew over, and Denise asked, "Are those songbirds too?"

"They can make lots of noise, but they don't sing pretty songs."

"I like songbirds," Denise said. "They're fun to listen to."

Just then, King soared overhead and Denise exclaimed, "That's really a big bird! I'm afraid. Could he pick me up and carry me away?"

"Yes, he could, but so far, he's been our friend. He saved my life one night when he killed another pterodactyl that was about to attack me."

"Were you afraid?"

"It happened so fast that it was over before I had time to be afraid."

"Will he protect me too?"

"I hope so, but if he doesn't, your father and I will."

Satisfied with Connie's answer, Denise continued to stare at the big pterodactyl that was still circling South Bay gazing down on all the activity. Noting her daughter's continuing interest, Connie said, "His name is King, and he lives on Western Island."

A second pterodactyl arrived on the scene, and Denise asked, "Does that one live on Western Island too?"

"Her name is Queen, and she does live on Western Island. King and Queen are mates, and they have a baby they're taking care of."

"They're sure taking a close look at everything going on here," commented Michelle. "But they don't seem to be alarmed by it."

"They've always been curious about us, but we've never given them any reason to think of us as enemies."

"How can we be sure that they aren't trying to decide which one of us would be a good breakfast?"

"We can't be certain, but these two are so skilled at catching fish that they don't need to view us as possible prey."

"Are you saying that we don't need to fear them as long as we don't threaten them in any way?"

"They've never acted threatening toward us, but they are wild creatures, and they are very capable killing machines."

"Fortunately, the most dramatic demonstration of that ability was when it was used to save your life."

"But we don't know if King intended to save my life or was simply killing an enemy."

"Whichever, the effect is the same; you and Dianne are still alive."

"While the effect is the same; the implications are very different."

"I can't argue with that. If King was protecting you, we might have a pair of flying guard dogs. But why would they want to be our protectors? They are wild creatures who are very skilled at taking care of themselves. What do they need us for?"

"A few days after our arrival, we solved a big problem for them."

"Are you suggesting that King was paying a debt?"

"Maybe, but they've also spent lots of time observing us. If they have any intelligence at all and are capable of elementary reasoning, they would have to conclude that we are vastly superior to them and that it might be to their advantage to be friends with us. They may even have decided that we could easily kill them if we wanted to."

"If they've concluded that we could kill them, why don't they just fly off to another part of the planet far away from here?" Michelle asked.

"Maybe they like us, or maybe they think of us as benevolent gods. After all, they've seen our shuttles and para-wings descend out of the heavens, and they've seen our shuttles ascend back into the heavens. Maybe they think it's to their advantage to try to win our appreciation, so that we'll help them if they ever again need us."

"It seems like the answers to all of our questions about them begin with *if* or *maybe*," Michelle said.

"Unfortunately, that's true. We just don't have any concrete answers, and until we do, we have no choice but to respect the fact that they are wild creatures with awesome killing ability."

Michelle looked up at the huge flying creatures and was impressed by how graceful they were in flight. She watched them circle South Bay one last time before flying off toward the southeast. Then, she said, "I guess they've satisfied their curiosity."

"Either that or they're hungry and looking for a fish breakfast."

"I could go for that myself," responded Michelle. "It's been a few years since I've eaten real fish."

"I haven't had any since yesterday," stated Connie, smugly.

"You couldn't resist saying that, could you?"

Connie smiled in response, and Michelle said, "If you're not yet hungry for more fish, I'll eat your share."

"That won't be necessary; my appetite's been pretty good. In fact, it seems like I'm always hungry."

"Maybe you're pregnant."

"Not at the moment, but Jerry and I have been thinking about getting pregnant soon."

"Mike and I have been talking about that too. And I've also heard others talking about it."

"It sounds like we might have a baby boom in nine to twelve months," commented Connie.

"They've all been waiting for several years to start their families. And we've been waiting for several years to expand ours."

"Hopefully, we'll have our homes built by then."

"A large permanent home would be helpful in raising a family," commented Michelle. "The prefabricated temporary shelters we'll be living in while we're building our permanent homes will be comfortable, but they'll be small. The floor space will only be 16 X 32."

"That might not be a problem," Connie said. "We'll be outside most of the time, and when we go inside, we'll have a bedroom, a bathroom, and a kitchen. Plus, we'll have electricity and indoor plumbing."

"That's true, but all the rooms will be small."

"Even so, I think they'll be adequate for two people, but for you and for us, there'll be three people. For the sake of privacy, I'd sure like to have a small second bedroom for Denise to sleep in."

"Mike and I've talked about that. We've considered several interior arrangements, and we've figured out a way to have a second bedroom. It'll be tiny but adequate for a child to sleep in."

"I'd like to see that floor plan."

"I'll sketch it out for you while we're eating breakfast."

"Okay," replied Connie.

Matthew insistently tugged at one of Michelle's hands and asked, "May I play in the water?"

Michelle glanced at South Bay. Then, she gazed at the vastness of Clear Lake and wondered what dangers it might contain. After considering that four of her fellow pioneers had been swimming in this lake for several weeks, Michelle looked into her son's eyes and noted how eager he was to have fun in the water, so she said, "Okay, but don't go out very far."

Denise grabbed one of Connie's hands. "I want to play in the water too."

Believing that it was safe for the children to play in the shallow water along the sandy beach, Connie said, "Okay, but let's head toward the elevator, so we can go eat breakfast."

Matthew and Denise repeatedly ran into and out of the lake, gleefully splashing water on each other. When they arrived at the elevator, they were soaked. Michelle opened her luggage and removed two towels and some dry clothing for them. After drying off and changing clothes, Denise stared at the open elevator cage and its rugged rustic structure and said, "The Challenger has better elevators."

"Is this one safe?" Matthew asked, appearing worried.

"We use it every day," replied Connie.

Filled with anxiety, the children continued to stare at the elevator. But at the urging of their mothers, they reluctantly stepped into the open cage.

Connie was about to start the elevator's ascent but stopped when she heard, "wait for us," and recognized Jerry's voice. A few moments later, Jerry and Mike boarded the elevator, and all six headed for the plateau.

As the elevator car steadily gained height, it wiggled and creaked renewing Denise's and Matthew's concern. Jerry assured them that it was safe, but the continued wiggling and creaking scared them. As the open elevator cage continued its ascent, Matthew and Denise looked down at the beach, now more than 100 feet below them. The perception of great height added to the anxiety they felt. However, even though they were fearful for their safety, they couldn't help enjoying the thrill of ascending the face of a vertical cliff in an open-air elevator. But when the elevator car reached the plateau, Matthew and Denise were the first to step off.

Dianne greeted them. "Did you enjoy the ride?"

Instantly, both children exclaimed, "It was scary!"

After a moment of thought, Denise repeated her earlier comment, "The Challenger has better elevators."

"But was it fun?" demanded Dianne.

"Yes, but it was scary," they repeated.

"Want to have some more fun?" Dianne asked.

Feeling uneasy, but not wanting to miss out on anything, Matthew hesitantly said, "Yes." Denise followed his lead and also said, "Yes."

"Okay, I'll give you an ATV ride."

Both children looked at the ATV. "I've never had a ride in anything like that," Denise said. "Is it fun?"

Before Dianne could answer the question, Matthew said, "I think it'll be fun." Then, he eagerly ran toward the ATV. Afraid that she might miss out on some excitement, Denise charged after him.

Michelle turned to Dianne. "If you could entertain your eager passengers for a few minutes, I'd appreciate it. I want to look around before we head for camp."

"That should be easy. I'll just give them a ride and answer their questions."

"That could keep you busy all day."

"I don't mind. They're so eager to learn that teaching them is fun."

When Dianne started walking toward the ATV, Connie said, "I'll go with you and field some of their questions."

Mike turned to Jerry. "Why don't we walk to camp? That will give me time to look at the plateau and give us a chance to discuss today's plans."

"Good idea," replied Jerry.

"Would you like to join us?" Mike asked Michelle.

"Thanks for the invite, but I need to stay here and silently enjoy the scenery for a few minutes. I need to bond with our new home."

"I'm not comfortable with leaving you alone," replied Mike.

"I should be safe here on the plateau. Anyway, I have my weapons, and I'll stay alert."

Mike considered Michelle's comments while looking around. Then, he gave her an affectionate hug. "I think you're right, but I will be looking back in this direction occasionally."

"Thank you for your concern."

Mike smiled at his wife reassuringly; then, he and Jerry headed toward camp. For a few moments, Michelle watched them walk away. Then, she slowly turned, looking in all directions. As she leisurely feasted her eyes on the scenic beauty surrounding her, a deep joyful happiness welled up inside her and filled her entire being.

She stepped to the edge of the plateau and looked down at the nuclear powered shuttles anchored in the bay. She focused her attention on the big cargo shuttle and recalled how she had become a part of this mission by hiding in it with Mike for a few days. She recalled the night on the Challenger's observation deck when Mike showed her the spectacular beauty of the universe. She remembered how he had patiently waited for her to become enthralled by the glittering beauty surrounding her. He then used his masculine charm to entice her into forever leaving the comfortable, secure life she had known on Earth in return for the uncertainties of being an interstellar pioneer. That night, long ago, Alpha Centauri A was nothing more than an unusually bright star that stood out prominently against the stellar background.

Michelle fleetingly glanced at Alpha Centauri A and thought, now, it's no longer just a bright star; it's as brilliant as the Sun is back on Earth, and here on Alcent, it is my source of heat, light, and life itself. Now, it's the Sun that's nothing more than a bright star in the nighttime sky, and Earth is so far away that we cannot see it even with the Challenger's most powerful telescope. Earth is now so far away that two-way communication is even difficult, because it takes 4.35 years for a transmission to reach them and another 4.35 years for a response to reach us. Practically speaking, I've been cut off from my birthplace. This is now my home!

Her attention shifted to Zeb who was down on the beach sitting in his wheelchair watching the activities of the newcomers. Michelle thought, when I left Earth, I never imagined that we'd discover a race of technologically advanced humans or that I'd write a biography for one of them. Perhaps, I should also write biographies for Rex and Shannon. Three life stories taken together should give us pretty good insight into life on B-2 and here for that matter. We now know about three earth-like planets. I wonder why humans evolved on Earth and B-2 but not here. Maybe I should stop calling it B-2 and call it Zebron. That is the name given to it by the people who live there.

Michelle's gaze shifted to the now empty barge that was being moved back to the cargo shuttle for a second load. She noticed that Zeb was looking up at her. She yelled to him. "Want to join us for breakfast?"

Zeb responded with an eager, "Yes," and headed toward the elevator, which Michelle sent down.

While Zeb rode up on the elevator, Michelle took another look at the panoramic view and thought, what a wonderful place to live. I am glad I came here. By the time Zeb arrived, the ATV and its occupants had returned. Michelle gazed at the children and saw that they were wildly excited. "What did you do to them?" she asked Dianne.

Wearing a naughty grin, Dianne said, "Well, it's possible that I may've driven a little too fast, and maybe I might've turned some corners with a little too much speed."

Dianne had hardly finished speaking, when Connie exclaimed, "That's a gross understatement! She came close to being a reckless driver, but I must admit that it was thrilling."

"She's exaggerating with her reckless driving charge," countered Dianne. "We were never in any danger. I was just showing the children how much fun riding an ATV can be."

"She definitely accomplished that," stated Connie.

Michelle turned her attention to the children and again noted how delighted they were. But before she could question them, Denise said, "It was scary, but it was fun."

Michelle turned to Matthew, who said, "Living here is more fun than living on the Challenger."

Michelle beamed when she heard her son's comment. She turned to Connie. "I think we were unnecessarily concerned when we were worried about them adjusting to their new home."

"They are definitely thrilled about being here," responded Connie.

The naughty grin returned to Dianne's face. "You can thank me for giving them their latest thrill."

"I think I should thank you for not killing us!" exclaimed Connie. "That was a wild ride!"

509

Dianne looked at Connie, but before she could respond to her bantering remarks, Matthew said, "I'm hungry. When can we eat?"

"I'm hungry too," stated Michelle. Then, she turned to Dianne. "Is it safe for me to ride the ATV, or should I walk to camp?"

"It's fun, Mom! Hop in!" Matthew exclaimed.

"Does that answer your question?" Dianne asked Michelle.

"Well, I guess I could take a chance," commented Michelle as she joined Dianne, Connie, and the children in the ATV and headed for camp.

After about a minute had gone by, Michelle asked Dianne, "Why are you driving so slowly?"

"I don't want you and Connie to feel like your lives are in danger. Besides that, I have to go slow, so Zeb can keep up with us in his wheelchair."

"Going fast is more fun," stated Matthew.

Meanwhile, Mike and Jerry were leisurely walking to camp and once again, Mike said, "This wide open space sure feels good. It seems like I've been cooped up inside a spaceship forever."

"Well, it was a rather long journey."

"That has to be the understatement of the year. I've been in space nearly seven years, and I've traveled 25 trillion miles at nearly 3/4 of light speed, and you call it a rather long journey."

"Well, it was a rather long journey."

"It was an incredibly long journey, and I'm glad I'm finally here."

"I'm glad you're here too, but I still remember when you shocked me by requesting that you be taken off the mission."

"I do too, and you don't know how happy I am that I didn't have to stay behind."

"If you had been unable to persuade Michelle to leave Earth, would you really have passed up going on the greatest adventure in history?"

"I was prepared to do that, but I was confident I wouldn't have to."

"But you weren't certain, because you did arrange for a replacement."

"I had to do that to make the stowaway plan work. And it all worked out very well. I have my wife and son here with me, and you were able to get your best friend on the ship."

"It's possible that my wonderful wife is alive only because of that replacement request you made years ago."

"What do you mean?" Mike asked.

"Remember the attack by the saber-toothed cats?"

"That was a close call."

"The first cat attacked Charlie, and that attack was so sudden the cat might've been able to kill Connie if Charlie hadn't been there."

"Now, I see what you're getting at. Building Charlie was Moose's idea, and if Moose weren't here, then Charlie might not have been built."

"It's possible someone else might've come up with the idea, but I pre-

510

fer to give Moose the credit for saving Connie's life."

Mike chuckled softly.

"What are you laughing at?" Jerry asked.

"I was just thinking about how upset some of the NIEA bureaucrats were at you for putting Moose on the ship in my place."

Mike noticed that Jerry was laughing in a seemingly self-satisfied way, so he asked, "Why do I get the feeling that you enjoyed ignoring their multitudes of rules and procedures and acting on your own?"

"Cooperating with slow-moving bureaucracies has never been one of my strong points, and thumbing my nose at them was fun. Anyway, putting Moose on the ship was a spur of the moment idea that I wanted to implement, and it was impossible to do that working within the system. I had to bypass them."

"As it turns out, you made the right choice. It's possible that Connie is alive only because you bypassed the normal channels of authority and acted on your own."

After walking in silence and looking around for a few minutes, Mike said, "I'd sure like to take this entire day and do nothing except explore this place and go sailing for a few hours, but that's going to have to wait until we get our projects done."

"There's only one project we should do today, and that's assemble our community bathroom. But that should be an easy one-day job. The building consists of prefabricated panels that we just snap together, and the floor panels have short adjustable legs for easy leveling. The sinks, toilets, and showers were designed for quick, easy installation."

"Besides sticking that stuff together, all we have to do is hook up the waste processing tanks, water supply, and electricity. I think we'll have the facility operational by early afternoon."

"I think you're being very optimistic," Jerry said.

"I don't think so. We have a highly motivated group of workers who want lots of time to explore the island today. During recent days, we formed crews to perform specific tasks. As much as possible, different parts of the project will be done at the same time. As we speak, the components for the facility are being unloaded and brought up. If you'll look back toward the elevator, you'll see that the trailer for hauling the components is already being assembled."

Jerry stopped walking and looked back toward the elevator. "They are busy, and between hauling people and towing that trailer, our ATVs are going to be busy too."

"We thought about bringing another one down, but there wasn't room for it. In addition to the bathroom facility and trailer, we brought down tents, camp equipment, and personal items. Both shuttles were stuffed."

"How much vacation time do you think we should have before we start building temporary homes?" Jerry asked.

"We've been in space for so long that I think everyone will be content to live in tents for a few weeks in order to have ample time to enjoy outdoor recreational activities and do some exploring."

"That sounds reasonable. During that time, we can divide this plateau into lots and draw numbers out of a hat to decide who gets which lot."

"I like that idea," Mike said. "While we're vacationing, we can get acquainted with our property and start making plans as to what we want to do with it. It'll be fun to look at a piece of land and think about where to build a home, where to plant a garden, where to plant fruit trees."

"Home building is more than just fun; it's actually the beginning of our future."

"You're right about that."

"Maybe tomorrow, Moose and I'll take the cargo shuttle up to the Challenger and start bringing down the materials we need to build our temporary homes."

"If you're going up to the Challenger, you might consider bringing down the other two ATVs. Also, there's another trailer up there that might be convenient to have down here. And don't forget the water glider that we built. It could add a lot of fun to our vacation. It will carry two people, and with any wind at all, it should zip around on this lake like a speed boat. It would provide a quick convenient way for people to take a look at the surrounding countryside."

"If I bring all that down, I'm not going to have much room for building materials," Jerry said.

"That's true, because everyone will probably have a list of items they'll want brought down."

"I think Moose and I'll make two trips up there, and I'll ask for a couple volunteers to go with us to help load the shuttle."

"What if no one wants to interrupt their vacation to go with you?"

"Then, I'll have to offer them an incentive."

"What do you have in mind?" Mike asked.

"The two volunteers will be the first to use the water glider. It'll be theirs for four hours."

"It'll be theirs for four hours after you and I check it out to make sure that it's working properly."

"Of course, after all, we can't put our people at risk with an untried piece of equipment."

"I smell fish frying," Mike said. "And it smells so good that it's making my stomach growl."

"The seafood here is delicious. You're in for a gourmet treat."

After breakfast, Jerry and Mike selected a site for the community bathroom and construction started immediately. As Mike had predicted, the workers were eager to get the project done and worked with utmost speed and efficiency. The prefabricated pieces of the facility were quickly put together, and by early afternoon, the project was complete. Everyone stepped back and admired the new building.

Matthew got Mike's attention and asked, "Does it work? I need to go to the bathroom."

"Go in and try it out," Mike replied. "Use this side. It's for boys; the other side is for girls."

While Matthew went into the building to put it to the test, Michelle asked, "How long will it be before we have hot water? I'd like to try out one of the showers?"

"It won't be long," responded Mike. "We have lots of power right now. With a clear sky, we're getting peak solar power, and the breeze out of the south is strong enough for the wind turbine to generate a generous power output."

"This breeze is very warm, almost hot," commented Michelle.

"It is hot," stated Mike. "Current temperature is 91 degrees. Why don't you forget about taking a shower. Let's just go swimming."

"That's a good idea, but let's wait for Matthew."

A few minutes later, Matthew emerged from the new bathroom and said, "It works." Then, he looked around, and sounding concerned, he asked, "Where are we going to sleep tonight?"

"We're going to sleep in a tent," Mike answered.

"That's camping out, isn't it?"

"Yes, it is."

"That will be fun!" Matthew exclaimed. But then, an expression of concern appeared on his face. "Will we be safe from dinosaurs in our tent?" he asked.

"There aren't any dinosaurs on this island," replied Mike.

Matthew thought about the reply for a few moments. Seemingly satisfied, he went on to the next question, "How big will our tent be?"

"It'll be large enough for us."

"I want to see it. Can I help you set it up?"

"Yes, you can." Turning to Michelle, Mike said, "Let's set up our tent and then go swimming."

Mike and Michelle selected a site 40 yards from the bathroom and with Matthew helping, proceeded to set up their tent. Forty-five minutes later, the tent was set up, air mattress beds were laid out, and personal items were stashed inside.

While Matthew was inside checking out his bed, Mike and Michelle were outside taking a look at their handiwork. "It looks pretty good as far as tents go," commented Michelle.

"It's going to be our home for a while," stated Mike.

"I feel like I'm on a camping trip, except I've never had this large a tent on any of my campouts."

"Ten by twenty is also larger than any tent I ever had on a camping trip, but all of my campouts were backpack trips."

"The thing I like most about this tent is the panel floor supported a few inches above ground by plastic rails. We don't have to worry about having a wet floor when it rains, and our beds will be flat and comfortable, no bumps under the air mattresses."

"I like the sturdy construction. The material is tough, and the frame is strong. This tent will withstand some pretty stormy weather."

"Also, it looks like it won't be hot inside on a warm day like today," commented Michelle. "The material is very reflective, and the tent has large screened openings on all sides."

"I'm happy with it. Let's get Matthew and go swimming."

Michelle looked into the tent to see why Matthew hadn't yet come out. She turned to Mike. "It looks like Matthew is happy with it too. He's sound asleep in there."

"I don't think we should wake him. There are enough people here to keep an eye on him. Let's go swimming without him and take him later."

"Good idea. He got up as early as the rest of us, and he's been active. As fast as he passed out, he must be exhausted."

Michelle found Connie, who said, "Denise is taking a nap too. She ran out of energy, stretched out on our bed, and fell asleep instantly."

"They've both been very active," Michelle said.

"And curious, I'm pleased with how interested they are in everything they encounter."

"This is a big new world for them," stated Michelle.

"I can't wait to take them for a submarine ride and show them the underwater world," responded Connie.

"Maybe we should do that before we teach them how to swim. It'll give them some insight into the water world they'll be playing in."

"I am first on the list for the submarine," stated Mike. "We have a 4:00 P.M. reservation."

"How did you get the first reservation?" Michelle asked.

"We drew numbers, and I drew the third spot. Then, I managed to talk the first place people into trading with me."

"How did you do that?"

"They were in last place for use of the ATV that's down on the beach. I drew second place, so we did some trading."

"I like the trade. A trip into the underwater world and some sailing will be worth the delay in driving around the island."

"I think so too. Besides that, in a couple days, we'll probably have the other two ATVs down here anyway."

"I'm hot and sweaty," stated Michelle. "I need a refreshing swim."

"I do too," Mike said.

"I'll wake the children for our 4:00 o'clock cruise," Connie said, "and we'll meet you on the beach. So just relax and enjoy your swim."

Michelle smiled. "I will. I haven't been in years, and it's a great day for it."

An hour later, Jerry, Connie, Denise, and Matthew stepped into the ATV and headed for South Bay. "Are we going swimming?" Denise asked.

"We're going for a submarine ride," replied Jerry. "I want to show you the underwater world."

"That's where fish live," stated Matthew.

"Will we see fish?" Denise asked.

"Yes, we will," replied Jerry.

"How deep is the water?" Matthew asked.

"In some places, it is as deep as this plateau is long," replied Jerry.

"That's really deep," stated Matthew.

"Is it scary that deep down?" Denise asked.

"Our submarine is rugged. It will protect us, and you'll have fun."

A short time later, Jerry, Connie, Denise, Mike, Michelle, and Matthew were on the submarine sailing out of South Bay. Before leaving the bay, Jerry took the submarine down to about ten feet off the bottom.

Denise and Matthew stared at the exotic underwater scenery in wide-eyed fascination. For them, this was like a journey into fantasyland, because they had never experienced anything like this underwater world teeming with life. They asked questions faster than the adults could answer them, and it took a full hour of underwater cruising to satisfy their curiosity. Then, hunger took over, and they asked for dinner.

Honoring their request, Jerry said, "Let's surface and do some sailing. While we're doing that, we can eat dinner."

"I'm ready to hoist the sail and play the wind," stated Mike.

After surfacing, Jerry and Mike rigged the boat for sailing while Connie and Michelle prepared dinner. Everyone ate except Mike, who was having fun sailing the boat.

A little later, when first sunset was only a half-hour away, Michelle said, "I think we should head for home. I'd like to see my first double sunset from the plateau." Mike agreed with his wife's suggestion and set course for South Bay.

Twenty-five minutes later, they stepped off the elevator onto the plateau, and Mike said, "We're here right on time. Alpha Centauri A is lying on the horizon."

Everyone watched Alpha Centauri A gradually drop out of sight. Then, the orange light of Alpha Centauri B dominated the area.

For Matthew and Denise, this was truly amazing. They had never seen a sunset, let alone, a double sunset. As had been the case so many times on this day, they watched in spellbound fascination.

While looking concerned by what was happening, Denise asked, "Is the orange sun going to go away too?"

"Pretty soon, it will set too," responded Connie.

"But then it will be dark," commented Denise. "On our starship, it only got dark when we turned out the lights."

"Here it gets dark after both of our suns set."

"Will our suns come back?"

Connie pointed to the east. "Tomorrow morning both of our suns will rise over there, and a new day will begin."

Denise appeared puzzled by the fact that night and day would no longer be controlled by the flick of a switch. "Will we still have lights to see with at night?" she asked.

"Yes."

Matthew turned to Mike. "Will we have lights in our tent?"

"Yes."

Matthew and Denise continued asking questions until Alpha Centauri B set. Then, the pioneers headed for camp, which now looked like a tent campground back on Earth, including a large blazing campfire.

When they arrived in camp, Michelle said, "This has been a long day, and I'm ready for ten hours of sleep. But first, I'm going to take a shower and relax next to the campfire. If my energy holds up, I'll stay up for first and second moonrise."

"I like that plan," Mike said. "And since I haven't had dinner yet, I'm going to roast some of Moose's smoked sausage over the campfire."

"That sounds like a good old-fashioned wiener roast," stated Jerry.

"Kind of, except I won't be roasting wieners, I'll be roasting dinosaur sausage."

"I think you'll find that it tastes better than wieners," commented Jerry. "Moose did a good job making that sausage. The seasoning is excellent, the texture is good, and the smoke flavor is great."

"You're making me even hungrier," Mike said. "I'm going to eat dinner now and take my shower later."

"Save some for me," Michelle said, as she headed for the shower.

"I'll have one ready for you."

Twenty minutes later, feeling refreshed, Michelle joined Mike and Matthew by the campfire. Mike immediately handed her a roasted sausage in a bun. "Taste this."

Michelle did as directed. "This is very good! Can I have it?"

"It's yours. I'll make another."

"Can I have one more?" Matthew asked.

"You sure can," replied Mike.

Jerry turned to Connie. "It appears that the new arrivals like the food here."

Before Connie could comment, Moose said, "It seems like my culinary talents are once again being recognized."

"That almost sounds like bragging," Mike said to Jerry. "But all of his creations have tasted so good that I cannot dispute his claim."

"I think it's his insatiable appetite that makes him a natural at food research and development."

"He does like to eat," agreed Mike. "It probably won't be long and he'll figure out how to make a good pizza using only local ingredients."

"That's a great idea," Moose said. "I'll start working on that tomorrow, but it's going to be a couple weeks before the wild rice is ripe. At the moment, that's my only possible local source of flour. The   t o m a t o based sauce will also be a problem."

"It sounds like you've already thought about this," commented Jerry.

"Of course, pizza is one of my favorite foods."

While munching on a piece of sausage, Michelle said to Moose, "If your pizza turns out as good as this sausage, you're going to have lots of contented customers."

"I'll experiment with it until it is good," stated Moose.

"Your confidence is justified," commented Michelle. "I've eaten a big variety of excellent food today, and nearly all of it came from here."

"I can't take credit for all of it," responded Moose. "Finding good food was a team effort."

"I'm amazed with what the four of you have accomplished. You landed on an alien planet, and in less than thirty days, you've not only explored this area and turned it into a home, but you've also identified and tested enough local foods to make us independent of our food synthesizers."

"We have accomplished a lot," agreed Connie. "But I'm especially pleased that we've suffered no serious illnesses or infections."

"That is something to be thankful for," Michelle said.

"While it is something to be thankful for, we must keep in mind that we've only been here four weeks," stated Connie. "I think it's too soon to disregard the dangers posed by microorganisms, but it's encouraging to note that our experience to date indicates that they won't be anymore of a problem here than they were back on Earth."

"The fact that Zeb has survived here for a long time with an immune system similar to ours adds validity to that opinion," Dianne said.

"But he was near death when we found him, and even though dangerous microorganisms are probably rare, they do exist. Finding them will continue to be one of my most important research projects."

"You will have help," Dianne said.

"That's good, because it's a life-long project."

"I have a big project too," stated Mike. "But hopefully, it won't take the rest of my life to complete."

"What project are you talking about?" Connie asked.

"It's an important project. It will be hard work, but it will be fun."

"That doesn't answer my question. What is the project?"

"I'm talking about designing and building a house."

Noticeably excited, Michelle said, "I'd like to help. When can we start?"

"First, we need to build our temporary home, and I'd like to get that done in the next two weeks. By then, we'll be tired of living in our tent."

"That's true," agreed Michelle. "But our tent is sturdy and quite spacious as far as camping tents go, and I think we should relocate it next to our temporary home and use it for dry storage. Since our temporary home will be small, we'll need the extra space."

"I agree, and the fact that our temporary home will be small leads into my concept for our permanent home. Basically, we need to gain living space quickly in the interest of being comfortable, and the quickest way to do that is to add a room to our temporary home. But adding a room can be more than just adding a room. It can be the first step in building our permanent home."

Michelle thought about Mike's comments. "If I understand you correctly, you're planning to design a home that can be built in sections rather than all at the same time."

"That's correct, but in addition, I plan to make our temporary home an integral part of the design for our permanent home. By doing it that way, we will actually be building the first section of our permanent home when we set up our prefabricated temporary home."

"I like the idea," Michelle said. "Each section we build will give us additional living space long before the entire structure is complete."

"That's the objective," stated Mike. "Considering the number of homes that we need to build, it will take years to complete all of them. However, building homes a section at a time will quickly provide additional space."

"That is a good idea," agreed Jerry. "Have you thought about what materials you're going to build your home with?"

"I'm thinking about building the walls with rocks and the roof with some good solid timber."

"Are you building a house or a fortress?" asked Moose.

"I intend for my house to be my fortress. When I go to bed at night, I like to sleep peacefully."

"Does that mean you'll have trouble sleeping in a tent?" Connie asked.

"No, we'll have guards on duty besides all of our other security measures. But eventually, we'll be living in permanent homes, and I think they should be rugged enough, so we can dispense with the guards."

"But there aren't any large animals on this plateau," stated Dianne.

"You haven't lived here long enough to know that's always going to be the case. Besides, weren't you almost killed by a pterodactyl?"

"Both of your points are true," admitted Dianne.

"I like the idea of our home being a fortress," Michelle said. "When we're in our home, we should be able to relax and not worry about danger."

518

"That's my objective," stated Mike.

"Can we build a rugged home that also looks good?" Michelle asked.

"Earlier today, I looked at the rockslide at the north end of this plateau. I was impressed by the colors and color patterns in some of the rocks. With some careful picking and choosing, we should be able to build a very attractive home."

"What kind of mortar are we going to set the rocks in?" Michelle asked.

"Our plastics technology is so good that we can easily manufacture resins with any characteristics we want, and we have plenty of sand on our beaches. We can make a mortar that is as strong as the rocks themselves. Also, we can add pigment to make the mortar whatever color we want, or we can go with the natural sand color."

"Talking about this is getting me excited," stated Michelle. "I'd like to start building tomorrow."

"First, we'll have to find out which piece of land is going to be ours, so we'll have a place to build."

Michelle turned to Jerry who anticipated her question. "Tomorrow morning, we'll divide the plateau into public and private land," he said. "Then, we'll divide the private land into lots and have a drawing to decide who gets which lot. Anyone who isn't happy with the lot they get will be free to trade with whomever they're able to make a deal with."

"How could anyone be unhappy with any lot here on the plateau?" Michelle asked. "All lots will be choice view property. I feel like we're living in paradise."

"We did look at the entire planet before choosing this location," noted Connie.

"Based on what I've seen today, I think we made the best possible choice," stated Michelle.

"When we find out which part of this plateau is ours, I want to start turning it into our home," Michelle said to Mike. "We can start by deciding where we want to build our house, plant a garden, and grow some fruit trees. We can even start gathering rocks for our house."

Mike grinned at Michelle. "You're awfully ambitious; considering that just a little while ago, you told me you needed ten hours of sleep."

"Well, it's beautiful here, and this is going to be our home. I'm excited about it! We're fortunate to have such a picturesque place to live. When you think about how far we've traveled and all that we've been through, we really have a lot to be thankful for. In fact, I think we should celebrate this day every year in thanksgiving for our safe arrival and our good fortune of finding such a wonderful place to live."

"This day could also be viewed as the beginning of our civilization," commented Jerry. "When four of us arrived here a month ago, it wasn't certain that we could live here, but now, we are confident that our immune systems can defend us against this planet's microbes. Consequently, we've brought everyone down, and we're ready to build a new civilization, the first to be totally independent of Earth."

"We have a big job ahead of us," stated Connie.

"It will be a lifelong challenge," added Jerry.

"Looking at the big picture, it's much more than that," stated Connie. "Building a new civilization is a process that will continue for many generations. For each generation, it will be a lifelong challenge that must be successfully met."

"That's true," agreed Jerry. "But our challenge is to get our new civilization off to a good solid start. We must build a solid foundation for it, something that each succeeding generation can build on. We are the founding fathers."

"And the founding mothers," declared Connie.

With Michelle nodding in agreement, Dianne said to Connie, "Thank you for including us."

With Connie, Michelle, Dianne, Mike and Moose staring at him, Jerry felt like he was on the proverbial hot seat and quickly said, "I was using the term *founding fathers* in a gender-neutral way. I had no intention of excluding the most important people in our lives."

"I am so happy you feel that way," responded Connie, while giving her husband a hug. "Starting a new society requires a team effort over a long period of time. But with any luck at all, most of us should still be alive and healthy 60 to 70 years from now. That'll give us plenty of time."

"I think making intelligent choices in our daily lives is far more important than relying on good luck," stated Jerry.

"I agree," Connie said. "However, a little good luck now and then sure won't hurt anything."

"That's true," Jerry replied. "But I think lots of good luck is the natural outcome of making intelligent choices, and the more that we learn about Alcent in general and our local environment in particular, the better equipped we'll be to do that."

"I can't argue with that," responded Connie. "Knowledge is definitely the key to our success, both gaining new knowledge and preserving for future generations the knowledge and technology we brought with us."

"That's all very important, but there's more to it than that," stated Moose. "When I was a kid, I made lots of bad choices that almost ruined my life. I had a bad attitude toward most of the people around me and toward society in general. Fortunately, I was able to pull myself out of it. If our society is going to be successful, I believe we must instill in our children a sense of right and wrong and a sense of responsibility toward themselves and those around them, so they'll make responsible choices."

"That just might be essential," stated Jerry. "From what I've seen, the greatest nations on Earth are the ones that allow the most individual freedom. But freedom can only exist when individuals make responsible choices in their daily lives. When people abuse their freedom by making bad choices, laws are usually enacted to deal with them. As more and more laws get passed, personal freedom gradually disappears and personal initiative becomes stifled. Eventually, society becomes so bogged down with laws and regulations that little progress is made."

Connie listened attentively. She smiled at Jerry. "You sure use lots of words to say that the success of our society depends on maximum individual freedom and that preserving individual freedom depends on individuals making responsible choices in daily living."

"I've always admired you for being able to get right to the point," stated Jerry.

"Is that why you married me?"

"I remember a morning in the medical lab when you needed very little time to get right to the point, and we did get married soon after that."

Connie glowed as she recalled what happened in the medical lab shortly after leaving Earth. "I definitely got better results from that physical than any other I've ever given."

"I hope you've never given another physical like that one," teased Jerry.

"I definitely haven't," responded Connie, as she leaned toward Jerry who met her halfway with a warm kiss.

Connie noticed Michelle smiling. "What are you so happy about?"

"While I wasn't in the medical lab with you that morning, I did help you prepare for that physical. Naturally, I'm pleased that everything worked out so well for you. You ended up with a wonderful husband and a beautiful daughter who gets along very well with my son."

"Your son is a healthy child with a pleasant attitude toward life. He is easy to get along with."

"Since Denise is also that way, it's easy for our children to be good playmates."

"There is a key word in your appraisal of Matthew," Jerry said to Connie.

"Which word got your attention?" Connie asked.

"Attitude."

"Why did that word attract your attention?"

"I believe that the success of our society is dependent on the kind of attitude that individuals in our society have. Specifically, as our children grow and develop into adults, I believe that it is very important to constantly nurture the development of a strong positive attitude in each of them. As our children become adults, it is important that each individual take responsibility for his or her own state of well-being. We must guard against them developing a frame of mind that allows them to readily blame others for personal shortcomings."

Jerry had barely finished speaking, when Moose said, "The last part of what you said hits me squarely in the head. When I was a rebellious teenager involved in illegal gang activity, I found it very easy to blame others and society in general for my lawless lifestyle. It took a long time, and it was difficult, but eventually I figured out that my high-risk, unruly lifestyle was no one's fault but my own. My dangerous lifestyle was the direct result of me making bad choices in my day-to-day life. When I started taking responsibility for my activities and making wise choices, my life turned around rather quickly."

Jerry grinned at Moose. "You sure use a lot of words to say that you agree with me."

"Would you prefer that I simply say that I know from painful personal experience that you are right?"

"Actually, I didn't mind hearing your long-winded account of your lawless days."

"I don't mean to change the subject." stated Michelle. "But since we're planning to live here for the rest of our lives, there is a mystery that we need to solve."

"What do you have in mind?" Jerry asked.

"For our own peace of mind, we need to know if we're alone on this planet. We need to know what happened to the people who deserted Zeb. Are they alive? Are they a threat to us?"

"I agree with you," responded Jerry.

"Also, Zeb would like to know if Zonya is still alive, where she is, and what her situation is."

"I'm planning to go up to the Challenger tomorrow," stated Jerry. "I'll invite Zeb to come along, so he can do a telepathic search."

"He'll like that," stated Michelle, as she turned to Zeb to give him the good news.

Zeb quickly became very excited at the prospect of finding his beloved Zonya. Even though, he realized there was a good chance that she might no longer be alive, he welcomed the opportunity to search for her. Speaking to Michelle, he said, "Tell Jerry, Thank You!"

Upon hearing the response, Jerry made eye contact with Zeb, nodded, and smiled.

After getting Jerry's attention, Dianne said, "There is something else we need to do as soon as we can."

"What do you have in mind?" Jerry asked.

"We need to go to Aphrodite and explore it."

"We are planning to explore Nocturne and Aphrodite."

"But we need to go to Aphrodite soon."

"Why the urgency?"

"Last night when Moose and I were looking at Aphrodite, a strange feeling came over me. I sensed that there is life on that moon that is in desperate need of help. It's almost like I could hear them crying out for help."

"But how could there be life there? Aphrodite has no atmosphere."

"I don't know anything more than what I sensed last night, but the feeling was strong, and I won't sleep well at night until we check this out."

"Okay, I've learned to trust you in what you sense, so the day after tomorrow, we'll go there and take a look."

"Thanks, I appreciate that."

With the serious business taken care of, the pioneers shifted their conversation to lighter subjects to just simply enjoy the beginning of their future. As they continued their fireside conversation, Nocturne rose above the eastern horizon and flooded the plateau with moonlight. Matthew and Denise viewed their first moonrise ever with total amazement and asked numerous questions about it.

Before Nocturne rose very high in the sky, both children were overcome by fatigue from their long active day. After putting Matthew to bed, Mike and Michelle took a leisurely stroll around the plateau to enjoy their new home by moonlight. By the time they returned to their tent, Aphrodite was peeking above the eastern horizon.

"What a novel sight to see a moonrise when we already have a moon hanging in the sky," Michelle said, while looking at it.

"It looks rather bizarre, but I like it," commented Mike.

"I think exotic is a better description than bizarre."

"I wonder how long we'll have to live here before the things that seem so peculiar now start to feel ordinary."

While gazing across the peaceful water of Clear Lake toward the two moons hanging in the eastern sky, Michelle said, "I don't know, but for right now, this alien scene is having a special romantic effect on me."

"Are you suggesting that we take advantage of the mood you're in?"

"I'd like that, and Matthew does need some brothers and sisters. Also, children are the building blocks in the foundation for our new civilization, and I think we should do our share in the building of that foundation."

Mike put his arms around Michelle and whispered, "You don't have to convince me. I'm in the same mood you're in, so let's find a secluded, moonlit area not too far away from the guards and celebrate the end of our first day here and the beginning of our future."

Pointing toward the east, Michelle said, "There's a grassy area on the other side of those bushes."

"That looks good. Let's take a blanket with us."

A few minutes later, Mike and Michelle arrived at the secluded area they had selected. After spreading out the blanket and making herself comfortable on it, Michelle said, "This is some unusual grass. It's thick and not very tall. It feels like we have a well-padded carpet under our blanket."

Mike stretched out on the blanket beside Michelle. "This really is comfortable. I think I could easily sleep here tonight."

Michelle gracefully moved into a provocative pose. "Don't go to sleep just yet; I need your attention for a while."

Mike sat up and gazed at Michelle. As his eyes roamed over her, his imagination became intensely fired up by the seductive way that she was presenting herself to him. In just a few moments, Mike's pulse quickened as his body prepared for action. "It seems like I don't feel sleepy anymore," Mike said huskily.

Greatly pleased with Mike's reaction to her alluring pose, Michelle smiled in satisfaction and reached out for him with open arms. Mike eagerly accepted her invitation, and for quite some time, they passionately enjoyed themselves in this exotic, romantic setting in their new home.

After they had satisfied their desire for each other's love, they sat up and gazed out across the water of Clear Lake. The peaceful, moonlit scene now seemed to have a very special romantic feel to it. Feeling content and happy, Michelle said, "I think our love for each other is really something precious. I hope we never lose these feelings."

"I will never forget that you left a life on Earth that you were very happy with because of your love for me."

"I didn't have any choice. I had to leave the security of that life for the uncertainties inherent in being on this mission."

"Why?"

"Because I am a hopeless romantic."

"What do you mean?"

"Don't you remember what happened on the observation deck long ago when we were still in orbit around Earth?"

"I do, but tell me about it anyway."

"The observation deck was really an exotic, romantic setting. With the spectacular beauty of the universe as a backdrop, you fired up my imagination and stimulated my desire to be a part of the greatest adventure in history. You also got me sexually aroused. Then, you took me to your apartment, and we made love with such fervent passion that it was more satisfying than any sexual experience I'd had in my life up to that time. That night, I realized that I could not be truly happy without you and that neither one of us could be truly happy if I took you off this mission by insisting that we stay on Earth. I simply could not stand between you and your lifelong dream."

"If you had decided to stay on Earth, I would've stayed with you, and I would've done my best to make our lives happy."

"I know, but it would never have been the same as being here."

"I am happy that we're here," stated Mike.

"I am too, and tomorrow, we can start building our future."

Mike stood up and gazed across the lake. Then, he looked around the moonlit plateau and down at Michelle. "Do you think we should sleep here on this blanket tonight?" he asked.

"That would be fun, and with the guards on duty, it would be reasonably safe, but if Matthew wakes up during the might, he'll be worried if we aren't there."

524

"You're right. We need to make sure that he always feels safe and secure."

A few minutes later, Mike and Michelle entered their tent. They went to bed filled with joy and high expectations for the future, and they quickly dropped into a sound, peaceful sleep.

Please note:

This story continues in *Alcent Adventures*, the second book in the Alcent series. *Alcent Adventures* will entertain you with daring outdoor adventure, suspense, conflict, romance, and mysteries to solve. You will not find any profanity or crude vulgar language in this book. If *Alcent Adventures* isn't in your local bookstore, you can contact the author and find out where to pick up a copy of it.

Contact the Author

If you would like to share your thoughts about this story with the author, he can be reached by e-mail at DLPekarek@aol.com or by U.S. Mail: Dan Pekarek, Alcent Adventures, P.O. Box 23781, Federal Way, WA 98093-0781